THE MAN *who* LAUGHS

MONCREIFFE
PRESS

THE MAN *who* LAUGHS

By VICTOR HUGO

TRANSLATION BY
ANONYMOUS

1869

UNITED STATES

CONTENTS

PRELIMINARY CHAPTER

URSUS

I.

Ursus and Homo were fast friends. Ursus was a man, Homo a wolf. Their dispositions tallied. It was the man who had christened the wolf: probably he had also chosen his own name. Having found *Ursus* fit for himself, he had found *Homo* fit for the beast. Man and wolf turned their partnership to account at fairs, at village fêtes, at the corners of streets where passers-by throng, and out of the need which people seem to feel everywhere to listen to idle gossip and to buy quack medicine. The wolf, gentle and courteously subordinate, diverted the crowd. It is a pleasant thing to behold the tameness of animals. Our greatest delight is to see all the varieties of domestication parade before us. This it is which collects so many folks on the road of royal processions.

Ursus and Homo went about from cross-road to cross-road, from the High Street of Aberystwith to the High Street of Jedburgh, from country-side to country-side, from shire to shire, from town to town. One market exhausted, they went on to another. Ursus lived in a small van upon wheels, which Homo was civilized enough to draw by day and guard by night. On bad roads, up hills, and where there were too many ruts, or there was too much mud, the man buckled the trace round his neck and pulled fraternally, side by side with the wolf. They had thus grown old together. They encamped at haphazard on a common, in the glade of a wood, on the waste patch of grass where roads intersect, at the outskirts of villages, at the gates of towns, in market-places, in public walks, on the borders of parks, before the entrances of churches. When the cart drew up on a fair green, when the gossips ran up open-mouthed and the curious made a circle round the pair, Ursus harangued and Homo approved. Homo, with a bowl in his mouth, politely made a collection among the audience. They gained their livelihood. The wolf was lettered, likewise the man. The wolf had been trained by the man, or had trained himself unassisted, to divers wolfish arts, which swelled the receipts. "Above all things, do not degenerate into a man," his friend would say to him.

Never did the wolf bite: the man did now and then. At least, to bite was the intent of Ursus. He was a misanthrope, and to italicize his misanthropy he had made himself a juggler. To live, also; for the stomach has to be consulted. Moreover, this juggler-misanthrope, whether to add to the complexity of his being or to perfect it, was a doctor. To be a doctor is little: Ursus was a ventriloquist. You heard him speak without his moving his lips. He counterfeited, so as to deceive you, any one's accent or pronunciation. He imitated voices so exactly that you believed you heard the people themselves. All alone he simulated the murmur of a crowd, and this gave him a right to the title of Engastrimythos, which he took. He reproduced all sorts of cries of birds, as of the thrush, the wren, the pipit lark, otherwise called the gray cheeper, and the ring ousel, all travellers like himself: so that at times when the fancy struck him, he made you aware either of a public thoroughfare filled with the uproar of men, or of a meadow loud with the voices of beasts—at one time stormy as a multitude, at another fresh and serene as the dawn. Such gifts, although rare, exist. In the last century a man called Touzel, who imitated the mingled utterances of men and animals, and who counterfeited all the cries of beasts, was attached to the person of Buffon—to serve as a menagerie.

Ursus was sagacious, contradictory, odd, and inclined to the singular expositions which we term fables. He had the appearance of believing in them, and this impudence was a part of his humour. He read people's hands, opened books at random and drew conclusions, told fortunes, taught that it is perilous to meet a black mare, still more perilous, as you start for a journey, to hear yourself accosted by one who knows not whither you are going; and he called himself a dealer in superstitions. He used to say: "There is one difference between me and the Archbishop of Canterbury: I avow what I am." Hence it was that the archbishop, justly indignant, had him one day before him; but Ursus cleverly disarmed his grace by reciting a sermon he had composed upon Christmas Day, which the delighted archbishop learnt by heart, and delivered from the pulpit as his own. In consideration thereof the archbishop pardoned Ursus.

As a doctor, Ursus wrought cures by some means or other. He made use of aromatics; he was versed in simples; he made the most of the immense power which lies in a heap of neglected plants, such as the hazel, the catkin, the white alder, the white bryony, the mealy-tree, the traveller's joy, the buckthorn. He treated phthisis with the sundew; at opportune moments he would use the leaves of the spurge, which plucked at the bottom are a purgative and plucked at the top, an emetic. He cured sore throat by means of the vegetable excrescence called Jew's ear. He knew the rush which cures the ox and the mint which cures the horse. He was well acquainted with the beauties and virtues of the herb mandragora, which, as every one knows, is of both sexes. He had many recipes. He cured burns with the salamander wool, of which, according to Pliny, Nero had a napkin. Ursus possessed a retort and a flask; he effected transmutations; he sold panaceas. It was said of him that he had once been for a short time in Bedlam; they had done him the honour to take him for a madman, but had set him free on discovering that he was only a poet. This story was probably not true; we have all to submit to some such legend about us.

The fact is, Ursus was a bit of a savant, a man of taste, and an old Latin poet. He was learned in two forms; he Hippocratized and he Pindarized. He could have vied in bombast with Rapin and Vida. He could have composed Jesuit tragedies in a style not less triumphant than that of Father Bouhours. It followed from his familiarity with the venerable rhythms and metres of the ancients, that he had peculiar figures of speech, and a whole family of classical metaphors. He would say of a mother followed by her two daughters, *There is a dactyl;* of a father preceded by his two sons, *There is an anapæst;* and of a little child walking between its grandmother and grandfather, *There is an amphimacer*. So much knowledge could only end in starvation. The school of Salerno says, "Eat little and often." Ursus ate little and seldom, thus obeying one half the precept and disobeying the other; but this was the fault of the public, who did not always flock to him, and who did not often buy.

Ursus was wont to say: "The expectoration of a sentence is a relief. The wolf is comforted by its howl, the sheep by its wool, the forest by its finch, woman by her love, and the philosopher by his epiphonema." Ursus at a pinch composed comedies, which, in recital, he all but acted; this helped to sell the drugs. Among other works, he had composed an heroic pastoral in honour of Sir Hugh Middleton, who in 1608 brought a river to London. The river was lying peacefully in Hertfordshire, twenty miles from London: the knight came and took possession of it. He brought a brigade of six hundred men, armed with shovels and pickaxes; set to breaking up the ground, scooping it out in one place, raising it in another—now thirty feet high, now twenty feet deep; made wooden aqueducts high in air; and at different points constructed eight hundred bridges of stone, bricks, and timber. One fine morning the river entered London, which was short of water. Ursus transformed all these vulgar details into a fine Eclogue between the Thames and the New River, in which the former invited the latter to come to him, and offered her his bed, saying, "I am too old to please women, but I am rich enough to pay them"—an ingenious and gallant conceit to indicate how Sir Hugh Middleton had completed thc work at his own expense.

Ursus was great in soliloquy. Of a disposition at once unsociable and talkative, desiring to see no one, yet wishing to converse with some one, he got out of the difficulty by talking to himself. Any one who has lived a solitary life knows how deeply seated monologue is in one's nature. Speech imprisoned frets to find a vent. To harangue space is an outlet. To speak out aloud when alone is as it were to have a dialogue with the divinity which is within. It was, as is well known, a custom of Socrates; he declaimed to himself. Luther did the same. Ursus took after those great men. He had the hermaphrodite faculty of being his own audience. He questioned himself, answered himself, praised himself, blamed himself. You heard him in the street soliloquizing in his van. The passers-by, who have their own way of appreciating clever people, used to say: He is an idiot. As we have just observed, he abused himself at times; but there were times also when he rendered himself justice. One day, in one of these allocutions addressed to himself, he was heard to cry out, "I have studied vegetation in all its mysteries—in the stalk, in the bud, in the sepal, in the stamen, in the carpel, in the ovule, in the spore, in the theca, and in the apothecium. I have thoroughly sifted chromatics, osmosy, and chymosy—that is to say, the formation of colours, of smell, and of taste." There was something fatuous, doubtless, in this certificate which Ursus gave to Ursus; but let those who have not thoroughly sifted chromatics, osmosy, and chymosy cast the first stone at him.

Fortunately Ursus had never gone into the Low Countries; there they would certainly have weighed him, to ascertain whether he was of the normal weight, above or below which a man is a sorcerer. In Holland this weight was sagely fixed by law. Nothing was simpler or more ingenious. It was a clear test. They put you in a scale, and the evidence was conclusive if you broke the equilibrium. Too heavy, you were hanged; too light, you were burned. To this day the scales in which sorcerers were weighed may be seen at Oudewater, but they are now used for weighing cheeses; how religion has degenerated! Ursus would certainly have had a crow to pluck with those scales. In his travels he kept away from Holland, and he did well. Indeed, we believe that he used never to leave the United Kingdom.

However this may have been, he was very poor and morose, and having made the acquaintance of Homo in a wood, a taste for a wandering life had come over him. He had taken the wolf into partnership, and with him had gone forth on the highways, living in the open air the great life of chance. He had a great deal of industry and of reserve, and great skill in everything connected with healing operations, restoring the sick to health, and in working wonders peculiar to himself. He was considered a clever mountebank and a good doctor. As may be imagined, he passed for a wizard as well—not much indeed; only a little, for it was unwholesome in those days to be considered a friend of the devil. To tell the truth, Ursus, by his passion for pharmacy and his love of plants, laid himself open to suspicion, seeing that he often went to gather herbs in rough thickets where grew Lucifer's salads, and where, as has been proved by the Counsellor De l'Ancre, there is a risk of meeting in the evening mist a man who comes out of the earth, "blind of the right eye, barefooted, without a cloak, and a sword by his side." But for the matter of that, Ursus, although eccentric in manner and disposition, was too good a fellow to invoke or disperse hail, to make faces appear, to kill a man with the torment of excessive dancing, to suggest dreams fair or foul and full of terror, and to cause the birth of cocks with four wings. He had no such mischievous tricks. He was incapable of certain abominations, such as, for instance, speaking German, Hebrew, or Greek, without having learned them, which is a sign of unpardonable wickedness, or of a natural infirmity proceeding from a morbid humour. If Ursus spoke Latin, it was because he knew it. He would never have allowed himself to speak Syriac, which he did not know. Besides, it is asserted that Syriac is the language spoken in the midnight meetings at which uncanny people worship the devil. In medicine he justly preferred Galen to Cardan; Cardan, although a learned man, being but an earthworm to Galen.

To sum up, Ursus was not one of those persons who live in fear of the police. His van was long enough and wide enough to allow of his lying down in it on a box containing his not very sumptuous apparel. He owned a lantern, several wigs, and some utensils suspended from nails, among which were musical instruments. He possessed, besides, a bearskin with which he covered himself on his days of grand performance. He called this putting on full dress. He used to say, "I have two skins; this is the real one," pointing to the bearskin.

The little house on wheels belonged to himself and to the wolf. Besides his house, his retort, and his wolf, he had a flute and a violoncello on which he played prettily. He concocted his own elixirs. His wits yielded him enough to sup on sometimes. In the top of his van was a hole, through which passed the pipe of a cast-iron stove; so close to his box as to scorch the wood of it. The stove had two compartments; in one of them Ursus cooked his chemicals, and in the other his potatoes. At night the wolf slept under the van, amicably secured by a chain. Homo's hair was black, that of Ursus, gray; Ursus was fifty, unless, indeed, he was sixty. He accepted his destiny, to such an extent that, as we have just seen, he ate potatoes, the trash on which at that time they fed pigs and convicts. He ate them indignant, but resigned. He was not tall—he was long. He was bent and melancholy. The bowed frame of an old man is the settlement in the architecture of life. Nature had formed him for sadness. He found it difficult to smile, and he had never been able to weep, so that he was deprived of the consolation of tears as well as of the palliative of joy. An old man is a thinking ruin; and such a ruin was Ursus. He had the loquacity of a charlatan, the leanness of a prophet, the irascibility of a charged mine: such was Ursus. In his youth he had been a philosopher in the house of a lord.

This was 180 years ago, when men were more like wolves than they are now.

Not so very much though.

II.

Homo was no ordinary wolf. From his appetite for medlars and potatoes he might have been taken for a prairie wolf; from his dark hide, for a lycaon; and from his howl prolonged into a bark, for a dog of Chili. But no one has as yet observed the eyeball of a dog of Chili sufficiently to enable us to determine whether he be not a fox, and Homo was a real wolf. He was five feet long, which is a fine length for a wolf, even in Lithuania; he was very strong; he looked at you askance, which was not his fault; he had a soft tongue, with which he occasionally licked Ursus; he had a narrow brush of short bristles on his backbone, and he was lean with the wholesome leanness of a forest life. Before he knew Ursus and had a carriage to draw, he thought nothing of doing his fifty miles a night. Ursus meeting him in a thicket near a stream of running water, had conceived a high opinion of him from seeing the skill and sagacity with which he fished out crayfish, and welcomed him as an honest and genuine Koupara wolf of the kind called crab-eater.

As a beast of burden, Ursus preferred Homo to a donkey. He would have felt repugnance to having his hut drawn by an ass; he thought too highly of the ass for that. Moreover he had observed that the ass, a four-legged thinker little understood by men, has a habit of cocking his ears uneasily when philosophers talk nonsense. In life the ass is a third person between our thoughts and ourselves, and acts as a restraint. As a friend, Ursus preferred Homo to a dog, considering that the love of a wolf is more rare.

Hence it was that Homo sufficed for Ursus. Homo was for Ursus more than a companion, he was an analogue. Ursus used to pat the wolf's empty ribs, saying: "I have found the second volume of myself!" Again he said, "When I am dead, any one wishing to know me need only study Homo. I shall leave a true copy behind me."

The English law, not very lenient to beasts of the forest, might have picked a quarrel with the wolf, and have put him to trouble for his assurance in going freely about the towns: but Homo took advantage of the immunity granted by a statute of Edward IV. to servants: "Every servant in attendance on his master is free to come and go." Besides, a certain relaxation of the law had resulted with regard to wolves, in consequence of its being the fashion of the ladies of the Court, under the later Stuarts, to have, instead of dogs, little wolves, called adives, about the size of cats, which were brought from Asia at great cost.

Ursus had communicated to Homo a portion of his talents: such as to stand upright, to restrain his rage into sulkiness, to growl instead of howling, etc.; and on his part, the wolf had taught the man what *he* knew—to do without a roof, without bread and fire, to prefer hunger in the woods to slavery in a palace.

The van, hut, and vehicle in one, which traversed so many different roads, without, however, leaving Great Britain, had four wheels, with shafts for the wolf and a splinter-bar for the man. The splinter-bar came into use when the roads were bad. The van was strong, although it was built of light boards like a dove-cot. In front there was a glass door with a little balcony used for orations, which had something of the character of the platform tempered by an air of the pulpit. At the back there was a door with a practicable panel. By lowering the three steps which turned on a hinge below the door, access was gained to the hut, which at night was securely fastened with bolt and lock. Rain and snow had fallen plentifully on it; it had been painted, but of what colour it was difficult to say, change of season being to vans what changes of reign are to courtiers. In front, outside, was a board, a kind of frontispiece, on which the following inscription might once have been deciphered; it was in black letters on a white ground, but by degrees the characters had become confused and blurred:—

"By friction gold loses every year a fourteen hundredth part of its bulk. This is what is called the Wear. Hence it follows that on fourteen hundred millions of gold in circulation throughout the world, one million is lost annually. This million dissolves into dust, flies away, floats about, is reduced to atoms, charges, drugs, weighs down consciences, amalgamates with the souls of the rich whom it renders proud, and with those of the poor whom it renders brutish."

The inscription, rubbed and blotted by the rain and by the kindness of nature, was fortunately illegible, for it is possible that its philosophy concerning the inhalation of gold, at the same time both enigmatical and lucid, might not have been to the taste of the sheriffs, the provost-marshals, and other big-wigs of the law. English legislation did not trifle in those days. It did not take much to make a man a felon. The magistrates were ferocious by tradition, and cruelty was a matter of routine. The judges of assize increased and multiplied. Jeffreys had become a breed.

III.

In the interior of the van there were two other inscriptions. Above the box, on a whitewashed plank, a hand had written in ink as follows:—

"THE ONLY THINGS NECESSARY TO KNOW.

"The Baron, peer of England, wears a cap with six pearls. The coronet begins with the rank of Viscount. The Viscount wears a coronet of which the pearls are without number. The Earl a coronet with the pearls upon points, mingled with strawberry leaves placed low between. The Marquis, one with pearls and leaves on the same level. The Duke, one with strawberry leaves alone—no pearls. The Royal Duke, a circlet of crosses and fleurs de lys. The Prince of Wales, crown like that of the King, but unclosed.

"The Duke is a most high and most puissant prince, the Marquis and Earl most noble and puissant lord, the Viscount noble and puissant lord, the Baron a trusty lord. The Duke is his Grace; the other Peers their Lordships. *Most honourable* is higher than *right honourable.*

"Lords who are peers are lords in their own right. Lords who are not peers are lords by courtesy:—there are no real lords, excepting such as are peers.

"The House of Lords is a chamber and a court, *Concilium et Curia*, legislature and court of justice. The Commons, who are the people, when ordered to the bar of the Lords, humbly present themselves bareheaded before the peers, who remain covered. The Commons send up their bills by forty members, who present the bill with three low bows. The Lords send their bills to the Commons by a mere clerk. In case of disagreement, the two Houses confer in the Painted Chamber, the Peers seated and covered, the Commons standing and bareheaded.

"Peers go to parliament in their coaches in file; the Commons do not. Some peers go to Westminster in open four-wheeled chariots. The use of these and of coaches emblazoned with coats of arms and coronets is allowed only to peers, and forms a portion of their dignity.

"Barons have the same rank as bishops. To be a baron peer of England, it is necessary to be in possession of a tenure from the king *per Baroniam integram*, by full barony. The full barony consists of thirteen knights' fees and one third part, each knight's fee being of the value of £20 sterling, which makes in all 400 marks. The head of a barony (*Caput baroniæ*) is a castle disposed by inheritance, as England herself, that is to say, descending to daughters if there be no sons, and in that case going to the eldest daughter, *cæteris filiabus aliundè satisfactis.*[1]

"Barons have the degree of lord: in Saxon, *laford; dominus* in high Latin; *Lordus* in low Latin. The eldest and younger sons of viscounts and barons are the first esquires in the kingdom. The eldest sons of peers take precedence of knights of the garter. The younger sons do not. The eldest son of a viscount comes after all barons, and precedes all baronets. Every daughter of a peer is a *Lady*. Other English girls are plain *Mistress.*

"All judges rank below peers. The serjeant wears a lambskin tippet; the judge one of patchwork, *de minuto vario*, made up of a variety of little white furs, always excepting ermine. Ermine is reserved for peers and the king.

"A lord never takes an oath, either to the crown or the law. His word suffices; he says, Upon my honour.

"By a law of Edward the Sixth, peers have the privilege of committing manslaughter. A peer who kills a man without premeditation is not prosecuted.

"The persons of peers are inviolable.

"A peer cannot be held in durance, save in the Tower of London.

"A writ of supplicavit cannot be granted against a peer.

"A peer sent for by the king has the right to kill one or two deer in the royal park.

"A peer holds in his castle a baron's court of justice.

"It is unworthy of a peer to walk the street in a cloak, followed by two footmen. He should only show himself attended by a great train of gentlemen of his household.

"A peer can be amerced only by his peers, and never to any greater amount than five pounds, excepting in the case of a duke, who can be amerced ten.

"A peer may retain six aliens born, any other Englishman but four.

"A peer can have wine custom-free; an earl eight tuns.

"A peer is alone exempt from presenting himself before the sheriff of the circuit.

"A peer cannot be assessed towards the militia.

"When it pleases a peer he raises a regiment and gives it to the king; thus have done their graces the Dukes of Athol, Hamilton, and Northumberland.

"A peer can hold only of a peer.

"In a civil cause he can demand the adjournment of the case, if there be not at least one knight on the jury.

"A peer nominates his own chaplains. A baron appoints three chaplains; a viscount four; an earl and a marquis five; a duke six.

"A peer cannot be put to the rack, even for high treason. A peer cannot be branded on the hand. A peer is a clerk, though he knows not how to read. In law he knows.

"A duke has a right to a canopy, or cloth of state, in all places where the king is not present; a viscount may have one in his house; a baron has a cover of assay, which may be held under his cup while he drinks. A baroness has the right to have her train borne by a man in the presence of a viscountess.

"Eighty-six tables, with five hundred dishes, are served every day in the royal palace at each meal.

"If a plebeian strike a lord, his hand is cut off.

"A lord is very nearly a king.

"The king is very nearly a god.

"The earth is a lordship.

"The English address God as my lord!"

Opposite this writing was written a second one, in the same fashion, which ran thus:—

"SATISFACTION WHICH MUST SUFFICE THOSE WHO HAVE NOTHING.

"Henry Auverquerque, Earl of Grantham, who sits in the House of Lords between the Earl of Jersey and the Earl of Greenwich, has a hundred thousand a year. To his lordship belongs the palace of Grantham Terrace, built all of marble and famous for what is called the labyrinth of passages—a curiosity which contains the scarlet corridor in marble of Sarancolin, the brown corridor in lumachel of Astracan, the white corridor in marble of Lani, the black corridor in marble of Alabanda, the gray corridor in marble of Staremma, the yellow corridor in marble of Hesse, the green corridor in marble of the Tyrol, the red corridor, half cherry-spotted marble of Bohemia, half lumachel of Cordova, the blue corridor in turquin of Genoa, the violet in granite of Catalonia, the mourning-hued corridor veined black and white in slate of Murviedro, the pink corridor in cipolin of the Alps, the pearl corridor in lumachel of Nonetta, and the corridor of all colours, called the courtiers' corridor, in motley.

"Richard Lowther, Viscount Lonsdale, owns Lowther in Westmorland, which has a magnificent approach, and a flight of entrance steps which seem to invite the ingress of kings.

"Richard, Earl of Scarborough, Viscount and Baron Lumley of Lumley Castle, Viscount Lumley of Waterford in Ireland, and Lord Lieutenant and Vice-Admiral of the county of Northumberland and of Durham, both city and county, owns the double castleward of old and new Sandbeck, where you admire a superb railing, in the form of a semicircle, surrounding the basin of a matchless fountain. He has, besides, his castle of Lumley.

"Robert Darcy, Earl of Holderness, has his domain of Holderness, with baronial towers, and large gardens laid out in French fashion, where he drives in his coach-and-six, preceded by two outriders, as becomes a peer of England.

"Charles Beauclerc, Duke of St. Albans, Earl of Burford, Baron Hedington, Grand Falconer of England, has an abode at Windsor, regal even by the side of the king's.

"Charles Bodville Robartes, Baron Robartes of Truro, Viscount Bodmin and Earl of Radnor, owns Wimpole in Cambridgeshire, which is as three palaces in one, having three façades, one bowed and two triangular. The approach is by an avenue of trees four deep.

"The most noble and most puissant Lord Philip, Baron Herbert of Cardiff, Earl of Montgomery and of Pembroke, Ross of Kendall, Parr, Fitzhugh, Marmion, St. Quentin, and Herbert of Shurland, Warden of the Stannaries in the counties of Cornwall and Devon, hereditary visitor of Jesus College, possesses the wonderful gardens at Wilton, where there are two sheaf-like fountains, finer than those of his most Christian Majesty King Louis XIV. at Versailles.

"Charles Somerset, Duke of Somerset, owns Somerset House on the Thames, which is equal to the Villa Pamphili at Rome. On the chimney-piece are seen two porcelain vases of the dynasty of the Yuens, which are worth half a million in French money.

"In Yorkshire, Arthur, Lord Ingram, Viscount Irwin, has Temple Newsain, which is entered under a triumphal arch and which has large wide roofs resembling Moorish terraces.

"Robert, Lord Ferrers of Chartly, Bourchier, and Lonvaine, has Staunton Harold in Leicestershire, of which the park is geometrically planned in the shape of a temple with a façade, and in front of the piece of water is the great church with the square belfry, which belongs to his lordship.

"In the county of Northampton, Charles Spencer, Earl of Sunderland, member of his Majesty's Privy Council, possesses Althorp, at the entrance of which is a railing with four columns surmounted by groups in marble.

"Laurence Hyde, Earl of Rochester, has, in Surrey, New Park, rendered magnificent by its sculptured pinnacles, its circular lawn belted by trees, and its woodland, at the extremity of which is a little mountain, artistically rounded, and surmounted by a large oak, which can be seen from afar.

"Philip Stanhope, Earl of Chesterfield, possesses Bretby Hall in Derbyshire, with a splendid clock tower, falconries, warrens, and very fine sheets of water, long, square, and oval, one of which is shaped like a mirror, and has two jets, which throw the water to a great height.

"Charles Cornwallis, Baron Cornwallis of Eye, owns Broome Hall, a palace of the fourteenth century.

"The most noble Algernon Capel, Viscount Maiden, Earl of Essex, has Cashiobury in Hertfordshire, a seat which has the shape of a capital H, and which rejoices sportsmen with its abundance of game.

"Charles, Lord Ossulston, owns Darnley in Middlesex, approached by Italian gardens.

"James Cecil, Earl of Salisbury, has, seven leagues from London, Hatfield House, with its four lordly pavilions, its belfry in the centre, and its grand courtyard of black and white slabs, like that of St. Germain. This palace, which has a frontage 272 feet in length, was built in the reign of James I. by the Lord High Treasurer of England, the great-grandfather of the present earl. To be seen there is the bed of one of the Countesses of Salisbury: it is of inestimable value and made entirely of Brazilian wood, which is a panacea against the bites of serpents, and which is called *milhombres*—that is to say, a thousand men. On this bed is inscribed, *Honi soit qui mal y pense.*

"Edward Rich, Earl of Warwick and Holland, is owner of Warwick Castle, where whole oaks are burnt in the fireplaces.

"In the parish of Sevenoaks, Charles Sackville, Baron Buckhurst, Baron Cranfield, Earl of Dorset and Middlesex, is owner of Knowle, which is as large as a town and is composed of three palaces standing parallel one behind the other, like ranks of infantry. There are six covered flights of steps on the principal frontage, and a gate under a keep with four towers.

"Thomas Thynne, Baron Thynne of Warminster, and Viscount Weymouth, possesses Longleat, in which there are as many chimneys, cupolas, pinnacles, pepper-boxes pavilions, and turrets as at Chambord, in France, which belongs to the king.

"Henry Howard, Earl of Suffolk, owns, twelve leagues from London, the palace of Audley End in Essex, which in grandeur and dignity scarcely yields the palm to the Escorial of the King of Spain.

"In Bedfordshire, Wrest House and Park, which is a whole district, enclosed by ditches, walls, woodlands, rivers, and hills, belongs to Henry, Marquis of Kent.

"Hampton Court, in Herefordshire, with its strong embattled keep, and its gardens bounded by a piece of water which divides them from the forest, belongs to Thomas, Lord Coningsby.

"Grimsthorp, in Lincolnshire, with its long façade intersected by turrets in pale, its park, its fish-ponds, its pheasantries, its sheepfolds, its lawns, its grounds planted with rows of trees, its groves, its walks, its shrubberies, its flower-beds and borders, formed in square and lozenge-shape, and resembling great carpets; its racecourses, and the majestic sweep for carriages to turn in at the entrance of the house—belongs to Robert, Earl Lindsey, hereditary lord of the forest of Waltham.

"Up Park, in Sussex, a square house, with two symmetrical belfried pavilions on each side of the great courtyard, belongs to the Right Honourable Forde, Baron Grey of Werke, Viscount Glendale and Earl of Tankerville.

"Newnham Paddox, in Warwickshire, which has two quadrangular fish-ponds and a gabled archway with a large window of four panes, belongs to the Earl of Denbigh, who is also Count von Rheinfelden, in Germany.

"Wytham Abbey, in Berkshire, with its French garden in which there are four curiously trimmed arbours, and its great embattled towers, supported by two bastions, belongs to Montague, Earl of Abingdon, who also owns Rycote, of which he is Baron, and the principal door of which bears the device *Virtus ariete fortior.*

"William Cavendish, Duke of Devonshire, has six dwelling-places, of which Chatsworth (two storied, and of the finest order of Grecian architecture) is one.

"The Viscount of Kinalmeaky, who is Earl of Cork, in Ireland, is owner of Burlington House, Piccadilly, with its extensive gardens, reaching to the fields outside London; he is also owner of Chiswick, where there are nine magnificent lodges; he also owns Londesborough, which is a new house by the side of an old palace.

"The Duke of Beaufort owns Chelsea, which contains two Gothic buildings, and a Florentine one; he has also Badminton, in Gloucestershire, a residence from which a number of avenues branch out like rays from a star. The most noble and puissant Prince Henry, Duke of Beaufort, is also Marquis and Earl of Worcester, Earl of Glamorgan, Viscount Grosmont, and Baron Herbert of Chepstow, Ragland, and Gower, Baron Beaufort of Caldecott Castle, and Baron de Bottetourt.

"John Holies, Duke of Newcastle, and Marquis of Clare, owns Bolsover, with its majestic square keeps; his also is Haughton, in Nottinghamshire, where a round pyramid, made to imitate the Tower of Babel, stands in the centre of a basin of water.

"William, Earl of Craven, Viscount Uffington, and Baron Craven of Hamstead Marshall, owns Combe Abbey in Warwickshire, where is to be seen the finest water-jet in England; and in Berkshire two baronies, Hamstead Marshall, on the façade of which are five Gothic lanterns sunk in the wall, and Ashdown Park, which is a country seat situate at the point of intersection of cross-roads in a forest.

"Linnæus, Lord Clancharlie, Baron Clancharlie and Hunkerville, Marquis of Corleone in Sicily, derives his title from the castle of Clancharlie, built in 912 by Edward the Elder, as a defence against the Danes. Besides Hunkerville House, in London, which is a palace, he has Corleone Lodge at Windsor, which is another, and eight castlewards, one at Burton-on-Trent, with a royalty on the carriage of plaster of Paris; then Grumdaith Humble, Moricambe, Trewardraith, Hell-Kerters (where there is a miraculous well), Phillinmore, with its turf bogs, Reculver, near the ancient city Vagniac, Vinecaunton, on the Moel-eulle Mountain; besides nineteen boroughs and villages with reeves, and the whole of Penneth chase, all of which bring his lordship £40,000 a year.

"The 172 peers enjoying their dignities under James II. possess among them altogether a revenue of £1,272,000 sterling a year, which is the eleventh part of the revenue of England."

In the margin, opposite the last name (that of Linnæus, Lord Clancharlie), there was a note in the handwriting of Ursus: *Rebel; in exile; houses, lands, and chattels sequestrated. It is well.*

IV.

Ursus admired Homo. One admires one's like. It is a law. To be always raging inwardly and grumbling outwardly was the normal condition of Ursus. He was the malcontent of creation. By nature he was a man ever in opposition. He took the world unkindly; he gave his satisfecit to no one and to nothing. The bee did not atone, by its honey-making, for its sting; a full-blown rose did not absolve the sun for yellow fever and black vomit. It is probable that in secret Ursus criticized Providence a good deal. "Evidently," he would say, "the devil works by a spring, and the wrong that God does is having let go the trigger." He approved of none but princes, and he had his own peculiar way of expressing his approbation. One day, when James II. made a gift to the Virgin in a Catholic chapel in Ireland of a massive gold lamp, Ursus, passing that way with Homo, who was more indifferent to such things, broke out in admiration before the crowd, and exclaimed, "It is certain that the blessed Virgin wants a lamp much more than these barefooted children there require shoes."

Such proofs of his loyalty, and such evidences of his respect for established powers, probably contributed in no small degree to make the magistrates tolerate his vagabond life and his low alliance with a wolf. Sometimes of an evening, through the weakness of friendship, he allowed Homo to stretch his limbs and wander at liberty about the caravan. The wolf was incapable of an abuse of confidence, and behaved in society, that is to say among men, with the discretion of a poodle. All the same, if bad-tempered officials had to be dealt with, difficulties might have arisen; so Ursus kept the honest wolf chained up as much as possible.

From a political point of view, his writing about gold, not very intelligible in itself, and now become undecipherable, was but a smear, and gave no handle to the enemy. Even after the time of James II., and under the "respectable" reign of William and Mary, his caravan might have been seen peacefully going its rounds of the little English country towns. He travelled freely from one end of Great Britain to the other, selling his philtres and phials, and sustaining, with the assistance of his wolf, his quack mummeries; and he passed with ease through the meshes of the nets which the police at that period had spread all over England in order to sift wandering gangs, and especially to stop the progress of the Comprachicos.

This was right enough. Ursus belonged to no gang. Ursus lived with Ursus, a *tête-à-tête*, into which the wolf gently thrust his nose. If Ursus could have had his way, he would have been a Caribbee; that being impossible, he preferred to be alone. The solitary man is a modified savage, accepted by civilization. He who wanders most is most alone; hence his continual change of place. To remain anywhere long suffocated him with the sense of being tamed. He passed his life in passing on his way. The sight of towns increased his taste for brambles, thickets, thorns, and holes in the rock. His home was the forest. He did not feel himself much out of his element in the murmur of crowded streets, which is like enough to the bluster of trees. The crowd to some extent satisfies our taste for the desert. What he disliked in his van was its having a door and windows, and thus resembling a house. He would have realized his ideal, had he been able to put a cave on four wheels and travel in a den.

He did not smile, as we have already said, but he used to laugh; sometimes, indeed frequently, a bitter laugh. There is consent in a smile, while a laugh is often a refusal.

His great business was to hate the human race. He was implacable in that hate. Having made it clear that human life is a dreadful thing; having observed the superposition of evils, kings on the people, war on kings, the plague on war, famine on the plague, folly on everything; having proved a certain measure of chastisement in the mere fact of existence; having recognized that, death is a deliverance—when they brought him a sick man he cured him; he had cordials and beverages to prolong the lives of the old. He put lame cripples on their legs again, and hurled this sarcasm at them, "There, you are on your paws once more; may you walk long in this valley of tears!" When he saw a poor man dying of hunger, he gave him all the pence he had about him, growling out, "Live on, you wretch! eat! last a long time! It is not I who would shorten your penal servitude." After which, he would rub his hands and say, "I do men all the harm I can."

Through the little window at the back, passers-by could read on the ceiling of the van these words, written within, but visible from without, inscribed with charcoal, in big letters,—

URSUS, PHILOSOPHER.

ANOTHER PRELIMINARY CHAPTER

THE COMPRACHICOS

I.

Who now knows the word Comprachicos, and who knows its meaning?

The Comprachicos, or Comprapequeños, were a hideous and nondescript association of wanderers, famous in the 17th century, forgotten in the 18th, unheard of in the 19th. The Comprachicos are like the "succession powder," an ancient social characteristic detail. They are part of old human ugliness. To the great eye of history, which sees everything collectively, the Comprachicos belong to the colossal fact of slavery. Joseph sold by his brethren is a chapter in their story. The Comprachicos have left their traces in the penal laws of Spain and England. You find here and there in the dark confusion of English laws the impress of this horrible truth, like the foot-print of a savage in a forest.

Comprachicos, the same as Comprapequeños, is a compound Spanish word signifying Child-buyers.

The Comprachicos traded in children. They bought and sold them. They did not steal them. The kidnapping of children is another branch of industry. And what did they make of these children?

Monsters.

Why monsters?

To laugh at.

The populace must needs laugh, and kings too. The mountebank is wanted in the streets, the jester at the Louvre. The one is called a Clown, the other a Fool.

The efforts of man to procure himself pleasure are at times worthy of the attention of the philosopher.

What are we sketching in these few preliminary pages? A chapter in the most terrible of books; a book which might be entitled—*The farming of the unhappy by the happy*.

II.

A child destined to be a plaything for men—such a thing has existed; such a thing exists even now. In simple and savage times such a thing constituted an especial trade. The 17th century, called the great century, was of those times. It was a century very Byzantine in tone. It combined corrupt simplicity with delicate ferocity—a curious variety of civilization. A tiger with a simper. Madame de Sevigné minces on the subject of the fagot and the wheel. That century traded a good deal in children. Flattering historians have concealed the sore, but have divulged the remedy, Vincent de Paul.

In order that a human toy should succeed, he must be taken early. The dwarf must be fashioned when young. We play with childhood. But a well-formed child is not very amusing; a hunchback is better fun.

Hence grew an art. There were trainers who took a man and made him an abortion; they took a face and made a muzzle; they stunted growth; they kneaded the features. The artificial production of teratological cases had its rules. It was quite a science—what one can imagine as the antithesis of orthopedy. Where God had put a look, their art put a squint; where God had made harmony, they made discord; where God had made the perfect picture, they re-established the sketch; and, in the eyes of connoisseurs, it was the sketch which was perfect. They debased animals as well; they invented piebald horses. Turenne rode a piebald horse. In our own days do they not dye dogs blue and green? Nature is our canvas. Man has always wished to add something to God's work. Man retouches creation, sometimes for better, sometimes for worse. The Court buffoon was nothing but an attempt to lead back man to the monkey. It was a progress the wrong way. A masterpiece in retrogression. At the same time they tried to make a man of the monkey. Barbara, Duchess of Cleveland and Countess of Southampton, had a marmoset for a page. Frances Sutton, Baroness Dudley, eighth peeress in the bench of barons, had tea served by a baboon clad in cold brocade, which her ladyship called My Black. Catherine Sedley, Countess of Dorchester, used to go and take her seat in Parliament in a coach with armorial bearings, behind which stood, their muzzles stuck up in the air, three Cape monkeys in grand livery. A Duchess of Medina-Celi, whose toilet Cardinal Pole witnessed, had her stockings put on by an orang-outang. These monkeys raised in the scale were a counterpoise to men brutalized and bestialized. This promiscuousness of man and beast, desired by the great, was especially prominent in the case of the dwarf and the dog. The dwarf never quitted the dog, which was always bigger than himself. The dog was the pair of the dwarf; it was as if they were coupled with a collar. This juxtaposition is authenticated by a mass of domestic records—notably by the portrait of Jeffrey Hudson, dwarf of Henrietta of France, daughter of Henri IV., and wife of Charles I.

To degrade man tends to deform him. The suppression of his state was completed by disfigurement. Certain vivisectors of that period succeeded marvellously well in effacing from the human face the divine effigy. Doctor Conquest, member of the Amen Street College, and judicial visitor of the chemists' shops of London, wrote a book in Latin on this pseudo-surgery, the processes of which he describes. If we are to believe Justus of Carrickfergus, the inventor of this branch of surgery was a monk named Avonmore—an Irish word signifying Great River.

The dwarf of the Elector Palatine, Perkeo, whose effigy—or ghost—springs from a magical box in the cave of Heidelberg, was a remarkable specimen of this science, very varied in its applications. It fashioned beings the law of whose existence was hideously simple: it permitted them to suffer, and commanded them to amuse.

III.

The manufacture of monsters was practised on a large scale, and comprised various branches.

The Sultan required them, so did the Pope; the one to guard his women, the other to say his prayers. These were of a peculiar kind, incapable of reproduction. Scarcely human beings, they were useful to voluptuousness and to religion. The seraglio and the Sistine Chapel utilized the same species of monsters; fierce in the former case, mild in the latter.

They knew how to produce things in those days which are not produced now; they had talents which we lack, and it is not without reason that some good folk cry out that the decline has come. We no longer know how to sculpture living human flesh; this is consequent on the loss of the art of torture. Men were once virtuosi in that respect, but are so no longer; the art has become so simplified that it will soon disappear altogether. In cutting the limbs of living men, in opening their bellies and in dragging out their entrails, phenomena were grasped on the moment and discoveries made. We are obliged to renounce these experiments now, and are thus deprived of the progress which surgery made by aid of the executioner.

The vivisection of former days was not limited to the manufacture of phenomena for the market-place, of buffoons for the palace (a species of augmentative of the courtier), and eunuchs for sultans and popes. It abounded in varieties. One of its triumphs was the manufacture of cocks for the king of England.

It was the custom, in the palace of the kings of England, to have a sort of watchman, who crowed like a cock. This watcher, awake while all others slept, ranged the palace, and raised from hour to hour the cry of the farmyard, repeating it as often as was necessary, and thus supplying a clock. This man, promoted to be cock, had in childhood undergone the operation of the pharynx, which was part of the art described by Dr. Conquest. Under Charles II. the salivation inseparable to the operation having disgusted the Duchess of Portsmouth, the appointment was indeed preserved, so that the splendour of the crown should not be tarnished, but they got an unmutilated man to represent the cock. A retired officer was generally selected for this honourable employment. Under James II. the functionary was named William Sampson, Cock, and received for his crow £9, 2s. 6d. annually.

The memoirs of Catherine II. inform us that at St. Petersburg, scarcely a hundred years since, whenever the czar or czarina was displeased with a Russian prince, he was forced to squat down in the great antechamber of the palace, and to remain in that posture a certain number of days, mewing like a cat, or clucking like a sitting hen, and pecking his food from the floor.

These fashions have passed away; but not so much, perhaps, as one might imagine. Nowadays, courtiers slightly modify their intonation in clucking to please their masters. More than one picks up from the ground—we will not say from the mud—what he eats.

It is very fortunate that kings cannot err. Hence their contradictions never perplex us. In approving always, one is sure to be always right—which is pleasant. Louis XIV. would not have liked to see at Versailles either an officer acting the cock, or a prince acting the turkey. That which raised the royal and imperial dignity in England and Russia would have seemed to Louis the Great incompatible with the crown of St. Louis. We know what his displeasure was when Madame Henriette forgot herself so far as to see a hen in a dream—which was, indeed, a grave breach of good manners in a lady of the court. When one is of the court, one should not dream of the courtyard. Bossuet, it may be remembered, was nearly as scandalized as Louis XIV.

IV.

The commerce in children in the 17th century, as we have explained, was connected with a trade. The Comprachicos engaged in the commerce, and carried on the trade. They bought children, worked a little on the raw material, and resold them afterwards.

The venders were of all kinds: from the wretched father, getting rid of his family, to the master, utilizing his stud of slaves. The sale of men was a simple matter. In our own time we have had fighting to maintain this right. Remember that it is less than a century ago since the Elector of Hesse sold his subjects to the King of England, who required men to be killed in America. Kings went to the Elector of Hesse as we go to the butcher to buy meat. The Elector had food for powder in stock, and hung up his subjects in his shop. Come buy; it is for sale. In England, under Jeffreys, after the tragical episode of Monmouth, there were many lords and gentlemen beheaded and quartered. Those who were executed left wives and daughters, widows and orphans, whom James II. gave to the queen, his wife. The queen sold these ladies to William Penn. Very likely the king had so much per cent. on the transaction. The extraordinary thing is, not that James II. should have sold the women, but that William Penn should have bought them. Penn's purchase is excused, or explained, by the fact that having a desert to sow with men, he needed women as farming implements.

Her Gracious Majesty made a good business out of these ladies. The young sold dear. We may imagine, with the uneasy feeling which a complicated scandal arouses, that probably some old duchesses were thrown in cheap.

The Comprachicos were also called the Cheylas, a Hindu word, which conveys the image of harrying a nest.

For a long time the Comprachicos only partially concealed themselves. There is sometimes in the social order a favouring shadow thrown over iniquitous trades, in which they thrive. In our own day we have seen an association of the kind in Spain, under the direction of the ruffian Ramon Selles, last from 1834 to 1866, and hold three provinces under terror for thirty years—Valencia, Alicante, and Murcia.

Under the Stuarts, the Comprachicos were by no means in bad odour at court. On occasions they were used for reasons of state. For James II. they were almost an *instrumentum regni*. It was a time when families, which were refractory or in the way, were dismembered; when a descent was cut short; when heirs were suddenly suppressed. At times one branch was defrauded to the profit of another. The Comprachicos had a genius for disfiguration which recommended them to state policy. To disfigure is better than to kill. There was, indeed, the Iron Mask, but that was a mighty measure. Europe could not be peopled with iron masks, while deformed tumblers ran about the streets without creating any surprise. Besides, the iron mask is removable; not so the mask of flesh. You are masked for ever by your own flesh—what can be more ingenious? The Comprachicos worked on man as the Chinese work on trees. They had their secrets, as we have said; they had tricks which are now lost arts. A sort of fantastic stunted thing left their hands; it was ridiculous and wonderful. They would touch up a little being with such skill that its father could not have known it. *Et que méconnaîtrait l'oeil même de son père*, as Racine says in bad French. Sometimes they left the spine straight and remade the face. They unmarked a child as one might unmark a pocket-handkerchief. Products, destined for tumblers, had their joints dislocated in a masterly manner—you would have said they had been boned. Thus gymnasts were made.

Not only did the Comprachicos take away his face from the child, they also took away his memory. At least they took away all they could of it; the child had no consciousness of the mutilation to which he had been subjected. This frightful surgery left its traces on his countenance, but not on his mind. The most he could recall was that one day he had been seized by men, that next he had fallen asleep, and then that he had been cured. Cured of what? He did not know. Of burnings by sulphur and incisions by the iron he remembered nothing. The Comprachicos deadened the little patient by means of a stupefying powder which was thought to be magical, and suppressed all pain. This powder has been known from time immemorial in China, and is still employed there in the present day. The Chinese have been beforehand with us in all our inventions—printing, artillery, aerostation, chloroform. Only the discovery which in Europe at once takes life and birth, and becomes a prodigy and a wonder, remains a chrysalis in China, and is preserved in a deathlike state. China is a museum of embryos.

Since we are in China, let us remain there a moment to note a peculiarity. In China, from time immemorial, they have possessed a certain refinement of industry and art. It is the art of moulding a living man. They take a child, two or three years old, put him in a porcelain vase, more or less grotesque, which is made without top or bottom, to allow egress for the head and feet. During the day the vase is set upright, and at night is laid down to allow the child to sleep. Thus the child thickens without growing taller, filling up with his compressed flesh and distorted bones the reliefs in the vase. This development in a bottle continues many years. After a certain time it becomes irreparable. When they consider that this is accomplished, and the monster made, they break the vase. The child comes out—and, behold, there is a man in the shape of a mug!

This is convenient: by ordering your dwarf betimes you are able to have it of any shape you wish.

V.

James II. tolerated the Comprachicos for the good reason that he made use of them; at least it happened that he did so more than once. We do not always disdain to use what we despise. This low trade, an excellent expedient sometimes for the higher one which is called state policy, was willingly left in a miserable state, but was not persecuted. There was no surveillance, but a certain amount of attention. Thus much might be useful—the law closed one eye, the king opened the other.

Sometimes the king went so far as to avow his complicity. These are audacities of monarchical terrorism. The disfigured one was marked with the fleur-de-lis; they took from him the mark of God; they put on him the mark of the king. Jacob Astley, knight and baronet, lord of Melton Constable, in the county of Norfolk, had in his family a child who had been sold, and upon whose forehead the dealer had imprinted a fleur-de-lis with a hot iron. In certain cases in which it was held desirable to register for some reason the royal origin of the new position made for the child, they used such means. England has always done us the honour to utilize, for her personal service, the fleur-de-lis.

The Comprachicos, allowing for the shade which divides a trade from a fanaticism, were analogous to the Stranglers of India. They lived among themselves in gangs, and to facilitate their progress, affected somewhat of the merry-andrew. They encamped here and there, but they were grave and religious, bearing no affinity to other nomads, and incapable of theft. The people for a long time wrongly confounded them with the Moors of Spain and the Moors of China. The Moors of Spain were coiners, the Moors of China were thieves. There was nothing of the sort about the Comprachicos; they were honest folk. Whatever you may think of them, they were sometimes sincerely scrupulous. They pushed open a door, entered, bargained for a child, paid, and departed. All was done with propriety.

They were of all countries. Under the name of Comprachicos fraternized English, French, Castilians, Germans, Italians. A unity of idea, a unity of superstition, the pursuit of the same calling, make such fusions. In this fraternity of vagabonds, those of the Mediterranean seaboard represented the East, those of the Atlantic seaboard the West. Many Basques conversed with many Irishmen. The Basque and the Irishman understand each other—they speak the old Punic jargon; add to this the intimate relations of Catholic Ireland with Catholic Spain—relations such that they terminated by bringing to the gallows in London one almost King of Ireland, the Celtic Lord de Brany; from which resulted the conquest of the county of Leitrim.

The Comprachicos were rather a fellowship than a tribe; rather a residuum than a fellowship. It was all the riffraff of the universe, having for their trade a crime. It was a sort of harlequin people, all composed of rags. To recruit a man was to sew on a tatter.

To wander was the Comprachicos' law of existence—to appear and disappear. What is barely tolerated cannot take root. Even in the kingdoms where their business supplied the courts, and, on occasions, served as an auxiliary to the royal power, they were now and then suddenly ill-treated. Kings made use of their art, and sent the artists to the galleys. These inconsistencies belong to the ebb and flow of royal caprice. "For such is our pleasure."

A rolling stone and a roving trade gather no moss. The Comprachicos were poor. They might have said what the lean and ragged witch observed, when she saw them setting fire to the stake, "Le jeu n'en vaut pas la chandelle." It is possible, nay probable (their chiefs remaining unknown), that the wholesale contractors in the trade were rich. After the lapse of two centuries, it would be difficult to throw any light on this point.

It was, as we have said, a fellowship. It had its laws, its oaths, its formulæ—it had almost its cabala. Any one nowadays wishing to know all about the Comprachicos need only go into Biscaya or Galicia; there were many Basques among them, and it is in those mountains that one hears their history. To this day the Comprachicos are spoken of at Oyarzun, at Urbistondo, at Leso, at Astigarraga. *Aguardate niño, que voy a llamar al Comprachicos*—Take care, child, or I'll call the Comprachicos—is the cry with which mothers frighten their children in that country.

The Comprachicos, like the Zigeuner and the Gipsies, had appointed places for periodical meetings. From time to time their leaders conferred together. In the seventeenth century they had four principal points of rendezvous: one in Spain—the pass of Pancorbo; one in Germany—the glade called the Wicked Woman, near Diekirsch, where there are two enigmatic bas-reliefs, representing a woman with a head and a man without one; one in France—the hill where was the colossal statue of Massue-la-Promesse in the old sacred wood of Borvo Tomona, near Bourbonne les Bains; one in England—behind the garden wall of William Challoner, Squire of Gisborough in Cleveland, Yorkshire, behind the square tower and the great wing which is entered by an arched door.

VI.

The laws against vagabonds have always been very rigorous in England. England, in her Gothic legislation, seemed to be inspired with this principle, *Homo errans fera errante pejor.* One of the special statutes classifies the man without a home as "more dangerous than the asp, dragon, lynx, or basilisk" (*atrocior aspide, dracone, lynce, et basilico*). For a long time England troubled herself as much concerning the gipsies, of whom she wished to be rid as about the wolves of which she had been cleared. In that the Englishman differed from the Irishman, who prayed to the saints for the health of the wolf, and called him "my godfather."

English law, nevertheless, in the same way as (we have just seen) it tolerated the wolf, tamed, domesticated, and become in some sort a dog, tolerated the regular vagabond, become in some sort a subject. It did not trouble itself about either the mountebank or the travelling barber, or the quack doctor, or the peddler, or the open-air scholar, as long as they had a trade to live by. Further than this, and with these exceptions, the description of freedom which exists in the wanderer terrified the law. A tramp was a possible public enemy. That modern thing, the lounger, was then unknown; that ancient thing, the vagrant, was alone understood. A suspicious appearance, that indescribable something which all understand and none can define, was sufficient reason that society should take a man by the collar. "Where do you live? How do you get your living?" And if he could not answer, harsh penalties awaited him. Iron and fire were in the code: the law practised the cauterization of vagrancy.

Hence, throughout English territory, a veritable "loi des suspects" was applicable to vagrants (who, it must be owned, readily became malefactors), and particularly to gipsies, whose expulsion has erroneously been compared to the expulsion of the Jews and the Moors from Spain, and the Protestants from France. As for us, we do not confound a battue with a persecution.

The Comprachicos, we insist, had nothing in common with the gipsies. The gipsies were a nation; the Comprachicos were a compound of all nations—the lees of a horrible vessel full of filthy waters. The Comprachicos had not, like the gipsies, an idiom of their own; their jargon was a promiscuous collection of idioms: all languages were mixed together in their language; they spoke a medley. Like the gipsies, they had come to be a people winding through the peoples; but their common tie was association, not race. At all epochs in history one finds in the vast liquid mass which constitutes humanity some of these streams of venomous men exuding poison around them. The gipsies were a tribe; the Comprachicos a freemasonry—a masonry having not a noble aim, but a hideous handicraft. Finally, their religions differ—the gipsies were Pagans, the Comprachicos were Christians, and more than that, good Christians, as became an association which, although a mixture of all nations, owed its birth to Spain, a devout land.

They were more than Christians, they were Catholics; they were more than Catholics, they were Romans, and so touchy in their faith, and so pure, that they refused to associate with the Hungarian nomads of the comitate of Pesth, commanded and led by an old man, having for sceptre a wand with a silver ball, surmounted by the double-headed Austrian eagle. It is true that these Hungarians were schismatics, to the extent of celebrating the Assumption on the 29th August, which is an abomination.

In England, so long as the Stuarts reigned, the confederation of the Comprachicos was (for motives of which we have already given you a glimpse) to a certain extent protected. James II., a devout man, who persecuted the Jews and trampled out the gipsies, was a good prince to the Comprachicos. We have seen why. The Comprachicos were buyers of the human wares in which he was dealer. They excelled in disappearances. Disappearances are occasionally necessary for the good of the state. An inconvenient heir of tender age whom they took and handled lost his shape. This facilitated confiscation; the tranfer of titles to favourites was simplified. The Comprachicos were, moreover, very discreet and very taciturn. They bound themselves to silence, and kept their word, which is necessary in affairs of state. There was scarcely an example of their having betrayed the secrets of the king. This was, it is true, for their interest; and if the king had lost confidence in them, they would have been in great danger. They were thus of use in a political point of view. Moreover these artists furnished singers for the Holy Father. The Comprachicos were useful for the *Miserere* of Allegri. They were particularly devoted to Mary. All this pleased the papistry of the Stuarts. James II. could not be hostile to holy men who pushed their devotion to the Virgin to the extent of manufacturing eunuchs. In 1688 there was a change of dynasty in England: Orange supplanted Stuart. William III. replaced James II.

James II. went away to die in exile, miracles were performed on his tomb, and his relics cured the Bishop of Autun of fistula—a worthy recompense of the Christian virtues of the prince.

William, having neither the same ideas nor the same practices as James, was severe to the Comprachicos. He did his best to crush out the vermin.

A statute of the early part of William and Mary's reign hit the association of child-buyers hard. It was as the blow of a club to the Comprachicos, who were from that time pulverized. By the terms of this statute those of the fellowship taken and duly convicted were to be branded with a red-hot iron, imprinting R. on the shoulder, signifying rogue; on the left hand T, signifying thief; and on the right hand M, signifying man-slayer. The chiefs, "supposed to be rich, although beggars in appearance," were to be punished in the *collistrigium*—that is, the pillory—and branded on the forehead with a P, besides having their goods confiscated, and the trees in their woods rooted up. Those who did not inform against the Comprachicos were to be punished by confiscation and imprisonment for life, as for the crime of misprision. As for the women found among these men, they were to suffer the cucking-stool—this is a tumbrel, the name of which is composed of the French word *coquine*, and the German *stuhl*. English law being endowed with a strange longevity, this punishment still exists in English legislation for quarrelsome women. The cucking-stool is suspended over a river or a pond, the woman seated on it. The chair is allowed to drop into the water, and then pulled out. This dipping of the woman is repeated three times, "to cool her anger," says the commentator, Chamberlayne.

PART I.

BOOK THE FIRST

NIGHT NOT SO BLACK AS MAN

CHAPTER I.

PORTLAND BILL

An obstinate north wind blew without ceasing over the mainland of Europe, and yet more roughly over England, during all the month of December, 1689, and all the month of January, 1690. Hence the disastrous cold weather, which caused that winter to be noted as "memorable to the poor," on the margin of the old Bible in the Presbyterian chapel of the Nonjurors in London. Thanks to the lasting qualities of the old monarchical parchment employed in official registers, long lists of poor persons, found dead of famine and cold, are still legible in many local repositories, particularly in the archives of the Liberty of the Clink, in the borough of Southwark, of Pie Powder Court (which signifies Dusty Feet Court), and in those of Whitechapel Court, held in the village of Stepney by the bailiff of the Lord of the Manor. The Thames was frozen over—a thing which does not happen once in a century, as the ice forms on it with difficulty owing to the action of the sea. Coaches rolled over the frozen river, and a fair was held with booths, bear-baiting, and bull-baiting. An ox was roasted whole on the ice. This thick ice lasted two months. The hard year 1690 surpassed in severity even the famous winters at the beginning of the seventeenth century, so minutely observed by Dr. Gideon Delane—the same who was, in his quality of apothecary to King James, honoured by the city of London with a bust and a pedestal.

One evening, towards the close of one of the most bitter days of the month of January, 1690, something unusual was going on in one of the numerous inhospitable bights of the bay of Portland, which caused the sea-gulls and wild geese to scream and circle round its mouth, not daring to re-enter.

In this creek, the most dangerous of all which line the bay during the continuance of certain winds, and consequently the most lonely—convenient, by reason of its very danger, for ships in hiding—a little vessel, almost touching the cliff, so deep was the water, was moored to a point of rock. We are wrong in saying, The night falls; we should say the night rises, for it is from the earth that obscurity comes. It was already night at the bottom of the cliff; it was still day at top. Any one approaching the vessel's moorings would have recognized a Biscayan hooker.

The sun, concealed all day by the mist, had just set. There was beginning to be felt that deep and sombrous melancholy which might be called anxiety for the absent sun. With no wind from the sea, the water of the creek was calm.

This was, especially in winter, a lucky exception. Almost all the Portland creeks have sand-bars; and in heavy weather the sea becomes very rough, and, to pass in safety, much skill and practice are necessary. These little ports (ports more in appearance than fact) are of small advantage. They are hazardous to enter, fearful to leave. On this evening, for a wonder, there was no danger.

The Biscay hooker is of an ancient model, now fallen into disuse. This kind of hooker, which has done service even in the navy, was stoutly built in its hull—a boat in size, a ship in strength. It figured in the Armada. Sometimes the war-hooker attained to a high tonnage; thus the Great Griffin, bearing a captain's flag, and commanded by Lopez de Medina, measured six hundred and fifty good tons, and carried forty guns. But the merchant and contraband hookers were very feeble specimens. Sea-folk held them at their true value, and esteemed the model a very sorry one, The rigging of the hooker was made of hemp, sometimes with wire inside, which was probably intended as a means, however unscientific, of obtaining indications, in the case of magnetic tension. The lightness of this rigging did not exclude the use of heavy tackle, the cabrias of the Spanish galleon, and the cameli of the Roman triremes. The helm was very long, which gives the advantage of a long arm of leverage, but the disadvantage of a small arc of effort. Two wheels in two pulleys at the end of the rudder corrected this defect, and compensated, to some extent, for the loss of strength. The compass was well housed in a case perfectly square, and well balanced by its two copper frames placed horizontally, one in the other, on little bolts, as in Cardan's lamps. There was science and cunning in the construction of the hooker, but it was ignorant science and barbarous cunning. The hooker was primitive, just like the praam and the canoe; was kindred to the praam in stability, and to the canoe in swiftness; and, like all vessels born of the instinct of the pirate and fisherman, it had remarkable sea qualities: it was equally well suited to landlocked and to open waters. Its system of sails, complicated in stays, and very peculiar, allowed of its navigating trimly in the close bays of Asturias (which are little more than enclosed basins, as Pasages, for instance), and also freely out at sea. It could sail round a lake, and sail round the world—a strange craft with two objects, good for a pond and good for a storm. The hooker is among vessels what the wagtail is among birds—one of the smallest and one of the boldest. The wagtail perching on a reed scarcely bends it, and, flying away, crosses the ocean.

These Biscay hookers, even to the poorest, were gilt and painted. Tattooing is part of the genius of those charming people, savages to some degree. The sublime colouring of their mountains, variegated by snows and meadows, reveals to them the rugged spell which ornament possesses in itself. They are poverty-stricken and magnificent; they put coats-of-arms on their cottages; they have huge asses, which they bedizen with bells, and huge oxen, on which they put head-dresses of feathers. Their coaches, which you can hear grinding the wheels two leagues off, are illuminated, carved, and hung with ribbons. A cobbler has a bas-relief on his door: it is only St. Crispin and an old shoe, but it is in stone. They trim their leathern jackets with lace. They do not mend their rags, but they embroider them.

Vivacity profound and superb! The Basques are, like the Greeks, children of the sun; while the Valencian drapes himself, bare and sad, in his russet woollen rug, with a hole to pass his head through, the natives of Galicia and Biscay have the delight of fine linen shirts, bleached in the dew. Their thresholds and their windows teem with faces fair and fresh, laughing under garlands of maize; a joyous and proud serenity shines out in their ingenious arts, in their trades, in their customs, in the dress of their maidens, in their songs. The mountain, that colossal ruin, is all aglow in Biscay: the sun's rays go in and out of every break. The wild Jaïzquivel is full of idylls. Biscay is Pyrenean grace as Savoy is Alpine grace. The dangerous bays—the neighbours of St. Sebastian, Leso, and Fontarabia—with storms, with clouds, with spray flying over the capes, with the rages of the waves and the winds, with terror, with uproar, mingle boat-women crowned with roses. He who has seen the Basque country wishes to see it again. It is the blessed land. Two harvests a year; villages resonant and gay; a stately poverty; all Sunday the sound of guitars, dancing, castanets, love-making; houses clean and bright; storks in the belfries.

Let us return to Portland—that rugged mountain in the sea.

The peninsula of Portland, looked at geometrically, presents the appearance of a bird's head, of which the bill is turned towards the ocean, the back of the head towards Weymouth; the isthmus is its neck.

Portland, greatly to the sacrifice of its wildness, exists now but for trade. The coasts of Portland were discovered by quarrymen and plasterers towards the middle of the seventeenth century. Since that period what is called Roman cement has been made of the Portland stone—a useful industry, enriching the district, and disfiguring the bay. Two hundred years ago these coasts were eaten away as a cliff; to-day, as a quarry. The pick bites meanly, the wave grandly; hence a diminution of beauty. To the magnificent ravages of the ocean have succeeded the measured strokes of men. These measured strokes have worked away the creek where the Biscay hooker was moored. To find any vestige of the little anchorage, now destroyed, the eastern side of the peninsula should be searched, towards the point beyond Folly Pier and Dirdle Pier, beyond Wakeham even, between the place called Church Hope and the place called Southwell.

The creek, walled in on all sides by precipices higher than its width, was minute by minute becoming more overshadowed by evening. The misty gloom, usual at twilight, became thicker; it was like a growth of darkness at the bottom of a well. The opening of the creek seaward, a narrow passage, traced on the almost night-black interior a pallid rift where the waves were moving. You must have been quite close to perceive the hooker moored to the rocks, and, as it were, hidden by the great cloaks of shadow. A plank thrown from on board on to a low and level projection of the cliff, the only point on which a landing could be made, placed the vessel in communication with the land. Dark figures were crossing and recrossing each other on this tottering gangway, and in the shadow some people were embarking.

It was less cold in the creek than out at sea, thanks to the screen of rock rising over the north of the basin, which did not, however, prevent the people from shivering. They were hurrying. The effect of the twilight defined the forms as though they had been punched out with a tool. Certain indentations in their clothes were visible, and showed that they belonged to the class called in England the ragged.

The twisting of the pathway could be distinguished vaguely in the relief of the cliff. A girl who lets her stay-lace hang down trailing over the back of an armchair, describes, without being conscious of it, most of the paths of cliffs and mountains. The pathway of this creek, full of knots and angles, almost perpendicular, and better adapted for goats than men, terminated on the platform where the plank was placed. The pathways of cliffs ordinarily imply a not very inviting declivity; they offer themselves less as a road than as a fall; they sink rather than incline. This one—probably some ramification of a road on the plain above—was disagreeable to look at, so vertical was it. From underneath you saw it gain by zigzag the higher layer of the cliff where it passed out through deep passages on to the high plateau by a cutting in the rock; and the passengers for whom the vessel was waiting in the creek must have come by this path.

Excepting the movement of embarkation which was being made in the creek, a movement visibly scared and uneasy, all around was solitude; no step, no noise, no breath was heard. At the other side of the roads, at the entrance of Ringstead Bay, you could just perceive a flotilla of shark-fishing boats, which were evidently out of their reckoning. These polar boats had been driven from Danish into English waters by the whims of the sea. Northerly winds play these tricks on fishermen. They had just taken refuge in the anchorage of Portland—a sign of bad weather expected and danger out at sea. They were engaged in casting anchor: the chief boat, placed in front after the old manner of Norwegian flotillas, all her rigging standing out in black, above the white level of the sea; and in front might be perceived the hook-iron, loaded with all kinds of hooks and harpoons, destined for the Greenland shark, the dogfish, and the spinous shark, as well as the nets to pick up the sunfish.

Except a few other craft, all swept into the same corner, the eye met nothing living on the vast horizon of Portland—not a house, not a ship. The coast in those days was not inhabited, and the roads, at that season, were not safe.

Whatever may have been the appearance of the weather, the beings who were going to sail away in the Biscayan urca pressed on the hour of departure all the same. They formed a busy and confused group, in rapid movement on the shore. To distinguish one from another was difficult; impossible to tell whether they were old or young. The indistinctness of evening intermixed and blurred them; the mask of shadow was over their faces. They were sketches in the night. There were eight of them, and there were seemingly among them one or two women, hard to recognize under the rags and tatters in which the group was attired—clothes which were no longer man's or woman's. Rags have no sex.

A smaller shadow, flitting to and fro among the larger ones, indicated either a dwarf or a child.

It was a child.

CHAPTER II.

LEFT ALONE

This is what an observer close at hand might have noted.

All wore long cloaks, torn and patched, but covering them, and at need concealing them up to the eyes; useful alike against the north wind and curiosity. They moved with ease under these cloaks. The greater number wore a handkerchief rolled round the head—a sort of rudiment which marks the commencement of the turban in Spain. This headdress was nothing unusual in England. At that time the South was in fashion in the North; perhaps this was connected with the fact that the North was beating the South. It conquered and admired. After the defeat of the Armada, Castilian was considered in the halls of Elizabeth to be elegant court talk. To speak English in the palace of the Queen of England was held almost an impropriety. Partially to adopt the manners of those upon whom we impose our laws is the habit of the conquering barbarian towards conquered civilization. The Tartar contemplates and imitates the Chinese. It was thus Castilian fashions penetrated into England; in return, English interests crept into Spain.

One of the men in the group embarking appeared to be a chief. He had sandals on his feet, and was bedizened with gold lace tatters and a tinsel waistcoat, shining under his cloak like the belly of a fish. Another pulled down over his face a huge piece of felt, cut like a sombrero; this felt had no hole for a pipe, thus indicating the wearer to be a man of letters.

On the principle that a man's vest is a child's cloak, the child was wrapped over his rags in a sailor's jacket, which descended to his knees.

By his height you would have guessed him to be a boy of ten or eleven; his feet were bare.

The crew of the hooker was composed of a captain and two sailors.

The hooker had apparently come from Spain, and was about to return thither. She was beyond a doubt engaged in a stealthy service from one coast to the other.

The persons embarking in her whispered among themselves.

The whispering interchanged by these creatures was of composite sound—now a word of Spanish, then of German, then of French, then of Gaelic, at times of Basque. It was either a patois or a slang. They appeared to be of all nations, and yet of the same band.

The motley group appeared to be a company of comrades, perhaps a gang of accomplices.

The crew was probably of their brotherhood. Community of object was visible in the embarkation.

Had there been a little more light, and if you could have looked at them attentively, you might have perceived on these people rosaries and scapulars half hidden under their rags; one of the semi-women mingling in the group had a rosary almost equal for the size of its beads to that of a dervish, and easy to recognize for an Irish one made at Llanymthefry, which is also called Llanandriffy.

You might also have observed, had it not been so dark, a figure of Our Lady and Child carved and gilt on the bow of the hooker. It was probably that of the Basque Notre Dame, a sort of Panagia of the old Cantabri. Under this image, which occupied the position of a figurehead, was a lantern, which at this moment was not lighted—an excess of caution which implied an extreme desire of concealment. This lantern was evidently for two purposes. When alight it burned before the Virgin, and at the same time illumined the sea—a beacon doing duty as a taper.

Under the bowsprit the cutwater, long, curved, and sharp, came out in front like the horn of a crescent. At the top of the cutwater, and at the feet of the Virgin, a kneeling angel, with folded wings, leaned her back against the stem, and looked through a spyglass at the horizon. The angel was gilded like Our Lady. In the cutwater were holes and openings to let the waves pass through, which afforded an opportunity for gilding and arabesques.

Under the figure of the Virgin was written, in gilt capitals, the word *Matutina*—the name of the vessel, not to be read just now on account of the darkness.

Amid the confusion of departure there were thrown down in disorder, at the foot of the cliff, the goods which the voyagers were to take with them, and which, by means of a plank serving as a bridge across, were being passed rapidly from the shore to the boat. Bags of biscuit, a cask of stock fish, a case of portable soup, three barrels—one of fresh water, one of malt, one of tar—four or five bottles of ale, an old portmanteau buckled up by straps, trunks, boxes, a ball of tow for torches and signals—such was the lading. These ragged people had valises, which seemed to indicate a roving life. Wandering rascals are obliged to own something; at times they would prefer to fly away like birds, but they cannot do so without abandoning the means of earning a livelihood. They of necessity possess boxes of tools and instruments of labour, whatever their errant trade may be. Those of whom we speak were dragging their baggage with them, often an encumbrance.

It could not have been easy to bring these movables to the bottom of the cliff. This, however, revealed the intention of a definite departure.

No time was lost; there was one continued passing to and fro from the shore to the vessel, and from the vessel to the shore; each one took his share of the work—one carried a bag, another a chest. Those amidst the promiscuous company who were possibly or probably women worked like the rest. They overloaded the child.

It was doubtful if the child's father or mother were in the group; no sign of life was vouchsafed him. They made him work, nothing more. He appeared not a child in a family, but a slave in a tribe. He waited on every one, and no one spoke to him.

However, he made haste, and, like the others of this mysterious troop, he seemed to have but one thought—to embark as quickly as possible. Did he know why? probably not: he hurried mechanically because he saw the others hurry.

The hooker was decked. The stowing of the lading in the hold was quickly finished, and the moment to put off arrived. The last case had been carried over the gangway, and nothing was left to embark but the men. The two objects among the group who seemed women were already on board; six, the child among them, were still on the low platform of the cliff. A movement of departure was made in the vessel: the captain seized the helm, a sailor took up an axe to cut the hawser—to cut is an evidence of haste; when there is time it is unknotted.

"Andamos," said, in a low voice, he who appeared chief of the six, and who had the spangles on his tatters. The child rushed towards the plank in order to be the first to pass. As he placed his foot on it, two of the men hurried by, at the risk of throwing him into the water, got in before him, and passed on; the fourth drove him back with his fist and followed the third; the fifth, who was the chief, bounded into rather than entered the vessel, and, as he jumped in, kicked back the plank, which fell into the sea, a stroke of the hatchet cut the moorings, the helm was put up, the vessel left the shore, and the child remained on land.

CHAPTER III.

ALONE

The child remained motionless on the rock, with his eyes fixed—no calling out, no appeal. Though this was unexpected by him, he spoke not a word. The same silence reigned in the vessel. No cry from the child to the men—no farewell from the men to the child. There was on both sides a mute acceptance of the widening distance between them. It was like a separation of ghosts on the banks of the Styx. The child, as if nailed to the rock, which the high tide was beginning to bathe, watched the departing bark. It seemed as if he realized his position. What did he realize? Darkness.

A moment later the hooker gained the neck of the crook and entered it. Against the clear sky the masthead was visible, rising above the split blocks between which the strait wound as between two walls. The truck wandered to the summit of the rocks, and appeared to run into them. Then it was seen no more—all was over—the bark had gained the sea.

The child watched its disappearance—he was astounded but dreamy. His stupefaction was complicated by a sense of the dark reality of existence. It seemed as if there were experience in this dawning being. Did he, perchance, already exercise judgment? Experience coming too early constructs, sometimes, in the obscure depths of a child's mind, some dangerous balance—we know not what—in which the poor little soul weighs God.

Feeling himself innocent, he yielded. There was no complaint—the irreproachable does not reproach.

His rough expulsion drew from him no sign; he suffered a sort of internal stiffening. The child did not bow under this sudden blow of fate, which seemed to put an end to his existence ere it had well begun; he received the thunderstroke standing.

It would have been evident to any one who could have seen his astonishment unmixed with dejection, that in the group which abandoned him there was nothing which loved him, nothing which he loved.

Brooding, he forgot the cold. Suddenly the wave wetted his feet—the tide was flowing; a gust passed through his hair—the north wind was rising. He shivered. There came over him, from head to foot, the shudder of awakening.

He cast his eyes about him.

He was alone.

Up to this day there had never existed for him any other men than those who were now in the hooker. Those men had just stolen away.

Let us add what seems a strange thing to state. Those men, the only ones he knew, were unknown to him.

He could not have said who they were. His childhood had been passed among them, without his having the consciousness of being of them. He was in juxtaposition to them, nothing more.

He had just been—forgotten—by them.

He had no money about him, no shoes to his feet, scarcely a garment to his body, not even a piece of bread in his pocket.

It was winter—it was night. It would be necessary to walk several leagues before a human habitation could be reached.

He did not know where he was.

He knew nothing, unless it was that those who had come with him to the brink of the sea had gone away without him.

He felt himself put outside the pale of life.

He felt that man failed him.

He was ten years old.

The child was in a desert, between depths where he saw the night rising and depths where he heard the waves murmur.

He stretched his little thin arms and yawned.

Then suddenly, as one who makes up his mind, bold, and throwing off his numbness—with the agility of a squirrel, or perhaps of an acrobat—he turned his back on the creek, and set himself to climb up the cliff. He escaladed the path, left it, returned to it, quick and venturous. He was hurrying landward, just as though he had a destination marked out; nevertheless he was going nowhere.

He hastened without an object—a fugitive before Fate.

To climb is the function of a man; to clamber is that of an animal—he did both. As the slopes of Portland face southward, there was scarcely any snow on the path; the intensity of cold had, however, frozen that snow into dust very troublesome to the walker. The child freed himself of it. His man's jacket, which was too big for him, complicated matters, and got in his way. Now and then on an overhanging crag or in a declivity he came upon a little ice, which caused him to slip down. Then, after hanging some moments over the precipice, he would catch hold of a dry branch or projecting stone. Once he came on a vein of slate, which suddenly gave way under him, letting him down with it. Crumbling slate is treacherous. For some seconds the child slid like a tile on a roof; he rolled to the extreme edge of the decline; a tuft of grass which he clutched at the right moment saved him. He was as mute in sight of the abyss as he had been in sight of the men; he gathered himself up and re-ascended silently. The slope was steep; so he had to tack in ascending. The precipice grew in the darkness; the vertical rock had no ending. It receded before the child in the distance of its height. As the child ascended, so seemed the summit to ascend. While he clambered he looked up at the dark entablature placed like a barrier between heaven and him. At last he reached the top.

He jumped on the level ground, or rather landed, for he rose from the precipice.

Scarcely was he on the cliff when he began to shiver. He felt in his face that bite of the night, the north wind. The bitter north-wester was blowing; he tightened his rough sailor's jacket about his chest.

It was a good coat, called in ship language a sou-'wester, because that sort of stuff allows little of the south-westerly rain to penetrate.

The child, having gained the tableland, stopped, placed his feet firmly on the frozen ground, and looked about him.

Behind him was the sea; in front the land; above, the sky—but a sky without stars; an opaque mist masked the zenith.

On reaching the summit of the rocky wall he found himself turned towards the land, and looked at it attentively. It lay before him as far as the sky-line, flat, frozen, and covered with snow. Some tufts of heather shivered in the wind. No roads were visible—nothing, not even a shepherd's cot. Here and there pale spiral vortices might be seen, which were whirls of fine snow, snatched from the ground by the wind and blown away. Successive undulations of ground, become suddenly misty, rolled themselves into the horizon. The great dull plains were lost under the white fog. Deep silence. It spread like infinity, and was hush as the tomb.

The child turned again towards the sea.

The sea, like the land, was white—the one with snow, the other with foam. There is nothing so melancholy as the light produced by this double whiteness.

Certain lights of night are very clearly cut in their hardness; the sea was like steel, the cliff like ebony. From the height where the child was the bay of Portland appeared almost like a geographical map, pale, in a semicircle of hills. There was something dreamlike in that nocturnal landscape—a wan disc belted by a dark crescent. The moon sometimes has a similar appearance. From cape to cape, along the whole coast, not a single spark indicating a hearth with a fire, not a lighted window, not an inhabited house, was to be seen. As in heaven, so on earth—no light. Not a lamp below, not a star above. Here and there came sudden risings in the great expanse of waters in the gulf, as the wind disarranged and wrinkled the vast sheet. The hooker was still visible in the bay as she fled.

It was a black triangle gliding over the livid waters.

Far away the waste of waters stirred confusedly in the ominous clear-obscure of immensity. The *Matutina* was making quick way. She seemed to grow smaller every minute. Nothing appears so rapid as the flight of a vessel melting into the distance of ocean.

Suddenly she lit the lantern at her prow. Probably the darkness falling round her made those on board uneasy, and the pilot thought it necessary to throw light on the waves. This luminous point, a spark seen from afar, clung like a corpse light to the high and long black form. You would have said it was a shroud raised up and moving in the middle of the sea, under which some one wandered with a star in his hand.

A storm threatened in the air; the child took no account of it, but a sailor would have trembled. It was that moment of preliminary anxiety when it seems as though the elements are changing into persons, and one is about to witness the mysterious transfiguration of the wind into the wind-god. The sea becomes Ocean: its power reveals itself as Will: that which one takes for a thing is a soul. It will become visible; hence the terror. The soul of man fears to be thus confronted with the soul of nature.

Chaos was about to appear. The wind rolling back the fog, and making a stage of the clouds behind, set the scene for that fearful drama of wave and winter which is called a Snowstorm. Vessels putting back hove in sight. For some minutes past the roads had no longer been deserted. Every instant troubled barks hastening towards an anchorage appeared from behind the capes; some were doubling Portland Bill, the others St. Alban's Head. From afar ships were running in. It was a race for refuge. Southwards the darkness thickened, and clouds, full of night, bordered on the sea. The weight of the tempest hanging overhead made a dreary lull on the waves. It certainly was no time to sail. Yet the hooker had sailed.

She had made the south of the cape. She was already out of the gulf, and in the open sea. Suddenly there came a gust of wind. The *Matutina*, which was still clearly in sight, made all sail, as if resolved to profit by the hurricane. It was the nor'-wester, a wind sullen and angry. Its weight was felt instantly. The hooker, caught broadside on, staggered, but recovering held her course to sea. This indicated a flight rather than a voyage, less fear of sea than of land, and greater heed of pursuit from man than from wind.

The hooker, passing through every degree of diminution, sank into the horizon. The little star which she carried into shadow paled. More and more the hooker became amalgamated with the night, then disappeared.

This time for good and all.

At least the child seemed to understand it so: he ceased to look at the sea. His eyes turned back upon the plains, the wastes, the hills, towards the space where it might not be impossible to meet something living.

Into this unknown he set out.

CHAPTER IV.

QUESTIONS

What kind of band was it which had left the child behind in its flight?

Were those fugitives Comprachicos?

We have already seen the account of the measures taken by William III. and passed by Parliament against the malefactors, male and female, called Comprachicos, otherwise Comprapequeños, otherwise Cheylas.

There are laws which disperse. The law acting against the Comprachicos determined, not only the Comprachicos, but vagabonds of all sorts, on a general flight.

It was the devil take the hindmost. The greater number of the Comprachicos returned to Spain—many of them, as we have said, being Basques.

The law for the protection of children had at first this strange result: it caused many children to be abandoned.

The immediate effect of the penal statute was to produce a crowd of children, found or rather lost. Nothing is easier to understand. Every wandering gang containing a child was liable to suspicion. The mere fact of the child's presence was in itself a denunciation.

"They are very likely Comprachicos." Such was the first idea of the sheriff, of the bailiff, of the constable. Hence arrest and inquiry. People simply unfortunate, reduced to wander and to beg, were seized with a terror of being taken for Comprachicos although they were nothing of the kind. But the weak have grave misgivings of possible errors in justice. Besides, these vagabond families are very easily scared. The accusation against the Comprachicos was that they traded in other people's children. But the promiscuousness caused by poverty and indigence is such that at times it might have been difficult for a father and mother to prove a child their own.

How came you by this child? how were they to prove that they held it from God? The child became a peril—they got rid of it. To fly unencumbered was easier; the parents resolved to lose it—now in a wood, now on a strand, now down a well.

Children were found drowned in cisterns.

Let us add that, in imitation of England, all Europe henceforth hunted down the Comprachicos. The impulse of pursuit was given. There is nothing like belling the cat. From this time forward the desire to seize them made rivalry and emulation among the police of all countries, and the alguazil was not less keenly watchful than the constable.

One could still read, twenty-three years ago, on a stone of the gate of Otero, an untranslatable inscription—the words of the code outraging propriety. In it, however, the shade of difference which existed between the buyers and the stealers of children is very strongly marked. Here is part of the inscription in somewhat rough Castillan, *Aqui quedan las orejas de los Comprachicos, y las bolsas de los robaniños, mientras que se van ellos al trabajo de mar.* You see the confiscation of ears, etc., did not prevent the owners going to the galleys. Whence followed a general rout among all vagabonds. They started frightened; they arrived trembling. On every shore in Europe their furtive advent was watched. Impossible for such a band to embark with a child, since to disembark with one was dangerous.

To lose the child was much simpler of accomplishment.

And this child, of whom we have caught a glimpse in the shadow of the solitudes of Portland, by whom had he been cast away?

To all appearance by Comprachicos.

CHAPTER V.

THE TREE OF HUMAN INVENTION

It might be about seven o'clock in the evening. The wind was now diminishing—a sign, however, of a violent recurrence impending. The child was on the table-land at the extreme south point of Portland.

Portland is a peninsula; but the child did not know what a peninsula is, and was ignorant even of the name of Portland. He knew but one thing, which is, that one can walk until one drops down. An idea is a guide; he had no idea. They had brought him there and left him there. *They* and *there*—these two enigmas represented his doom. *They* were humankind. *There* was the universe. For him in all creation there was absolutely no other basis to rest on but the little piece of ground where he placed his heel, ground hard and cold to his naked feet. In the great twilight world, open on all sides, what was there for the child? Nothing.

He walked towards this Nothing. Around him was the vastness of human desertion.

He crossed the first plateau diagonally, then a second, then a third. At the extremity of each plateau the child came upon a break in the ground. The slope was sometimes steep, but always short; the high, bare plains of Portland resemble great flagstones overlapping each other. The south side seems to enter under the protruding slab, the north side rises over the next one; these made ascents, which the child stepped over nimbly. From time to time he stopped, and seemed to hold counsel with himself. The night was becoming very dark. His radius of sight was contracting. He now only saw a few steps before him.

All of a sudden he stopped, listened for an instant, and with an almost imperceptible nod of satisfaction turned quickly and directed his steps towards an eminence of moderate height, which he dimly perceived on his right, at the point of the plain nearest the cliff. There was on the eminence a shape which in the mist looked like a tree. The child had just heard a noise in this direction, which was the noise neither of the wind nor of the sea, nor was it the cry of animals. He thought that some one was there, and in a few strides he was at the foot of the hillock.

In truth, some one was there.

That which had been indistinct on the top of the eminence was now visible. It was something like a great arm thrust straight out of the ground; at the upper extremity of the arm a sort of forefinger, supported from beneath, by the thumb, pointed out horizontally; the arm, the thumb, and the forefinger drew a square against the sky. At the point of juncture of this peculiar finger and this peculiar thumb there was a line, from which hung something black and shapeless. The line moving in the wind sounded like a chain. This was the noise the child had heard. Seen closely the line was that which the noise indicated, a chain—a single chain cable.

By that mysterious law of amalgamation which throughout nature causes appearances to exaggerate realities, the place, the hour, the mist, the mournful sea, the cloudy turmoils on the distant horizon, added to the effect of this figure, and made it seem enormous.

The mass linked to the chain presented the appearance of a scabbard. It was swaddled like a child and long like a man. There was a round thing at its summit, about which the end of the chain was rolled. The scabbard was riven asunder at the lower end, and shreds of flesh hung out between the rents.

A feeble breeze stirred the chain, and that which hung to it swayed gently. The passive mass obeyed the vague motions of space. It was an object to inspire indescribable dread. Horror, which disproportions everything, blurred its dimensions while retaining its shape. It was a condensation of darkness, which had a defined form. Night was above and within the spectre; it was a prey of ghastly exaggeration. Twilight and moonrise, stars setting behind the cliff, floating things in space, the clouds, winds from all quarters, had ended by penetrating into the composition of this visible nothing. The species of log hanging in the wind partook of the impersonality diffused far over sea and sky, and the darkness completed this phase of the *thing* which had once been a man.

It was that which is no longer.

To be naught but a remainder! Such a thing is beyond the power of language to express. To exist no more, yet to persist; to be in the abyss, yet out of it; to reappear above death as if indissoluble—there is a certain amount of impossibility mixed with such reality. Thence comes the inexpressible. This being—was it a being? This black witness was a remainder, and an awful remainder—a remainder of what? Of nature first, and then of society. Naught, and yet total.

The lawless inclemency of the weather held it at its will; the deep oblivion of solitude environed it; it was given up to unknown chances; it was without defence against the darkness, which did with it what it willed. It was for ever the patient; it submitted; the hurricane (that ghastly conflict of winds) was upon it.

The spectre was given over to pillage. It underwent the horrible outrage of rotting in the open air; it was an outlaw of the tomb. There was no peace for it even in annihilation: in the summer it fell away into dust, in the winter into mud. Death should be veiled, the grave should have its reserve. Here was neither veil nor reserve, but cynically avowed putrefaction. It is effrontery in death to display its work; it offends all the calmness of shadow when it does its task outside its laboratory, the grave.

This dead thing had been stripped. To strip one already stripped—relentless act! His marrow was no longer in his bones; his entrails were no longer in his body; his voice no longer in his throat. A corpse is a pocket which death turns inside out and empties. If he ever had a Me, where was the Me? There still, perchance, and this was fearful to think of. Something wandering about something in chains—can one imagine a more mournful lineament in the darkness?

Realities exist here below which serve as issues to the unknown, which seem to facilitate the egress of speculation, and at which hypothesis snatches. Conjecture has its *compelle intrare*. In passing by certain places and before certain objects one cannot help stopping—a prey to dreams into the realms of which the mind enters. In the invisible there are dark portals ajar. No one could have met this dead man without meditating.

In the vastness of dispersion he was wearing silently away. He had had blood which had been drunk, skin which had been eaten, flesh which had been stolen. Nothing had passed him by without taking somewhat from him. December had borrowed cold of him; midnight, horror; the iron, rust; the plague, miasma; the flowers, perfume. His slow disintegration was a toll paid to all—a toll of the corpse to the storm, to the rain, to the dew, to the reptiles, to the birds. All the dark hands of night had rifled the dead.

He was, indeed, an inexpressibly strange tenant, a tenant of the darkness. He was on a plain and on a hill, and *he was not.* He was palpable, yet vanished. He was a shadow accruing to the night. After the disappearance of day into the vast of silent obscurity, he became in lugubrious accord with all around him. By his mere presence he increased the gloom of the tempest and the calm of stars. The unutterable which is in the desert was condensed in him. Waif of an unknown fate, he commingled with all the wild secrets of the night. There was in his mystery a vague reverberation of all enigmas.

About him life seemed sinking to its lowest depths. Certainty and confidence appeared to diminish in his environs. The shiver of the brushwood and the grass, a desolate melancholy, an anxiety in which a conscience seemed to lurk, appropriated with tragic force the whole landscape to that black figure suspended by the chain. The presence of a spectre in the horizon is an aggravation of solitude.

He was a Sign. Having unappeasable winds around him, he was implacable. Perpetual shuddering made him terrible. Fearful to say, he seemed to be a centre in space, with something immense leaning on him. Who can tell? Perhaps that equity, half seen and set at defiance, which transcends human justice. There was in his unburied continuance the vengeance of men and his own vengeance. He was a testimony in the twilight and the waste. He was in himself a disquieting substance, since we tremble before the substance which is the ruined habitation of the soul. For dead matter to trouble us, it must once have been tenanted by spirit. He denounced the law of earth to the law of Heaven. Placed there by man, he there awaited God. Above him floated, blended with all the vague distortions of the cloud and the wave, boundless dreams of shadow.

Who could tell what sinister mysteries lurked behind this phantom? The illimitable, circumscribed by naught, nor tree, nor roof, nor passer-by, was around the dead man. When the unchangeable broods over us—when Heaven, the abyss, the life, grave, and eternity appear patent—then it is we feel that all is inaccessible, all is forbidden, all is sealed. When infinity opens to us, terrible indeed is the closing of the gate behind.

CHAPTER VI.

STRUGGLE BETWEEN DEATH AND LIFE

The child was before this thing, dumb, wondering, and with eyes fixed.

To a man it would have been a gibbet; to the child it was an apparition.

Where a man would have seen a corpse the child saw a spectre.

Besides, he did not understand.

The attractions of the obscure are manifold. There was one on the summit of that hill. The child took a step, then another; he ascended, wishing all the while to descend; and approached, wishing all the while to retreat.

Bold, yet trembling, he went close up to survey the spectre.

When he got close under the gibbet, he looked up and examined it.

The spectre was tarred; here and there it shone. The child distinguished the face. It was coated over with pitch; and this mask, which appeared viscous and sticky, varied its aspect with the night shadows. The child saw the mouth, which was a hole; the nose, which was a hole; the eyes, which were holes. The body was wrapped, and apparently corded up, in coarse canvas, soaked in naphtha. The canvas was mouldy and torn. A knee protruded through it. A rent disclosed the ribs—partly corpse, partly skeleton. The face was the colour of earth; slugs, wandering over it, had traced across it vague ribbons of silver. The canvas, glued to the bones, showed in reliefs like the robe of a statue. The skull, cracked and fractured, gaped like a rotten fruit. The teeth were still human, for they retained a laugh. The remains of a cry seemed to murmur in the open mouth. There were a few hairs of beard on the cheek. The inclined head had an air of attention.

Some repairs had recently been done; the face had been tarred afresh, as well as the ribs and the knee which protruded from the canvas. The feet hung out below.

Just underneath, in the grass, were two shoes, which snow and rain had rendered shapeless. These shoes had fallen from the dead man.

The barefooted child looked at the shoes.

The wind, which had become more and more restless, was now and then interrupted by those pauses which foretell the approach of a storm. For the last few minutes it had altogether ceased to blow. The corpse no longer stirred; the chain was as motionless as a plumb line.

Like all newcomers into life, and taking into account the peculiar influences of his fate, the child no doubt felt within him that awakening of ideas characteristic of early years, which endeavours to open the brain, and which resembles the pecking of the young bird in the egg. But all that there was in his little consciousness just then was resolved into stupor. Excess of sensation has the effect of too much oil, and ends by putting out thought. A man would have put himself questions; the child put himself none—he only looked.

The tar gave the face a wet appearance; drops of pitch, congealed in what had once been the eyes, produced the effect of tears. However, thanks to the pitch, the ravage of death, if not annulled, was visibly slackened and reduced to the least possible decay. That which was before the child was a thing of which care was taken: the man was evidently precious. They had not cared to keep him alive, but they cared to keep him dead.

The gibbet was old, worm-eaten, although strong, and had been in use many years.

It was an immemorial custom in England to tar smugglers. They were hanged on the seaboard, coated over with pitch and left swinging. Examples must be made in public, and tarred examples last longest. The tar was mercy: by renewing it they were spared making too many fresh examples. They placed gibbets from point to point along the coast, as nowadays they do beacons. The hanged man did duty as a lantern. After his fashion, he guided his comrades, the smugglers. The smugglers from far out at sea perceived the gibbets. There is one, first warning; another, second warning. It did not stop smuggling; but public order is made up of such things. The fashion lasted in England up to the beginning of this century. In 1822 three men were still to be seen hanging in front of Dover Castle. But, for that matter, the preserving process was employed not only with smugglers. England turned robbers, incendiaries, and murderers to the same account. Jack Painter, who set fire to the government storehouses at Portsmouth, was hanged and tarred in 1776. L'Abbé Coyer, who describes him as Jean le Peintre, saw him again in 1777. Jack Painter was hanging above the ruin he had made, and was re-tarred from time to time. His corpse lasted—I had almost said lived—nearly fourteen years. It was still doing good service in 1788; in 1790, however, they were obliged to replace it by another. The Egyptians used to value the mummy of the king; a plebeian mummy can also, it appears, be of service.

The wind, having great power on the hill, had swept it of all its snow. Herbage reappeared on it, interspersed here and there with a few thistles; the hill was covered by that close short grass which grows by the sea, and causes the tops of cliffs to resemble green cloth. Under the gibbet, on the very spot over which hung the feet of the executed criminal, was a long and thick tuft, uncommon on such poor soil. Corpses, crumbling there for centuries past, accounted for the beauty of the grass. Earth feeds on man.

A dreary fascination held the child; he remained there open-mouthed. He only dropped his head a moment when a nettle, which felt like an insect, stung his leg; then he looked up again—he looked above him at the face which looked down on him. It appeared to regard him the more steadfastly because it had no eyes. It was a comprehensive glance, having an indescribable fixedness in which there were both light and darkness, and which emanated from the skull and teeth, as well as the empty arches of the brow. The whole head of a dead man seems to have vision, and this is awful. No eyeball, yet we feel that we are looked at. A horror of worms.

Little by little the child himself was becoming an object of terror. He no longer moved. Torpor was coming over him. He did not perceive that he was losing consciousness—he was becoming benumbed and lifeless. Winter was silently delivering him over to night. There is something of the traitor in winter. The child was all but a statue. The coldness of stone was penetrating his bones; darkness, that reptile, was crawling over him. The drowsiness resulting from snow creeps over a man like a dim tide. The child was being slowly invaded by a stagnation resembling that of the corpse. He was falling asleep.

On the hand of sleep is the finger of death. The child felt himself seized by that hand. He was on the point of falling under the gibbet. He no longer knew whether he was standing upright.

The end always impending, no transition between to be and not to be, the return into the crucible, the slip possible every minute—such is the precipice which is Creation.

Another instant, the child and the dead, life in sketch and life in ruin, would be confounded in the same obliteration.

The spectre appeared to understand, and not to wish it. Of a sudden it stirred. One would have said it was warning the child. It was the wind beginning to blow again. Nothing stranger than this dead man in movement.

The corpse at the end of the chain, pushed by the invisible gust, took an oblique attitude; rose to the left, then fell back, reascended to the right, and fell and rose with slow and mournful precision. A weird game of see-saw. It seemed as though one saw in the darkness the pendulum of the clock of Eternity.

This continued for some time. The child felt himself waking up at the sight of the dead; through his increasing numbness he experienced a distinct sense of fear.

The chain at every oscillation made a grinding sound, with hideous regularity. It appeared to take breath, and then to resume. This grinding was like the cry of a grasshopper.

An approaching squall is heralded by sudden gusts of wind. All at once the breeze increased into a gale. The corpse emphasized its dismal oscillations. It no longer swung, it tossed; the chain, which had been grinding, now shrieked. It appeared that its shriek was heard. If it was an appeal, it was obeyed. From the depths of the horizon came the sound of a rushing noise.

It was the noise of wings.

An incident occurred, a stormy incident, peculiar to graveyards and solitudes. It was the arrival of a flight of ravens. Black flying specks pricked the clouds, pierced through the mist, increased in size, came near, amalgamated, thickened, hastening towards the hill, uttering cries. It was like the approach of a Legion. The winged vermin of the darkness alighted on the gibbet; the child, scared, drew back.

Swarms obey words of command: the birds crowded on the gibbet; not one was on the corpse. They were talking among themselves. The croaking was frightful. The howl, the whistle and the roar, are signs of life; the croak is a satisfied acceptance of putrefaction. In it you can fancy you hear the tomb breaking silence. The croak is night-like in itself.

The child was frozen even more by terror than by cold.

Then the ravens held silence. One of them perched on the skeleton. This was a signal: they all precipitated themselves upon it. There was a cloud of wings, then all their feathers closed up, and the hanged man disappeared under a swarm of black blisters struggling in the obscurity. Just then the corpse moved. Was it the corpse? Was it the wind? It made a frightful bound. The hurricane, which was increasing, came to its aid. The phantom fell into convulsions.

The squall, already blowing with full lungs, laid hold of it, and moved it about in all directions.

It became horrible; it began to struggle. An awful puppet, with a gibbet chain for a string. Some humorist of night must have seized the string and been playing with the mummy. It turned and leapt as if it would fain dislocate itself; the birds, frightened, flew off. It was like an explosion of all those unclean creatures. Then they returned, and a struggle began.

The dead man seemed possessed with hideous vitality. The winds raised him as though they meant to carry him away. He seemed struggling and making efforts to escape, but his iron collar held him back. The birds adapted themselves to all his movements, retreating, then striking again, scared but desperate. On one side a strange flight was attempted, on the other the pursuit of a chained man. The corpse, impelled by every spasm of the wind, had shocks, starts, fits of rage: it went, it came, it rose, it fell, driving back the scattered swarm. The dead man was a club, the swarms were dust. The fierce, assailing flock would not leave their hold, and grew stubborn; the man, as if maddened by the cluster of beaks, redoubled his blind chastisement of space. It was like the blows of a stone held in a sling. At times the corpse was covered by talons and wings; then it was free. There were disappearances of the horde, then sudden furious returns—a frightful torment continuing after life was past. The birds seemed frenzied. The air-holes of hell must surely give passage to such swarms. Thrusting of claws, thrusting of beaks, croakings, rendings of shreds no longer flesh, creakings of the gibbet, shudderings of the skeleton, jingling of the chain, the voices of the storm and tumult—what conflict more fearful? A hobgoblin warring with devils! A combat with a spectre!

At times the storm redoubling its violence, the hanged man revolved on his own pivot, turning every way at once towards the swarm, as if he wished to run after the birds; his teeth seemed to try and bite them. The wind was for him, the chain against him. It was as if black deities were mixing themselves up in the fray. The hurricane was in the battle. As the dead man turned himself about, the flock of birds wound round him spirally. It was a whirl in a whirlwind. A great roar was heard from below. It was the sea.

The child saw this nightmare. Suddenly he trembled in all his limbs; a shiver thrilled his frame; he staggered, tottered, nearly fell, recovered himself, pressed both hands to his forehead, as if he felt his forehead a support; then, haggard, his hair streaming in the wind, descending the hill with long strides, his eyes closed, himself almost a phantom, he took flight, leaving behind that torment in the night.

CHAPTER VII.

THE NORTH POINT OF PORTLAND

He ran until he was breathless, at random, desperate, over the plain into the snow, into space. His flight warmed him. He needed it. Without the run and the fright he had died.

When his breath failed him he stopped, but he dared not look back. He fancied that the birds would pursue him, that the dead man had undone his chain and was perhaps hurrying behind him, and no doubt the gibbet itself was descending the hill, running after the dead man; he feared to see these things if he turned his head.

When he had somewhat recovered his breath he resumed his flight.

To account for facts does not belong to childhood. He received impressions which were magnified by terror, but he did not link them together in his mind, nor form any conclusion on them. He was going on, no matter how or where; he ran in agony and difficulty as one in a dream. During the three hours or so since he had been deserted, his onward progress, still vague, had changed its purpose. At first it was a search; now it was a flight. He no longer felt hunger nor cold—he felt fear. One instinct had given place to another. To escape was now his whole thought—to escape from what? From everything. On all sides life seemed to enclose him like a horrible wall. If he could have fled from all things, he would have done so. But children know nothing of that breaking from prison which is called suicide. He was running. He ran on for an indefinite time; but fear dies with lack of breath.

All at once, as if seized by a sudden accession of energy and intelligence, he stopped. One would have said he was ashamed of running away. He drew himself up, stamped his foot, and, with head erect, looked round. There was no longer hill, nor gibbet, nor flights of crows. The fog had resumed possession of the horizon. The child pursued his way: he now no longer ran but walked. To say that meeting with a corpse had made a man of him would be to limit the manifold and confused impression which possessed him. There was in his impression much more and much less. The gibbet, a mighty trouble in the rudiment of comprehension, nascent in his mind, still seemed to him an apparition; but a trouble overcome is strength gained, and he felt himself stronger. Had he been of an age to probe self, he would have detected within him a thousand other germs of meditation; but the reflection of children is shapeless, and the utmost they feel is the bitter aftertaste of that which, obscure to them, the man later on calls indignation. Let us add that a child has the faculty of quickly accepting the conclusion of a sensation; the distant fading boundaries which amplify painful subjects escape him. A child is protected by the limit of feebleness against emotions which are too complex. He sees the fact, and little else beside. The difficulty of being satisfied by half-ideas does not exist for him. It is not until later that experience comes, with its brief, to conduct the lawsuit of life. *Then* he confronts groups of facts which have crossed his path; the understanding, cultivated and enlarged, draws comparisons; the memories of youth reappear under the passions, like the traces of a palimpsest under the erasure; these memories form the bases of logic, and that which was a vision in the child's brain becomes a syllogism in the man's. Experience is, however, various, and turns to good or evil according to natural disposition. With the good it ripens, with the bad it rots.

The child had run quite a quarter of a league, and walked another quarter, when suddenly he felt the craving of hunger. A thought which altogether eclipsed the hideous apparition on the hill occurred to him forcibly—that he must eat. Happily there is in man a brute which serves to lead him back to reality.

But what to eat, where to eat, how to eat?

He felt his pockets mechanically, well knowing that they were empty. Then he quickened his steps, without knowing whither he was going. He hastened towards a possible shelter. This faith in an inn is one of the convictions enrooted by God in man. To believe in a shelter is to believe in God.

However, in that plain of snow there was nothing like a roof. The child went on, and the waste continued bare as far as eye could see. There had never been a human habitation on the tableland. It was at the foot of the cliff, in holes in the rocks, that, lacking wood to build themselves huts, had dwelt long ago the aboriginal inhabitants, who had slings for arms, dried cow-dung for firing, for a god the idol Heil standing in a glade at Dorchester, and for trade the fishing of that false gray coral which the Gauls called *plin*, and the Greeks *isidis plocamos*.

The child found his way as best he could. Destiny is made up of cross-roads. An option of path is dangerous. This little being had an early choice of doubtful chances.

He continued to advance, but although the muscles of his thighs seemed to be of steel, he began to tire. There were no tracks in the plain; or if there were any, the snow had obliterated them. Instinctively he inclined eastwards. Sharp stones had wounded his heels. Had it been daylight pink stains made by his blood might have been seen in the footprints he left in the snow.

He recognized nothing. He was crossing the plain of Portland from south to north, and it is probable that the band with which he had come, to avoid meeting any one, had crossed it from east to west; they had most likely sailed in some fisherman's or smuggler's boat, from a point on the coast of Uggescombe, such as St. Catherine's Cape or Swancry, to Portland to find the hooker which awaited them; and they must have landed in one of the creeks of Weston, and re-embarked in one of those of Easton. That direction was intersected by the one the child was now following. It was impossible for him to recognize the road.

On the plain of Portland there are, here and there, raised strips of land, abruptly ended by the shore and cut perpendicular to the sea. The wandering child reached one of these culminating points and stopped on it, hoping that a larger space might reveal further indications. He tried to see around him. Before him, in place of a horizon, was a vast livid opacity. He looked at this attentively, and under the fixedness of his glance it became less indistinct. At the base of a distant fold of land towards the east, in the depths of that opaque lividity (a moving and wan sort of precipice, which resembled a cliff of the night), crept and floated some vague black rents, some dim shreds of vapour. The pale opacity was fog, the black shreds were smoke. Where there is smoke there are men. The child turned his steps in that direction.

He saw some distance off a descent, and at the foot of the descent, among shapeless conformations of rock, blurred by the mist, what seemed to be either a sandbank or a tongue of land, joining probably to the plains of the horizon the tableland he had just crossed. It was evident he must pass that way.

He had, in fact, arrived at the Isthmus of Portland, a diluvian alluvium which is called Chess Hill.

He began to descend the side of the plateau.

The descent was difficult and rough. It was (with less of ruggedness, however) the reverse of the ascent he had made on leaving the creek. Every ascent is balanced by a decline. After having clambered up he crawled down.

He leapt from one rock to another at the risk of a sprain, at the risk of falling into the vague depths below. To save himself when he slipped on the rock or on the ice, he caught hold of handfuls of weeds and furze, thick with thorns, and their points ran into his fingers. At times he came on an easier declivity, taking breath as he descended; then came on the precipice again, and each step necessitated an expedient. In descending precipices, every movement solves a problem. One must be skilful under pain of death. These problems the child solved with an instinct which would have made him the admiration of apes and mountebanks. The descent was steep and long. Nevertheless he was coming to the end of it.

Little by little it was drawing nearer the moment when he should land on the Isthmus, of which from time to time he caught a glimpse. At intervals, while he bounded or dropped from rock to rock, he pricked up his ears, his head erect, like a listening deer. He was hearkening to a diffused and faint uproar, far away to the left, like the deep note of a clarion. It was a commotion of winds, preceding that fearful north blast which is heard rushing from the pole, like an inroad of trumpets. At the same time the child felt now and then on his brow, on his eyes, on his cheeks, something which was like the palms of cold hands being placed on his face. These were large frozen flakes, sown at first softly in space, then eddying, and heralding a snowstorm. The child was covered with them. The snowstorm, which for the last hour had been on the sea, was beginning to gain the land. It was slowly invading the plains. It was entering obliquely, by the north-west, the tableland of Portland.

BOOK THE SECOND

THE HOOKER AT SEA

CHAPTER I.

SUPERHUMAN LAWS

The snowstorm is one of the mysteries of the ocean. It is the most obscure of things meteorological—obscure in every sense of the word. It is a mixture of fog and storm; and even in our days we cannot well account for the phenomenon. Hence many disasters.

We try to explain all things by the action of wind and wave; yet in the air there is a force which is not the wind, and in the waters a force which is not the wave. That force, both in the air and in the water, is effluvium. Air and water are two nearly identical liquid masses, entering into the composition of each other by condensation and dilatation, so that to breathe is to drink. Effluvium alone is fluid. The wind and the wave are only impulses; effluvium is a current. The wind is visible in clouds, the wave is visible in foam; effluvium is invisible. From time to time, however, it says, "I am here." Its "I am here" is a clap of thunder.

The snowstorm offers a problem analogous to the dry fog. If the solution of the *callina* of the Spaniards and the *quobar* of the Ethiopians be possible, assuredly that solution will be achieved by attentive observation of magnetic effluvium.

Without effluvium a crowd of circumstances would remain enigmatic. Strictly speaking, the changes in the velocity of the wind, varying from 3 feet per second to 220 feet, would supply a reason for the variations of the waves rising from 3 inches in a calm sea to 36 feet in a raging one. Strictly speaking, the horizontal direction of the winds, even in a squall, enables us to understand how it is that a wave 30 feet high can be 1,500 feet long. But why are the waves of the Pacific four times higher near America than near Asia; that is to say, higher in the East than in the West? Why is the contrary true of the Atlantic? Why, under the Equator, are they highest in the middle of the sea? Wherefore these deviations in the swell of the ocean? This is what magnetic effluvium, combined with terrestrial rotation and sidereal attraction, can alone explain.

Is not this mysterious complication needed to explain an oscillation of the wind veering, for instance, by the west from south-east to north-east, then suddenly returning in the same great curve from north-east to south-east, so as to make in thirty-six hours a prodigious circuit of 560 degrees? Such was the preface to the snowstorm of March 17, 1867.

The storm-waves of Australia reach a height of 80 feet; this fact is connected with the vicinity of the Pole. Storms in those latitudes result less from disorder of the winds than from submarine electrical discharges. In the year 1866 the transatlantic cable was disturbed at regular intervals in its working for two hours in the twenty-four—from noon to two o'clock—by a sort of intermittent fever. Certain compositions and decompositions of forces produce phenomena, and impose themselves on the calculations of the seaman under pain of shipwreck. The day that navigation, now a routine, shall become a mathematic; the day we shall, for instance, seek to know why it is that in our regions hot winds come sometimes from the north, and cold winds from the south; the day we shall understand that diminutions of temperature are proportionate to oceanic depths; the day we realize that the globe is a vast loadstone polarized in immensity, with two axes—an axis of rotation and an axis of effluvium—intersecting each other at the centre of the earth, and that the magnetic poles turn round the geographical poles; when those who risk life will choose to risk it scientifically; when men shall navigate assured from studied uncertainty; when the captain shall be a meteorologist; when the pilot shall be a chemist; then will many catastrophes be avoided. The sea is magnetic as much as aquatic: an ocean of unknown forces floats in the ocean of the waves, or, one might say, on the surface. Only to behold in the sea a mass of water is not to see it at all: the sea is an ebb and flow of fluid, as much as a flux and reflux of liquid. It is, perhaps, complicated by attractions even more than by hurricanes; molecular adhesion, manifested among other phenomena by capillary attraction, although microscopic, takes in ocean its place in the grandeur of immensity; and the wave of effluvium sometimes aids, sometimes counteracts, the wave of the air and the wave of the waters. He who is ignorant of electric law is ignorant of hydraulic law; for the one intermixes with the other. It is true there is no study more difficult nor more obscure; it verges on empiricism, just as astronomy verges on astrology; and yet without this study there is no navigation. Having said this much we will pass on.

One of the most dangerous components of the sea is the snowstorm. The snowstorm is above all things magnetic. The pole produces it as it produces the aurora borealis. It is in the fog of the one as in the light of the other; and in the flake of snow as in the streak of flame effluvium is visible.

Storms are the nervous attacks and delirious frenzies of the sea. The sea has its ailments. Tempests may be compared to maladies. Some are mortal, others not; some may be escaped, others not. The snowstorm is supposed to be generally mortal. Jarabija, one of the pilots of Magellan, termed it "a cloud issuing from the devil's sore side."[2]

The old Spanish navigators called this kind of squall *la nevada*, when it came with snow; *la helada*, when it came with hail. According to them, bats fell from the sky, with the snow.

Snowstorms are characteristic of polar latitudes; nevertheless, at times they glide—one might almost say tumble—into our climates; so much ruin is mingled with the chances of the air.

The *Matutina*, as we have seen, plunged resolutely into the great hazard of the night, a hazard increased by the impending storm. She had encountered its menace with a sort of tragic audacity; nevertheless, it must be remembered that she had received due warning.

CHAPTER II.

OUR FIRST ROUGH SKETCHES FILLED IN

While the hooker was in the gulf of Portland, there was but little sea on; the ocean, if gloomy, was almost still, and the sky was yet clear. The wind took little effect on the vessel; the hooker hugged the cliff as closely as possible; it served as a screen to her.

There were ten on board the little Biscayan felucca—three men in crew, and seven passengers, of whom two were women. In the light of the open sea (which broadens twilight into day) all the figures on board were clearly visible. Besides they were not hiding now—they were all at ease; each one reassumed his freedom of manner, spoke in his own note, showed his face; departure was to them a deliverance.

The motley nature of the group shone out. The women were of no age. A wandering life produces premature old age, and indigence is made up of wrinkles. One of them was a Basque of the Dry-ports. The other, with the large rosary, was an Irishwoman. They wore that air of indifference common to the wretched. They had squatted down close to each other when they got on board, on chests at the foot of the mast. They talked to each other. Irish and Basque are, as we have said, kindred languages. The Basque woman's hair was scented with onions and basil. The skipper of the hooker was a Basque of Guipuzcoa. One sailor was a Basque of the northern slope of the Pyrenees, the other was of the southern slope—that is to say, they were of the same nation, although the first was French and the latter Spanish. The Basques recognize no official country. *Mi madre se llama Montaña*, my mother is called the mountain, as Zalareus, the muleteer, used to say. Of the five men who were with the two women, one was a Frenchman of Languedoc, one a Frenchman of Provence, one a Genoese; one, an old man, he who wore the sombrero without a hole for a pipe, appeared to be a German. The fifth, the chief, was a Basque of the Landes from Biscarrosse. It was he who, just as the child was going on board the hooker, had, with a kick of his heel, cast the plank into the sea. This man, robust, agile, sudden in movement, covered, as may be remembered, with trimmings, slashings, and glistening tinsel, could not keep in his place; he stooped down, rose up, and continually passed to and fro from one end of the vessel to the other, as if debating uneasily on what had been done and what was going to happen.

This chief of the band, the captain and the two men of the crew, all four Basques, spoke sometimes Basque, sometimes Spanish, sometimes French—these three languages being common on both slopes of the Pyrenees. But generally speaking, excepting the women, all talked something like French, which was the foundation of their slang. The French language about this period began to be chosen by the peoples as something intermediate between the excess of consonants in the north and the excess of vowels in the south. In Europe, French was the language of commerce, and also of felony. It will be remembered that Gibby, a London thief, understood Cartouche.

The hooker, a fine sailer, was making quick way; still, ten persons, besides their baggage, were a heavy cargo for one of such light draught.

The fact of the vessel's aiding the escape of a band did not necessarily imply that the crew were accomplices. It was sufficient that the captain of the vessel was a Vascongado, and that the chief of the band was another. Among that race mutual assistance is a duty which admits of no exception. A Basque, as we have said, is neither Spanish nor French; he is Basque, and always and everywhere he must succour a Basque. Such is Pyrenean fraternity.

All the time the hooker was in the gulf, the sky, although threatening, did not frown enough to cause the fugitives any uneasiness. They were flying, they were escaping, they were brutally gay. One laughed, another sang; the laugh was dry but free, the song was low but careless.

The Languedocian cried, "*Caoucagno!*" "*Cocagne*" expresses the highest pitch of satisfaction in Narbonne. He was a longshore sailor, a native of the waterside village of Gruissan, on the southern side of the Clappe, a bargeman rather than a mariner, but accustomed to work the reaches of the inlet of Bages, and to draw the drag-net full of fish over the salt sands of St. Lucie. He was of the race who wear a red cap, make complicated signs of the cross after the Spanish fashion, drink wine out of goat-skins, eat scraped ham, kneel down to blaspheme, and implore their patron saint with threats—"Great saint, grant me what I ask, or I'll throw a stone at thy head, *ou té feg un pic.*" He might be, at need, a useful addition to the crew.

The Provençal in the caboose was blowing up a turf fire under an iron pot, and making broth. The broth was a kind of puchero, in which fish took the place of meat, and into which the Provençal threw chick peas, little bits of bacon cut in squares, and pods of red pimento—concessions made by the eaters of *bouillabaisse* to the eaters of *olla podrida.* One of the bags of provisions was beside him unpacked. He had lighted over his head an iron lantern, glazed with talc, which swung on a hook from the ceiling. By its side, on another hook, swung the weather-cock halcyon. There was a popular belief in those days that a dead halcyon, hung by the beak, always turned its breast to the quarter whence the wind was blowing. While he made the broth, the Provençal put the neck of a gourd into his mouth, and now and then swallowed a draught of aguardiente. It was one of those gourds covered with wicker, broad and flat, with handles, which used to be hung to the side by a strap, and which were then called hip-gourds. Between each gulp he mumbled one of those country songs of which the subject is nothing at all: a hollow road, a hedge; you see in the meadow, through a gap in the bushes, the shadow of a horse and cart, elongated in the sunset, and from time to time, above the hedge, the end of a fork loaded with hay appears and disappears—you want no more to make a song.

A departure, according to the bent of one's mind, is a relief or a depression. All seemed lighter in spirits excepting the old man of the band, the man with the hat that had no pipe.

This old man, who looked more German than anything else, although he had one of those unfathomable faces in which nationality is lost, was bald, and so grave that his baldness might have been a tonsure. Every time he passed before the Virgin on the prow, he raised his felt hat, so that you could see the swollen and senile veins of his skull. A sort of full gown, torn and threadbare, of brown Dorchester serge, but half hid his closely fitting coat, tight, compact, and hooked up to the neck like a cassock. His hands inclined to cross each other, and had the mechanical junction of habitual prayer. He had what might be called a wan countenance; for the countenance is above all things a reflection, and it is an error to believe that idea is colourless. That countenance was evidently the surface of a strange inner state, the result of a composition of contradictions, some tending to drift away in good, others in evil, and to an observer it was the revelation of one who was less and more than human—capable of falling below the scale of the tiger, or of rising above that of man. Such chaotic souls exist. There was something inscrutable in that face. Its secret reached the abstract. You felt that the man had known the foretaste of evil which is the calculation, and the after-taste which is the zero. In his impassibility, which was perhaps only on the surface, were imprinted two petrifactions—the petrifaction of the heart proper to the hangman, and the petrifaction of the mind proper to the mandarin. One might have said (for the monstrous has its mode of being complete) that all things were possible to him, even emotion. In every savant there is something of the corpse, and this man was a savant. Only to see him you caught science imprinted in the gestures of his body and in the folds of his dress. His was a fossil face, the serious cast of which was counteracted by that wrinkled mobility of the polyglot which verges on grimace. But a severe man withal; nothing of the hypocrite, nothing of the cynic. A tragic dreamer. He was one of those whom crime leaves pensive; he had the brow of an incendiary tempered by the eyes of an archbishop. His sparse gray locks turned to white over his temples. The Christian was evident in him, complicated with the fatalism of the Turk. Chalkstones deformed his fingers, dissected by leanness. The stiffness of his tall frame was grotesque. He had his sea-legs, he walked slowly about the deck, not looking at any one, with an air decided and sinister. His eyeballs were vaguely filled with the fixed light of a soul studious of the darkness and afflicted by reapparitions of conscience.

From time to time the chief of the band, abrupt and alert, and making sudden turns about the vessel, came to him and whispered in his ear. The old man answered by a nod. It might have been the lightning consulting the night.

CHAPTER III.

TROUBLED MEN
ON THE TROUBLED SEA

Two men on board the craft were absorbed in thought—the old man, and the skipper of the hooker, who must not be mistaken for the chief of the band. The captain was occupied by the sea, the old man by the sky. The former did not lift his eyes from the waters; the latter kept watch on the firmament. The skipper's anxiety was the state of the sea; the old man seemed to suspect the heavens. He scanned the stars through every break in the clouds.

It was the time when day still lingers, but some few stars begin faintly to pierce the twilight. The horizon was singular. The mist upon it varied. Haze predominated on land, clouds at sea.

The skipper, noting the rising billows, hauled all taut before he got outside Portland Bay. He would not delay so doing until he should pass the headland. He examined the rigging closely, and satisfied himself that the lower shrouds were well set up, and supported firmly the futtock-shrouds—precautions of a man who means to carry on with a press of sail, at all risks.

The hooker was not trimmed, being two feet by the head. This was her weak point.

The captain passed every minute from the binnacle to the standard compass, taking the bearings of objects on shore. The *Matutina* had at first a soldier's wind which was not unfavourable, though she could not lie within five points of her course. The captain took the helm as often as possible, trusting no one but himself to prevent her from dropping to leeward, the effect of the rudder being influenced by the steerage-way.

The difference between the true and apparent course being relative to the way on the vessel, the hooker seemed to lie closer to the wind than she did in reality. The breeze was not a-beam, nor was the hooker close-hauled; but one cannot ascertain the true course made, except when the wind is abaft. When you perceive long streaks of clouds meeting in a point on the horizon, you may be sure that the wind is in that quarter; but this evening the wind was variable; the needle fluctuated; the captain distrusted the erratic movements of the vessel. He steered carefully but resolutely, luffed her up, watched her coming to, prevented her from yawing, and from running into the wind's eye: noted the leeway, the little jerks of the helm: was observant of every roll and pitch of the vessel, of the difference in her speed, and of the variable gusts of wind. For fear of accidents, he was constantly on the lookout for squalls from off the land he was hugging, and above all he was cautious to keep her full; the direction of the breeze indicated by the compass being uncertain from the small size of the instrument. The captain's eyes, frequently lowered, remarked every change in the waves.

Once nevertheless he raised them towards the sky, and tried to make out the three stars of Orion's belt. These stars are called the three magi, and an old proverb of the ancient Spanish pilots declares that, "He who sees the three magi is not far from the Saviour."

This glance of the captain's tallied with an aside growled out, at the other end of the vessel, by the old man, "We don't even see the pointers, nor the star Antares, red as he is. Not one is distinct."

No care troubled the other fugitives.

Still, when the first hilarity they felt in their escape had passed away, they could not help remembering that they were at sea in the month of January, and that the wind was frozen. It was impossible to establish themselves in the cabin. It was much too narrow and too much encumbered by bales and baggage. The baggage belonged to the passengers, the bales to the crew, for the hooker was no pleasure boat, and was engaged in smuggling. The passengers were obliged to settle themselves on deck, a condition to which these wanderers easily resigned themselves. Open-air habits make it simple for vagabonds to arrange themselves for the night. The open air (*la belle étoile*) is their friend, and the cold helps them to sleep—sometimes to die.

This night, as we have seen, there was no *belle étoile*.

The Languedocian and the Genoese, while waiting for supper, rolled themselves up near the women, at the foot of the mast, in some tarpaulin which the sailors had thrown them.

The old man remained at the bow motionless, and apparently insensible to the cold.

The captain of the hooker, from the helm where he was standing, uttered a sort of guttural call somewhat like the cry of the American bird called the exclaimer; at his call the chief of the brand drew near, and the captain addressed him thus,—

"Etcheco Jaüna." These two words, which mean "tiller of the mountain," form with the old Cantabri a solemn preface to any subject which should command attention.

Then the captain pointed the old man out to the chief, and the dialogue continued in Spanish; it was not, indeed, a very correct dialect, being that of the mountains. Here are the questions and answers.

"Etcheco jaüna, que es este hombre?"

"Un hombre."

"Que lenguas habla?"

"Todas."

"Que cosas sabe?"

"Todas."

"Quai païs?"

"Ningun, y todos."

"Qual dios?"

"Dios."

"Como le llamas?"

"El tonto."

"Como dices que le llamas?"

"El sabio."

"En vuestre tropa que esta?"
"Esta lo que esta."
"El gefe?"
"No."
"Pues que esta?"
"La alma."[3]

The chief and the captain parted, each reverting to his own meditation, and a little while afterwards the *Matutina* left the gulf.

Now came the great rolling of the open sea. The ocean in the spaces between the foam was slimy in appearance. The waves, seen through the twilight in indistinct outline, somewhat resembled plashes of gall. Here and there a wave floating flat showed cracks and stars, like a pane of glass broken by stones; in the centre of these stars, in a revolving orifice, trembled a phosphorescence, like that feline reflection, of vanished light which shines in the eyeballs of owls.

Proudly, like a bold swimmer, the *Matutina* crossed the dangerous Shambles shoal. This bank, a hidden obstruction at the entrance of Portland roads, is not a barrier; it is an amphitheatre—a circus of sand under the sea, its benches cut out by the circling of the waves—an arena, round and symmetrical, as high as a Jungfrau, only drowned—a coliseum of the ocean, seen by the diver in the vision-like transparency which engulfs him,—such is the Shambles shoal. There hydras fight, leviathans meet. There, says the legend, at the bottom of the gigantic shaft, are the wrecks of ships, seized and sunk by the huge spider Kraken, also called the fish-mountain. Such things lie in the fearful shadow of the sea.

These spectral realities, unknown to man, are manifested at the surface by a slight shiver.

In this nineteenth century, the Shambles bank is in ruins; the breakwater recently constructed has overthrown and mutilated, by the force of its surf, that high submarine architecture, just as the jetty, built at the Croisic in 1760, changed, by a quarter of an hour, the course of the tides. And yet the tide is eternal. But eternity obeys man more than man imagines.

CHAPTER IV.

A CLOUD DIFFERENT FROM THE OTHERS ENTERS ON THE SCENE

The old man whom the chief of the band had named first the Madman, then the Sage, now never left the forecastle. Since they crossed the Shambles shoal, his attention had been divided between the heavens and the waters. He looked down, he looked upwards, and above all watched the north-east.

The skipper gave the helm to a sailor, stepped over the after hatchway, crossed the gangway, and went on to the forecastle. He approached the old man, but not in front. He stood a little behind, with elbows resting on his hips, with outstretched hands, the head on one side, with open eyes and arched eyebrows, and a smile in the corners of his mouth—an attitude of curiosity hesitating between mockery and respect.

The old man, either that it was his habit to talk to himself, or that hearing some one behind incited him to speech, began to soliloquize while he looked into space.

"The meridian, from which the right ascension is calculated, is marked in this century by four stars—the Polar, Cassiopeia's Chair, Andromeda's Head, and the star Algenib, which is in Pegasus. But there is not one visible."

These words followed each other mechanically, confused, and scarcely articulated, as if he did not care to pronounce them. They floated out of his mouth and dispersed. Soliloquy is the smoke exhaled by the inmost fires of the soul.

The skipper broke in, "My lord!"

The old man, perhaps rather deaf as well as very thoughtful, went on,—

"Too few stars, and too much wind. The breeze continually changes its direction and blows inshore; thence it rises perpendicularly. This results from the land being warmer than the water. Its atmosphere is lighter. The cold and dense wind of the sea rushes in to replace it. From this cause, in the upper regions the wind blows towards the land from every quarter. It would be advisable to make long tacks between the true and apparent parallel. When the latitude by observation differs from the latitude by dead reckoning by not more than three minutes in thirty miles, or by four minutes in sixty miles, you are in the true course."

The skipper bowed, but the old man saw him not. The latter, who wore what resembled an Oxford or Gottingen university gown, did not relax his haughty and rigid attitude. He observed the waters as a critic of waves and of men. He studied the billows, but almost as if he was about to demand his turn to speak amidst their turmoil, and teach them something. There was in him both pedagogue and soothsayer. He seemed an oracle of the deep.

He continued his soliloquy, which was perhaps intended to be heard.

"We might strive if we had a wheel instead of a helm. With a speed of twelve miles an hour, a force of twenty pounds exerted on the wheel produces three hundred thousand pounds' effect on the course. And more too. For in some cases, with a double block and runner, they can get two more revolutions."

The skipper bowed a second time, and said, "My lord!"

The old man's eye rested on him; he had turned his head without moving his body.

"Call me Doctor."

"Master Doctor, I am the skipper."

"Just so," said the doctor.

The doctor, as henceforward we shall call him, appeared willing to converse.

"Skipper, have you an English sextant?"

"No."

"Without an English sextant you cannot take an altitude at all."

"The Basques," replied the captain, "took altitudes before there were any English."

"Be careful you are not taken aback."

"I keep her away when necessary."

"Have you tried how many knots she is running?"

"Yes."

"When?"

"Just now."

"How?"

"By the log."

"Did you take the trouble to look at the triangle?"

"Yes."

"Did the sand run through the glass in exactly thirty seconds?"

"Yes."

"Are you sure that the sand has not worn the hole between the globes?"

"Yes."

"Have you proved the sand-glass by the oscillations of a bullet?"

"Suspended by a rope yarn drawn out from the top of a coil of soaked hemp? Undoubtedly."

"Have you waxed the yarn lest it should stretch?"

"Yes."

"Have you tested the log?"

"I tested the sand-glass by the bullet, and checked the log by a round shot."

"Of what size was the shot?"

"One foot in diameter."

"Heavy enough?"

"It is an old round shot of our war hooker, La Casse de Par-Grand."

"Which was in the Armada?"

"Yes."

"And which carried six hundred soldiers, fifty sailors, and twenty-five guns?"

"Shipwreck knows it."

"How did you compute the resistance of the water to the shot?"

"By means of a German scale."

"Have you taken into account the resistance of the rope supporting the shot to the waves?"

"Yes."
"What was the result?"
"The resistance of the water was 170 pounds."
"That's to say she is running four French leagues an hour."
"And three Dutch leagues."
"But that is the difference merely of the vessel's way and the rate at which the sea is running?"
"Undoubtedly."
"Whither are you steering?"
"For a creek I know, between Loyola and St. Sebastian."
"Make the latitude of the harbour's mouth as soon as possible."
"Yes, as near as I can."
"Beware of gusts and currents. The first cause the second."
"Traidores."[4]
"No abuse. The sea understands. Insult nothing. Rest satisfied with watching."
"I have watched, and I do watch. Just now the tide is running against the wind; by-and-by, when it turns, we shall be all right."
"Have you a chart?"
"No; not for this channel."
"Then you sail by rule of thumb?"
"Not at all. I have a compass."
"The compass is one eye, the chart the other."
"A man with one eye can see."
"How do you compute the difference between the true and apparent course?"
"I've got my standard compass, and I make a guess."
"To guess is all very well. To know for certain is better."
"Christopher guessed."
"When there is a fog and the needle revolves treacherously, you can never tell on which side you should look out for squalls, and the end of it is that you know neither the true nor apparent day's work. An ass with his chart is better off than a wizard with his oracle."
"There is no fog in the breeze yet, and I see no cause for alarm."
"Ships are like flies in the spider's web of the sea."
"Just now both winds and waves are tolerably favourable."
"Black specks quivering on the billows—such are men on the ocean."
"I dare say there will be nothing wrong to-night."
"You may get into such a mess that you will find it hard to get out of it."
"All goes well at present."
The doctor's eyes were fixed on the north-east. The skipper continued,—
"Let us once reach the Gulf of Gascony, and I answer for our safety. Ah! I should say I am at home there. I know it well, my Gulf of Gascony. It is a little basin, often very boisterous; but there, I know every sounding in it and the nature of the bottom—mud opposite San Cipriano, shells opposite Cizarque, sand off Cape Peñas, little pebbles off Boncaut de Mimizan, and I know the colour of every pebble."
The skipper broke off; the doctor was no longer listening.

The doctor gazed at the north-east. Over that icy face passed an extraordinary expression. All the agony of terror possible to a mask of stone was depicted there. From his mouth escaped this word, "Good!"

His eyeballs, which had all at once become quite round like an owl's, were dilated with stupor on discovering a speck on the horizon. He added,—

"It is well. As for me, I am resigned."

The skipper looked at him. The doctor went on talking to himself, or to some one in the deep,—

"I say, Yes."

Then he was silent, opened his eyes wider and wider with renewed attention on that which he was watching, and said,—

"It is coming from afar, but not the less surely will it come."

The arc of the horizon which occupied the visual rays and thoughts of the doctor, being opposite to the west, was illuminated by the transcendent reflection of twilight, as if it were day. This arc, limited in extent, and surrounded by streaks of grayish vapour, was uniformly blue, but of a leaden rather than cerulean blue. The doctor, having completely returned to the contemplation of the sea, pointed to this atmospheric arc, and said,—

"Skipper, do you see?"

"What?"

"That."

"What?"

"Out there."

"A blue spot? Yes."

"What is it?"

"A niche in heaven."

"For those who go to heaven; for those who go elsewhere it is another affair." And he emphasized these enigmatical words with an appalling expression which was unseen in the darkness.

A silence ensued. The skipper, remembering the two names given by the chief to this man, asked himself the question,—

"Is he a madman, or is he a sage?"

The stiff and bony finger of the doctor remained immovably pointing, like a sign-post, to the misty blue spot in the sky.

The skipper looked at this spot.

"In truth," he growled out, "it is not sky but clouds."

"A blue cloud is worse than a black cloud," said the doctor; "and," he added, "it's a snow-cloud."

"La nube de la nieve," said the skipper, as if trying to understand the word better by translating it.

"Do you know what a snow-cloud is?" asked the doctor.

"No."

"You'll know by-and-by."

The skipper again turned his attention to the horizon.

Continuing to observe the cloud, he muttered between his teeth,—

"One month of squalls, another of wet; January with its gales, February with its rains—that's all the winter we Asturians get. Our rain even is warm. We've no snow but on the mountains. Ay, ay; look out for the avalanche. The avalanche is no respecter of persons. The avalanche is a brute."

"And the waterspout is a monster," said the doctor, adding, after a pause, "Here it comes." He continued, "Several winds are getting up together—a strong wind from the west, and a gentle wind from the east."

"That last is a deceitful one," said the skipper.

The blue cloud was growing larger.

"If the snow," said the doctor, "is appalling when it slips down the mountain, think what it is when it falls from the Pole!"

His eye was glassy. The cloud seemed to spread over his face and simultaneously over the horizon. He continued, in musing tones,—

"Every minute the fatal hour draws nearer. The will of Heaven is about to be manifested."

The skipper asked himself again this question,—"Is he a madman?"

"Skipper," began the doctor, without taking his eyes off the cloud, "have you often crossed the Channel?"

"This is the first time."

The doctor, who was absorbed by the blue cloud, and who, as a sponge can take up but a definite quantity of water, had but a definite measure of anxiety, displayed no more emotion at this answer of the skipper than was expressed by a slight shrug of his shoulders.

"How is that?"

"Master Doctor, my usual cruise is to Ireland. I sail from Fontarabia to Black Harbour or to the Achill Islands. I go sometimes to Braich-y-Pwll, a point on the Welsh coast. But I always steer outside the Scilly Islands. I do not know this sea at all."

"That's serious. Woe to him who is inexperienced on the ocean! One ought to be familiar with the Channel—the Channel is the Sphinx. Look out for shoals."

"We are in twenty-five fathoms here."

"We ought to get into fifty-five fathoms to the west, and avoid even twenty fathoms to the east."

"We'll sound as we get on."

"The Channel is not an ordinary sea. The water rises fifty feet with the spring tides, and twenty-five with neap tides. Here we are in slack water. I thought you looked scared."

"We'll sound to-night."

"To sound you must heave to, and that you cannot do."

"Why not?"

"On account of the wind."

"We'll try."

"The squall is close on us."

"We'll sound, Master Doctor."

"You could not even bring to."

"Trust in God."

"Take care what you say. Pronounce not lightly the awful name."

"I will sound, I tell you."

"Be sensible; you will have a gale of wind presently."

"I say that I will try for soundings."

"The resistance of the water will prevent the lead from sinking, and the line will break. Ah! so this is your first time in these waters?"

"The first time."

"Very well; in that case listen, skipper."

The tone of the word "listen" was so commanding that the skipper made an obeisance.

"Master Doctor, I am all attention."

"Port your helm, and haul up on the starboard tack."

"What do you mean?"

"Steer your course to the west."

"Caramba!"

"Steer your course to the west."

"Impossible."

"As you will. What I tell you is for the others' sake. As for myself, I am indifferent."

"But, Master Doctor, steer west?"

"Yes, skipper."

"The wind will be dead ahead."

"Yes, skipper."

"She'll pitch like the devil."

"Moderate your language. Yes, skipper."

"The vessel would be in irons."

"Yes, skipper."

"That means very likely the mast will go."

"Possibly."

"Do you wish me to steer west?"

"Yes."

"I cannot."

"In that case settle your reckoning with the sea."

"The wind ought to change."

"It will not change all night."

"Why not?"

"Because it is a wind twelve hundred leagues in length."

"Make headway against such a wind! Impossible."

"To the west, I tell you."

"I'll try, but in spite of everything she will fall off."

"That's the danger."

"The wind sets us to the east."

"Don't go to the east."

"Why not?"

"Skipper, do you know what is for us the word of death?"

"No."

"Death is the east."

"I'll steer west."

This time the doctor, having turned right round, looked the skipper full in the face, and with his eyes resting on him, as though to implant the idea in his head, pronounced slowly, syllable by syllable, these words,—

"If to-night out at sea we hear the sound of a bell, the ship is lost."

The skipper pondered in amaze.

"What do you mean?"

The doctor did not answer. His countenance, expressive for a moment, was now reserved. His eyes became vacuous. He did not appear to hear the skipper's wondering question. He was now attending to his own monologue. His lips let fall, as if mechanically, in a low murmuring tone, these words,—

"The time has come for sullied souls to purify themselves."

The skipper made that expressive grimace which raises the chin towards the nose.

"He is more madman than sage," he growled, and moved off.

Nevertheless he steered west.

But the wind and the sea were rising.

CHAPTER V.

HARDQUANONNE

The mist was deformed by all sorts of inequalities, bulging out at once on every point of the horizon, as if invisible mouths were busy puffing out the bags of wind. The formation of the clouds was becoming ominous. In the west, as in the east, the sky's depths were now invaded by the blue cloud: it advanced in the teeth of the wind. These contradictions are part of the wind's vagaries.

The sea, which a moment before wore scales, now wore a skin—such is the nature of that dragon. It was no longer a crocodile: it was a boa. The skin, lead-coloured and dirty, looked thick, and was crossed by heavy wrinkles. Here and there, on its surface, bubbles of surge, like pustules, gathered and then burst. The foam was like a leprosy. It was at this moment that the hooker, still seen from afar by the child, lighted her signal.

A quarter of an hour elapsed.

The skipper looked for the doctor: he was no longer on deck. Directly the skipper had left him, the doctor had stooped his somewhat ungainly form under the hood, and had entered the cabin; there he had sat down near the stove, on a block. He had taken a shagreen ink-bottle and a cordwain pocket-book from his pocket; he had extracted from his pocket-book a parchment folded four times, old, stained, and yellow; he had opened the sheet, taken a pen out of his ink-case, placed the pocket-book flat on his knee, and the parchment on the pocket-book; and by the rays of the lantern, which was lighting the cook, he set to writing on the back of the parchment. The roll of the waves inconvenienced him. He wrote thus for some time.

As he wrote, the doctor remarked the gourd of aguardiente, which the Provençal tasted every time he added a grain of pimento to the puchero, as if he were consulting it in reference to the seasoning. The doctor noticed the gourd, not because it was a bottle of brandy, but because of a name which was plaited in the wickerwork with red rushes on a background of white. There was light enough in the cabin to permit of his reading the name.

The doctor paused, and spelled it in a low voice,—

"Hardquanonne."

Then he addressed the cook.

"I had not observed that gourd before; did it belong to Hardquanonne?"

"Yes," the cook answered; "to our poor comrade, Hardquanonne."

The doctor went on,—

"To Hardquanonne, the Fleming of Flanders?"

"Yes."

"Who is in prison?"

"Yes."

"In the dungeon at Chatham?"

"It is his gourd," replied the cook; "and he was my friend. I keep it in remembrance of him. When shall we see him again? It is the bottle he used to wear slung over his hip."

The doctor took up his pen again, and continued laboriously tracing somewhat straggling lines on the parchment. He was evidently anxious that his handwriting should be very legible; and at length, notwithstanding the tremulousness of the vessel and the tremulousness of age, he finished what he wanted to write.

It was time, for suddenly a sea struck the craft, a mighty rush of waters besieged the hooker, and they felt her break into that fearful dance in which ships lead off with the tempest.

The doctor arose and approached the stove, meeting the ship's motion with his knees dexterously bent, dried as best he could, at the stove where the pot was boiling, the lines he had written, refolded the parchment in the pocket-book, and replaced the pocket-book and the inkhorn in his pocket.

The stove was not the least ingenious piece of interior economy in the hooker. It was judiciously isolated. Meanwhile the pot heaved—the Provençal was watching it.

"Fish broth," said he.

"For the fishes," replied the doctor. Then he went on deck again.

CHAPTER VI.

THEY THINK THAT HELP IS AT HAND

Through his growing preoccupation the doctor in some sort reviewed the situation; and any one near to him might have heard these words drop from his lips,—

"Too much rolling, and not enough pitching."

Then recalled to himself by the dark workings of his mind, he sank again into thought, as a miner into his shaft. His meditation in nowise interfered with his watch on the sea. The contemplation of the sea is in itself a reverie.

The dark punishment of the waters, eternally tortured, was commencing. A lamentation arose from the whole main. Preparations, confused and melancholy, were forming in space. The doctor observed all before him, and lost no detail. There was, however, no sign of scrutiny in his face. One does not scrutinize hell.

A vast commotion, yet half latent, but visible through the turmoils in space, increased and irritated, more and more, the winds, the vapours, the waves. Nothing is so logical and nothing appears so absurd as the ocean. Self-dispersion is the essence of its sovereignty, and is one of the elements of its redundance. The sea is ever for and against. It knots that it may unravel itself; one of its slopes attacks, the other relieves. No apparition is so wonderful as the waves. Who can paint the alternating hollows and promontories, the valleys, the melting bosoms, the sketches? How render the thickets of foam, blendings of mountains and dreams? The indescribable is everywhere there—in the rending, in the frowning, in the anxiety, in the perpetual contradiction, in the chiaroscuro, in the pendants of the cloud, in the keys of the ever-open vault, in the disaggregation without rupture, in the funereal tumult caused by all that madness!

The wind had just set due north. Its violence was so favourable and so useful in driving them away from England that the captain of the *Matutina* had made up his mind to set all sail. The hooker slipped through the foam as at a gallop, the wind right aft, bounding from wave to wave in a gay frenzy. The fugitives were delighted, and laughed; they clapped their hands, applauded the surf, the sea, the wind, the sails, the swift progress, the flight, all unmindful of the future. The doctor appeared not to see them, and dreamt on.

Every vestige of day had faded away. This was the moment when the child, watching from the distant cliff, lost sight of the hooker. Up to then his glance had remained fixed, and, as it were, leaning on the vessel. What part had that look in fate? When the hooker was lost to sight in the distance, and when the child could no longer see aught, the child went north and the ship went south.

All were plunged in darkness.

CHAPTER VII.

SUPERHUMAN HORRORS

On their part it was with wild jubilee and delight that those on board the hooker saw the hostile land recede and lessen behind them. By degrees the dark ring of ocean rose higher, dwarfing in twilight Portland, Purbeck, Tineham, Kimmeridge, the Matravers, the long streaks of dim cliffs, and the coast dotted with lighthouses.

England disappeared. The fugitives had now nothing round them but the sea.

All at once night grew awful.

There was no longer extent nor space; the sky became blackness, and closed in round the vessel. The snow began to fall slowly; a few flakes appeared. They might have been ghosts. Nothing else was visible in the course of the wind. They felt as if yielded up. A snare lurked in every possibility.

It is in this cavernous darkness that in our climate the Polar waterspout makes its appearance.

A great muddy cloud, like to the belly of a hydra, hung over ocean, and in places its lividity adhered to the waves. Some of these adherences resembled pouches with holes, pumping the sea, disgorging vapour, and refilling themselves with water. Here and there these suctions drew up cones of foam on the sea.

The boreal storm hurled itself on the hooker. The hooker rushed to meet it. The squall and the vessel met as though to insult each other.

In the first mad shock not a sail was clewed up, not a jib lowered, not a reef taken in, so much is flight a delirium. The mast creaked and bent back as if in fear.

Cyclones, in our northern hemisphere, circle from left to right, in the same direction as the hands of a watch, with a velocity which is sometimes as much as sixty miles an hour. Although she was entirely at the mercy of that whirling power, the hooker behaved as if she were out in moderate weather, without any further precaution than keeping her head on to the rollers, with the wind broad on the bow so as to avoid being pooped or caught broadside on. This semi-prudence would have availed her nothing in case of the wind's shifting and taking her aback.

A deep rumbling was brewing up in the distance. The roar of the abyss, nothing can be compared to it. It is the great brutish howl of the universe. What we call matter, that unsearchable organism, that amalgamation of incommensurable energies, in which can occasionally be detected an almost imperceptible degree of intention which makes us shudder, that blind, benighted cosmos, that enigmatical Pan, has a cry, a strange cry, prolonged, obstinate, and continuous, which is less than speech and more than thunder. That cry is the hurricane. Other voices, songs, melodies, clamours, tones, proceed from nests, from broods, from pairings, from nuptials, from homes. This one, a trumpet, comes out of the Naught, which is All. Other voices express the soul of the universe; this one expresses the monster. It is the howl of the formless. It is the inarticulate finding utterance in the indefinite. A thing it is full of pathos and terror. Those clamours converse above and beyond man. They rise, fall, undulate, determine waves of sound, form all sorts of wild surprises for the mind, now burst close to the ear with the importunity of a peal of trumpets, now assail us with the rumbling hoarseness of distance. Giddy uproar which resembles a language, and which, in fact, is a language. It is the effort which the world makes to speak. It is the lisping of the wonderful. In this wail is manifested vaguely all that the vast dark palpitation endures, suffers, accepts, rejects. For the most part it talks nonsense; it is like an access of chronic sickness, and rather an epilepsy diffused than a force employed; we fancy that we are witnessing the descent of supreme evil into the infinite. At moments we seem to discern a reclamation of the elements, some vain effort of chaos to reassert itself over creation. At times it is a complaint. The void bewails and justifies itself. It is as the pleading of the world's cause. We can fancy that the universe is engaged in a lawsuit; we listen—we try to grasp the reasons given, the redoubtable for and against. Such a moaning of the shadows has the tenacity of a syllogism. Here is a vast trouble for thought. Here is the *raison d'être* of mythologies and polytheisms. To the terror of those great murmurs are added superhuman outlines melting away as they appear—Eumenides which are almost distinct, throats of Furies shaped in the clouds, Plutonian chimeras almost defined. No horrors equal those sobs, those laughs, those tricks of tumult, those inscrutable questions and answers, those appeals to unknown aid. Man knows not what to become in the presence of that awful incantation. He bows under the enigma of those Draconian intonations. What latent meaning have they? What do they signify? What do they threaten? What do they implore? It would seem as though all bonds were loosened. Vociferations from precipice to precipice, from air to water, from the wind to the wave, from the rain to the rock, from the zenith to the nadir, from the stars to the foam—the abyss unmuzzled—such is that tumult, complicated by some mysterious strife with evil consciences.

The loquacity of night is not less lugubrious than its silence. One feels in it the anger of the unknown.

Night is a presence. Presence of what?

For that matter we must distinguish between night and the shadows. In the night there is the absolute; in the darkness the multiple. Grammar, logic as it is, admits of no singular for the shadows. The night is one, the shadows are many.[5]

This mist of nocturnal mystery is the scattered, the fugitive, the crumbling, the fatal; one feels earth no longer, one feels the other reality.

In the shadow, infinite and indefinite, lives something or some one; but that which lives there forms part of our death. After our earthly passage, when that shadow shall be light for us, the life which is beyond our life shall seize us. Meanwhile it appears to touch and try us. Obscurity is a pressure. Night is, as it were, a hand placed on our soul. At certain hideous and solemn hours we feel that which is beyond the wall of the tomb encroaching on us.

Never does this proximity of the unknown seem more imminent than in storms at sea. The horrible combines with the fantastic. The possible interrupter of human actions, the old Cloud compeller, has it in his power to mould, in whatsoever shape he chooses, the inconsistent element, the limitless incoherence, the force diffused and undecided of aim. That mystery the tempest every instant accepts and executes some unknown changes of will, apparent or real.

Poets have, in all ages, called this the caprice of the waves. But there is no such thing as caprice. The disconcerting enigmas which in nature we call caprice, and in human life chance, are splinters of a law revealed to us in glimpses.

CHAPTER VIII.

NIX ET NOX

The characteristic of the snowstorm is its blackness. Nature's habitual aspect during a storm, the earth or sea black and the sky pale, is reversed; the sky is black, the ocean white, foam below, darkness above; a horizon walled in with smoke; a zenith roofed with crape. The tempest resembles a cathedral hung with mourning, but no light in that cathedral: no phantom lights on the crests of the waves, no spark, no phosphorescence, naught but a huge shadow. The polar cyclone differs from the tropical cyclone, inasmuch as the one sets fire to every light, and the other extinguishes them all. The world is suddenly converted into the arched vault of a cave. Out of the night falls a dust of pale spots, which hesitate between sky and sea. These spots, which are flakes of snow, slip, wander, and flow. It is like the tears of a winding-sheet putting themselves into lifelike motion. A mad wind mingles with this dissemination. Blackness crumbling into whiteness, the furious into the obscure, all the tumult of which the sepulchre is capable, a whirlwind under a catafalque—such is the snowstorm. Underneath trembles the ocean, forming and re-forming over portentous unknown depths.

In the polar wind, which is electrical, the flakes turn suddenly into hailstones, and the air becomes filled with projectiles; the water crackles, shot with grape.

No thunderstrokes: the lightning of boreal storms is silent. What is sometimes said of the cat, "it swears," may be applied to this lightning. It is a menace proceeding from a mouth half open and strangely inexorable. The snowstorm is a storm blind and dumb; when it has passed, the ships also are often blind and the sailors dumb.

To escape from such an abyss is difficult.

It would be wrong, however, to believe shipwreck to be absolutely inevitable. The Danish fishermen of Disco and the Balesin; the seekers of black whales; Hearn steering towards Behring Strait, to discover the mouth of Coppermine River; Hudson, Mackenzie, Vancouver, Ross, Dumont D'Urville, all underwent at the Pole itself the wildest hurricanes, and escaped out of them.

It was into this description of tempest that the hooker had entered, triumphant and in full sail—frenzy against frenzy. When Montgomery, escaping from Rouen, threw his galley, with all the force of its oars, against the chain barring the Seine at La Bouille, he showed similar effrontery.

The *Matutina* sailed on fast; she bent so much under her sails that at moments she made a fearful angle with the sea of fifteen degrees; but her good bellied keel adhered to the water as if glued to it. The keel resisted the grasp of the hurricane. The lantern at the prow cast its light ahead.

The cloud, full of winds, dragging its tumour over the deep, cramped and eat more and more into the sea round the hooker. Not a gull, not a sea-mew, nothing but snow. The expanse of the field of waves was becoming contracted and terrible; only three or four gigantic ones were visible.

Now and then a tremendous flash of lightning of a red copper colour broke out behind the obscure superposition of the horizon and the zenith; that sudden release of vermilion flame revealed the horror of the clouds; that abrupt conflagration of the depths, to which for an instant the first tiers of clouds and the distant boundaries of the celestial chaos seemed to adhere, placed the abyss in perspective. On this ground of fire the snow-flakes showed black—they might have been compared to dark butterflies flying about in a furnace—then all was extinguished.

The first explosion over, the squall, still pursuing the hooker, began to roar in thorough bass. This phase of grumbling is a perilous diminution of uproar. Nothing is so terrifying as this monologue of the storm. This gloomy recitative appears to serve as a moment of rest to the mysterious combating forces, and indicates a species of patrol kept in the unknown.

The hooker held wildly on her course. Her two mainsails especially were doing fearful work. The sky and sea were as of ink with jets of foam running higher than the mast. Every instant masses of water swept the deck like a deluge, and at each roll of the vessel the hawse-holes, now to starboard, now to larboard, became as so many open mouths vomiting back the foam into the sea. The women had taken refuge in the cabin, but the men remained on deck; the blinding snow eddied round, the spitting surge mingled with it. All was fury.

At that moment the chief of the band, standing abaft on the stern frames, holding on with one hand to the shrouds, and with the other taking off the kerchief he wore round his head and waving it in the light of the lantern, gay and arrogant, with pride in his face, and his hair in wild disorder, intoxicated by all the darkness, cried out,—

"We are free!"

"Free, free, free," echoed the fugitives, and the band, seizing hold of the rigging, rose up on deck.

"Hurrah!" shouted the chief.

And the band shouted in the storm,—

"Hurrah!"

Just as this clamour was dying away in the tempest, a loud solemn voice rose from the other end of the vessel, saying,—

"Silence!"

All turned their heads. The darkness was thick, and the doctor was leaning against the mast so that he seemed part of it, and they could not see him.

The voice spoke again,—

"Listen!"

All were silent.

Then did they distinctly hear through the darkness the toll of a bell.

CHAPTER IX.

THE CHARGE CONFIDED TO A RAGING SEA

The skipper, at the helm, burst out laughing,—

"A bell! that's good. We are on the larboard tack. What does the bell prove? Why, that we have land to starboard."

The firm and measured voice of the doctor replied,—

"You have not land to starboard."

"But we have," shouted the skipper.

"No!"

"But that bell tolls from the land."

"That bell," said the doctor, "tolls from the sea."

A shudder passed over these daring men. The haggard faces of the two women appeared above the companion like two hobgoblins conjured up. The doctor took a step forward, separating his tall form from the mast. From the depth of the night's darkness came the toll of the bell.

The doctor resumed,—

"There is in the midst of the sea, halfway between Portland and the Channel Islands, a buoy, placed there as a caution; that buoy is moored by chains to the shoal, and floats on the top of the water. On the buoy is fixed an iron trestle, and across the trestle a bell is hung. In bad weather heavy seas toss the buoy, and the bell rings. That is the bell you hear."

The doctor paused to allow an extra violent gust of wind to pass over, waited until the sound of the bell reasserted itself, and then went on,—

"To hear that bell in a storm, when the nor'-wester is blowing, is to be lost. Wherefore? For this reason: if you hear the bell, it is because the wind brings it to you. But the wind is nor'-westerly, and the breakers of Aurigny lie east. You hear the bell only because you are between the buoy and the breakers. It is on those breakers the wind is driving you. You are on the wrong side of the buoy. If you were on the right side, you would be out at sea on a safe course, and you would not hear the bell. The wind would not convey the sound to you. You would pass close to the buoy without knowing it. We are out of our course. That bell is shipwreck sounding the tocsin. Now, look out!"

As the doctor spoke, the bell, soothed by a lull of the storm, rang slowly stroke by stroke, and its intermitting toll seemed to testify to the truth of the old man's words. It was as the knell of the abyss.

All listened breathless, now to the voice, now to the bell.

CHAPTER X.

THE COLOSSAL SAVAGE, THE STORM.

In the meantime the skipper had caught up his speaking-trumpet.

"Strike every sail, my lads; let go the sheets, man the down-hauls, lower ties and brails. Let us steer to the west, let us regain the high sea; head for the buoy, steer for the bell—there's an offing down there. We've yet a chance."

"Try," said the doctor.

Let us remark here, by the way, that this ringing buoy, a kind of bell tower on the deep, was removed in 1802. There are yet alive very old mariners who remember hearing it. It forewarned, but rather too late.

The orders of the skipper were obeyed. The Languedocian made a third sailor. All bore a hand. Not satisfied with brailing up, they furled the sails, lashed the earrings, secured the clew-lines, bunt-lines, and leech-lines, and clapped preventer-shrouds on the block straps, which thus might serve as back-stays. They fished the mast. They battened down the ports and bulls'-eyes, which is a method of walling up a ship. These evolutions, though executed in a lubberly fashion, were, nevertheless, thoroughly effective. The hooker was stripped to bare poles. But in proportion as the vessel, stowing every stitch of canvas, became more helpless, the havoc of both winds and waves increased. The seas ran mountains high. The hurricane, like an executioner hastening to his victim, began to dismember the craft. There came, in the twinkling of an eye, a dreadful crash: the top-sails were blown from the bolt-ropes, the chess-trees were hewn asunder, the deck was swept clear, the shrouds were carried away, the mast went by the board, all the lumber of the wreck was flying in shivers. The main shrouds gave out although they were turned in, and stoppered to four fathoms.

The magnetic currents common to snowstorms hastened the destruction of the rigging. It broke as much from the effect of effluvium as the violence of the wind. Most of the chain gear, fouled in the blocks, ceased to work. Forward the bows, aft the quarters, quivered under the terrific shocks. One wave washed overboard the compass and its binnacle. A second carried away the boat, which, like a box slung under a carriage, had been, in accordance with the quaint Asturian custom, lashed to the bowsprit. A third breaker wrenched off the spritsail yard. A fourth swept away the figurehead and signal light. The rudder only was left.

To replace the ship's bow lantern they set fire to, and suspended at the stem, a large block of wood covered with oakum and tar.

The mast, broken in two, all bristling with quivering splinters, ropes, blocks, and yards, cumbered the deck. In falling it had stove in a plank of the starboard gunwale. The skipper, still firm at the helm, shouted,—

"While we can steer we have yet a chance. The lower planks hold good. Axes, axes! Overboard with the mast! Clear the decks!"

Both crew and passengers worked with the excitement of despair. A few strokes of the hatchets, and it was done. They pushed the mast over the side. The deck was cleared.

"Now," continued the skipper, "take a rope's end and lash me to the helm." To the tiller they bound him.

While they were fastening him he laughed, and shouted,—

"Blow, old hurdy-gurdy, bellow. I've seen your equal off Cape Machichaco."

And when secured he clutched the helm with that strange hilarity which danger awakens.

"All goes well, my lads. Long live our Lady of Buglose! Let us steer west."

An enormous wave came down abeam, and fell on the vessel's quarter. There is always in storms a tiger-like wave, a billow fierce and decisive, which, attaining a certain height, creeps horizontally over the surface of the waters for a time, then rises, roars, rages, and falling on the distressed vessel tears it limb from limb.

A cloud of foam covered the entire poop of the *Matutina.*

There was heard above the confusion of darkness and waters a crash.

When the spray cleared off, when the stern again rose in view, the skipper and the helm had disappeared. Both had been swept away.

The helm and the man they had but just secured to it had passed with the wave into the hissing turmoil of the hurricane.

The chief of the band, gazing intently into the darkness, shouted,—

"*Te burlas de nosotros?*"

To this defiant exclamation there followed another cry,—

"Let go the anchor. Save the skipper."

They rushed to the capstan and let go the anchor.

Hookers carry but one. In this case the anchor reached the bottom, but only to be lost. The bottom was of the hardest rock. The billows were raging with resistless force. The cable snapped like a thread.

The anchor lay at the bottom of the sea. At the cutwater there remained but the cable end protruding from the hawse-hole.

From this moment the hooker became a wreck. The *Matutina* was irrevocably disabled. The vessel, just before in full sail, and almost formidable in her speed, was now helpless. All her evolutions were uncertain and executed at random. She yielded passively and like a log to the capricious fury of the waves. That in a few minutes there should be in place of an eagle a useless cripple, such a transformation is to be witnessed only at sea.

The howling of the wind became more and more frightful. A hurricane has terrible lungs; it makes unceasingly mournful additions to darkness, which cannot be intensified. The bell on the sea rang despairingly, as if tolled by a weird hand.

The *Matutina* drifted like a cork at the mercy of the waves. She sailed no longer—she merely floated. Every moment she seemed about to turn over on her back, like a dead fish. The good condition and perfectly water-tight state of the hull alone saved her from this disaster. Below the water-line not a plank had started. There was not a cranny, chink, nor crack; and she had not made a single drop of water in the hold. This was lucky, as the pump, being out of order, was useless.

The hooker pitched and roared frightfully in the seething billows. The vessel had throes as of sickness, and seemed to be trying to belch forth the unhappy crew.

Helpless they clung to the standing rigging, to the transoms, to the shank painters, to the gaskets, to the broken planks, the protruding nails of which tore their hands, to the warped riders, and to all the rugged projections of the stumps of the masts. From time to time they listened. The toll of the bell came over the waters fainter and fainter; one would have thought that it also was in distress. Its ringing was no more than an intermittent rattle. Then this rattle died away. Where were they? At what distance from the buoy? The sound of the bell had frightened them; its silence terrified them. The north-wester drove them forward in perhaps a fatal course. They felt themselves wafted on by maddened and ever-recurring gusts of wind. The wreck sped forward in the darkness. There is nothing more fearful than being hurried forward blindfold. They felt the abyss before them, over them, under them. It was no longer a run, it was a rush.

Suddenly, through the appalling density of the snowstorm, there loomed a red light.

"A lighthouse!" cried the crew.

CHAPTER XI.

THE CASKETS

It was indeed the Caskets light.

A lighthouse of the nineteenth century is a high cylinder of masonry, surmounted by scientifically constructed machinery for throwing light. The Caskets lighthouse in particular is a triple white tower, bearing three light-rooms. These three chambers revolve on clockwork wheels, with such precision that the man on watch who sees them from sea can invariably take ten steps during their irradiation, and twenty-five during their eclipse. Everything is based on the focal plan, and on the rotation of the octagon drum, formed of eight wide simple lenses in range, having above and below it two series of dioptric rings; an algebraic gear, secured from the effects of the beating of winds and waves by glass a millimetre thick[6], yet sometimes broken by the sea-eagles, which dash themselves like great moths against these gigantic lanterns. The building which encloses and sustains this mechanism, and in which it is set, is also mathematically constructed. Everything about it is plain, exact, bare, precise, correct. A lighthouse is a mathematical figure.

In the seventeenth century a lighthouse was a sort of plume of the land on the seashore. The architecture of a lighthouse tower was magnificent and extravagant. It was covered with balconies, balusters, lodges, alcoves, weathercocks. Nothing but masks, statues, foliage, volutes, reliefs, figures large and small, medallions with inscriptions. *Pax in bello*, said the Eddystone lighthouse. We may as well observe, by the way, that this declaration of peace did not always disarm the ocean. Winstanley repeated it on a lighthouse which he constructed at his own expense, on a wild spot near Plymouth. The tower being finished, he shut himself up in it to have it tried by the tempest. The storm came, and carried off the lighthouse and Winstanley in it. Such excessive adornment gave too great a hold to the hurricane, as generals too brilliantly equipped in battle draw the enemy's fire. Besides whimsical designs in stone, they were loaded with whimsical designs in iron, copper, and wood. The ironwork was in relief, the woodwork stood out. On the sides of the lighthouse there jutted out, clinging to the walls among the arabesques, engines of every description, useful and useless, windlasses, tackles, pulleys, counterpoises, ladders, cranes, grapnels. On the pinnacle around the light delicately-wrought ironwork held great iron chandeliers, in which were placed pieces of rope steeped in resin; wicks which burned doggedly, and which no wind extinguished; and from top to bottom the tower was covered by a complication of sea-standards, banderoles, banners, flags, pennons, colours which rose from stage to stage, from story to story, a medley of all hues, all shapes, all heraldic devices, all signals, all confusion, up to the light chamber, making, in the storm, a gay riot of tatters about the blaze. That insolent light on the brink of the abyss showed like a defiance, and inspired shipwrecked men with a spirit of daring. But the Caskets light was not after this fashion.

It was, at that period, merely an old barbarous lighthouse, such as Henry I. had built it after the loss of the *White Ship*—a flaming pile of wood under an iron trellis, a brazier behind a railing, a head of hair flaming in the wind.

The only improvement made in this lighthouse since the twelfth century was a pair of forge-bellows worked by an indented pendulum and a stone weight, which had been added to the light chamber in 1610.

The fate of the sea-birds who chanced to fly against these old lighthouses was more tragic than those of our days. The birds dashed against them, attracted by the light, and fell into the brazier, where they could be seen struggling like black spirits in a hell, and at times they would fall back again between the railings upon the rock, red hot, smoking, lame, blind, like half-burnt flies out of a lamp.

To a full-rigged ship in good trim, answering readily to the pilot's handling, the Caskets light is useful; it cries, "Look out;" it warns her of the shoal. To a disabled ship it is simply terrible. The hull, paralyzed and inert, without resistance, without defence against the impulse of the storm or the mad heaving of the waves, a fish without fins, a bird without wings, can but go where the wind wills. The lighthouse shows the end—points out the spot where it is doomed to disappear—throws light upon the burial. It is the torch of the sepulchre.

To light up the inexorable chasm, to warn against the inevitable, what more tragic mockery!

CHAPTER XII.

FACE TO FACE WITH THE ROCK

The wretched people in distress on board the *Matutina* understood at once the mysterious derision which mocked their shipwreck. The appearance of the lighthouse raised their spirits at first, then overwhelmed them. Nothing could be done, nothing attempted. What has been said of kings, we may say of the waves—we are their people, we are their prey. All that they rave must be borne. The nor'-wester was driving the hooker on the Caskets. They were nearing them; no evasion was possible. They drifted rapidly towards the reef; they felt that they were getting into shallow waters; the lead, if they could have thrown it to any purpose, would not have shown more than three or four fathoms. The shipwrecked people heard the dull sound of the waves being sucked within the submarine caves of the steep rock. They made out, under the lighthouse, like a dark cutting between two plates of granite, the narrow passage of the ugly wild-looking little harbour, supposed to be full of the skeletons of men and carcasses of ships. It looked like the mouth of a cavern, rather than the entrance of a port. They could hear the crackling of the pile on high within the iron grating. A ghastly purple illuminated the storm; the collision of the rain and hail disturbed the mist. The black cloud and the red flame fought, serpent against serpent; live ashes, reft by the wind, flew from the fire, and the sudden assaults of the sparks seemed to drive the snowflakes before them. The breakers, blurred at first in outline, now stood out in bold relief, a medley of rocks with peaks, crests, and vertebræ. The angles were formed by strongly marked red lines, and the inclined planes in blood-like streams of light. As they neared it, the outline of the reefs increased and rose—sinister.

One of the women, the Irishwoman, told her beads wildly.

In place of the skipper, who was the pilot, remained the chief, who was the captain. The Basques all know the mountain and the sea. They are bold on the precipice, and inventive in catastrophes.

They neared the cliff. They were about to strike. Suddenly they were so close to the great north rock of the Caskets that it shut out the lighthouse from them. They saw nothing but the rock and the red light behind it. The huge rock looming in the mist was like a gigantic black woman with a hood of fire.

That ill-famed rock is called the Biblet. It faces the north side the reef, which on the south is faced by another ridge, L'Etacq-aux-giulmets. The chief looked at the Biblet, and shouted,—

"A man with a will to take a rope to the rock! Who can swim?"

No answer.

No one on board knew how to swim, not even the sailors—an ignorance not uncommon among seafaring people.

A beam nearly free of its lashings was swinging loose. The chief clasped it with both hands, crying, "Help me."

They unlashed the beam. They had now at their disposal the very thing they wanted. From the defensive, they assumed the offensive.

It was a longish beam of heart of oak, sound and strong, useful either as a support or as an engine of attack—a lever for a burden, a ram against a tower.

"Ready!" shouted the chief.

All six, getting foothold on the stump of the mast, threw their weight on the spar projecting over the side, straight as a lance towards a projection of the cliff.

It was a dangerous manoeuvre. To strike at a mountain is audacity indeed. The six men might well have been thrown into the water by the shock.

There is variety in struggles with storms. After the hurricane, the shoal; after the wind, the rock. First the intangible, then the immovable, to be encountered.

Some minutes passed, such minutes as whiten men's hair.

The rock and the vessel were about to come in collision. The rock, like a culprit, awaited the blow.

A resistless wave rushed in; it ended the respite. It caught the vessel underneath, raised it, and swayed it for an instant as the sling swings its projectile.

"Steady!" cried the chief; "it is only a rock, and we are men."

The beam was couched, the six men were one with it, its sharp bolts tore their arm-pits, but they did not feel them.

The wave dashed the hooker against the rock.

Then came the shock.

It came under the shapeless cloud of foam which always hides such catastrophes.

When this cloud fell back into the sea, when the waves rolled back from the rock, the six men were tossing about the deck, but the *Matutina* was floating alongside the rock—clear of it. The beam had stood and turned the vessel; the sea was running so fast that in a few seconds she had left the Caskets behind.

Such things sometimes occur. It was a straight stroke of the bowsprit that saved Wood of Largo at the mouth of the Tay. In the wild neighbourhood of Cape Winterton, and under the command of Captain Hamilton, it was the appliance of such a lever against the dangerous rock, Branodu-um, that saved the *Royal Mary* from shipwreck, although she was but a Scotch built frigate. The force of the waves can be so abruptly discomposed that changes of direction can be easily managed, or at least are possible even in the most violent collisions. There is a brute in the tempest. The hurricane is a bull, and can be turned.

The whole secret of avoiding shipwreck is to try and pass from the secant to the tangent.

Such was the service rendered by the beam to the vessel. It had done the work of an oar, had taken the place of a rudder. But the manoeuvre once performed could not be repeated. The beam was overboard; the shock of the collision had wrenched it out of the men's hands, and it was lost in the waves. To loosen another beam would have been to dislocate the hull.

The hurricane carried off the *Matutina.* Presently the Caskets showed as a harmless encumbrance on the horizon. Nothing looks more out of countenance than a reef of rocks under such circumstances. There are in nature, in its obscure aspects, in which the visible blends with the invisible, certain motionless, surly profiles, which seem to express that a prey has escaped.

Thus glowered the Caskest while the *Matutina* fled.

The lighthouse paled in distance, faded, and disappeared.

There was something mournful in its extinction. Layers of mist sank down upon the now uncertain light. Its rays died in the waste of waters; the flame floated, struggled, sank, and lost its form. It might have been a drowning creature. The brasier dwindled to the snuff of a candle; then nothing; more but a weak, uncertain flutter. Around it spread a circle of extravasated glimmer; it was like the quenching of: light in the pit of night.

The bell which had threatened was dumb. The lighthouse which had threatened had melted away. And yet it was more awful now that they had ceased to threaten. One was a voice, the other a torch. There was something human about them.

They were gone, and nought remained but the abyss.

CHAPTER XIII.

FACE TO FACE WITH NIGHT

Again was the hooker running with the shadow into immeasurable darkness.

The *Matutina*, escaped from the Caskets, sank and rose from billow to billow. A respite, but in chaos.

Spun round by the wind, tossed by all the thousand motions of the wave, she reflected every mad oscillation of the sea. She scarcely pitched at all—a terrible symptom of a ship's distress. Wrecks merely roll. Pitching is a convulsion of the strife. The helm alone can turn a vessel to the wind.

In storms, and more especially in the meteors of snow, sea and night end by melting into amalgamation, resolving into nothing but a smoke. Mists, whirlwinds, gales, motion in all directions, no basis, no shelter, no stop. Constant recommencement, one gulf succeeding another. No horizon visible; intense blackness for background. Through all these the hooker drifted.

To have got free of the Caskets, to have eluded the rock, was a victory for the shipwrecked men; but it was a victory which left them in stupor. They had raised no cheer: at sea such an imprudence is not repeated twice. To throw down a challenge where they could not cast the lead, would have been too serious a jest.

The repulse of the rock was an impossibility achieved. They were petrified by it. By degrees, however, they began to hope again. Such are the insubmergable mirages of the soul! There is no distress so complete but that even in the most critical moments the inexplicable sunrise of hope is seen in its depths. These poor wretches were ready to acknowledge to themselves that they were saved. It was on their lips.

But suddenly something terrible appeared to them in the darkness.

On the port bow arose, standing stark, cut out on the background of mist, a tall, opaque mass, vertical, right-angled, a tower of the abyss. They watched it open-mouthed.

The storm was driving them towards it.

They knew not what it was. It was the Ortach rock.

CHAPTER XIV.

ORTACH

The reef reappeared. After the Caskets comes Ortach. The storm is no artist; brutal and all-powerful, it never varies its appliances. The darkness is inexhaustible. Its snares and perfidies never come to an end. As for man, he soon comes to the bottom of his resources. Man expends his strength, the abyss never.

The shipwrecked men turned towards the chief, their hope. He could only shrug his shoulders. Dismal contempt of helplessness.

A pavement in the midst of the ocean—such is the Ortach rock. The Ortach, all of a piece, rises up in a straight line to eighty feet above the angry beating of the waves. Waves and ships break against it. An immovable cube, it plunges its rectilinear planes apeak into the numberless serpentine curves of the sea.

At night it stands an enormous block resting on the folds of a huge black sheet. In time of storm it awaits the stroke of the axe, which is the thunder-clap.

But there is never a thunder-clap during the snowstorm. True, the ship has the bandage round her eyes; darkness is knotted about her; she is like one prepared to be led to the scaffold. As for the thunderbolt, which makes quick ending, it is not to be hoped for.

The *Matutina*, nothing better than a log upon the waters, drifted towards this rock as she had drifted towards the other. The poor wretches on board, who had for a moment believed themselves saved, relapsed into their agony. The destruction they had left behind faced them again. The reef reappeared from the bottom of the sea. Nothing had been gained.

The Caskets are a figuring iron[7] with a thousand compartments. The Ortach is a wall. To be wrecked on the Caskets is to be cut into ribbons; to strike on the Ortach is to be crushed into powder.

Nevertheless, there was one chance.

On a straight frontage such as that of the Ortach neither the wave nor the cannon ball can ricochet. The operation is simple: first the flux, then the reflux; a wave advances, a billow returns.

In such cases the question of life and death is balanced thus: if the wave carries the vessel on the rock, she breaks on it and is lost; if the billow retires before the ship has touched, she is carried back, she is saved.

It was a moment of great anxiety; those on board saw through the gloom the great decisive wave bearing down on them. How far was it going to drag them? If the wave broke upon the ship, they were carried on the rock and dashed to pieces. If it passed under the ship....

The wave *did* pass under.

They breathed again.

But what of the recoil? What would the surf do with them? The surf carried them back. A few minutes later the *Matutina* was free of the breakers. The Ortach faded from their view, as the Caskets had done. It was their second victory. For the second time the hooker had verged on destruction, and had drawn back in time

CHAPTER XV.

PORTENTOSUM MARE

Meanwhile a thickening mist had descended on the drifting wretches. They were ignorant of their whereabouts, they could scarcely see a cable's length around. Despite a furious storm of hail which forced them to bend down their heads, the women had obstinately refused to go below again. No one, however hopeless, but wishes, if shipwreck be inevitable, to meet it in the open air. When so near death, a ceiling above one's head seems like the first outline of a coffin.

They were now in a short and chopping sea. A turgid sea indicates its constraint. Even in a fog the entrance into a strait may be known by the boiling-like appearance of the waves. And thus it was, for they were unconsciously coasting Aurigny. Between the west of Ortach and the Caskets and the east of Aurigny the sea is hemmed in and cramped, and the uneasy position determines locally the condition of storms. The sea suffers like others, and when it suffers it is irritable. That channel is a thing to fear.

The *Matutina* was in it.

Imagine under the sea a tortoise shell as big as Hyde Park or the Champs Elysées, of which every striature is a shallow, and every embossment a reef. Such is the western approach of Aurigny. The sea covers and conceals this ship-wrecking apparatus. On this conglomeration of submarine breakers the cloven waves leap and foam—in calm weather, a chopping sea; in storms, a chaos.

The shipwrecked men observed this new complication without endeavouring to explain it to themselves. Suddenly they understood it. A pale vista broadened in the zenith; a wan tinge overspread the sea; the livid light revealed on the port side a long shoal stretching eastward, towards which the power of the rushing wind was driving the vessel. The shoal was Aurigny.

What was that shoal? They shuddered. They would have shuddered even more had a voice answered them—Aurigny.

No isle so well defended against man's approach as Aurigny. Below and above water it is protected by a savage guard, of which Ortach is the outpost. To the west, Burhou, Sauteriaux, Anfroque, Niangle, Fond du Croc, Les Jumelles, La Grosse, La Clanque, Les Eguillons, Le Vrac, La Fosse-Malière; to the east, Sauquet, Hommeau Floreau, La Brinebetais, La Queslingue, Croquelihou, La Fourche, Le Saut, Noire Pute, Coupie, Orbue. These are hydra-monsters of the species reef.

One of these reefs is called Le But, the goal, as if to imply that every voyage ends there.

This obstruction of rocks, simplified by night and sea, appeared to the shipwrecked men in the shape of a single dark band, a sort of black blot on the horizon.

Shipwreck is the ideal of helplessness; to be near land, and unable to reach it; to float, yet not to be able to do so in any desired direction; to rest the foot on what seems firm and is fragile; to be full of life, when o'ershadowed by death; to be the prisoner of space; to be walled in between sky and ocean; to have the infinite overhead like a dungeon; to be encompassed by the eluding elements of wind and waves; and to be seized, bound, paralyzed—such a load of misfortune stupefies and crushes us. We imagine that in it we catch a glimpse of the sneer of the opponent who is beyond our reach. That which holds you fast is that which releases the birds and sets the fishes free. It appears nothing, and is everything. We are dependent on the air which is ruffled by our mouths; we are dependent on the water which we catch in the hollow of our hands. Draw a glassful from the storm, and it is but a cup of bitterness—a mouthful is nausea, a waveful is extermination. The grain of sand in the desert, the foam-flake on the sea, are fearful symptoms. Omnipotence takes no care to hide its atom, it changes weakness into strength, fills naught with all; and it is with the infinitely little that the infinitely great crushes you. It is with its drops the ocean dissolves you. You feel you are a plaything.

A plaything—ghastly epithet!

The *Matutina* was a little above Aurigny, which was not an unfavourable position; but she was drifting towards its northern point, which was fatal. As a bent bow discharges its arrow, the nor'-wester was shooting the vessel towards the northern cape. Off that point, a little beyond the harbour of Corbelets, is that which the seamen of the Norman archipelago call a "*singe*."

The "*singe*," or race, is a furious kind of current. A wreath of funnels in the shallows produces in the waves a wreath of whirlpools. You escape one to fall into another. A ship caught hold of by the race, winds round and round until some sharp rock cleaves her hull; then the shattered vessel stops, her stern rises from the waves, the stem completes the revolution in the abyss, the stern sinks in, and all is sucked down. A circle of foam broadens and floats, and nothing more is seen on the surface of the waves but a few bubbles here and there rising from the smothered breathings below.

The three most dangerous races in the whole Channel are one close to the well-known Girdler Sands, one at Jersey between the Pignonnet and the Point of Noirmont, and the race of Aurigny.

Had a local pilot been on board the *Matutina*, he could have warned them of their fresh peril. In place of a pilot, they had their instinct. In situations of extreme danger men are endowed with second sight. High contortions of foam were flying along the coast in the frenzied raid of the wind. It was the spitting of the race. Many a bark has been swamped in that snare. Without knowing what awaited them, they approached the spot with horror.

How to double that cape? There were no means of doing it.

Just as they had seen, first the Caskets, then Ortach, rise before them, they now saw the point of Aurigny, all of steep rock. It was like a number of giants, rising up one after another—a series of frightful duels.

Charybdis and Scylla are but two; the Caskets, Ortach, and Aurigny are three.

The phenomenon of the horizon being invaded by the rocks was thus repeated with the grand monotony of the abyss. The battles of the ocean have the same sublime tautology as the combats of Homer.

Each wave, as they neared it, added twenty cubits to the cape, awfully magnified by the mist; the fast decreasing distance seemed more inevitable—they were touching the skirts of the race! The first fold which seized them would drag them in—another wave surmounted, and all would be over.

Suddenly the hooker was driven back, as by the blow of a Titan's fist. The wave reared up under the vessel and fell back, throwing the waif back in its mane of foam. The *Matutina*, thus impelled, drifted away from Aurigny.

She was again on the open sea.

Whence had come the succour? From the wind. The breath of the storm had changed its direction.

The wave had played with them; now it was the wind's turn. They had saved themselves from the Caskets. Off Ortach it was the wave which had been their friend. Now it was the wind. The wind had suddenly veered from north to south. The sou'-wester had succeeded the nor'-wester.

The current is the wind in the waters; the wind is the current in the air. These two forces had just counteracted each other, and it had been the wind's will to snatch its prey from the current.

The sudden fantasies of ocean are uncertain. They are, perhaps, an embodiment of the perpetual, when at their mercy man must neither hope nor despair. They do and they undo. The ocean amuses itself. Every shade of wild, untamed ferocity is phased in the vastness of that cunning sea, which Jean Bart used to call the "great brute." To its claws and their gashings succeed soft intervals of velvet paws. Sometimes the storm hurries on a wreck, at others it works out the problem with care; it might almost be said that it caresses it. The sea can afford to take its time, as men in their agonies find out.

We must own that occasionally these lulls of the torture announce deliverance. Such cases are rare. However this may be, men in extreme peril are quick to believe in rescue; the slightest pause in the storm's threats is sufficient; they tell themselves that they are out of danger. After believing themselves buried, they declare their resurrection; they feverishly embrace what they do not yet possess; it is clear that the bad luck has turned; they declare themselves satisfied; they are saved; they cry quits with God. They should not be in so great a hurry to give receipts to the Unknown.

The sou'-wester set in with a whirlwind. Shipwrecked men have never any but rough helpers. The *Matutina* was dragged rapidly out to sea by the remnant of her rigging—like a dead woman trailed by the hair. It was like the enfranchisement granted by Tiberius, at the price of violation.

The wind treated with brutality those whom it saved; it rendered service with fury; it was help without pity.

The wreck was breaking up under the severity of its deliverers.

Hailstones, big and hard enough to charge a blunderbuss, smote the vessel; at every rotation of the waves these hailstones rolled about the deck like marbles. The hooker, whose deck was almost flush with the water, was being beaten out of shape by the rolling masses of water and its sheets of spray. On board it each man was for himself.

They clung on as best they could. As each sea swept over them, it was with a sense of surprise they saw that all were still there. Several had their faces torn by splinters.

Happily despair has stout hands. In terror a child's hand has the grasp of a giant. Agony makes a vice of a woman's fingers. A girl in her fright can almost bury her rose-coloured fingers in a piece of iron. With hooked fingers they hung on somehow, as the waves dashed on and passed off them; but every wave brought them the fear of being swept away.

Suddenly they were relieved.

CHAPTER XVI.

THE PROBLEM SUDDENLY WORKS IN SILENCE

The hurricane had just stopped short. There was no longer in the air sou'-wester or nor'-wester. The fierce clarions of space were mute. The whole of the waterspout had poured from the sky without any warning of diminution, as if it had slided perpendicularly into a gulf beneath. None knew what had become of it; flakes replaced the hailstones, the snow began to fall slowly. No more swell: the sea flattened down.

Such sudden cessations are peculiar to snowstorms. The electric effluvium exhausted, all becomes still, even the wave, which in ordinary storms often remains agitated for a long time. In snowstorms it is not so. No prolonged anger in the deep. Like a tired-out worker it becomes drowsy directly, thus almost giving the lie to the laws of statics, but not astonishing old seamen, who know that the sea is full of unforeseen surprises.

The same phenomenon takes place, although very rarely, in ordinary storms. Thus, in our time, on the occasion of the memorable hurricane of July 27th, 1867, at Jersey the wind, after fourteen hours' fury, suddenly relapsed into a dead calm.

In a few minutes the hooker was floating in sleeping waters.

At the same time (for the last phase of these storms resembles the first) they could distinguish nothing; all that had been made visible in the convulsions of the meteoric cloud was again dark. Pale outlines were fused in vague mist, and the gloom of infinite space closed about the vessel. The wall of night—that circular occlusion, that interior of a cylinder the diameter of which was lessening minute by minute—enveloped the *Matutina*, and, with the sinister deliberation of an encroaching iceberg, was drawing in dangerously. In the zenith nothing—a lid of fog closing down. It was as if the hooker were at the bottom of the well of the abyss.

In that well the sea was a puddle of liquid lead. No stir in the waters—ominous immobility! The ocean is never less tamed than when it is still as a pool.

All was silence, stillness, blindness.

Perchance the silence of inanimate objects is taciturnity.

The last ripples glided along the hull. The deck was horizontal, with an insensible slope to the sides. Some broken planks were shifting about irresolutely. The block on which they had lighted the tow steeped in tar, in place of the signal light which had been swept away, swung no longer at the prow, and no longer let fall burning drops into the sea. What little breeze remained in the clouds was noiseless. The snow fell thickly, softly, with scarce a slant. No foam of breakers could be heard. The peace of shadows was over all.

This repose succeeding all the past exasperations and paroxysms was, for the poor creatures so long tossed about, an unspeakable comfort. It was as though the punishment of the rack had ceased. They caught a glimpse about them and above them of something which seemed like a consent, that they should be saved. They regained confidence. All that had been fury was now tranquillity. It appeared to them a pledge of peace. Their wretched hearts dilated. They were able to let go the end of rope or beam to which they had clung, to rise, hold themselves up, stand, walk, move about. They felt inexpressibly calmed. There are in the depths of darkness such phases of paradise, preparations for other things. It was clear that they were delivered out of the storm, out of the foam, out of the wind, out of the uproar. Henceforth all the chances were in their favour. In three or four hours it would be sunrise. They would be seen by some passing ship; they would be rescued. The worst was over; they were re-entering life. The important feat was to have been able to keep afloat until the cessation of the tempest. They said to themselves, "It is all over this time."

Suddenly they found that all was indeed over.

One of the sailors, the northern Basque, Galdeazun by name, went down into the hold to look for a rope, then came above again and said,—

"The hold is full."

"Of what?" asked the chief.

"Of water," answered the sailor.

The chief cried out,—

"What does that mean?"

"It means," replied Galdeazun, "that in half an hour we shall founder."

CHAPTER XVII.

THE LAST RESOURCE

There was a hole in the keel. A leak had been sprung. When it happened no one could have said. Was it when they touched the Caskets? Was it off Ortach? Was it when they were whirled about the shallows west of Aurigny? It was most probable that they had touched some rock there. They had struck against some hidden buttress which they had not felt in the midst of the convulsive fury of the wind which was tossing them. In tetanus who would feel a prick?

The other sailor, the southern Basque, whose name was Ave Maria, went down into the hold, too, came on deck again, and said,—

"There are two varas of water in the hold."

About six feet.

Ave Maria added, "In less than forty minutes we shall sink."

Where was the leak? They couldn't find it. It was hidden by the water which was filling up the hold. The vessel had a hole in her hull somewhere under the water-line, quite forward in the keel. Impossible to find it—impossible to check it. They had a wound which they could not stanch. The water, however, was not rising very fast.

The chief called out,

"We must work the pump."

Galdeazun replied, "We have no pump left."

"Then," said the chief, "we must make for land."

"Where is the land?"

"I don't know."

"Nor I."

"But it must be somewhere."

"True enough."

"Let some one steer for it."

"We have no pilot."

"Stand to the tiller yourself."

"We have lost the tiller."

"Let's rig one out of the first beam we can lay hands on. Nails—a hammer—quick—some tools."

"The carpenter's box is overboard, we have no tools."

"We'll steer all the same, no matter where."

"The rudder is lost."

"Where is the boat? We'll get in and row."

"The boat is lost."

"We'll row the wreck."

"We have lost the oars."

"We'll sail."

"We have lost the sails and the mast."

"We'll rig one up with a pole and a tarpaulin for sail Let's get clear of this and trust in the wind."

"There is no wind."

The wind, indeed, had left them, the storm had fled; and its departure, which they had believed to mean safety, meant, in fact, destruction. Had the sou'-wester continued it might have driven them wildly on some shore—might have beaten the leak in speed—might, perhaps, have carried them to some propitious sandbank, and cast them on it before the hooker foundered. The swiftness of the storm, bearing them away, might have enabled them to reach land; but no more wind, no more hope. They were going to die because the hurricane was over.

The end was near!

Wind, hail, the hurricane, the whirlwind—these are wild combatants that may be overcome; the storm can be taken in the weak point of its armour; there are resources against the violence which continually lays itself open, is off its guard, and often hits wide. But nothing is to be done against a calm; it offers nothing to the grasp of which you can lay hold.

The winds are a charge of Cossacks: stand your ground and they disperse. Calms are the pincers of the executioner.

The water, deliberate and sure, irrepressible and heavy, rose in the hold, and as it rose the vessel sank—it was happening slowly.

Those on board the wreck of the *Matutina* felt that most hopeless of catastrophes—an inert catastrophe undermining them. The still and sinister certainty of their fate petrified them. No stir in the air, no movement on the sea. The motionless is the inexorable. Absorption was sucking them down silently. Through the depths of the dumb waters—without anger, without passion, not willing, not knowing, not caring—the fatal centre of the globe was attracting them downwards. Horror in repose amalgamating them with itself. It was no longer the wide open mouth of the sea, the double jaw of the wind and the wave, vicious in its threat, the grin of the waterspout, the foaming appetite of the breakers—it was as if the wretched beings had under them the black yawn of the infinite.

They felt themselves sinking into Death's peaceful depths. The height between the vessel and the water was lessening—that was all. They could calculate her disappearance to the moment. It was the exact reverse of submersion by the rising tide. The water was not rising towards them; they were sinking towards it. They were digging their own grave. Their own weight was their sexton.

They were being executed, not by the law of man, but by the law of things.

The snow was falling, and as the wreck was now motionless, this white lint made a cloth over the deck and covered the vessel as with a winding-sheet.

The hold was becoming fuller and deeper—no means of getting at the leak. They struck a light and fixed three or four torches in holes as best they could. Galdeazun brought some old leathern buckets, and they tried to bale the hold out, standing in a row to pass them from hand to hand; but the buckets were past use, the leather of some was unstitched, there were holes in the bottoms of the others, and the buckets emptied themselves on the way. The difference in quantity between the water which was making its way in and that which they returned to the sea was ludicrous—for a ton that entered a glassful was baled out; they did not improve their condition. It was like the expenditure of a miser, trying to exhaust a million, halfpenny by halfpenny.

The chief said, "Let us lighten the wreck."

During the storm they had lashed together the few chests which were on deck. These remained tied to the stump of the mast. They undid the lashings and rolled the chests overboard through a breach in the gunwale. One of these trunks belonged to the Basque woman, who could not repress a sigh.

"Oh, my new cloak lined with scarlet! Oh, my poor stockings of birchen-bark lace! Oh, my silver ear-rings to wear at mass on May Day!"

The deck cleared, there remained the cabin to be seen to. It was greatly encumbered; in it were, as may be remembered, the luggage belonging to the passengers, and the bales belonging to the sailors. They took the luggage, and threw it over the gunwale. They carried up the bales and cast them into the sea.

Thus they emptied the cabin. The lantern, the cap, the barrels, the sacks, the bales, and the water-butts, the pot of soup, all went over into the waves.

They unscrewed the nuts of the iron stove, long since extinguished: they pulled it out, hoisted it on deck, dragged it to the side, and threw it out of the vessel.

They cast overboard everything they could pull out of the deck—chains, shrouds, and torn rigging.

From time to time the chief took a torch, and throwing its light on the figures painted on the prow to show the draught of water, looked to see how deep the wreck had settled down.

CHAPTER XVIII.

THE HIGHEST RESOURCE

The wreck being lightened, was sinking more slowly, but none the less surely.

The hopelessness of their situation was without resource—without mitigation; they had exhausted their last expedient.

"Is there anything else we can throw overboard?"

The doctor, whom every one had forgotten, rose from the companion, and said,

"Yes."

"What?" asked the chief.

The doctor answered, "Our Crime."

They shuddered, and all cried out,—

"Amen."

The doctor standing up, pale, raised his hand to heaven, saying,—

"Kneel down."

They wavered—to waver is the preface to kneeling down.

The doctor went on,—

"Let us throw our crimes into the sea, they weigh us down; it is they that are sinking the ship. Let us think no more of safety—let us think of salvation. Our last crime, above all, the crime which we committed, or rather completed, just now—O wretched beings who are listening to me—it is that which is overwhelming us. For those who leave intended murder behind them, it is an impious insolence to tempt the abyss. He who sins against a child, sins against God. True, we were obliged to put to sea, but it was certain perdition. The storm, warned by the shadow of our crime, came on. It is well. Regret nothing, however. There, not far off in the darkness, are the sands of Vauville and Cape la Hogue. It is France. There was but one possible shelter for us, which was Spain. France is no less dangerous to us than England. Our deliverance from the sea would have led but to the gibbet. Hanged or drowned—we had no alternative. God has chosen for us; let us give Him thanks. He has vouchsafed us the grave which cleanses. Brethren, the inevitable hand is in it. Remember that it was we who just now did our best to send on high that child, and that at this very moment, now as I speak, there is perhaps, above our heads, a soul accusing us before a Judge whose eye is on us. Let us make the best use of this last respite; let us make an effort, if we still may, to repair, as far as we are able, the evil that we have wrought. If the child survives us, let us come to his aid; if he is dead, let us seek his forgiveness. Let us cast our crime from us. Let us ease our consciences of its weight. Let us strive that our souls be not swallowed up before God, for that is the awful shipwreck. Bodies go to the fishes, souls to the devils. Have pity on yourselves. Kneel down, I tell you. Repentance is the bark which never sinks. You have lost your compass! You are wrong! You still have prayer."

The wolves became lambs—such transformations occur in last agonies; tigers lick the crucifix; when the dark portal opens ajar, belief is difficult, unbelief impossible. However imperfect may be the different sketches of religion essayed by man, even when his belief is shapeless, even when the outline of the dogma is not in harmony with the lineaments of the eternity he foresees, there comes in his last hour a trembling of the soul. There is something which will begin when life is over; this thought impresses the last pang.

A man's dying agony is the expiration of a term. In that fatal second he feels weighing on him a diffused responsibility. That which has been complicates that which is to be. The past returns and enters into the future. What is known becomes as much an abyss as the unknown. And the two chasms, the one which is full by his faults, the other of his anticipations, mingle their reverberations. It is this confusion of the two gulfs which terrifies the dying man.

They had spent their last grain of hope on the direction of life; hence they turned in the other. Their only remaining chance was in its dark shadow. They understood it. It came on them as a lugubrious flash, followed by the relapse of horror. That which is intelligible to the dying man is as what is perceived in the lightning. Everything, then nothing; you see, then all is blindness. After death the eye will reopen, and that which was a flash will become a sun.

They cried out to the doctor,—

"Thou, thou, there is no one but thee. We will obey thee, what must we do? Speak."

The doctor answered,—

"The question is how to pass over the unknown precipice and reach the other bank of life, which is beyond the tomb. Being the one who knows the most, my danger is greater than yours. You do well to leave the choice of the bridge to him whose burden is the heaviest."

He added,—

"Knowledge is a weight added to conscience."

He continued,—

"How much time have we still?"

Galdeazun looked at the water-mark, and answered,—

"A little more than a quarter of an hour."

"Good," said the doctor.

The low hood of the companion on which he leant his elbows made a sort of table; the doctor took from his pocket his inkhorn and pen, and his pocket-book out of which he drew a parchment, the same one on the back of which he had written, a few hours before, some twenty cramped and crooked lines.

"A light," he said.

The snow, falling like the spray of a cataract, had extinguished the torches one after another; there was but one left. Ave Maria took it out of the place where it had been stuck, and holding it in his hand, came and stood by the doctor's side.

The doctor replaced his pocket-book in his pocket, put down the pen and inkhorn on the hood of the companion, unfolded the parchment, and said,—

"Listen."

Then in the midst of the sea, on the failing bridge (a sort of shuddering flooring of the tomb), the doctor began a solemn reading, to which all the shadows seemed to listen. The doomed men bowed their heads around him. The flaming of the torch intensified their pallor. What the doctor read was written in English. Now and then, when one of those woebegone looks seemed to ask an explanation, the doctor would stop, to repeat—whether in French, or Spanish, Basque, or Italian—the passage he had just read. Stifled sobs and hollow beatings of the breast were heard. The wreck was sinking more and more.

The reading over, the doctor placed the parchment flat on the companion, seized his pen, and on a clear margin which he had carefully left at the bottom of what he had written, he signed himself, GERNARDUS GEESTEMUNDE: Doctor.

Then, turning towards the others, he said,—

"Come, and sign."

The Basque woman approached, took the pen, and signed herself, ASUNCION.

She handed the pen to the Irish woman, who, not knowing how to write, made a cross.

The doctor, by the side of this cross, wrote, BARBARA FERMOY, *of Tyrrif Island, in the Hebrides.*

Then he handed the pen to the chief of the band.

The chief signed, GAIZDORRA: *Captal.*

The Genoese signed himself under the chief's name. GIANGIRATE.

The Languedocian signed, JACQUES QUARTOURZE: *alias, the Narbonnais.*

The Provençal signed, LUC-PIERRE CAPGAROUPE, *of the Galleys of Mahon.*

Under these signatures the doctor added a note:—

"Of the crew of three men, the skipper having been washed overboard by a sea, but two remain, and they have signed."

The two sailors affixed their names underneath the note. The northern Basque signed himself, GALDEAZUN.

The southern Basque signed, AVE MARIA: *Robber.*

Then the doctor said,—

"Capgaroupe."

"Here," said the Provençal.

"Have you Hardquanonne's flask?"

"Yes."

"Give it me."

Capgaroupe drank off the last mouthful of brandy, and handed the flask to the doctor.

The water was rising in the hold; the wreck was sinking deeper and deeper into the sea. The sloping edges of the ship were covered by a thin gnawing wave, which was rising. All were crowded on the centre of the deck.

The doctor dried the ink on the signatures by the heat of the torch, and folding the parchment into a narrower compass than the diameter of the neck, put it into the flask. He called for the cork.

"I don't know where it is," said Capgaroupe.

"Here is a piece of rope," said Jacques Quartourze.

The doctor corked the flask with a bit of rope, and asked for some tar. Galdeazun went forward, extinguished the signal light with a piece of tow, took the vessel in which it was contained from the stern, and brought it, half full of burning tar, to the doctor.

The flask holding the parchment which they had all signed was corked and tarred over.

"It is done," said the doctor.

And from out all their mouths, vaguely stammered in every language, came the dismal utterances of the catacombs.

"Ainsi soit-il!"

"Mea culpa!"

"Asi sea!"

"Aro raï!"

"Amen!"

It was as though the sombre voices of Babel were scattered through the shadows as Heaven uttered its awful refusal to hear them.

The doctor turned away from his companions in crime and distress, and took a few steps towards the gunwale. Reaching the side, he looked into space, and said, in a deep voice,—

"Bist du bei mir?"[8]

Perchance he was addressing some phantom.

The wreck was sinking.

Behind the doctor all the others were in a dream. Prayer mastered them by main force. They did not bow, they were bent. There was something involuntary in their condition; they wavered as a sail flaps when the breeze fails. And the haggard group took by degrees, with clasping of hands and prostration of foreheads, attitudes various, yet of humiliation. Some strange reflection of the deep seemed to soften their villainous features.

The doctor returned towards them. Whatever had been his past, the old man was great in the presence of the catastrophe.

The deep reserve of nature which enveloped him preoccupied without disconcerting him. He was not one to be taken unawares. Over him was the calm of a silent horror: on his countenance the majesty of God's will comprehended.

This old and thoughtful outlaw unconsciously assumed the air of a pontiff.

He said,—

"Attend to me."

He contemplated for a moment the waste of water, and added,—

"Now we are going to die."

Then he took the torch from the hands of Ave Maria, and waved it.

A spark broke from it and flew into the night.

Then the doctor cast the torch into the sea.

The torch was extinguished: all light disappeared. Nothing left but the huge, unfathomable shadow. It was like the filling up of the grave.

In the darkness the doctor was heard saying,—

"Let us pray."

All knelt down.

It was no longer on the snow, but in the water, that they knelt.

They had but a few minutes more.

The doctor alone remained standing.

The flakes of snow falling on him had sprinkled him with white tears, and made him visible on the background of darkness. He might have been the speaking statue of the shadow.

The doctor made the sign of the cross and raised his voice, while beneath his feet he felt that almost imperceptible oscillation which prefaces the moment in which a wreck is about to founder. He said,—

"Pater noster qui es in coelis."

The Provençal repeated in French,—

"Notre Père qui êtes aux cieux."

The Irishwoman repeated in Gaelic, understood by the Basque woman,—

"Ar nathair ata ar neamh."

The doctor continued,—

"Sanctificetur nomen tuum."

"Que votre nom soit sanctifié," said the Provençal.

"Naomhthar hainm," said the Irishwoman.

"Adveniat regnum tuum," continued the doctor.

"Que votre règne arrive," said the Provençal.

"Tigeadh do rioghachd," said the Irishwoman.

As they knelt, the waters had risen to their shoulders. The doctor went on,—

"Fiat voluntas tua."

"Que votre volonté soit faite," stammered the Provençal.

And the Irishwoman and Basque woman cried,—

"Deuntar do thoil ar an Hhalàmb."

"Sicut in coelo, sicut in terra," said the doctor.

No voice answered him.

He looked down. All their heads were under water. They had let themselves be drowned on their knees.

The doctor took in his right hand the flask which he had placed on the companion, and raised it above his head.

The wreck was going down. As he sank, the doctor murmured the rest of the prayer.

For an instant his shoulders were above water, then his head, then nothing remained but his arm holding up the flask, as if he were showing it to the Infinite.

His arm disappeared; there was no greater fold on the deep sea than there would have been on a tun of oil. The snow continued falling.

One thing floated, and was carried by the waves into the darkness. It was the tarred flask, kept afloat by its osier cover.

BOOK THE THIRD

THE CHILD IN THE SHADOW

CHAPTER I.

CHESIL

The storm was no less severe on land than on sea. The same wild enfranchisement of the elements had taken place around the abandoned child. The weak and innocent become their sport in the expenditure of the unreasoning rage of their blind forces. Shadows discern not, and things inanimate have not the clemency they are supposed to possess.

On the land there was but little wind. There was an inexplicable dumbness in the cold. There was no hail. The thickness of the falling snow was fearful.

Hailstones strike, harass, bruise, stun, crush. Snowflakes do worse: soft and inexorable, the snowflake does its work in silence; touch it, and it melts. It is pure, even as the hypocrite is candid. It is by white particles slowly heaped upon each other that the flake becomes an avalanche and the knave a criminal.

The child continued to advance into the mist. The fog presents but a soft obstacle; hence its danger. It yields, and yet persists. Mist, like snow, is full of treachery. The child, strange wrestler at war with all these risks, had succeeded in reaching the bottom of the descent, and had gained Chesil. Without knowing it he was on an isthmus, with the ocean on each side; so that he could not lose his way in the fog, in the snow, or in the darkness, without falling into the deep waters of the gulf on the right hand, or into the raging billows of the high sea on the left. He was travelling on, in ignorance, between these two abysses.

The Isthmus of Portland was at this period singularly sharp and rugged. Nothing remains at this date of its past configuration. Since the idea of manufacturing Portland stone into Roman cement was first seized, the whole rock has been subjected to an alteration which has completely changed its original appearance. Calcareous lias, slate, and trap are still to be found there, rising from layers of conglomerate, like teeth from a gum; but the pickaxe has broken up and levelled those bristling, rugged peaks which were once the fearful perches of the ossifrage. The summits exist no longer where the labbes and the skua gulls used to flock together, soaring, like the envious, to sully high places. In vain might you seek the tall monolith called Godolphin, an old British word, signifying "white eagle." In summer you may still gather on those surfaces, pierced and perforated like a sponge, rosemary, pennyroyal, wild hyssop, and sea-fennel which when infused makes a good cordial, and that herb full of knots, which grows in the sand and from which they make matting; but you no longer find gray amber, or black tin, or that triple species of slate—one sort green, one blue, and the third the colour of sage-leaves. The foxes, the badgers, the otters, and the martens have taken themselves off; on the cliffs of Portland, as well as at the extremity of Cornwall, where there were at one time chamois, none remain. They still fish in some inlets for plaice and pilchards; but the scared salmon no longer ascend the Wey, between Michaelmas and Christmas, to spawn. No more are seen there, as during the reign of Elizabeth, those old unknown birds as large as hawks, who could cut an apple in two, but ate only the pips. You never meet those crows with yellow beaks, called Cornish choughs in English, *pyrrocorax* in Latin, who, in their mischief, would drop burning twigs on thatched roofs. Nor that magic bird, the fulmar, a wanderer from the Scottish archipelago, dropping from his bill an oil which the islanders used to burn in their lamps. Nor do you ever find in the evening, in the plash of the ebbing tide, that ancient, legendary neitse, with the feet of a hog and the bleat of a calf. The tide no longer throws up the whiskered seal, with its curled ears and sharp jaws, dragging itself along on its nailless paws. On that Portland—nowadays so changed as scarcely to be recognized—the absence of forests precluded nightingales; but now the falcon, the swan, and the wild goose have fled. The sheep of Portland, nowadays, are fat and have fine wool; the few scattered ewes, which nibbled the salt grass there two centuries ago, were small and tough and coarse in the fleece, as became Celtic flocks brought there by garlic-eating shepherds, who lived to a hundred, and who, at the distance of half a mile, could pierce a cuirass with their yard-long arrows. Uncultivated land makes coarse wool. The Chesil of to-day resembles in no particular the Chesil of the past, so much has it been disturbed by man and by those furious winds which gnaw the very stones.

At present this tongue of land bears a railway, terminating in a pretty square of houses, called Chesilton, and there is a Portland station. Railway carriages roll where seals used to crawl.

The Isthmus of Portland two hundred years ago was a back of sand, with a vertebral spine of rock.

The child's danger changed its form. What he had had to fear in the descent was falling to the bottom of the precipice; in the isthmus, it was falling into the holes. After dealing with the precipice, he must deal with the pitfalls. Everything on the sea-shore is a trap—the rock is slippery, the strand is quicksand. Resting-places are but snares. It is walking on ice which may suddenly crack and yawn with a fissure, through which you disappear. The ocean has false stages below, like a well-arranged theatre.

The long backbone of granite, from which fall away both slopes of the isthmus, is awkward of access. It is difficult to find there what, in scene-shifters' language, are termed *practicables*. Man has no hospitality to hope for from the ocean; from the rock no more than from the wave. The sea is provident for the bird and the fish alone. Isthmuses are especially naked and rugged; the wave, which wears and mines them on either side, reduces them to the simplest form. Everywhere there were sharp relief ridges, cuttings, frightful fragments of torn stone, yawning with many points, like the jaws of a shark; breaknecks of wet moss, rapid slopes of rock ending in the sea. Whosoever undertakes to pass over an isthmus meets at every step misshapen blocks, as large as houses, in the forms of shin-bones, shoulder-blades, and thigh-bones, the hideous anatomy of dismembered rocks. It is not without reason that these *striæ* of the sea-shore are called *côtes*.[9]

The wayfarer must get out as he best can from the confusion of these ruins. It is like journeying over the bones of an enormous skeleton.

Put a child to this labour of Hercules.

Broad daylight might have aided him. It was night. A guide was necessary. He was alone. All the vigour of manhood would not have been too much. He had but the feeble strength of a child. In default of a guide, a footpath might have aided him; there was none.

By instinct he avoided the sharp ridge of the rocks, and kept to the strand as much as possible. It was there that he met with the pitfalls. They were multiplied before him under three forms: the pitfall of water, the pitfall of snow, and the pitfall of sand. This last is the most dangerous of all, because the most illusory. To know the peril we face is alarming; to be ignorant of it is terrible. The child was fighting against unknown dangers. He was groping his way through something which might, perhaps, be the grave.

He did not hesitate. He went round the rocks, avoided the crevices, guessed at the pitfalls, obeyed the twistings and turnings caused by such obstacles, yet he went on. Though unable to advance in a straight line, he walked with a firm step. When necessary, he drew back with energy. He knew how to tear himself in time from the horrid bird-lime of the quicksands. He shook the snow from about him. He entered the water more than once up to the knees. Directly that he left it, his wet knees were frozen by the intense cold of the night. He walked rapidly in his stiffened garments; yet he took care to keep his sailor's coat dry and warm on his chest. He was still tormented by hunger.

The chances of the abyss are illimitable. Everything is possible in it, even salvation. The issue may be found, though it be invisible. How the child, wrapped in a smothering winding-sheet of snow, lost on a narrow elevation between two jaws of an abyss, managed to cross the isthmus is what he could not himself have explained. He had slipped, climbed, rolled, searched, walked, persevered, that is all. Such is the secret of all triumphs. At the end of somewhat less than half an hour he felt that the ground was rising. He had reached the other shore. Leaving Chesil, he had gained terra firma.

The bridge which now unites Sandford Castle with Smallmouth Sands did not then exist. It is probable that in his intelligent groping he had reascended as far as Wyke Regis, where there was then a tongue of sand, a natural road crossing East Fleet.

He was saved from the isthmus; but he found himself again face to face with the tempest, with the cold, with the night.

Before him once more lay the plain, shapeless in the density of impenetrable shadow. He examined the ground, seeking a footpath. Suddenly he bent down. He had discovered, in the snow, something which seemed to him a track.

It was indeed a track—the print of a foot. The print was cut out clearly in the whiteness of the snow, which rendered it distinctly visible. He examined it. It was a naked foot; too small for that of a man, too large for that of a child.

It was probably the foot of a woman. Beyond that mark was another, then another, then another. The footprints followed each other at the distance of a step, and struck across the plain to the right. They were still fresh, and slightly covered with little snow. A woman had just passed that way.

This woman was walking in the direction in which the child had seen the smoke. With his eyes fixed on the footprints, he set himself to follow them.

CHAPTER II.

THE EFFECT OF SNOW

He journeyed some time along this course. Unfortunately the footprints were becoming less and less distinct. Dense and fearful was the falling of the snow. It was the time when the hooker was so distressed by the snow-storm at sea.

The child, in distress like the vessel, but after another fashion, had, in the inextricable intersection of shadows which rose up before him, no resource but the footsteps in the snow, and he held to it as the thread of a labyrinth.

Suddenly, whether the snow had filled them up or for some other reason, the footsteps ceased. All became even, level, smooth, without a stain, without a detail. There was now nothing but a white cloth drawn over the earth and a black one over the sky. It seemed as if the foot-passenger had flown away. The child, in despair, bent down and searched; but in vain.

As he arose he had a sensation of hearing some indistinct sound, but he could not be sure of it. It resembled a voice, a breath, a shadow. It was more human than animal; more sepulchral than living. It was a sound, but the sound of a dream.

He looked, but saw nothing.

Solitude, wide, naked and livid, was before him. He listened. That which he had thought he heard had faded away. Perhaps it had been but fancy. He still listened. All was silent.

There was illusion in the mist.

He went on his way again. He walked forward at random, with nothing henceforth to guide him.

As he moved away the noise began again. This time he could doubt it no longer. It was a groan, almost a sob.

He turned. He searched the darkness of space with his eyes. He saw nothing. The sound arose once more. If limbo could cry out, it would cry in such a tone.

Nothing so penetrating, so piercing, so feeble as the voice—for it was a voice. It arose from a soul. There was palpitation in the murmur. Nevertheless, it seemed uttered almost unconsciously. It was an appeal of suffering, not knowing that it suffered or that it appealed.

The cry—perhaps a first breath, perhaps a last sigh—was equally distant from the rattle which closes life and the wail with which it commences. It breathed, it was stifled, it wept, a gloomy supplication from the depths of night. The child fixed his attention everywhere, far, near, on high, below. There was no one. There was nothing. He listened. The voice arose again. He perceived it distinctly. The sound somewhat resembled the bleating of a lamb.

Then he was frightened, and thought of flight.

The groan again. This was the fourth time. It was strangely miserable and plaintive. One felt that after that last effort, more mechanical than voluntary, the cry would probably be extinguished. It was an expiring exclamation, instinctively appealing to the amount of aid held in suspense in space. It was some muttering of agony, addressed to a possible Providence.

The child approached in the direction from whence the sound came.

Still he saw nothing.

He advanced again, watchfully.

The complaint continued. Inarticulate and confused as it was, it had become clear—almost vibrating. The child was near the voice; but where was it?

He was close to a complaint. The trembling of a cry passed by his side into space. A human moan floated away into the darkness. This was what he had met. Such at least was his impression, dim as the dense mist in which he was lost.

Whilst he hesitated between an instinct which urged him to fly and an instinct which commanded him to remain, he perceived in the snow at his feet, a few steps before him, a sort of undulation of the dimensions of a human body—a little eminence, low, long, and narrow, like the mould over a grave—a sepulchre in a white churchyard.

At the same time the voice cried out. It was from beneath the undulation that it proceeded. The child bent down, crouching before the undulation, and with both his hands began to clear it away.

Beneath the snow which he removed a form grew under his hands; and suddenly in the hollow he had made there appeared a pale face.

The cry had not proceeded from that face. Its eyes were shut, and the mouth open but full of snow.

It remained motionless; it stirred not under the hands of the child. The child, whose fingers were numbed with frost, shuddered when he touched its coldness. It was that of a woman. Her dishevelled hair was mingled with the snow. The woman was dead.

Again the child set himself to sweep away the snow. The neck of the dead woman appeared; then her shoulders, clothed in rags. Suddenly he felt something move feebly under his touch. It was something small that was buried, and which stirred. The child swiftly cleared away the snow, discovering a wretched little body—thin, wan with cold, still alive, lying naked on the dead woman's naked breast.

It was a little girl.

It had been swaddled up, but in rags so scanty that in its struggles it had freed itself from its tatters. Under it its attenuated limbs, and above it its breath, had somewhat melted the snow. A nurse would have said that it was five or six months old, but perhaps it might be a year, for growth, in poverty, suffers heart-breaking reductions which sometimes even produce rachitis. When its face was exposed to the air it gave a cry, the continuation of its sobs of distress. For the mother not to have heard that sob, proved her irrevocably dead.

The child took the infant in his arms. The stiffened body of the mother was a fearful sight; a spectral light proceeded from her face. The mouth, apart and without breath, seemed to form in the indistinct language of shadows her answer to the questions put to the dead by the invisible. The ghastly reflection of the icy plains was on that countenance. There was the youthful forehead under the brown hair, the almost indignant knitting of the eyebrows, the pinched nostrils, the closed eyelids, the lashes glued together by the rime, and from the corners of the eyes to the corners of the mouth a deep channel of tears. The snow lighted up the corpse. Winter and the tomb are not adverse. The corpse is the icicle of man. The nakedness of her breasts was pathetic. They had fulfilled their purpose. On them was a sublime blight of the life infused into one being by another from whom life has fled, and maternal majesty was there instead of virginal purity. At the point of one of the nipples was a white pearl. It was a drop of milk frozen.

Let us explain at once. On the plains over which the deserted boy was passing in his turn a beggar woman, nursing her infant and searching for a refuge, had lost her way a few hours before. Benumbed with cold she had sunk under the tempest, and could not rise again. The falling snow had covered her. So long as she was able she had clasped her little girl to her bosom, and thus died.

The infant had tried to suck the marble breast. Blind trust, inspired by nature, for it seems that it is possible for a woman to suckle her child even after her last sigh.

But the lips of the infant had been unable to find the breast, where the drop of milk, stolen by death, had frozen, whilst under the snow the child, more accustomed to the cradle than the tomb, had wailed.

The deserted child had heard the cry of the dying child.

He disinterred it.

He took it in his arms.

When she felt herself in his arms she ceased crying. The faces of the two children touched each other, and the purple lips of the infant sought the cheek of the boy, as it had been a breast. The little girl had nearly reached the moment when the congealed blood stops the action of the heart. Her mother had touched her with the chill of her own death—a corpse communicates death; its numbness is infectious. Her feet, hands, arms, knees, seemed paralyzed by cold. The boy felt the terrible chill. He had on him a garment dry and warm—his pilot jacket. He placed the infant on the breast of the corpse, took off his jacket, wrapped the infant in it, took it up again in his arms, and now, almost naked, under the blast of the north wind which covered him with eddies of snow-flakes, carrying the infant, he pursued his journey.

The little one having succeeded in finding the boy's cheek, again applied her lips to it, and, soothed by the warmth, she slept. First kiss of those two souls in the darkness.

The mother lay there, her back to the snow, her face to the night; but perhaps at the moment when the little boy stripped himself to clothe the little girl, the mother saw him from the depths of infinity.

CHAPTER III.

A BURDEN MAKES A ROUGH ROAD ROUGHER

It was little more than four hours since the hooker had sailed from the creek of Portland, leaving the boy on the shore. During the long hours since he had been deserted, and had been journeying onwards, he had met but three persons of that human society into which he was, perchance, about to enter—a man, the man on the hill; a woman, the woman in the snow; and the little girl whom he was carrying in his arms.

He was exhausted by fatigue and hunger, yet advanced more resolutely than ever, with less strength and an added burden. He was now almost naked. The few rags which remained to him, hardened by the frost, were sharp as glass, and cut his skin. He became colder, but the infant was warmer. That which he lost was not thrown away, but was gained by her. He found out that the poor infant enjoyed the comfort which was to her the renewal of life. He continued to advance.

From time to time, still holding her securely, he bent down, and taking a handful of snow he rubbed his feet with it, to prevent their being frost-bitten. At other times, his throat feeling as if it were on fire, he put a little snow in his mouth and sucked it; this for a moment assuaged his thirst, but changed it into fever—a relief which was an aggravation.

The storm had become shapeless from its violence. Deluges of snow are possible. This was one. The paroxysm scourged the shore at the same time that it uptore the depths of ocean. This was, perhaps, the moment when the distracted hooker was going to pieces in the battle of the breakers.

He travelled under this north wind, still towards the east, over wide surfaces of snow. He knew not how the hours had passed. For a long time he had ceased to see the smoke. Such indications are soon effaced in the night; besides, it was past the hour when fires are put out. Or he had, perhaps, made a mistake, and it was possible that neither town nor village existed in the direction in which he was travelling. Doubting, he yet persevered.

Two or three times the little infant cried. Then he adopted in his gait a rocking movement, and the child was soothed and silenced. She ended by falling into a sound sleep. Shivering himself, he felt her warm. He frequently tightened the folds of the jacket round the babe's neck, so that the frost should not get in through any opening, and that no melted snow should drop between the garment and the child.

The plain was unequal. In the declivities into which it sloped the snow, driven by the wind into the dips of the ground, was so deep, in comparison with a child so small, that it almost engulfed him, and he had to struggle through it half buried. He walked on, working away the snow with his knees.

Having cleared the ravine, he reached the high lands swept by the winds, where the snow lay thin. Then he found the surface a sheet of ice. The little girl's lukewarm breath, playing on his face, warmed it for a moment, then lingered, and froze in his hair, stiffening it into icicles.

He felt the approach of another danger. He could not afford to fall. He knew that if he did so he should never rise again. He was overcome by fatigue, and the weight of the darkness would, as with the dead woman, have held him to the ground, and the ice glued him alive to the earth.

He had tripped upon the slopes of precipices, and had recovered himself; he had stumbled into holes, and had got out again. Thenceforward the slightest fall would be death; a false step opened for him a tomb. He must not slip. He had not strength to rise even to his knees. Now everything was slippery; everywhere there was rime and frozen snow. The little creature whom he carried made his progress fearfully difficult. She was not only a burden, which his weariness and exhaustion made excessive, but was also an embarrassment. She occupied both his arms, and to him who walks over ice both arms are a natural and necessary balancing power.

He was obliged to do without this balance.

He did without it and advanced, bending under his burden, not knowing what would become of him.

This little infant was the drop causing the cup of distress to overflow.

He advanced, reeling at every step, as if on a spring board, and accomplishing, without spectators, miracles of equilibrium. Let us repeat that he was, perhaps, followed on this path of pain by eyes unsleeping in the distances of the shadows—the eyes of the mother and the eyes of God. He staggered, slipped, recovered himself, took care of the infant, and, gathering the jacket about her, he covered up her head; staggered again, advanced, slipped, then drew himself up. The cowardly wind drove against him. Apparently, he made much more way than was necessary. He was, to all appearance, on the plains where Bincleaves Farm was afterwards established, between what are now called Spring Gardens and the Parsonage House. Homesteads and cottages occupy the place of waste lands. Sometimes less than a century separates a steppe from a city.

Suddenly, a lull having occurred in the icy blast which was blinding him, he perceived, at a short distance in front of him, a cluster of gables and of chimneys shown in relief by the snow. The reverse of a silhouette—a city painted in white on a black horizon, something like what we call nowadays a negative proof. Roofs—dwellings—shelter! He had arrived somewhere at last. He felt the ineffable encouragement of hope. The watch of a ship which has wandered from her course feels some such emotion when he cries, "Land ho!"

He hurried his steps.

At length, then, he was near mankind. He would soon be amidst living creatures. There was no longer anything to fear. There glowed within him that sudden warmth—security; that out of which he was emerging was over; thenceforward there would no longer be night, nor winter, nor tempest. It seemed to him that he had left all evil chances behind him. The infant was no longer a burden. He almost ran.

His eyes were fixed on the roofs. There was life there. He never took his eyes off them. A dead man might gaze thus on what might appear through the half-opened lid of his sepulchre. There were the chimneys of which he had seen the smoke.

No smoke arose from them now. He was not long before he reached the houses. He came to the outskirts of a town—an open street. At that period bars to streets were falling into disuse.

The street began by two houses. In those two houses neither candle nor lamp was to be seen; nor in the whole street; nor in the whole town, so far as eye could reach. The house to the right was a roof rather than a house; nothing could be more mean. The walls were of mud, the roof was of straw, and there was more thatch than wall. A large nettle, springing from the bottom of the wall, reached the roof. The hovel had but one door, which was like that of a dog-kennel; and a window, which was but a hole. All was shut up. At the side an inhabited pig-sty told that the house was also inhabited.

The house on the left was large, high, built entirely of stone, with a slated roof. It was also closed. It was the rich man's home, opposite to that of the pauper.

The boy did not hesitate. He approached the great mansion. The double folding-door of massive oak, studded with large nails, was of the kind that leads one to expect that behind it there is a stout armoury of bolts and locks. An iron knocker was attached to it. He raised the knocker with some difficulty, for his benumbed hands were stumps rather than hands. He knocked once.

No answer.

He struck again, and two knocks.

No movement was heard in the house.

He knocked a third time.

There was no sound. He saw that they were all asleep, and did not care to get up.

Then he turned to the hovel. He picked up a pebble from the snow, and knocked against the low door.

There was no answer.

He raised himself on tiptoe, and knocked with his pebble against the pane too softly to break the glass, but loud enough to be heard.

No voice was heard; no step moved; no candle was lighted.

He saw that there, as well, they did not care to awake.

The house of stone and the thatched hovel were equally deaf to the wretched.

The boy decided on pushing on further, and penetrating the strait of houses which stretched away in front of him, so dark that it seemed more like a gulf between two cliffs than the entrance to a town.

CHAPTER IV.

ANOTHER FORM OF DESERT

It was Weymouth which he had just entered. Weymouth then was not the respectable and fine Weymouth of to-day.

Ancient Weymouth did not present, like the present one, an irreproachable rectangular quay, with an inn and a statue in honour of George III. This resulted from the fact that George III. had not yet been born. For the same reason they had not yet designed on the slope of the green hill towards the east, fashioned flat on the soil by cutting away the turf and leaving the bare chalk to the view, the white horse, an acre long, bearing the king upon his back, and always turning, in honour of George III., his tail to the city. These honours, however, were deserved. George III., having lost in his old age the intellect he had never possessed in his youth, was not responsible for the calamities of his reign. He was an innocent. Why not erect statues to him?

Weymouth, a hundred and eighty years ago, was about as symmetrical as a game of spillikins in confusion. In legends it is said that Astaroth travelled over the world, carrying on her back a wallet which contained everything, even good women in their houses. A pell-mell of sheds thrown from her devil's bag would give an idea of that irregular Weymouth—the good women in the sheds included. The Music Hall remains as a specimen of those buildings. A confusion of wooden dens, carved and eaten by worms (which carve in another fashion)—shapeless, overhanging buildings, some with pillars, leaning one against the other for support against the sea wind, and leaving between them awkward spaces of narrow and winding channels, lanes, and passages, often flooded by the equinoctial tides; a heap of old grandmother houses, crowded round a grandfather church—such was Weymouth; a sort of old Norman village thrown up on the coast of England.

The traveller who entered the tavern, now replaced by the hotel, instead of paying royally his twenty-five francs for a fried sole and a bottle of wine, had to suffer the humiliation of eating a pennyworth of soup made of fish—which soup, by-the-bye, was very good. Wretched fare!

The deserted child, carrying the foundling, passed through the first street, then the second, then the third. He raised his eyes, seeking in the higher stories and in the roofs a lighted window-pane; but all were closed and dark. At intervals he knocked at the doors. No one answered. Nothing makes the heart so like a stone as being warm between sheets. The noise and the shaking had at length awakened the infant. He knew this because he felt her suck his cheek. She did not cry, believing him her mother.

He was about to turn and wander long, perhaps, in the intersections of the Scrambridge lanes, where there were then more cultivated plots than dwellings, more thorn hedges than houses; but fortunately he struck into a passage which exists to this day near Trinity schools. This passage led him to a water-brink, where there was a roughly built quay with a parapet, and to the right he made out a bridge. It was the bridge over the Wey, connecting Weymouth with Melcombe Regis, and under the arches of which the Backwater joins the harbour.

Weymouth, a hamlet, was then the suburb of Melcombe Regis, a city and port. Now Melcombe Regis is a parish of Weymouth. The village has absorbed the city. It was the bridge which did the work. Bridges are strange vehicles of suction, which inhale the population, and sometimes swell one river-bank at the expense of its opposite neighbour.

The boy went to the bridge, which at that period was a covered timber structure. He crossed it. Thanks to its roofing, there was no snow on the planks. His bare feet had a moment's comfort as they crossed them. Having passed over the bridge, he was in Melcombe Regis. There were fewer wooden houses than stone ones there. He was no longer in the village; he was in the city.

The bridge opened on a rather fine street called St. Thomas's Street. He entered it. Here and there were high carved gables and shop-fronts. He set to knocking at the doors again: he had no strength left to call or shout.

At Melcombe Regis, as at Weymouth, no one was stirring. The doors were all carefully double-locked, The windows were covered by their shutters, as the eyes by their lids. Every precaution had been taken to avoid being roused by disagreeable surprises. The little wanderer was suffering the indefinable depression made by a sleeping town. Its silence, as of a paralyzed ants' nest, makes the head swim. All its lethargies mingle their nightmares, its slumbers are a crowd, and from its human bodies lying prone there arises a vapour of dreams. Sleep has gloomy associates beyond this life: the decomposed thoughts of the sleepers float above them in a mist which is both of death and of life, and combine with the possible, which has also, perhaps, the power of thought, as it floats in space. Hence arise entanglements. Dreams, those clouds, interpose their folds and their transparencies over that star, the mind. Above those closed eyelids, where vision has taken the place of sight, a sepulchral disintegration of outlines and appearances dilates itself into impalpability. Mysterious, diffused existences amalgamate themselves with life on that border of death, which sleep is. Those larvæ and souls mingle in the air. Even he who sleeps not feels a medium press upon him full of sinister life. The surrounding chimera, in which he suspects a reality, impedes him. The waking man, wending his way amidst the sleep phantoms of others, unconsciously pushes back passing shadows, has, or imagines that he has, a vague fear of adverse contact with the invisible, and feels at every moment the obscure pressure of a hostile encounter which immediately dissolves. There is something of the effect of a forest in the nocturnal diffusion of dreams.

This is what is called being afraid without reason.

What a man feels a child feels still more.

The uneasiness of nocturnal fear, increased by the spectral houses, increased the weight of the sad burden under which he was struggling.

He entered Conycar Lane, and perceived at the end of that passage the Backwater, which he took for the ocean. He no longer knew in what direction the sea lay. He retraced his steps, struck to the left by Maiden Street, and returned as far as St. Alban's Row.

There, by chance and without selection, he knocked violently at any house that he happened to pass. His blows, on which he was expending his last energies, were jerky and without aim; now ceasing altogether for a time, now renewed as if in irritation. It was the violence of his fever striking against the doors.

One voice answered.

That of Time.

Three o'clock tolled slowly behind him from the old belfry of St. Nicholas.

Then all sank into silence again.

That no inhabitant should have opened a lattice may appear surprising. Nevertheless that silence is in a great measure to be explained. We must remember that in January 1790 they were just over a somewhat severe outbreak of the plague in London, and that the fear of receiving sick vagabonds caused a diminution of hospitality everywhere. People would not even open their windows for fear of inhaling the poison.

The child felt the coldness of men more terribly than the coldness of night. The coldness of men is intentional. He felt a tightening on his sinking heart which he had not known on the open plains. Now he had entered into the midst of life, and remained alone. This was the summit of misery. The pitiless desert he had understood; the unrelenting town was too much to bear.

The hour, the strokes of which he had just counted, had been another blow. Nothing is so freezing in certain situations as the voice of the hour. It is a declaration of indifference. It is Eternity saying, "What does it matter to me?"

He stopped, and it is not certain that, in that miserable minute, he did not ask himself whether it would not be easier to lie down there and die. However, the little infant leaned her head against his shoulder, and fell asleep again.

This blind confidence set him onwards again. He whom all supports were failing felt that he was himself a basis of support. Irresistible summons of duty!

Neither such ideas nor such a situation belonged to his age. It is probable that he did not understand them. It was a matter of instinct. He did what he chanced to do.

He set out again in the direction of Johnstone Row. But now he no longer walked; he dragged himself along. He left St. Mary's Street to the left, made zigzags through lanes, and at the end of a winding passage found himself in a rather wide open space. It was a piece of waste land not built upon—probably the spot where Chesterfield Place now stands. The houses ended there. He perceived the sea to the right, and scarcely anything more of the town to his left.

What was to become of him? Here was the country again. To the east great inclined planes of snow marked out the wide slopes of Radipole. Should he continue this journey? Should he advance and re-enter the solitudes? Should he return and re-enter the streets? What was he to do between those two silences—the mute plain and the deaf city? Which of the two refusals should he choose?

There is the anchor of mercy. There is also the look of piteousness. It was that look which the poor little despairing wanderer threw around him.

All at once he heard a menace.

CHAPTER V.

MISANTHROPY PLAYS ITS PRANKS

A strange and alarming grinding of teeth reached him through the darkness.

It was enough to drive one back: he advanced. To those to whom silence has become dreadful a howl is comforting.

That fierce growl reassured him; that threat was a promise. There was there a being alive and awake, though it might be a wild beast. He advanced in the direction whence came the snarl.

He turned the corner of a wall, and, behind in the vast sepulchral light made by the reflection of snow and sea, he saw a thing placed as if for shelter. It was a cart, unless it was a hovel. It had wheels—it was a carriage. It had a roof—it was a dwelling. From the roof arose a funnel, and out of the funnel smoke. This smoke was red, and seemed to imply a good fire in the interior. Behind, projecting hinges indicated a door, and in the centre of this door a square opening showed a light inside the caravan. He approached.

Whatever had growled perceived his approach, and became furious. It was no longer a growl which he had to meet; it was a roar. He heard a sharp sound, as of a chain violently pulled to its full length, and suddenly, under the door, between the hind wheels, two rows of sharp white teeth appeared. At the same time as the mouth between the wheels a head was put through the window.

"Peace there!" said the head.

The mouth was silent.

The head began again,—

"Is any one there?"

The child answered,—

"Yes."

"Who?"

"I."

"You? Who are you? whence do you come?"

"I am weary," said the child.

"What o'clock is it?"

"I am cold."

"What are you doing there?"

"I am hungry."

The head replied,—

"Every one cannot be as happy as a lord. Go away."

The head was withdrawn and the window closed.

The child bowed his forehead, drew the sleeping infant closer in his arms, and collected his strength to resume his journey. He had taken a few steps, and was hurrying away.

However, at the same time that the window closed the door had opened; a step had been let down; the voice which had spoken to the child cried out angrily from the inside of the van,—

"Well! why do you not enter?"

The child turned back.

"Come in," resumed the voice. "Who has sent me a fellow like this, who is hungry and cold, and who does not come in?"

The child, at once repulsed and invited, remained motionless.

The voice continued,—

"You are told to come in, you young rascal."

He made up his mind, and placed one foot on the lowest step.

There was a great growl under the van. He drew back. The gaping jaws appeared.

"Peace!" cried the voice of the man.

The jaws retreated, the growling ceased.

"Come up!" continued the man.

The child with difficulty climbed up the three steps. He was impeded by the infant, so benumbed, rolled up and enveloped in the jacket that nothing could be distinguished of her, and she was but a little shapeless mass.

He passed over the three steps; and having reached the threshold, stopped.

No candle was burning in the caravan, probably from the economy of want. The hut was lighted only by a red tinge, arising from the opening at the top of the stove, in which sparkled a peat fire. On the stove were smoking a porringer and a saucepan, containing to all appearance something to eat. The savoury odour was perceptible. The hut was furnished with a chest, a stool, and an unlighted lantern which hung from the ceiling. Besides, to the partition were attached some boards on brackets and some hooks, from which hung a variety of things. On the boards and nails were rows of glasses, coppers, an alembic, a vessel rather like those used for graining wax, which are called granulators, and a confusion of strange objects of which the child understood nothing, and which were utensils for cooking and chemistry. The caravan was oblong in shape, the stove being in front. It was not even a little room; it was scarcely a big box. There was more light outside from the snow than inside from the stove. Everything in the caravan was indistinct and misty. Nevertheless, a reflection of the fire on the ceiling enabled the spectator to read in large letters,—

URSUS, PHILOSOPHER.

The child, in fact, was entering the house of Homo and Ursus. The one he had just heard growling, the other speaking.

The child having reached the threshold, perceived near the stove a man, tall, smooth, thin and old, dressed in gray, whose head, as he stood, reached the roof. The man could not have raised himself on tiptoe. The caravan was just his size.

"Come in!" said the man, who was Ursus.

The child entered.

"Put down your bundle."

The child placed his burden carefully on the top of the chest, for fear of awakening and terrifying it.

The man continued,—

"How gently you put it down! You could not be more careful were it a case of relics. Is it that you are afraid of tearing a hole in your rags? Worthless vagabond! in the streets at this hour! Who are you? Answer! But no. I forbid you to answer. There! You are cold. Warm yourself as quick as you can," and he shoved him by the shoulders in front of the fire.

"How wet you are! You're frozen through! A nice state to come into a house! Come, take off those rags, you villain!" and as with one hand, and with feverish haste, he dragged off the boy's rags which tore into shreds, with the other he took down from a nail a man's shirt, and one of those knitted jackets which are up to this day called kiss-me-quicks.

"Here are clothes."

He chose out of a heap a woollen rag, and chafed before the fire the limbs of the exhausted and bewildered child, who at that moment, warm and naked, felt as if he were seeing and touching heaven. The limbs having been rubbed, he next wiped the boy's feet.

"Come, you limb; you have nothing frost-bitten! I was a fool to fancy you had something frozen, hind legs or fore paws. You will not lose the use of them this time. Dress yourself!"

The child put on the shirt, and the man slipped the knitted jacket over it.

"Now...."

The man kicked the stool forward and made the little boy sit down, again shoving him by the shoulders; then he pointed with his finger to the porringer which was smoking upon the stove. What the child saw in the porringer was again heaven to him—namely, a potato and a bit of bacon.

"You are hungry; eat!"

The man took from the shelf a crust of hard bread and an iron fork, and handed them to the child.

The boy hesitated.

"Perhaps you expect me to lay the cloth," said the man, and he placed the porringer on the child's lap.

"Gobble that up."

Hunger overcame astonishment. The child began to eat. The poor boy devoured rather than ate. The glad sound of the crunching of bread filed the hut. The man grumbled,—

"Not so quick, you horrid glutton! Isn't he a greedy scoundrel? When such scum are hungry, they eat in a revolting fashion. You should see a lord sup. In my time I have seen dukes eat. They don't eat; that's noble. They drink, however. Come, you pig, stuff yourself!"

The absence of ears, which is the concomitant of a hungry stomach, caused the child to take little heed of these violent epithets, tempered as they were by charity of action involving a contradiction resulting in his benefit. For the moment he was absorbed by two exigencies and by two ecstasies—food and warmth.

Ursus continued his imprecations, muttering to himself,—

"I have seen King James supping *in propriâ personâ* in the Banqueting House, where are to be admired the paintings of the famous Rubens. His Majesty touched nothing. This beggar here browses: browses, a word derived from brute. What put it into my head to come to this Weymouth seven times devoted to the infernal deities? I have sold nothing since morning I have harangued the snow. I have played the flute to the hurricane. I have not pocketed a farthing; and now, to-night, beggars drop in. Horrid place! There is battle, struggle, competition between the fools in the street and myself. They try to give me nothing but farthings. I try to give them nothing but drugs. Well, to-day I've made nothing. Not an idiot on the highway, not a penny in the till. Eat away, hell-born boy! Tear and crunch! We have fallen on times when nothing can equal the cynicism of spongers. Fatten at my expense, parasite! This wretched boy is more than hungry; he is mad. It is not appetite, it is ferocity. He is carried away by a rabid virus. Perhaps he has the plague. Have you the plague, you thief? Suppose he were to give it to Homo! No, never! Let the populace die, but not my wolf. But by-the-bye I am hungry myself. I declare that this is all very disagreeable. I have worked far into the night. There are seasons in a man's life when he is hard pressed. I was to-night, by hunger. I was alone. I made a fire. I had but one potato, one crust of bread, a mouthful of bacon, and a drop of milk, and I put it to warm. I said to myself, 'Good.' I think I am going to eat, and bang! this crocodile falls upon me at the very moment. He installs himself clean between my food and myself. Behold, how my larder is devastated! Eat, pike, eat! You shark! how many teeth have you in your jaws? Guzzle, wolf-cub; no, I withdraw that word. I respect wolves. Swallow up my food, boa. I have worked all day, and far into the night, on an empty stomach; my throat is sore, my pancreas in distress, my entrails torn; and my reward is to see another eat. 'Tis all one, though! We will divide. He shall have the bread, the potato, and the bacon; but I will have the milk."

Just then a wail, touching and prolonged, arose in the hut. The man listened.

"You cry, sycophant! Why do you cry?"

The boy turned towards him. It was evident that it was not he who cried. He had his mouth full.

The cry continued.

The man went to the chest.

"So it is your bundle that wails! Vale of Jehoshaphat! Behold a vociferating parcel! What the devil has your bundle got to croak about?"

He unrolled the jacket. An infant's head appeared, the mouth open and crying.

"Well, who goes there?" said the man. "Here is another of them. When is this to end? Who is there? To arms! Corporal, call out the guard! Another bang! What have you brought me, thief! Don't you see it is thirsty? Come! the little one must have a drink. So now I shall not have even the milk!"

He took down from the things lying in disorder on the shelf a bandage of linen, a sponge and a phial, muttering savagely, "What an infernal place!"

Then he looked at the little infant. "'Tis a girl! one can tell that by her scream, and she is drenched as well." He dragged away, as he had done from the boy, the tatters in which she was knotted up rather than dressed, and swathed her in a rag, which, though of coarse linen, was clean and dry. This rough and sudden dressing made the infant angry.

"She mews relentlessly," said he.

He bit off a long piece of sponge, tore from the roll a square piece of linen, drew from it a bit of thread, took the saucepan containing the milk from the stove, filled the phial with milk, drove down the sponge halfway into its neck, covered the sponge with linen, tied this cork in with the thread, applied his cheeks to the phial to be sure that it was not too hot, and seized under his left arm the bewildered bundle which was still crying. "Come! take your supper, creature! Let me suckle you," and he put the neck of the bottle to its mouth.

The little infant drank greedily.

He held the phial at the necessary incline, grumbling, "They are all the same, the cowards! When they have all they want they are silent."

The child had drunk so ravenously, and had seized so eagerly this breast offered by a cross-grained providence, that she was taken with a fit of coughing.

"You are going to choke!" growled Ursus. "A fine gobbler this one, too!"

He drew away the sponge which she was sucking, allowed the cough to subside, and then replaced the phial to her lips, saying, "Suck, you little wretch!"

In the meantime the boy had laid down his fork. Seeing the infant drink had made him forget to eat. The moment before, while he ate, the expression in his face was satisfaction; now it was gratitude. He watched the infant's renewal of life; the completion of the resurrection begun by himself filled his eyes with an ineffable brilliancy. Ursus went on muttering angry words between his teeth. The little boy now and then lifted towards Ursus his eyes moist with the unspeakable emotion which the poor little being felt, but was unable to express. Ursus addressed him furiously.

"Well, will you eat?"

"And you?" said the child, trembling all over, and with tears in his eyes. "You will have nothing!"

"Will you be kind enough to eat it all up, you cub? There is not too much for you, since there was not enough for me."

The child took up his fork, but did not eat.

"Eat," shouted Ursus. "What has it got to do with me? Who speaks of me? Wretched little barefooted clerk of Penniless Parish, I tell you, eat it all up! You are here to eat, drink, and sleep—eat, or I will kick you out, both of you."

The boy, under this menace, began to eat again. He had not much trouble in finishing what was left in the porringer. Ursus muttered, "This building is badly joined. The cold comes in by the window pane." A pane had indeed been broken in front, either by a jolt of the caravan or by a stone thrown by some mischievous boy. Ursus had placed a star of paper over the fracture, which had become unpasted. The blast entered there.

He was half seated on the chest. The infant in his arms, and at the same time on his lap, was sucking rapturously at the bottle, in the happy somnolency of cherubim before their Creator, and infants at their mothers' breast.

"She is drunk," said Ursus; and he continued, "After this, preach sermons on temperance!"

The wind tore from the pane the plaster of paper, which flew across the hut; but this was nothing to the children, who were entering life anew. Whilst the little girl drank, and the little boy ate, Ursus grumbled,—

"Drunkenness begins in the infant in swaddling clothes. What useful trouble Bishop Tillotson gives himself, thundering against excessive drinking. What an odious draught of wind! And then my stove is old. It allows puffs of smoke to escape enough to give you trichiasis. One has the inconvenience of cold, and the inconvenience of fire. One cannot see clearly. That being over there abuses my hospitality. Well, I have not been able to distinguish the animal's face yet. Comfort is wanting here. By Jove! I am a great admirer of exquisite banquets in well closed rooms. I have missed my vocation. I was born to be a sensualist. The greatest of stoics was Philoxenus, who wished to possess the neck of a crane, so as to be longer in tasting the pleasures of the table. Receipts to-day, naught. Nothing sold all day. Inhabitants, servants, and tradesmen, here is the doctor, here are the drugs. You are losing your time, old friend. Pack up your physic. Every one is well down here. It's a cursed town, where every one is well! The skies alone have diarrhoea—what snow! Anaxagoras taught that the snow was black; and he was right, cold being blackness. Ice is night. What a hurricane! I can fancy the delight of those at sea. The hurricane is the passage of demons. It is the row of the tempest fiends galloping and rolling head over heels above our bone-boxes. In the cloud this one has a tail, that one has horns, another a flame for a tongue, another claws to its wings, another a lord chancellor's paunch, another an academician's pate. You may observe a form in every sound. To every fresh wind a fresh demon. The ear hears, the eye sees, the crash is a face. Zounds! There are folks at sea—that is certain. My friends, get through the storm as best you can. I have enough to do to get through life. Come now, do I keep an inn, or do I not? Why should I trade with these travellers? The universal distress sends its spatterings even as far as my poverty. Into my cabin fall hideous drops of the far-spreading mud of mankind. I am given up to the voracity of travellers. I am a prey—the prey of those dying of hunger. Winter, night, a pasteboard hut, an unfortunate friend below and without, the storm, a potato, a fire as big as my fist, parasites, the wind penetrating through every cranny, not a halfpenny, and bundles which set to howling. I open them and find beggars inside. Is this fair? Besides, the laws are violated. Ah! vagabond with your vagabond child! Mischievous pick-pocket, evil-minded abortion, so you walk the streets after curfew? If our good king only knew it, would he not have you thrown into the bottom of a ditch, just to teach you better? My gentleman walks out at night with my lady, and with the glass at fifteen degrees of frost, bare-headed and bare-footed. Understand that such things are forbidden. There are rules and regulations, you lawless wretches. Vagabonds are punished, honest folks who have houses are guarded and protected. Kings are the fathers of their people. I have my own house. You would have been whipped in the public street had you chanced to have been met, and quite right, too. There must be order in an established city. For my own part, I did wrong not to denounce you to the constable. But I am such a fool! I understand what is right and do what is wrong. O the ruffian! to come here in such a state! I did not see the snow upon them when they came in; it had melted, and here's my whole house swamped. I have an inundation in my home. I shall have to burn an incredible amount of coals to dry up this lake—coals at twelve farthings the miners' standard! How am I going to manage to fit three into this caravan? Now it is over; I enter the nursery; I am going to have in my house the weaning of the future beggardom of England. I shall have for employment, office, and function, to fashion the miscarried fortunes of that colossal prostitute, Misery, to bring to perfection future gallows' birds, and to give young thieves the forms of philosophy. The tongue of the wolf is the warning of God. And to think that if I had not been eaten up by creatures of this kind for the last thirty years, I should be rich; Homo would be fat; I should have a medicine-chest full of rarities; as many surgical instruments as Doctor Linacre, surgeon to King Henry VIII.; divers animals of all kinds; Egyptian mummies, and similar curiosities; I should be a member of the College of Physicians, and have the right of using the library, built in 1652 by the celebrated Hervey, and of studying in the lantern of that dome, whence you can see the whole of London. I could continue my observations of solar obfuscation, and prove that a caligenous vapour arises from the planet. Such was the opinion of John Kepler, who was born the year before the Massacre of St. Bartholomew, and who was mathematician to the emperor. The sun is a chimney which sometimes smokes; so does my stove. My stove is no better than the sun. Yes, I should have made my fortune; my part would have been a different one—I should not be the insignificant fellow I am. I should not degrade science in the highways, for the crowd is not worthy of the doctrine, the crowd being nothing better than a confused mixture of all sorts of ages, sexes, humours, and conditions, that wise men of all periods have not hesitated to despise, and whose extravagance and passion the most moderate men in their justice detest. Oh, I am weary of existence! After all, one does not live long! The human life is soon done with. But no—it is long. At intervals, that we should not become too discouraged, that we may have the stupidity to consent to bear our being, and not profit by the magnificent opportunities to hang ourselves which cords and nails afford, nature puts on an air of taking a little care of man—not to-night, though. The rogue causes the wheat to spring up, ripens the grape, gives her song to the nightingale. From time to time a ray of morning or a glass of gin, and that is what we call happiness! It is a narrow border of good round a huge winding-sheet of evil. We have a destiny of which the devil has woven the stuff and God has sewn the hem. In the meantime, you have eaten my supper, you thief!"

In the meantime the infant whom he was holding all the time in his arms very tenderly whilst he was vituperating, shut its eyes languidly; a sign of repletion. Ursus examined the phial, and grumbled,—

"She has drunk it all up, the impudent creature!"

He arose, and sustaining the infant with his left arm, with his right he raised the lid of the chest and drew from beneath it a bear-skin—the one he called, as will be remembered, his real skin. Whilst he was doing this he heard the other child eating, and looked at him sideways.

"It will be something to do if, henceforth, I have to feed that growing glutton. It will be a worm gnawing at the vitals of my industry."

He spread out, still with one arm, the bear-skin on the chest, working his elbow and managing his movements so as not to disturb the sleep into which the infant was just sinking.

Then he laid her down on the fur, on the side next the fire. Having done so, he placed the phial on the stove, and exclaimed,—

"I'm thirsty, if you like!"

He looked into the pot. There were a few good mouthfuls of milk left in it; he raised it to his lips. Just as he was about to drink, his eye fell on the little girl. He replaced the pot on the stove, took the phial, uncorked it, poured into it all the milk that remained, which was just sufficient to fill it, replaced the sponge and the linen rag over it, and tied it round the neck of the bottle.

"All the same, I'm hungry and thirsty," he observed.

And he added,—

"When one cannot eat bread, one must drink water."

Behind the stove there was a jug with the spout off. He took it and handed it to the boy.

"Will you drink?"

The child drank, and then went on eating.

Ursus seized the pitcher again, and conveyed it to his mouth. The temperature of the water which it contained had been unequally modified by the proximity of the stove.

He swallowed some mouthfuls and made a grimace.

"Water! pretending to be pure, thou resemblest false friends. Thou art warm at the top and cold at bottom."

In the meantime the boy had finished his supper. The porringer was more than empty; it was cleaned out. He picked up and ate pensively a few crumbs caught in the folds of the knitted jacket on his lap.

Ursus turned towards him.

"That is not all. Now, a word with you. The mouth is not made only for eating; it is made for speaking. Now that you are warmed and stuffed, you beast, take care of yourself. You are going to answer my questions. Whence do you come?"

The child replied,—

"I do not know."

"How do you mean? you don't know?"

"I was abandoned this evening on the sea-shore."

"You little scamp! what's your name? He is so good for nothing that his relations desert him."

"I have no relations."

"Give in a little to my tastes, and observe that I do not like those who sing to a tune of fibs. Thou must have relatives since you have a sister."

"It is not my sister."

"It is not your sister?"

"No."

"Who is it then?"

"It is a baby that I found."

"Found?"

"Yes."

"What! did you pick her up?"

"Yes."

"Where? If you lie I will exterminate you."

"On the breast of a woman who was dead in the snow."

"When?"

"An hour ago."

"Where?"

"A league from here."

The arched brow of Ursus knitted and took that pointed shape which characterizes emotion on the brow of a philosopher.

"Dead! Lucky for her! We must leave her in the snow. She is well off there. In which direction?"

"In the direction of the sea."

"Did you cross the bridge?"

"Yes."

Ursus opened the window at the back and examined the view.

The weather had not improved. The snow was falling thickly and mournfully.

He shut the window.

He went to the broken glass; he filled the hole with a rag; he heaped the stove with peat; he spread out as far as he could the bear-skin on the chest; took a large book which he had in a corner, placed it under the skin for a pillow, and laid the head of the sleeping infant on it.

Then he turned to the boy.

"Lie down there."

The boy obeyed, and stretched himself at full length by the side of the infant.

Ursus rolled the bear-skin over the two children, and tucked it under their feet.

He took down from a shelf, and tied round his waist, a linen belt with a large pocket containing, no doubt, a case of instruments and bottles of restoratives.

Then he took the lantern from where it hung to the ceiling and lighted it. It was a dark lantern. When lighted it still left the children in shadow.

Ursus half opened the door, and said,—

"I am going out; do not be afraid. I shall return. Go to sleep."

Then letting down the steps, he called Homo. He was answered by a loving growl.

Ursus, holding the lantern in his hand, descended. The steps were replaced, the door was reclosed. The children remained alone.

From without, a voice, the voice of Ursus, said,—

"You, boy, who have just eaten up my supper, are you already asleep?"

"No," replied the child.

"Well, if she cries, give her the rest of the milk."

The clinking of a chain being undone was heard, and the sound of a man's footsteps, mingled with that of the pads of an animal, died off in the distance. A few minutes after, both children slept profoundly.

The little boy and girl, lying naked side by side, were joined through the silent hours, in the seraphic promiscuousness of the shadows; such dreams as were possible to their age floated from one to the other; beneath their closed eyelids there shone, perhaps, a starlight; if the word marriage were not inappropriate to the situation, they were husband and wife after the fashion of the angels. Such innocence in such darkness, such purity in such an embrace; such foretastes of heaven are possible only to childhood, and no immensity approaches the greatness of little children. Of all gulfs this is the deepest. The fearful perpetuity of the dead chained beyond life, the mighty animosity of the ocean to a wreck, the whiteness of the snow over buried bodies, do not equal in pathos two children's mouths meeting divinely in sleep,[10] and the meeting of which is not even a kiss. A betrothal perchance, perchance a catastrophe. The unknown weighs down upon their juxtaposition. It charms, it terrifies; who knows which? It stays the pulse. Innocence is higher than virtue. Innocence is holy ignorance. They slept. They were in peace. They were warm. The nakedness of their bodies, embraced each in each, amalgamated with the virginity of their souls. They were there as in the nest of the abyss.

CHAPTER VI.

THE AWAKING

The beginning of day is sinister. A sad pale light penetrated the hut. It was the frozen dawn. That wan light which throws into relief the mournful reality of objects which are blurred into spectral forms by the night, did not awake the children, so soundly were they sleeping. The caravan was warm. Their breathings alternated like two peaceful waves. There was no longer a hurricane without. The light of dawn was slowly taking possession of the horizon. The constellations were being extinguished, like candles blown out one after the other. Only a few large stars resisted. The deep-toned song of the Infinite was coming from the sea.

The fire in the stove was not quite out. The twilight broke, little by little, into daylight. The boy slept less heavily than the girl. At length, a ray brighter than the others broke through the pane, and he opened his eyes. The sleep of childhood ends in forgetfulness. He lay in a state of semi-stupor, without knowing where he was or what was near him, without making an effort to remember, gazing at the ceiling, and setting himself an aimless task as he gazed dreamily at the letters of the inscription—"Ursus, Philosopher"—which, being unable to read, he examined without the power of deciphering.

The sound of the key turning in the lock caused him to turn his head.

The door turned on its hinges, the steps were let down. Ursus was returning. He ascended the steps, his extinguished lantern in his hand. At the same time the pattering of four paws fell upon the steps. It was Homo, following Ursus, who had also returned to his home.

The boy awoke with somewhat of a start. The wolf, having probably an appetite, gave him a morning yawn, showing two rows of very white teeth. He stopped when he had got halfway up the steps, and placed both forepaws within the caravan, leaning on the threshold, like a preacher with his elbows on the edge of the pulpit. He sniffed the chest from afar, not being in the habit of finding it occupied as it then was. His wolfine form, framed by the doorway, was designed in black against the light of morning. He made up his mind, and entered. The boy, seeing the wolf in the caravan, got out of the bear-skin, and, standing up, placed himself in front of the little infant, who was sleeping more soundly than ever.

Ursus had just hung the lantern up on a nail in the ceiling. Silently, and with mechanical deliberation, he unbuckled the belt in which was his case, and replaced it on the shelf. He looked at nothing, and seemed to see nothing. His eyes were glassy. Something was moving him deeply in his mind. His thoughts at length found breath, as usual, in a rapid outflow of words. He exclaimed,—

"Happy, doubtless! Dead! stone dead!"

He bent down, and put a shovelful of turf mould into the stove; and as he poked the peat he growled out,—

"I had a deal of trouble to find her. The mischief of the unknown had buried her under two feet of snow. Had it not been for Homo, who sees as clearly with his nose as Christopher Columbus did with his mind, I should be still there, scratching at the avalanche, and playing hide and seek with Death. Diogenes took his lantern and sought for a man; I took my lantern and sought for a woman. He found a sarcasm, and I found mourning. How cold she was! I touched her hand—a stone! What silence in her eyes! How can any one be such a fool as to die and leave a child behind? It will not be convenient to pack three into this box. A pretty family I have now! A boy and a girl!"

Whilst Ursus was speaking, Homo sidled up close to the stove. The hand of the sleeping infant was hanging down between the stove and the chest. The wolf set to licking it. He licked it so softly that he did not awake the little infant.

Ursus turned round.

"Well done, Homo. I shall be father, and you shall be uncle."

Then he betook himself again to arranging the fire with philosophical care, without interrupting his aside.

"Adoption! It is settled; Homo is willing."

He drew himself up.

"I should like to know who is responsible for that woman's death? Is it man? or...."

He raised his eyes, but looked beyond the ceiling, and his lips murmured,—

"Is it Thou?"

Then his brow dropped, as if under a burden, and he continued,—

"The night took the trouble to kill the woman."

Raising his eyes, they met those of the boy, just awakened, who was listening. Ursus addressed him abruptly,—

"What are you laughing about?"

The boy answered,—

"I am not laughing."

Ursus felt a kind of shock, looked at him fixedly for a few minutes, and said,—

"Then you are frightful."

The interior of the caravan, on the previous night, had been so dark that Ursus had not yet seen the boy's face. The broad daylight revealed it. He placed the palms of his hands on the two shoulders of the boy, and, examining his countenance more and more piercingly, exclaimed,—

"Do not laugh any more!"

"I am not laughing," said the child.

Ursus was seized with a shudder from head to foot.

"You do laugh, I tell you."

Then seizing the child with a grasp which would have been one of fury had it not been one of pity, he asked him: roughly,—

"Who did that to you?"

The child replied,—

"I don't know what you mean."

"How long have you had that laugh?"

"I have always been thus," said the child.

Ursus turned towards the chest, saying in a low voice,—

"I thought that work was out of date."

He took from the top of it, very softly, so as not to awaken the infant, the book which he had placed there for a pillow.

"Let us see Conquest," he murmured.

It was a bundle of paper in folio, bound in soft parchment. He turned the pages with his thumb, stopped at a certain one, opened the book wide on the stove, and read,—

"'*De Denasatis*,' it is here."

And he continued,—

"*Bucca fissa usque ad aures, genezivis denudatis, nasoque murdridato, masca eris, et ridebis semper.*"

"There it is for certain."

Then he replaced the book on one of the shelves, growling.

"It might not be wholesome to inquire too deeply into a case of the kind. We will remain on the surface. Laugh away, my boy!"

Just then the little girl awoke. Her good-day was a cry.

"Come, nurse, give her the breast," said Ursus.

The infant sat up. Ursus taking the phial from the stove gave it to her to suck.

Then the sun arose. He was level with the horizon. His red rays gleamed through the glass, and struck against the face of the infant, which was turned towards him. Her eyeballs, fixed on the sun, reflected his purple orbit like two mirrors. The eyeballs were immovable, the eyelids also.

"See!" said Ursus. "She is blind."

PART II.

BOOK THE FIRST

THE EVERLASTING PRESENCE OF THE PAST:MAN REFLECTS MAN

CHAPTER I.

LORD CLANCHARLIE

I.

There was, in those days, an old tradition.

That tradition was Lord Linnæus Clancharlie.

Linnæus Baron Clancharlie, a contemporary of Cromwell, was one of the peers of England—few in number, be it said—who accepted the republic. The reason of his acceptance of it might, indeed, for want of a better, be found in the fact that for the time being the republic was triumphant. It was a matter of course that Lord Clancharlie should adhere to the republic, as long as the republic had the upper hand; but after the close of the revolution and the fall of the parliamentary government, Lord Clancharlie had persisted in his fidelity to it. It would have been easy for the noble patrician to re-enter the reconstituted upper house, repentance being ever well received on restorations, and Charles II. being a kind prince enough to those who returned to their allegiance to him; but Lord Clancharlie had failed to understand what was due to events. While the nation overwhelmed with acclamation the king come to retake possession of England, while unanimity was recording its verdict, while the people were bowing their salutation to the monarchy, while the dynasty was rising anew amidst a glorious and triumphant recantation, at the moment when the past was becoming the future, and the future becoming the past, that nobleman remained refractory. He turned his head away from all that joy, and voluntarily exiled himself. While he could have been a peer, he preferred being an outlaw. Years had thus passed away. He had grown old in his fidelity to the dead republic, and was therefore crowned with the ridicule which is the natural reward of such folly.

He had retired into Switzerland, and dwelt in a sort of lofty ruin on the banks of the Lake of Geneva. He had chosen his dwelling in the most rugged nook of the lake, between Chillon, where is the dungeon of Bonnivard, and Vevay, where is Ludlow's tomb. The rugged Alps, filled with twilight, winds, and clouds, were around him; and he lived there, hidden in the great shadows that fall from the mountains. He was rarely met by any passer-by. The man was out of his country, almost out of his century. At that time, to those who understood and were posted in the affairs of the period, no resistance to established things was justifiable. England was happy; a restoration is as the reconciliation of husband and wife, prince and nation return to each other, no state can be more graceful or more pleasant. Great Britain beamed with joy; to have a king at all was a good deal—but furthermore, the king was a charming one. Charles II. was amiable—a man of pleasure, yet able to govern; and great, if not after the fashion of Louis XIV. He was essentially a gentleman. Charles II. was admired by his subjects. He had made war in Hanover for reasons best known to himself; at least, no one else knew them. He had sold Dunkirk to France, a manoeuvre of state policy. The Whig peers, concerning whom Chamberlain says, "The cursed republic infected with its stinking breath several of the high nobility," had had the good sense to bow to the inevitable, to conform to the times, and to resume their seats in the House of Lords. To do so, it sufficed that they should take the oath of allegiance to the king. When these facts were considered—the glorious reign, the excellent king, august princes given back by divine mercy to the people's love; when it was remembered that persons of such consideration as Monk, and, later on, Jeffreys, had rallied round the throne; that they had been properly rewarded for their loyalty and zeal by the most splendid appointments and the most lucrative offices; that Lord Clancharlie could not be ignorant of this, and that it only depended on himself to be seated by their side, glorious in his honours; that England had, thanks to her king, risen again to the summit of prosperity; that London was all banquets and carousals; that everybody was rich and enthusiastic, that the court was gallant, gay, and magnificent;—if by chance, far from these splendours, in some melancholy, indescribable half-light, like nightfall, that old man, clad in the same garb as the common people, was observed pale, absent-minded, bent towards the grave, standing on the shore of the lake, scarce heeding the storm and the winter, walking as though at random, his eye fixed, his white hair tossed by the wind of the shadow, silent, pensive, solitary, who could forbear to smile?

It was the sketch of a madman.

Thinking of Lord Clancharlie, of what he might have been and what he was, a smile was indulgent; some laughed out aloud, others could not restrain their anger. It is easy to understand that men of sense were much shocked by the insolence implied by his isolation.

One extenuating circumstance: Lord Clancharlie had never had any brains. Every one agreed on that point.

II.

It is disagreeable to see one's fellows practise obstinacy. Imitations of Regulus are not popular, and public opinion holds them in some derision. Stubborn people are like reproaches, and we have a right to laugh at them.

Besides, to sum up, are these perversities, these rugged notches, virtues? Is there not in these excessive advertisements of self-abnegation and of honour a good deal of ostentation? It is all parade more than anything else. Why such exaggeration of solitude and exile? to carry nothing to extremes is the wise man's maxim. Be in opposition if you choose, blame if you will, but decently, and crying out all the while "Long live the King." The true virtue is common sense—what falls ought to fall, what succeeds ought to succeed. Providence acts advisedly, it crowns him who deserves the crown; do you pretend to know better than Providence? When matters are settled—when one rule has replaced another—when success is the scale in which truth and falsehood are weighed, in one side the catastrophe, in the other the triumph; then doubt is no longer possible, the honest man rallies to the winning side, and although it may happen to serve his fortune and his family, he does not allow himself to be influenced by that consideration, but thinking only of the public weal, holds out his hand heartily to the conqueror.

What would become of the state if no one consented to serve it? Would not everything come to a standstill? To keep his place is the duty of a good citizen. Learn to sacrifice your secret preferences. Appointments must be filled, and some one must necessarily sacrifice himself. To be faithful to public functions is true fidelity. The retirement of public officials would paralyse the state. What! banish yourself!—how weak! As an example?—what vanity! As a defiance?—what audacity! What do you set yourself up to be, I wonder? Learn that we are just as good as you. If we chose we too could be intractable and untameable and do worse things than you; but we prefer to be sensible people. Because I am a Trimalcion, you think that I could not be a Cato! What nonsense!

III.

Never was a situation more clearly defined or more decisive than that of 1660. Never had a course of conduct been more plainly indicated to a well-ordered mind. England was out of Cromwell's grasp. Under the republic many irregularities had been committed. British preponderance had been created. With the aid of the Thirty Years' War, Germany had been overcome; with the aid of the Fronde, France had been humiliated; with the aid of the Duke of Braganza, the power of Spain had been lessened. Cromwell had tamed Mazarin; in signing treaties the Protector of England wrote his name above that of the King of France. The United Provinces had been put under a fine of eight millions; Algiers and Tunis had been attacked; Jamaica conquered; Lisbon humbled; French rivalry encouraged in Barcelona, and Masaniello in Naples; Portugal had been made fast to England; the seas had been swept of Barbary pirates from Gibraltar to Crete; maritime domination had been founded under two forms, Victory and Commerce. On the 10th of August, 1653, the man of thirty-three victories, the old admiral who called himself the sailors' grandfather, Martin Happertz van Tromp, who had beaten the Spanish, had been destroyed by the English fleet. The Atlantic had been cleared of the Spanish navy, the Pacific of the Dutch, the Mediterranean of the Venetian, and by the patent of navigation, England had taken possession of the sea-coast of the world. By the ocean she commanded the world; at sea the Dutch flag humbly saluted the British flag. France, in the person of the Ambassador Mancini, bent the knee to Oliver Cromwell; and Cromwell played with Calais and Dunkirk as with two shuttlecocks on a battledore. The Continent had been taught to tremble, peace had been dictated, war declared, the British Ensign raised on every pinnacle. By itself the Protector's regiment of Ironsides weighed in the fears of Europe against an army. Cromwell used to say, "*I wish the Republic of England to be respected, as was respected the Republic of Rome.*" No longer were delusions held sacred; speech was free, the press was free. In the public street men said what they listed; they printed what they pleased without control or censorship. The equilibrium of thrones had been destroyed. The whole order of European monarchy, in which the Stuarts formed a link, had been overturned. But at last England had emerged from this odious order of things, and had won its pardon.

The indulgent Charles II. had granted the declaration of Breda. He had conceded to England oblivion of the period in which the son of the Huntingdon brewer placed his foot on the neck of Louis XIV. England said its mea culpa, and breathed again. The cup of joy was, as we have just said, full; gibbets for the regicides adding to the universal delight. A restoration is a smile; but a few gibbets are not out of place, and satisfaction is due to the conscience of the public. To be good subjects was thenceforth the people's sole ambition. The spirit of lawlessness had been expelled. Royalty was reconstituted. Men had recovered from the follies of politics. They mocked at revolution, they jeered at the republic, and as to those times when such strange words as *Right, Liberty, Progress*, had been in the mouth—why, they laughed at such bombast! Admirable was the return to common sense. England had been in a dream. What joy to be quit of such errors! Was ever anything so mad? Where should we be if every one had his rights? Fancy every one's having a hand in the government? Can you imagine a city ruled by its citizens? Why, the citizens are the team, and the team cannot be driver. To put to the vote is to throw to the winds. Would you have states driven like clouds? Disorder cannot build up order. With chaos for an architect, the edifice would be a Babel. And, besides, what tyranny is this pretended liberty! As for me, I wish to enjoy myself; not to govern. It is a bore to have to vote; I want to dance. A prince is a providence, and takes care of us all. Truly the king is generous to take so much trouble for our sakes. Besides, he is to the manner born. He knows what it is. It's his business. Peace, War, Legislation, Finance—what have the people to do with such things? Of course the people have to pay; of course the people have to serve; but that should suffice them. They have a place in policy; from them come two essential things, the army and the budget. To be liable to contribute, and to be liable to serve; is not that enough? What more should they want? They are the military and the financial arm. A magnificent *rôle*. The king reigns for them, and they must reward him accordingly. Taxation and the civil list are the salaries paid by the peoples and earned by the prince. The people give their blood and their money, in return for which they are led. To wish to lead themselves! what an absurd idea! They require a guide; being ignorant, they are blind. Has not the blind man his dog? Only the people have a lion, the king, who consents to act the dog. How kind of him! But why are the people ignorant? because it is good for them. Ignorance is the guardian of Virtue. Where there is no perspective there is no ambition. The ignorant man is in useful darkness, which, suppressing sight, suppresses covetousness: whence innocence. He who reads, thinks; who thinks, reasons. But not to reason is duty; and happiness as well. These truths are incontestable; society is based on them.

Thus had sound social doctrines been re-established in England; thus had the nation been reinstated. At the same time a correct taste in literature was reviving. Shakespeare was despised, Dryden admired. "*Dryden is the greatest poet of England, and of the century*," said Atterbury, the translator of "Achitophel." It was about the time when M. Huet, Bishop of Avranches, wrote to Saumaise, who had done the author of "Paradise Lost" the honour to refute and abuse him, "*How can you trouble yourself about so mean a thing as that Milton?*" Everything was falling into its proper place: Dryden above, Shakespeare below; Charles II. on the throne, Cromwell on the gibbet. England was raising herself out of the shame and the excesses of the past. It is a great happiness for nations to be led back by monarchy to good order in the state and good taste in letters.

That such benefits should be misunderstood is difficult to believe. To turn the cold shoulder to Charles II., to reward with ingratitude the magnanimity which he displayed in ascending the throne—was not such conduct abominable? Lord Linnæus Clancharlie had inflicted this vexation upon honest men. To sulk at his country's happiness, alack, what aberration!

We know that in 1650 Parliament had drawn up this form of declaration: "*I promise to remain faithful to the republic, without king, sovereign, or lord.*" Under pretext of having taken this monstrous oath, Lord Clancharlie was living out of the kingdom, and, in the face of the general joy, thought that he had the right to be sad. He had a morose esteem for that which was no more, and was absurdly attached to things which had been.

To excuse him was impossible. The kindest-hearted abandoned him; his friends had long done him the honour to believe that he had entered the republican ranks only to observe the more closely the flaws in the republican armour, and to smite it the more surely, when the day should come, for the sacred cause of the king. These lurkings in ambush for the convenient hour to strike the enemy a death-blow in the back are attributes to loyalty. Such a line of conduct had been expected of Lord Clancharlie, so strong was the wish to judge him favourably; but, in the face of his strange persistence in republicanism, people were obliged to lower their estimate. Evidently Lord Clancharlie was confirmed in his convictions—that is to say, an idiot!

The explanation given by the indulgent, wavered between puerile stubbornness and senile obstinacy.

The severe and the just went further; they blighted the name of the renegade. Folly has its rights, but it has also its limits. A man may be a brute, but he has no right to be a rebel. And, after all, what was this Lord Clancharlie? A deserter. He had fled his camp, the aristocracy, for that of the enemy, the people. This faithful man was a traitor. It is true that he was a traitor to the stronger, and faithful to the weaker; it is true that the camp repudiated by him was the conquering camp, and the camp adopted by him, the conquered; it is true that by his treason he lost everything—his political privileges and his domestic hearth, his title and his country. He gained nothing but ridicule, he attained no benefit but exile. But what does all this prove?—that he was a fool. Granted.

Plainly a dupe and traitor in one. Let a man be as great a fool as he likes, so that he does not set a bad example. Fools need only be civil, and in consideration thereof they may aim at being the basis of monarchies. The narrowness of Clancharlie's mind was incomprehensible. His eyes were still dazzled by the phantasmagoria of the revolution. He had allowed himself to be taken in by the republic—yes; and cast out. He was an affront to his country. The attitude he assumed was downright felony. Absence was an insult. He held aloof from the public joy as from the plague. In his voluntary banishment he found some indescribable refuge from the national rejoicing. He treated loyalty as a contagion; over the widespread gladness at the revival of the monarchy, denounced by him as a lazaretto, he was the black flag. What! could he look thus askance at order reconstituted, a nation exalted, and a religion restored? Over such serenity why cast his shadow? Take umbrage at England's contentment! Must he be the one blot in the clear blue sky! Be as a threat! Protest against a nation's will! refuse his Yes to the universal consent! It would be disgusting, if it were not the part of a fool. Clancharlie could not have taken into account the fact that it did not matter if one had taken the wrong turn with Cromwell, as long as one found one's way back into the right path with Monk.

Take Monk's case. He commands the republican army. Charles II., having been informed of his honesty, writes to him. Monk, who combines virtue with tact, dissimulates at first, then suddenly at the head of his troops dissolves the rebel parliament, and re-establishes the king on the throne. Monk is created Duke of Albemarle, has the honour of having saved society, becomes very rich, sheds a glory over his own time, is created Knight of the Garter, and has the prospect of being buried in Westminster Abbey. Such glory is the reward of British fidelity!

Lord Clancharlie could never rise to a sense of duty thus carried out. He had the infatuation and obstinacy of an exile. He contented himself with hollow phrases. He was tongue-tied by pride. The words conscience and dignity are but words, after all. One must penetrate to the depths. These depths Lord Clancharlie had not reached. His "eye was single," and before committing an act he wished to observe it so closely as to be able to judge it by more senses than one. Hence arose absurd disgust to the facts examined. No man can be a statesman who gives way to such overstrained delicacy. Excess of conscientiousness degenerates into infirmity. Scruple is one-handed when a sceptre is to be seized, and a eunuch when fortune is to be wedded. Distrust scruples; they drag you too far. Unreasonable fidelity is like a ladder leading into a cavern—one step down, another, then another, and there you are in the dark. The clever reascend; fools remain in it. Conscience must not be allowed to practise such austerity. If it be, it will fall until, from transition to transition, it at length reaches the deep gloom of political prudery. Then one is lost. Thus it was with Lord Clancharlie.

Principles terminate in a precipice.

He was walking, his hands behind him, along the shores of the Lake of Geneva. A fine way of getting on!

In London they sometimes spoke of the exile. He was accused before the tribunal of public opinion. They pleaded for and against him. The cause having been heard, he was acquitted on the ground of stupidity.

Many zealous friends of the former republic had given their adherence to the Stuarts. For this they deserve praise. They naturally calumniated him a little. The obstinate are repulsive to the compliant. Men of sense, in favour and good places at Court, weary of his disagreeable attitude, took pleasure in saying, "*If he has not rallied to the throne, it is because he has not been sufficiently paid*," *etc.* "*He wanted the chancellorship which the king has given to Hyde.*" One of his old friends went so far as to whisper, "*He told me so himself.*" Remote as was the solitude of Linnæus Clancharlie, something of this talk would reach him through the outlaws he met, such as old regicides like Andrew Broughton, who lived at Lausanne. Clancharlie confined himself to an imperceptible shrug of the shoulders, a sign of profound deterioration. On one occasion he added to the shrug these few words, murmured in a low voice, "I pity those who believe such things."

IV.

Charles II., good man! despised him. The happiness of England under Charles II. was more than happiness, it was enchantment. A restoration is like an old oil painting, blackened by time, and revarnished. All the past reappeared, good old manners returned, beautiful women reigned and governed. Evelyn notices it. We read in his journal, "Luxury, profaneness, contempt of God. I saw the king on Sunday evening with his courtesans, Portsmouth, Cleveland, Mazarin, and two or three others, all nearly naked, in the gaming-room." We feel that there is ill-nature in this description, for Evelyn was a grumbling Puritan, tainted with republican reveries. He did not appreciate the profitable example given by kings in those grand Babylonian gaieties, which, after all, maintain luxury. He did not understand the utility of vice. Here is a maxim: Do not extirpate vice, if you want to have charming women; if you do you are like idiots who destroy the chrysalis whilst they delight in the butterfly.

Charles II., as we have said, scarcely remembered that a rebel called Clancharlie existed; but James II. was more heedful. Charles II. governed gently, it was his way; we may add, that he did not govern the worse on that account. A sailor sometimes makes on a rope intended to baffle the wind, a slack knot which he leaves to the wind to tighten. Such is the stupidity of the storm and of the people.

The slack knot very soon becomes a tight one. So did the government of Charles II.

Under James II. the throttling began; a necessary throttling of what remained of the revolution. James II. had a laudable ambition to be an efficient king. The reign of Charles II. was, in his opinion, but a sketch of restoration. James wished for a still more complete return to order. He had, in 1660, deplored that they had confined themselves to the hanging of ten regicides. He was a more genuine reconstructor of authority. He infused vigour into serious principles. He installed true justice, which is superior to sentimental declamations, and attends, above all things, to the interests of society. In his protecting severities we recognize the father of the state. He entrusted the hand of justice to Jeffreys, and its sword to Kirke. That useful Colonel, one day, hung and rehung the same man, a republican, asking him each time, "Will you renounce the republic?" The villain, having each time said "No," was dispatched. "*I hanged him four times*," said Kirke, with satisfaction. The renewal of executions is a great sign of power in the executive authority. Lady Lisle, who, though she had sent her son to fight against Monmouth, had concealed two rebels in her house, was executed; another rebel, having been honourable enough to declare that an Anabaptist female had given him shelter, was pardoned, and the woman was burned alive. Kirke, on another occasion, gave a town to understand that he knew its principles to be republican, by hanging nineteen burgesses. These reprisals were certainly legitimate, for it must be remembered that, under Cromwell, they cut off the noses and ears of the stone saints in the churches. James II., who had had the sense to choose Jeffreys and Kirke, was a prince imbued with true religion; he practised mortification in the ugliness of his mistresses; he listened to le Père la Colombière, a preacher almost as unctuous as le Père Cheminais, but with more fire, who had the glory of being, during the first part of his life, the counsellor of James II., and, during the latter, the inspirer of Mary Alcock. It was, thanks to this strong religious nourishment, that, later on, James II. was enabled to bear exile with dignity, and to exhibit, in his retirement at Saint Germain, the spectacle of a king rising superior to adversity, calmly touching for king's evil, and conversing with Jesuits.

It will be readily understood that such a king would trouble himself to a certain extent about such a rebel as Lord Linnæus Clancharlie. Hereditary peerages have a certain hold on the future, and it was evident that if any precautions were necessary with regard to that lord, James II. was not the man to hesitate.

CHAPTER II.

LORD DAVID DIRRY-MOIR

I.

Lord Linnæus Clancharlie had not always been old and proscribed; he had had his phase of youth and passion. We know from Harrison and Pride that Cromwell, when young, loved women and pleasure, a taste which, at times (another reading of the text "Woman"), betrays a seditious man. Distrust the loosely-clasped girdle. *Male proecinctam juvenem cavete.* Lord Clancharlie, like Cromwell, had had his wild hours and his irregularities. He was known to have had a natural child, a son. This son was born in England in the last days of the republic, just as his father was going into exile. Hence he had never seen his father. This bastard of Lord Clancharlie had grown up as page at the court of Charles II. He was styled Lord David Dirry-Moir: he was a lord by courtesy, his mother being a woman of quality. The mother, while Lord Clancharlie was becoming an owl in Switzerland, made up her mind, being a beauty, to give over sulking, and was forgiven that Goth, her first lover, by one undeniably polished and at the same time a royalist, for it was the king himself.

She had been but a short time the mistress of Charles II., sufficiently long however to have made his Majesty—who was delighted to have won so pretty a woman from the republic—bestow on the little Lord David, the son of his conquest, the office of keeper of the stick, which made that bastard officer, boarded at the king's expense, by a natural revulsion of feeling, an ardent adherent of the Stuarts. Lord David was for some time one of the hundred and seventy wearing the great sword, while afterwards, entering the corps of pensioners, he became one of the forty who bear the gilded halberd. He had, besides being one of the noble company instituted by Henry VIII. as a bodyguard, the privilege of laying the dishes on the king's table. Thus it was that whilst his father was growing gray in exile, Lord David prospered under Charles II.

After which he prospered under James II.

The king is dead. Long live the king! It is the *non deficit alter, aureus.*

It was on the accession of the Duke of York that he obtained permission to call himself Lord David Dirry-Moir, from an estate which his mother, who had just died, had left him, in that great forest of Scotland, where is found the krag, a bird which scoops out a nest with its beak in the trunk of the oak.

II.

James II. was a king, and affected to be a general. He loved to surround himself with young officers. He showed himself frequently in public on horseback, in a helmet and cuirass, with a huge projecting wig hanging below the helmet and over the cuirass—a sort of equestrian statue of imbecile war. He took a fancy to the graceful mien of the young Lord David. He liked the royalist for being the son of a republican. The repudiation of a father does not damage the foundation of a court fortune. The king made Lord David gentleman of the bedchamber, at a salary of a thousand a year.

It was a fine promotion. A gentleman of the bedchamber sleeps near the king every night, on a bed which is made up for him. There are twelve gentlemen who relieve each other.

Lord David, whilst he held that post, was also head of the king's granary, giving out corn for the horses and receiving a salary of £260. Under him were the five coachmen of the king, the five postilions of the king, the five grooms of the king, the twelve footmen of the king, and the four chair-bearers of the king. He had the management of the race-horses which the king kept at Newmarket, and which cost his Majesty £600 a year. He worked his will on the king's wardrobe, from which the Knights of the Garter are furnished with their robes of ceremony. He was saluted to the ground by the usher of the Black Rod, who belongs to the king. That usher, under James II., was the knight of Duppa. Mr. Baker, who was clerk of the crown, and Mr. Brown, who was clerk of the Parliament, kotowed to Lord David. The court of England, which is magnificent, is a model of hospitality. Lord David presided, as one of the twelve, at banquets and receptions. He had the glory of standing behind the king on offertory days, when the king give to the church the golden *byzantium;* on collar-days, when the king wears the collar of his order; on communion days, when no one takes the sacrament excepting the king and the princes. It was he who, on Holy Thursday, introduced into his Majesty's presence the twelve poor men to whom the king gives as many silver pence as the years of his age, and as many shillings as the years of his reign. The duty devolved on him when the king was ill, to call to the assistance of his Majesty the two grooms of the almonry, who are priests, and to prevent the approach of doctors without permission from the council of state. Besides, he was lieutenant-colonel of the Scotch regiment of Guards, the one which plays the Scottish march. As such, he made several campaigns, and with glory, for he was a gallant soldier. He was a brave lord, well-made, handsome, generous, and majestic in look and in manner. His person was like his quality. He was tall in stature as well as high in birth.

At one time he stood a chance of being made groom of the stole, which would have given him the privilege of putting the king's shirt on his Majesty: but to hold that office it was necessary to be either prince or peer. Now, to create a peer is a serious thing; it is to create a peerage, and that makes many people jealous. It is a favour; a favour which gives the king one friend and a hundred enemies, without taking into account that the one friend becomes ungrateful. James II., from policy, was indisposed to create peerages, but he transferred them freely. The transfer of a peerage produces no sensation. It is simply the continuation of a name. The order is little affected by it.

The goodwill of royalty had no objection to raise Lord David Dirry-Moir to the Upper House so long as it could do so by means of a substituted peerage.

Nothing would have pleased his majesty better than to transform Lord David Dirry-Moir, lord by courtesy, into a lord by right.

III.

The opportunity occurred.

One day it was announced that several things had happened to the old exile, Lord Clancharlie, the most important of which was that he was dead. Death does just this much good to folks: it causes a little talk about them. People related what they knew, or what they thought they knew, of the last years of Lord Linnæus. What they said was probably legend and conjecture. If these random tales were to be credited, Lord Clancharlie must have had his republicanism intensified towards the end of his life, to the extent of marrying (strange obstinacy of the exile!) Ann Bradshaw, the daughter of a regicide; they were precise about the name. She had also died, it was said, but in giving birth to a boy. If these details should prove to be correct, his child would of course be the legitimate and rightful heir of Lord Clancharlie. These reports, however, were extremely vague in form, and were rumours rather than facts. Circumstances which happened in Switzerland, in those days, were as remote from the England of that period as those which take place in China from the England of to-day. Lord Clancharlie must have been fifty-nine at the time of his marriage, they said, and sixty at the birth of his son, and must have died shortly after, leaving his infant orphaned both of father and mother. This was possible, perhaps, but improbable. They added that the child was beautiful as the day,—just as we read in all the fairy tales. King James put an end to these rumours, evidently without foundation, by declaring, one fine morning, Lord David Dirry-Moir sole and positive heir *in default of legitimate issue*, and by his royal pleasure, of Lord Linnæus Clancharlie, his natural father, *the absence of all other issue and descent being established*, patents of which grant were registered in the House of Lords. By these patents the king instituted Lord David Dirry-Moir in the titles, rights, and prerogatives of the late Lord Linnæus Clancharlie, on the sole condition that Lord David should wed, when she attained a marriageable age, a girl who was, at that time, a mere infant a few months old, and whom the king had, in her cradle, created a duchess, no one knew exactly why; or, rather, every one knew why. This little infant was called the Duchess Josiana.

The English fashion then ran on Spanish names. One of Charles II.'s bastards was called Carlos, Earl of Plymouth. It is likely that Josiana was a contraction for Josefa-y-Ana. Josiana, however, may have been a name—the feminine of Josias. One of Henry VIII.'s gentlemen was called Josias du Passage.

It was to this little duchess that the king granted the peerage of Clancharlie. She was a peeress till there should be a peer; the peer should be her husband. The peerage was founded on a double castleward, the barony of Clancharlie and the barony of Hunkerville; besides, the barons of Clancharlie were, in recompense of an ancient feat of arms, and by royal licence, Marquises of Corleone, in Sicily.

Peers of England cannot bear foreign titles; there are, nevertheless, exceptions; thus—Henry Arundel, Baron Arundel of Wardour, was, as well as Lord Clifford, a Count of the Holy Roman Empire, of which Lord Cowper is a prince. The Duke of Hamilton is Duke of Chatelherault, in France; Basil Fielding, Earl of Denbigh, is Count of Hapsburg, of Lauffenberg, and of Rheinfelden, in Germany. The Duke of Marlborough was Prince of Mindelheim, in Suabia, just as the Duke of Wellington was Prince of Waterloo, in Belgium. The same Lord Wellington was a Spanish Duke of Ciudad Rodrigo, and Portuguese Count of Vimiera.

There were in England, and there are still, lands both noble and common. The lands of the Lords of Clancharlie were all noble. These lands, burghs, bailiwicks, fiefs, rents, freeholds, and domains, adherent to the peerage of Clancharlie-Hunkerville, belonged provisionally to Lady Josiana, and the king declared that, once married to Josiana, Lord David Dirry-Moir should be Baron Clancharlie.

Besides the Clancharlie inheritance, Lady Josiana had her own fortune. She possessed great wealth, much of which was derived from the gifts of *Madame sans queue* to the Duke of York. *Madame sans queue* is short for Madame. Henrietta of England, Duchess of Orleans, the lady of highest rank in France after the queen, was thus called.

IV.

Having prospered under Charles and James, Lord David prospered under William. His Jacobite feeling did not reach to the extent of following James into exile. While he continued to love his legitimate king, he had the good sense to serve the usurper; he was, moreover, although sometimes disposed to rebel against discipline, an excellent officer. He passed from the land to the sea forces, and distinguished himself in the White Squadron. He rose in it to be what was then called captain of a light frigate. Altogether he made a very fine fellow, carrying to a great extent the elegancies of vice: a bit of a poet, like every one else; a good servant of the state, a good servant to the prince; assiduous at feasts, at galas, at ladies' receptions, at ceremonies, and in battle; servile in a gentlemanlike way; very haughty; with eyesight dull or keen, according to the object examined; inclined to integrity; obsequious or arrogant, as occasion required; frank and sincere on first acquaintance, with the power of assuming the mask afterwards; very observant of the smiles and frowns of the royal humour; careless before a sword's point; always ready to risk his life on a sign from his Majesty with heroism and complacency, capable of any insult but of no impoliteness; a man of courtesy and etiquette, proud of kneeling at great regal ceremonies; of a gay valour; a courtier on the surface, a paladin below; quite young at forty-five. Lord David sang French songs, an elegant gaiety which had delighted Charles II. He loved eloquence and fine language. He greatly admired those celebrated discourses which are called the funeral orations of Bossuet.

From his mother he had inherited almost enough to live on, about £10,000 a year. He managed to get on with it—by running into debt. In magnificence, extravagance, and novelty he was without a rival. Directly he was copied he changed his fashion. On horseback he wore loose boots of cow-hide, which turned over, with spurs. He had hats like nobody else's, unheard-of lace, and bands of which he alone had the pattern.

CHAPTER III.

THE DUCHESS JOSIANA

Towards 1705, although Lady Josiana was twenty-three and Lord David forty-four, the wedding had not yet taken place, and that for the best reasons in the world. Did they hate each other? Far from it; but what cannot escape from you inspires you with no haste to obtain it. Josiana wanted to remain free, David to remain young. To have no tie until as late as possible appeared to him to be a prolongation of youth. Middle-aged young men abounded in those rakish times. They grew gray as young fops. The wig was an accomplice: later on, powder became the auxiliary. At fifty-five Lord Charles Gerrard, Baron Gerrard, one of the Gerrards of Bromley, filled London with his successes. The young and pretty Duchess of Buckingham, Countess of Coventry, made a fool of herself for love of the handsome Thomas Bellasys, Viscount Falconberg, who was sixty-seven. People quoted the famous verses of Corneille, the septuagenarian, to a girl of twenty—"*Marquise, si mon visage.*" Women, too, had their successes in the autumn of life. Witness Ninon and Marion. Such were the models of the day.

Josiana and David carried on a flirtation of a particular shade. They did not love, they pleased, each other. To be at each other's side sufficed them. Why hasten the conclusion? The novels of those days carried lovers and engaged couples to that kind of stage which was the most becoming. Besides, Josiana, while she knew herself to be a bastard, felt herself a princess, and carried her authority over him with a high tone in all their arrangements. She had a fancy for Lord David. Lord David was handsome, but that was over and above the bargain. She considered him to be fashionable.

To be fashionable is everything. Caliban, fashionable and magnificent, would distance Ariel, poor. Lord David was handsome, so much the better. The danger in being handsome is being insipid; and that he was not. He betted, boxed, ran into debt. Josiana thought great things of his horses, his dogs, his losses at play, his mistresses. Lord David, on his side, bowed down before the fascinations of the Duchess Josiana—a maiden without spot or scruple, haughty, inaccessible, and audacious. He addressed sonnets to her, which Josiana sometimes read. In these sonnets he declared that to possess Josiana would be to rise to the stars, which did not prevent his always putting the ascent off to the following year. He waited in the antechamber outside Josiana's heart; and this suited the convenience of both. At court all admired the good taste of this delay. Lady Josiana said, "It is a bore that I should be obliged to marry Lord David; I, who would desire nothing better than to be in love with him!"

Josiana was "the flesh." Nothing could be more resplendent. She was very tall—too tall. Her hair was of that tinge which might be called red gold. She was plump, fresh, strong, and rosy, with immense boldness and wit. She had eyes which were too intelligible. She had neither lovers nor chastity. She walled herself round with pride. Men! oh, fie! a god only would be worthy of her, or a monster. If virtue consists in the protection of an inaccessible position, Josiana possessed all possible virtue, but without any innocence. She disdained intrigues; but she would not have been displeased had she been supposed to have engaged in some, provided that the objects were uncommon, and proportioned to the merits of one so highly placed. She thought little of her reputation, but much of her glory. To appear yielding, and to be unapproachable, is perfection. Josiana felt herself majestic and material. Hers was a cumbrous beauty. She usurped rather than charmed. She trod upon hearts. She was earthly. She would have been as much astonished at being proved to have a soul in her bosom as wings on her back. She discoursed on Locke; she was polite; she was suspected of knowing Arabic.

To be "the flesh" and to be woman are two different things. Where a woman is vulnerable, on the side of pity, for instance, which so readily turns to love, Josiana was not. Not that she was unfeeling. The ancient comparison of flesh to marble is absolutely false. The beauty of flesh consists in not being marble: its beauty is to palpitate, to tremble, to blush, to bleed, to have firmness without hardness, to be white without being cold, to have its sensations and its infirmities; its beauty is to be life, and marble is death.

Flesh, when it attains a certain degree of beauty, has almost a claim to the right of nudity; it conceals itself in its own dazzling charms as in a veil. He who might have looked upon Josiana nude would have perceived her outlines only through a surrounding glory. She would have shown herself without hesitation to a satyr or a eunuch. She had the self-possession of a goddess. To have made her nudity a torment, ever eluding a pursuing Tantalus, would have been an amusement to her.

The king had made her a duchess, and Jupiter a Nereid—a double irradiation of which the strange, brightness of this creature was composed. In admiring her you felt yourself becoming a pagan and a lackey. Her origin had been bastardy and the ocean. She appeared to have emerged from the foam. From the stream had risen the first jet of her destiny; but the spring was royal. In her there was something of the wave, of chance, of the patrician, and of the tempest. She was well read and accomplished. Never had a passion approached her, yet she had sounded them all. She had a disgust for realizations, and at the same time a taste for them. If she had stabbed herself, it would, like Lucretia, not have been until afterwards. She was a virgin stained with every defilement in its visionary stage. She was a possible Astarte in a real Diana. She was, in the insolence of high birth, tempting and inaccessible. Nevertheless, she might find it amusing to plan a fall for herself. She dwelt in a halo of glory, half wishing to descend from it, and perhaps feeling curious to know what a fall was like. She was a little too heavy for her cloud. To err is a diversion. Princely unconstraint has the privilege of experiment, and what is frailty in a plebeian is only frolic in a duchess. Josiana was in everything—in birth, in beauty, in irony, in brilliancy—almost a queen. She had felt a moment's enthusiasm for Louis de Boufflers, who used to break horseshoes between his fingers. She regretted that Hercules was dead. She lived in some undefined expectation of a voluptuous and supreme ideal.

Morally, Josiana brought to one's mind the line—

"Un beau torse de femme en hydre se termine."

Hers was a noble neck, a splendid bosom, heaving harmoniously over a royal heart, a glance full of life and light, a countenance pure and haughty, and who knows? below the surface was there not, in a semi-transparent and misty depth, an undulating, supernatural prolongation, perchance deformed and dragon-like—a proud virtue ending in vice in the depth of dreams.

II.

With all that she was a prude.

It was the fashion.

Remember Elizabeth.

Elizabeth was of a type that prevailed in England for three centuries—the sixteenth, seventeenth, and eighteenth. Elizabeth was more than English—she was Anglican. Hence the deep respect of the Episcopalian Church for that queen—respect resented by the Church of Rome, which counterbalanced it with a dash of excommunication. In the mouth of Sixtus V., when anathematizing Elizabeth, malediction turned to madrigal. "*Un gran cervello di principessa*," he says. Mary Stuart, less concerned with the church and more with the woman part of the question, had little respect for her sister Elizabeth, and wrote to her as queen to queen and coquette to prude: "Your disinclination to marriage arises from your not wishing to lose the liberty of being made love to." Mary Stuart played with the fan, Elizabeth with the axe. An uneven match. They were rivals, besides, in literature. Mary Stuart composed French verses; Elizabeth translated Horace. The ugly Elizabeth decreed herself beautiful; liked quatrains and acrostics; had the keys of towns presented to her by cupids; bit her lips after the Italian fashion, rolled her eyes after the Spanish; had in her wardrobe three thousand dresses and costumes, of which several were for the character of Minerva and Amphitrite; esteemed the Irish for the width of their shoulders; covered her farthingale with braids and spangles; loved roses; cursed, swore, and stamped; struck her maids of honour with her clenched fists; used to send Dudley to the devil; beat Burleigh, the Chancellor, who would cry—poor old fool! spat on Matthew; collared Hatton; boxed the ears of Essex; showed her legs to Bassompierre; and was a virgin.

What she did for Bassompierre the Queen of Sheba had done for Solomon;[11] consequently she was right, Holy Writ having created the precedent. That which is biblical may well be Anglican. Biblical precedent goes so far as to speak of a child who was called Ebnehaquem or Melilechet—that is to say, the Wise Man's son.

Why object to such manners? Cynicism is at least as good as hypocrisy.

Nowadays England, whose Loyola is named Wesley, casts down her eyes a little at the remembrance of that past age. She is vexed at the memory, yet proud of it.

These fine ladies, moreover, knew Latin. From the 16th century this had been accounted a feminine accomplishment. Lady Jane Grey had carried fashion to the point of knowing Hebrew. The Duchess Josiana Latinized. Then (another fine thing) she was secretly a Catholic; after the manner of her uncle, Charles II., rather than her father, James II. James II. had lost his crown for his Catholicism, and Josiana did not care to risk her peerage. Thus it was that while a Catholic amongst her intimate friends and the refined of both sexes, she was outwardly a Protestant for the benefit of the riffraff.

This is the pleasant view to take of religion. You enjoy all the good things belonging to the official Episcopalian church, and later on you die, like Grotius, in the odour of Catholicity, having the glory of a mass being said for you by le Père Petau.

Although plump and healthy, Josiana was, we repeat, a perfect prude.

At times her sleepy and voluptuous way of dragging out the end of her phrases was like the creeping of a tiger's paws in the jungle.

The advantage of prudes is that they disorganize the human race. They deprive it of the honour of their adherence. Beyond all, keep the human species at a distance. This is a point of the greatest importance.

When one has not got Olympus, one must take the Hôtel de Rambouillet. Juno resolves herself into Araminta. A pretension to divinity not admitted creates affectation. In default of thunderclaps there is impertinence. The temple shrivels into the boudoir. Not having the power to be a goddess, she is an idol.

There is besides, in prudery, a certain pedantry which is pleasing to women. The coquette and the pedant are neighbours. Their kinship is visible in the fop. The subtile is derived from the sensual. Gluttony affects delicacy, a grimace of disgust conceals cupidity. And then woman feels her weak point guarded by all that casuistry of gallantry which takes the place of scruples in prudes. It is a line of circumvallation with a ditch. Every prude puts on an air of repugnance. It is a protection. She will consent, but she disdains—for the present.

Josiana had an uneasy conscience. She felt such a leaning towards immodesty that she was a prude. The recoils of pride in the direction opposed to our vices lead us to those of a contrary nature. It was the excessive effort to be chaste which made her a prude. To be too much on the defensive points to a secret desire for attack; the shy woman is not strait-laced. She shut herself up in the arrogance of the exceptional circumstances of her rank, meditating, perhaps, all the while, some sudden lapse from it.

It was the dawn of the eighteenth century. England was a sketch of what France was during the regency. Walpole and Dubois are not unlike. Marlborough was fighting against his former king, James II., to whom it was said he had sold his sister, Miss Churchill. Bolingbroke was in his meridian, and Richelieu in his dawn. Gallantry found its convenience in a certain medley of ranks. Men were equalized by the same vices as they were later on, perhaps, by the same ideas. Degradation of rank, an aristocratic prelude, began what the revolution was to complete. It was not very far off the time when Jelyotte was seen publicly sitting, in broad daylight, on the bed of the Marquise d'Epinay. It is true (for manners re-echo each other) that in the sixteenth century Smeton's nightcap had been found under Anne Boleyn's pillow.

If the word woman signifies fault, as I forget what Council decided, never was woman so womanlike as then. Never, covering her frailty by her charms, and her weakness by her omnipotence, has she claimed absolution more imperiously. In making the forbidden the permitted fruit, Eve fell; in making the permitted the forbidden fruit, she triumphs. That is the climax. In the eighteenth century the wife bolts out her husband. She shuts herself up in Eden with Satan. Adam is left outside.

III.

All Josiana's instincts impelled her to yield herself gallantly rather than to give herself legally. To surrender on the score of gallantry implies learning, recalls Menalcas and Amaryllis, and is almost a literary act. Mademoiselle de Scudéry, putting aside the attraction of ugliness for ugliness' sake, had no other motive for yielding to Pélisson.

The maiden a sovereign, the wife a subject, such was the old English notion. Josiana was deferring the hour of this subjection as long as she could. She must eventually marry Lord David, since such was the royal pleasure. It was a necessity, doubtless; but what a pity! Josiana appreciated Lord David, and showed him off. There was between them a tacit agreement neither to conclude nor to break off the engagement. They eluded each other. This method of making love, one step in advance and two back, is expressed in the dances of the period, the minuet and the gavotte.

It is unbecoming to be married—fades one's ribbons and makes one look old. An espousal is a dreary absorption of brilliancy. A woman handed over to you by a notary, how commonplace! The brutality of marriage creates definite situations; suppresses the will; kills choice; has a syntax, like grammar; replaces inspiration by orthography; makes a dictation of love; disperses all life's mysteries; diminishes the rights both of sovereign and subject; by a turn of the scale destroys the charming equilibrium of the sexes, the one robust in bodily strength, the other all-powerful in feminine weakness—strength on one side, beauty on the other; makes one a master and the other a servant, while without marriage one is a slave, the other a queen.

To make Love prosaically decent, how gross! to deprive it of all impropriety, how dull!

Lord David was ripening. Forty; 'tis a marked period. He did not perceive this, and in truth he looked no more than thirty. He considered it more amusing to desire Josiana than to possess her. He possessed others. He had mistresses. On the other hand, Josiana had dreams.

The Duchess Josiana had a peculiarity, less rare than it is supposed. One of her eyes was blue and the other black. Her pupils were made for love and hate, for happiness and misery. Night and day were mingled in her look.

Her ambition was this—to show herself capable of impossibilities. One day she said to Swift, "You people fancy that you know what scorn is." "You people" meant the human race.

She was a skin-deep Papist. Her Catholicism did not exceed the amount necessary for fashion. She would have been a Puseyite in the present day. She wore great dresses of velvet, satin, or moire, some composed of fifteen or sixteen yards of material, with embroideries of gold and silver; and round her waist many knots of pearls, alternating with other precious stones. She was extravagant in gold lace. Sometimes she wore an embroidered cloth jacket like a bachelor. She rode on a man's saddle, notwithstanding the invention of side-saddles, introduced into

England in the fourteenth century by Anne, wife of Richard II. She washed her face, arms, shoulders, and neck, in sugar-candy, diluted in white of egg, after the fashion of Castile. There came over her face, after any one had spoken wittily in her presence, a reflective smile of singular grace. She was free from malice, and rather good-natured than otherwise.

CHAPTER IV.

THE LEADER OF FASHION

Josiana was bored. The fact is so natural as to be scarcely worth mentioning.

Lord David held the position of judge in the gay life of London. He was looked up to by the nobility and gentry. Let us register a glory of Lord David's. He was daring enough to wear his own hair. The reaction against the wig was beginning. Just as in 1824 Eugene Deveria was the first to allow his beard to grow, so in 1702 Prince Devereux was the first to risk wearing his own hair in public disguised by artful curling. For to risk one's hair was almost to risk one's head. The indignation was universal. Nevertheless Prince Devereux was Viscount Hereford, and a peer of England. He was insulted, and the deed was well worth the insult. In the hottest part of the row Lord David suddenly appeared without his wig and in his own hair. Such conduct shakes the foundations of society. Lord David was insulted even more than Viscount Hereford. He held his ground. Prince Devereux was the first, Lord David Dirry-Moir the second. It is sometimes more difficult to be second than first. It requires less genius, but more courage. The first, intoxicated by the novelty, may ignore the danger; the second sees the abyss, and rushes into it. Lord David flung himself into the abyss of no longer wearing a wig. Later on these lords found imitators. Following these two revolutionists, men found sufficient audacity to wear their own hair, and powder was introduced as an extenuating circumstance.

In order to establish, before we pass on, an important period of history, we should remark that the first blow in the war of wigs was really struck by a Queen, Christina of Sweden, who wore man's clothes, and had appeared in 1680, in her hair of golden brown, powdered, and brushed up from her head. She had, besides, says Misson, a slight beard. The Pope, on his part, by a bull of March 1694, had somewhat let down the wig, by taking it from the heads of bishops and priests, and in ordering churchmen to let their hair grow.

Lord David, then, did not wear a wig, and did wear cowhide boots. Such great things made him a mark for public admiration. There was not a club of which he was not the leader, not a boxing match in which he was not desired as referee. The referee is the arbitrator.

He had drawn up the rules of several clubs in high life. He founded several resorts of fashionable society, of which one, the Lady Guinea, was still in existence in Pall Mall in 1772. The Lady Guinea was a club in which all the youth of the peerage congregated. They gamed there. The lowest stake allowed was a rouleau of fifty guineas, and there was never less than 20,000 guineas on the table. By the side of each player was a little stand on which to place his cup of tea, and a gilt bowl in which to put the rouleaux of guineas. The players, like servants when cleaning knives, wore leather sleeves to save their lace, breastplates of leather to protect their ruffles, shades on their brows to shelter their eyes from the great glare of the lamps, and, to keep their curls in order, broad-brimmed hats covered with flowers. They were masked to conceal their excitement, especially when playing the game of *quinze*. All, moreover, had their coats turned the wrong way, for luck. Lord David was a member of the Beefsteak Club, the Surly Club, and of the Splitfarthing Club, of the Cross Club, the Scratchpenny Club, of the Sealed Knot, a Royalist Club, and of the Martinus Scribblerus, founded by Swift, to take the place of the Rota, founded by Milton.

Though handsome, he belonged to the Ugly Club. This club was dedicated to deformity. The members agreed to fight, not about a beautiful woman, but about an ugly man. The hall of the club was adorned by hideous portraits—Thersites, Triboulet, Duns, Hudibras, Scarron; over the chimney was Æsop, between two men, each blind of an eye, Cocles and Camoëns (Cocles being blind of the left, Camoëns of the right eye), so arranged that the two profiles without eyes were turned to each other. The day that the beautiful Mrs. Visart caught the small pox the Ugly Club toasted her. This club was still in existence in the beginning of the nineteenth century, and Mirabeau was elected an honorary member.

Since the restoration of Charles II. revolutionary clubs had been abolished. The tavern in the little street by Moorfields, where the Calf's Head Club was held, had been pulled down; it was so called because on the 30th of January, the day on which the blood of Charles I. flowed on the scaffold, the members had drunk red wine out of the skull of a calf to the health of Cromwell. To the republican clubs had succeeded monarchical clubs. In them people amused themselves with decency.

* * * * * *

There was the Hell-fire Club, where they played at being impious. It was a joust of sacrilege. Hell was at auction there to the highest bidder in blasphemy.

There was the Butting Club, so called from its members butting folks with their heads. They found some street porter with a wide chest and a stupid countenance. They offered him, and compelled him, if necessary, to accept a pot of porter, in return for which he was to allow them to butt him with their heads four times in the chest, and on this they betted. One day a man, a great brute of a Welshman named Gogangerdd, expired at the third butt. This looked serious. An inquest was held, and the jury returned the following verdict: "Died of an inflation of the heart, caused by excessive drinking." Gogangerdd had certainly drunk the contents of the pot of porter.

There was the Fun Club. *Fun* is like *cant*, like *humour*, a word which is untranslatable. Fun is to farce what pepper is to salt. To get into a house and break a valuable mirror, slash the family portraits, poison the dog, put the cat in the aviary, is called "cutting a bit of fun." To give bad news which is untrue, whereby people put on mourning by mistake, is fun. It was fun to cut a square hole in the Holbein at Hampton Court. Fun would have been proud to have broken the arm of the Venus of Milo. Under James II. a young millionaire lord who had during the night set fire to a thatched cottage—a feat which made all London burst with laughter—was proclaimed the King of Fun. The poor devils in the cottage were saved in their night clothes. The members of the Fun Club, all of the highest aristocracy, used to run about London during the hours when the citizens were asleep, pulling the hinges from the shutters, cutting off the pipes of pumps, filling up cisterns, digging up cultivated plots of ground, putting out lamps, sawing through the beams which supported houses, breaking the window panes, especially in the poor quarters of the town. It was the rich who acted thus towards the poor. For this reason no complaint was possible. That was the best of the joke. Those manners have not altogether disappeared. In many places in England and in English possessions—at Guernsey, for instance—your house is now and then somewhat damaged during the night, or a fence is broken, or the knocker twisted off your door. If it were poor people who did these things, they would be sent to jail; but they are done by pleasant young gentlemen.

The most fashionable of the clubs was presided over by an emperor, who wore a crescent on his forehead, and was called the Grand Mohawk. The Mohawk surpassed the Fun. Do evil for evil's sake was the programme. The Mohawk Club had one great object—to injure. To fulfil this duty all means were held good. In becoming a Mohawk the members took an oath to be hurtful. To injure at any price, no matter when, no matter whom, no matter where, was a matter of duty. Every member of the Mohawk Club was bound to possess an accomplishment. One was "a dancing master;" that is to say he made the rustics frisk about by pricking the calves of their legs with the point of his sword. Others knew how to make a man sweat; that is to say, a circle of gentlemen with drawn rapiers would surround a poor wretch, so that it was impossible for him not to turn his back upon some one. The gentleman behind him chastised him for this by a prick of his sword, which made him spring round; another prick in the back warned the fellow that one of noble blood was behind him, and so on, each one wounding him in his turn. When the man, closed round by the circle of swords and covered with blood, had turned and danced about enough, they ordered their servants to beat him with sticks, to change the course of his ideas. Others "hit the lion"—that is, they gaily stopped a passenger, broke his nose with a blow of the fist, and then shoved both thumbs into his eyes. If his eyes were gouged out, he was paid for them.

Such were, towards the beginning of the eighteenth century, the pastimes of the rich idlers of London. The idlers of Paris had theirs. M. de Charolais was firing his gun at a citizen standing on his own threshold. In all times youth has had its amusements.

Lord David Dirry-Moir brought into all these institutions his magnificent and liberal spirit. Just like any one else, he would gaily set fire to a cot of woodwork and thatch, and just scorch those within; but he would rebuild their houses in stone. He insulted two ladies. One was unmarried—he gave her a portion; the other was married—he had her husband appointed chaplain.

Cockfighting owed him some praiseworthy improvements. It was marvellous to see Lord David dress a cock for the pit. Cocks lay hold of each other by the feathers, as men by the hair. Lord David, therefore, made his cock as bald as possible. With a pair of scissors he cut off all the feathers from the tail and from the head to the shoulders, and all those on the neck. So much less for the enemy's beak, he used to say. Then he extended the cock's wings, and cut each feather, one after another, to a point, and thus the wings were furnished with darts. So much for the enemy's eyes, he would say. Then he scraped its claws with a penknife, sharpened its nails, fitted it with spurs of sharp steel, spat on its head, spat on its neck, anointed it with spittle, as they used to rub oil over athletes; then set it down in the pit, a redoubtable champion, exclaiming, "That's how to make a cock an eagle, and a bird of the poultry yard a bird of the mountain."

Lord David attended prize-fights, and was their living law. On occasions of great performances it was he who had the stakes driven in and ropes stretched, and who fixed the number of feet for the ring. When he was a second, he followed his man step by step, a bottle in one hand, a sponge in the other, crying out to him to *hit hard*, suggesting stratagems, advising him as he fought, wiping away the blood, raising him when overthrown, placing him on his knee, putting the mouth of the bottle between his teeth, and from his own mouth, filled with water, blowing a fine rain into his eyes and ears—a thing which reanimates even a dying man. If he was referee, he saw that there was no foul play, prevented any one, whosoever he might be, from assisting the combatants, excepting the seconds, declare the man beaten who did not fairly face his opponent, watched that the time between the rounds did not exceed half a minute, prevented butting, and declared whoever resorted to it beaten, and forbade a man's being hit when down. All this science, however, did not render him a pedant, nor destroy his ease of manner in society.

When he was referee, rough, pimple-faced, unshorn friends of either combatant never dared to come to the aid of their failing man, nor, in order to upset the chances of the betting, jumped over the barrier, entered the ring, broke the ropes, pulled down the stakes, and violently interposed in the battle. Lord David was one of the few referees whom they dared not thrash.

No one could train like him. The pugilist whose trainer he consented to become was sure to win. Lord David would choose a Hercules—massive as a rock, tall as a tower—and make him his child. The problem was to turn that human rock from a defensive to an offensive state. In this he excelled. Having once adopted the Cyclops, he never left him. He became his nurse; he measured out his wine, weighed his meat, and counted his hours of sleep. It was he who invented the athlete's admirable rules, afterwards reproduced by Morley. In the mornings, a raw egg and a glass of sherry; at twelve, some slices of a leg of mutton, almost raw, with tea; at four, toast and tea; in the evening, pale ale and toast; after which he undressed his man, rubbed him, and put him to bed. In the street he never allowed him to leave his sight, keeping him out of every danger—runaway horses, the wheels of carriages, drunken soldiers, pretty girls. He watched over his virtue. This maternal solicitude continually brought some new perfection into the pupil's education. He taught him the blow with the fist which breaks the teeth, and the twist of the thumb which gouges out the eye. What could be more touching?

Thus he was preparing himself for public life to which he was to be called later on. It is no easy matter to become an accomplished gentleman.

Lord David Dirry-Moir was passionately fond of open-air exhibitions, of shows, of circuses with wild beasts, of the caravans of mountebanks, of clowns, tumblers, merrymen, open-air farces, and the wonders of a fair. The true noble is he who smacks of the people. Therefore it was that Lord David frequented the taverns and low haunts of London and the Cinque Ports. In order to be able at need, and without compromising his rank in the white squadron, to be cheek-by-jowl with a topman or a calker, he used to wear a sailor's jacket when he went into the slums. For such disguise his not wearing a wig was convenient; for even under Louis XIV. the people kept to their hair like the lion to his mane. This gave him great freedom of action. The low people whom Lord David used to meet in the stews, and with whom he mixed, held him in high esteem, without ever dreaming that he was a lord. They called him Tom-Jim-Jack. Under this name he was famous and very popular amongst the dregs of the people. He played the blackguard in a masterly style: when necessary, he used his fists. This phase of his fashionable life was highly appreciated by Lady Josiana.

CHAPTER V.

QUEEN ANNE

I.

Above this couple there was Anne, Queen of England. An ordinary woman was Queen Anne. She was gay, kindly, august—to a certain extent. No quality of hers attained to virtue, none to vice. Her stoutness was bloated, her fun heavy, her good-nature stupid. She was stubborn and weak. As a wife she was faithless and faithful, having favourites to whom she gave up her heart, and a husband for whom she kept her bed. As a Christian she was a heretic and a bigot. She had one beauty—the well-developed neck of a Niobe. The rest of her person was indifferently formed. She was a clumsy coquette and a chaste one. Her skin was white and fine; she displayed a great deal of it. It was she who introduced the fashion of necklaces of large pearls clasped round the throat. She had a narrow forehead, sensual lips, fleshy cheeks, large eyes, short sight. Her short sight extended to her mind. Beyond a burst of merriment now and then, almost as ponderous as her anger, she lived in a sort of taciturn grumble and a grumbling silence. Words escaped from her which had to be guessed at. She was a mixture of a good woman and a mischievous devil. She liked surprises, which is extremely woman-like. Anne was a pattern—just sketched roughly—of the universal Eve. To that sketch had fallen that chance, the throne. She drank. Her husband was a Dane, thoroughbred. A Tory, she governed by the Whigs—like a woman, like a mad woman. She had fits of rage. She was violent, a brawler. Nobody more awkward than Anne in directing affairs of state. She allowed events to fall about as they might chance. Her whole policy was cracked. She excelled in bringing about great catastrophes from little causes. When a whim of authority took hold of her, she called it giving a stir with the poker. She would say with an air of profound thought, "No peer may keep his hat on before the king except De Courcy, Baron Kingsale, an Irish peer;" or, "It would be an injustice were my husband not to be Lord High Admiral, since my father was." And she made George of Denmark High Admiral of England and of all her Majesty's plantations. She was perpetually perspiring bad humour; she did not explain her thought, she exuded it. There was something of the Sphinx in this goose.

She rather liked fun, teasing, and practical jokes. Could she have made Apollo a hunchback, it would have delighted her. But she would have left him a god. Good-natured, her ideal was to allow none to despair, and to worry all. She had often a rough word in her mouth; a little more, and she would have sworn like Elizabeth. From time to time she would take from a man's pocket, which she wore in her skirt, a little round box, of chased silver, on which was her portrait, in profile, between the two letters Q.A.; she would open this box, and take from it, on her finger, a little pomade, with which she reddened her lips, and, having coloured her mouth, would laugh. She was greedily fond of the flat Zealand gingerbread cakes. She was proud of being fat.

More of a Puritan than anything else, she would, nevertheless, have liked to devote herself to stage plays. She had an absurd academy of music, copied after that of France. In 1700 a Frenchman, named Foretroche, wanted to build a royal circus at Paris, at a cost of 400,000 francs, which scheme was opposed by D'Argenson. This Forteroche passed into England, and proposed to Queen Anne, who was immediately charmed by the idea, to build in London a theatre with machinery, with a fourth under-stage finer than that of the King of France. Like Louis XIV., she liked to be driven at a gallop. Her teams and relays would sometimes do the distance between London and Windsor in less than an hour and a quarter.

II.

In Anne's time no meeting was allowed without the permission of two justices of the peace. The assembly of twelve persons, were it only to eat oysters and drink porter, was a felony. Under her reign, otherwise relatively mild, pressing for the fleet was carried on with extreme violence—a gloomy evidence that the Englishman is a subject rather than a citizen. For centuries England suffered under that process of tyranny which gave the lie to all the old charters of freedom, and out of which France especially gathered a cause of triumph and indignation. What in some degree diminishes the triumph is, that while sailors were pressed in England, soldiers were pressed in France. In every great town of France, any able-bodied man, going through the streets on his business, was liable to be shoved by the crimps into a house called the oven. There he was shut up with others in the same plight; those fit for service were picked out, and the recruiters sold them to the officers. In 1695 there were thirty of these ovens in Paris.

The laws against Ireland, emanating from Queen Anne, were atrocious. Anne was born in 1664, two years before the great fire of London, on which the astrologers (there were some left, and Louis XIV. was born with the assistance of an astrologer, and swaddled in a horoscope) predicted that, being the elder sister of fire, she would be queen. And so she was, thanks to astrology and the revolution of 1688. She had the humiliation of having only Gilbert, Archbishop of Canterbury, for godfather. To be godchild of the Pope was no longer possible in England. A mere primate is but a poor sort of godfather. Anne had to put up with one, however. It was her own fault. Why was she a Protestant?

Denmark had paid for her virginity (*virginitas empta*, as the old charters expressed it) by a dowry of £6,250 a year, secured on the bailiwick of Wardinburg and the island of Fehmarn. Anne followed, without conviction, and by routine, the traditions of William. The English under that royalty born of a revolution possessed as much liberty as they could lay hands on between the Tower of London, into which they put orators, and the pillory, into which they put writers. Anne spoke a little Danish in her private chats with her husband, and a little French in her private chats with Bolingbroke. Wretched gibberish; but the height of English fashion, especially at court, was to talk French. There was never a *bon mot* but in French. Anne paid a deal of attention to her coins, especially to copper coins, which are the low and popular ones; she wanted to cut a great figure on them. Six farthings were struck during her reign. On the back of the first three she had merely a throne struck, on the back of the fourth she ordered a triumphal chariot, and on the back of the sixth a goddess holding a sword in one hand and an olive branch in the other, with the scroll, *Bello et pace*. Her father, James II., was candid and cruel; she was brutal.

At the same time she was mild at bottom. A contradiction which only appears such. A fit of anger metamorphosed her. Heat sugar and it will boil.

Anne was popular. England liked feminine rulers. Why? France excludes them. There is a reason at once. Perhaps there is no other. With English historians Elizabeth embodies grandeur, Anne good-nature. As they will. Be it so. But there is nothing delicate in the reigns of these women. The lines are heavy. It is gross grandeur and gross good-nature. As to their immaculate virtue, England is tenacious of it, and we are not going to oppose the idea. Elizabeth was a virgin tempered by Essex; Anne, a wife complicated by Bolingbroke.

III.

One idiotic habit of the people is to attribute to the king what they do themselves. They fight. Whose the glory? The king's. They pay. Whose the generosity? The king's. Then the people love him for being so rich. The king receives a crown from the poor, and returns them a farthing. How generous he is! The colossus which is the pedestal contemplates the pigmy which is the statue. How great is this myrmidon! he is on my back. A dwarf has an excellent way of being taller than a giant: it is to perch himself on his shoulders. But that the giant should allow it, there is the wonder; and that he should admire the height of the dwarf, there is the folly. Simplicity of mankind! The equestrian statue, reserved for kings alone, is an excellent figure of royalty: the horse is the people. Only that the horse becomes transfigured by degrees. It begins in an ass; it ends in a lion. Then it throws its rider, and you have 1642 in England and 1789 in France; and sometimes it devours him, and you have in England 1649, and in France 1793. That the lion should relapse into the donkey is astonishing; but it is so. This was occurring in England. It had resumed the pack-saddle, idolatry of the crown. Queen Anne, as we have just observed, was popular. What was she doing to be so? Nothing. Nothing!—that is all that is asked of the sovereign of England. He receives for that nothing £1,250,000 a year. In 1705, England which had had but thirteen men of war under Elizabeth, and thirty-six under James I., counted a hundred and fifty in her fleet. The English had three armies, 5,000 men in Catalonia; 10,000 in Portugal; 50,000 in Flanders; and besides, was paying £1,666,666 a year to monarchical and diplomatic Europe, a sort of prostitute the English people has always had in keeping. Parliament having voted a patriotic loan of thirty-four million francs of annuities, there had been a crush at the Exchequer to subscribe it. England was sending a squadron to the East Indies, and a squadron to the West of Spain under Admiral Leake, without mentioning the reserve of four hundred sail, under Admiral Sir Cloudesley Shovel. England had lately annexed Scotland. It was the interval between Hochstadt and Ramillies, and the first of these victories was foretelling the second. England, in its cast of the net at Hochstadt, had made prisoners of twenty-seven battalions and four regiments of dragoons, and deprived France of one hundred leagues of country—France drawing back dismayed from the Danube to the Rhine. England was stretching her hand out towards Sardinia and the Balearic Islands. She was bringing into her ports in triumph ten Spanish line-of-battle ships, and many a galleon laden with gold. Hudson Bay and Straits were already half given over by Louis XIV. It was felt that he was about to give up his hold over Acadia, St. Christopher, and Newfoundland, and that he would be but too happy if England would only tolerate the King of France fishing for cod at Cape Breton. England was about to impose upon him the shame of demolishing himself the fortifications of Dunkirk. Meanwhile, she had taken Gibraltar, and was taking Barcelona. What great things accomplished! How was it possible to refuse Anne admiration for taking the trouble of living at the period?

From a certain point of view, the reign of Anne appears a reflection of the reign of Louis XIV. Anne, for a moment even with that king in the race which is called history, bears to him the vague resemblance of a reflection. Like him, she plays at a great reign; she has her monuments, her arts, her victories, her captains, her men of letters, her privy purse to pension celebrities, her gallery of chefs-d'oeuvre, side by side with those of his Majesty. Her court, too, was a cortège, with the features of a triumph, an order and a march. It was a miniature copy of all the great men of Versailles, not giants themselves. In it there is enough to deceive the eye; add God save the Queen, which might have been taken from Lulli, and the ensemble becomes an illusion. Not a personage is missing. Christopher Wren is a very passable Mansard; Somers is as good as Lamoignon; Anne has a Racine in Dryden, a Boileau in Pope, a Colbert in Godolphin, a Louvois in Pembroke, and a Turenne in Marlborough. Heighten the wigs and lower the foreheads. The whole is solemn and pompous, and the Windsor of the time has a faded resemblance to Marly. Still the whole was effeminate, and Anne's Père Tellier was called Sarah Jennings. However, there is an outline of incipient irony, which fifty years later was to turn to philosophy, in the literature of the age, and the Protestant Tartuffe is unmasked by Swift just in the same way as the Catholic Tartuffe is denounced by Molière. Although the England of the period quarrels and fights France, she imitates her and draws enlightenment from her; and the light on the façade of England is French light. It is a pity that Anne's reign lasted but twelve years, or the English would not hesitate to call it the century of Anne, as we say the century of Louis XIV. Anne appeared in 1702, as Louis XIV. declined. It is one of the curiosities of history, that the rise of that pale planet coincides with the setting of the planet of purple, and that at the moment in which France had the king Sun, England should have had the queen Moon.

A detail to be noted. Louis XIV., although they made war with him, was greatly admired in England. "He is the kind of king they want in France," said the English. The love of the English for their own liberty is mingled with a certain acceptance of servitude for others. That favourable regard of the chains which bind their neighbours sometimes attains to enthusiasm for the despot next door.

To sum up, Anne rendered her people *hureux*, as the French translator of Beeverell's book repeats three times, with graceful reiteration at the sixth and ninth page of his dedication and the third of his preface.

IV.

Queen Anne bore a little grudge to the Duchess Josiana, for two reasons. Firstly, because she thought the Duchess Josiana handsome. Secondly, because she thought the Duchess Josiana's betrothed handsome. Two reasons for jealousy are sufficient for a woman. One is sufficient for a queen. Let us add that she bore her a grudge for being her sister. Anne did not like women to be pretty. She considered it against good morals. As for herself, she was ugly. Not from choice, however. A part of her religion she derived from that ugliness. Josiana, beautiful and philosophical, was a cause of vexation to the queen. To an ugly queen, a pretty duchess is not an agreeable sister.

There was another grievance, Josiana's "improper" birth. Anne was the daughter of Anne Hyde, a simple gentlewoman, legitimately, but vexatiously, married by James II. when Duke of York. Anne, having this inferior blood in her veins, felt herself but half royal, and Josiana, having come into the world quite irregularly, drew closer attention to the incorrectness, less great, but really existing, in the birth of the queen. The daughter of *mésalliance* looked without love upon the daughter of bastardy, so near her. It was an unpleasant resemblance. Josiana had a right to say to Anne, "My mother was at least as good as yours." At court no one said so, but they evidently thought it. This was a bore for her royal Majesty. Why this Josiana? What had put it into her head to be born? What good was a Josiana? Certain relationships are detrimental. Nevertheless, Anne smiled on Josiana. Perhaps she might even have liked her, had she not been her sister.

CHAPTER VI.

BARKILPHEDRO.

It is useful to know what people do, and a certain surveillance is wise. Josiana had Lord David watched by a little creature of hers, in whom she reposed confidence, and whose name was Barkilphedro.

Lord David had Josiana discreetly observed by a creature of his, of whom he was sure, and whose name was Barkilphedro.

Queen Anne, on her part, kept herself secretly informed of the actions and conduct of the Duchess Josiana, her bastard sister, and of Lord David, her future brother-in-law by the left hand, by a creature of hers, on whom she counted fully, and whose name was Barkilphedro.

This Barkilphedro had his fingers on that keyboard—Josiana, Lord David, a queen. A man between two women. What modulations possible! What amalgamation of souls!

Barkilphedro had not always held the magnificent position of whispering into three ears.

He was an old servant of the Duke of York. He had tried to be a churchman but had failed. The Duke of York, an English and a Roman prince, compounded of royal Popery and legal Anglicanism, had his Catholic house and his Protestant house, and might have pushed Barkilphedro in one or the other hierarchy; but he did not judge him to be Catholic enough to make him almoner, or Protestant enough to make him chaplain. So that between two religions, Barkilphedro found himself with his soul on the ground.

Not a bad posture, either, for certain reptile souls.

Certain ways are impracticable, except by crawling flat on the belly.

An obscure but fattening servitude had long made up Barkilphedro's whole existence. Service is something; but he wanted power besides. He was, perhaps, about to reach it when James II. fell. He had to begin all over again. Nothing to do under William III., a sullen prince, and exercising in his mode of reigning a prudery which he believed to be probity. Barkilphedro, when his protector, James II., was dethroned, did not lapse all at once into rags. There is a something which survives deposed princes, and which feeds and sustains their parasites. The remains of the exhaustible sap causes leaves to live on for two or three days on the branches of the uprooted tree; then, all at once, the leaf yellows and dries up: and thus it is with the courtier.

Thanks to that embalming which is called legitimacy, the prince himself, although fallen and cast away, lasts and keeps preserved; it is not so with the courtier, much more dead than the king. The king, beyond there, is a mummy; the courtier, here, is a phantom. To be the shadow of a shadow is leanness indeed. Hence Barkilphedro became famished. Then he took up the character of a man of letters.

But he was thrust back even from the kitchens. Sometimes he knew not where to sleep. "Who will give me shelter?" he would ask. He struggled on. All that is interesting in patience in distress he possessed. He had, besides, the talent of the termite—knowing how to bore a hole from the bottom to the top. By dint of making use of the name of James II., of old memories, of fables of fidelity, of touching stories, he pierced as far as the Duchess Josiana's heart.

Josiana took a liking to this man of poverty and wit, an interesting combination. She presented him to Lord Dirry-Moir, gave him a shelter in the servants' hall among her domestics, retained him in her household, was kind to him, and sometimes even spoke to him. Barkilphedro felt neither hunger nor cold again. Josiana addressed him in the second person; it was the fashion for great ladies to do so to men of letters, who allowed it. The Marquise de Mailly received Roy, whom she had never seen before, in bed, and said to him, "C'est toi qui as fait l'Année galante! Bonjour." Later on, the men of letters returned the custom. The day came when Fabre d'Eglantine said to the Duchesse de Rohan, "N'est-tu pas la Chabot?"

For Barkilphedro to be "thee'd" and "thou'd" was a success; he was overjoyed by it. He had aspired to this contemptuous familiarity. "Lady Josiana thees-and-thous me," he would say to himself. And he would rub his hands. He profited by this theeing-and-thouing to make further way. He became a sort of constant attendant in Josiana's private rooms; in no way troublesome; unperceived; the duchess would almost have changed her shift before him. All this, however, was precarious. Barkilphedro was aiming at a position. A duchess was half-way; an underground passage which did not lead to the queen was having bored for nothing.

One day Barkilphedro said to Josiana,—

"Would your Grace like to make my fortune?".

"What dost thou want?"

"An appointment."

"An appointment? for thee!"

"Yes, madam."

"What an idea! *thou* to ask for an appointment! thou, who art good for nothing."

"That's just the reason."

Josiana burst out laughing.

"Among the offices to which thou art unsuited, which dost thou desire?"

"That of cork drawer of the bottles of the ocean."

Josiana's laugh redoubled.

"What meanest thou? Thou art fooling."

"No, madam."

"To amuse myself, I shall answer you seriously," said the duchess. "What dost thou wish to be? Repeat it."

"Uncorker of the bottles of the ocean."

"Everything is possible at court. Is there an appointment of that kind?"

"Yes, madam."

"This is news to me. Go on."

"There is such an appointment."

"Swear it on the soul which thou dost not possess."

"I swear it."

"I do not believe thee."

"Thank you, madam."

"Then thou wishest? Begin again."

"To uncork the bottles of the ocean."

"That is a situation which can give little trouble. It is like grooming a bronze horse."

"Very nearly."

"Nothing to do. Well 'tis a situation to suit thee. Thou art good for that much."

"You see I am good for something."

"Come! thou art talking nonsense. Is there such an appointment?"

Barkilphedro assumed an attitude of deferential gravity. "Madam, you had an august father, James II., the king, and you have an illustrious brother-in-law, George of Denmark, Duke of Cumberland; your father was, and your brother is, Lord High Admiral of England—"

"Is what thou tellest me fresh news? I know all that as well as thou."

"But here is what your Grace does not know. In the sea there are three kinds of things: those at the bottom, *lagan;* those which float, *flotsam;* those which the sea throws up on the shore, *jetsam.*"

"And then?"

"These three things—*lagan*, *flotsam*, and *jetsam*—belong to the Lord High Admiral."

"And then?"

"Your Grace understands."

"No."

"All that is in the sea, all that sinks, all that floats, all that is cast ashore—all belongs to the Admiral of England."

"Everything! Really? And then?"

"Except the sturgeon, which belongs to the king."

"I should have thought," said Josiana, "all that would have belonged to Neptune."

"Neptune is a fool. He has given up everything. He has allowed the English to take everything."

"Finish what thou wert saying."

"'Prizes of the sea' is the name given to such *treasure trove.*"

"Be it so."

"It is boundless: there is always something floating, something being cast up. It is the contribution of the sea—the tax which the ocean pays to England."

"With all my heart. But pray conclude."

"Your Grace understands that in this way the ocean creates a department."

"Where?"

"At the Admiralty."

"What department?"

"The Sea Prize Department."

"Well?"

"The department is subdivided into three offices—Lagan, Flotsam, and Jetsam—and in each there is an officer."

"And then?"

"A ship at sea writes to give notice on any subject to those on land—that it is sailing in such a latitude; that it has met a sea monster; that it is in sight of shore; that it is in distress; that it is about to founder; that it is lost, etc. The captain takes a bottle, puts into it a bit of paper on which he has written the information, corks up the flask, and casts it into the sea. If the bottle goes to the bottom, it is in the department of the lagan officer; if it floats, it is in the department of the flotsam officer; if it be thrown upon shore, it concerns the jetsam officer."

"And wouldst thou like to be the jetsam officer?"

"Precisely so."

"And that is what thou callest uncorking the bottles of the ocean?"

"Since there is such an appointment."

"Why dost thou wish for the last-named place in preference to both the others?"

"Because it is vacant just now."

"In what does the appointment consist?"

"Madam, in 1598 a tarred bottle, picked up by a man, conger-fishing on the strand of Epidium Promontorium, was brought to Queen Elizabeth; and a parchment drawn out of it gave information to England that Holland had taken, without saying anything about it, an unknown country, Nova Zembla; that the capture had taken place in June, 1596; that in that country people were eaten by bears; and that the manner of passing the winter was described on a paper enclosed in a musket-case hanging in the chimney of the wooden house built in the island, and left by the Dutchmen, who were all dead: and that the chimney was built of a barrel with the end knocked out, sunk into the roof."

"I don't understand much of thy rigmarole."

"Be it so. Elizabeth understood. A country the more for Holland was a country the less for England. The bottle which had given the information was held to be of importance; and thenceforward an order was issued that anybody who should find a sealed bottle on the sea-shore should take it to the Lord High Admiral of England, under pain of the gallows. The admiral entrusts the opening of such bottles to an officer, who presents the contents to the queen, if there be reason for so doing."

"Are many such bottles brought to the Admiralty?"

"But few. But it's all the same. The appointment exists. There is for the office a room and lodgings at the Admiralty."

"And for that way of doing nothing, how is one paid?"

"One hundred guineas a year."

"And thou wouldst trouble me for that much?"

"It is enough to live upon."

"Like a beggar."

"As it becomes one of my sort."

"One hundred guineas! It's a bagatelle."

"What keeps you for a minute, keeps us for a year. That's the advantage of the poor."

"Thou shalt have the place."

A week afterwards, thanks to Josiana's exertions, thanks to the influence of Lord David Dirry-Moir, Barkilphedro—safe thenceforward, drawn out of his precarious existence, lodged, and boarded, with a salary of a hundred guineas—was installed at the Admiralty.

CHAPTER VII.

BARKILPHEDRO GNAWS HIS WAY.

There is one thing the most pressing of all: to be ungrateful.

Barkilphedro was not wanting therein.

Having received so many benefits from Josiana, he had naturally but one thought—to revenge himself on her. When we add that Josiana was beautiful, great, young, rich, powerful, illustrious, while Barkilphedro was ugly, little, old, poor, dependent, obscure, he must necessarily revenge himself for all this as well.

When a man is made out of night, how is he to forgive so many beams of light?

Barkilphedro was an Irishman who had denied Ireland—a bad species.

Barkilphedro had but one thing in his favour—that he had a very big belly. A big belly passes for a sign of kind-heartedness. But his belly was but an addition to Barkilphedro's hypocrisy; for the man was full of malice.

What was Barkilphedro's age? None. The age necessary for his project of the moment. He was old in his wrinkles and gray hairs, young in the activity of his mind. He was active and ponderous; a sort of hippopotamus-monkey. A royalist, certainly; a republican—who knows? a Catholic, perhaps; a Protestant, without doubt. For Stuart, probably; for Brunswick, evidently. To be For is a power only on the condition of being at the same time Against. Barkilphedro practised this wisdom.

The appointment of drawer of the bottles of the ocean was not as absurd as Barkilphedro had appeared to make out. The complaints, which would in these times be termed declamations, of Garcia Fernandez in his "Chart-Book of the Sea," against the robbery of jetsam, called right of wreck, and against the pillage of wreck by the inhabitants of the coast, had created a sensation in England, and had obtained for the shipwrecked this reform—that their goods, chattels, and property, instead of being stolen by the country-people, were confiscated by the Lord High Admiral. All the *débris* of the sea cast upon the English shore—merchandise, broken hulls of ships, bales, chests, etc.—belonged to the Lord High Admiral; but—and here was revealed the importance of the place asked for by Barkilphedro—the floating receptacles containing messages and declarations awakened particularly the attention of the Admiralty. Shipwrecks are one of England's gravest cares. Navigation being her life, shipwreck is her anxiety. England is kept in perpetual care by the sea. The little glass bottle thrown to the waves by the doomed ship, contains final intelligence, precious from every point of view. Intelligence concerning the ship, intelligence concerning the crew, intelligence concerning the place, the time, the manner of loss, intelligence concerning the winds which have broken up the vessel, intelligence concerning the currents which bore the floating flask ashore. The situation filled by Barkilphedro has been abolished more than a century, but it had its real utility. The last holder was William Hussey, of Doddington, in Lincolnshire. The man who held it was a sort of guardian of the things of the sea. All the closed and sealed-up vessels, bottles, flasks, jars, thrown upon the English coast by the tide were brought to him. He alone had the right to open them; he was first in the secrets of their contents; he put them in order, and ticketed them with his signature. The expression "*loger un papier au greffe*," still used in the Channel Islands, is thence derived. However, one precaution was certainly taken. Not one of these bottles could be unsealed except in the presence of two jurors of the Admiralty sworn to secrecy, who signed, conjointly with the holder of the jetsam office, the official report of the opening. But these jurors being held to secrecy, there resulted for Barkilphedro a certain discretionary latitude; it depended upon him, to a certain extent, to suppress a fact or bring it to light.

These fragile floating messages were far from being what Barkilphedro had told Josiana, rare and insignificant. Some times they reached land with little delay; at others, after many years. That depended on the winds and the currents. The fashion of casting bottles on the surface of the sea has somewhat passed away, like that of vowing offerings, but in those religious times, those who were about to die were glad thus to send their last thought to God and to men, and at times these messages from the sea were plentiful at the Admiralty. A parchment preserved in the hall at Audlyene (ancient spelling), with notes by the Earl of Suffolk, Grand Treasurer of England under James I., bears witness that in the one year, 1615, fifty-two flasks, bladders, and tarred vessels, containing mention of sinking ships, were brought and registered in the records of the Lord High Admiral.

Court appointments are the drop of oil in the widow's cruse, they ever increase. Thus it is that the porter has become chancellor, and the groom, constable. The special officer charged with the appointment desired and obtained by Barkilphedro was invariably a confidential man. Elizabeth had wished that it should be so. At court, to speak of confidence is to speak of intrigue, and to speak of intrigue is to speak of advancement. This functionary had come to be a personage of some consideration. He was a clerk, and ranked directly after the two grooms of the almonry. He had the right of entrance into the palace, but we must add, what was called the humble entrance—*humilis introïtus*—and even into the bed-chamber. For it was the custom that he should inform the monarch, on occasions of sufficient importance, of the objects found, which were often very curious: the wills of men in despair, farewells cast to fatherland, revelations of falsified logs, bills of lading, and crimes committed at sea, legacies to the crown, etc., that he should maintain his records in communication with the court, and should account, from time to time, to the king or queen, concerning the opening of these ill-omened bottles. It was the black cabinet of the ocean.

Elizabeth, who was always glad of an opportunity of speaking Latin, used to ask Tonfield, of Coley in Berkshire, jetsam officer of her day, when he brought her one of these papers cast up by the sea, "Quid mihi scribit Neptunus?" (What does Neptune write me?)

The way had been eaten, the insect had succeeded. Barkilphedro approached the queen.

This was all he wanted.

To make his fortune?

No.

To unmake that of others?

A greater happiness.

To hurt is to enjoy.

To have within one the desire of injuring, vague but implacable, and never to lose sight of it, is not given to all.

Barkilphedro possessed that fixity of intention.

As the bulldog holds on with his jaws, so did his thought.

To feel himself inexorable gave him a depth of gloomy satisfaction. As long as he had a prey under his teeth, or in his soul, a certainty of evil-doing, he wanted nothing.

He was happy, shivering in the cold which his neighbour was suffering. To be malignant is an opulence. Such a man is believed to be poor, and, in truth, is so; but he has all his riches in malice, and prefers having them so. Everything is in what contents one. To do a bad turn, which is the same as a good turn, is better than money. Bad for him who endures, good for him who does it. Catesby, the colleague of Guy Fawkes, in the Popish powder plot, said: "To see Parliament blown upside down, I wouldn't miss it for a million sterling."

What was Barkilphedro? That meanest and most terrible of things—an envious man.

Envy is a thing ever easily placed at court.

Courts abound in impertinent people, in idlers, in rich loungers hungering for gossip, in those who seek for needles in trusses of hay, in triflers, in banterers bantered, in witty ninnies, who cannot do without converse with an envious man.

What a refreshing thing is the evil spoken to you of others.

Envy is good stuff to make a spy. There is a profound analogy between that natural passion, envy, and that social function, espionage. The spy hunts on others' account, like the dog. The envious man hunts on his own, like the cat.

A fierce Myself, such is the envious man.

He had other qualities. Barkilphedro was discreet, secret, concrete. He kept in everything and racked himself with his hate. Enormous baseness implies enormous vanity. He was liked by those whom he amused, and hated by all others; but he felt that he was disdained by those who hated him, and despised by those who liked him. He restrained himself. All his gall simmered noiselessly in his hostile resignation. He was indignant, as if rogues had the right to be so. He was the furies' silent prey. To swallow everything was his talent. There were deaf wraths within him, frenzies of interior rage, black and brooding flames unseen; he was a *smoke-consuming* man of passion. The surface was smiling. He was kind, prompt, easy, amiable, obliging. Never mind to whom, never mind where, he bowed. For a breath of wind he inclined to the earth. What a source of fortune to have a reed for a spine! Such concealed and venomous beings are not so rare as is believed. We live surrounded by ill-omened crawling things. Wherefore the malevolent? A keen question! The dreamer constantly proposes it to himself, and the thinker never resolves it. Hence the sad eye of the philosophers ever fixed upon that mountain of darkness which is destiny, and from the top of which the colossal spectre of evil casts handfuls of serpents over the earth.

Barkilphedro's body was obese and his face lean. A fat bust and a bony countenance. His nails were channelled and short, his fingers knotted, his thumbs flat, his hair coarse, his temples wide apart, and his forehead a murderer's, broad and low. The littleness of his eye was hidden under his bushy eyebrows. His nose, long, sharp, and flabby, nearly met his mouth. Barkilphedro, properly attired, as an emperor, would have somewhat resembled Domitian. His face of muddy yellow might have been modelled in slimy paste—his immovable cheeks were like putty; he had all kinds of ugly refractory wrinkles; the angle of his jaw was massive, his chin heavy, his ear underbred. In repose, and seen in profile, his upper lip was raised at an acute angle, showing two teeth. Those teeth seemed to look at you. The teeth can look, just as the eye can bite.

Patience, temperance, continence, reserve, self-control, amenity, deference, gentleness, politeness, sobriety, chastity, completed and finished Barkilphedro. He culumniated those virtues by their possession.

In a short time Barkilphedro took a foothold at court.

CHAPTER VIII.

INFERI

There are two ways of making a footing at court. In the clouds, and you are august; in the mud, and you are powerful.

In the first case, you belong to Olympus.

In the second case, you belong to the private closet.

He who belongs to Olympus has but the thunderbolt, he who is of the private closet has the police.

The private closet contains all the instruments of government, and sometimes, for it is a traitor, its chastisement. Heliogabalus goes there to die. Then it is called the latrines.

Generally it is less tragic. It is there that Alberoni admires Vendôme. Royal personages willingly make it their place of audience. It takes the place of the throne. Louis XIV. receives the Duchess of Burgundy there. Philip V. is shoulder to shoulder there with the queen. The priest penetrates into it. The private closet is sometimes a branch of the confessional. Therefore it is that at court there are underground fortunes—not always the least. If, under Louis XI., you would be great, be Pierre de Rohan, Marshal of France; if you would be influential, be Olivier le Daim, the barber; if you would, under Mary de Medicis, be glorious, be Sillery, the Chancellor; if you would be a person of consideration, be La Hannon, the maid; if you would, under Louis XV., be illustrious, be Choiseul, the minister; if you would be formidable, be Lebel, the valet. Given, Louis XIV., Bontemps, who makes his bed, is more powerful than Louvois, who raises his armies, and Turenne, who gains his victories. From Richelieu, take Père Joseph, and you have Richelieu nearly empty. There is the mystery the less. His Eminence in scarlet is magnificent; his Eminence in gray is terrible. What power in being a worm! All the Narvaez amalgamated with all the O'Donnells do less work than one Sõr Patrocinio.

Of course the condition of this power is littleness. If you would remain powerful, remain petty. Be Nothingness. The serpent in repose, twisted into a circle, is a figure at the same time of the infinite and of naught.

One of these viper-like fortunes had fallen to Barkilphedro.

He had crawled where he wanted.

Flat beasts can get in everywhere. Louis XIV. had bugs in his bed and Jesuits in his policy.

The incompatibility is nil.

In this world everything is a clock. To gravitate is to oscillate. One pole is attracted to the other. Francis I. is attracted by Triboulet; Louis XIV. is attracted by Lebel. There exists a deep affinity between extreme elevation and extreme debasement.

It is abasement which directs. Nothing is easier of comprehension. It is he who is below who pulls the strings. No position more convenient. He is the eye, and has the ear. He is the eye of the government; he has the ear of the king. To have the eye of the king is to draw and shut, at one's whim, the bolt of the royal conscience, and to throw into that conscience whatever one wishes. The mind of the king is his cupboard; if he be a rag-picker, it is his basket. The ears of kings belong not to kings, and therefore it is that, on the whole, the poor devils are not altogether responsible for their actions. He who does not possess his own thought does not possess his own deed. A king obeys—what? Any evil spirit buzzing from outside in his ear; a noisome fly of the abyss.

This buzzing commands. A reign is a dictation.

The loud voice is the sovereign; the low voice, sovereignty. Those who know how to distinguish, in a reign, this low voice, and to hear what it whispers to the loud, are the real historians.

CHAPTER IX.

HATE IS AS STRONG AS LOVE

Queen Anne had several of these low voices about her. Barkilphedro was one.

Besides the queen, he secretly worked, influenced, and plotted upon Lady Josiana and Lord David. As we have said, he whispered in three ears, one more than Dangeau. Dangeau whispered in but two, in the days when, thrusting himself between Louis XIV., in love with Henrietta, his sister-in-law, and Henrietta, in love with Louis XIV., her brother-in-law, he being Louis's secretary, without the knowledge of Henrietta, and Henrietta's without the knowledge of Louis, he wrote the questions and answers of both the love-making marionettes.

Barkilphedro was so cheerful, so accepting, so incapable of taking up the defence of anybody, possessing so little devotion at bottom, so ugly, so mischievous, that it was quite natural that a regal personage should come to be unable to do without him. Once Anne had tasted Barkilphedro she would have no other flatterer. He flattered her as they flattered Louis the Great, by stinging her neighbours. "The king being ignorant," says Madame de Montchevreuil, "one is obliged to mock at the savants."

To poison the sting, from time to time, is the acme of art. Nero loves to see Locusta at work.

Royal palaces are very easily entered; these madrepores have a way in soon guessed at, contrived, examined, and scooped out at need by the gnawing thing which is called the courtier. A pretext to enter is sufficient. Barkilphedro, having found this pretext, his position with the queen soon became the same as that with the Duchess Josiana—that of an indispensable domestic animal. A witticism risked one day by him immediately led to his perfect understanding of the queen and how to estimate exactly her kindness of heart. The queen was greatly attached to her Lord Steward, William Cavendish, Duke of Devonshire, who was a great fool. This lord, who had obtained every Oxford degree and did not know how to spell, one fine morning committed the folly of dying. To die is a very imprudent thing at court, for there is then no further restraint in speaking of you. The queen, in the presence of Barkilphedro, lamented the event, finally exclaiming, with a sigh,—

"It is a pity that so many virtues should have been borne and served by so poor an intellect."

"Dieu veuille avoir son âne!" whispered Barkilphedro, in a low voice, and in French.

The queen smiled. Barkilphedro noted the smile. His conclusion was that biting pleased. Free licence had been given to his spite. From that day he thrust his curiosity everywhere, and his malignity with it. He was given his way, so much was he feared. He who can make the king laugh makes the others tremble. He was a powerful buffoon. Every day he worked his way forward—underground.

Barkilphedro became a necessity. Many great people honoured him with their confidence, to the extent of charging him, when they required him, with their disgraceful commissions.

There are wheels within wheels at court. Barkilphedro became the motive power. Have you remarked, in certain mechanisms, the smallness of the motive wheel?

Josiana, in particular, who, as we have explained, made use of Barkilphedro's talents as a spy, reposed such confidence in him that she had not hesitated to entrust him with one of the master-keys of her apartments, by means of which he was able to enter them at any hour. This excessive licence of insight into private life was in fashion in the seventeenth century. It was called "giving the key." Josiana had given two of these confidential keys—Lord David had one, Barkilphedro the other. However, to enter straight into a bedchamber was, in the old code of manners, a thing not in the least out of the way. Thence resulted incidents. La Ferté, suddenly drawing back the bed curtains of Mademoiselle Lafont, found inside Sainson, the black musketeer, etc., etc.

Barkilphedro excelled in making the cunning discoveries which place the great in the power of the little. His walk in the dark was winding, soft, clever. Like every perfect spy, he was composed of the inclemency of the executioner and the patience of a micograph. He was a born courtier. Every courtier is a noctambulist. The courtier prowls in the night, which is called power. He carries a dark lantern in his hand. He lights up the spot he wishes, and remains in darkness himself. What he seeks with his lantern is not a man, it is a fool. What he finds is the king.

Kings do not like to see those about them pretend to greatness. Irony aimed at any one except themselves has a charm for them. The talent of Barkilphedro consisted in a perpetual dwarfing of the peers and princes to the advantage of her Majesty's stature, thus increased in proportion. The master-key held by Barkilphedro was made with two sets of wards, one at each end, so as to open the inner apartments in both Josiana's favourite residences—Hunkerville House in London, Corleone Lodge at Windsor. These two houses were part of the Clancharlie inheritance. Hunkerville House was close to Oldgate. Oldgate was a gate of London, which was entered by the Harwich road, and on which was displayed a statue of Charles II., with a painted angel on his head, and beneath his feet a carved lion and unicorn. From Hunkerville House, in an easterly wind, you heard the peals of St. Marylebone. Corleone Lodge was a Florentine palace of brick and stone, with a marble colonnade, built on pilework, at Windsor, at the head of the wooden bridge, and having one of the finest courts in England.

In the latter palace, near Windsor Castle, Josiana was within the queen's reach. Nevertheless, Josiana liked it.

Scarcely anything in appearance, everything in the root, such was the influence of Barkilphedro over the queen. There is nothing more difficult than to drag up these bad grasses of the court—they take a deep root, and offer no hold above the surface. To root out a Roquelaure, a Triboulet, or a Brummel, is almost impossible.

From day to day, and more and more, did the queen take Barkilphedro into her good graces. Sarah Jennings is famous; Barkilphedro is unknown. His existence remains ignored. The name of Barkilphedro has not reached as far as history. All the moles are not caught by the mole-trapper.

Barkilphedro, once a candidate for orders, had studied a little of everything. Skimming all things leaves naught for result. One may be victim of the *omnis res scibilis*. Having the vessel of the Danaïdes in one's head is the misfortune of a whole race of learned men, who may be termed the sterile. What Barkilphedro had put into his brain had left it empty.

The mind, like nature, abhors vacuum. Into emptiness nature puts love; the mind often puts hate. Hate occupies.

Hate for hate's sake exists. Art for art's sake exists in nature more than is believed. A man hates—he must do something. Gratuitous hate—formidable word! It means hate which is itself its own payment. The bear lives by licking his claws. Not indefinitely, of course. The claws must be revictualled—something must be put under them.

Hate indistinct is sweet, and suffices for a time; but one must end by having an object. An animosity diffused over creation is exhausting, like every solitary pleasure. Hate without an object is like a shooting-match without a target. What lends interest to the game is a heart to be pierced. One cannot hate solely for honour; some seasoning is necessary—a man, a woman, somebody, to destroy. This service of making the game interesting; of offering an end; of throwing passion into hate by fixing it on an object; of of amusing the hunter by the sight of his living prey; giving the watcher the hope of the smoking and boiling blood about to flow; of amusing the bird-catcher by the credulity of the uselessly-winged lark; of being a victim, unknowingly reared for murder by a master-mind—all this exquisite and horrible service, of which the person rendering it is unconscious, Josiana rendered Barkilphedro.

Thought is a projectile. Barkilphedro had, from the first day, begun to aim at Josiana the evil intentions which were in his mind. An intention and a carbine are alike. Barkilphedro aimed at Josiana, directing against the duchess all his secret malice. That astonishes you! What has the bird done at which you fire? You want to eat it, you say. And so it was with Barkilphedro.

Josiana could not be struck in the heart—the spot where the enigma lies is hard to wound; but she could be struck in the head—that is, in her pride. It was there that she thought herself strong, and that she was weak.

Barkilphedro had found it out. If Josiana had been able to see clearly through the night of Barkilphedro, if she had been able to distinguish what lay in ambush behind his smile, that proud woman, so highly situated, would have trembled. Fortunately for the tranquillity of her sleep, she was in complete ignorance of what was in the man.

The unexpected spreads, one knows not whence. The profound depths of life are dangerous. There is no small hate. Hate is always enormous. It preserves its stature in the smallest being, and remains a monster. An elephant hated by a worm is in danger.

Even before he struck, Barkilphedro felt, with joy, the foretaste of the evil action which he was about to commit. He did not as yet know what he was going to do to Josiana; but he had made up his mind to do something. To have come to this decision was a great step taken. To crush Josiana utterly would have been too great a triumph. He did not hope for so much; but to humiliate her, lessen her, bring her grief, redden her proud eyes with tears of rage—what a success! He counted on it. Tenacious, diligent, faithful to the torment of his neighbour, not to be torn from his purpose, nature had not formed him for nothing. He well understood how to find the flaw in Josiana's golden armour, and how to make the blood of that Olympian flow.

What benefit, we ask again, would accrue to him in so doing? An immense benefit—doing evil to one who had done good to him. What is an envious man? An ungrateful one. He hates the light which lights and warms him. Zoilus hated that benefit to man, Homer. To inflict on Josiana what would nowadays be called vivisection—to place her, all convulsed, on his anatomical table; to dissect her alive, at his leisure, in some surgery; to cut her up, as an amateur, while she should scream—this dream delighted Barkilphedro!

To arrive at this result it was necessary to suffer somewhat himself; he did so willingly. We may pinch ourselves with our own pincers. The knife as it shuts cuts our fingers. What does it matter? That he should partake of Josiana's torture was a matter of little moment. The executioner handling the red-hot iron, when about to brand a prisoner, takes no heed of a little burn. Because another suffers much, he suffers nothing. To see the victim's writhings takes all pain from the inflicter.

Do harm, whatever happens.

To plan evil for others is mingled with an acceptance of some hazy responsibility. We risk ourselves in the danger which we impel towards another, because the chain of events sometimes, of course, brings unexpected accidents. This does not stop the man who is truly malicious. He feels as much joy as the patient suffers agony. He is tickled by the laceration of the victim. The malicious man blooms in hideous joy. Pain reflects itself on him in a sense of welfare. The Duke of Alva used to warm his hands at the stake. The pile was torture, the reflection of it pleasure. That such transpositions should be possible makes one shudder. Our dark side is unfathomable. *Supplice exquis* (exquisite torture)—the expression is in Bodin[12]—has perhaps this terrible triple sense: search for the torture; suffering of the tortured; delight of the torturer.

Ambition, appetite—all such words signify some one sacrificed to some one satiated. It is sad that hope should be wicked. Is it that the outpourings of our wishes flow naturally to the direction to which we most incline—that of evil? One of the hardest labours of the just man is to expunge from his soul a malevolence which it is difficult to efface. Almost all our desires, when examined, contain what we dare not avow.

In the completely wicked man this exists in hideous perfection. So much the worse for others, signifies so much the better for himself. The shadows of the caverns of man's mind.

Josiana, in a plenitude of security the fruit of ignorant pride, had a contempt for all danger. The feminine faculty of disdain is extraordinary. Josiana's disdain, unreasoning, involuntary, and confident. Barkilphedro was to her so contemptible that she would have been astonished had any one remarked to her that such a creature existed. She went, and came, and laughed before this man who was looking at her with evil eyes. Thoughtful, he bided his time.

In proportion as he waited, his determination to cast a despair into this woman's life augmented. Inexorable high tide of malice.

In the meantime he gave himself excellent reasons for his determination. It must not be thought that scoundrels are deficient in self-esteem. They enter into details with themselves in their lofty monologues, and they take matters with a high hand. How? This Josiana had bestowed charity on him! She had thrown some crumbs of her enormous wealth to him, as to a beggar. She had nailed and riveted him to an office which was unworthy him. Yes; that he, Barkilphedro, almost a clergyman, of varied and profound talent, a learned man, with the material in him for a bishop, should have for employ the registration of nasty patience-trying shards, that he should have to pass his life in the garret of a register-office, gravely uncorking stupid bottles, incrusted with all the nastiness of the sea, deciphering musty parchments, like filthy conjuring-books, dirty wills, and other illegible stuff of the kind, was the fault of this Josiana. Worst of all, this creature "thee'd" and "thou'd" him! And he should not revenge himself—he should not punish such conduct! Well, in that case there would no longer be justice on earth!

CHAPTER X.

THE FLAME WHICH WOULD BE SEEN IF MAN WERE TRANSPARENT

What! this woman, this extravagant thing, this libidinous dreamer, a virgin until the opportunity occurred, this bit of flesh as yet unfreed, this bold creature under a princess's coronet; this Diana by pride, as yet untaken by the first comer, just because chance had so willed it; this bastard of a low-lived king who had not the intellect to keep his place; this duchess by a lucky hit, who, being a fine lady, played the goddess, and who, had she been poor, would have been a prostitute; this lady, more or less, this robber of a proscribed man's goods, this overbearing strumpet, because one day he, Barkilphedro, had not money enough to buy his dinner, and to get a lodging—she had had the impudence to seat him in her house at the corner of a table, and to put him up in some hole in her intolerable palace. Where? never mind where. Perhaps in the barn, perhaps in the cellar; what does it matter? A little better than her valets, a little worse than her horses. She had abused his distress—his, Barkilphedro's—in hastening to do him treacherous good; a thing which the rich do in order to humiliate the poor, and to tie them, like curs led by a string. Besides, what did the service she rendered him cost her? A service is worth what it costs. She had spare rooms in her house. She came to Barkilphedro's aid! A great thing, indeed. Had she eaten a spoonful the less of turtle soup for it? had she deprived herself of anything in the hateful overflowing of her superfluous luxuries? No. She had added to it a vanity, a luxury, a good action like a ring on her finger, the relief of a man of wit, the patronization of a clergyman. She could give herself airs: say, "I lavish kindness; I fill the mouths of men of letters; I am his benefactress. How lucky the wretch was to find me out! What a patroness of the arts I am!" All for having set up a truckle bed in a wretched garret in the roof. As for the place in the Admiralty, Barkilphedro owed it to Josiana; by Jove, a pretty appointment! Josiana had made Barkilphedro what he was. She had created him. Be it so. Yes, created nothing—less than nothing. For in his absurd situation he felt borne down, tongue-tied, disfigured. What did he owe Josiana? The thanks due from a hunchback to the mother who bore him deformed. Behold your privileged ones, your folks overwhelmed with fortune, your parvenus, your favourites of that horrid stepmother Fortune! And that man of talent, Barkilphedro, was obliged to stand on staircases, to bow to footmen, to climb to the top of the house at night, to be courteous, assiduous, pleasant, respectful, and to have ever on his muzzle a respectful grimace! Was not it enough to make him gnash his teeth with rage! And all the while she was putting pearls round her neck, and making amorous poses to her fool, Lord David Dirry-Moir; the hussy!

Never let any one do you a service. They will abuse the advantage it gives them. Never allow yourself to be taken in the act of inanition. They would relieve you. Because he was starving, this woman had found it a sufficient pretext to give him bread. From that moment he was her servant; a craving of the stomach, and there is a chain for life! To be obliged is to be sold. The happy, the powerful, make use of the moment you stretch out your hand to place a penny in it, and at the crisis of your weakness make you a slave, and a slave of the worst kind, the slave of an act of charity—a slave forced to love the enslaver. What infamy! what want of delicacy! what an assault on your self-respect! Then all is over. You are sentenced for life to consider this man good, that woman beautiful; to remain in the back rows; to approve, to applaud, to admire, to worship, to prostrate yourself, to blister your knees by long genuflections, to sugar your words when you are gnawing your lips with anger, when you are biting down your cries of fury, and when you have within you more savage turbulence and more bitter foam than the ocean!

It is thus that the rich make prisoners of the poor.

This slime of a good action performed towards you bedaubs and bespatters you with mud for ever.

An alms is irremediable. Gratitude is paralysis. A benefit is a sticky and repugnant adherence which deprives you of free movement. Those odious, opulent, and spoiled creatures whose pity has thus injured you are well aware of this. It is done—you are their creature. They have bought you—and how? By a bone taken from their dog and cast to you. They have flung that bone at your head. You have been stoned as much as benefited. It is all one. Have you gnawed the bone—yes or no? You have had your place in the dog-kennel as well. Then be thankful—be ever thankful. Adore your masters. Kneel on indefinitely. A benefit implies an understood inferiority accepted by you. It means that you feel them to be gods and yourself a poor devil. Your diminution augments them. Your bent form makes theirs more upright. In the tones of their voices there is an impertinent inflexion. Their family matters—their marriages, their baptisms, their child-bearings, their progeny—all concern you. A wolf cub is born to them. Well, you have to compose a sonnet. You are a poet because you are low. Isn't it enough to make the stars fall! A little more, and they would make you wear their old shoes.

"Who have you got there, my dear? How ugly he is! Who is that man?"

"I do not know. A sort of scholar, whom I feed."

Thus converse these idiots, without even lowering their voice. You hear, and remain mechanically amiable. If you are ill, your masters will send for the doctor—not their own. Occasionally they may even inquire after you. Being of a different species from you, and at an inaccessible height above you, they are affable. Their height makes them easy. They know that equality is impossible. By force of disdain they are polite. At table they give you a little nod. Sometimes they absolutely know how your name is spelt! They only show that they are your protectors by walking unconsciously over all the delicacy and susceptibility you possess. They treat you with good-nature. Is all this to be borne?

No doubt he was eager to punish Josiana. He must teach her with whom she had to deal!

O my rich gentry, because you cannot eat up everything, because opulence produces indigestion seeing that your stomachs are no bigger than ours, because it is, after all, better to distribute the remainder than to throw it away, you exalt a morsel flung to the poor into an act of magnificence. Oh, you give us bread, you give us shelter, you give us clothes, you give us employment, and you push audacity, folly, cruelty, stupidity, and absurdity to the pitch of believing that we are grateful! The bread is the bread of servitude, the shelter is a footman's bedroom, the clothes are a livery, the employment is ridiculous, paid for, it is true, but brutalizing.

Oh, you believe in the right to humiliate us with lodging and nourishment, and you imagine that we are your debtors, and you count on our gratitude! Very well; we will eat up your substance, we will devour you alive and gnaw your heart-strings with our teeth.

This Josiana! Was it not absurd? What merit had she? She had accomplished the wonderful work of coming into the world as a testimony of the folly of her father and the shame of her mother. She had done us the favour to exist, and for her kindness in becoming a public scandal they paid her millions; she had estates and castles, warrens, parks, lakes, forests, and I know not what besides, and with all that she was making a fool of herself, and verses were addressed to her! And Barkilphedro, who had studied and laboured and taken pains, and stuffed his eyes and his brain with great books, who had grown mouldy in old works and in science, who was full of wit, who could command armies, who could, if he would, write tragedies like Otway and Dryden, who was made to be an emperor—Barkilphedro had been reduced to permit this nobody to prevent him from dying of hunger. Could the usurpation of the rich, the hateful elect of chance, go further? They put on the semblance of being generous to us, of protecting us, and of smiling on us, and we would drink their blood and lick our lips after it! That this low woman of the court should have the odious power of being a benefactress, and that a man so superior should be condemned to pick up such bribes falling from such a hand, what a frightful iniquity! And what social system is this which has for its base disproportion and injustice? Would it not be best to take it by the four corners, and to throw pell-mell to the ceiling the damask tablecloth, and the festival, and the orgies, and the tippling and drunkenness, and the guests, and those with their elbows on the table, and those with their paws under it, and the insolent who give and the idiots who accept, and to spit it all back again in the face of Providence, and fling all the earth to the heavens? In the meantime let us stick our claws into Josiana.

Thus dreamed Barkilphedro. Such were the ragings of his soul. It is the habit of the envious man to absolve himself, amalgamating with his personal grievance the public wrongs.

All the wild forms of hateful passions went and came in the intellect of this ferocious being. At the corners of old maps of the world of the fifteenth century are great vague spaces without shape or name, on which are written these three words, *Hic sunt leones*. Such a dark corner is there also in man. Passions grow and growl somewhere within us, and we may say of an obscure portion of our souls, "There are lions here."

Is this scaffolding of wild reasoning absolutely absurd? does it lack a certain justice? We must confess it does not.

It is fearful to think that judgment within us is not justice. Judgment is the relative, justice is the absolute. Think of the difference between a judge and a just man.

Wicked men lead conscience astray with authority. There are gymnastics of untruth. A sophist is a forger, and this forger sometimes brutalizes good sense.

A certain logic, very supple, very implacable, and very agile, is at the service of evil, and excels in stabbing truth in the dark. These are blows struck by the devil at Providence.

The worst of it was that Barkilphedro had a presentiment. He was undertaking a heavy task, and he was afraid that after all the evil achieved might not be proportionate to the work.

To be corrosive as he was, to have within himself a will of steel, a hate of diamond, a burning curiosity for the catastrophe, and to burn nothing, to decapitate nothing, to exterminate nothing; to be what he was, a force of devastation, a voracious animosity, a devourer of the happiness of others, to have been created (for there is a creator, whether God or devil), to have been created Barkilphedro all over, and to inflict perhaps after all but a fillip of the finger—could this be possible? could it be that Barkilphedro should miss his aim? To be a lever powerful enough to heave great masses of rock, and when sprung to the utmost power to succeed only in giving an affected woman a bump in the forehead—to be a catapult dealing ruin on a pole-kitten! To accomplish the task of Sisyphus, to crush an ant; to sweat all over with hate, and for nothing at all. Would not this be humiliating, when he felt himself a mechanism of hostility capable of reducing the world to powder! To put into movement all the wheels within wheels, to work in the darkness all the mechanism of a Marly machine, and to succeed perhaps in pinching the end of a little rosy finger! He was to turn over and over blocks of marble, perchance with the result of ruffling a little the smooth surface of the court! Providence has a way of thus expending forces grandly. The movement of a mountain often only displaces a molehill.

Besides this, when the court is the dangerous arena, nothing is more dangerous than to aim at your enemy and miss him. In the first place, it unmasks you and irritates him; but besides and above all, it displeases the master. Kings do not like the unskilful. Let us have no contusions, no ugly gashes. Kill anybody, but give no one a bloody nose. He who kills is clever, he who wounds awkward. Kings do not like to see their servants lamed. They are displeased if you chip a porcelain jar on their chimney-piece or a courtier in their cortège. The court must be kept neat. Break and replace; that does not matter. Besides, all this agrees perfectly with the taste of princes for scandal. Speak evil, do none; or if you do, let it be in grand style.

Stab, do not scratch, unless the pin be poisoned. This would be an extenuating circumstance, and was, we may remember, the case with Barkilphedro.

Every malicious pigmy is a phial in which is enclosed the dragon of Solomon. The phial is microscopic, the dragon immense. A formidable condensation, awaiting the gigantic hour of dilation! Ennui consoled by the premeditation of explosion! The prisoner is larger than the prison. A latent giant! how wonderful! A minnow in which is contained a hydra. To be this fearful magical box, to contain within him a leviathan, is to the dwarf both a torture and a delight.

Nor would anything have caused Barkilphedro to let go his hold. He awaited his time. Was it to come? What mattered that? He watched for it. Self-love is mixed up in the malice of the very wicked man. To make holes and gaps in a court fortune higher than your own, to undermine it at all risks and perils, while encased and concealed yourself, is, we repeat, exceedingly interesting. The player at such a game becomes eager, even to passion. He throws himself into the work as if he were composing an epic. To be very mean, and to attack that which is great, is in itself a brilliant action. It is a fine thing to be a flea on a lion.

The noble beast feels the bite, and expends his mighty anger against the atom. An encounter with a tiger would weary him less; see how the actors exchange their parts. The lion, humiliated, feels the sting of the insect; and the flea can say, "I have in my veins the blood of a lion."

However, these reflections but half appeased the cravings of Barkilphedro's pride. Consolations, palliations at most. To vex is one thing; to torment would be infinitely better. Barkilphedro had a thought which returned to him without ceasing: his success might not go beyond just irritating the epidermis of Josiana. What could he hope for more—he so obscure against her so radiant? A scratch is worth but little to him who longs to see the crimson blood of his flayed victim, and to hear her cries as she lies before him more than naked, without even that garment the skin! With such a craving, how sad to be powerless!

Alas, there is nothing perfect!

However, he resigned himself. Not being able to do better, he only dreamed half his dream. To play a treacherous trick is an object after all.

What a man is he who revenges himself for a benefit received! Barkilphedro was a giant among such men. Usually, ingratitude is forgetfulness. With this man, patented in wickedness, it was fury. The vulgar ingrate is full of ashes; what was within Barkilphedro? A furnace—furnace walled round by hate, silence, and rancour, awaiting Josiana for fuel. Never had a man abhorred a woman to such a point without reason. How terrible! She was his dream, his preoccupation, his ennui, his rage.

Perhaps he was a little in love with her.

CHAPTER XI.

BARKILPHEDRO IN AMBUSCADE

To find the vulnerable spot in Josiana, and to strike her there, was, for all the causes we have just mentioned, the imperturbable determination of Barkilphedro. The wish is sufficient; the power is required. How was he to set about it? There was the question.

Vulgar vagabonds set the scene of any wickedness they intend to commit with care. They do not feel themselves strong enough to seize the opportunity as it passes, to take possession of it by fair means or foul, and to constrain it to serve them. Deep scoundrels disdain preliminary combinations. They start from their villainies alone, merely arming themselves all round, prepared to avail themselves of various chances which may occur, and then, like Barkilphedro, await the opportunity. They know that a ready-made scheme runs the risk of fitting ill into the event which may present itself. It is not thus that a man makes himself master of possibilities and guides them as one pleases. You can come to no previous arrangement with destiny. To-morrow will not obey you. There is a certain want of discipline in chance.

Therefore they watch for it, and summon it suddenly, authoritatively, on the spot. No plan, no sketch, no rough model; no ready-made shoe ill-fitting the unexpected. They plunge headlong into the dark. To turn to immediate and rapid profit any circumstance that can aid him is the quality which distinguishes the able scoundrel, and elevates the villain into the demon. To strike suddenly at fortune, *that* is true genius.

The true scoundrel strikes you from a sling with the first stone he can pick up. Clever malefactors count on the unexpected, that senseless accomplice of so many crimes. They grasp the incident and leap on it; there is no better *Ars Poetica* for this species of talent. Meanwhile be sure with whom you have to deal. Survey the ground.

With Barkilphedro the ground was Queen Anne. Barkilphedro approached the queen, and so close that sometimes he fancied he heard the monologues of her Majesty. Sometimes he was present unheeded at conversations between the sisters. Neither did they forbid his sliding in a word. He profited by this to lessen himself—a way of inspiring confidence. Thus one day in the garden at Hampton Court, being behind the duchess, who was behind the queen, he heard Anne, following the fashion, awkwardly enunciating sentiments.

"Animals are happy," said the queen. "They run no risk of going to hell."

"They are there already," replied Josiana.

This answer, which bluntly substituted philosophy for religion, displeased the queen. If, perchance, there was depth in the observation, Anne felt shocked.

"My dear," said she to Josiana, "we talk of hell like a couple of fools. Ask Barkilphedro all about it. He ought to know such things."

"As a devil?" said Josiana.

"As a beast," replied Barkilphedro, with a bow.

"Madam," said the queen to Josiana, "he is cleverer than we."

For a man like Barkilphedro to approach the queen was to obtain a hold on her. He could say, "I hold her." Now, he wanted a means of taking advantage of his power for his own benefit. He had his foothold in the court. To be settled there was a fine thing. No chance could now escape him. More than once he had made the queen smile maliciously. This was having a licence to shoot. But was there any preserved game? Did this licence to shoot permit him to break the wing or the leg of one like the sister of her Majesty? The first point to make clear was, did the queen love her sister? One false step would lose all. Barkilphedro watched.

Before he plays the player looks at the cards. What trumps has he? Barkilphedro began by examining the age of the two women. Josiana, twenty-three; Anne, forty-one. So far so good. He held trumps. The moment that a woman ceases to count by springs, and begins to count by winters, she becomes cross. A dull rancour possesses her against the time of which she carries the proofs. Fresh-blown beauties, perfumes for others, are to such a one but thorns. Of the roses she feels but the prick. It seems as if all the freshness is stolen from her, and that beauty decreases in her because it increases in others.

To profit by this secret ill-humour, to dive into the wrinkle on the face of this woman of forty, who was a queen, seemed a good game for Barkilphedro.

Envy excels in exciting jealousy, as a rat draws the crocodile from its hole.

Barkilphedro fixed his wise gaze on Anne. He saw into the queen as one sees into a stagnant pool. The marsh has its transparency. In dirty water we see vices, in muddy water we see stupidity; Anne was muddy water.

Embryos of sentiments and larvæ of ideas moved in her thick brain. They were not distinct; they had scarcely any outline. But they were realities, however shapeless. The queen thought this; the queen desired that. To decide what was the difficulty. The confused transformations which work in stagnant water are difficult to study. The queen, habitually obscure, sometimes made sudden and stupid revelations. It was on these that it was necessary to seize. He must take advantage of them on the moment. How did the queen feel towards the Duchess Josiana? Did she wish her good or evil?

Here was the problem. Barkilphedro set himself to solve it. This problem solved, he might go further.

Divers chances served Barkilphedro—his tenacity at the watch above all.

Anne was, on her husband's side, slightly related to the new Queen of Prussia, wife of the king with the hundred chamberlains. She had her portrait painted on enamel, after the process of Turquet of Mayerne. This Queen of Prussia had also a younger illegitimate sister, the Baroness Drika.

One day, in the presence of Barkilphedro, Anne asked the Russian ambassador some question about this Drika.

"They say she is rich?"

"Very rich."

"She has palaces?"

"More magnificent than those of her sister, the queen."

"Whom will she marry?"

"A great lord, the Count Gormo."

"Pretty?"

"Charming."

"Is she young?"

"Very young."

"As beautiful as the queen?"

The ambassador lowered his voice, and replied,—

"More beautiful."

"That is insolent," murmured Barkilphedro.

The queen was silent; then she exclaimed,—

"Those bastards!"

Barkilphedro noticed the plural.

Another time, when the queen was leaving the chapel, Barkilphedro kept pretty close to her Majesty, behind the two grooms of the almonry. Lord David Dirry-Moir, crossing the ranks of women, made a sensation by his handsome appearance. As he passed there was an explosion of feminine exclamations.

"How elegant! How gallant! What a noble air! How handsome!"

"How disagreeable!" grumbled the queen.

Barkilphedro overheard this; it decided him.

He could hurt the duchess without displeasing the queen. The first problem was solved; but now the second presented itself.

What could he do to harm the duchess? What means did his wretched appointment offer to attain so difficult an object?

Evidently none.

CHAPTER XII.

SCOTLAND, IRELAND, AND ENGLAND

Let us note a circumstance. Josiana had *le tour*.

This is easy to understand when we reflect that she was, although illegitimate, the queen's sister—that is to say, a princely personage.

To have *le tour*—what does it mean?

Viscount St. John, otherwise Bolingbroke, wrote as follows to Thomas Lennard, Earl of Sussex:—

"Two things mark the great—in England, they have *le tour;* in France, *le pour.*"

When the King of France travelled, the courier of the court stopped at the halting-place in the evening, and assigned lodgings to his Majesty's suite.

Amongst the gentlemen some had an immense privilege. "They have *le pour*" says the *Journal Historique* for the year 1694, page 6; "which means that the courier who marks the billets puts '*pour*' before their names—as, '*Pour* M. le Prince de Soubise;' instead of which, when he marks the lodging of one who is not royal, he does not put *pour*, but simply the name—as, 'Le Duc de Gesvres, le Duc de Mazarin.'" This *pour* on a door indicated a prince or a favourite. A favourite is worse than a prince. The king granted *le pour*, like a blue ribbon or a peerage.

Avoir le tour in England was less glorious but more real. It was a sign of intimate communication with the sovereign. Whoever might be, by birth or favour, in a position to receive direct communications from majesty, had in the wall of their bedchamber a shaft in which was adjusted a bell. The bell sounded, the shaft opened, a royal missive appeared on a gold plate or on a cushion of velvet, and the shaft closed. This was intimate and solemn, the mysterious in the familiar. The shaft was used for no other purpose. The sound of the bell announced a royal message. No one saw who brought it. It was of course merely the page of the king or the queen. Leicester *avait le tour* under Elizabeth; Buckingham under James I. Josiana had it under Anne, though not much in favour. Never was a privilege more envied.

This privilege entailed additional servility. The recipient was more of a servant. At court that which elevates, degrades. *Avoir le tour* was said in French; this circumstance of English etiquette having, probably, been borrowed from some old French folly.

Lady Josiana, a virgin peeress as Elizabeth had been a virgin queen, led—sometimes in the City, and sometimes in the country, according to the season—an almost princely life, and kept nearly a court, at which Lord David was courtier, with many others.

Not being married, Lord David and Lady Josiana could show themselves together in public without exciting ridicule, and they did so frequently. They often went to plays and racecourses in the same carriage, and sat together in the same box. They were chilled by the impending marriage, which was not only permitted to them, but imposed upon them; but they felt an attraction for each other's society. The privacy permitted to the engaged has a frontier easily passed. From this they abstained; that which is easy is in bad taste.

The best pugilistic encounters then took place at Lambeth, a parish in which the Lord Archbishop of Canterbury has a palace though the air there is unhealthy, and a rich library open at certain hours to decent people.

One evening in winter there was in a meadow there, the gates of which were locked, a fight, at which Josiana, escorted by Lord David, was present. She had asked,—

"Are women admitted?"

And David had responded,—

"*Sunt fœminae magnates!*"

Liberal translation, "Not shopkeepers." Literal translation, "Great ladies exist. A duchess goes everywhere!"

This is why Lady Josiana saw a boxing match.

Lady Josiana made only this concession to propriety—she dressed as a man, a very common custom at that period. Women seldom travelled otherwise. Out of every six persons who travelled by the coach from Windsor, it was rare that there were not one or two amongst them who were women in male attire; a certain sign of high birth.

Lord David, being in company with a woman, could not take any part in the match himself, and merely assisted as one of the audience.

Lady Josiana betrayed her quality in one way; she had an opera-glass, then used by gentlemen only.

This encounter in the noble science was presided over by Lord Germaine, great-grandfather, or grand-uncle, of that Lord Germaine who, towards the end of the eighteenth century, was colonel, ran away in a battle, was afterwards made Minister of War, and only escaped from the bolts of the enemy, to fall by a worse fate, shot through and through by the sarcasm of Sheridan.

Many gentlemen were betting. Harry Bellew, of Carleton, who had claims to the extinct peerage of Bella-aqua, with Henry, Lord Hyde, member of Parliament for the borough of Dunhivid, which is also called Launceston; the Honourable Peregrine Bertie, member for the borough of Truro, with Sir Thomas Colpepper, member for Maidstone; the Laird of Lamyrbau, which is on the borders of Lothian, with Samuel Trefusis, of the borough of Penryn; Sir Bartholomew Gracedieu, of the borough of Saint Ives, with the Honourable Charles Bodville, who was called Lord Robartes, and who was Custos Rotulorum of the county of Cornwall; besides many others.

Of the two combatants, one was an Irishman, named after his native mountain in Tipperary, Phelem-ghe-Madone, and the other a Scot, named Helmsgail.

They represented the national pride of each country. Ireland and Scotland were about to set to; Erin was going to fisticuff Gajothel. So that the bets amounted to over forty thousand guineas, besides the stakes.

The two champions were naked, excepting short breeches buckled over the hips, and spiked boots laced as high as the ankles.

Helmsgail, the Scot, was a youth scarcely nineteen, but he had already had his forehead sewn up, for which reason they laid 2 1/3 to 1 on him. The month before he had broken the ribs and gouged out the eyes of a pugilist named Sixmileswater. This explained the enthusiasm he created. He had won his backers twelve thousand pounds. Besides having his forehead sewn up Helmsgail's jaw had been broken. He was neatly made and active. He was about the height of a small woman, upright, thick-set, and of a stature low and threatening. And nothing had been lost of the advantages given him by nature; not a muscle which was not trained to its object, pugilism. His firm chest was compact, and brown and shining like brass. He smiled, and three teeth which he had lost added to his smile.

His adversary was tall and overgrown—that is to say, weak.

He was a man of forty years of age, six feet high, with the chest of a hippopotamus, and a mild expression of face. The blow of his fist would break in the deck of a vessel, but he did not know how to use it.

The Irishman, Phelem-ghe-Madone, was all surface, and seemed to have entered the ring to receive rather than to give blows. Only it was felt that he would take a deal of punishment. Like underdone beef, tough to chew, and impossible to swallow. He was what was termed, in local slang, raw meat. He squinted. He seemed resigned.

The two men had passed the preceding night in the same bed, and had slept together. They had each drunk port wine from the same glass, to the three-inch mark.

Each had his group of seconds—men of savage expression, threatening the umpires when it suited their side. Amongst Helmsgail's supporters was to be seen John Gromane, celebrated for having carried an ox on his back; and one called John Bray, who had once carried on his back ten bushels of flour, at fifteen pecks to the bushel, besides the miller himself, and had walked over two hundred paces under the weight. On the side of Phelem-ghe-Madone, Lord Hyde had brought from Launceston a certain Kilter, who lived at Green Castle, and could throw a stone weighing twenty pounds to a greater height than the highest tower of the castle.

These three men, Kilter, Bray, and Gromane, were Cornishmen by birth, and did honour to their county.

The other seconds were brutal fellows, with broad backs, bowed legs, knotted fists, dull faces; ragged, fearing nothing, nearly all jail-birds.

Many of them understood admirably how to make the police drunk. Each profession should have its peculiar talents.

The field chosen was farther off than the bear garden, where they formerly baited bears, bulls, and dogs; it was beyond the line of the farthest houses, by the side of the ruins of the Priory of Saint Mary Overy, dismantled by Henry VIII. The wind was northerly, and biting; a small rain fell, which was instantly frozen into ice. Some gentlemen present were evidently fathers of families, recognized as such by their putting up their umbrellas.

On the side of Phelem-ghe-Madone was Colonel Moncreif, as umpire; and Kilter, as second, to support him on his knee.

On the side of Helmsgail, the Honourable Pughe Beaumaris was umpire, with Lord Desertum, from Kilcarry, as bottle-holder, to support him on his knee.

The two combatants stood for a few seconds motionless in the ring, whilst the watches were being compared. They then approached each other and shook hands.

Phelem-ghe-Madone said to Helmsgail,—

"I should prefer going home."

Helmsgail answered, handsomely,—

"The gentlemen must not be disappointed, on any account."

Naked as they were, they felt the cold. Phelem-ghe-Madone shook. His teeth chattered.

Dr. Eleanor Sharpe, nephew of the Archbishop of York, cried out to them,—

"Set to, boys; it will warm you."

Those friendly words thawed them.

They set to.

But neither one nor the other was angry. There were three ineffectual rounds. The Rev. Doctor Gumdraith, one of the forty Fellows of All Souls' College, cried,—

"Spirit them up with gin."

But the two umpires and the two seconds adhered to the rule. Yet it was exceedingly cold.

First blood was claimed.

They were again set face to face.

They looked at each other, approached, stretched their arms, touched each other's fists, and then drew back.

All at once, Helmsgail, the little man, sprang forward. The real fight had begun.

Phelem-ghe-Madone was struck in the face, between the Ryes. His whole face streamed with blood. The crowd cried,—

"Helmsgail has tapped his claret!"

There was applause. Phelem-ghe-Madone, turning his arms like the sails of a windmill, struck out at random.

The Honourable Peregrine Bertie said, "Blinded;" but he was not blind yet.

Then Helmsgail heard on all sides these encouraging words,—

"Bung up his peepers!"

On the whole, the two champions were really well matched; and, notwithstanding the unfavourable weather, it was seen that the fight would be a success.

The great giant, Phelem-ghe-Madone, had to bear the inconveniences of his advantages; he moved heavily. His arms were massive as clubs; but his chest was a mass. His little opponent ran, struck, sprang, gnashed his teeth; redoubling vigour by quickness, from knowledge of the science.

On the one side was the primitive blow of the fist—savage, uncultivated, in a state of ignorance; on the other side, the civilized blow of the fist. Helmsgail fought as much with his nerves as with his muscles, and with as much intention as force. Phelem-ghe-Madone was a kind of sluggish mauler—somewhat mauled himself, to begin with. It was art against nature. It was cultivated ferocity against barbarism.

It was clear that the barbarian would be beaten, but not very quickly. Hence the interest.

A little man against a big one, and the chances are in favour of the little one. The cat has the best of it with a dog. Goliaths are always vanquished by Davids.

A hail of exclamations followed the combatants.

"Bravo, Helmsgail! Good! Well done, Highlander! Now, Phelem!"

And the friends of Helmsgail repeated their benevolent exhortation,—

"Bung up his peepers!"

Helmsgail did better. Rapidly bending down and back again, with the undulation of a serpent, he struck Phelem-ghe-Madone in the sternum. The Colossus staggered.

"Foul blow!" cried Viscount Barnard.

Phelem-ghe-Madone sank down on the knee of his second, saying,—

"I am beginning to get warm."

Lord Desertum consulted the umpires, and said,—

"Five minutes before time is called."

Phelem-ghe-Madone was becoming weaker. Kilter wiped the blood from his face and the sweat from his body with a flannel, and placed the neck of a bottle to his mouth. They had come to the eleventh round. Phelem, besides the scar on his forehead, had his breast disfigured by blows, his belly swollen, and the fore part of the head scarified. Helmsgail was untouched.

A kind of tumult arose amongst the gentlemen.

Lord Barnard repeated, "Foul blow."

"Bets void!" said the Laird of Lamyrbau.

"I claim my stake!" replied Sir Thomas Colpepper.

And the honourable member for the borough of Saint Ives, Sir Bartholomew Gracedieu, added, "Give me back my five hundred guineas, and I will go. Stop the fight."

Phelem arose, staggering like a drunken man, and said,—

"Let us go on fighting, on one condition—that I also shall have the right to give one foul blow."

They cried "Agreed!" from all parts of the ring. Helmsgail shrugged his shoulders. Five minutes elapsed, and they set to again.

The fighting, which was agony to Phelem, was play to Helmsgail. Such are the triumphs of science.

The little man found means of putting the big one into chancery—that is to say, Helmsgail suddenly took under his left arm, which was bent like a steel crescent, the huge head of Phelem-ghe-Madone, and held it there under his armpits, the neck bent and twisted, whilst Helmsgail's right fist fell again and again like a hammer on a nail, only from below and striking upwards, thus smashing his opponent's face at his ease. When Phelem, released at length, lifted his head, he had no longer a face.

That which had been a nose, eyes, and a mouth now looked only like a black sponge, soaked in blood. He spat, and on the ground lay four of his teeth.

Then he fell. Kilter received him on his knee.

Helmsgail was hardly touched: he had some insignificant bruises and a scratch on his collar bone.

No one was cold now. They laid sixteen and a quarter to one on Helmsgail.

Harry Carleton cried out,—

"It is all over with Phelem-ghe-Madone. I will lay my peerage of Bella-aqua, and my title of Lord Bellew, against the Archbishop of Canterbury's old wig, on Helmsgail."

"Give me your muzzle," said Kilter to Phelem-ghe-Madone. And stuffing the bloody flannel into the bottle, he washed him all over with gin. The mouth reappeared, and he opened one eyelid. His temples seemed fractured.

"One round more, my friend," said Kilter; and he added, "for the honour of the low town."

The Welsh and the Irish understand each other, still Phelem made no sign of having any power of understanding left.

Phelem arose, supported by Kilter. It was the twenty-fifth round. From the way in which this Cyclops, for he had but one eye, placed himself in position, it was evident that this was the last round, for no one doubted his defeat. He placed his guard below his chin, with the awkwardness of a failing man.

Helmsgail, with a skin hardly sweating, cried out,—

"I'll back myself, a thousand to one."

Helmsgail, raising his arm, struck out; and, what was strange, both fell. A ghastly chuckle was heard. It was Phelem-ghe-Madone's expression of delight. While receiving the terrible blow given him by Helmsgail on the skull, he had given him a foul blow on the navel.

Helmsgail, lying on his back, rattled in his throat.

The spectators looked at him as he lay on the ground, and said, "Paid back!" All clapped their hands, even those who had lost. Phelem-ghe-Madone had given foul blow for foul blow, and had only asserted his right.

They carried Helmsgail off on a hand-barrow. The opinion was that he would not recover.

Lord Robartes exclaimed, "I win twelve hundred guineas."

Phelem-ghe-Madone was evidently maimed for life.

As she left, Josiana took the arm of Lord David, an act which was tolerated amongst people "engaged." She said to him,—

"It is very fine, but—"

"But what?"

"I thought it would have driven away my spleen. It has not."

Lord David stopped, looked at Josiana, shut his mouth, and inflated his cheeks, whilst he nodded his head, which signified attention, and said to the duchess,—

"For spleen there is but one remedy."

"What is it?"

"Gwynplaine."

The duchess asked,—

"And who is Gwynplaine?"

BOOK THE SECOND

GWYNPLAINE AND DEA

CHAPTER I.

WHEREIN WE SEE THE FACE OF HIM OF WHOM WE HAVE HITHERTO SEEN ONLY THE ACTS

Nature had been prodigal of her kindness to Gwynplaine. She had bestowed on him a mouth opening to his ears, ears folding over to his eyes, a shapeless nose to support the spectacles of the grimace maker, and a face that no one could look upon without laughing.

We have just said that nature had loaded Gwynplaine with her gifts. But was it nature? Had she not been assisted?

Two slits for eyes, a hiatus for a mouth, a snub protuberance with two holes for nostrils, a flattened face, all having for the result an appearance of laughter; it is certain that nature never produces such perfection single-handed.

But is laughter a synonym of joy?

If, in the presence of this mountebank—for he was one—the first impression of gaiety wore off, and the man were observed with attention, traces of art were to be recognized. Such a face could never have been created by chance; it must have resulted from intention. Such perfect completeness is not in nature. Man can do nothing to create beauty, but everything to produce ugliness. A Hottentot profile cannot be changed into a Roman outline, but out of a Grecian nose you may make a Calmuck's. It only requires to obliterate the root of the nose and to flatten the nostrils. The dog Latin of the Middle Ages had a reason for its creation of the verb *denasare.* Had Gwynplaine when a child been so worthy of attention that his face had been subjected to transmutation? Why not? Needed there a greater motive than the speculation of his future exhibition? According to all appearance, industrious manipulators of children had worked upon his face. It seemed evident that a mysterious and probably occult science, which was to surgery what alchemy was to chemistry, had chiselled his flesh, evidently at a very tender age, and manufactured his countenance with premeditation. That science, clever with the knife, skilled in obtusions and ligatures, had enlarged the mouth, cut away the lips, laid bare the gums, distended the ears, cut the cartilages, displaced the eyelids and the cheeks, enlarged the zygomatic muscle, pressed the scars and cicatrices to a level, turned back the skin over the lesions whilst the face was thus stretched, from all which resulted that powerful and profound piece of sculpture, the mask, Gwynplaine.

Man is not born thus.

However it may have been, the manipulation of Gwynplaine had succeeded admirably. Gwynplaine was a gift of Providence to dispel the sadness of man.

Of what providence? Is there a providence of demons as well as of God? We put the question without answering it.

Gwynplaine was a mountebank. He showed himself on the platform. No such effect had ever before been produced. Hypochondriacs were cured by the sight of him alone. He was avoided by folks in mourning, because they were compelled to laugh when they saw him, without regard to their decent gravity. One day the executioner came, and Gwynplaine made him laugh. Every one who saw Gwynplaine held his sides; he spoke, and they rolled on the ground. He was removed from sadness as is pole from pole. Spleen at the one; Gwynplaine at the other.

Thus he rose rapidly in the fair ground and at the cross roads to the very satisfactory renown of a horrible man.

It was Gwynplaine's laugh which created the laughter of others, yet he did not laugh himself. His face laughed; his thoughts did not. The extraordinary face which chance or a special and weird industry had fashioned for him, laughed alone. Gwynplaine had nothing to do with it. The outside did not depend on the interior. The laugh which he had not placed, himself, on his brow, on his eyelids, on his mouth, he could not remove. It had been stamped for ever on his face. It was automatic, and the more irresistible because it seemed petrified. No one could escape from this rictus. Two convulsions of the face are infectious; laughing and yawning. By virtue of the mysterious operation to which Gwynplaine had probably been subjected in his infancy, every part of his face contributed to that rictus; his whole physiognomy led to that result, as a wheel centres in the nave. All his emotions, whatever they might have been, augmented his strange face of joy, or to speak more correctly, aggravated it. Any astonishment which might seize him, any suffering which he might feel, any anger which might take possession of him, any pity which might move him, would only increase this hilarity of his muscles. If he wept, he laughed; and whatever Gwynplaine was, whatever he wished to be, whatever he thought, the moment that he raised his head, the crowd, if crowd there was, had before them one impersonation: an overwhelming burst of laughter.

It was like a head of Medusa, but Medusa hilarious. All feeling or thought in the mind of the spectator was suddenly put to flight by the unexpected apparition, and laughter was inevitable. Antique art formerly placed on the outsides of the Greek theatre a joyous brazen face, called comedy. It laughed and occasioned laughter, but remained pensive. All parody which borders on folly, all irony which borders on wisdom, were condensed and amalgamated in that face. The burden of care, of disillusion, anxiety, and grief were expressed in its impassive countenance, and resulted in a lugubrious sum of mirth. One corner of the mouth was raised, in mockery of the human race; the other side, in blasphemy of the gods. Men confronted that model of the ideal sarcasm and exemplification of the irony which each one possesses within him; and the crowd, continually renewed round its fixed laugh, died away with delight before its sepulchral immobility of mirth.

One might almost have said that Gwynplaine was that dark, dead mask of ancient comedy adjusted to the body of a living man. That infernal head of implacable hilarity he supported on his neck. What a weight for the shoulders of a man—an everlasting laugh!

An everlasting laugh!

Let us understand each other; we will explain. The Manichæans believed the absolute occasionally gives way, and that God Himself sometimes abdicates for a time. So also of the will. We do not admit that it can ever be utterly powerless. The whole of existence resembles a letter modified in the postscript. For Gwynplaine the postscript was this: by the force of his will, and by concentrating all his attention, and on condition that no emotion should come to distract and turn away the fixedness of his effort, he could manage to suspend the everlasting rictus of his face, and to throw over it a kind of tragic veil, and then the spectator laughed no longer; he shuddered.

This exertion Gwynplaine scarcely ever made. It was a terrible effort, and an insupportable tension. Moreover, it happened that on the slightest distraction, or the slightest emotion, the laugh, driven back for a moment, returned like a tide with an impulse which was irresistible in proportion to the force of the adverse emotion.

With this exception, Gwynplaine's laugh was everlasting.

On seeing Gwynplaine, all laughed. When they had laughed they turned away their heads. Women especially shrank from him with horror. The man was frightful. The joyous convulsion of laughter was as a tribute paid; they submitted to it gladly, but almost mechanically. Besides, when once the novelty of the laugh had passed over, Gwynplaine was intolerable for a woman to see, and impossible to contemplate. But he was tall, well made, and agile, and no way deformed, excepting in his face.

This led to the presumption that Gwynplaine was rather a creation of art than a work of nature. Gwynplaine, beautiful in figure, had probably been beautiful in face. At his birth he had no doubt resembled other infants. They had left the body intact, and retouched only the face.

Gwynplaine had been made to order—at least, that was probable. They had left him his teeth; teeth are necessary to a laugh. The death's head retains them. The operation performed on him must have been frightful. That he had no remembrance of it was no proof that it had not taken place. Surgical sculpture of the kind could never have succeeded except on a very young child, and consequently on one having little consciousness of what happened to him, and who might easily take a wound for a sickness. Besides, we must remember that they had in those times means of putting patients to sleep, and of suppressing all suffering; only then it was called magic, while now it is called anæsthesia.

Besides this face, those who had brought him up had given him the resources of a gymnast and an athlete. His articulations usefully displaced and fashioned to bending the wrong way, had received the education of a clown, and could, like the hinges of a door, move backwards and forwards. In appropriating him to the profession of mountebank nothing had been neglected. His hair had been dyed with ochre once for all; a secret which has been rediscovered at the present day. Pretty women use it, and that which was formerly considered ugly is now considered an embellishment. Gwynplaine had yellow hair. His hair having probably been dyed with some corrosive preparation, had left it woolly and rough to the touch. Its yellow bristles, rather a mane than a head of hair, covered and concealed a lofty brow, evidently made to contain thought. The operation, whatever it had been, which had deprived his features of harmony, and put all their flesh into disorder, had had no effect on the bony structure of his head. The facial angle was powerful and surprisingly grand. Behind his laugh there was a soul, dreaming, as all our souls dream.

However, his laugh was to Gwynplaine quite a talent. He could do nothing with it, so he turned it to account. By means of it he gained his living.

Gwynplaine, as you have doubtless already guessed, was the child abandoned one winter evening on the coast of Portland, and received into a poor caravan at Weymouth.

CHAPTER II.

DEA

That boy was at this time a man. Fifteen years had elapsed. It was in 1705. Gwynplaine was in his twenty-fifth year.

Ursus had kept the two children with him. They were a group of wanderers. Ursus and Homo had aged. Ursus had become quite bald. The wolf was growing gray. The age of wolves is not ascertained like that of dogs. According to Molière, there are wolves which live to eighty, amongst others the little koupara, and the rank wolf, the *Canis nubilus* of Say.

The little girl found on the dead woman was now a tall creature of sixteen, with brown hair, slight, fragile, almost trembling from delicacy, and almost inspiring fear lest she should break; admirably beautiful, her eyes full of light, yet blind. That fatal winter night which threw down the beggar woman and her infant in the snow had struck a double blow. It had killed the mother and blinded the child. Gutta serena had for ever paralysed the eyes of the girl, now become woman in her turn. On her face, through which the light of day never passed, the depressed corners of the mouth indicated the bitterness of the privation. Her eyes, large and clear, had a strange quality: extinguished for ever to her, to others they were brilliant. They were mysterious torches lighting only the outside. They gave light but possessed it not. These sightless eyes were resplendent. A captive of shadow, she lighted up the dull place she inhabited. From the depth of her incurable darkness, from behind the black wall called blindness, she flung her rays. She saw not the sun without, but her soul was perceptible from within.

In her dead look there was a celestial earnestness. She was the night, and from the irremediable darkness with which she was amalgamated she came out a star.

Ursus, with his mania for Latin names, had christened her Dea. He had taken his wolf into consultation. He had said to him, "You represent man, I represent the beasts. We are of the lower world; this little one shall represent the world on high. Such feebleness is all-powerful. In this manner the universe shall be complete in our hut in its three orders—human, animal, and Divine." The wolf made no objection. Therefore the foundling was called Dea.

As to Gwynplaine, Ursus had not had the trouble of inventing a name for him. The morning of the day on which he had realized the disfigurement of the little boy and the blindness of the infant he had asked him, "Boy, what is your name?" and the boy had answered, "They call me Gwynplaine." "Be Gwynplaine, then," said Ursus.

Dea assisted Gwynplaine in his performances. If human misery could be summed up, it might have been summed up in Gwynplaine and Dea. Each seemed born in a compartment of the sepulchre; Gwynplaine in the horrible, Dea in the darkness. Their existences were shadowed by two different kinds of darkness, taken from the two formidable sides of night. Dea had that shadow in her, Gwynplaine had it on him. There was a phantom in Dea, a spectre in Gwynplaine. Dea was sunk in the mournful, Gwynplaine in something worse. There was for Gwynplaine, who could see, a heartrending possibility that existed not for Dea, who was blind; he could compare himself with other men. Now, in a situation such as that of Gwynplaine, admitting that he should seek to examine it, to compare himself with others was to understand himself no more. To have, like Dea, empty sight from which the world is absent, is a supreme distress, yet less than to be an enigma to oneself; to feel that something is wanting here as well, and that something, oneself; to see the universe and not to see oneself. Dea had a veil over her, the night; Gwynplaine a mask, his face. Inexpressible fact, it was by his own flesh that Gwynplaine was masked! What his visage had been, he knew not. His face had vanished. They had affixed to him a false self. He had for a face, a disappearance. His head lived, his face was dead. He never remembered to have seen it. Mankind was for Gwynplaine, as for Dea, an exterior fact. It was far-off. She was alone, he was alone. The isolation of Dea was funereal, she saw nothing; that of Gwynplaine sinister, he saw all things. For Dea creation never passed the bounds of touch and hearing; reality was bounded, limited, short, immediately lost. Nothing was infinite to her but darkness. For Gwynplaine to live was to have the crowd for ever before him and outside him. Dea was the proscribed from light, Gwynplaine the banned of life. They were beyond the pale of hope, and had reached the depth of possible calamity; they had sunk into it, both of them. An observer who had watched them would have felt his reverie melt into immeasurable pity. What must they not have suffered! The decree of misfortune weighed visibly on these human creatures, and never had fate encompassed two beings who had done nothing to deserve it, and more clearly turned destiny into torture, and life into hell.

They were in a Paradise.

They were in love.

Gwynplaine adored Dea. Dea idolized Gwynplaine.

"How beautiful you are!" she would say to him.

CHAPTER III.

"OCULOS NON HABET, ET VIDET"

Only one woman on earth saw Gwynplaine. It was the blind girl. She had learned what Gwynplaine had done for her, from Ursus, to whom he had related his rough journey from Portland to Weymouth, and the many sufferings which he had endured when deserted by the gang. She knew that when an infant dying upon her dead mother, suckling a corpse, a being scarcely bigger than herself had taken her up; that this being, exiled, and, as it were, buried under the refusal of the universe to aid him, had heard her cry; that all the world being deaf to him, he had not been deaf to her; that the child, alone, weak, cast off, without resting-place here below, dragging himself over the waste, exhausted by fatigue, crushed, had accepted from the hands of night a burden, another child: that he, who had nothing to expect in that obscure distribution which we call fate, had charged himself with a destiny; that naked, in anguish and distress, he had made himself a Providence; that when Heaven had closed he had opened his heart; that, himself lost, he had saved; that having neither roof-tree nor shelter, he had been an asylum; that he had made himself mother and nurse; that he who was alone in the world had responded to desertion by adoption; that lost in the darkness he had given an example; that, as if not already sufficiently burdened, he had added to his load another's misery; that in this world, which seemed to contain nothing for him, he had found a duty; that where every one else would have hesitated, he had advanced; that where every one else would have drawn back, he consented; that he had put his hand into the jaws of the grave and drawn out her—Dea. That, himself half naked, he had given her his rags, because she was cold; that famished, he had thought of giving her food and drink; that for one little creature, another little creature had combated death; that he had fought it under every form; under the form of winter and snow, under the form of solitude, under the form of terror, under the form of cold, hunger, and thirst, under the form of whirlwind, and that for her, Dea, this Titan of ten had given battle to the immensity of night. She knew that as a child he had done this, and that now as a man, he was strength to her weakness, riches to her poverty, healing to her sickness, and sight to her blindness. Through the mist of the unknown by which she felt herself encompassed, she distinguished clearly his devotion, his abnegation, his courage. Heroism in immaterial regions has an outline; she distinguished this sublime outline. In the inexpressible abstraction in which thought lives unlighted by the sun, Dea perceived this mysterious lineament of virtue. In the surrounding of dark things put in motion, which was the only impression made on her by reality; in the uneasy stagnation of a creature, always passive, yet always on the watch for possible evil; in the sensation of being ever defenceless, which is the life of the blind—she felt Gwynplaine above her; Gwynplaine never cold, never absent, never obscured; Gwynplaine sympathetic, helpful, and sweet-tempered. Dea quivered with certainty and gratitude, her anxiety changed into ecstasy, and with her shadowy eyes she contemplated on the zenith from the depth of her abyss the rich light of his goodness. In the ideal, kindness is the sun; and Gwynplaine dazzled Dea.

To the crowd, which has too many heads to have a thought, and too many eyes to have a sight—to the crowd who, superficial themselves, judge only of the surface, Gwynplaine was a clown, a merry-andrew, a mountebank, a creature grotesque, a little more and a little less than a beast. The crowd knew only the face.

For Dea, Gwynplaine was the saviour, who had gathered her into his arms in the tomb, and borne her out of it; the consoler, who made life tolerable; the liberator, whose hand, holding her own, guided her through that labyrinth called blindness. Gwynplaine was her brother, friend, guide, support; the personification of heavenly power; the husband, winged and resplendent. Where the multitude saw the monster, Dea recognized the archangel. It was that Dea, blind, perceived his soul.

CHAPTER IV.

WELL-MATCHED LOVERS

Ursus being a philosopher understood. He approved of the fascination of Dea. He said, The blind see the invisible. He said, Conscience is vision. Then, looking at Gwynplaine, he murmured, Semi-monster, but demi-god.

Gwynplaine, on the other hand, was madly in love with Dea.

There is the invisible eye, the spirit, and the visible eye, the pupil. He saw her with the visible eye. Dea was dazzled by the ideal; Gwynplaine, by the real. Gwynplaine was not ugly; he was frightful. He saw his contrast before him: in proportion as he was terrible, Dea was sweet. He was horror; she was grace. Dea was his dream. She seemed a vision scarcely embodied. There was in her whole person, in her Grecian form, in her fine and supple figure, swaying like a reed; in her shoulders, on which might have been invisible wings; in the modest curves which indicated her sex, to the soul rather than to the senses; in her fairness, which amounted almost to transparency; in the august and reserved serenity of her look, divinely shut out from earth; in the sacred innocence of her smile—she was almost an angel, and yet just a woman.

Gwynplaine, we have said, compared himself and compared Dea.

His existence, such as it was, was the result of a double and unheard-of choice. It was the point of intersection of two rays—one from below and one from above—a black and a white ray. To the same crumb, perhaps pecked at at once by the beaks of evil and good, one gave the bite, the other the kiss. Gwynplaine was this crumb—an atom, wounded and caressed. Gwynplaine was the product of fatality combined with Providence. Misfortune had placed its finger on him;

happiness as well. Two extreme destinies composed his strange lot. He had on him an anathema and a benediction. He was the elect, cursed. Who was he? He knew not. When he looked at himself, he saw one he knew not; but this unknown was a monster. Gwynplaine lived as it were beheaded, with a face which did not belong to him. This face was frightful, so frightful that it was absurd. It caused as much fear as laughter. It was a hell-concocted absurdity. It was the shipwreck of a human face into the mask of an animal. Never had been seen so total an eclipse of humanity in a human face; never parody more complete; never had apparition more frightful grinned in nightmare; never had everything repulsive to woman been more hideously amalgamated in a man. The unfortunate heart, masked and calumniated by the face, seemed for ever condemned to solitude under it, as under a tombstone.

Yet no! Where unknown malice had done its worst, invisible goodness had lent its aid. In the poor fallen one, suddenly raised up, by the side of the repulsive, it had placed the attractive; on the barren shoal it had set the loadstone; it had caused a soul to fly with swift wings towards the deserted one; it had sent the dove to console the creature whom the thunderbolt had overwhelmed, and had made beauty adore deformity. For this to be possible it was necessary that beauty should not see the disfigurement. For this good fortune, misfortune was required. Providence had made Dea blind.

Gwynplaine vaguely felt himself the object of a redemption. Why had he been persecuted? He knew not. Why redeemed? He knew not. All he knew was that a halo had encircled his brand. When Gwynplaine had been old enough to understand, Ursus had read and explained to him the text of Doctor Conquest *de Denasatis*, and in another folio, Hugo Plagon, the passage, *Naves habensmutilas;* but Ursus had prudently abstained from "hypotheses," and had been reserved in his opinion of what it might mean. Suppositions were possible. The probability of violence inflicted on Gwynplaine when an infant was hinted at, but for Gwynplaine the result was the only evidence. His destiny was to live under a stigma. Why this stigma? There was no answer.

Silence and solitude were around Gwynplaine. All was uncertain in the conjectures which could be fitted to the tragical reality; excepting the terrible fact, nothing was certain. In his discouragement Dea intervened a sort of celestial interposition between him and despair. He perceived, melted and inspirited by the sweetness of the beautiful girl who turned to him, that, horrible as he was, a beautified wonder affected his monstrous visage. Having been fashioned to create dread, he was the object of a miraculous exception, that it was admired and adored in the ideal by the light; and, monster that he was, he felt himself the contemplation of a star.

Gwynplaine and Dea were united, and these two suffering hearts adored each other. One nest and two birds—that was their story. They had begun to feel a universal law—to please, to seek, and to find each other.

Thus hatred had made a mistake. The persecutors of Gwynplaine, whoever they might have been—the deadly enigma, from wherever it came—had missed their aim. They had intended to drive him to desperation; they had succeeded in driving him into enchantment. They had affianced him beforehand to a healing wound. They had predestined him for consolation by an infliction. The pincers of the executioner had softly changed into the delicately-moulded hand of a girl. Gwynplaine was horrible—artificially horrible—made horrible by the hand of man. They had hoped to exile him for ever: first, from his family, if his family existed, and then from humanity. When an infant, they had made him a ruin; of this ruin Nature had repossessed herself, as she does of all ruins. This solitude Nature had consoled, as she consoles all solitudes. Nature comes to the succour of the deserted; where all is lacking, she gives back her whole self. She flourishes and grows green amid ruins; she has ivy for the stones and love for man.

Profound generosity of the shadows!

CHAPTER V.

THE BLUE SKY THROUGH THE BLACK CLOUD

Thus lived these unfortunate creatures together—Dea, relying; Gwynplaine, accepted. These orphans were all in all to each other, the feeble and the deformed. The widowed were betrothed. An inexpressible thanksgiving arose out of their distress. They were grateful. To whom? To the obscure immensity. Be grateful in your own hearts. That suffices. Thanksgiving has wings, and flies to its right destination. Your prayer knows its way better than you can.

How many men have believed that they prayed to Jupiter, when they prayed to Jehovah! How many believers in amulets are listened to by the Almighty! How many atheists there are who know not that, in the simple fact of being good and sad, they pray to God!

Gwynplaine and Dea were grateful. Deformity is expulsion. Blindness is a precipice. The expelled one had been adopted; the precipice was habitable.

Gwynplaine had seen a brilliant light descending on him, in an arrangement of destiny which seemed to put, in the perspective of a dream, a white cloud of beauty having the form of a woman, a radiant vision in which there was a heart; and the phantom, almost a cloud and yet a woman, clasped him; and the apparition embraced him; and the heart desired him. Gwynplaine was no longer deformed. He was beloved. The rose demanded the caterpillar in marriage, feeling that within the caterpillar there was a divine butterfly. Gwynplaine the rejected was chosen. To have one's desire is everything. Gwynplaine had his, Dea hers.

The abjection of the disfigured man was exalted and dilated into intoxication, into delight, into belief; and a hand was stretched out towards the melancholy hesitation of the blind girl, to guide her in her darkness.

It was the penetration of two misfortunes into the ideal which absorbed them. The rejected found a refuge in each other. Two blanks, combining, filled each other up. They held together by what they lacked: in that in which one was poor, the other was rich. The misfortune of the one made the treasure of the other. Had Dea not been blind, would she have chosen Gwynplaine? Had Gwynplaine not been disfigured, would he have preferred Dea? She would probably have rejected the deformed, as he would have passed by the infirm. What happiness for Dea that Gwynplaine was hideous! What good fortune for Gwynplaine that Dea was blind! Apart from their providential matching, they were impossible to each other. A mighty want of each other was at the bottom of their loves, Gwynplaine saved Dea. Dea saved Gwynplaine. Apposition of misery produced adherence. It was the embrace of those swallowed in the abyss; none closer, none more hopeless, none more exquisite.

Gwynplaine had a thought—"What should I be without her?" Dea had a thought—"What should I be without him?" The exile of each made a country for both. The two incurable fatalities, the stigmata of Gwynplaine and the blindness of Dea, joined them together in contentment. They sufficed to each other. They imagined nothing beyond each other. To speak to one another was a delight, to approach was beatitude; by force of reciprocal intuition they became united in the same reverie, and thought the same thoughts. In Gwynplaine's tread Dea believed that she heard the step of one deified. They tightened their mutual grasp in a sort of sidereal *chiaroscuro*, full of perfumes, of gleams, of music, of the luminous architecture of dreams. They belonged to each other; they knew themselves to be for ever united in the same joy and the same ecstasy; and nothing could be stranger than this construction of an Eden by two of the damned.

They were inexpressibly happy. In their hell they had created heaven. Such was thy power, O Love! Dea heard Gwynplaine's laugh; Gwynplaine saw Dea's smile. Thus ideal felicity was found, the perfect joy of life was realized, the mysterious problem of happiness was solved; and by whom? By two outcasts.

For Gwynplaine, Dea was splendour. For Dea, Gwynplaine was presence. Presence is that profound mystery which renders the invisible world divine, and from which results that other mystery—confidence. In religions this is the only thing which is irreducible; but this irreducible thing suffices. The great motive power is not seen; it is felt.

Gwynplaine was the religion of Dea. Sometimes, lost in her sense of love towards him, she knelt, like a beautiful priestess before a gnome in a pagoda, made happy by her adoration.

Imagine to yourself an abyss, and in its centre an oasis of light, and in this oasis two creatures shut out of life, dazzling each other. No purity could be compared to their loves. Dea was ignorant what a kiss might be, though perhaps she desired it; because blindness, especially in a woman, has its dreams, and though trembling at the approaches of the unknown, does not fear them all. As to Gwynplaine, his sensitive youth made him pensive. The more delirious he felt, the more timid he became. He might have dared anything with this companion of his early youth, with this creature as innocent of fault as of the light, with this blind girl who saw but one thing—that she adored him! But he would have thought it a theft to take what she might have given; so he resigned himself with a melancholy satisfaction to love angelically, and the conviction of his deformity resolved itself into a proud purity.

These happy creatures dwelt in the ideal. They were spouses in it at distances as opposite as the spheres. They exchanged in its firmament the deep effluvium which is in infinity attraction, and on earth the sexes. Their kisses were the kisses of souls.

They had always lived a common life. They knew themselves only in each other's society. The infancy of Dea had coincided with the youth of Gwynplaine. They had grown up side by side. For a long time they had slept in the same bed, for the hut was not a large bedchamber. They lay on the chest, Ursus on the floor; that was the arrangement. One fine day, whilst Dea was still very little, Gwynplaine felt himself grown up, and it was in the youth that shame arose. He said to Ursus, "I will also sleep on the floor." And at night he stretched himself, with the old man, on the bear skin. Then Dea wept. She cried for her bed-fellow; but Gwynplaine, become restless because he had begun to love, decided to remain where he was. From that time he always slept by the side of Ursus on the planks. In the summer, when the nights were fine, he slept outside with Homo.

When thirteen, Dea had not yet become resigned to the arrangement. Often in the evening she said, "Gwynplaine, come close to me; that will put me to sleep." A man lying by her side was a necessity to her innocent slumbers.

Nudity is to see that one is naked. She ignored nudity. It was the ingenuousness of Arcadia or Otaheite. Dea untaught made Gwynplaine wild. Sometimes it happened that Dea, when almost reaching youth, combed her long hair as she sat on her bed—her chemise unfastened and falling off revealed indications of a feminine outline, and a vague commencement of Eve—and would call Gwynplaine. Gwynplaine blushed, lowered his eyes, and knew not what to do in presence of this innocent creature. Stammering, he turned his head, feared, and fled. The Daphnis of darkness took flight before the Chloe of shadow.

Such was the idyll blooming in a tragedy.

Ursus said to them,—"Old brutes, adore each other!"

CHAPTER VI.

URSUS AS TUTOR, AND URSUS AS GUARDIAN

Ursus added,—

"Some of these days I will play them a nasty trick. I will marry them."

Ursus taught Gwynplaine the theory of love. He said to him,—

"Do you know how the Almighty lights the fire called love? He places the woman underneath, the devil between, and the man at the top. A match—that is to say, a look—and behold, it is all on fire."

"A look is unnecessary," answered Gwynplaine, thinking of Dea.

And Ursus replied,—

"Booby! Do souls require mortal eyes to see each other?"

Ursus was a good fellow at times. Gwynplaine, sometimes madly in love with Dea, became melancholy, and made use of the presence of Ursus as a guard on himself. One day Ursus said to him,—

"Bah! do not put yourself out. When in love, the cock shows himself."

"But the eagle conceals himself," replied Gwynplaine.

At other times Ursus would say to himself, apart,—

"It is wise to put spokes in the wheels of the Cytherean car. They love each other too much. This may have its disadvantages. Let us avoid a fire. Let us moderate these hearts."

Then Ursus had recourse to warnings of this nature, speaking to Gwynplaine when Dea slept, and to Dea when Gwynplaine's back was turned:—

"Dea, you must not be so fond of Gwynplaine. To live in the life of another is perilous. Egoism is a good root of happiness. Men escape from women. And then Gwynplaine might end by becoming infatuated with you. His success is so great! You have no idea how great his success is!"

"Gwynplaine, disproportions are no good. So much ugliness on one side and so much beauty on another ought to compel reflection. Temper your ardour, my boy. Do not become too enthusiastic about Dea. Do you seriously consider that you are made for her? Just think of your deformity and her perfection! See the distance between her and yourself. She has everything, this Dea. What a white skin! What hair! Lips like strawberries! And her foot! her hand! Those shoulders, with their exquisite curve! Her expression is sublime. She walks diffusing light; and in speaking, the grave tone of her voice is charming. But for all this, to think that she is a woman! She would not be such a fool as to be an angel. She is absolute beauty. Repeat all this to yourself, to calm your ardour."

These speeches redoubled the love of Gwynplaine and Dea, and Ursus was astonished at his want of success, just as one who should say, "It is singular that with all the oil I throw on fire I cannot extinguish it."

Did he, then, desire to extinguish their love, or to cool it even?

Certainly not. He would have been well punished had he succeeded. At the bottom of his heart this love, which was flame for them and warmth for him, was his delight.

But it is natural to grate a little against that which charms us; men call it wisdom.

Ursus had been, in his relations with Gwynplaine and Dea, almost a father and a mother. Grumbling all the while, he had brought them up; grumbling all the while, he had nourished them. His adoption of them had made the hut roll more heavily, and he had been oftener compelled to harness himself by Homo's side to help to draw it.

We may observe, however, that after the first few years, when Gwynplaine was nearly grown up, and Ursus had grown quite old, Gwynplaine had taken his turn, and drawn Ursus.

Ursus, seeing that Gwynplaine was becoming a man, had cast the horoscope of his deformity. "*It has made your fortune!*" he had told him.

This family of an old man and two children, with a wolf, had become, as they wandered, a group more and more intimately united. There errant life had not hindered education. "To wander is to grow," Ursus said. Gwynplaine was evidently made to exhibit at fairs. Ursus had cultivated in him feats of dexterity, and had encrusted him as much as possible with all he himself possessed of science and wisdom.

Ursus, contemplating the perplexing mask of Gwynplaine's face, often growled,—

"He has begun well." It was for this reason that he had perfected him with every ornament of philosophy and wisdom.

He repeated constantly to Gwynplaine,—

"Be a philosopher. To be wise is to be invulnerable. You see what I am, I have never shed a tears. This is the result of my wisdom. Do you think that occasion for tears has been wanting, had I felt disposed to weep?"

Ursus, in one of his monologues in the hearing of the wolf, said,—

"I have taught Gwynplaine everything, Latin included. I have taught Dea nothing, music included."

He had taught them both to sing. He had himself a pretty talent for playing on the oaten reed, a little flute of that period. He played on it agreeably, as also on the *chiffonie*, a sort of beggar's hurdy-gurdy, mentioned in the Chronicle of Bertrand Duguesclin as the "truant instrument," which started the symphony. These instruments attracted the crowd. Ursus would show them the chiffonie, and say, "It is called organistrum in Latin."

He had taught Dea and Gwynplaine to sing, according to the method of Orpheus and of Egide Binchois. Frequently he interrupted the lessons with cries of enthusiasm, such as "Orpheus, musician of Greece! Binchois, musician of Picardy!"

These branches of careful culture did not occupy the children so as to prevent their adoring each other. They had mingled their hearts together as they grew up, as two saplings planted near mingle their branches as they become trees.

"No matter," said Ursus. "I will marry them."

Then he grumbled to himself,—

"They are quite tiresome with their love."

The past—their little past, at least—had no existence for Dea and Gwynplaine. They knew only what Ursus had told them of it. They called Ursus father. The only remembrance which Gwynplaine had of his infancy was as of a passage of demons over his cradle. He had an impression of having been trodden in the darkness under deformed feet. Was this intentional or not? He was ignorant on this point. That which he remembered clearly and to the slightest detail were his tragical adventures when deserted at Portland. The finding of Dea made that dismal night a radiant date for him.

The memory of Dea, even more than that of Gwynplaine, was lost in clouds. In so young a child all remembrance melts away. She recollected her mother as something cold. Had she ever seen the sun? Perhaps so. She made efforts to pierce into the blank which was her past life.

"The sun!—what was it?"

She had some vague memory of a thing luminous and warm, of which Gwynplaine had taken the place.

They spoke to each other in low tones. It is certain that cooing is the most important thing in the world. Dea often said to Gwynplaine,—

"Light means that you are speaking."

Once, no longer containing himself, as he saw through a muslin sleeve the arm of Dea, Gwynplaine brushed its transparency with his lips—ideal kiss of a deformed mouth! Dea felt a deep delight; she blushed like a rose. This kiss from a monster made Aurora gleam on that beautiful brow full of night. However, Gwynplaine sighed with a kind of terror, and as the neckerchief of Dea gaped, he could not refrain from looking at the whiteness visible through that glimpse of Paradise.

Dea pulled up her sleeve, and stretching towards Gwynplaine her naked arm, said,—

"Again!"

Gwynplaine fled.

The next day the game was renewed, with variations.

It was a heavenly subsidence into that sweet abyss called love.

At such things heaven smiles philosophically.

CHAPTER VII.

BLINDNESS GIVES LESSONS IN CLAIRVOYANCE

At times Gwynplaine reproached himself. He made his happiness a case of conscience. He fancied that to allow a woman who could not see him to love him was to deceive her.

What would she have said could she have suddenly obtained her sight? How she would have felt repulsed by what had previously attracted her! How she would have recoiled from her frightful loadstone! What a cry! What covering of her face! What a flight! A bitter scruple harassed him. He told himself that such a monster as he had no right to love. He was a hydra idolized by a star. It was his duty to enlighten the blind star.

One day he said to Dea,—

"You know that I am very ugly."

"I know that you are sublime," she answered.

He resumed,—

"When you hear all the world laugh, they laugh at me because I am horrible."

"I love you," said Dea.

After a silence, she added,—

"I was in death; you brought me to life. When you are here, heaven is by my side. Give me your hand, that I may touch heaven."

Their hands met and grasped each other. They spoke no more, but were silent in the plenitude of love.

Ursus, who was crabbed, had overheard this. The next day, when the three were together, he said,—

"For that matter, Dea is ugly also."

The word produced no effect. Dea and Gwynplaine were not listening. Absorbed in each other, they rarely heeded such exclamations of Ursus. Their depth was a dead loss.

This time, however, the precaution of Ursus, "Dea is also ugly," indicated in this learned man a certain knowledge of women. It is certain that Gwynplaine, in his loyalty, had been guilty of an imprudence. To have said, *I am ugly*, to any other blind girl than Dea might have been dangerous. To be blind, and in love, is to be twofold blind. In such a situation dreams are dreamt. Illusion is the food of dreams. Take illusion from love, and you take from it its aliment. It is compounded of every enthusiasm, of both physical and moral admiration.

Moreover, you should never tell a woman a word difficult to understand. She will dream about it, and she often dreams falsely. An enigma in a reverie spoils it. The shock caused by the fall of a careless word displaces that against which it strikes. At times it happens, without our knowing why, that because we have received the obscure blow of a chance word the heart empties itself insensibly of love. He who loves perceives a decline in his happiness. Nothing is to be feared more than this slow exudation from the fissure in the vase.

Happily, Dea was not formed of such clay. The stuff of which other women are made had not been used in her construction. She had a rare nature. The frame, but not the heart, was fragile. A divine perseverance in love was in the heart of her being.

The whole disturbance which the word used by Gwynplaine had produced in her ended in her saying one day,—

"To be ugly—what is it? It is to do wrong. Gwynplaine only does good. He is handsome."

Then, under the form of interrogation so familiar to children and to the blind, she resumed,—

"To see—what is it that you call seeing? For my own part, I cannot see; I know. It seems that *to see* means to hide."

"What do you mean?" said Gwynplaine.

Dea answered,—

"To see is a thing which conceals the true."

"No," said Gwynplaine.

"But yes," replied Dea, "since you say you are ugly."

She reflected a moment, and then said, "Story-teller!"

Gwynplaine felt the joy of having confessed and of not being believed. Both his conscience and his love were consoled.

Thus they had reached, Dea sixteen, Gwynplaine nearly twenty-five. They were not, as it would now be expressed, "more advanced" than the first day. Less even; for it may be remembered that on their wedding night she was nine months and he ten years old. A sort of holy childhood had continued in their love. Thus it sometimes happens that the belated nightingale prolongs her nocturnal song till dawn.

Their caresses went no further than pressing hands, or lips brushing a naked arm. Soft, half-articulate whispers sufficed them.

Twenty-four and sixteen! So it happened that Ursus, who did not lose sight of the ill turn he intended to do them, said,—

"One of these days you must choose a religion."

"Wherefore?" inquired Gwynplaine.

"That you may marry."

"That is already done," said Dea.

Dea did not understand that they could be more man and wife than they were already.

At bottom, this chimerical and virginal content, this innocent union of souls, this celibacy taken for marriage, was not displeasing to Ursus.

Besides, were they not already married? If the indissoluble existed anywhere, was it not in their union? Gwynplaine and Dea! They were creatures worthy of the love they mutually felt, flung by misfortune into each other's arms. And as if they were not enough in this first link, love had survened on misfortune, and had attached them, united and bound them together. What power could ever break that iron chain, bound with knots of flowers? They were indeed bound together.

Dea had beauty, Gwynplaine had sight. Each brought a dowry. They were more than coupled—they were paired: separated solely by the sacred interposition of innocence.

Though dream as Gwynplaine would, however, and absorb all meaner passions as he could in the contemplation of Dea and before the tribunal of conscience, he was a man. Fatal laws are not to be eluded. He underwent, like everything else in nature, the obscure fermentations willed by the Creator. At times, therefore, he looked at the women who were in the crowd, but he immediately felt that the look was a sin, and hastened to retire, repentant, into his own soul.

Let us add that he met with no encouragement. On the face of every woman who looked upon him he saw aversion antipathy, repugnance, and rejection. It was clear that no other than Dea was possible for him. This aided his repentance.

CHAPTER VIII.

NOT ONLY HAPPINESS, BUT PROSPERITY

What true things are told in stories! The burnt scar of the invisible fiend who has touched you is remorse for a wicked thought. In Gwynplaine evil thoughts never ripened, and he had therefore no remorse. Sometimes he felt regret.

Vague mists of conscience.

What was this?

Nothing.

Their happiness was complete—so complete that they were no longer even poor.

From 1680 to 1704 a great change had taken place.

It happened sometimes, in the year 1704, that as night fell on some little village on the coast, a great, heavy van, drawn by a pair of stout horses, made its entry. It was like the shell of a vessel reversed—the keel for a roof, the deck for a floor, placed on four wheels. The wheels were all of the same size, and high as wagon wheels. Wheels, pole, and van were all painted green, with a rhythmical gradation of shades, which ranged from bottle green for the wheels to apple green for the roofing. This green colour had succeeded in drawing attention to the carriage, which was known in all the fair grounds as The Green Box. The Green Box had but two windows, one at each extremity, and at the back a door with steps to let down. On the roof, from a tube painted green like the rest, smoke arose. This moving house was always varnished and washed afresh. In front, on a ledge fastened to the van, with the window for a door, behind the horses and by the side of an old man who held the reins and directed the team, two gipsy women, dressed as goddesses, sounded their trumpets. The astonishment with which the villagers regarded this machine was overwhelming.

This was the old establishment of Ursus, its proportions augmented by success, and improved from a wretched booth into a theatre. A kind of animal, between dog and wolf, was chained under the van. This was Homo. The old coachman who drove the horses was the philosopher himself.

Whence came this improvement from the miserable hut to the Olympic caravan?

From this—Gwynplaine had become famous.

It was with a correct scent of what would succeed amongst men that Ursus had said to Gwynplaine,—

"They made your fortune."

Ursus, it may be remembered, had made Gwynplaine his pupil. Unknown people had worked upon his face; he, on the other hand, had worked on his mind, and behind this well-executed mask he had placed all that he could of thought. So soon as the growth of the child had rendered him fitted for it, he had brought him out on the stage—that is, he had produced him in front of the van.

The effect of his appearance had been surprising. The passers-by were immediately struck with wonder. Never had anything been seen to be compared to this extraordinary mimic of laughter. They were ignorant how the miracle of infectious hilarity had been obtained. Some believed it to be natural, others declared it to be artificial, and as conjecture was added to reality, everywhere, at every cross-road on the journey, in all the grounds of fairs and fêtes, the crowd ran after Gwynplaine. Thanks to this great attraction, there had come into the poor purse of the wandering group, first a rain of farthings, then of heavy pennies, and finally of shillings. The curiosity of one place exhausted, they passed on to another. Rolling does not enrich a stone but it enriches a caravan; and year by year, from city to city, with the increased growth of Gwynplaine's person and of his ugliness, the fortune predicted by Ursus had come.

"What a good turn they did you there, my boy!" said Ursus.

This "fortune" had allowed Ursus, who was the administrator of Gwynplaine's success, to have the chariot of his dreams constructed—that is to say, a caravan large enough to carry a theatre, and to sow science and art in the highways. Moreover, Ursus had been able to add to the group composed of himself, Homo, Gwynplaine, and Dea, two horses and two women, who were the goddesses of the troupe, as we have just said, and its servants. A mythological frontispiece was, in those days, of service to a caravan of mountebanks.

"We are a wandering temple," said Ursus.

These two gipsies, picked up by the philosopher from amongst the vagabondage of cities and suburbs, were ugly and young, and were called, by order of Ursus, the one Phoebe, and the other Venus.

For these read Fibi and Vinos, that we may conform to English pronunciation.

Phoebe cooked; Venus scrubbed the temple.

Moreover, on days of performance they dressed Dea.

Mountebanks have their public life as well as princes, and on these occasions Dea was arrayed, like Fibi and Vinos, in a Florentine petticoat of flowered stuff, and a woman's jacket without sleeves, leaving the arms bare. Ursus and Gwynplaine wore men's jackets, and, like sailors on board a man-of-war, great loose trousers. Gwynplaine had, besides, for his work and for his feats of strength, round his neck and over his shoulders, an esclavine of leather. He took charge of the horses. Ursus and Homo took charge of each other.

Dea, being used to the Green Box, came and went in the interior of the wheeled house, with almost as much ease and certainty as those who saw.

The eye which could penetrate within this structure and its internal arrangements might have perceived in a corner, fastened to the planks, and immovable on its four wheels, the old hut of Ursus, placed on half-pay, allowed to rust, and from thenceforth dispensed the labour of rolling as Ursus was relieved from the labour of drawing it.

This hut, in a corner at the back, to the right of the door, served as bedchamber and dressing-room to Ursus and Gwynplaine. It now contained two beds. In the opposite corner was the kitchen.

The arrangement of a vessel was not more precise and concise than that of the interior of the Green Box. Everything within it was in its place—arranged, foreseen, and intended.

The caravan was divided into three compartments, partitioned from each other. These communicated by open spaces without doors. A piece of stuff fell over them, and answered the purpose of concealment. The compartment behind belonged to the men, the compartment in front to the women; the compartment in the middle, separating the two sexes, was the stage. The instruments of the orchestra and the properties were kept in the kitchen. A loft under the arch of the roof contained the scenes, and on opening a trap-door lamps appeared, producing wonders of light.

Ursus was the poet of these magical representations; he wrote the pieces. He had a diversity of talents; he was clever at sleight of hand. Besides the voices he imitated, he produced all sorts of unexpected things—shocks of light and darkness; spontaneous formations of figures or words, as he willed, on the partition; vanishing figures in chiaroscuro; strange things, amidst which he seemed to meditate, unmindful of the crowd who marvelled at him.

One day Gwynplaine said to him,—

"Father, you look like a sorcerer!"

And Ursus replied,—

"Then I look, perhaps, like what I am."

The Green Box, built on a clear model of Ursus's, contained this refinement of ingenuity—that between the fore and hind wheels the central panel of the left side turned on hinges by the aid of chains and pulleys, and could be let down at will like a drawbridge. As it dropped it set at liberty three legs on hinges, which supported the panel when let down, and which placed themselves straight on the ground like the legs of a table, and supported it above the earth like a platform. This exposed the stage, which was thus enlarged by the platform in front.

This opening looked for all the world like a "mouth of hell," in the words of the itinerant Puritan preachers, who turned away from it with horror. It was, perhaps, for some such pious invention that Solon kicked out Thespis.

For all that Thespis has lasted much longer than is generally believed. The travelling theatre is still in existence. It was on those stages on wheels that, in the sixteenth and seventeenth centuries, they performed in England the ballets and dances of Amner and Pilkington; in France, the pastorals of Gilbert Colin; in Flanders, at the annual fairs, the double choruses of Clement, called Non Papa; in Germany, the "Adam and Eve" of Theiles; and, in Italy, the Venetian exhibitions of Animuccia and of Cafossis, the "Silvæ" of Gesualdo, the "Prince of Venosa," the "Satyr" of Laura Guidiccioni, the "Despair of Philene," the "Death of Ugolina," by Vincent Galileo, father of the astronomer, which Vincent Galileo sang his own music, and accompanied himself on his *viol de gamba;* as well as all the first attempts of the Italian opera which, from 1580, substituted free inspiration for the madrigal style.

The chariot, of the colour of hope, which carried Ursus, Gwynplaine, and their fortunes, and in front of which Fibi and Vinos trumpeted like figures of Fame, played its part of this grand Bohemian and literary brotherhood. Thespis would no more have disowned Ursus than Congrio would have disowned Gwynplaine.

Arrived at open spaces in towns or villages, Ursus, in the intervals between the too-tooing of Fibi and Vinos, gave instructive revelations as to the trumpetings.

"This symphony is Gregorian," he would exclaim. "Citizens and townsmen, the Gregorian form of worship, this great progress, is opposed in Italy to the Ambrosial ritual, and in Spain to the Mozarabic ceremonial, and has achieved its triumph over them with difficulty."

After which the Green Box drew up in some place chosen by Ursus, and evening having fallen, and the panel stage having been let down, the theatre opened, and the performance began.

The scene of the Green Box represented a landscape painted by Ursus; and as he did not know how to paint, it represented a cavern just as well as a landscape. The curtain, which we call drop nowadays, was a checked silk, with squares of contrasted colours.

The public stood without, in the street, in the fair, forming a semicircle round the stage, exposed to the sun and the showers; an arrangement which made rain less desirable for theatres in those days than now. When they could, they acted in an inn yard, on which occasions the windows of the different stories made rows of boxes for the spectators. The theatre was thus more enclosed, and the audience a more paying one. Ursus was in everything—in the piece, in the company, in the kitchen, in the orchestra. Vinos beat the drum, and handled the sticks with great dexterity. Fibi played on the *morache*, a kind of guitar. The wolf had been promoted to be a utility gentleman, and played, as occasion required, his little parts. Often when they appeared side by side on the stage—Ursus in his tightly-laced bear's skin, Homo with his wolf's skin fitting still better—no one could tell which was the beast. This flattered Ursus.

CHAPTER IX.

ABSURDITIES WHICH FOLKS WITHOUT TASTE CALL POETRY

The pieces written by Ursus were interludes—a kind of composition out of fashion nowadays. One of these pieces, which has not come down to us, was entitled "Ursus Rursus." It is probable that he played the principal part himself. A pretended exit, followed by a reappearance, was apparently its praiseworthy and sober subject. The titles of the interludes of Ursus were sometimes Latin, as we have seen, and the poetry frequently Spanish. The Spanish verses written by Ursus were rhymed, as was nearly all the Castilian poetry of that period. This did not puzzle the people. Spanish was then a familiar language; and the English sailors spoke Castilian even as the Roman sailors spoke Carthaginian (see Plautus). Moreover, at a theatrical representation, as at mass, Latin, or any other language unknown to the audience, is by no means a subject of care with them. They get out of the dilemma by adapting to the sounds familiar words. Our old Gallic France was particularly prone to this manner of being devout. At church, under cover of an *Immolatus*, the faithful chanted, "I will make merry;" and under a *Sanctus*, "Kiss me, sweet."

The Council of Trent was required to put an end to these familiarities.

Ursus had composed expressly for Gwynplaine an interlude, with which he was well pleased. It was his best work. He had thrown his whole soul into it. To give the sum of all one's talents in the production is the greatest triumph that any one can achieve. The toad which produces a toad achieves a grand success. You doubt it? Try, then, to do as much.

Ursus had carefully polished this interlude. This bear's cub was entitled "Chaos Vanquished." Here it was:—A night scene. When the curtain drew up, the crowd, massed around the Green Box, saw nothing but blackness. In this blackness three confused forms moved in the reptile state—wolf, a bear, and a man. The wolf acted the wolf; Ursus, the bear; Gwynplaine, the man. The wolf and the bear represented the ferocious forces of Nature—unreasoning hunger and savage ignorance. Both rushed on Gwynplaine. It was chaos combating man. No face could be distinguished. Gwynplaine fought infolded, in a winding-sheet, and his face was covered by his thickly-falling locks. All else was shadow. The bear growled, the wolf gnashed his teeth, the man cried out. The man was down; the beasts overwhelmed him. He cried for aid and succour; he hurled to the unknown an agonized appeal. He gave a death-rattle. To witness this agony of the prostrate man, now scarcely distinguishable from the brutes, was appalling. The crowd looked on breathless; in one minute more the wild beasts would triumph, and chaos reabsorb man. A struggle—cries—howlings; then, all at once, silence.

A song in the shadows. A breath had passed, and they heard a voice. Mysterious music floated, accompanying this chant of the invisible; and suddenly, none knowing whence or how, a white apparition arose. This apparition was a light; this light was a woman; this woman was a spirit. Dea—calm, fair, beautiful, formidable in her serenity and sweetness—appeared in the centre of a luminous mist. A profile of brightness in a dawn! She was a voice—a voice light, deep, indescribable. She sang in the new-born light—she, invisible, made visible. They thought that they heard the hymn of an angel or the song of a bird. At this apparition the man, starting up in his ecstasy, struck the beasts with his fists, and overthrew them.

Then the vision, gliding along in a manner difficult to understand, and therefore the more admired, sang these words in Spanish sufficiently pure for the English sailors who were present:—

"Ora! llora!
De palabra
Nace razon.
De luz el son."[13]

Then looking down, as if she saw a gulf beneath, she went on,—

"Noche, quita te de alli!
El alba canta hallali."[14]

As she sang, the man raised himself by degrees; instead of lying he was now kneeling, his hands elevated towards the vision, his knees resting on the beasts, which lay motionless, and as if thunder-stricken.

She continued, turning towards him,—

"Es menester a cielos ir,
Y tu que llorabas reir."[15]

And approaching him with the majesty of a star, she added,—

"Gebra barzon;
Deja, monstruo,
A tu negro
Caparazon."[16]

And she put hot hand on his brow. Then another voice arose, deeper, and consequently still sweeter—a voice broken and enwrapt with a gravity both tender and wild. It was the human chant responding to the chant of the stars. Gwynplaine, still in obscurity, his head under Dea's hand, and kneeling on the vanquished bear and wolf, sang,—

"O ven! ama!
Eres alma,
Soy corazon."[17]

And suddenly from the shadow a ray of light fell full upon Gwynplaine. Then, through the darkness, was the monster full exposed.

To describe the commotion of the crowd is impossible.

A sun of laughter rising, such was the effect. Laughter springs from unexpected causes, and nothing could be more unexpected than this termination. Never was sensation comparable to that produced by the ray of light striking on that mask, at once ludicrous and terrible. They laughed all around his laugh. Everywhere—above, below, behind, before, at the uttermost distance; men, women, old gray-heads, rosy-faced children; the good, the wicked, the gay, the sad, everybody. And even in the streets, the passers-by who could see nothing, hearing the laughter, laughed also. The laughter ended in clapping of hands and stamping of feet. The curtain dropped: Gwynplaine was recalled with frenzy. Hence an immense success. Have you seen "Chaos Vanquished?" Gwynplaine was run after. The listless came to laugh, the melancholy came to laugh, evil consciences came to laugh—a laugh so irresistible that it seemed almost an epidemic. But there is a pestilence from which men do not fly, and that is the contagion of joy. The success, it must be admitted, did not rise higher than the populace. A great crowd means a crowd of nobodies. "Chaos Vanquished" could be seen for a penny. Fashionable people never go where the price of admission is a penny.

Ursus thought a good deal of his work, which he had brooded over for a long time. "It is in the style of one Shakespeare," he said modestly.

The juxtaposition of Dea added to the indescribable effect produced by Gwynplaine. Her white face by the side of the gnome represented what might have been called divine astonishment. The audience regarded Dea with a sort of mysterious anxiety. She had in her aspect the dignity of a virgin and of a priestess, not knowing man and knowing God. They saw that she was blind, and felt that she could see. She seemed to stand on the threshold of the supernatural. The light that beamed on her seemed half earthly and half heavenly. She had come to work on earth, and to work as heaven works, in the radiance of morning. Finding a hydra, she formed a soul. She seemed like a creative power, satisfied but astonished at the result of her creation; and the audience fancied that they could see in the divine surprise of that face desire of the cause and wonder at the result. They felt that she loved this monster. Did she know that he was one? Yes; since she touched him. No; since she accepted him. This depth of night and this glory of day united, formed in the mind of the spectator a chiaroscuro in which appeared endless perspectives. How much divinity exists in the germ, in what manner the penetration of the soul into matter is accomplished, how the solar ray is an umbilical cord, how the disfigured is transfigured, how the deformed becomes heavenly—all these glimpses of mysteries added an almost cosmical emotion to the convulsive hilarity produced by Gwynplaine. Without going too deep—for spectators do not like the fatigue of seeking below the surface—something more was understood than was perceived. And this strange spectacle had the transparency of an avatar.

As to Dea, what she felt cannot be expressed by human words. She knew that she was in the midst of a crowd, and knew not what a crowd was. She heard a murmur, that was all. For her the crowd was but a breath. Generations are passing breaths. Man respires, aspires, and expires. In that crowd Dea felt herself alone, and shuddering as one hanging over a precipice. Suddenly, in this trouble of innocence in distress, prompt to accuse the unknown, in her dread of a possible fall, Dea, serene notwithstanding, and superior to the vague agonies of peril, but inwardly shuddering at her isolation, found confidence and support. She had seized her thread of safety in the universe of shadows; she put her hand on the powerful head of Gwynplaine.

Joy unspeakable! she placed her rosy fingers on his forest of crisp hair. Wool when touched gives an impression of softness. Dea touched a lamb which she knew to be a lion. Her whole heart poured out an ineffable love. She felt out of danger—she had found her saviour. The public believed that they saw the contrary. To the spectators the being loved was Gwynplaine, and the saviour was Dea. What matters? thought Ursus, to whom the heart of Dea was visible. And Dea, reassured, consoled and delighted, adored the angel whilst the people contemplated the monster, and endured, fascinated herself as well, though in the opposite sense, that dread Promethean laugh.

True love is never weary. Being all soul it cannot cool. A brazier comes to be full of cinders; not so a star. Her exquisite impressions were renewed every evening for Dea, and she was ready to weep with tenderness whilst the audience was in convulsions of laughter. Those around her were but joyful; she was happy.

The sensation of gaiety due to the sudden shock caused by the rictus of Gwynplaine was evidently not intended by Ursus. He would have preferred more smiles and less laughter, and more of a literary triumph. But success consoles. He reconciled himself every evening to his excessive triumph, as he counted how many shillings the piles of farthings made, and how many pounds the piles of shillings; and besides, he said, after all, when the laugh had passed, "Chaos Vanquished" would be found in the depths of their minds, and something of it would remain there.

Perhaps he was not altogether wrong: the foundations of a work settle down in the mind of the public. The truth is, that the populace, attentive to the wolf, the bear, to the man, then to the music, to the howlings governed by harmony, to the night dissipated by dawn, to the chant releasing the light, accepted with a confused, dull sympathy, and with a certain emotional respect, the dramatic poem of "Chaos Vanquished," the victory of spirit over matter, ending with the joy of man.

Such were the vulgar pleasures of the people.

They sufficed them. The people had not the means of going to the noble matches of the gentry, and could not, like lords and gentlemen, bet a thousand guineas on Helmsgail against Phelem-ghe-madone.

CHAPTER X.

AN OUTSIDER'S VIEW OF MEN AND THINGS

Man has a notion of revenging himself on that which pleases him. Hence the contempt felt for the comedian.

This being charms me, diverts, distracts, teaches, enchants, consoles me; flings me into an ideal world, is agreeable and useful to me. What evil can I do him in return? Humiliate him. Disdain is a blow from afar. Let us strike the blow. He pleases me, therefore he is vile. He serves me, therefore I hate him. Where can I find a stone to throw at him? Priest, give me yours. Philosopher, give me yours. Bossuet, excommunicate him. Rousseau, insult him. Orator, spit the pebbles from your mouth at him. Bear, fling your stone. Let us cast stones at the tree, hit the fruit and eat it. "Bravo!" and "Down with him!" To repeat poetry is to be infected with the plague. Wretched playactor, we will put him in the pillory for his success. Let him follow up his triumph with our hisses. Let him collect a crowd and create a solitude. Thus it is that the wealthy, termed the higher classes, have invented for the actor that form of isolation, applause.

The crowd is less brutal. They neither hated nor despised Gwynplaine. Only the meanest calker of the meanest crew of the meanest merchantman, anchored in the meanest English seaport, considered himself immeasurably superior to this amuser of the "scum," and believed that a calker is as superior to an actor as a lord is to a calker.

Gwynplaine was, therefore, like all comedians, applauded and kept at a distance. Truly, all success in this world is a crime, and must be expiated. He who obtains the medal has to take its reverse side as well.

For Gwynplaine there was no reverse. In this sense, both sides of his medal pleased him. He was satisfied with the applause, and content with the isolation. In applause he was rich, in isolation happy.

To be rich in his low estate means to be no longer wretchedly poor—to have neither holes in his clothes, nor cold at his hearth, nor emptiness in his stomach. It is to eat when hungry and drink when thirsty. It is to have everything necessary, including a penny for a beggar. This indigent wealth, enough for liberty, was possessed by Gwynplaine. So far as his soul was concerned, he was opulent. He had love. What more could he want? Nothing.

You may think that had the offer been made to him to remove his deformity he would have grasped at it. Yet he would have refused it emphatically. What! to throw off his mask and have his former face restored; to be the creature he had perchance been created, handsome and charming? No, he would never have consented to it. For what would he have to support Dea? What would have become of that poor child, the sweet blind girl who loved him? Without his rictus, which made him a clown without parallel, he would have been a mountebank, like any other; a common athlete, a picker up of pence from the chinks in the pavement, and Dea would perhaps not have had bread every day. It was with deep and tender pride that he felt himself the protector of the helpless and heavenly creature. Night, solitude, nakedness, weakness, ignorance, hunger, and thirst—seven yawning jaws of misery—were raised around her, and he was the St. George fighting the dragon. He triumphed over poverty. How? By his deformity. By his deformity he was useful, helpful, victorious, great. He had but to show himself, and money poured in. He was a master of crowds, the sovereign of the mob. He could do everything for Dea. Her wants he foresaw; her desires, her tastes, her fancies, in the limited sphere in which wishes are possible to the blind, he fulfilled. Gwynplaine and Dea were, as we have already shown, Providence to each other. He felt himself raised on her wings; she felt herself carried in his arms. To protect the being who loves you, to give what she requires to her who shines on you as your star, can anything be sweeter? Gwynplaine possessed this supreme happiness, and he owed it to his deformity. His deformity had raised him above all. By it he had gained the means of life for himself and others; by it he had gained independence, liberty, celebrity, internal satisfaction and pride. In his deformity he was inaccessible. The Fates could do nothing beyond this blow in which they had spent their whole force, and which he had turned into a triumph. This lowest depth of misfortune had become the summit of Elysium. Gwynplaine was imprisoned in his deformity, but with Dea. And this was, as we have already said, to live in a dungeon of paradise. A wall stood between them and the living world. So much the better. This wall protected as well as enclosed them. What could affect Dea, what could affect Gwynplaine, with such a fortress around them? To take from him his success was impossible. They would have had to deprive him of his face. Take from him his love. Impossible. Dea could not see him. The blindness of Dea was divinely incurable. What harm did his deformity do Gwynplaine? None. What advantage did it give him? Every advantage. He was beloved, notwithstanding its horror, and perhaps for that very cause. Infirmity and deformity had by instinct been drawn towards and coupled with each other. To be beloved, is not that everything? Gwynplaine thought of his disfigurement only with gratitude. He was blessed in the stigma. With joy he felt that it was irremediable and eternal. What a blessing that it was so! While there were highways and fairgrounds, and journeys to take, the people below and the sky above, they would be sure to live, Dea would want nothing, and they should have love. Gwynplaine would not have changed faces with Apollo. To be a monster was his form of happiness.

Thus, as we said before, destiny had given him all, even to overflowing. He who had been rejected had been preferred.

He was so happy that he felt compassion for the men around him. He pitied the rest of the world. It was, besides, his instinct to look about him, because no one is always consistent, and a man's nature is not always theoretic; he was delighted to live within an enclosure, but from time to time he lifted his head above the wall. Then he retreated again with more joy into his loneliness with Dea, having drawn his comparisons. What did he see around him?

What were those living creatures of which his wandering life showed him so many specimens, changed every day? Always new crowds, always the same multitude, ever new faces, ever the same miseries. A jumble of ruins. Every evening every phase of social misfortune came and encircled his happiness.

The Green Box was popular.

Low prices attract the low classes. Those who came were the weak, the poor, the little. They rushed to Gwynplaine as they rushed to gin. They came to buy a pennyworth of forgetfulness. From the height of his platform Gwynplaine passed those wretched people in review. His spirit was enwrapt in the contemplation of every succeeding apparition of widespread misery. The physiognomy of man is modelled by conscience, and by the tenor of life, and is the result of a crowd of mysterious excavations. There was never a suffering, not an anger, not a shame, not a despair, of which Gwynplaine did not see the wrinkle. The mouths of those children had not eaten. That man was a father, that woman a mother, and behind them their families might be guessed to be on the road to ruin. There was a face already marked by vice, on the threshold of crime, and the reasons were plain—ignorance and indigence. Another showed the stamp of original goodness, obliterated by social pressure, and turned to hate. On the face of an old woman he saw starvation; on that of a girl, prostitution. The same fact, and although the girl had the resource of her youth, all the sadder for that! In the crowd were arms without tools; the workers asked only for work, but the work was wanting. Sometimes a soldier came and seated himself by the workmen, sometimes a wounded pensioner; and Gwynplaine saw the spectre of war. Here Gwynplaine read want of work; there man-farming, slavery. On certain brows he saw an indescribable ebbing back towards animalism, and that slow return of man to beast, produced on those below by the dull pressure of the happiness of those above. There was a break in the gloom for Gwynplaine. He and Dea had a loophole of happiness; the rest was damnation. Gwynplaine felt above him the thoughtless trampling of the powerful, the rich, the magnificent, the great, the elect of chance. Below he saw the pale faces of the disinherited. He saw himself and Dea, with their little happiness, so great to themselves, between two worlds. That which was above went and came, free, joyous, dancing, trampling under foot; above him the world which treads, below the world which is trodden upon. It is a fatal fact, and one indicating a profound social evil, that light should crush the shadow! Gwynplaine thoroughly grasped this dark evil. What! a destiny so reptile? Shall a man drag himself thus along with such adherence to dust and corruption, with such vicious tastes, such an abdication of right, or such abjectness that one feels inclined to crush him under foot? Of what butterfly is, then, this earthly life the grub?

What! in the crowd which hungers and which denies everywhere, and before all, the questions of crime and shame (the inflexibility of the law producing laxity of conscience), is there no child that grows but to be stunted, no virgin but matures for sin, no rose that blooms but for the slime of the snail?

His eyes at times sought everywhere, with the curiosity of emotion, to probe the depths of that darkness, in which there died away so many useless efforts, and in which there struggled so much weariness: families devoured by society, morals tortured by the laws, wounds gangrened by penalties, poverty gnawed by taxes, wrecked intelligence swallowed up by ignorance, rafts in distress alive with the famished, feuds, dearth, death-rattles, cries, disappearances. He felt the vague oppression of a keen, universal suffering. He saw the vision of the foaming wave of misery dashing over the crowd of humanity. He was safe in port himself, as he watched the wreck around him. Sometimes he laid his disfigured head in his hands and dreamed.

What folly to be happy! How one dreams! Ideas were born within him. Absurd notions crossed his brain.

Because formerly he had succoured an infant, he felt a ridiculous desire to succour the whole world. The mists of reverie sometimes obscured his individuality, and he lost his ideas of proportion so far as to ask himself the question, "What can be done for the poor?" Sometimes he was so absorbed in his subject as to express it aloud. Then Ursus shrugged his shoulders and looked at him fixedly. Gwynplaine continued his reverie.

"Oh; were I powerful, would I not aid the wretched? But what am I? An atom. What can I do? Nothing."

He was mistaken. He was able to do a great deal for the wretched. He could make them laugh; and, as we have said, to make people laugh is to make them forget. What a benefactor on earth is he who can bestow forgetfulness!

CHAPTER XI.

GWYNPLAINE THINKS JUSTICE, AND URSUS TALKS TRUTH

A philosopher is a spy. Ursus, a watcher of dreams, studied his pupil.

Our monologues leave on our brows a faint reflection, distinguishable to the eye of a physiognomist. Hence what occurred to Gwynplaine did not escape Ursus. One day, as Gwynplaine was meditating, Ursus pulled him by his jacket, and exclaimed,—

"You strike me as being an observer! You fool! Take care; it is no business of yours. You have one thing to do—to love Dea. You have two causes of happiness—the first is, that the crowd sees your muzzle; the second is, that Dea does not. You have no right to the happiness you possess, for no woman who saw your mouth would consent to your kiss; and that mouth which has made your fortune, and that face which has given you riches, are not your own. You were not born with that countenance. It was borrowed from the grimace which is at the bottom of the infinite. You have stolen your mask from the devil. You are hideous; be satisfied with having drawn that prize in the lottery. There are in this world (and a very good thing too) the happy by right and the happy by luck. You are happy by luck. You are in a cave wherein a star is enclosed. The poor star belongs to you. Do not seek to leave the cave, and guard your star, O spider! You have in your web the carbuncle, Venus. Do me the favour to be satisfied. I see your dreams are troubled. It is idiotic of you. Listen; I am going to speak to you in the language of true poetry. Let Dea eat beefsteaks and mutton chops, and in six months she will be as strong as a Turk; marry her immediately, give her a child, two children, three children, a long string of children. That is what I call philosophy. Moreover, it is happiness, which is no folly. To have children is a glimpse of heaven. Have brats—wipe them, blow their noses, dirt them, wash them, and put them to bed. Let them swarm about you. If they laugh, it is well; if they howl, it is better—to cry is to live. Watch them suck at six months, crawl at a year, walk at two, grow tall at fifteen, fall in love at twenty. He who has these joys has everything For myself, I lacked the advantage; and that is the reason why I am a brute. God, a composer of beautiful poems and the first of men of letters, said to his fellow-workman, Moses, 'Increase and multiply.' Such is the text. Multiply, you beast! As to the world, it is as it is; you cannot make nor mar it. Do not trouble yourself about it. Pay no attention to what goes on outside. Leave the horizon alone. A comedian is made to be looked at, not to look. Do you know what there is outside? The happy by right. You, I repeat, are the happy by chance. You are the pickpocket of the happiness of which they are the proprietors. They are the legitimate possessors; you are the intruder. You live in concubinage with luck. What do you want that you have not already? Shibboleth help me! This fellow is a rascal. To multiply himself by Dea would be pleasant, all the same. Such happiness is like a swindle. Those above who possess happiness by privilege do not like folks below them to have so much enjoyment. If they ask you what right you have to be happy, you will not know what to answer. You have no patent, and they have. Jupiter, Allah, Vishnu, Sabaoth, it does not matter who, has given them the passport to happiness. Fear them. Do not meddle with them, lest they should meddle with you. Wretch! do you know what the man is who is happy by right? He is a terrible being. He is a lord. A lord! He must have intrigued pretty well in the devil's unknown country before he was born, to enter life by the door he did. How difficult it must have been to him to be born! It is the only trouble he has given himself; but, just heavens, what a one!—to obtain from destiny, the blind blockhead, to mark him in his cradle a master of men. To bribe the box-keeper to give him the best place at the show. Read the memoranda in the old hut, which I have placed on half-pay. Read that breviary of my wisdom, and you will see what it is to be a lord. A lord is one who has all and is all. A lord is one who exists above his own nature. A lord is one who has when young the rights of an old man; when old, the success in intrigue of a young one; if vicious, the homage of respectable people; if a coward, the command of brave men; if a do-nothing, the fruits of labour; if ignorant, the diploma of Cambridge or Oxford; if a fool, the admiration of poets; if ugly, the smiles of women; if a Thersites, the helm of Achilles; if a hare, the skin of a lion. Do not misunderstand my words. I do not say that a lord must necessarily be ignorant, a coward, ugly, stupid, or old. I only mean that he may be all those things without any detriment to himself. On the contrary. Lords are princes. The King of England is only a lord, the first peer of the peerage; that is all, but it is much. Kings were formerly called lords—the Lord of Denmark, the Lord of Ireland, the Lord of the Isles. The Lord of Norway was first called king three hundred years ago. Lucius, the most ancient king in England, was spoken to by Saint Telesphonis as my Lord Lucius. The lords are peers—that is to say, equals—of whom? Of the king. I do not commit the mistake of confounding the lords with parliament. The assembly of the people which the Saxons before the Conquest called *wittenagemote*, the Normans, after the Conquest, entitled *parliamentum*. By degrees the people were turned out. The king's letters clause convoking the Commons, addressed formerly *ad concilium impendendum*, are now addressed *ad consentiendum*. To say yes is their liberty. The peers can say no; and the proof is that they have said it. The peers can cut off the king's head. The people cannot. The stroke of the hatchet which decapitated Charles I. is an encroachment, not on the king, but on the peers, and it was well to place on the gibbet the carcass of Cromwell. The lords have power. Why? Because they have riches. Who has turned over the leaves of the Doomsday Book? It is the proof that the lords possess England. It is the registry of the estates of subjects, compiled under William the Conqueror; and it is in the charge of the Chancellor of the Exchequer. To copy anything in it you have to pay twopence a line. It is a proud book. Do you know that I was domestic doctor to a lord, who was called Marmaduke, and who had thirty-six thousand a year? Think of that, you hideous idiot! Do you know that, with rabbits only from the warrens of Earl Lindsay, they could feed all the riffraff of the Cinque Ports? And the good order kept! Every poacher is hung. For two long furry ears sticking out of a game bag I saw the father of six children hanging on the gibbet. Such is the peerage. The rabbit of a great lord is of more importance than God's image in a man.

"Lords exist, you trespasser, do you see? and we must think it good that they do; and even if we do not, what harm will it do them? The people object, indeed! Why? Plautus himself would never have attained the comicality of such an idea. A philosopher would be jesting if he advised the poor devil of the masses to cry out against the size and weight of the lords. Just as well might the gnat dispute with the foot of an elephant. One day I saw a hippopotamus tread upon a molehill; he crushed it utterly. He was innocent. The great soft-headed fool of a mastodon did not even know of the existence of moles. My son, the moles that are trodden on are the human race. To crush is a law. And do you think that the mole himself crushes nothing? Why, it is the mastodon of the fleshworm, who is the mastodon of the globeworm. But let us cease arguing. My boy, there are coaches in the world; my lord is inside, the people under the wheels; the philosopher gets out of the way. Stand aside, and let them pass. As to myself, I love lords, and shun them. I lived with one; the beauty of my recollections suffices me. I remember his country house, like a glory in a cloud. My dreams are all retrospective. Nothing could be more admirable than Marmaduke Lodge in grandeur, beautiful symmetry, rich avenues, and the ornaments and surroundings of the edifice. The houses, country seats, and palaces of the lords present a selection of all that is greatest and most magnificent in this flourishing kingdom. I love our lords. I thank them for being opulent, powerful, and prosperous. I myself am clothed in shadow, and I look with interest upon the shred of heavenly blue which is called a lord. You enter Marmaduke Lodge by an exceedingly spacious courtyard, which forms an oblong square, divided into eight spaces, each surrounded by a balustrade; on each side is a wide approach, and a superb hexagonal fountain plays in the midst; this fountain is formed of two basins, which are surmounted by a dome of exquisite openwork, elevated on six columns. It was there that I knew a learned Frenchman, Monsieur l'Abbé du Cros, who belonged to the Jacobin monastery in the Rue Saint Jacques. Half the library of Erpenius is at Marmaduke Lodge, the other half being at the theological gallery at Cambridge. I used to read the books, seated under the ornamented portal. These things are only shown to a select number of curious travellers. Do you know, you ridiculous boy, that William North, who is Lord Grey of Rolleston, and sits fourteenth on the bench of Barons, has more forest trees on his mountains than you have hairs on your horrible noddle? Do you know that Lord Norreys of Rycote, who is Earl of Abingdon, has a square keep a hundred feet high, having this device—*Virtus ariete fortior;* which you would think meant that virtue is stronger than a ram, but which really means, you idiot, that courage is stronger than a battering-machine. Yes, I honour, accept, respect, and revere our lords. It is the lords who, with her royal Majesty, work to procure and preserve the advantages of the nation. Their consummate wisdom shines in intricate junctures. Their precedence over others I wish they had not; but they have it. What is called principality in Germany, grandeeship in Spain, is called peerage in England and France. There being a fair show of reason for considering the world a wretched place enough, heaven felt where the burden was most galling, and to prove that it knew how to make happy people, created lords for the satisfaction of philosophers. This acts as a set-off, and gets heaven out of the scrape, affording it a decent escape from a false position. The great are great. A peer, speaking of himself, says *we*. A peer is a plural. The king qualifies the peer *consanguinei nostri*. The peers have made a multitude of wise laws; amongst others, one which condemns to death any one who cuts down a three-year-old poplar tree. Their supremacy is such that they have a language of their own. In heraldic style, black, which is called sable for gentry, is called saturne for princes, and diamond for peers. Diamond dust, a night thick with stars, such is the night of the happy! Even amongst themselves these high and mighty lords have their own distinctions. A baron cannot wash with a viscount without his permission. These are indeed excellent things, and safeguards to the nation. What a fine thing it is for the people to have twenty-five dukes, five marquises, seventy-six earls, nine viscounts, and sixty-one barons, making altogether a hundred and seventy-six peers, of which some are your grace, and some my lord! What matter a few rags here and there, withal: everybody cannot be dressed in gold. Let the rags be. Cannot you see the purple? One balances the other. A thing must be built of something. Yes, of course, there are the poor—what of them! They line the happiness of the wealthy. Devil take it! our lords are our glory! The pack of hounds belonging to Charles, Baron Mohun, costs him as much as the hospital for lepers in Moorgate, and for Christ's Hospital, founded for children, in 1553, by Edward VI. Thomas Osborne, Duke of Leeds, spends yearly on his liveries five thousand golden guineas. The Spanish grandees have a guardian appointed by law to prevent their ruining themselves. That is cowardly. Our lords are extravagant and magnificent. I esteem them for it. Let us not abuse them like envious folks. I feel happy when a beautiful vision passes. I have not the light, but I have the reflection. A reflection thrown on my ulcer, you will say. Go to the devil! I am a Job, delighted in the contemplation of Trimalcion. Oh, that beautiful and radiant planet up there! But the moonlight is something. To suppress the lords was an idea which Orestes, mad as he was, would not have dared to entertain. To say that the lords are mischievous or useless is as much as to say that the state should be revolutionized, and that men are not made to live like cattle, browsing the grass and bitten by the dog. The field is shorn by the sheep, the sheep by the shepherd. It is all one to me. I am a philosopher, and I care about life as much as a fly. Life is but a lodging. When I think that Henry Bowes Howard, Earl of Berkshire, has in his stable twenty-four state carriages, of which one is mounted in silver and another in gold—good heavens! I know that every one has not got twenty-four state carriages; but there is no need to complain for all that. Because you were cold one night, what was that to him? It concerns you only. Others besides you suffer cold and hunger. Don't you know that without that cold, Dea would not have been blind, and if Dea were not blind she would not love you? Think of that, you fool! And, besides, if all the people who are lost were to complain, there would be a pretty tumult! Silence is the rule. I have no doubt that heaven imposes silence on the damned, otherwise heaven itself would be punished by their everlasting cry. The happiness of Olympus is bought by the silence of Cocytus. Then, people, be silent! I do better myself; I approve and admire. Just now I was enumerating the lords, and I ought to add to the list two archbishops and twenty-four bishops. Truly, I am quite affected when I think of it! I remember to have seen at the tithe-gathering of the Rev. Dean of Raphoe, who combined the peerage with the church, a great tithe of beautiful wheat taken from the peasants in the neighbourhood, and which the dean had not been at the trouble of growing. This left him time to say his prayers. Do you know that Lord Marmaduke, my master, was Lord Grand Treasurer of Ireland, and High Seneschal of the sovereignty of Knaresborough in the county of York? Do you know that the Lord High Chamberlain, which is an office hereditary in the family of the Dukes of Ancaster, dresses the king for his coronation, and receives for his trouble forty yards of crimson velvet, besides the bed on which the king has slept; and that the Usher of the Black Rod is his deputy? I should like to see you deny this, that the senior viscount of England is Robert Brent, created a viscount by Henry V. The lords' titles imply sovereignty over land, except that of Earl Rivers, who takes his title from his family name. How admirable is the right which they have to tax others, and to levy, for instance, four shillings in the pound sterling income-tax, which has just been continued for another year! And all the time taxes on distilled spirits, on the excise of wine and beer, on tonnage and poundage, on cider, on perry, on mum, malt, and prepared barley, on coals, and on a hundred things besides. Let us venerate things as they are. The clergy themselves depend on the lords. The Bishop of Man is subject to the Earl of Derby. The lords have wild beasts of their own, which they place in their armorial bearings. God not having made enough, they have invented others. They have created the heraldic wild boar, who is as much above the wild boar as the wild boar is above the domestic pig and the lord is above the priest. They have created the griffin, which is an eagle to lions, and a lion to eagles, terrifying lions by his wings, and eagles by his mane. They have the guivre, the unicorn, the serpent, the salamander, the tarask, the dree, the dragon, and the hippogriff. All these things, terrible to us, are to them but an ornament and an embellishment. They have a menagerie which they call the blazon, in which unknown beasts roar. The prodigies of the forest are nothing compared to the inventions of their pride. Their vanity is full of phantoms which move as in a sublime night, armed with helm and cuirass, spurs on their heels and the sceptres in their hands, saying in a grave voice, 'We are the ancestors!' The canker-worms eat the roots, and panoplies eat the people. Why not? Are we to change the laws? The peerage is part of the order of society. Do you know that there is a duke in Scotland who can ride ninety miles without leaving his own estate? Do you know that the Archbishop of Canterbury has a revenue of £40,000 a year? Do you know that her Majesty has £700,000 sterling from the civil list, besides castles, forests, domains, fiefs, tenancies, freeholds, prebendaries, tithes, rent, confiscations, and fines, which bring in over a million sterling? Those who are not satisfied are hard to please."

"Yes," murmured Gwynplaine sadly, "the paradise of the rich is made out of the hell of the poor."

CHAPTER XII.

URSUS THE POET DRAGS ON URSUS THE PHILOSOPHER

Then Dea entered. He looked at her, and saw nothing but her. This is love; one may be carried away for a moment by the importunity of some other idea, but the beloved one enters, and all that does not appertain to her presence immediately fades away, without her dreaming that perhaps she is effacing in us a world.

Let us mention a circumstance. In "Chaos Vanquished," the word *monstruo*, addressed to Gwynplaine, displeased Dea. Sometimes, with the smattering of Spanish which every one knew at the period, she took it into her head to replace it by *quiero*, which signifies, "I wish it." Ursus tolerated, although not without an expression of impatience, this alteration in his text. He might have said to Dea, as in our day Moessard said to Vissot, *Tu manques de respect au repertoire.*

"The Laughing Man."

Such was the form of Gwynplaine's fame. His name, Gwynplaine, little known at any time, had disappeared under his nickname, as his face had disappeared under its grin.

His popularity was like his visage—a mask.

His name, however, was to be read on a large placard in front of the Green Box, which offered the crowd the following narrative composed by Ursus:—

"Here is to be seen Gwynplaine, deserted at the age of ten, on the night of the 29th of January, 1690, by the villainous Comprachicos, on the coast of Portland. The little boy has grown up, and is called now, THE LAUGHING MAN."

The existence of these mountebanks was as an existence of lepers in a leper-house, and of the blessed in one of the Pleiades. There was every day a sudden transition from the noisy exhibition outside, into the most complete seclusion. Every evening they made their exit from this world. They were like the dead, vanishing on condition of being reborn next day. A comedian is a revolving light, appearing one moment, disappearing the next, and existing for the public but as a phantom or a light, as his life circles round. To exhibition succeeded isolation. When the performance was finished, whilst the audience were dispersing, and their murmur of satisfaction was dying away in the streets, the Green Box shut up its platform, as a fortress does its drawbridge, and all communication with mankind was cut off. On one side, the universe; on the other, the caravan; and this caravan contained liberty, clear consciences, courage, devotion, innocence, happiness, love—all the constellations.

Blindness having sight and deformity beloved sat side by side, hand pressing hand, brow touching brow, and whispered to each other, intoxicated with love.

The compartment in the middle served two purposes—for the public it was a stage, for the actors a dining-room.

Ursus, ever delighting in comparisons, profited by the diversity of its uses to liken the central compartment in the Green Box to the arradach in an Abyssinian hut.

Ursus counted the receipts, then they supped. In love all is ideal. In love, eating and drinking together affords opportunities for many sweet promiscuous touches, by which a mouthful becomes a kiss. They drank ale or wine from the same glass, as they might drink dew out of the same lily. Two souls in love are as full of grace as two birds. Gwynplaine waited on Dea, cut her bread, poured out her drink, approached her too close.

"Hum!" cried Ursus, and he turned away, his scolding melting into a smile.

The wolf supped under the table, heedless of everything which did actually not concern his bone.

Fibi and Vinos shared the repast, but gave little trouble. These vagabonds, half wild and as uncouth as ever, spoke in the gipsy language to each other.

At length Dea re-entered the women's apartment with Fibi and Vinos. Ursus chained up Homo under the Green Box; Gwynplaine looked after the horses, the lover becoming a groom, like a hero of Homer's or a paladin of Charlemagne's. At midnight, all were asleep, except the wolf, who, alive to his responsibility, now and then opened an eye. The next morning they met again. They breakfasted together, generally on ham and tea. Tea was introduced into England in 1678. Then Dea, after the Spanish fashion, took a siesta, acting on the advice of Ursus, who considered her delicate, and slept some hours, while Gwynplaine and Ursus did all the little jobs of work, without and within, which their wandering life made necessary. Gwynplaine rarely wandered away from the Green Box, except on unfrequented roads and in solitary places. In cities he went out only at night, disguised in a large, slouched hat, so as not to exhibit his face in the street.

His face was to be seen uncovered only on the stage.

The Green Box had frequented cities but little. Gwynplaine at twenty-four had never seen towns larger than the Cinque Ports. His renown, however, was increasing. It began to rise above the populace, and to percolate through higher ground. Amongst those who were fond of, and ran after, strange foreign curiosities and prodigies, it was known that there was somewhere in existence, leading a wandering life, now here, now there, an extraordinary monster. They talked about him, they sought him, they asked where he was. The laughing man was becoming decidedly famous. A certain lustre was reflected on "Chaos Vanquished."

So much so, that, one day, Ursus, being ambitious, said,—

"We must go to London."

BOOK THE THIRD

THE BEGINNING OF THE FISSURE

CHAPTER I.

THE TADCASTER INN.

At that period London had but one bridge—London Bridge, with houses built upon it. This bridge united London to Southwark, a suburb which was paved with flint pebbles taken from the Thames, divided into small streets and alleys, like the City, with a great number of buildings, houses, dwellings, and wooden huts jammed together, a pell-mell mixture of combustible matter, amidst which fire might take its pleasure, as 1666 had proved. Southwark was then pronounced Soudric, it is now pronounced Sousouorc, or near it; indeed, an excellent way of pronouncing English names is not to pronounce them. Thus, for Southampton, say Stpntn.

It was the time when "Chatham" was pronounced *je t'aime*.

The Southwark of those days resembles the Southwark of to-day about as much as Vaugirard resembles Marseilles. It was a village—it is a city. Nevertheless, a considerable trade was carried on there. The long old Cyclopean wall by the Thames was studded with rings, to which were anchored the river barges.

This wall was called the Effroc Wall, or Effroc Stone. York, in Saxon times, was called Effroc. The legend related that a Duke of Effroc had been drowned at the foot of the wall. Certainly the water there was deep enough to drown a duke. At low water it was six good fathoms. The excellence of this little anchorage attracted sea vessels, and the old Dutch tub, called the *Vograat*, came to anchor at the Effroc Stone. The *Vograat* made the crossing from London to Rotterdam, and from Rotterdam to London, punctually once a week. Other barges started twice a day, either for Deptford, Greenwich, or Gravesend, going down with one tide and returning with the next. The voyage to Gravesend, though twenty miles, was performed in six hours.

The *Vograat* was of a model now no longer to be seen, except in naval museums. It was almost a junk. At that time, while France copied Greece, Holland copied China. The *Vograat*, a heavy hull with two masts, was partitioned perpendicularly, so as to be water-tight, having a narrow hold in the middle, and two decks, one fore and the other aft. The decks were flush as in the iron turret-vessels of the present day, the advantage of which is that in foul weather, the force of the wave is diminished, and the inconvenience of which is that the crew is exposed to the action of the sea, owing to there being no bulwarks. There was nothing to save any one on board from falling over. Hence the frequent falls overboard and the losses of men, which have caused the model to fall into disuse. The *Vograat* went to Holland direct, and did not even call at Gravesend.

An old ridge of stones, rock as much as masonry, ran along the bottom of the Effroc Stone, and being passable at all tides, was used as a passage on board the ships moored to the wall. This wall was, at intervals, furnished with steps. It marked the southern point of Southwark. An embankment at the top allowed the passers-by to rest their elbows on the Effroc Stone, as on the parapet of a quay. Thence they could look down on the Thames; on the other side of the water London dwindled away into fields.

Up the river from the Effroc Stone, at the bend of the Thames which is nearly opposite St. James's Palace, behind Lambeth House, not far from the walk then called Foxhall (Vauxhall, probably), there was, between a pottery in which they made porcelain, and a glass-blower's, where they made ornamental bottles, one of those large unenclosed spaces covered with grass, called formerly in France *cultures* and *mails*, and in England bowling-greens. Of bowling-green, a green on which to roll a ball, the French have made *boulingrin*. Folks have this green inside their houses nowadays, only it is put on the table, is a cloth instead of turf, and is called billiards.

It is difficult to see why, having boulevard (boule-vert), which is the same word as bowling-green, the French should have adopted *boulingrin*. It is surprising that a person so grave as the Dictionary should indulge in useless luxuries.

The bowling-green of Southwark was called Tarrinzeau Field, because it had belonged to the Barons Hastings, who are also Barons Tarrinzeau and Mauchline. From the Lords Hastings the Tarrinzeau Field passed to the Lords Tadcaster, who had made a speculation of it, just as, at a later date, a Duke of Orleans made a speculation of the Palais Royal. Tarrinzeau Field afterwards became waste ground and parochial property.

Tarrinzeau Field was a kind of permanent fair ground covered with jugglers, athletes, mountebanks, and music on platforms; and always full of "fools going to look at the devil," as Archbishop Sharp said. To look at the devil means to go to the play.

Several inns, which harboured the public and sent them to these outlandish exhibitions, were established in this place, which kept holiday all the year round, and thereby prospered. These inns were simply stalls, inhabited only during the day. In the evening the tavern-keeper put into his pocket the key of the tavern and went away.

One only of these inns was a house, the only dwelling in the whole bowling-green, the caravans of the fair ground having the power of disappearing at any moment, considering the absence of any ties in the vagabond life of all mountebanks.

Mountebanks have no roots to their lives.

This inn, called the Tadcaster, after the former owners of the ground, was an inn rather than a tavern, an hotel rather than an inn, and had a carriage entrance and a large yard.

The carriage entrance, opening from the court on the field, was the legitimate door of the Tadcaster Inn, which had, beside it, a small bastard door, by which people entered. To call it bastard is to mean preferred. This lower door was the only one used, It opened into the tavern, properly so called, which was a large taproom, full of tobacco smoke, furnished with tables, and low in the ceiling. Over it was a window on the first floor, to the iron bars of which was fastened and hung the sign of the inn. The principal door was barred and bolted, and always remained closed.

It was thus necessary to cross the tavern to enter the courtyard.

At the Tadcaster Inn there was a landlord and a boy. The landlord was called Master Nicless, the boy Govicum. Master Nicless—Nicholas, doubtless, which the English habit of contraction had made Nicless, was a miserly widower, and one who respected and feared the laws. As to his appearance, he had bushy eyebrows and hairy hands. The boy, aged fourteen, who poured out drink, and answered to the name of Govicum, wore a merry face and an apron. His hair was cropped close, a sign of servitude.

He slept on the ground floor, in a nook in which they formerly kept a dog. This nook had for window a bull's-eye looking on the bowling-green.

CHAPTER II.

OPEN-AIR ELOQUENCE

One very cold and windy evening, on which there was every reason why folks should hasten on their way along the street, a man, who was walking in Tarrinzeau Field close under the walls of the tavern, stopped suddenly. It was during the last months of winter between 1704 and 1705. This man, whose dress indicated a sailor, was of good mien and fine figure, things imperative to courtiers, and not forbidden to common folk.

Why did he stop? To listen. What to? To a voice apparently speaking in the court on the other side of the wall, a voice a little weakened by age, but so powerful notwithstanding that it reached the passer-by in the street. At the same time might be heard in the enclosure, from which the voice came, the hubbub of a crowd.

This voice said,—

"Men and women of London, here I am! I cordially wish you joy of being English. You are a great people. I say more: you are a great populace. Your fisticuffs are even better than your sword thrusts. You have an appetite. You are the nation which eats other nations—a magnificent function! This suction of the world makes England preeminent. As politicians and philosophers, in the management of colonies, populations, and industry, and in the desire to do others any harm which may turn to your own good, you stand alone. The hour will come when two boards will be put up on earth—inscribed on one side, Men; on the other, Englishmen. I mention this to your glory, I, who am neither English nor human, having the honour to be a bear. Still more—I am a doctor. That follows. Gentlemen, I teach. What? Two kinds of things—things which I know, and things which I do not. I sell my drugs and I sell my ideas. Approach and listen. Science invites you. Open your ear; if it is small, it will hold but little truth; if large, a great deal of folly will find its way in. Now, then, attention! I teach the Pseudoxia Epidemica. I have a comrade who will make you laugh, but I can make you think. We live in the same box, laughter being of quite as old a family as thought. When people asked Democritus, 'How do you know?' he answered, 'I laugh.' And if I am asked, 'Why do you laugh?' I shall answer, 'I know.' However, I am not laughing. I am the rectifier of popular errors. I take upon myself the task of cleaning your intellects. They require it. Heaven permits people to deceive themselves, and to be deceived. It is useless to be absurdly modest. I frankly avow that I believe in Providence, even where it is wrong. Only when I see filth—errors are filth—I sweep them away. How am I sure of what I know? That concerns only myself. Every one catches wisdom as he can. Lactantius asked questions of, and received answers from, a bronze head of Virgil. Sylvester II. conversed with birds. Did the birds speak? Did the Pope twitter? That is a question. The dead child of the Rabbi Elcazer talked to Saint Augustine. Between ourselves, I doubt all these facts except the last. The dead child might perhaps talk, because under its tongue it had a gold plate, on which were engraved divers constellations. Thus he deceived people. The fact explains itself. You see my moderation. I separate the true from the false. See! here are other errors in which, no doubt, you partake, poor ignorant folks that you are, and from which I wish to free you. Dioscorides believed that there was a god in the henbane; Chrysippus in the cynopaste; Josephus in the root bauras; Homer in the plant moly. They were all wrong. The spirits in herbs are not gods but devils. I have tested this fact. It is not true that the serpent which tempted Eve had a human face, as Cadmus relates. Garcias de Horto, Cadamosto, and John Hugo, Archbishop of Treves, deny that it is sufficient to saw down a tree to catch an elephant. I incline to their opinion. Citizens, the efforts of Lucifer are the cause of all false impressions. Under the reign of such a prince it is natural that meteors of error and of perdition should arise. My friends, Claudius Pulcher did not die because the fowls refused to come out of the fowl house. The fact is, that Lucifer, having foreseen the death of Claudius Pulcher, took care to prevent the birds feeding. That Beelzebub gave the Emperor Vespasian the virtue of curing the lame and giving sight to the blind, by his touch, was an act praiseworthy in itself, but of which the motive was culpable. Gentlemen, distrust those false doctors, who sell the root of the bryony and the white snake, and who make washes with honey and the blood of a cock. See clearly through that which is false. It is not quite true that Orion was the result of a natural function of Jupiter. The truth is that it was Mercury who produced this star in that way. It is not true that Adam had a navel. When St. George killed the dragon he had not the daughter of a saint standing by his side. St. Jerome had not a clock on the chimney-piece of his study; first, because living in a cave, he had no study; secondly, because he had no chimney-piece; thirdly, because clocks were not yet invented. Let us put these things right. Put them right. O gentlefolks, who listen to me, if any one tells you that a lizard will be born in your head if you smell the herb valerian; that the rotting carcase of the ox changes into bees, and that of the horse into hornets; that a man weighs more when dead than when alive; that the blood of the he-goat dissolves emeralds; that a caterpillar, a fly, and a spider, seen on the same tree, announces famine, war, and pestilence; that the falling sickness is to be cured by a worm found in the head of a buck—do not believe him. These things are errors. But now listen to truths. The skin of a sea-calf is a safeguard against thunder. The toad feeds upon earth, which causes a stone to come into his head. The rose of Jericho blooms on Christmas Eve. Serpents cannot endure the shadow of the ash tree. The elephant has no joints, and sleeps resting upright against a tree. Make a toad sit upon a cock's egg, and he will hatch a scorpion which will become a salamander. A blind person will recover sight by putting one hand on the left side of the altar and the other on his eyes. Virginity does not hinder maternity. Honest people, lay these truths to heart. Above all, you can believe in Providence in either of two ways, either as thirst believes in the orange, or as the ass believes in the whip. Now I am going to introduce you to my family."

Here a violent gust of wind shook the window-frames and shutters of the inn, which stood detached. It was like a prolonged murmur of the sky. The orator paused a moment, and then resumed.

"An interruption; very good. Speak, north wind. Gentlemen, I am not angry. The wind is loquacious, like all solitary creatures. There is no one to keep him company up there, so he jabbers. I resume the thread of my discourse. Here you see associated artists. We are four—*a lupo principium.* I begin by my friend, who is a wolf. He does not conceal it. See him! He is educated, grave, and sagacious. Providence, perhaps, entertained for a moment the idea of making him a doctor of the university; but for that one must be rather stupid, and that he is not. I may add that he has no prejudices, and is not aristocratic. He chats sometimes with bitches; he who, by right, should consort only with she-wolves. His heirs, if he have any, will no doubt gracefully combine the yap of their mother with the howl of their father. Because he does howl. He howls in sympathy with men. He barks as well, in condescension to civilization—a magnanimous concession. Homo is a dog made perfect. Let us venerate the dog. The dog—curious animal! sweats with its tongue and smiles with its tail. Gentlemen, Homo equals in wisdom, and surpasses in cordiality, the hairless wolf of Mexico, the wonderful xoloïtzeniski. I may add that he is humble. He has the modesty of a wolf who is useful to men. He is helpful and charitable, and says nothing about it. His left paw knows not the good which his right paw does. These are his merits. Of the other, my second friend, I have but one word to say. He is a monster. You will admire him. He was formerly abandoned by pirates on the shores of the wild ocean. This third one is blind. Is she an exception? No, we are all blind. The miser is blind; he sees gold, and he does not see riches. The prodigal is blind; he sees the beginning, and does not see the end. The coquette is blind; she does not see her wrinkles. The learned man is blind; he does not see his own ignorance. The honest man is blind; he does not see the thief. The thief is blind; he does not see God. God is blind; the day that he created the world He did not see the devil manage to creep into it. I myself am blind; I speak, and do not see that you are deaf. This blind girl who accompanies us is a mysterious priestess. Vesta has confided to her her torch. She has in her character depths as soft as a division in the wool of a sheep. I believe her to be a king's daughter, though I do not assert it as a fact. A laudable distrust is the attribute of wisdom. For my own part, I reason and I doctor, I think and I heal. *Chirurgus sum.* I cure fevers, miasmas, and plagues. Almost all our melancholy and sufferings are issues, which if carefully treated relieve us quietly from other evils which might be worse. All the same I do not recommend you to have an anthrax, otherwise called carbuncle. It is a stupid malady, and serves no good end. One dies of it—that is all. I am neither uncultivated nor rustic. I honour eloquence and poetry, and live in an innocent union with these goddesses. I conclude by a piece of advice. Ladies and gentlemen, on the sunny side of your dispositions, cultivate virtue, modesty, honesty, probity, justice, and love. Each one here below may thus have his little pot of flowers on his window-sill. My lords and gentlemen, I have spoken. The play is about to begin."

The man who was apparently a sailor, and who had been listening outside, entered the lower room of the inn, crossed it, paid the necessary entrance money, reached the courtyard which was full of people, saw at the bottom of it a caravan on wheels, wide open, and on the platform an old man dressed in a bearskin, a young man looking like a mask, a blind girl, and a wolf.

"Gracious heaven!" he cried, "what delightful people!"

CHAPTER III.

WHERE THE PASSER-BY REAPPEARS

The Green Box, as we have just seen, had arrived in London. It was established at Southwark. Ursus had been tempted by the bowling-green, which had one great recommendation, that it was always fair-day there, even in winter.

The dome of St. Paul's was a delight to Ursus.

London, take it all in all, has some good in it. It was a brave thing to dedicate a cathedral to St. Paul. The real cathedral saint is St. Peter. St. Paul is suspected of imagination, and in matters ecclesiastical imagination means heresy. St. Paul is a saint only with extenuating circumstances. He entered heaven only by the artists' door.

A cathedral is a sign. St. Peter is the sign of Rome, the city of the dogma; St. Paul that of London, the city of schism.

Ursus, whose philosophy had arms so long that it embraced everything, was a man who appreciated these shades of difference, and his attraction towards London arose, perhaps, from a certain taste of his for St. Paul.

The yard of the Tadcaster Inn had taken the fancy of Ursus. It might have been ordered for the Green Box. It was a theatre ready-made. It was square, with three sides built round, and a wall forming the fourth. Against this wall was placed the Green Box, which they were able to draw into the yard, owing to the height of the gate. A large wooden balcony, roofed over, and supported on posts, on which the rooms of the first story opened, ran round the three fronts of the interior façade of the house, making two right angles. The windows of the ground floor made boxes, the pavement of the court the pit, and the balcony the gallery. The Green Box, reared against the wall, was thus in front of a theatre. It was very like the Globe, where they played "Othello," "King Lear," and "The Tempest."

In a corner behind the Green Box was a stable.

Ursus had made his arrangements with the tavern keeper, Master Nicless, who, owing to his respect for the law, would not admit the wolf without charging him extra.

The placard, "Gwynplaine, the Laughing Man," taken from its nail in the Green Box, was hung up close to the sign of the inn. The sitting-room of the tavern had, as we have seen, an inside door which opened into the court. By the side of the door was constructed off-hand, by means of an empty barrel, a box for the money-taker, who was sometimes Fibi and sometimes Vinos. This was managed much as at present. Pay and pass in. Under the placard announcing the Laughing Man was a piece of wood, painted white, hung on two nails, on which was written in charcoal in large letters the title of Ursus's grand piece, "Chaos Vanquished."

In the centre of the balcony, precisely opposite the Green Box, and in a compartment having for entrance a window reaching to the ground, there had been partitioned off a space "for the nobility." It was large enough to hold, in two rows, ten spectators.

"We are in London," said Ursus. "We must be prepared for the gentry."

He had furnished this box with the best chairs in the inn, and had placed in the centre a grand arm-chair of yellow Utrecht velvet, with a cherry-coloured pattern, in case some alderman's wife should come.

They began their performances. The crowd immediately flocked to them, but the compartment for the nobility remained empty. With that exception their success became so great that no mountebank memory could recall its parallel. All Southwark ran in crowds to admire the Laughing Man.

The merry-andrews and mountebanks of Tarrinzeau Field were aghast at Gwynplaine. The effect he caused was as that of a sparrow-hawk flapping his wings in a cage of goldfinches, and feeding in their seed-trough. Gwynplaine ate up their public.

Besides the small fry, the swallowers of swords and the grimace makers, real performances took place on the green. There was a circus of women, ringing from morning till night with a magnificent peal of all sorts of instruments—psalteries, drums, rebecks, micamons, timbrels, reeds, dulcimers, gongs, chevrettes, bagpipes, German horns, English eschaqueils, pipes, flutes, and flageolets.

In a large round tent were some tumblers, who could not have equalled our present climbers of the Pyrenees—Dulma, Bordenave, and Meylonga—who from the peak of Pierrefitte descend to the plateau of Limaçon, an almost perpendicular height. There was a travelling menagerie, where was to be seen a performing tiger, who, lashed by the keeper, snapped at the whip and tried to swallow the lash. Even this comedian of jaws and claws was eclipsed in success.

Curiosity, applause, receipts, crowds, the Laughing Man monopolized everything. It happened in the twinkling of an eye. Nothing was thought of but the Green Box.

"'Chaos Vanquished' is 'Chaos Victor,'" said Ursus, appropriating half Gwynplaine's success, and taking the wind out of his sails, as they say at sea. That success was prodigious. Still it remained local. Fame does not cross the sea easily. It took a hundred and thirty years for the name of Shakespeare to penetrate from England into France. The sea is a wall; and if Voltaire—a thing which he very much regretted when it was too late—had not thrown a bridge over to Shakespeare, Shakespeare might still be in England, on the other side of the wall, a captive in insular glory.

The glory of Gwynplaine had not passed London Bridge. It was not great enough yet to re-echo throughout the city. At least not at first. But Southwark ought to have sufficed to satisfy the ambition of a clown. Ursus said,—

"The money bag grows palpably bigger."

They played "Ursus Rursus" and "Chaos Vanquished."

Between the acts Ursus exhibited his power as an engastrimist, and executed marvels of ventriloquism. He imitated every cry which occurred in the audience—a song, a cry, enough to startle, so exact the imitation, the singer or the crier himself; and now and then he copied the hubbub of the public, and whistled as if there were a crowd of people within him. These were remarkable talents. Besides this he harangued like Cicero, as we have just seen, sold his drugs, attended sickness, and even healed the sick.

Southwark was enthralled.

Ursus was satisfied with the applause of Southwark, but by no means astonished.

"They are the ancient Trinobantes," he said.

Then he added, "I must not mistake them, for delicacy of taste, for the Atrobates, who people Berkshire, or the Belgians, who inhabited Somersetshire, nor for the Parisians, who founded York."

At every performance the yard of the inn, transformed into a pit, was filled with a ragged and enthusiastic audience. It was composed of watermen, chairmen, coachmen, and bargemen, and sailors, just ashore, spending their wages in feasting and women. In it there were felons, ruffians, and blackguards, who were soldiers condemned for some crime against discipline to wear their red coats, which were lined with black, inside out, and from thence the name of blackguard, which the French turn into *blagueurs*. All these flowed from the street into the theatre, and poured back from the theatre into the tap. The emptying of tankards did not decrease their success.

Amidst what it is usual to call the scum, there was one taller than the rest, bigger, stronger, less poverty-stricken, broader in the shoulders; dressed like the common people, but not ragged.

Admiring and applauding everything to the skies, clearing his way with his fists, wearing a disordered periwig, swearing, shouting, joking, never dirty, and, at need, ready to blacken an eye or pay for a bottle.

This frequenter was the passer-by whose cheer of enthusiasm has been recorded.

This connoisseur was suddenly fascinated, and had adopted the Laughing Man. He did not come every evening, but when he came he led the public—applause grew into acclamation—success rose not to the roof, for there was none, but to the clouds, for there were plenty of them. Which clouds (seeing that there was no roof) sometimes wept over the masterpiece of Ursus.

His enthusiasm caused Ursus to remark this man, and Gwynplaine to observe him.

They had a great friend in this unknown visitor.

Ursus and Gwynplaine wanted to know him; at least, to know who he was.

One evening Ursus was in the side scene, which was the kitchen-door of the Green Box, seeing Master Nicless standing by him, showed him this man in the crowd, and asked him,—

"Do you know that man?"

"Of course I do."

"Who is he?"

"A sailor."

"What is his name?" said Gwynplaine, interrupting.

"Tom-Jim-Jack," replied the inn-keeper.

Then as he redescended the steps at the back of the Green Box, to enter the inn, Master Nicless let fall this profound reflection, so deep as to be unintelligible,—

"What a pity that he should not be a lord. He would make a famous scoundrel."

Otherwise, although established in the tavern, the group in the Green Box had in no way altered their manner of living, and held to their isolated habits. Except a few words exchanged now and then with the tavern-keeper, they held no communication with any of those who were living, either permanently or temporarily, in the inn; and continued to keep to themselves.

Since they had been at Southwark, Gwynplaine had made it his habit, after the performance and the supper of both family and horses—when Ursus and Dea had gone to bed in their respective compartments—to breathe a little the fresh air of the bowling-green, between eleven o'clock and midnight.

A certain vagrancy in our spirits impels us to take walks at night, and to saunter under the stars. There is a mysterious expectation in youth. Therefore it is that we are prone to wander out in the night, without an object.

At that hour there was no one in the fair-ground, except, perhaps, some reeling drunkard, making staggering shadows in dark corners. The empty taverns were shut up, and the lower room in the Tadcaster Inn was dark, except where, in some corner, a solitary candle lighted a last reveller. An indistinct glow gleamed through the window-shutters of the half-closed tavern, as Gwynplaine, pensive, content, and dreaming, happy in a haze of divine joy, passed backwards and forwards in front of the half-open door.

Of what was he thinking? Of Dea—of nothing—of everything—of the depths.

He never wandered far from the Green Box, being held, as by a thread, to Dea. A few steps away from it was far enough for him.

Then he returned, found the whole Green Box asleep, and went to bed himself.

CHAPTER IV.

CONTRARIES FRATERNIZE IN HATE

Success is hateful, especially to those whom it overthrows. It is rare that the eaten adore the eaters.

The Laughing Man had decidedly made a hit. The mountebanks around were indignant. A theatrical success is a syphon—it pumps in the crowd and creates emptiness all round. The shop opposite is done for. The increased receipts of the Green Box caused a corresponding decrease in the receipts of the surrounding shows. Those entertainments, popular up to that time, suddenly collapsed. It was like a low-water mark, showing inversely, but in perfect concordance, the rise here, the fall there. Theatres experience the effect of tides: they rise in one only on condition of falling in another. The swarming foreigners who exhibited their talents and their trumpetings on the neighbouring platforms, seeing themselves ruined by the Laughing Man, were despairing, yet dazzled. All the grimacers, all the clowns, all the merry-andrews envied Gwynplaine. How happy he must be with the snout of a wild beast! The buffoon mothers and dancers on the tight-rope, with pretty children, looked at them in anger, and pointing out Gwynplaine, would say, "What a pity you have not a face like that!" Some beat their babes savagely for being pretty. More than one, had she known the secret, would have fashioned her son's face in the Gwynplaine style. The head of an angel, which brings no money in, is not as good as that of a lucrative devil. One day the mother of a little child who was a marvel of beauty, and who acted a cupid, exclaimed,—

"Our children are failures! They only succeeded with Gwynplaine." And shaking her fist at her son, she added, "If I only knew your father, wouldn't he catch it!"

Gwynplaine was the goose with the golden eggs! What a marvellous phenomenon! There was an uproar through all the caravans. The mountebanks, enthusiastic and exasperated, looked at Gwynplaine and gnashed their teeth. Admiring anger is called envy. Then it howls! They tried to disturb "Chaos Vanquished;" made a cabal, hissed, scolded, shouted! This was an excuse for Ursus to make out-of-door harangues to the populace, and for his friend Tom-Jim-Jack to use his fists to re-establish order. His pugilistic marks of friendship brought him still more under the notice and regard of Ursus and Gwynplaine. At a distance, however, for the group in the Green Box sufficed to themselves, and held aloof from the rest of the world, and because Tom-Jim-Jack, this leader of the mob, seemed a sort of supreme bully, without a tie, without a friend; a smasher of windows, a manager of men, now here, now gone, hail-fellow-well-met with every one, companion of none.

This raging envy against Gwynplaine did not give in for a few friendly hits from Tom-Jim-Jack. The outcries having miscarried, the mountebanks of Tarrinzeau Field fell back on a petition. They addressed to the authorities. This is the usual course. Against an unpleasant success we first try to stir up the crowd and then we petition the magistrate.

With the merry-andrews the reverends allied themselves. The Laughing Man had inflicted a blow on the preachers. There were empty places not only in the caravans, but in the churches. The congregations in the churches of the five parishes in Southwark had dwindled away. People left before the sermon to go to Gwynplaine. "Chaos Vanquished," the Green Box, the Laughing Man, all the abominations of Baal, eclipsed the eloquence of the pulpit. The voice crying in the desert, *vox clamantis in deserto*, is discontented, and is prone to call for the aid of the authorities. The clergy of the five parishes complained to the Bishop of London, who complained to her Majesty.

The complaint of the merry-andrews was based on religion. They declared it to be insulted. They described Gwynplaine as a sorcerer, and Ursus as an atheist. The reverend gentlemen invoked social order. Setting orthodoxy aside they took action on the fact that Acts of Parliament were violated. It was clever. Because it was the period of Mr. Locke, who had died but six months previously—28th October, 1704—and when scepticism, which Bolingbroke had imbibed from Voltaire, was taking root. Later on Wesley came and restored the Bible, as Loyola restored the papacy.

Thus the Green Box was battered on both sides; by the merry-andrews, in the name of the Pentateuch, and by chaplains in the name of the police. In the name of Heaven and of the inspectors of nuisances. The Green Box was denounced by the priests as an obstruction, and by the jugglers as sacrilegious.

Had they any pretext? Was there any excuse? Yes. What was the crime? This: there was the wolf. A dog was allowable; a wolf forbidden. In England the wolf is an outlaw. England admits the dog which barks, but not the dog which howls—a shade of difference between the yard and the woods.

The rectors and vicars of the five parishes of Southwark called attention in their petitions to numerous parliamentary and royal statutes putting the wolf beyond the protection of the law. They moved for something like the imprisonment of Gwynplaine and the execution of the wolf, or at any rate for their banishment. The question was one of public importance, the danger to persons passing, etc. And on this point, they appealed to the Faculty. They cited the opinion of the Eighty physicians of London, a learned body which dates from Henry VIII., which has a seal like that of the State, which can raise sick people to the dignity of being amenable to their jurisdiction, which has the right to imprison those who infringe its law and contravene its ordinances, and which, amongst other useful regulations for the health of the citizens, put beyond doubt this fact acquired by science; that if a wolf sees a man first, the man becomes hoarse for life. Besides, he may be bitten.

Homo, then, was a pretext.

Ursus heard of these designs through the inn-keeper. He was uneasy. He was afraid of two claws—the police and the justices. To be afraid of the magistracy, it is sufficient to be afraid, there is no need to be guilty. Ursus had no desire for contact with sheriffs, provosts, bailiffs, and coroners. His eagerness to make their acquaintance amounted to nil. His curiosity to see the magistrates was about as great as the hare's to see the greyhound.

He began to regret that he had come to London. "'Better' is the enemy of 'good,'" murmured he apart. "I thought the proverb was ill-considered. I was wrong. Stupid truths are true truths."

Against the coalition of powers—merry-andrews taking in hand the cause of religion, and chaplains, indignant in the name of medicine—the poor Green Box, suspected of sorcery in Gwynplaine and of hydrophobia in Homo, had only one thing in its favour (but a thing of great power in England), municipal inactivity. It is to the local authorities letting things take their own course that Englishmen owe their liberty. Liberty in England behaves very much as the sea around England. It is a tide. Little by little manners surmount the law. A cruel system of legislation drowned under the wave of custom; a savage code of laws still visible through the transparency of universal liberty: such is England.

The Laughing Man, "Chaos Vanquished," and Homo might have mountebanks, preachers, bishops, the House of Commons, the House of Lords, her Majesty, London, and the whole of England against them, and remain undisturbed so long as Southwark permitted.

The Green Box was the favourite amusement of the suburb, and the local authorities seemed disinclined to interfere. In England, indifference is protection. So long as the sheriff of the county of Surrey, to the jurisdiction of which Southwark belongs, did not move in the matter, Ursus breathed freely, and Homo could sleep on his wolf's ears.

So long as the hatred which it excited did not occasion acts of violence, it increased success. The Green Box was none the worse for it, for the time. On the contrary, hints were scattered that it contained something mysterious. Hence the Laughing Man became more and more popular. The public follow with gusto the scent of anything contraband. To be suspected is a recommendation. The people adopt by instinct that at which the finger is pointed. The thing which is denounced is like the savour of forbidden fruit; we rush to eat it. Besides, applause which irritates some one, especially if that some one is in authority, is sweet. To perform, whilst passing a pleasant evening, both an act of kindness to the oppressed and of opposition to the oppressor is agreeable. You are protecting at the same time that you are being amused. So the theatrical caravans on the bowling-green continued to howl and to cabal against the Laughing Man. Nothing could be better calculated to enhance his success. The shouts of one's enemies are useful and give point and vitality to one's triumph. A friend wearies sooner in praise than an enemy in abuse. To abuse does not hurt. Enemies are ignorant of this fact. They cannot help insulting us, and this constitutes their use. They cannot hold their tongues, and thus keep the public awake.

The crowds which flocked to "Chaos Vanquished" increased daily.

Ursus kept what Master Nicless had said of intriguers and complaints in high places to himself, and did not tell Gwynplaine, lest it should trouble the ease of his acting by creating anxiety. If evil was to come, he would be sure to know it soon enough.

CHAPTER V.

THE WAPENTAKE

Once, however, he thought it his duty to derogate from this prudence, for prudence' sake, thinking that it might be well to make Gwynplaine uneasy. It is true that this idea arose from a circumstance much graver, in the opinion of Ursus, than the cabals of the fair or of the church.

Gwynplaine, as he picked up a farthing which had fallen when counting the receipts, had, in the presence of the innkeeper, drawn a contrast between the farthing, representing the misery of the people, and the die, representing, under the figure of Anne, the parasitical magnificence of the throne—an ill-sounding speech. This observation was repeated by Master Nicless, and had such a run that it reached to Ursus through Fibi and Vinos. It put Ursus into a fever. Seditious words, lèse Majesté. He took Gwynplaine severely to task. "Watch over your abominable jaws. There is a rule for the great—to do nothing; and a rule for the small—to say nothing. The poor man has but one friend, silence. He should only pronounce one syllable: 'Yes.' To confess and to consent is all the right he has. 'Yes,' to the judge; 'yes,' to the king. Great people, if it pleases them to do so, beat us. I have received blows from them. It is their prerogative; and they lose nothing of their greatness by breaking our bones. The ossifrage is a species of eagle. Let us venerate the sceptre, which is the first of staves. Respect is prudence, and mediocrity is safety. To insult the king is to put oneself in the same danger as a girl rashly paring the nails of a lion. They tell me that you have been prattling about the farthing, which is the same thing as the liard, and that you have found fault with the august medallion, for which they sell us at market the eighth part of a salt herring. Take care; let us be serious. Consider the existence of pains and penalties. Suck in these legislative truths. You are in a country in which the man who cuts down a tree three years old is quietly taken off to the gallows. As to swearers, their feet are put into the stocks. The drunkard is shut up in a barrel with the bottom out, so that he can walk, with a hole in the top, through which his head is passed, and with two in the bung for his hands, so that he cannot lie down. He who strikes another one in Westminster Hall is imprisoned for life and has his goods confiscated. Whoever strikes any one in the king's palace has his hand struck off. A fillip on the nose chances to bleed, and, behold! you are maimed for life. He who is convicted of heresy in the bishop's court is burnt alive. It was for no great matter that Cuthbert Simpson was quartered on a turnstile. Three years since, in 1702, which is not long ago, you see, they placed in the pillory a scoundrel, called Daniel Defoe, who had had the audacity to print the names of the Members of Parliament who had spoken on the previous evening. He who commits high treason is disembowelled alive, and they tear out his heart and buffet his cheeks with it. Impress on yourself notions of right and justice. Never allow yourself to speak a word, and at the first cause of anxiety, run for it. Such is the bravery which I counsel and which I practise. In the way of temerity, imitate the birds; in the way of talking, imitate the fishes. England has one admirable point in her favour, that her legislation is very mild."

His admonition over, Ursus remained uneasy for some time. Gwynplaine not at all. The intrepidity of youth arises from want of experience. However, it seemed that Gwynplaine had good reason for his easy mind, for the weeks flowed on peacefully, and no bad consequences seemed to have resulted from his observations about the queen.

Ursus, we know, lacked apathy, and, like a roebuck on the watch, kept a lookout in every direction. One day, a short time after his sermon to Gwynplaine, as he was looking out from the window in the wall which commanded the field, he became suddenly pale.

"Gwynplaine?"

"What?"

"Look."

"Where?"

"In the field."

"Well."

"Do you see that passer-by?"

"The man in black?"

"Yes."

"Who has a kind of mace in his hand?"

"Yes."

"Well?"

"Well, Gwynplaine, that man is a wapentake."

"What is a wapentake?"

"He is the bailiff of the hundred."

"What is the bailiff of the hundred?"

"He is the *proepositus hundredi.*"

"And what is the *proepositus hundredi?*"

"He is a terrible officer."

"What has he got in his hand?"

"The iron weapon."

"What is the iron weapon?"

"A thing made of iron."

"What does he do with that?"

"First of all, he swears upon it. It is for that reason that he is called the wapentake."

"And then?"

"Then he touches you with it."

"With what?"

"With the iron weapon."

"The wapentake touches you with the iron weapon?"

"Yes."

"What does that mean?"

"That means, follow me."

"And must you follow?"

"Yes."

"Whither?"

"How should I know?"

"But he tells you where he is going to take you?"

"No."

"How is that?"

"He says nothing, and you say nothing."

"But—"

"He touches you with the iron weapon. All is over then. You must go."

"But where?"

"After him."

"But where?"

"Wherever he likes, Gwynplaine."

"And if you resist?"

"You are hanged."

Ursus looked out of the window again, and drawing a long breath, said,—

"Thank God! He has passed. He was not coming here."

Ursus was perhaps unreasonably alarmed about the indiscreet remark, and the consequences likely to result from the unconsidered words of Gwynplaine.

Master Nicless, who had heard them, had no interest in compromising the poor inhabitants of the Green Box. He was amassing, at the same time as the Laughing Man, a nice little fortune. "Chaos Vanquished" had succeeded in two ways. While it made art triumph on the stage, it made drunkenness prosper in the tavern.

CHAPTER VI.

THE MOUSE EXAMINED BY THE CATS

Ursus was soon afterwards startled by another alarming circumstance. This time it was he himself who was concerned. He was summoned to Bishopsgate before a commission composed of three disagreeable countenances. They belonged to three doctors, called overseers. One was a Doctor of Theology, delegated by the Dean of Westminster; another, a Doctor of Medicine, delegated by the College of Surgeons; the third, a Doctor in History and Civil Law, delegated by Gresham College. These three experts *in omni re scibili* had the censorship of everything said in public throughout the bounds of the hundred and thirty parishes of London, the seventy-three of Middlesex, and, by extension, the five of Southwark.

Such theological jurisdictions still subsist in England, and do good service. In December, 1868, by sentence of the Court of Arches, confirmed by the decision of the Privy Council, the Reverend Mackonochie was censured, besides being condemned in costs, for having placed lighted candles on a table. The liturgy allows no jokes.

Ursus, then, one fine day received from the delegated doctors an order to appear before them, which was, luckily, given into his own hands, and which he was therefore enabled to keep secret. Without saying a word, he obeyed the citation, shuddering at the thought that he might be considered culpable to the extent of having the appearance of being suspected of a certain amount of rashness. He who had so recommended silence to others had here a rough lesson. *Garrule, sana te ipsum.*

The three doctors, delegated and appointed overseers, sat at Bishopsgate, at the end of a room on the ground floor, in three armchairs covered with black leather, with three busts of Minos, Æacus, and Rhadamanthus, in the wall above their heads, a table before them, and at their feet a form for the accused.

Ursus, introduced by a tipstaff, of placid but severe expression, entered, perceived the doctors, and immediately in his own mind, gave to each of them the name of the judge of the infernal regions represented by the bust placed above his head. Minos, the president, the representative of theology, made him a sign to sit down on the form.

Ursus made a proper bow—that is to say, bowed to the ground; and knowing that bears are charmed by honey, and doctors by Latin, he said, keeping his body still bent respectfully,—

"*Tres faciunt capitulum!*"

Then, with head inclined (for modesty disarms) he sat down on the form.

Each of the three doctors had before him a bundle of papers, of which he was turning the leaves.

Minos began.

"You speak in public?"
"Yes," replied Ursus.
"By what right?"
"I am a philosopher."
"That gives no right."
"I am also a mountebank," said Ursus.
"That is a different thing."
Ursus breathed again, but with humility.
Minos resumed,—
"As a mountebank, you may speak; as a philosopher, you must keep silence."
"I will try," said Ursus.
Then he thought to himself.
"I may speak, but I must be silent. How complicated."
He was much alarmed.
The same overseer continued,—
"You say things which do not sound right. You insult religion. You deny the most evident truths. You propagate revolting errors. For instance, you have said that the fact of virginity excludes the possibility of maternity."
Ursus lifted his eyes meekly, "I did not say that. I said that the fact of maternity excludes the possibility of virginity."
Minos was thoughtful, and mumbled, "True, that is the contrary."
It was really the same thing. But Ursus had parried the first blow.
Minos, meditating on the answer just given by Ursus, sank into the depths of his own imbecility, and kept silent.
The overseer of history, or, as Ursus called him, Rhadamanthus, covered the retreat of Minos by this interpolation, "Accused! your audacity and your errors are of two sorts. You have denied that the battle of Pharsalia would have been lost because Brutus and Cassius had met a negro."
"I said," murmured Ursus "that there was something in the fact that Cæsar was the better captain."
The man of history passed, without transition, to mythology.
"You have excused the infamous acts of Actæon."
"I think," said Ursus, insinuatingly, "that a man is not dishonoured by having seen a naked woman."
"Then you are wrong," said the judge severely. Rhadamanthus returned to history.
"Apropos of the accidents which happened to the cavalry of Mithridates, you have contested the virtues of herbs and plants. You have denied that a herb like the securiduca, could make the shoes of horses fall off."
"Pardon me," replied Ursus. "I said that the power existed only in the herb sferra cavallo. I never denied the virtue of any herb," and he added, in a low voice, "nor of any woman."
By this extraneous addition to his answer Ursus proved to himself that, anxious as he was, he was not disheartened. Ursus was a compound of terror and presence of mind.

"To continue," resumed Rhadamanthus; "you have declared that it was folly in Scipio, when he wished to open the gates of Carthage, to use as a key the herb æthiopis, because the herb æthiopis has not the property of breaking locks."

"I merely said that he would have done better to have used the herb lunaria."

"That is a matter of opinion," murmured Rhadamanthus, touched in his turn. And the man of history was silent.

The theologian, Minos, having returned to consciousness, questioned Ursus anew. He had had time to consult his notes.

"You have classed orpiment amongst the products of arsenic, and you have said that it is a poison. The Bible denies this."

"The Bible denies, but arsenic affirms it," sighed Ursus.

The man whom Ursus called Æacus, and who was the envy of medicine, had not yet spoken, but now looking down on Ursus, with proudly half-closed eyes, he said,—

"The answer is not without some show of reason."

Ursus thanked him with his most cringing smile. Minos frowned frightfully. "I resume," said Minos. "You have said that it is false that the basilisk is the king of serpents, under the name of cockatrice."

"Very reverend sir," said Ursus, "so little did I desire to insult the basilisk that I have given out as certain that it has a man's head."

"Be it so," replied Minos severely; "but you added that Poerius had seen one with the head of a falcon. Can you prove it?"

"Not easily," said Ursus.

Here he had lost a little ground.

Minos, seizing the advantage, pushed it.

"You have said that a converted Jew has not a nice smell."

"Yes. But I added that a Christian who becomes a Jew has a nasty one."

Minos lost his eyes over the accusing documents.

"You have affirmed and propagated things which are impossible. You have said that Elien had seen an elephant write sentences."

"Nay, very reverend gentleman! I simply said that Oppian had heard a hippopotamus discuss a philosophical problem."

"You have declared that it is not true that a dish made of beech-wood will become covered of itself with all the viands that one can desire."

"I said, that if it has this virtue, it must be that you received it from the devil."

"That I received it!"

"No, most reverend sir. I, nobody, everybody!"

Aside, Ursus thought, "I don't know what I am saying."

But his outward confusion, though extreme, was not distinctly visible. Ursus struggled with it.

"All this," Minos began again, "implies a certain belief in the devil."

Ursus held his own.

"Very reverend sir, I am not an unbeliever with regard to the devil. Belief in the devil is the reverse side of faith in God. The one proves the other. He who does not believe a little in the devil, does not believe much in God. He who believes in the sun must believe in the shadow. The devil is the night of God. What is night? The proof of day."

Ursus here extemporized a fathomless combination of philosophy and religion. Minos remained pensive, and relapsed into silence.

Ursus breathed afresh.

A sharp onslaught now took place. Æacus, the medical delegate, who had disdainfully protected Ursus against the theologian, now turned suddenly from auxiliary into assailant. He placed his closed fist on his bundle of papers, which was large and heavy. Ursus received this apostrophe full in the breast,—

"It is proved that crystal is sublimated ice, and that the diamond is sublimated crystal. It is averred that ice becomes crystal in a thousand years, and crystal diamond in a thousand ages. You have denied this."

"Nay," replied Ursus, with sadness, "I only said that in a thousand years ice had time to melt, and that a thousand ages were difficult to count."

The examination went on; questions and answers clashed like swords.

"You have denied that plants can talk."

"Not at all. But to do so they must grow under a gibbet."

"Do you own that the mandragora cries?"

"No; but it sings."

"You have denied that the fourth finger of the left hand has a cordial virtue."

"I only said that to sneeze to the left was a bad sign."

"You have spoken rashly and disrespectfully of the phoenix."

"Learned judge, I merely said that when he wrote that the brain of the phoenix was a delicate morsel, but that it produced headache, Plutarch was a little out of his reckoning, inasmuch as the phoenix never existed."

"A detestable speech! The cinnamalker which makes its nest with sticks of cinnamon, the rhintacus that Parysatis used in the manufacture of his poisons, the manucodiatas which is the bird of paradise, and the semenda, which has a threefold beak, have been mistaken for the phoenix; but the phoenix has existed."

"I do not deny it."

"You are a stupid ass."

"I desire to be thought no better."

"You have confessed that the elder tree cures the quinsy, but you added that it was not because it has in its root a fairy excrescence."

"I said it was because Judas hung himself on an elder tree."

"A plausible opinion," growled the theologian, glad to strike his little blow at Æacus.

Arrogance repulsed soon turns to anger. Æacus was enraged.

"Wandering mountebank! you wander as much in mind as with your feet. Your tendencies are out of the way and suspicious. You approach the bounds of sorcery. You have dealings with unknown animals. You speak to the populace of things that exist but for you alone, and the nature of which is unknown, such as the hoemorrhoüs."

"The hoemorrhoüs is a viper which was seen by Tremellius."

This repartee produced a certain disorder in the irritated science of Doctor Æacus.

Ursus added, "The existence of the hoemorrhoüs is quite as true as that of the odoriferous hyena, and of the civet described by Castellus."

Æacus got out of the difficulty by charging home.

"Here are your own words, and very diabolical words they are. Listen."

With his eyes on his notes, Æacus read,—

"Two plants, the thalagssigle and the aglaphotis, are luminous in the evening, flowers by day, stars by night;" and looking steadily at Ursus, "What have you to say to that?"

Ursus answered,—

"Every plant is a lamp. Its perfume is its light." Æacus turned over other pages.

"You have denied that the vesicles of the otter are equivalent to castoreum."

"I merely said that perhaps it may be necessary to receive the teaching of Ætius on this point with some reserve."

Æacus became furious.

"You practise medicine?"

"I practise medicine," sighed Ursus timidly.

"On living things?"

"Rather than on dead ones," said Ursus.

Ursus defended himself stoutly, but dully; an admirable mixture, in which meekness predominated. He spoke with such gentleness that Doctor Æacus felt that he must insult him.

"What are you murmuring there?" said he rudely.

Ursus was amazed, and restricted himself to saying,—

"Murmurings are for the young, and moans for the aged. Alas, I moan!"

Æacus replied,—

"Be assured of this—if you attend a sick person, and he dies, you will be punished by death."

Ursus hazarded a question.

"And if he gets well?"

"In that case," said the doctor, softening his voice, "you will be punished by death."

"There is little difference," said Ursus.

The doctor replied,—

"If death ensues, we punish gross ignorance; if recovery, we punish presumption. The gibbet in either case."

"I was ignorant of the circumstance," murmured Ursus. "I thank you for teaching me. One does not know all the beauties of the law."

"Take care of yourself."

"Religiously," said Ursus.

"We know what you are about."

"As for me," thought Ursus, "that is more than I always know myself."

"We could send you to prison."

"I see that perfectly, gentlemen."

"You cannot deny your infractions nor your encroachments."

"My philosophy asks pardon."

"Great audacity has been attributed to you."

"That is quite a mistake."

"It is said that you have cured the sick."

"I am the victim of calumny."

The three pairs of eyebrows which were so horribly fixed on Ursus contracted. The three wise faces drew near to each other, and whispered. Ursus had the vision of a vague fool's cap sketched out above those three empowered heads. The low and requisite whispering of the trio was of some minutes' duration, during which time Ursus felt all the ice and all the scorch of agony. At length Minos, who was president, turned to him and said angrily,—

"Go away!"

Ursus felt something like Jonas when he was leaving the belly of the whale.

Minos continued,—

"You are discharged."

Ursus said to himself,—

"They won't catch me at this again. Good-bye, medicine!"

And he added in his innermost heart,—

"From henceforth I will carefully allow them to die."

Bent double, he bowed everywhere; to the doctors, to the busts, the tables, the walls, and retiring backwards through the door, disappeared almost as a shadow melting into air.

He left the hall slowly, like an innocent man, and rushed from the street rapidly, like a guilty one. The officers of justice are so singular and obscure in their ways that even when acquitted one flies from them.

As he fled he mumbled,—

"I am well out of it. I am the savant untamed; they the savants civilized. Doctors cavil at the learned. False science is the excrement of the true, and is employed to the destruction of philosophers. Philosophers, as they produce sophists, produce their own scourge. Of the dung of the thrush is born the mistletoe, with which is made birdlime, with which the thrush is captured. *Turdus sibi malum cacat.*"

We do not represent Ursus as a refined man. He was imprudent enough to use words which expressed his thoughts. He had no more taste than Voltaire.

When Ursus returned to the Green Box, he told Master Nicless that he had been delayed by following a pretty woman, and let not a word escape him concerning his adventure.

Except in the evening when he said in a low voice to Homo,—

"See here, I have vanquished the three heads of Cerberus."

CHAPTER VII.

WHY SHOULD A GOLD PIECE LOWER ITSELF BY MIXING WITH A HEAP OF PENNIES?

An event happened.

The Tadcaster Inn became more and more a furnace of joy and laughter. Never was there more resonant gaiety. The landlord and his boy were become insufficient to draw the ale, stout, and porter. In the evening in the lower room, with its windows all aglow, there was not a vacant table. They sang, they shouted; the great old hearth, vaulted like an oven, with its iron bars piled with coals, shone out brightly. It was like a house of fire and noise.

In the yard—that is to say, in the theatre—the crowd was greater still.

Crowds as great as the suburb of Southwark could supply so thronged the performances of "Chaos Vanquished" that directly the curtain was raised—that is to say, the platform of the Green Box was lowered—every place was filled. The windows were alive with spectators, the balcony was crammed. Not a single paving-stone in the paved yard was to be seen. It seemed paved with faces.

Only the compartment for the nobility remained empty.

There was thus a space in the centre of the balcony, a black hole, called in metaphorical slang, an oven. No one there. Crowds everywhere except in that one spot.

One evening it was occupied.

It was on a Saturday, a day on which the English make all haste to amuse themselves before the *ennui* of Sunday. The hall was full.

We say *hall.* Shakespeare for a long time had to use the yard of an inn for a theatre, and he called it *hall.*

Just as the curtain rose on the prologue of "Chaos Vanquished," with Ursus, Homo, and Gwynplaine on the stage, Ursus, from habit, cast a look at the audience, and felt a sensation.

The compartment for the nobility was occupied. A lady was sitting alone in the middle of the box, on the Utrecht velvet arm-chair. She was alone, and she filled the box. Certain beings seem to give out light. This lady, like Dea, had a light in herself, but a light of a different character.

Dea was pale, this lady was pink. Dea was the twilight, this lady, Aurora. Dea was beautiful, this lady was superb. Dea was innocence, candour, fairness, alabaster—this woman was of the purple, and one felt that she did not fear the blush. Her irradiation overflowed the box, she sat in the midst of it, immovable, in the spreading majesty of an idol.

Amidst the sordid crowd she shone out grandly, as with the radiance of a carbuncle. She inundated it with so much light that she drowned it in shadow, and all the mean faces in it underwent eclipse. Her splendour blotted out all else.

Every eye was turned towards her.

Tom-Jim-Jack was in the crowd. He was lost like the rest in the nimbus of this dazzling creature.

The lady at first absorbed the whole attention of the public, who had crowded to the performance, thus somewhat diminishing the opening effects of "Chaos Vanquished."

Whatever might be the air of dreamland about her, for those who were near she was a woman; perchance too much a woman.

She was tall and amply formed, and showed as much as possible of her magnificent person. She wore heavy earrings of pearls, with which were mixed those whimsical jewels called "keys of England." Her upper dress was of Indian muslin, embroidered all over with gold—a great luxury, because those muslin dresses then cost six hundred crowns. A large diamond brooch closed her chemise, the which she wore so as to display her shoulders and bosom, in the immodest fashion of the time; the chemisette was made of that lawn of which Anne of Austria had sheets so fine that they could be passed through a ring. She wore what seemed like a cuirass of rubies—some uncut, but polished, and precious stones were sewn all over the body of her dress. Then, her eyebrows were blackened with Indian ink; and her arms, elbows, shoulders, chin, and nostrils, with the top of her eyelids, the lobes of her ears, the palms of her hands, the tips of her fingers, were tinted with a glowing and provoking touch of colour. Above all, she wore an expression of implacable determination to be beautiful. This reached the point of ferocity. She was like a panther, with the power of turning cat at will, and caressing. One of her eyes was blue, the other black.

Gwynplaine, as well as Ursus, contemplated her.

The Green Box somewhat resembled a phantasmagoria in its representations. "Chaos Vanquished" was rather a dream than a piece; it generally produced on the audience the effect of a vision. Now, this effect was reflected on the actors. The house took the performers by surprise, and they were thunderstruck in their turn. It was a rebound of fascination.

The woman watched them, and they watched her.

At the distance at which they were placed, and in that luminous mist which is the half-light of a theatre, details were lost and it was like a hallucination. Of course it was a woman, but was it not a chimera as well? The penetration of her light into their obscurity stupefied them. It was like the appearance of an unknown planet. It came from a world of the happy. Her irradiation amplified her figure. The lady was covered with nocturnal glitterings, like a milky way. Her precious stones were stars. The diamond brooch was perhaps a pleiad. The splendid beauty of her bosom seemed supernatural. They felt, as they looked upon the star-like creature, the momentary but thrilling approach of the regions of felicity. It was out of the heights of a Paradise that she leant towards their mean-looking Green Box, and revealed to the gaze of its wretched audience her expression of inexorable serenity. As she satisfied her unbounded curiosity, she fed at the same time the curiosity of the public.

It was the Zenith permitting the Abyss to look at it.

Ursus, Gwynplaine, Vinos, Fibi, the crowd, every one had succumbed to her dazzling beauty, except Dea, ignorant in her darkness.

An apparition was indeed before them; but none of the ideas usually evoked by the word were realized in the lady's appearance.

There was nothing about her diaphanous, nothing undecided, nothing floating, no mist. She was an apparition; rose-coloured and fresh, and full of health. Yet, under the optical condition in which Ursus and Gwynplaine were placed, she looked like a vision. There are fleshy phantoms, called vampires. Such a queen as she, though a spirit to the crowd, consumes twelve hundred thousand a year, to keep her health.

Behind the lady, in the shadow, her page was to be perceived, *el mozo*, a little child-like man, fair and pretty, with a serious face. A very young and very grave servant was the fashion at that period. This page was dressed from top to toe in scarlet velvet, and had on his skull-cap, which was embroidered with gold, a bunch of curled feathers. This was the sign of a high class of service, and indicated attendance on a very great lady.

The lackey is part of the lord, and it was impossible not to remark, in the shadow of his mistress, the train-bearing page. Memory often takes notes unconsciously; and, without Gwynplaine's suspecting it, the round cheeks, the serious mien, the embroidered and plumed cap of the lady's page left some trace on his mind. The page, however, did nothing to call attention to himself. To do so is to be wanting in respect. He held himself aloof and passive at the back of the box, retiring as far as the closed door permitted.

Notwithstanding the presence of her train-bearer, the lady was not the less alone in the compartment, since a valet counts for nothing.

However powerful a diversion had been produced by this person, who produced the effect of a personage, the *dénouement* of "Chaos Vanquished" was more powerful still. The impression which it made was, as usual, irresistible. Perhaps, even, there occurred in the hall, on account of the radiant spectator (for sometimes the spectator is part of the spectacle), an increase of electricity. The contagion of Gwynplaine's laugh was more triumphant than ever. The whole audience fell into an indescribable epilepsy of hilarity, through which could be distinguished the sonorous and magisterial ha! ha! of Tom-Jim-Jack.

Only the unknown lady looked at the performance with the immobility of a statue, and with her eyes, like those of a phantom, she laughed not. A spectre, but sun-born.

The performance over, the platform drawn up, and the family reassembled in the Green Box, Ursus opened and emptied on the supper-table the bag of receipts. From a heap of pennies there slid suddenly forth a Spanish gold onza. "Hers!" cried Ursus.

The onza amidst the pence covered with verdigris was a type of the lady amidst the crowd.

"She has paid an onza for her seat," cried Ursus with enthusiasm.

Just then, the hotel-keeper entered the Green Box, and, passing his arm out of the window at the back of it, opened the loophole in the wall of which we have already spoken, which gave a view over the field, and which was level with the window; then he made a silent sign to Ursus to look out. A carriage, swarming with plumed footmen carrying torches and magnificently appointed, was driving off at a fast trot.

Ursus took the piece of gold between his forefinger and thumb respectfully, and, showing it to Master Nicless, said,—

"She is a goddess."

Then his eyes falling on the carriage which was about to turn the corner of the field, and on the imperial of which the footmen's torches lighted up a golden coronet, with eight strawberry leaves, he exclaimed,—

"She is more. She is a duchess."

The carriage disappeared: The rumbling of its wheels died away in the distance.

Ursus remained some moments in an ecstasy, holding the gold piece between his finger and thumb, as in a monstrance, elevating it as the priest elevates the host.

Then he placed it on the table, and, as he contemplated it, began to talk of "Madam."

The innkeeper replied,—

"She was a duchess." Yes. They knew her title. But her name? Of that they were ignorant. Master Nicless had been close to the carriage, and seen the coat of arms and the footmen covered with lace. The coachman had a wig on which might have belonged to a Lord Chancellor. The carriage was of that rare design called, in Spain, *cochetumbon*, a splendid build, with a top like a tomb, which makes a magnificent support for a coronet. The page was a man in miniature, so small that he could sit on the step of the carriage outside the door. The duty of those pretty creatures was to bear the trains of their mistresses. They also bore their messages. And did you remark the plumed cap of the page? How grand it was! You pay a fine if you wear those plumes without the right of doing so. Master Nicless had seen the lady, too, quite close. A kind of queen. Such wealth gives beauty. The skin is whiter, the eye more proud, the gait more noble, and grace more insolent. Nothing can equal the elegant impertinence of hands which never work. Master Nicless told the story of all the magnificence, of the white skin with the blue veins, the neck, the shoulders, the arms, the touch of paint everywhere, the pearl earrings, the head-dress powdered with gold; the profusion of stones, the rubies, the diamonds.

"Less brilliant than her eyes," murmured Ursus.

Gwynplaine said nothing.

Dea listened.

"And do you know," said the tavern-keeper, "the most wonderful thing of all?"

"What?" said Ursus.

"I saw her get into her carriage."

"What then?"

"She did not get in alone."

"Nonsense!"

"Some one got in with her."

"Who?"

"Guess."

"The king," said Ursus.

"In the first place," said Master Nicless, "there is no king at present. We are not living under a king. Guess who got into the carriage with the duchess."

"Jupiter," said Ursus.

The hotel-keeper replied,—

"Tom-Jim-Jack!"

Gwynplaine, who had not said a word, broke silence.

"Tom-Jim-Jack!" he cried.

There was a pause of astonishment, during which the low voice of Dea was heard to say,—

"Cannot this woman be prevented coming."

CHAPTER VIII.

SYMPTOMS OF POISONING

The "apparition" did not return. It did not reappear in the theatre, but it reappeared to the memory of Gwynplaine. Gwynplaine was, to a certain degree, troubled. It seemed to him that for the first time in his life he had seen a woman.

He made that first stumble, a strange dream. We should beware of the nature of the reveries that fasten on us. Reverie has in it the mystery and subtlety of an odour. It is to thought what perfume is to the tuberose. It is at times the exudation of a venomous idea, and it penetrates like a vapour. You may poison yourself with reveries, as with flowers. An intoxicating suicide, exquisite and malignant. The suicide of the soul is evil thought. In it is the poison. Reverie attracts, cajoles, lures, entwines, and then makes you its accomplice. It makes you bear your half in the trickeries which it plays on conscience. It charms; then it corrupts you. We may say of reverie as of play, one begins by being a dupe, and ends by being a cheat.

Gwynplaine dreamed.

He had never before seen Woman. He had seen the shadow in the women of the populace, and he had seen the soul in Dea.

He had just seen the reality.

A warm and living skin, under which one felt the circulation of passionate blood; an outline with the precision of marble and the undulation of the wave; a high and impassive mien, mingling refusal with attraction, and summing itself up in its own glory; hair of the colour of the reflection from a furnace; a gallantry of adornment producing in herself and in others a tremor of voluptuousness, the half-revealed nudity betraying a disdainful desire to be coveted at a distance by the crowd; an ineradicable coquetry; the charm of impenetrability, temptation seasoned by the glimpse of perdition, a promise to the senses and a menace to the mind; a double anxiety, the one desire, the other fear. He had just seen these things. He had just seen Woman.

He had seen more and less than a woman; he had seen a female.

And at the same time an Olympian. The female of a god.

The mystery of sex had just been revealed to him.

And where? On inaccessible heights—at an infinite distance.

O mocking destiny! The soul, that celestial essence, he possessed; he held it in his hand. It was Dea. Sex, that terrestrial embodiment, he perceived in the heights of heaven. It was that woman.

A duchess!

"More than a goddess," Ursus had said.

What a precipice! Even dreams dissolved before such a perpendicular height to escalade.

Was he going to commit the folly of dreaming about the unknown beauty?

He debated with himself.

He recalled all that Ursus had said of high stations which are almost royal. The philosopher's disquisitions, which had hitherto seemed so useless, now became landmarks for his thoughts. A very thin layer of forgetfulness often lies over our memory, through which at times we catch a glimpse of all beneath it. His fancy ran on that august world, the peerage, to which the lady belonged, and which was so inexorably placed above the inferior world, the common people, of which he was one.

And was he even one of the people? Was not he, the mountebank, below the lowest of the low? For the first time since he had arrived at the age of reflection, he felt his heart vaguely contracted by a sense of his baseness, and of that which we nowadays call abasement. The paintings and the catalogues of Ursus, his lyrical inventories, his dithyrambics of castles, parks, fountains, and colonnades, his catalogues of riches and of power, revived in the memory of Gwynplaine in the relief of reality mingled with mist. He was possessed with the image of this zenith. That a man should be a lord!—it seemed chimerical. It was so, however. Incredible thing! There were lords! But were they of flesh and blood, like ourselves? It seemed doubtful. He felt that he lay at the bottom of all darkness, encompassed by a wall, while he could just perceive in the far distance above his head, through the mouth of the pit, a dazzling confusion of azure, of figures, and of rays, which was Olympus. In the midst of this glory the duchess shone out resplendent.

He felt for this woman a strange, inexpressible longing, combined with a conviction of the impossibility of attainment. This poignant contradiction returned to his mind again and again, notwithstanding every effort. He saw near to him, even within his reach, in close and tangible reality, the soul; and in the unattainable—in the depths of the ideal—the flesh. None of these thoughts attained to certain shape. They were as a vapour within him, changing every instant its form, and floating away. But the darkness which the vapour caused was intense.

He did not form even in his dreams any hope of reaching the heights where the duchess dwelt. Luckily for him.

The vibration of such ladders of fancy, if ever we put our foot upon them, may render our brains dizzy for ever. Intending to scale Olympus, we reach Bedlam; any distinct feeling of actual desire would have terrified him. He entertained none of that nature.

Besides, was he likely ever to see the lady again? Most probably not. To fall in love with a passing light on the horizon, madness cannot reach to that pitch. To make loving eyes at a star even, is not incomprehensible. It is seen again, it reappears, it is fixed in the sky. But can any one be enamoured of a flash of lightning?

Dreams flowed and ebbed within him. The majestic and gallant idol at the back of the box had cast a light over his diffused ideas, then faded away. He thought, yet thought not of it; turned to other things—returned to it. It rocked about in his brain—nothing more. It broke his sleep for several nights. Sleeplessness is as full of dreams as sleep.

It is almost impossible to express in their exact limits the abstract evolutions of the brain. The inconvenience of words is that they are more marked in form than ideas. All ideas have indistinct boundary lines, words have not. A certain diffused phase of the soul ever escapes words. Expression has its frontiers, thought has none.

The depths of our secret souls are so vast that Gwynplaine's dreams scarcely touched Dea. Dea reigned sacred in the centre of his soul; nothing could approach her.

Still (for such contradictions make up the soul of man) there was a conflict within him. Was he conscious of it? Scarcely.

In his heart of hearts he felt a collision of desires. We all have our weak points. Its nature would have been clear to Ursus; but to Gwynplaine it was not.

Two instincts—one the ideal, the other sexual—were struggling within him. Such contests occur between the angels of light and darkness on the edge of the abyss.

At length the angel of darkness was overthrown. One day Gwynplaine suddenly thought no more of the unknown woman.

The struggle between two principles—the duel between his earthly and his heavenly nature—had taken place within his soul, and at such a depth that he had understood it but dimly. One thing was certain, that he had never for one moment ceased to adore Dea.

He had been attacked by a violent disorder, his blood had been fevered; but it was over. Dea alone remained.

Gwynplaine would have been much astonished had any one told him that Dea had ever been, even for a moment, in danger; and in a week or two the phantom which had threatened the hearts of both their souls faded away.

Within Gwynplaine nothing remained but the heart, which was the hearth, and the love, which was its fire.

Besides, we have just said that "the duchess" did not return.

Ursus thought it all very natural. "The lady with the gold piece" is a phenomenon. She enters, pays, and vanishes. It would be too much joy were she to return.

As to Dea, she made no allusion to the woman who had come and passed away. She listened, perhaps, and was sufficiently enlightened by the sighs of Ursus, and now and then by some significant exclamation, such as,—

"*One does not get ounces of gold every day!*"

She spoke no more of the "woman." This showed deep instinct. The soul takes obscure precautions, in the secrets of which it is not always admitted itself. To keep silence about any one seems to keep them afar off. One fears that questions may call them back. We put silence between us, as if we were shutting a door.

So the incident fell into oblivion.

Was it ever anything? Had it ever occurred? Could it be said that a shadow had floated between Gwynplaine and Dea? Dea did not know of it, nor Gwynplaine either. No; nothing had occurred. The duchess herself was blurred in the distant perspective like an illusion. It had been but a momentary dream passing over Gwynplaine, out of which he had awakened.

When it fades away, a reverie, like a mist, leaves no trace behind; and when the cloud has passed on, love shines out as brightly in the heart as the sun in the sky.

CHAPTER IX.

ABYSSUS ABYSSUM VOCAT

Another face, disappeared—Tom-Jim-Jack's. Suddenly he ceased to frequent the Tadcaster Inn.

Persons so situated as to be able to observe other phases of fashionable life in London, might have seen that about this time the *Weekly Gazette*, between two extracts from parish registers, announced the departure of Lord David Dirry-Moir, by order of her Majesty, to take command of his frigate in the white squadron then cruising off the coast of Holland.

Ursus, perceiving that Tom-Jim-Jack did not return, was troubled by his absence. He had not seen Tom-Jim-Jack since the day on which he had driven off in the same carriage with the lady of the gold piece. It was, indeed, an enigma who this Tom-Jim-Jack could be, who carried off duchesses under his arm. What an interesting investigation! What questions to propound! What things to be said. Therefore Ursus said not a word.

Ursus, who had had experience, knew the smart caused by rash curiosity. Curiosity ought always to be proportioned to the curious. By listening, we risk our ear; by watching, we risk our eye. Prudent people neither hear nor see. Tom-Jim-Jack had got into a princely carriage. The tavern-keeper had seen him. It appeared so extraordinary that the sailor should sit by the lady that it made Ursus circumspect. The caprices of those in high life ought to be sacred to the lower orders. The reptiles called the poor had best squat in their holes when they see anything out of the way. Quiescence is a power. Shut your eyes, if you have not the luck to be blind; stop up your ears, if you have not the good fortune to be deaf; paralyze your tongue, if you have not the perfection of being mute. The great do what they like, the little what they can. Let the unknown pass unnoticed. Do not importune mythology. Do not interrogate appearances. Have a profound respect for idols. Do not let us direct our gossiping towards the lessenings or increasings which take place in superior regions, of the motives of which we are ignorant. Such things are mostly optical delusions to us inferior creatures. Metamorphoses are the business of the gods: the transformations and the contingent disorders of great persons who float above us are clouds impossible to comprehend and perilous to study. Too much attention irritates the Olympians engaged in their gyrations of amusement or fancy; and a thunderbolt may teach you that the bull you are too curiously examining is Jupiter. Do not lift the folds of the stone-coloured mantles of those terrible powers. Indifference is intelligence. Do not stir, and you will be safe. Feign death, and they will not kill you. Therein lies the wisdom of the insect. Ursus practised it.

The tavern-keeper, who was puzzled as well, questioned Ursus one day.

"Do you observe that Tom-Jim-Jack never comes here now!"

"Indeed!" said Ursus. "I have not remarked it."

Master Nicless made an observation in an undertone, no doubt touching the intimacy between the ducal carriage and Tom-Jim-Jack—a remark which, as it might have been irreverent and dangerous, Ursus took care not to hear.

Still Ursus was too much of an artist not to regret Tom-Jim-Jack. He felt some disappointment. He told his feeling to Homo, of whose discretion alone he felt certain. He whispered into the ear of the wolf, "Since Tom-Jim-Jack ceased to come, I feel a blank as a man, and a chill as a poet." This pouring out of his heart to a friend relieved Ursus.

His lips were sealed before Gwynplaine, who, however, made no allusion to Tom-Jim-Jack. The fact was that Tom-Jim-Jack's presence or absence mattered not to Gwynplaine, absorbed as he was in Dea.

Forgetfulness fell more and more on Gwynplaine. As for Dea, she had not even suspected the existence of a vague trouble. At the same time, no more cabals or complaints against the Laughing Man were spoken of. Hate seemed to have let go its hold. All was tranquil in and around the Green Box. No more opposition from strollers, merry-andrews, nor priests; no more grumbling outside. Their success was unclouded. Destiny allows of such sudden serenity. The brilliant happiness of Gwynplaine and Dea was for the present absolutely cloudless. Little by little it had risen to a degree which admitted of no increase. There is one word which expresses the situation—apogee. Happiness, like the sea, has its high tide. The worst thing for the perfectly happy is that it recedes.

There are two ways of being inaccessible: being too high and being too low. At least as much, perhaps, as the first is the second to be desired. More surely than the eagle escapes the arrow, the animalcule escapes being crushed. This security of insignificance, if it had ever existed on earth, was enjoyed by Gwynplaine and Dea, and never before had it been so complete. They lived on, daily more and more ecstatically wrapt in each other. The heart saturates itself with love as with a divine salt that preserves it, and from this arises the incorruptible constancy of those who have loved each other from the dawn of their lives, and the affection which keeps its freshness in old age. There is such a thing as the embalmment of the heart. It is of Daphnis and Chloë that Philemon and Baucis are made. The old age of which we speak, evening resembling morning, was evidently reserved for Gwynplaine and Dea. In the meantime they were young.

Ursus looked on this love as a doctor examines his case. He had what was in those days termed a hippocratical expression of face. He fixed his sagacious eyes on Dea, fragile and pale, and growled out, "It is lucky that she is happy." At other times he said, "She is lucky for her health's sake." He shook his head, and at times read attentively a portion treating of heart-disease in Aviccunas, translated by Vossiscus Fortunatus, Louvain, 1650, an old worm-eaten book of his.

Dea, when fatigued, suffered from perspirations and drowsiness, and took a daily *siesta*, as we have already seen. One day, while she was lying asleep on the bearskin, Gwynplaine was out, and Ursus bent down softly and applied his ear to Dea's heart. He seemed to listen for a few minutes, and then stood up, murmuring, "She must not have any shock. It would find out the weak place."

The crowd continued to flock to the performance of "Chaos Vanquished." The success of the Laughing Man seemed inexhaustible. Every one rushed to see him; no longer from Southwark only, but even from other parts of London. The general public began to mingle with the usual audience, which no longer consisted of sailors and drivers only; in the opinion of Master Nicless, who was well acquainted with crowds, there were in the crowd gentlemen and baronets disguised as common people. Disguise is one of the pleasures of pride, and was much in fashion at that period. This mixing of the aristocratic element with the mob was a good sign, and showed that their popularity was extending to London. The fame of Gwynplaine has decidedly penetrated into the great world. Such was the fact. Nothing was talked of but the Laughing Man. He was talked about even at the Mohawk Club, frequented by noblemen.

In the Green Box they had no idea of all this. They were content to be happy. It was intoxication to Dea to feel, as she did every evening, the crisp and tawny head of Gwynplaine. In love there is nothing like habit. The whole of life is concentrated in it. The reappearance of the stars is the custom of the universe. Creation is nothing but a mistress, and the sun is a lover. Light is a dazzling caryatid supporting the world. Each day, for a sublime minute, the earth, covered by night, rests on the rising sun. Dea, blind, felt a like return of warmth and hope within her when she placed her hand on the head of Gwynplaine.

To adore each other in the shadows, to love in the plenitude of silence; who could not become reconciled to such an eternity?

One evening Gwynplaine, feeling within him that overflow of felicity which, like the intoxication of perfumes, causes a sort of delicious faintness, was strolling, as he usually did after the performance, in the meadow some hundred paces from the Green Box. Sometimes in those high tides of feeling in our souls we feel that we would fain pour out the sensations of the overflowing heart. The night was dark but clear. The stars were shining. The whole fair-ground was deserted. Sleep and forgetfulness reigned in the caravans which were scattered over Tarrinzeau Field.

One light alone was unextinguished. It was the lamp of the Tadcaster Inn, the door of which was left ajar to admit Gwynplaine on his return.

Midnight had just struck in the five parishes of Southwark, with the breaks and differences of tone of their various bells. Gwynplaine was dreaming of Dea. Of whom else should he dream? But that evening, feeling singularly troubled, and full of a charm which was at the same time a pang, he thought of Dea as a man thinks of a woman. He reproached himself for this. It seemed to be failing in respect to her. The husband's attack was forming dimly within him. Sweet and imperious impatience! He was crossing the invisible frontier, on this side of which is the virgin, on the other, the wife. He questioned himself anxiously. A blush, as it were, overspread his mind. The Gwynplaine of long ago had been transformed, by degrees, unconsciously in a mysterious growth. His old modesty was becoming misty and uneasy. We have an ear of light, into which speaks the spirit; and an ear of darkness, into which speaks the instinct. Into the latter strange voices were making their proposals. However pure-minded may be the youth who dreams of love, a certain grossness of the flesh eventually comes between his dream and him. Intentions lose their transparency. The unavowed desire implanted by nature enters into his conscience. Gwynplaine felt an indescribable yearning of the flesh, which abounds in all temptation, and Dea was scarcely flesh. In this fever, which he knew to be unhealthy, he transfigured Dea into a more material aspect, and tried to exaggerate her seraphic form into feminine loveliness. It is thou, O woman, that we require.

Love comes not to permit too much of paradise. It requires the fevered skin, the troubled life, the unbound hair, the kiss electrical and irreparable, the clasp of desire. The sidereal is embarrassing, the ethereal is heavy. Too much of the heavenly in love is like too much fuel on a fire: the flame suffers from it. Gwynplaine fell into an exquisite nightmare; Dea to be clasped in his arms—Dea clasped in them! He heard nature in his heart crying out for a woman. Like a Pygmalion in a dream modelling a Galathea out of the azure, in the depths of his soul he worked at the chaste contour of Dea—a contour with too much of heaven, too little of Eden. For Eden is Eve, and Eve was a female, a carnal mother, a terrestrial nurse; the sacred womb of generations; the breast of unfailing milk; the rocker of the cradle of the newborn world, and wings are incompatible with the bosom of woman. Virginity is but the hope of maternity. Still, in Gwynplaine's dreams, Dea, until now, had been enthroned above flesh. Now, however, he made wild efforts in thought to draw her downwards by that thread, sex, which ties every girl to earth. Not one of those birds is free. Dea, like all the rest, was within this law; and Gwynplaine, though he scarcely acknowledged it, felt a vague desire that she should submit to it. This desire possessed him in spite of himself, and with an ever-recurring relapse. He pictured Dea as woman. He came to the point of regarding her under a hitherto unheard-of form; as a creature no longer of ecstasy only, but of voluptuousness; as Dea, with her head resting on the pillow. He was ashamed of this visionary desecration. It was like an attempt at profanation. He resisted its assault. He turned from it, but it returned again. He felt as if he were committing a criminal assault. To him Dea was encompassed by a cloud. Cleaving that cloud, he shuddered, as though he were raising her chemise. It was in April. The spine has its dreams. He rambled at random with the uncertain step caused by solitude. To have no one by is a provocative to wander. Whither flew his thoughts? He would not have dared to own it to himself. To heaven? No. To a bed. You were looking down upon him, O ye stars.

Why talk of a man in love? Rather say a man possessed. To be possessed by the devil, is the exception; to be possessed by a woman, the rule. Every man has to bear this alienation of himself. What a sorceress is a pretty woman! The true name of love is captivity.

Man is made prisoner by the soul of a woman; by her flesh as well, and sometimes even more by the flesh than by the soul. The soul is the true love, the flesh, the mistress.

We slander the devil. It was not he who tempted Eve. It was Eve who tempted him. The woman began. Lucifer was passing by quietly. He perceived the woman, and became Satan.

The flesh is the cover of the unknown. It is provocative (which is strange) by its modesty. Nothing could be more distracting. It is full of shame, the hussey!

It was the terrible love of the surface which was then agitating Gwynplaine, and holding him in its power. Fearful the moment in which man covets the nakedness of woman! What dark things lurk beneath the fairness of Venus!

Something within him was calling Dea aloud, Dea the maiden, Dea the other half of a man, Dea flesh and blood, Dea with uncovered bosom. That cry was almost driving away the angel. Mysterious crisis through which all love must pass and in which the Ideal is in danger! Therein is the predestination of Creation. Moment of heavenly corruption! Gwynplaine's love of Dea was becoming nuptial. Virgin love is but a transition. The moment was come. Gwynplaine coveted the woman.

He coveted a woman!

Precipice of which one sees but the first gentle slope!

The indistinct summons of nature is inexorable. The whole of woman—what an abyss!

Luckily, there was no woman for Gwynplaine but Dea—the only one he desired, the only one who could desire him.

Gwynplaine felt that vague and mighty shudder which is the vital claim of infinity. Besides there was the aggravation of the spring. He was breathing the nameless odours of the starry darkness. He walked forward in a wild feeling of delight. The wandering perfumes of the rising sap, the heady irradiations which float in shadow, the distant opening of nocturnal flowers, the complicity of little hidden nests, the murmurs of waters and of leaves, soft sighs rising from all things, the freshness, the warmth, and the mysterious awakening of April and May, is the vast diffusion of sex murmuring, in whispers, their proposals of voluptuousness, till the soul stammers in answer to the giddy provocation. The ideal no longer knows what it is saying.

Any one observing Gwynplaine walk would have said, "See!—a drunken man!"

He almost staggered under the weight of his own heart, of spring, and of the night.

The solitude in the bowling-green was so peaceful that at times he spoke aloud. The consciousness that there is no listener induces speech.

He walked with slow steps, his head bent down, his hands behind him, the left hand in the right, the fingers open.

Suddenly he felt something slipped between his fingers.

He turned round quickly.

In his hand was a paper, and in front of him a man.

It was the man who, coming behind him with the stealth of a cat, had placed the paper in his fingers.

The paper was a letter.

The man, as he appeared pretty clearly in the starlight, was small, chubby-cheeked, young, sedate, and dressed in a scarlet livery, exposed from top to toe through the opening of a long gray cloak, then called a capenoche, a Spanish word contracted; in French it was *cape-de-nuit*. His head was covered by a crimson cap, like the skull-cap of a cardinal, on which servitude was indicated by a strip of lace. On this cap was a plume of tisserin feathers. He stood motionless before Gwynplaine, like a dark outline in a dream.

Gwynplaine recognized the duchess's page.

Before Gwynplaine could utter an exclamation of surprise, he heard the thin voice of the page, at once childlike and feminine in its tone, saying to him,—

"At this hour to-morrow, be at the corner of London Bridge. I will be there to conduct you—"

"Whither?" demanded Gwynplaine.

"Where you are expected."

Gwynplaine dropped his eyes on the letter, which he was holding mechanically in his hand.

When he looked up the page was no longer with him.

He perceived a vague form lessening rapidly in the distance. It was the little valet. He turned the corner of the street, and solitude reigned again.

Gwynplaine saw the page vanish, then looked at the letter. There are moments in our lives when what happens seems not to happen. Stupor keeps us for a moment at a distance from the fact.

Gwynplaine raised the letter to his eyes, as if to read it, but soon perceived that he could not do so for two reasons—first, because he had not broken the seal; and, secondly, because it was too dark.

It was some minutes before he remembered that there was a lamp at the inn. He took a few steps sideways, as if he knew not whither he was going.

A somnambulist, to whom a phantom had given a letter, might walk as he did.

At last he made up his mind. He ran rather than walked towards the inn, stood in the light which broke through the half-open door, and by it again examined the closed letter. There was no design on the seal, and on the envelope was written, "*To Gwynplaine*." He broke the seal, tore the envelope, unfolded the letter, put it directly under the light, and read as follows:—

"You are hideous; I am beautiful. You are a player; I am a duchess. I am the highest; you are the lowest. I desire you! I love you! Come!"

BOOK THE FOURTH

THE CELL OF TORTURE

CHAPTER I.

THE TEMPTATION OF ST. GWYNPLAINE

One jet of flame hardly makes a prick in the darkness; another sets fire to a volcano.

Some sparks are gigantic.

Gwynplaine read the letter, then he read it over again. Yes, the words were there, "I love you!"

Terrors chased each other through his mind.

The first was, that he believed himself to be mad.

He was mad; that was certain: He had just seen what had no existence. The twilight spectres were making game of him, poor wretch! The little man in scarlet was the will-o'-the-wisp of a dream. Sometimes, at night, nothings condensed into flame come and laugh at us. Having had his laugh out, the visionary being had disappeared, and left Gwynplaine behind him, mad.

Such are the freaks of darkness.

The second terror was, to find out that he was in his right senses.

A vision? Certainly not. How could that be? Had he not a letter in his hand? Did he not see an envelope, a seal, paper, and writing? Did he not know from whom that came? It was all clear enough. Some one took a pen and ink, and wrote. Some one lighted a taper, and sealed it with wax. Was not his name written on the letter—"*To Gwynplaine?*" The paper was scented. All was clear.

Gwynplaine knew the little man. The dwarf was a page. The gleam was a livery. The page had given him a rendezvous for the same hour on the morrow, at the corner of London Bridge.

Was London Bridge an illusion?

No, no. All was clear. There was no delirium. All was reality. Gwynplaine was perfectly clear in his intellect. It was not a phantasmagoria, suddenly dissolving above his head, and fading into nothingness. It was something which had really happened to him. No, Gwynplaine was not mad, nor was he dreaming. Again he read the letter.

Well, yes! But then?

That then was terror-striking.

There was a woman who desired him! If so, let no one ever again pronounce the word incredible! A woman desire him! A woman who had seen his face! A woman who was not blind! And who was this woman? An ugly one? No; a beauty. A gipsy? No; a duchess!

What was it all about, and what could it all mean? What peril in such a triumph! And how was he to help plunging into it headlong?

What! that woman! The siren, the apparition, the lady in the visionary box, the light in the darkness! It was she! Yes; it was she!

The crackling of the fire burst out in every part of his frame. It was the strange, unknown lady, she who had previously so troubled his thoughts; and his first tumultuous feelings about this woman returned, heated by the evil fire. Forgetfulness is nothing but a palimpsest: an incident happens unexpectedly, and all that was effaced revives in the blanks of wondering memory.

Gwynplaine thought that he had dismissed that image from his remembrance, and he found that it was still there; and she had put her mark in his brain, unconsciously guilty of a dream. Without his suspecting it, the lines of the engraving had been bitten deep by reverie. And now a certain amount of evil had been done, and this train of thought, thenceforth, perhaps, irreparable, he took up again eagerly. What! she desired him! What! the princess descend from her throne, the idol from its shrine, the statue from its pedestal, the phantom from its cloud! What! from the depths of the impossible had this chimera come! This deity of the sky! This irradiation! This nereid all glistening with jewels! This proud and unattainable beauty, from the height of her radiant throne, was bending down to Gwynplaine! What! had she drawn up her chariot of the dawn, with its yoke of turtle-doves and dragons, before Gwynplaine, and said to him, "Come!" What! this terrible glory of being the object of such abasement from the empyrean, for Gwynplaine! This woman, if he could give that name to a form so starlike and majestic, this woman proposed herself, gave herself, delivered herself up to him! Wonder of wonders! A goddess prostituting herself for him! The arms of a courtesan opening in a cloud to clasp him to the bosom of a goddess, and that without degradation! Such majestic creatures cannot be sullied. The gods bathe themselves pure in light; and this goddess who came to him knew what she was doing. She was not ignorant of the incarnate hideousness of Gwynplaine. She had seen the mask which was his face; and that mask had not caused her to draw back. Gwynplaine was loved notwithstanding it!

Here was a thing surpassing all the extravagance of dreams. He was loved in consequence of his mask. Far from repulsing the goddess, the mask attracted her. Gwynplaine was not only loved; he was desired. He was more than accepted; he was chosen. He, chosen!

What! there, where this woman dwelt, in the regal region of irresponsible splendour, and in the power of full, free will; where there were princes, and she could take a prince; nobles, and she could take a noble; where there were men handsome, charming, magnificent, and she could take an Adonis: whom did she take? Gnafron! She could choose from the midst of meteors and thunders, the mighty six-winged seraphim, and she chose the larva crawling in the slime. On one side were highnesses and peers, all grandeur, all opulence, all glory; on the other, a mountebank. The mountebank carried it! What kind of scales could there be in the heart of this woman? By what measure did she weigh her love? She took off her ducal coronet, and flung it on the platform of a clown! She took from her brow the Olympian aureola, and placed it on the bristly head of a gnome! The world had turned topsy-turvy. The insects swarmed on high, the stars were scattered below, whilst the wonder-stricken Gwynplaine, overwhelmed by a falling ruin of light, and lying in the dust, was enshrined in a glory. One all-powerful, revolting against beauty and splendour, gave herself to the damned of night; preferred Gwynplaine to Antinoüs; excited by curiosity, she entered the shadows, and descending within them, and from this abdication of goddess-ship was rising, crowned and prodigious, the royalty of the wretched. "You are hideous. I love you." These words touched Gwynplaine in the ugly spot of pride. Pride is the heel in which all heroes are vulnerable. Gwynplaine was flattered in his vanity as a monster. He was loved for his deformity. He, too, was the exception, as much and perhaps more than the Jupiters and the Apollos. He felt superhuman, and so much a monster as to be a god. Fearful bewilderment!

Now, who was this woman? What did he know about her? Everything and nothing. She was a duchess, that he knew; he knew, also, that she was beautiful and rich; that she had liveries, lackeys, pages, and footmen running with torches by the side of her coroneted carriage. He knew that she was in love with him; at least she said so. Of everything else he was ignorant. He knew her title, but not her name. He knew her thought; he knew not her life. Was she married, widow, maiden? Was she free? Of what family was she? Were there snares, traps, dangers about her? Of the gallantry existing on the idle heights of society; the caves on those summits, in which savage charmers dream amid the scattered skeletons of the loves which they have already preyed on; of the extent of tragic cynicism to which the experiments of a woman may attain who believes herself to be beyond the reach of man—of things such as these Gwynplaine had no idea. Nor had he even in his mind materials out of which to build up a conjecture, information concerning such things being very scanty in the social depths in which he lived. Still he detected a shadow; he felt that a mist hung over all this brightness. Did he understand it? No. Could he guess at it? Still less. What was there behind that letter? One pair of folding doors opening before him, another closing on him, and causing him a vague anxiety. On the one side an avowal; on the other an enigma—avowal and enigma, which, like two mouths, one tempting, the other threatening, pronounce the same word, Dare!

Never had perfidious chance taken its measures better, nor timed more fitly the moment of temptation. Gwynplaine, stirred by spring, and by the sap rising in all things, was prompt to dream the dream of the flesh. The old man who is not to be stamped out, and over whom none of us can triumph, was awaking in that backward youth, still a boy at twenty-four.

It was just then, at the most stormy moment of the crisis, that the offer was made him, and the naked bosom of the Sphinx appeared before his dazzled eyes. Youth is an inclined plane. Gwynplaine was stooping, and something pushed him forward. What? the season, and the night. Who? the woman.

Were there no month of April, man would be a great deal more virtuous. The budding plants are a set of accomplices! Love is the thief, Spring the receiver.

Gwynplaine was shaken.

There is a kind of smoke of evil, preceding sin, in which the conscience cannot breathe. The obscure nausea of hell comes over virtue in temptation. The yawning abyss discharges an exhalation which warns the strong and turns the weak giddy. Gwynplaine was suffering its mysterious attack.

Dilemmas, transient and at the same time stubborn, were floating before him. Sin, presenting itself obstinately again and again to his mind, was taking form. The morrow, midnight? London Bridge, the page? Should he go? "Yes," cried the flesh; "No," cried the soul.

Nevertheless, we must remark that, strange as it may appear at first sight, he never once put himself the question, "Should he go?" quite distinctly. Reprehensible actions are like over-strong brandies—you cannot swallow them at a draught. You put down your glass; you will see to it presently; there is a strange taste even about that first drop. One thing is certain: he felt something behind him pushing him, forward towards the unknown. And he trembled. He could catch a glimpse of a crumbling precipice, and he drew back, stricken by the terror encircling him. He closed his eyes. He tried hard to deny to himself that the adventure had ever occurred, and to persuade himself into doubting his reason. This was evidently his best plan; the wisest thing he could do was to believe himself mad.

Fatal fever! Every man, surprised by the unexpected, has at times felt the throb of such tragic pulsations. The observer ever listens with anxiety to the echoes resounding from the dull strokes of the battering-ram of destiny striking against a conscience.

Alas! Gwynplaine put himself questions. Where duty is clear, to put oneself questions is to suffer defeat.

There are invasions which the mind may have to suffer. There are the Vandals of the soul—evil thoughts coming to devastate our virtue. A thousand contrary ideas rushed into Gwynplaine's brain, now following each other singly, now crowding together. Then silence reigned again, and he would lean his head on his hands, in a kind of mournful attention, as of one who contemplates a landscape by night.

Suddenly he felt that he was no longer thinking. His reverie had reached that point of utter darkness in which all things disappear.

He remembered, too, that he had not entered the inn. It might be about two o'clock in the morning.

He placed the letter which the page had brought him in his side-pocket; but perceiving that it was next his heart, he drew it out again, crumpled it up, and placed it in a pocket of his hose. He then directed his steps towards the inn, which he entered stealthily, and without awaking little Govicum, who, while waiting up for him, had fallen asleep on the table, with his arms for a pillow. He closed the door, lighted a candle at the lamp, fastened the bolt, turned the key in the lock, taking, mechanically, all the precautions usual to a man returning home late, ascended the staircase of the Green Box, slipped into the old hovel which he used as a bedroom, looked at Ursus who was asleep, blew out his candle, and did not go to bed.

Thus an hour passed away. Weary, at length, and fancying that bed and sleep were one, he laid his head upon the pillow without undressing, making darkness the concession of closing his eyes. But the storm of emotions which assailed him had not waned for an instant. Sleeplessness is a cruelty which night inflicts on man. Gwynplaine suffered greatly. For the first time in his life, he was not pleased with himself. Ache of heart mingled with gratified vanity. What was he to do? Day broke at last; he heard Ursus get up, but did not raise his eyelids. No truce for him, however. The letter was ever in his mind. Every word of it came back to him in a kind of chaos. In certain violent storms within the soul thought becomes a liquid. It is convulsed, it heaves, and something rises from it, like the dull roaring of the waves. Flood and flow, sudden shocks and whirls, the hesitation of the wave before the rock; hail and rain clouds with the light shining through their breaks; the petty flights of useless foam; wild swell broken in an instant; great efforts lost; wreck appearing all around; darkness and universal dispersion—as these things are of the sea, so are they of man. Gwynplaine was a prey to such a storm.

At the acme of his agony, his eyes still closed, he heard an exquisite voice saying, "Are you asleep, Gwynplaine?" He opened his eyes with a start, and sat up. Dea was standing in the half-open doorway. Her ineffable smile was in her eyes and on her lips. She was standing there, charming in the unconscious serenity of her radiance. Then came, as it were, a sacred moment. Gwynplaine watched her, startled, dazzled, awakened. Awakened from what?—from sleep? no, from sleeplessness. It was she, it was Dea; and suddenly he felt in the depths of his being the indescribable wane of the storm and the sublime descent of good over evil; the miracle of the look from on high was accomplished; the blind girl, the sweet light-bearer, with no effort beyond her mere presence, dissipated all the darkness within him; the curtain of cloud was dispersed from the soul as if drawn by an invisible hand, and a sky of azure, as though by celestial enchantment, again spread over Gwynplaine's conscience. In a moment he became by the virtue of that angel, the great and good Gwynplaine, the innocent man. Such mysterious confrontations occur to the soul as they do to creation. Both were silent—she, who was the light; he, who was the abyss; she, who was divine; he, who was appeased; and over Gwynplaine's stormy heart Dea shone with the indescribable effect of a star shining on the sea.

CHAPTER II.

FROM GAY TO GRAVE

How simple is a miracle! It was breakfast hour in the Green Box, and Dea had merely come to see why Gwynplaine had not joined their little breakfast table.

"It is you!" exclaimed Gwynplaine; and he had said everything. There was no other horizon, no vision for him now but the heavens where Dea was. His mind was appeased—appeased in such a manner as he alone can understand who has seen the smile spread swiftly over the sea when the hurricane had passed away. Over nothing does the calm come so quickly as over the whirlpool. This results from its power of absorption. And so it is with the human heart. Not always, however.

Dea had but to show herself, and all the light that was in Gwynplaine left him and went to her, and behind the dazzled Gwynplaine there was but a flight of phantoms. What a peacemaker is adoration! A few minutes afterwards they were sitting opposite each other, Ursus between them, Homo at their feet. The teapot, hung over a little lamp, was on the table. Fibi and Vinos were outside, waiting.

They breakfasted as they supped, in the centre compartment. From the position in which the narrow table was placed, Dea's back was turned towards the aperture in the partition which was opposite the entrance door of the Green Box. Their knees were touching. Gwynplaine was pouring out tea for Dea. Dea blew gracefully on her cup. Suddenly she sneezed. Just at that moment a thin smoke rose above the flame of the lamp, and something like a piece of paper fell into ashes. It was the smoke which had caused Dea to sneeze.

"What was that?" she asked.

"Nothing," replied Gwynplaine.

And he smiled. He had just burnt the duchess's letter.

The conscience of the man who loves is the guardian angel of the woman whom he loves.

Unburdened of the letter, his relief was wondrous, and Gwynplaine felt his integrity as the eagle feels its wings.

It seemed to him as if his temptation had evaporated with the smoke, and as if the duchess had crumbled into ashes with the paper.

Taking up their cups at random, and drinking one after the other from the same one, they talked. A babble of lovers, a chattering of sparrows! Child's talk, worthy of Mother Goose or of Homer! With two loving hearts, go no further for poetry; with two kisses for dialogue, go no further for music.

"Do you know something?"

"No."

"Gwynplaine, I dreamt that we were animals, and had wings."

"Wings; that means birds," murmured Gwynplaine.

"Fools! it means angels," growled Ursus.

And their talk went on.

"If you did not exist, Gwynplaine?"

"What then?"

"It could only be because there was no God."

"The tea is too hot; you will burn yourself, Dea."

"Blow on my cup."

"How beautiful you are this morning!"

"Do you know that I have a great many things to say to you?"

"Say them."

"I love you."

"I adore you."

And Ursus said aside, "By heaven, they are polite!"

Exquisite to lovers are their moments of silence! In them they gather, as it were, masses of love, which afterwards explode into sweet fragments.

"Do you know! In the evening, when we are playing our parts, at the moment when my hand touches your forehead—oh, what a noble head is yours, Gwynplaine!—at the moment when I feel your hair under my fingers, I shiver; a heavenly joy comes over me, and I say to myself, In all this world of darkness which encompasses me, in this universe of solitude, in this great obscurity of ruin in which I am, in this quaking fear of myself and of everything, I have one prop; and he is there. It is he—it is you."

"Oh! you love me," said Gwynplaine. "I, too, have but you on earth. You are all in all to me. Dea, what would you have me do? What do you desire? What do you want?"

Dea answered,—

"I do not know. I am happy."

"Oh," replied Gwynplaine, "we are happy."

Ursus raised his voice severely,—

"Oh, you are happy, are you? That's a crime. I have warned you already. You are happy! Then take care you aren't seen. Take up as little room as you can. Happiness ought to stuff itself into a hole. Make yourselves still less than you are, if that can be. God measures the greatness of happiness by the littleness of the happy. The happy should conceal themselves like malefactors. Oh, only shine out like the wretched glowworms that you are, and you'll be trodden on; and quite right too! What do you mean by all that love-making nonsense? I'm no duenna, whose business it is to watch lovers billing and cooing. I'm tired of it all, I tell you; and you may both go to the devil."

And feeling that his harsh tones were melting into tenderness, he drowned his emotion in a loud grumble.

"Father," said Dea, "how roughly you scold!"

"It's because I don't like to see people too happy."

Here Homo re-echoed Ursus. His growl was heard from beneath the lovers' feet.

Ursus stooped down, and placed his hand on Homo's head.

"That's right; you're in bad humour, too. You growl. The bristles are all on end on your wolf's pate. You don't like all this love-making. That's because you are wise. Hold your tongue, all the same. You have had your say and given your opinion; be it so. Now be silent."

The wolf growled again. Ursus looked under the table at him.

"Be still, Homo! Come, don't dwell on it, you philosopher!"

But the wolf sat up, and looked towards the door, showing his teeth.

"What's wrong with you now?" said Ursus. And he caught hold of Homo by the skin of the neck.

Heedless of the wolf's growls, and wholly wrapped up in her own thoughts and in the sound of Gwynplaine's voice, which left its after-taste within her, Dea was silent, and absorbed by that kind of esctasy peculiar to the blind, which seems at times to give them a song to listen to in their souls, and to make up to them for the light which they lack by some strain of ideal music. Blindness is a cavern, to which reaches the deep harmony of the Eternal.

While Ursus, addressing Homo, was looking down, Gwynplaine had raised his eyes. He was about to drink a cup of tea, but did not drink it. He placed it on the table with the slow movement of a spring drawn back; his fingers remained open, his eyes fixed. He scarcely breathed.

A man was standing in the doorway, behind Dea. He was clad in black, with a hood. He wore a wig down to his eyebrows, and held in his hand an iron staff with a crown at each end. His staff was short and massive. He was like Medusa thrusting her head between two branches in Paradise.

Ursus, who had heard some one enter and raised his head without loosing his hold of Homo, recognized the terrible personage. He shook from head to foot, and whispered to Gwynplaine,—

"It's the wapentake."

Gwynplaine recollected. An exclamation of surprise was about to escape him, but he restrained it. The iron staff, with the crown at each end, was called the iron weapon. It was from this iron weapon, upon which the city officers of justice took the oath when they entered on their duties, that the old wapentakes of the English police derived their qualification.

Behind the man in the wig, the frightened landlord could just be perceived in the shadow.

Without saying a word, a personification of the Muta Themis of the old charters, the man stretched his right arm over the radiant Dea, and touched Gwynplaine on the shoulder with the iron staff, at the same time pointing with his left thumb to the door of the Green Box behind him. These gestures, all the more imperious for their silence, meant, "Follow me."

Pro signo exeundi, sursum trahe, says the old Norman record.

He who was touched by the iron weapon had no right but the right of obedience. To that mute order there was no reply. The harsh penalties of the English law threatened the refractory. Gwynplaine felt a shock under the rigid touch of the law; then he sat as though petrified.

If, instead of having been merely grazed on the shoulder, he had been struck a violent blow on the head with the iron staff, he could not have been more stunned. He knew that the police-officer summoned him to follow; but why? *That* he could not understand.

On his part Ursus, too, was thrown into the most painful agitation, but he saw through matters pretty distinctly. His thoughts ran on the jugglers and preachers, his competitors, on informations laid against the Green Box, on that delinquent the wolf, on his own affair with the three Bishopsgate commissioners, and who knows?—perhaps—but that would be too fearful—Gwynplaine's unbecoming and factious speeches touching the royal authority.

He trembled violently.

Dea was smiling.

Neither Gwynplaine nor Ursus pronounced a word. They had both the same thought—not to frighten Dea. It may have struck the wolf as well, for he ceased growling. True, Ursus did not loose him.

Homo, however, was a prudent wolf when occasion required. Who is there who has not remarked a kind of intelligent anxiety in animals? It may be that to the extent to which a wolf can understand mankind he felt that he was an outlaw.

Gwynplaine rose.

Resistance was impracticable, as Gwynplaine knew. He remembered Ursus's words, and there was no question possible. He remained standing in front of the wapentake. The latter raised the iron staff from Gwynplaine's shoulder, and drawing it back, held it out straight in an attitude of command—a constable's attitude which was well understood in those days by the whole people, and which expressed the following order: "Let this man, and no other, follow me. The rest remain where they are. Silence!"

No curious followers were allowed. In all times the police have had a taste for arrests of the kind. This description of seizure was termed sequestration of the person.

The wapentake turned round in one motion, like a piece of mechanism revolving on its own pivot, and with grave and magisterial step proceeded towards the door of the Green Box.

Gwynplaine looked at Ursus. The latter went through a pantomime composed as follows: he shrugged his shoulders, placed both elbows close to his hips, with his hands out, and knitted his brows into chevrons—all which signifies, "We must submit to the unknown."

Gwynplaine looked at Dea. She was in her dream. She was still smiling. He put the ends of his fingers to his lips, and sent her an unutterable kiss.

Ursus, relieved of some portion of his terror now that the wapentake's back was turned, seized the moment to whisper in Gwynplaine's ear,—

"On your life, do not speak until you are questioned."

Gwynplaine, with the same care to make no noise as he would have taken in a sickroom, took his hat and cloak from the hook on the partition, wrapped himself up to the eyes in the cloak, and pushed his hat over his forehead. Not having been to bed, he had his working clothes still on, and his leather esclavin round his neck. Once more he looked at Dea. Having reached the door, the wapentake raised his staff and began to descend the steps; then Gwynplaine set out as if the man was dragging him by an invisible chain. Ursus watched Gwynplaine leave the Green Box. At that moment the wolf gave a low growl; but Ursus silenced him, and whispered, "He is coming back."

In the yard, Master Nicless was stemming, with servile and imperious gestures, the cries of terror raised by Vinos and Fibi, as in great distress they watched Gwynplaine led away, and the mourning-coloured garb and the iron staff of the wapentake.

The two girls were like petrifactions: they were in the attitude of stalactites. Govicum, stunned, was looking open-mouthed out of a window.

The wapentake preceded Gwynplaine by a few steps, never turning round or looking at him, in that icy ease which is given by the knowledge that one is the law.

In death-like silence they both crossed the yard, went through the dark taproom, and reached the street. A few passers-by had collected about the inn door, and the justice of the quorum was there at the head of a squad of police. The idlers, stupefied, and without breathing a word, opened out and stood aside, with English discipline, at the sight of the constable's staff. The wapentake moved off in the direction of the narrow street then called the Little Strand, running by the Thames; and Gwynplaine, with the justice of the quorum's men in ranks on each side, like a double hedge, pale, without a motion except that of his steps, wrapped in his cloak as in a shroud, was leaving the inn farther and farther behind him as he followed the silent man, like a statue following a spectre.

CHAPTER III.

LEX, REX, FEX

Unexplained arrest, which would greatly astonish an Englishman nowadays, was then a very usual proceeding of the police. Recourse was had to it, notwithstanding the Habeas Corpus Act, up to George II.'s time, especially in such delicate cases as were provided for by *lettres de cachet* in France; and one of the accusations against which Walpole had to defend himself was that he had caused or allowed Neuhoff to be arrested in that manner. The accusation was probably without foundation, for Neuhoff, King of Corsica, was put in prison by his creditors.

These silent captures of the person, very usual with the Holy Væhme in Germany, were admitted by German custom, which rules one half of the old English laws, and recommended in certain cases by Norman custom, which rules the other half. Justinian's chief of the palace police was called "*silentiarius imperialis*." The English magistrates who practised the captures in question relied upon numerous Norman texts:—*Canes latrant, sergentes silent. Sergenter agere, id est tacere.* They quoted Lundulphus Sagax, paragraph 16: *Facit imperator silentium.* They quoted the charter of King Philip in 1307: *Multos tenebimus bastonerios qui, obmutescentes, sergentare valeant.* They quoted the statutes of Henry I. of England, cap. 53: *Surge signo jussus. Taciturnior esto. Hoc est esse in captione regis.* They took advantage especially of the following description, held to form part of the ancient feudal franchises of England:—"Sous les viscomtes sont les serjans de l'espée, lesquels doivent justicier vertueusement à l'espée tous ceux qui suient malveses compagnies, gens diffamez d'aucuns crimes, et gens fuites et forbannis.... et les doivent si vigoureusement et discrètement appréhender, que la bonne gent qui sont paisibles soient gardez paisiblement et que les malfeteurs soient espoantés." To be thus arrested was to be seized "à le glaive de l'espée." (*Vetus Consuetudo Normanniæ*, MS. part I, sect. I, ch. 11.) The jurisconsults referred besides "*in Charta Ludovici Hutum pro Normannis*, chapter *Servientes spathæ*." *Servientes spathæ*, in the gradual approach of base Latin to our idioms, became *sergentes spadæ*.

These silent arrests were the contrary of the *Clameur de Haro*, and gave warning that it was advisable to hold one's tongue until such time as light should be thrown upon certain matters still in the dark. They signified questions reserved, and showed in the operation of the police a certain amount of *raison d'état*.

The legal term "private" was applied to arrests of this description. It was thus that Edward III., according to some chroniclers, caused Mortimer to be seized in the bed of his mother, Isabella of France. This, again, we may take leave to doubt; for Mortimer sustained a siege in his town before being captured.

Warwick, the king-maker, delighted in practising this mode of "attaching people." Cromwell made use of it, especially in Connaught; and it was with this precaution of silence that Trailie Arcklo, a relation of the Earl of Ormond, was arrested at Kilmacaugh.

These captures of the body by the mere motion of justice represented rather the *mandat de comparution* than the warrant of arrest. Sometimes they were but processes of inquiry, and even argued, by the silence imposed upon all, a certain consideration for the person seized. For the mass of the people, little versed as they were in the estimate of such shades of difference, they had peculiar terrors.

It must not be forgotten that in 1705, and even much later, England was far from being what she is to-day. The general features of its constitution were confused and at times very oppressive. Daniel Defoe, who had himself had a taste of the pillory, characterizes the social order of England, somewhere in his writings, as the "iron hands of the law." There was not only the law; there was its arbitrary administration. We have but to recall Steele, ejected from Parliament; Locke, driven from his chair; Hobbes and Gibbon, compelled to flight; Charles Churchill, Hume, and Priestley, persecuted; John Wilkes sent to the Tower. The task would be a long one, were we to count over the victims of the statute against seditious libel. The Inquisition had, to some extent, spread its arrangements throughout Europe, and its police practice was taken as a guide. A monstrous attempt against all rights was possible in England. We have only to recall the *Gazetier Cuirassé*. In the midst of the eighteenth century, Louis XV. had writers, whose works displeased him, arrested in Piccadilly. It is true that George II. laid his hands on the Pretender in France, right in the middle of the hall at the opera. Those were two long arms—that of the King of France reaching London; that of the King of England, Paris! Such was the liberty of the period.

CHAPTER IV.

URSUS SPIES THE POLICE

As we have already said, according to the very severe laws of the police of those days, the summons to follow the wapentake, addressed to an individual, implied to all other persons present the command not to stir.

Some curious idlers, however, were stubborn, and followed from afar off the *cortège* which had taken Gwynplaine into custody.

Ursus was of them. He had been as nearly petrified as any one has a right to be. But Ursus, so often assailed by the surprises incident to a wandering life, and by the malice of chance, was, like a ship-of-war, prepared for action, and could call to the post of danger the whole crew—that is to say, the aid of all his intelligence.

He flung off his stupor and began to think. He strove not to give way to emotion, but to stand face to face with circumstances.

To look fortune in the face is the duty of every one not an idiot; to seek not to understand, but to act.

Presently he asked himself, What could he do?

Gwynplaine being taken, Ursus was placed between two terrors—a fear for Gwynplaine, which instigated him to follow; and a fear for himself, which urged him to remain where he was.

Ursus had the intrepidity of a fly and the impassibility of a sensitive plant. His agitation was not to be described. However, he took his resolution heroically, and decided to brave the law, and to follow the wapentake, so anxious was he concerning the fate of Gwynplaine.

His terror must have been great to prompt so much courage.

To what valiant acts will not fear drive a hare!

The chamois in despair jumps a precipice. To be terrified into imprudence is one of the forms of fear.

Gwynplaine had been carried off rather than arrested. The operation of the police had been executed so rapidly that the Fair field, generally little frequented at that hour of the morning, had scarcely taken cognizance of the circumstance.

Scarcely any one in the caravans had any idea that the wapentake had come to take Gwynplaine. Hence the smallness of the crowd.

Gwynplaine, thanks to his cloak and his hat, which nearly concealed his face, could not be recognized by the passers-by.

Before he went out to follow Gwynplaine, Ursus took a precaution. He spoke to Master Nicless, to the boy Govicum, and to Fibi and Vinos, and insisted on their keeping absolute silence before Dea, who was ignorant of everything. That they should not utter a syllable that could make her suspect what had occurred; that they should make her understand that the cares of the management of the Green Box necessitated the absence of Gwynplaine and Ursus; that, besides, it would soon be the time of her daily siesta, and that before she awoke he and Gwynplaine would have returned; that all that had taken place had arisen from a mistake; that it would be very easy for Gwynplaine and himself to clear themselves before the magistrate and police; that a touch of the finger would put the matter straight, after which they should both return; above all, that no one should say a word on the subject to Dea. Having given these directions he departed.

Ursus was able to follow Gwynplaine without being remarked. Though he kept at the greatest possible distance, he so managed as not to lose sight of him. Boldness in ambuscade is the bravery of the timid.

After all, notwithstanding the solemnity of the attendant circumstances, Gwynplaine might have been summoned before the magistrate for some unimportant infraction of the law.

Ursus assured himself that the question would be decided at once.

The solution of the mystery would be made under his very eyes by the direction taken by the *cortège* which took Gwynplaine from Tarrinzeau Field when it reached the entrance of the lanes of the Little Strand.

If it turned to the left, it would conduct Gwynplaine to the justice hall in Southwark. In that case there would be little to fear, some trifling municipal offence, an admonition from the magistrate, two or three shillings to pay, and Gwynplaine would be set at liberty, and the representation of "Chaos Vanquished" would take place in the evening as usual. In that case no one would know that anything unusual had happened.

If the *cortège* turned to the right, matters would be serious.

There were frightful places in that direction.

When the wapentake, leading the file of soldiers between whom Gwynplaine walked, arrived at the small streets, Ursus watched them breathlessly. There are moments in which a man's whole being passes into his eyes.

Which way were they going to turn?

They turned to the right.

Ursus, staggering with terror, leant against a wall that he might not fall.

There is no hypocrisy so great as the words which we say to ourselves, "*I wish to know the worst!*" At heart we do not wish it at all. We have a dreadful fear of knowing it. Agony is mingled with a dim effort not to see the end. We do not own it to ourselves, but we would draw back if we dared; and when we have advanced, we reproach ourselves for having done so.

Thus did Ursus. He shuddered as he thought,—

"Here are things going wrong. I should have found it out soon enough. What business had I to follow Gwynplaine?"

Having made this reflection, man being but self-contradiction, he increased his pace, and, mastering his anxiety, hastened to get nearer the *cortège*, so as not to break, in the maze of small streets, the thread between Gwynplaine and himself.

The *cortège* of police could not move quickly, on account of its solemnity.

The wapentake led it.

The justice of the quorum closed it.

This order compelled a certain deliberation of movement.

All the majesty possible in an official shone in the justice of the quorum. His costume held a middle place between the splendid robe of a doctor of music of

Oxford and the sober black habiliments of a doctor of divinity of Cambridge. He wore the dress of a gentleman under a long *godebert*, which is a mantle trimmed with the fur of the Norwegian hare. He was half Gothic and half modern, wearing a wig like Lamoignon, and sleeves like Tristan l'Hermite. His great round eye watched Gwynplaine with the fixedness of an owl's.

He walked with a cadence. Never did honest man look fiercer.

Ursus, for a moment thrown out of his way in the tangled skein of streets, overtook, close to Saint Mary Overy, the *cortège*, which had fortunately been retarded in the churchyard by a fight between children and dogs—a common incident in the streets in those days. "*Dogs and boys*," say the old registers of police, placing the dogs before the boys.

A man being taken before a magistrate by the police was, after all, an everyday affair, and each one having his own business to attend to, the few who had followed soon dispersed. There remained but Ursus on the track of Gwynplaine.

They passed before two chapels opposite to each other, belonging the one to the Recreative Religionists, the other to the Hallelujah League—sects which flourished then, and which exist to the present day.

Then the *cortège* wound from street to street, making a zigzag, choosing by preference lanes not yet built on, roads where the grass grew, and deserted alleys.

At length it stopped.

It was in a little lane with no houses except two or three hovels. This narrow alley was composed of two walls—one on the left, low; the other on the right, high. The high wall was black, and built in the Saxon style with narrow holes, scorpions, and large square gratings over narrow loopholes. There was no window on it, but here and there slits, old embrasures of *pierriers* and archegayes. At the foot of this high wall was seen, like the hole at the bottom of a rat-trap, a little wicket gate, very elliptical in its arch.

This small door, encased in a full, heavy girding of stone, had a grated peephole, a heavy knocker, a large lock, hinges thick and knotted, a bristling of nails, an armour of plates, and hinges, so that altogether it was more of iron than of wood.

There was no one in the lane—no shops, no passengers; but in it there was heard a continual noise, as if the lane ran parallel to a torrent. There was a tumult of voices and of carriages. It seemed as if on the other side of the black edifice there must be a great street, doubtless the principal street of Southwark, one end of which ran into the Canterbury road, and the other on to London Bridge.

All the length of the lane, except the *cortège* which surrounded Gwynplaine, a watcher would have seen no other human face than the pale profile of Ursus, hazarding a hall advance from the shadow of the corner of the wall—looking, yet fearing to see. He had posted himself behind the wall at a turn of the lane.

The constables grouped themselves before the wicket. Gwynplaine was in the centre, the wapentake and his baton of iron being now behind him.

The justice of the quorum raised the knocker, and struck the door three times. The loophole opened.

The justice of the quorum said,—

"By order of her Majesty."

The heavy door of oak and iron turned on its hinges, making a chilly opening, like the mouth of a cavern. A hideous depth yawned in the shadow.

Ursus saw Gwynplaine disappear within it.

CHAPTER V.

A FEARFUL PLACE

The wapentake entered behind Gwynplaine.

Then the justice of the quorum.

Then the constables.

The wicket was closed.

The heavy door swung to, closing hermetically on the stone sills, without any one seeing who had opened or shut it. It seemed as if the bolts re-entered their sockets of their own act. Some of these mechanisms, the inventions of ancient intimidation, still exist in old prisons—doors of which you saw no doorkeeper. With them the entrance to a prison becomes like the entrance to a tomb.

This wicket was the lower door of Southwark Jail.

There was nothing in the harsh and worm-eaten aspect of this prison to soften its appropriate air of rigour.

Originally a pagan temple, built by the Catieuchlans for the Mogons, ancient English gods, it became a palace for Ethelwolf and a fortress for Edward the Confessor; then it was elevated to the dignity of a prison, in 1199, by John Lackland. Such was Southwark Jail. This jail, at first intersected by a street, like Chenonceaux by a river, had been for a century or two a gate—that is to say, the gate of the suburb; the passage had then been walled up. There remain in England some prisons of this nature. In London, Newgate; at Canterbury, Westgate; at Edinburgh, Canongate. In France the Bastile was originally a gate.

Almost all the jails of England present the same appearance—a high wall without and a hive of cells within. Nothing could be more funereal than the appearance of those prisons, where spiders and justice spread their webs, and where John Howard, that ray of light, had not yet penetrated. Like the old Gehenna of Brussels, they might well have been designated Treurenberg—*the house of tears.*

Men felt before such buildings, at once so savage and inhospitable, the same distress that the ancient navigators suffered before the hell of slaves mentioned by Plautus, islands of creaking chains, *ferricrepiditæ insulæ*, when they passed near enough to hear the clank of the fetters.

Southwark Jail, an old place of exorcisms and torture, was originally used solely for the imprisonment of sorcerers, as was proved by two verses engraved on a defaced stone at the foot of the wicket,—

Sunt arreptitii, vexati dæmone multo

Est energumenus, quem dæmon possidet unus.

Lines which draw a subtle delicate distinction between the demoniac and man possessed by a devil.

At the bottom of this inscription, nailed flat against the wall, was a stone ladder, which had been originally of wood, but which had been changed into stone by being buried in earth of petrifying quality at a place called Apsley Gowis, near Woburn Abbey.

The prison of Southwark, now demolished, opened on two streets, between which, as a gate, it formerly served as means of communication. It had two doors. In the large street a door, apparently used by the authorities; and in the lane the door of punishment, used by the rest of the living and by the dead also, because when a prisoner in the jail died it was by that issue that his corpse was carried out. A liberation not to be despised. Death is release into infinity.

It was by the gate of punishment that Gwynplaine had been taken into prison. The lane, as we have said, was nothing but a little passage, paved with flints, confined between two opposite walls. There is one of the same kind at Brussels called *Rue d'une Personne*. The walls were unequal in height. The high one was the prison; the low one, the cemetery—the enclosure for the mortuary remains of the jail—was not higher than the ordinary stature of a man. In it was a gate almost opposite the prison wicket. The dead had only to cross the street; the cemetery was but twenty paces from the jail. On the high wall was affixed a gallows; on the low one was sculptured a Death's head. Neither of these walls made its opposite neighbour more cheerful.

CHAPTER VI.

THE KIND OF MAGISTRACY UNDER THE WIGS OF FORMER DAYS

Any one observing at that moment the other side of the prison—its façade—would have perceived the high street of Southwark, and might have remarked, stationed before the monumental and official entrance to the jail, a travelling carriage, recognized as such by its imperial. A few idlers surrounded the carriage. On it was a coat of arms, and a personage had been seen to descend from it and enter the prison. "Probably a magistrate," conjectured the crowd. Many of the English magistrates were noble, and almost all had the right of bearing arms. In France blazon and robe were almost contradictory terms. The Duke Saint-Simon says, in speaking of magistrates, "people of that class." In England a gentleman was not despised for being a judge.

There are travelling magistrates in England; they are called judges of circuit, and nothing was easier than to recognize the carriage as the vehicle of a judge on circuit. That which was less comprehensible was, that the supposed magistrate got down, not from the carriage itself, but from the box, a place which is not habitually occupied by the owner. Another unusual thing. People travelled at that period in England in two ways—by coach, at the rate of a shilling for five miles; and by post, paying three half-pence per mile, and twopence to the postillion after each stage. A private carriage, whose owner desired to travel by relays, paid as many shillings per horse per mile as the horseman paid pence. The carriage drawn up before the jail in Southwark had four horses and two postillions, which displayed princely state. Finally, that which excited and disconcerted conjectures to the utmost was the circumstance that the carriage was sedulously shut up. The blinds of the windows were closed up. The glasses in front were darkened by blinds; every opening by which the eye might have penetrated was masked. From without, nothing within could be seen, and most likely from within, nothing could be seen outside. However, it did not seem probable that there was any one in the carriage.

Southwark being in Surrey, the prison was within the jurisdiction of the sheriff of the county.

Such distinct jurisdictions were very frequent in England. Thus, for example, the Tower of London was not supposed to be situated in any county; that is to say, that legally it was considered to be in air. The Tower recognized no authority of jurisdiction except in its own constable, who was qualified as *custos turris.* The Tower had its jurisdiction, its church, its court of justice, and its government apart. The authority of its *custos*, or constable, extended, beyond London, over twenty-one hamlets. As in Great Britain legal singularities engraft one upon another the office of the master gunner of England was derived from the Tower of London. Other legal customs seem still more whimsical. Thus, the English Court of Admiralty consults and applies the laws of Rhodes and of Oleron, a French island which was once English.

The sheriff of a county was a person of high consideration. He was always an esquire, and sometimes a knight. He was called *spectabilis* in the old deeds, "a man to be looked at"—kind of intermediate title between *illustris* and *clarissimus;* less than the first, more than the second. Long ago the sheriffs of the counties were chosen by the people; but Edward II., and after him Henry VI., having claimed their nomination for the crown, the office of sheriff became a royal emanation.

They all received their commissions from majesty, except the sheriff of Westmoreland, whose office was hereditary, and the sheriffs of London and Middlesex, who were elected by the livery in the common hall. Sheriffs of Wales and Chester possessed certain fiscal prerogatives. These appointments are all still in existence in England, but, subjected little by little to the friction of manners and ideas, they have lost their old aspects. It was the duty of the sheriff of the county to escort and protect the judges on circuit. As we have two arms, he had two officers; his right arm the under-sheriff, his left arm the justice of the quorum. The justice of the quorum, assisted by the bailiff of the hundred, termed the wapentake, apprehended, examined, and, under the responsibility of the sheriff, imprisoned, for trial by the judges of circuit, thieves, murderers, rebels, vagabonds, and all sorts of felons.

The shade of difference between the under-sheriff and the justice of the quorum, in their hierarchical service towards the sheriff, was that the under-sheriff accompanied and the justice of the quorum assisted.

The sheriff held two courts—one fixed and central, the county court; and a movable court, the sheriff's turn. He thus represented both unity and ubiquity. He might as judge be aided and informed on legal questions by the serjeant of the coif, called *sergens coifæ*, who is a serjeant-at-law, and who wears under his black skull-cap a fillet of white Cambray lawn.

The sheriff delivered the jails. When he arrived at a town in his province, he had the right of summary trial of the prisoners, of which he might cause either their release or the execution. This was called a jail delivery. The sheriff presented bills of indictment to the twenty-four members of the grand jury. If they approved, they wrote above, *billa vera;* if the contrary, they wrote *ignoramus*. In the latter case the accusation was annulled, and the sheriff had the privilege of tearing up the bill. If during the deliberation a juror died, this legally acquitted the prisoner and made him innocent, and the sheriff, who had the privilege of arresting the accused, had also that of setting him at liberty.

That which made the sheriff singularly feared and respected was that he had the charge of executing all the orders of her Majesty—a fearful latitude. An arbitrary power lodges in such commissions.

The officers termed vergers, the coroners making part of the sheriff's *cortège*, and the clerks of the market as escort, with gentlemen on horseback and their servants in livery, made a handsome suite. The sheriff, says Chamberlayne, is the "life of justice, of law, and of the country."

In England an insensible demolition constantly pulverizes and dissevers laws and customs. You must understand in our day that neither the sheriff, the wapentake, nor the justice of the quorum could exercise their functions as they did then. There was in the England of the past a certain confusion of powers, whose ill-defined attributes resulted in their overstepping their real bounds at times—a thing which would be impossible in the present day. The usurpation of power by police and justices has ceased. We believe that even the word "wapentake" has changed its meaning. It implied a magisterial function; now it signifies a territorial division: it specified the centurion; it now specifies the hundred (*centum*).

Moreover, in those days the sheriff of the county combined with something more and something less, and condensed in his own authority, which was at once royal and municipal, the two magistrates formerly called in France the civil lieutenant of Paris and the lieutenant of police. The civil lieutenant of Paris, Monsieur, is pretty well described in an old police note: "The civil lieutenant has no dislike to domestic quarrels, because he always has the pickings" (22nd July 1704). As to the lieutenant of police, he was a redoubtable person, multiple and vague. The best personification of him was René d'Argenson, who, as was said by Saint-Simon, displayed in his face the three judges of hell united.

The three judges of hell sat, as has already been seen, at Bishopsgate, London.

CHAPTER VII.

SHUDDERING

When Gwynplaine heard the wicket shut, creaking in all its bolts, he trembled. It seemed to him that the door which had just closed was the communication between light and darkness—opening on one side on the living, human crowd, and on the other on a dead world; and now that everything illumined by the sun was behind him, that he had stepped over the boundary of life and was standing without it, his heart contracted. What were they going to do with him? What did it all mean? Where was he?

He saw nothing around him; he found himself in perfect darkness. The shutting of the door had momentarily blinded him. The window in the door had been closed as well. No loophole, no lamp. Such were the precautions of old times. It was forbidden to light the entrance to the jails, so that the newcomers should take no observations.

Gwynplaine extended his arms, and touched the wall on the right side and on the left. He was in a passage. Little by little a cavernous daylight exuding, no one knows whence, and which floats about dark places, and to which the dilatation of the pupil adjusts itself slowly, enabled him to distinguish a feature here and there, and the corridor was vaguely sketched out before him.

Gwynplaine, who had never had a glimpse of penal severities, save in the exaggerations of Ursus, felt as though seized by a sort of vague gigantic hand. To be caught in the mysterious toils of the law is frightful. He who is brave in all other dangers is disconcerted in the presence of justice. Why? Is it that the justice of man works in twilight, and the judge gropes his way? Gwynplaine remembered what Ursus had told him of the necessity for silence. He wished to see Dea again; he felt some discretionary instinct, which urged him not to irritate. Sometimes to wish to be enlightened is to make matters worse; on the other hand, however, the weight of the adventure was so overwhelming that he gave way at length, and could not restrain a question.

"Gentlemen," said he, "whither are you taking me?"

They made no answer.

It was the law of silent capture, and the Norman text is formal: *A silentiariis ostio, præpositis introducti sunt.*

This silence froze Gwynplaine. Up to that moment he had believed himself to be firm: he was self-sufficing. To be self-sufficing is to be powerful. He had lived isolated from the world, and imagined that being alone he was unassailable; and now all at once he felt himself under the pressure of a hideous collective force. How was he to combat that horrible anonyma, the law? He felt faint under the perplexity; a fear of an unknown character had found a fissure in his armour; besides, he had not slept, he had not eaten, he had scarcely moistened his lips with a cup of tea. The whole night had been passed in a kind of delirium, and the fever was still on him. He was thirsty; perhaps hungry. The craving of the stomach disorders everything. Since the previous evening all kinds of incidents had assailed him. The emotions which had tormented had sustained him. Without the storm a sail would be a rag. But his was the excessive feebleness of the rag, which the wind inflates till it tears it. He felt himself sinking. Was he about to fall without consciousness on the pavement? To faint is the resource of a woman, and the humiliation of a man. He hardened himself, but he trembled. He felt as one losing his footing.

CHAPTER VIII.

LAMENTATION

They began to move forward.

They advanced through the passage.

There was no preliminary registry, no place of record. The prisons in those times were not overburdened with documents. They were content to close round you without knowing why. To be a prison, and to hold prisoners, sufficed.

The procession was obliged to lengthen itself out, taking the form of the corridor. They walked almost in single file; first the wapentake, then Gwynplaine, then the justice of the quorum, then the constables, advancing in a group, and blocking up the passage behind Gwynplaine as with a bung. The passage narrowed. Now Gwynplaine touched the walls with both his elbows. In the roof, which was made of flints, dashed with cement, was a succession of granite arches jutting out, and still more contracting the passage. He had to stoop to pass under them. No speed was possible in that corridor. Any one trying to escape through it would have been compelled to move slowly. The passage twisted. All entrails are tortuous; those of a prison as well as those of a man. Here and there, sometimes to the right and sometimes to the left, spaces in the wall, square and closed by large iron gratings, gave glimpses of flights of stairs, some descending and some ascending.

They reached a closed door; it opened. They passed through, and it closed again. Then they came to a second door, which admitted them; then to a third, which also turned on its hinges. These doors seemed to open and shut of themselves. No one was to be seen. While the corridor contracted, the roof grew lower, until at length it was impossible to stand upright. Moisture exuded from the wall. Drops of water fell from the vault. The slabs that paved the corridor were clammy as an intestine. The diffused pallor that served as light became more and more a pall. Air was deficient, and, what was singularly ominous, the passage was a descent.

Close observation was necessary to perceive that there was such a descent. In darkness a gentle declivity is portentous. Nothing is more fearful than the vague evils to which we are led by imperceptible degrees.

It is awful to descend into unknown depths.

How long had they proceeded thus? Gwynplaine could not tell.

Moments passed under such crushing agony seem immeasurably prolonged.

Suddenly they halted.

The darkness was intense.

The corridor widened somewhat. Gwynplaine heard close to him a noise of which only a Chinese gong could give an idea; something like a blow struck against the diaphragm of the abyss. It was the wapentake striking his wand against a sheet of iron.

That sheet of iron was a door.

Not a door on hinges, but a door which was raised and let down.

Something like a portcullis.

There was a sound of creaking in a groove, and Gwynplaine was suddenly face to face with a bit of square light. The sheet of metal had just been raised into a slit in the vault, like the door of a mouse-trap.

An opening had appeared.

The light was not daylight, but glimmer; but on the dilated eyeballs of Gwynplaine the pale and sudden ray struck like a flash of lightning.

It was some time before he could see anything. To see with dazzled eyes is as difficult as to see in darkness.

At length, by degrees, the pupil of his eye became proportioned to the light, just as it had been proportioned to the darkness, and he was able to distinguish objects. The light, which at first had seemed too bright, settled into its proper hue and became livid. He cast a glance into the yawning space before him, and what he saw was terrible.

At his feet were about twenty steps, steep, narrow, worn, almost perpendicular, without balustrade on either side, a sort of stone ridge cut out from the side of a wall into stairs, entering and leading into a very deep cell. They reached to the bottom.

The cell was round, roofed by an ogee vault with a low arch, from the fault of level in the top stone of the frieze, a displacement common to cells under heavy edifices.

The kind of hole acting as a door, which the sheet of iron had just revealed, and on which the stairs abutted, was formed in the vault, so that the eye looked down from it as into a well.

The cell was large, and if it was the bottom of a well, it must have been a cyclopean one. The idea that the old word "*cul-de-basse-fosse*" awakens in the mind can only be applied to it if it were a lair of wild beasts.

The cell was neither flagged nor paved. The bottom was of that cold, moist earth peculiar to deep places.

In the midst of the cell, four low and disproportioned columns sustained a porch heavily ogival, of which the four mouldings united in the interior of the porch, something like the inside of a mitre. This porch, similar to the pinnacles under which sarcophagi were formerly placed, rose nearly to the top of the vault, and made a sort of central chamber in the cavern, if that could be called a chamber which had only pillars in place of walls.

From the key of the arch hung a brass lamp, round and barred like the window of a prison. This lamp threw around it—on the pillars, on the vault, on the circular wall which was seen dimly behind the pillars—a wan light, cut by bars of shadow.

This was the light which had at first dazzled Gwynplaine; now it threw out only a confused redness.

There was no other light in the cell—neither window, nor door, nor loophole.

Between the four pillars, exactly below the lamp, in the spot where there was most light, a pale and terrible form lay on the ground.

It was lying on its back; a head was visible, of which the eyes were shut; a body, of which the chest was a shapeless mass; four limbs belonging to the body, in the position of the cross of Saint Andrew, were drawn towards the four pillars by four chains fastened to each foot and each hand.

These chains were fastened to an iron ring at the base of each column. The form was held immovable, in the horrible position of being quartered, and had the icy look of a livid corpse.

It was naked. It was a man.

Gwynplaine, as if petrified, stood at the top of the stairs, looking down. Suddenly he heard a rattle in the throat.

The corpse was alive.

Close to the spectre, in one of the ogives of the door, on each side of a great seat, which stood on a large flat stone, stood two men swathed in long black cloaks; and on the seat an old man was sitting, dressed in a red robe—wan, motionless, and ominous, holding a bunch of roses in his hand.

The bunch of roses would have enlightened any one less ignorant that Gwynplaine. The right of judging with a nosegay in his hand implied the holder to be a magistrate, at once royal and municipal. The Lord Mayor of London still keeps up the custom. To assist the deliberations of the judges was the function of the earliest roses of the season.

The old man seated on the bench was the sheriff of the county of Surrey.

His was the majestic rigidity of a Roman dignitary.

The bench was the only seat in the cell.

By the side of it was a table covered with papers and books, on which lay the long, white wand of the sheriff. The men standing by the side of the sheriff were two doctors, one of medicine, the other of law; the latter recognizable by the Serjeant's coif over his wig. Both wore black robes—one of the shape worn by judges, the other by doctors.

Men of these kinds wear mourning for the deaths of which they are the cause.

Behind the sheriff, at the edge of the flat stone under the seat, was crouched—with a writing-table near to him, a bundle of papers on his knees, and a sheet of parchment on the bundle—a secretary, in a round wig, with a pen in his hand, in the attitude of a man ready to write.

This secretary was of the class called keeper of the bag, as was shown by a bag at his feet.

These bags, in former times employed in law processes, were termed bags of justice.

With folded arms, leaning against a pillar, was a man entirely dressed in leather, the hangman's assistant.

These men seemed as if they had been fixed by enchantment in their funereal postures round the chained man. None of them spoke or moved.

There brooded over all a fearful calm.

What Gwynplaine saw was a torture chamber. There were many such in England.

The crypt of Beauchamp Tower long served this purpose, as did also the cell in the Lollards' prison. A place of this nature is still to be seen in London, called "the Vaults of Lady Place." In this last-mentioned chamber there is a grate for the purpose of heating the irons.

All the prisons of King John's time (and Southwark Jail was one) had their chambers of torture.

The scene which is about to follow was in those days a frequent one in England, and might even, by criminal process, be carried out to-day, since the same laws are still unrepealed. England offers the curious sight of a barbarous code living on the best terms with liberty. We confess that they make an excellent family party.

Some distrust, however, might not be undesirable. In the case of a crisis, a return to the penal code would not be impossible. English legislation is a tamed tiger with a velvet paw, but the claws are still there. Cut the claws of the law, and you will do well. Law almost ignores right. On one side is penalty, on the other humanity. Philosophers protest; but it will take some time yet before the justice of man is assimilated to the justice of God.

Respect for the law: that is the English phrase. In England they venerate so many laws, that they never repeal any. They save themselves from the consequences of their veneration by never putting them into execution. An old law falls into disuse like an old woman, and they never think of killing either one or the other. They cease to make use of them; that is all. Both are at liberty to consider themselves still young and beautiful. They may fancy that they are as they were. This politeness is called respect.

Norman custom is very wrinkled. That does not prevent many an English judge casting sheep's eyes at her. They stick amorously to an antiquated atrocity, so long as it is Norman. What can be more savage than the gibbet? In 1867 a man was sentenced to be cut into four quarters and offered to a woman—the Queen.[18]

Still, torture was never practised in England. History asserts this as a fact. The assurance of history is wonderful.

Matthew of Westminster mentions that the "Saxon law, very clement and kind," did not punish criminals by death; and adds that "it limited itself to cutting off the nose and scooping out the eyes." That was all!

Gwynplaine, scared and haggard, stood at the top of the steps, trembling in every limb. He shuddered from head to foot. He tried to remember what crime he had committed. To the silence of the wapentake had succeeded the vision of torture to be endured. It was a step, indeed, forward; but a tragic one. He saw the dark enigma of the law under the power of which he felt himself increasing in obscurity.

The human form lying on the earth rattled in its throat again.

Gwynplaine felt some one touching him gently on his shoulder.

It was the wapentake.

Gwynplaine knew that meant that he was to descend.

He obeyed.

He descended the stairs step by step. They were very narrow, each eight or nine inches in height. There was no hand-rail. The descent required caution. Two steps behind Gwynplaine followed the wapentake, holding up his iron weapon; and at the same interval behind the wapentake, the justice of the quorum.

As he descended the steps, Gwynplaine felt an indescribable extinction of hope. There was death in each step. In each one that he descended there died a ray of the light within him. Growing paler and paler, he reached the bottom of the stairs.

The larva lying chained to the four pillars still rattled in its throat.

A voice in the shadow said,—

"Approach!"

It was the sheriff addressing Gwynplaine.

Gwynplaine took a step forward.

"Closer," said the sheriff.

The justice of the quorum murmured in the ear of Gwynplaine, so gravely that there was solemnity in the whisper, "You are before the sheriff of the county of Surrey."

Gwynplaine advanced towards the victim extended in the centre of the cell. The wapentake and the justice of the quorum remained where they were, allowing Gwynplaine to advance alone.

When Gwynplaine reached the spot under the porch, close to that miserable thing which he had hitherto perceived only from a distance, but which was a living man, his fear rose to terror. The man who was chained there was quite naked, except for that rag so hideously modest, which might be called the vineleaf of punishment, the *succingulum* of the Romans, and the *christipannus* of the Goths, of which the old Gallic jargon made *cripagne*. Christ wore but that shred on the cross.

The terror-stricken sufferer whom Gwynplaine now saw seemed a man of about fifty or sixty years of age. He was bald. Grizzly hairs of beard bristled on his chin. His eyes were closed, his mouth open. Every tooth was to be seen. His thin and bony face was like a death's-head. His arms and legs were fastened by chains to the four stone pillars in the shape of the letter X. He had on his breast and belly a plate of iron, and on this iron five or six large stones were laid. His rattle was at times a sigh, at times a roar.

The sheriff, still holding his bunch of roses, took from the table with the hand which was free his white wand, and standing up said, "Obedience to her Majesty."

Then he replaced the wand upon the table.

Then in words long-drawn as a knell, without a gesture, and immovable as the sufferer, the sheriff, raising his voice, said,—

"Man, who liest here bound in chains, listen for the last time to the voice of justice; you have been taken from your dungeon and brought to this jail. Legally summoned in the usual forms, *formaliis verbis pressus;* not regarding to lectures and communications which have been made, and which will now be repeated, to you; inspired by a bad and perverse spirit of tenacity, you have preserved silence, and refused to answer the judge. This is a detestable licence, which constitutes, among deeds punishable by cashlit, the crime and misdemeanour of overseness."

The serjeant of the coif on the right of the sheriff interrupted him, and said, with an indifference indescribably lugubrious in its effect, "*Overhernessa.* Laws of Alfred and of Godrun, chapter the sixth."

The sheriff resumed.

"The law is respected by all except by scoundrels who infest the woods where the hinds bear young."

Like one clock striking after another, the serjeant said,—

"*Qui faciunt vastum in foresta ubi damoe solent founinare.*"

"He who refuses to answer the magistrate," said the sheriff, "is suspected of every vice. He is reputed capable of every evil."

The serjeant interposed.

"*Prodigus, devorator, profusus, salax, ruffianus, ebriosus, luxuriosus, simulator, consumptor patrimonii, elluo, ambro, et gluto.*"

"Every vice," said the sheriff, "means every crime. He who confesses nothing, confesses everything. He who holds his peace before the questions of the judge is in fact a liar and a parricide."

"*Mendax et parricida,*" said the serjeant.

The sheriff said,—

"Man, it is not permitted to absent oneself by silence. To pretend contumaciousness is a wound given to the law. It is like Diomede wounding a goddess. Taciturnity before a judge is a form of rebellion. Treason to justice is high treason. Nothing is more hateful or rash. He who resists interrogation steals truth. The law has provided for this. For such cases, the English have always enjoyed the right of the foss, the fork, and chains."

"*Anglica Charta,* year 1088," said the serjeant. Then with the same mechanical gravity he added, "*Ferrum, et fossam, et furcas cum aliis libertatibus.*"

The sheriff continued,—

"Man! Forasmuch as you have not chosen to break silence, though of sound mind and having full knowledge in respect of the subject concerning which justice demands an answer, and forasmuch as you are diabolically refractory, you have necessarily been put to torture, and you have been, by the terms of the criminal statutes, tried by the '*Peine forte et dure.*' This is what has been done to you, for the law requires that I should fully inform you. You have been brought to this dungeon. You have been stripped of your clothes. You have been laid on your back naked on the ground, your limbs have been stretched and tied to the four pillars of the law; a sheet of iron has been placed on your chest, and as many stones as you can bear have been heaped on your belly, 'and more,' says the law."

"*Plusque,*" affirmed the serjeant.

The sheriff continued,—

"In this situation, and before prolonging the torture, a second summons to answer and to speak has been made you by me, sheriff of the county of Surrey, and you have satanically kept silent, though under torture, chains, shackles, fetters, and irons."

"*Attachiamenta legalia,*" said the serjeant.

"On your refusal and contumacy," said the sheriff, "it being right that the obstinacy of the law should equal the obstinacy of the criminal, the proof has been continued according to the edicts and texts. The first day you were given nothing to eat or drink."

"*Hoc est superjejunare,*" said the serjeant.

There was silence, the awful hiss of the man's breathing was heard from under the heap of stones.

The serjeant-at-law completed his quotation.

"*Adde augmentum abstinentiæ ciborum diminutione. Consuetudo brittanica,* art. 504."

The two men, the sheriff and the serjeant, alternated. Nothing could be more dreary than their imperturbable monotony. The mournful voice responded to the ominous voice; it might be said that the priest and the deacon of punishment were celebrating the savage mass of the law.

The sheriff resumed,—

"On the first day you were given nothing to eat or drink. On the second day you were given food, but nothing to drink. Between your teeth were thrust three mouthfuls of barley bread. On the third day they gave you to drink, but nothing to eat. They poured into your mouth at three different times, and in three different glasses, a pint of water taken from the common sewer of the prison. The fourth day is come. It is to-day. Now, if you do not answer, you will be left here till you die. Justice wills it."

The Serjeant, ready with his reply, appeared.

"*Mors rei homagium est bonæ legi.*"

"And while you feel yourself dying miserably," resumed the sheriff, "no one will attend to you, even when the blood rushes from your throat, your chin, and your armpits, and every pore, from the mouth to the loins."

"*A throtabolla,*" said the Serjeant, "*et pabu et subhircis et a grugno usque ad crupponum.*"

The sheriff continued,—

"Man, attend to me, because the consequences concern you. If you renounce your execrable silence, and if you confess, you will only be hanged, and you will have a right to the meldefeoh, which is a sum of money."

"*Damnum confitens,*" said the Serjeant, "*habeat le meldefeoh. Leges Inæ,* chapter the twentieth."

"Which sum," insisted the sheriff, "shall be paid in doitkins, suskins, and galihalpens, the only case in which this money is to pass, according to the terms of the statute of abolition, in the third of Henry V., and you will have the right and enjoyment of *scortum ante mortem*, and then be hanged on the gibbet. Such are the advantages of confession. Does it please you to answer to justice?"

The sheriff ceased and waited.

The prisoner lay motionless.

The sheriff resumed,—

"Man, silence is a refuge in which there is more risk than safety. The obstinate man is damnable and vicious. He who is silent before justice is a felon to the crown. Do not persist in this unfilial disobedience. Think of her Majesty. Do not oppose our gracious queen. When I speak to you, answer her; be a loyal subject."

The patient rattled in the throat.

The sheriff continued,—

"So, after the seventy-two hours of the proof, here we are at the fourth day. Man, this is the decisive day. The fourth day has been fixed by the law for the confrontation."

"*Quarta die, frontem ad frontem adduce,*" growled the Serjeant.

"The wisdom of the law," continued the sheriff, "has chosen this last hour to hold what our ancestors called 'judgment by mortal cold,' seeing that it is the moment when men are believed on their yes or their no."

The serjeant on the right confirmed his words.

"*Judicium pro frodmortell, quod homines credendi sint per suum ya et per suum no.* Charter of King Adelstan, volume the first, page one hundred and sixty-three."

There was a moment's pause; then the sheriff bent his stern face towards the prisoner.

"Man, who art lying there on the ground—"

He paused.

"Man," he cried, "do you hear me?"

The man did not move.

"In the name of the law," said the sheriff, "open your eyes."

The man's lids remained closed.

The sheriff turned to the doctor, who was standing on his left.

"Doctor, give your diagnostic."

"*Probe, da diagnosticum,*" said the serjeant.

The doctor came down with magisterial stiffness, approached the man, leant over him, put his ear close to the mouth of the sufferer, felt the pulse at the wrist, the armpit, and the thigh, then rose again.

"Well?" said the sheriff.

"He can still hear," said the doctor.

"Can he see?" inquired the sheriff.

The doctor answered, "He can see."

On a sign from the sheriff, the justice of the quorum and the wapentake advanced. The wapentake placed himself near the head of the patient. The justice of the quorum stood behind Gwynplaine.

The doctor retired a step behind the pillars.

Then the sheriff, raising the bunch of roses as a priest about to sprinkle holy water, called to the prisoner in a loud voice, and became awful.

"O wretched man, speak! The law supplicates before she exterminates you. You, who feign to be mute, remember how mute is the tomb. You, who appear deaf, remember that damnation is more deaf. Think of the death which is worse than your present state. Repent! You are about to be left alone in this cell. Listen! you who are my likeness; for I am a man! Listen, my brother, because I am a Christian! Listen, my son, because I am an old man! Look at me; for I am the master of your sufferings, and I am about to become terrible. The terrors of the law make up the majesty of the judge. Believe that I myself tremble before myself. My own power alarms me. Do not drive me to extremities. I am filled by the holy malice of chastisement. Feel, then, wretched man, the salutary and honest fear of justice, and obey me. The hour of confrontation is come, and you must answer. Do not harden yourself in resistance. Do not that which will be irrevocable. Think that your end belongs to me. Half man, half corpse, listen! At least, let it not be your determination to expire here, exhausted for hours, days, and weeks, by frightful agonies of hunger and foulness, under the weight of those stones, alone in this cell, deserted, forgotten, annihilated, left as food for the rats and the weasels, gnawed by creatures of darkness while the world comes and goes, buys and sells, whilst carriages roll in the streets above your head. Unless you would continue to draw painful breath without remission in the depths of this despair—grinding your teeth, weeping, blaspheming—without a doctor to appease the anguish of your wounds, without a priest to offer a divine draught of water to your soul. Oh! if only that you may not feel the frightful froth of the sepulchre ooze slowly from your lips, I adjure and conjure you to hear me. I call you to your own aid. Have pity on yourself. Do what is asked of you. Give way to justice. Open your eyes, and see if you recognize this man!"

The prisoner neither turned his head nor lifted his eyelids.

The sheriff cast a glance first at the justice of the quorum and then at the wapentake.

The justice of the quorum, taking Gwynplaine's hat and mantle, put his hands on his shoulders and placed him in the light by the side of the chained man. The face of Gwynplaine stood out clearly from the surrounding shadow in its strange relief.

At the same time, the wapentake bent down, took the man's temples between his hands, turned the inert head towards Gwynplaine, and with his thumbs and his first fingers lifted the closed eyelids.

The prisoner saw Gwynplaine. Then, raising his head voluntarily, and opening his eyes wide, he looked at him.

He quivered as much as a man can quiver with a mountain on his breast, and then cried out,—

"'Tis he! Yes; 'tis he!"

And he burst into a horrible laugh.

"'Tis he!" he repeated.

Then his head fell back on the ground, and he closed his eyes again.

"Registrar, take that down," said the justice.

Gwynplaine, though terrified, had, up to that moment, preserved a calm exterior. The cry of the prisoner, "'Tis he!" overwhelmed him completely. The words, "Registrar, take that down!" froze him. It seemed to him that a scoundrel had dragged him to his fate without his being able to guess why, and that the man's unintelligible confession was closing round him like the clasp of an iron collar. He fancied himself side by side with him in the posts of the same pillory. Gwynplaine lost his footing in his terror, and protested. He began to stammer incoherent words in the deep distress of an innocent man, and quivering, terrified, lost, uttered the first random outcries that rose to his mind, and words of agony like aimless projectiles.

"It is not true. It was not me. I do not know the man. He cannot know me, since I do not know him. I have my part to play this evening. What do you want of me? I demand my liberty. Nor is that all. Why have I been brought into this dungeon? Are there laws no longer? You may as well say at once that there are no laws. My Lord Judge, I repeat that it is not I. I am innocent of all that can be said. I know I am. I wish to go away. This is not justice. There is nothing between this man and me. You can find out. My life is not hidden up. They came and took me away like a thief. Why did they come like that? How could I know the man? I am a travelling mountebank, who plays farces at fairs and markets. I am the Laughing Man. Plenty of people have been to see me. We are staying in Tarrinzeau Field. I have been earning an honest livelihood these fifteen years. I am five-and-twenty. I lodge at the Tadcaster Inn. I am called Gwynplaine. My lord, let me out. You should not take advantage of the low estate of the unfortunate. Have compassion on a man who has done no harm, who is without protection and without defence. You have before you a poor mountebank."

"I have before me," said the sheriff, "Lord Fermain Clancharlie, Baron Clancharlie and Hunkerville, Marquis of Corleone in Sicily, and a peer of England."

Rising, and offering his chair to Gwynplaine, the sheriff added,—

"My lord, will your lordship deign to seat yourself?"

BOOK THE FIFTH

THE SEA AND FATE ARE MOVED BY THE SAME BREATH

CHAPTER I.

THE DURABILITY OF FRAGILE THINGS

Destiny sometimes proffers us a glass of madness to drink. A hand is thrust out of the mist, and suddenly hands us the mysterious cup in which is contained the latent intoxication.

Gwynplaine did not understand.

He looked behind him to see who it was who had been addressed.

A sound may be too sharp to be perceptible to the ear; an emotion too acute conveys no meaning to the mind. There is a limit to comprehension as well as to hearing.

The wapentake and the justice of the quorum approached Gwynplaine and took him by the arms. He felt himself placed in the chair which the sheriff had just vacated. He let it be done, without seeking an explanation.

When Gwynplaine was seated, the justice of the quorum and the wapentake retired a few steps, and stood upright and motionless, behind the seat.

Then the sheriff placed his bunch of roses on the stone table, put on spectacles which the secretary gave him, drew from the bundles of papers which covered the table a sheet of parchment, yellow, green, torn, and jagged in places, which seemed to have been folded in very small folds, and of which one side was covered with writing; standing under the light of the lamp, he held the sheet close to his eyes, and in his most solemn tone read as follows:—

"In the name of the Father, the Son, and the Holy Ghost.

"This present day, the twenty-ninth of January, one thousand six hundred and ninetieth year of our Lord.

"Has been wickedly deserted on the desert coast of Portland, with the intention of allowing him to perish of hunger, of cold, and of solitude, a child ten years old.

"That child was sold at the age of two years, by order of his most gracious Majesty, King James the Second.

"That child is Lord Fermain Clancharlie, the only legitimate son of Lord Linnæus Clancharlie, Baron Clancharlie and Hunkerville, Marquis of Corleone in Sicily, a peer of England, and of Ann Bradshaw, his wife, both deceased. That child is the inheritor of the estates and titles of his father. For this reason he was sold, mutilated, disfigured, and put out of the way by desire of his most gracious Majesty.

"That child was brought up, and trained to be a mountebank at markets and fairs.

"He was sold at the age of two, after the death of the peer, his father, and ten pounds sterling were given to the king as his purchase-money, as well as for divers concessions, tolerations, and immunities.

"Lord Fermain Clancharlie, at the age of two years, was bought by me, the undersigned, who write these lines, and mutilated and disfigured by a Fleming of Flanders, called Hardquanonne, who alone is acquainted with the secrets and modes of treatment of Doctor Conquest.

"The child was destined by us to be a laughing mask (*masca ridens*).

"With this intention Hardquanonne performed on him the operation, *Bucca fissa usque ad aures*, which stamps an everlasting laugh upon the face.

"The child, by means known only to Hardquanonne, was put to sleep and made insensible during its performance, knowing nothing of the operation which he underwent.

"He does not know that he is Lord Clancharlie.

"He answers to the name of Gwynplaine.

"This fact is the result of his youth, and the slight powers of memory he could have had when he was bought and sold, being then barely two years old.

"Hardquanonne is the only person who knows how to perform the operation *Bucca fissa*, and the said child is the only living subject upon which it has been essayed.

"The operation is so unique and singular that though after long years this child should have come to be an old man instead of a child, and his black locks should have turned white, he would be immediately recognized by Hardquanonne.

"At the time that I am writing this, Hardquanonne, who has perfect knowledge of all the facts, and participated as principal therein, is detained in the prisons of his highness the Prince of Orange, commonly called King William III. Hardquanonne was apprehended and seized as being one of the band of Comprachicos or Cheylas. He is imprisoned in the dungeon of Chatham.

"It was in Switzerland, near the Lake of Geneva, between Lausanne and Vevey, in the very house in which his father and mother died, that the child was, in obedience with the orders of the king, sold and given up by the last servant of the deceased Lord Linnæus, which servant died soon after his master, so that this secret and delicate matter is now unknown to any one on earth, excepting Hardquanonne, who is in the dungeon of Chatham, and ourselves, now about to perish.

"We, the undersigned, brought up and kept, for eight years, for professional purposes, the little lord bought by us of the king.

"To-day, flying from England to avoid Hardquanonne's ill-fortune, our fear of the penal indictments, prohibitions, and fulminations of Parliament has induced us to desert, at night-fall, on the coast of Portland, the said child Gwynplaine, who is Lord Fermain Clancharlie.

"Now, we have sworn secrecy to the king, but not to God.

"To-night, at sea, overtaken by a violent tempest by the will of Providence, full of despair and distress, kneeling before Him who could save our lives, and may, perhaps, be willing to save our souls, having nothing more to hope from men, but everything to fear from God, having for only anchor and resource repentance of our bad actions, resigned to death, and content if Divine justice be satisfied, humble, penitent, and beating our breasts, we make this declaration, and confide and deliver it to the furious ocean to use as it best may according to the will of God. And may the Holy Virgin aid us, Amen. And we attach our signatures."

The sheriff interrupted, saying,—"Here are the signatures. All in different handwritings."

And he resumed,—

"Doctor Gernardus Geestemunde.—Asuncion.—A cross, and at the side of it, Barbara Fermoy, from Tyrryf Isle, in the Hebrides; Gaizdorra, Captain; Giangirate; Jacques Quartourze, alias le Narbonnais; Luc-Pierre Capgaroupe, from the galleys of Mahon."

The sheriff, after a pause, resumed, a "note written in the same hand as the text and the first signature," and he read,—

"Of the three men comprising the crew, the skipper having been swept off by a wave, there remain but two, and we have signed, Galdeazun; Ave Maria, Thief."

The sheriff, interspersing his reading with his own observations, continued, "At the bottom of the sheet is written,—

"'At sea, on board of the *Matutina*, Biscay hooker, from the Gulf de Pasages.' This sheet," added the sheriff, "is a legal document, bearing the mark of King James the Second. On the margin of the declaration, and in the same handwriting there is this note, 'The present declaration is written by us on the back of the royal order, which was given us as our receipt when we bought the child. Turn the leaf and the order will be seen.'"

The sheriff turned the parchment, and raised it in his right hand, to expose it to the light.

A blank page was seen, if the word blank can be applied to a thing so mouldy, and in the middle of the page three words were written, two Latin words, *Jussu regis*, and a signature, *Jeffreys*.

"*Jussu regis, Jeffreys*," said the sheriff, passing from a grave voice to a clear one.

Gwynplaine was as a man on whose head a tile falls from the palace of dreams.

He began to speak, like one who speaks unconsciously.

"Gernardus, yes, the doctor. An old, sad-looking man. I was afraid of him. Gaizdorra, Captain, that means chief. There were women, Asuncion, and the other. And then the Provençal. His name was Capgaroupe. He used to drink out of a flat bottle on which there was a name written in red."

"Behold it," said the sheriff.

He placed on the table something which the secretary had just taken out of the bag. It was a gourd, with handles like ears, covered with wicker. This bottle had evidently seen service, and had sojourned in the water. Shells and seaweed adhered to it. It was encrusted and damascened over with the rust of ocean. There was a ring of tar round its neck, showing that it had been hermetically sealed. Now it was unsealed and open. They had, however, replaced in the flask a sort of bung made of tarred oakum, which had been used to cork it.

"It was in this bottle," said the sheriff, "that the men about to perish placed the declaration which I have just read. This message addressed to justice has been faithfully delivered by the sea."

The sheriff increased the majesty of his tones, and continued,—

"In the same way that Harrow Hill produces excellent wheat, which is turned into fine flour for the royal table, so the sea renders every service in its power to England, and when a nobleman is lost finds and restores him."

Then he resumed,—

"On this flask, as you say, there is a name written in red."

He raised his voice, turning to the motionless prisoner,—

"Your name, malefactor, is here. Such are the hidden channels by which truth, swallowed up in the gulf of human actions, floats to the surface."

The sheriff took the gourd, and turned to the light one of its sides, which had, no doubt, been cleaned for the ends of justice. Between the interstices of wicker was a narrow line of red reed, blackened here and there by the action of water and of time.

The reed, notwithstanding some breakages, traced distinctly in the wicker-work these twelve letters—Hardquanonne.

Then the sheriff, resuming that monotonous tone of voice which resembles nothing else, and which may be termed a judicial accent, turned towards the sufferer.

"Hardquanonne! when by us, the sheriff, this bottle, on which is your name, was for the first time shown, exhibited, and presented to you, you at once, and willingly, recognized it as having belonged to you. Then, the parchment being read to you which was contained, folded and enclosed within it, you would say no more; and in the hope, doubtless, that the lost child would never be recovered, and that you would escape punishment, you refuse to answer. As the result of your refusal, you have had applied to you the *peine forte et dure;* and the second reading of the said parchment, on which is written the declaration and confession of your accomplices, was made to you, but in vain.

"This is the fourth day, and that which is legally set apart for the confrontation, and he who was deserted on the twenty-ninth of January, one thousand six hundred and ninety, having been brought into your presence, your devilish hope has vanished, you have broken silence, and recognized your victim."

The prisoner opened his eyes, lifted his head, and, with a voice strangely resonant of agony, but which had still an indescribable calm mingled with its hoarseness, pronounced in excruciating accents, from under the mass of stones, words to pronounce each of which he had to lift that which was like the slab of a tomb placed upon him. He spoke,—

"I swore to keep the secret. I have kept it as long as I could. Men of dark lives are faithful, and hell has its honour. Now silence is useless. So be it! For this reason I speak. Well—yes; 'tis he! We did it between us—the king and I: the king, by his will; I, by my art!"

And looking at Gwynplaine,—

"Now laugh for ever!"

And he himself began to laugh.

This second laugh, wilder yet than the first, might have been taken for a sob.

The laughed ceased, and the man lay back. His eyelids closed.

The sheriff, who had allowed the prisoner to speak, resumed,—

"All which is placed on record."

He gave the secretary time to write, and then said,—

"Hardquanonne, by the terms of the law, after confrontation followed by identification, after the third reading of the declarations of your accomplices, since confirmed by your recognition and confession, and after your renewed avowal, you are about to be relieved from these irons, and placed at the good pleasure of her Majesty to be hung as *plagiary*."

"*Plagiary*," said the serjeant of the coif. "That is to say, a buyer and seller of children. Law of the Visigoths, seventh book, third

"'*Qui pueros vendis, plagiarius est tibi nomen*.'"

The sheriff placed the parchment on the table, laid down his spectacles, took up the nosegay, and said,—

"End of *la peine forte et dure*. Hardquanonne, thank her Majesty."

By a sign the justice of the quorum set in motion the man dressed in leather.

This man, who was the executioner's assistant, "groom of the gibbet," the old charters call him, went to the prisoner, took off the stones, one by one, from his chest, and lifted the plate of iron up, exposing the wretch's crushed sides. Then he freed his wrists and ankle-bones from the four chains that fastened him to the pillars.

The prisoner, released alike from stones and chains, lay flat on the ground, his eyes closed, his arms and legs apart, like a crucified man taken down from a cross.

"Hardquanonne," said the sheriff, "arise!"

The prisoner did not move.

The groom of the gibbet took up a hand and let it go; the hand fell back. The other hand, being raised, fell back likewise.

The groom of the gibbet seized one foot and then the other, and the heels fell back on the ground.

The fingers remained inert, and the toes motionless. The naked feet of an extended corpse seem, as it were, to bristle.

The doctor approached, and drawing from the pocket of his robe a little mirror of steel, put it to the open mouth of Hardquanonne. Then with his fingers he opened the eyelids. They did not close again; the glassy eyeballs remained fixed.

The doctor rose up and said,—

"He is dead."

And he added,—

"He laughed; that killed him."

"'Tis of little consequence," said the sheriff. "After confession, life or death is a mere formality."

Then pointing to Hardquanonne by a gesture with the nosegay of roses, the sheriff gave the order to the wapentake,—

"A corpse to be carried away to-night."

The wapentake acquiesced by a nod.

And the sheriff added,—

"The cemetery of the jail is opposite."

The wapentake nodded again.

The sheriff, holding in his left hand the nosegay and in his right the white wand, placed himself opposite Gwynplaine, who was still seated, and made him a low bow; then assuming another solemn attitude, he turned his head over his shoulder, and looking Gwynplaine in the face, said,—

"To you here present, we Philip Denzill Parsons, knight, sheriff of the county of Surrey, assisted by Aubrey Dominick, Esq., our clerk and registrar, and by our usual officers, duly provided by the direct and special commands of her Majesty, in virtue of our commission, and the rights and duties of our charge, and with authority from the Lord Chancellor of England, the affidavits having been drawn up and recorded, regard being had to the documents communicated by the Admiralty, after verification of attestations and signatures, after declarations read and heard, after confrontation made, all the statements and legal information having been completed, exhausted, and brought to a good and just issue—we signify and declare to you, in order that right may be done, that you are Fermain Clancharlie, Baron Clancharlie and Hunkerville, Marquis de Corleone in Sicily, and a peer of England; and God keep your lordship!"

And he bowed to him.

The serjeant on the right, the doctor, the justice of the quorum, the wapentake, the secretary, all the attendants except the executioner, repeated his salutation still more respectfully, and bowed to the ground before Gwynplaine.

"Ah," said Gwynplaine, "awake me!"

And he stood up, pale as death.

"I come to awake you indeed," said a voice which had not yet been heard.

A man came out from behind the pillars. As no one had entered the cell since the sheet of iron had given passage to the *cortège* of police, it was clear that this man had been there in the shadow before Gwynplaine had entered, that he had a regular right of attendance, and had been present by appointment and mission. The man was fat and pursy, and wore a court wig and a travelling cloak.

He was rather old than young, and very precise.

He saluted Gwynplaine with ease and respect—with the ease of a gentleman-in-waiting, and without the awkwardness of a judge.

"Yes," he said; "I have come to awaken you. For twenty-five years you have slept. You have been dreaming. It is time to awake. You believe yourself to be Gwynplaine; you are Clancharlie. You believe yourself to be one of the people; you belong to the peerage. You believe yourself to be of the lowest rank; you are of the highest. You believe yourself a player; you are a senator. You believe yourself poor; you are wealthy. You believe yourself to be of no account; you are important. Awake, my lord!"

Gwynplaine, in a low voice, in which a tremor of fear was to be distinguished, murmured,—

"What does it all mean?"

"It means, my lord," said the fat man, "that I am called Barkilphedro; that I am an officer of the Admiralty; that this waif, the flask of Hardquanonne, was found on the beach, and was brought to be unsealed by me, according to the duty and prerogative of my office; that I opened it in the presence of two sworn jurors of the Jetsam Office, both members of Parliament, William Brathwait, for the city of Bath, and Thomas Jervois, for Southampton; that the two jurors deciphered and attested the contents of the flask, and signed the necessary affidavit conjointly with me; that I made my report to her Majesty, and by order of the queen all necessary and legal formalities were carried out with the discretion necessary in a matter so delicate; that the last form, the confrontation, has just been carried out; that you have £40,000 a year; that you are a peer of the United Kingdom of Great Britain, a legislator and a judge, a supreme judge, a sovereign legislator, dressed in purple and ermine, equal to princes, like unto emperors; that you have on your brow the coronet of a peer, and that you are about to wed a duchess, the daughter of a king."

Under this transfiguration, overwhelming him like a series of thunderbolts, Gwynplaine fainted.

CHAPTER II.

THE WAIF KNOWS ITS OWN COURS

All this had occurred owing to the circumstance of a soldier having found a bottle on the beach. We will relate the facts. In all facts there are wheels within wheels.

One day one of the four gunners composing the garrison of Castle Calshor picked up on the sand at low water a flask covered with wicker, which had been cast up by the tide. This flask, covered with mould, was corked by a tarred bung. The soldier carried the waif to the colonel of the castle, and the colonel sent it to the High Admiral of England. The Admiral meant the Admiralty; with waifs, the Admiralty meant Barkilphedro.

Barkilphedro, having uncorked and emptied the bottle, carried it to the queen. The queen immediately took the matter into consideration.

Two weighty counsellors were instructed and consulted—namely, the Lord Chancellor, who is by law the guardian of the king's conscience; and the Lord Marshal, who is referee in Heraldry and in the pedigrees of the nobility. Thomas Howard, Duke of Norfolk, a Catholic peer, who is hereditary Earl Marshal of England, had sent word by his deputy Earl Marshal, Henry Howard, Earl Bindon, that he would agree with the Lord Chancellor. The Lord Chancellor was William Cowper. We must not confound this chancellor with his namesake and contemporary William Cowper, the anatomist and commentator on Bidloo, who published a treatise on muscles, in England, at the very time that Etienne Abeille published a history of bones, in France. A surgeon is a very different thing from a lord. Lord William Cowper is celebrated for having, with reference to the affair of Talbot Yelverton, Viscount Longueville, propounded this opinion: That in the English constitution the restoration of a peer is more important than the restoration of a king. The flask found at Calshor had awakened his interest in the highest degree. The author of a maxim delights in opportunities to which it may be applied. Here was a case of the restoration of a peer. Search was made. Gwynplaine, by the inscription over his door, was soon found. Neither was Hardquanonne dead. A prison rots a man, but preserves him—if to keep is to preserve. People placed in Bastiles were rarely removed. There is little more change in the dungeon than in the tomb. Hardquanonne was still in prison at Chatham. They had only to put their hands on him. He was transferred from Chatham to London. In the meantime information was sought in Switzerland. The facts were found to be correct. They obtained from the local archives at Vevey, at Lausanne, the certificate of Lord Linnæus's marriage in exile, the certificate of his child's birth, the certificate of the decease of the father and mother; and they had duplicates, duly authenticated, made to answer all necessary requirements.

All this was done with the most rigid secrecy, with what is called royal promptitude, and with that mole-like silence recommended and practised by Bacon, and later on made law by Blackstone, for affairs connected with the Chancellorship and the state, and in matters termed parliamentary. The *jussu regis* and the signature *Jeffreys* were authenticated. To those who have studied pathologically the cases of caprice called "our good will and pleasure," this *jussu regis* is very simple. Why should James II., whose credit required the concealment of such acts, have allowed that to be written which endangered their success? The answer is, cynicism—haughty indifference. Oh! you believe that effrontery is confined to abandoned women? The *raison d'état* is equally abandoned. *Et se cupit ante videri.* To commit a crime and emblazon it, there is the sum total of history. The king tattooes himself like the convict. Often when it would be to a man's greatest advantage to escape from the hands of the police or the records of history, he would seem to regret the escape so great is the love of notoriety. Look at my arm! Observe the design! *I* am Lacenaire! See, a temple of love and a burning heart pierced through with an arrow! *Jussu regis.* It is I, James the Second. A man commits a bad action, and places his mark upon it. To fill up the measure of crime by effrontery, to denounce himself, to cling to his misdeeds, is the insolent bravado of the criminal. Christina seized Monaldeschi, had him confessed and assassinated, and said,—

"I am the Queen of Sweden, in the palace of the King of France."

There is the tyrant who conceals himself, like Tiberius; and the tyrant who displays himself, like Philip II. One has the attributes of the scorpion, the other those rather of the leopard. James II. was of this latter variety. He had, we know, a gay and open countenance, differing so far from Philip. Philip was sullen, James jovial. Both were equally ferocious. James II. was an easy-minded tiger; like Philip II., his crimes lay light upon his conscience. He was a monster by the grace of God. Therefore he had nothing to dissimulate nor to extenuate, and his assassinations were by divine right. He, too, would not have minded leaving behind him those archives of Simancas, with all his misdeeds dated, classified, labelled, and put in order, each in its compartment, like poisons in the cabinet of a chemist. To set the sign-manual to crimes is right royal.

Every deed done is a draft drawn on the great invisible paymaster. A bill had just come due with the ominous endorsement, *Jussu regis.*

Queen Anne, in one particular unfeminine, seeing that she could keep a secret, demanded a confidential report of so grave a matter from the Lord Chancellor—one of the kind specified as "report to the royal ear." Reports of this kind have been common in all monarchies. At Vienna there was "a counsellor of the ear"—an aulic dignitary. It was an ancient Carlovingian office—the *auricularius* of the old palatine deeds. He who whispers to the emperor.

William, Baron Cowper, Chancellor of England, whom the queen believed in because he was short-sighted like herself, or even more so, had committed to writing a memorandum commencing thus: "Two birds were subject to Solomon—a lapwing, the hudbud, who could speak all languages; and an eagle, the simourganka, who covered with the shadow of his wings a caravan of twenty thousand men. Thus, under another form, Providence," etc. The Lord Chancellor proved the fact that the heir to a peerage had been carried off, mutilated, and then restored. He did not blame James II., who was, after all, the queen's father. He even went so far as to justify him. First, there are ancient monarchical maxims. *E senioratu eripimus. In roturagio cadat.* Secondly, there is a royal right of mutilation. Chamberlayne asserts the fact.[19] *Corpora et bona nostrorum subjectorum nostra sunt*, said James I., of glorious and learned memory. The eyes of dukes of the blood royal have been plucked out for the good of the kingdom. Certain princes, too near to the throne, have been conveniently stifled between mattresses, the cause of death being given out as apoplexy. Now to stifle is worse than to mutilate. The King of Tunis tore out the eyes of his father, Muley Assem, and his ambassadors have not been the less favourably received by the emperor. Hence the king may order the suppression of a limb like the suppression of a state, etc. It is legal. But one law does not destroy another. "If a drowned man is cast up by the water, and is not dead, it is an act of God readjusting one of the king. If the heir be found, let the coronet be given back to him. Thus was it done for Lord Alla, King of Northumberland, who was also a mountebank. Thus should be done to Gwynplaine, who is also a king, seeing that he is a peer. The lowness of the occupation which he has been obliged to follow, under constraint of superior power, does not tarnish the blazon: as in the case of Abdolmumen, who was a king, although he had been a gardener; that of Joseph, who was a saint, although he had been a carpenter; that of Apollo, who was a god, although he had been a shepherd."

In short, the learned chancellor concluded by advising the reinstatement, in all his estates and dignities, of Lord Fermain Clancharlie, miscalled Gwynplaine, on the sole condition that he should be confronted with the criminal Hardquanonne, and identified by the same. And on this point the chancellor, as constitutional keeper of the royal conscience, based the royal decision. The Lord Chancellor added in a postscript that if Hardquanonne refused to answer he should be subjected to the *peine forte et dure*, until the period called the *frodmortell*, according to the statute of King Athelstane, which orders the confrontation to take place on the fourth day. In this there is a certain inconvenience, for if the prisoner dies on the second or third day the confrontation becomes difficult; still the law must be obeyed. The inconvenience of the law makes part and parcel of it. In the mind of the Lord Chancellor, however, the recognition of Gwynplaine by Hardquanonne was indubitable.

Anne, having been made aware of the deformity of Gwynplaine, and not wishing to wrong her sister, on whom had been bestowed the estates of Clancharlie, graciously decided that the Duchess Josiana should be espoused by the new lord—that is to say, by Gwynplaine.

The reinstatement of Lord Fermain Clancharlie was, moreover, a very simple affair, the heir being legitimate, and in the direct line.

In cases of doubtful descent, and of peerages in abeyance claimed by collaterals, the House of Lords must be consulted. This (to go no further back) was done in 1782, in the case of the barony of Sydney, claimed by Elizabeth Perry; in 1798, in that of the barony of Beaumont, claimed by Thomas Stapleton; in 1803, in that of the barony of Stapleton; in 1803, in that of the barony of Chandos, claimed by the Reverend Tymewell Brydges; in 1813, in that of the earldom of Banbury, claimed by General Knollys, etc., etc. But the present was no similar case. Here there was no pretence for litigation; the legitimacy was undoubted, the right clear and certain. There was no point to submit to the House, and the Queen, assisted by the Lord Chancellor, had power to recognize and admit the new peer.

Barkilphedro managed everything.

The affair, thanks to him, was kept so close, the secret was so hermetically sealed, that neither Josiana nor Lord David caught sight of the fearful abyss which was being dug under them. It was easy to deceive Josiana, entrenched as she was behind a rampart of pride. She was self-isolated. As to Lord David, they sent him to sea, off the coast of Flanders. He was going to lose his peerage, and had no suspicion of it. One circumstance is noteworthy.

It happened that at six leagues from the anchorage of the naval station commanded by Lord David, a captain called Halyburton broke through the French fleet. The Earl of Pembroke, President of the Council, proposed that this Captain Halyburton should be made vice-admiral. Anne struck out Halyburton's name, and put Lord David Dirry-Moir's in its place, that he might, when no longer a peer, have the satisfaction of being a vice-admiral.

Anne was well pleased. A hideous husband for her sister, and a fine step for Lord David. Mischief and kindness combined.

Her Majesty was going to enjoy a comedy. Besides, she argued to herself that she was repairing an abuse of power committed by her august father. She was reinstating a member of the peerage. She was acting like a great queen; she was protecting innocence according to the will of God that Providence in its holy and impenetrable ways, etc., etc. It is very sweet to do a just action which is disagreeable to those whom we do not like.

To know that the future husband of her sister was deformed, sufficed the queen. In what manner Gwynplaine was deformed, and by what kind of ugliness, Barkilphedro had not communicated to the queen, and Anne had not deigned to inquire. She was proudly and royally disdainful. Besides, what could it matter? The House of Lords could not but be grateful. The Lord Chancellor, its oracle, had approved. To restore a peer is to restore the peerage. Royalty on this occasion had shown itself a good and scrupulous guardian of the privileges of the peerage. Whatever might be the face of the new lord, a face cannot be urged in objection to a right. Anne said all this to herself, or something like it, and went straight to her object, an object at once grand, womanlike, and regal—namely, to give herself a pleasure.

The queen was then at Windsor—a circumstance which placed a certain distance between the intrigues of the court and the public. Only such persons as were absolutely necessary to the plan were in the secret of what was taking place. As to Barkilphedro, he was joyful—a circumstance which gave a lugubrious expression to his face. If there be one thing in the world which can be more hideous than another, 'tis joy.

He had had the delight of being the first to taste the contents of Hardquanonne's flask. He seemed but little surprised, for astonishment is the attribute of a little mind. Besides, was it not all due to him, who had waited so long on duty at the gate of chance? Knowing how to wait, he had fairly won his reward.

This *nil admirari* was an expression of face. At heart we may admit that he was very much astonished. Any one who could have lifted the mask with which he covered his inmost heart even before God would have discovered this: that at the very time Barkilphedro had begun to feel finally convinced that it would be impossible—even to him, the intimate and most infinitesimal enemy of Josiana—to find a vulnerable point in her lofty life. Hence an access of savage animosity lurked in his mind. He had reached the paroxysm which is called discouragement. He was all the more furious, because despairing. To gnaw one's chain—how tragic and appropriate the expression! A villain gnawing at his own powerlessness!

Barkilphedro was perhaps just on the point of renouncing not his desire to do evil to Josiana, but his hope of doing it; not the rage, but the effort. But how degrading to be thus baffled! To keep hate thenceforth in a case, like a dagger in a museum! How bitter the humiliation!

All at once to a certain goal—Chance, immense and universal, loves to bring such coincidences about—the flask of Hardquanonne came, driven from wave to wave, into Barkilphedro's hands. There is in the unknown an indescribable fealty which seems to be at the beck and call of evil. Barkilphedro, assisted by two chance witnesses, disinterested jurors of the Admiralty, uncorked the flask, found the parchment, unfolded, read it. What words could express his devilish delight!

It is strange to think that the sea, the wind, space, the ebb and flow of the tide, storms, calms, breezes, should have given themselves so much trouble to bestow happiness on a scoundrel. That co-operation had continued for fifteen years. Mysterious efforts! During fifteen years the ocean had never for an instant ceased from its labours. The waves transmitted from one to another the floating bottle. The shelving rocks had shunned the brittle glass; no crack had yawned in the flask; no friction had displaced the cork; the sea-weeds had not rotted the osier; the shells had not eaten out the word "Hardquanonne;" the water had not penetrated into the waif; the mould had not rotted the parchment; the wet had hot effaced the writing. What trouble the abyss must have taken! Thus that which Gernardus had flung into darkness, darkness had handed back to Barkilphedro. The message sent to God had reached the devil. Space had committed an abuse of confidence, and a lurking sarcasm which mingles with events had so arranged that it had complicated the loyal triumph of the lost child's becoming Lord Clancharlie with a venomous victory: in doing a good action, it had mischievously placed justice at the service of iniquity. To save the victim of James II. was to give a prey to Barkilphedro. To reinstate Gwynplaine was to crush Josiana. Barkilphedro had succeeded, and it was for this that for so many years the waves, the surge, the squalls had buffeted, shaken, thrown, pushed, tormented, and respected this bubble of glass, which bore within it so many commingled fates. It was for this that there had been a cordial co-operation between the winds, the tides, and the tempests—a vast agitation of all prodigies for the pleasure of a scoundrel; the infinite co-operating with an earthworm! Destiny is subject to such grim caprices.

Barkilphedro was struck by a flash of Titanic pride. He said to himself that it had all been done to fulfil his intentions. He felt that he was the object and the instrument.

But he was wrong. Let us clear the character of chance.

Such was not the real meaning of the remarkable circumstance of which the hatred of Barkilphedro was to profit. Ocean had made itself father and mother to an orphan, had sent the hurricane against his executioners, had wrecked the vessel which had repulsed the child, had swallowed up the clasped hands of the storm-beaten sailors, refusing their supplications and accepting only their repentance; the tempest received a deposit from the hands of death. The strong vessel containing the crime was replaced by the fragile phial containing the reparation. The sea changed its character, and, like a panther turning nurse, began to rock the cradle, not of the child, but of his destiny, whilst he grew up ignorant of all that the depths of ocean were doing for him.

The waves to which this flask had been flung watching over that past which contained a future; the whirlwind breathing kindly on it; the currents directing the frail waif across the fathomless wastes of water; the caution exercised by seaweed, the swells, the rocks; the vast froth of the abyss, taking under its protection an innocent child; the wave imperturbable as a conscience; chaos re-establishing order; the worldwide shadows ending in radiance; darkness employed to bring to light the star of truth; the exile consoled in his tomb; the heir given back to his inheritance; the crime of the king repaired; divine premeditation obeyed; the little, the weak, the deserted child with infinity for a guardian—all this Barkilphedro might have seen in the event on which he triumphed. This is what he did not see. He did not believe that it had all been done for Gwynplaine. He fancied that it had been effected for Barkilphedro, and that he was well worth the trouble. Thus it is ever with Satan.

Moreover, ere we feel astonished that a waif so fragile should have floated for fifteen years undamaged, we should seek to understand the tender care of the ocean. Fifteen years is nothing. On the 4th of October 1867, on the coast of Morbihan, between the Isle de Croix, the extremity of the peninsula de Gavres, and the Rocher des Errants, the fishermen of Port Louis found a Roman amphora of the fourth century, covered with arabesques by the incrustations of the sea. That amphora had been floating fifteen hundred years.

Whatever appearance of indifference Barkilphedro tried to exhibit, his wonder had equalled his joy. Everything he could desire was there to his hand. All seemed ready made. The fragments of the event which was to satisfy his hate were spread out within his reach. He had nothing to do but to pick them up and fit them together—a repair which it was an amusement to execute. He was the artificer.

Gwynplaine! He knew the name. *Masca ridens.* Like every one else, he had been to see the Laughing Man. He had read the sign nailed up against the Tadcaster Inn as one reads a play-bill that attracts a crowd. He had noted it. He remembered it directly in its most minute details; and, in any case, it was easy to compare them with the original. That notice, in the electrical summons which arose in his memory, appeared in the depths of his mind, and placed itself by the side of the parchment signed by the shipwrecked crew, like an answer following a question, like the solution following an enigma; and the lines—"Here is to be seen Gwynplaine, deserted at the age of ten, on the 29th of January, 1690, on the coast at Portland"—suddenly appeared to his eyes in the splendour of an apocalypse. His vision was the light of *Mene, Tekel, Upharsin*, outside a booth. Here was the destruction of the edifice which made the existence of Josiana. A sudden earthquake. The lost child was found. There was a Lord Clancharlie; David Dirry-Moir was nobody. Peerage, riches, power, rank—all these things left Lord David and entered Gwynplaine. All the castles, parks, forests, town houses, palaces, domains, Josiana included, belonged to Gwynplaine. And what a climax for Josiana! What had she now before her? Illustrious and haughty, a player; beautiful, a monster. Who could have hoped for this? The truth was that the joy of Barkilphedro had become enthusiastic. The most hateful combinations are surpassed by the infernal munificence of the unforeseen. When reality likes, it works masterpieces. Barkilphedro found that all his dreams had been nonsense; reality were better.

The change he was about to work would not have seemed less desirable had it been detrimental to him. Insects exist which are so savagely disinterested that they sting, knowing that to sting is to die. Barkilphedro was like such vermin.

But this time he had not the merit of being disinterested. Lord David Dirry-Moir owed him nothing, and Lord Fermain Clancharlie was about to owe him everything. From being a *protégé* Barkilphedro was about to become a protector. Protector of whom? Of a peer of England. He was going to have a lord of his own, and a lord who would be his creature. Barkilphedro counted on giving him his first impressions. His peer would be the morganatic brother-in-law of the queen. His ugliness would please the queen in the same proportion as it displeased Josiana. Advancing by such favour, and assuming grave and modest airs, Barkilphedro might become a somebody. He had always been destined for the church. He had a vague longing to be a bishop.

Meanwhile he was happy.

Oh, what a great success! and what a deal of useful work had chance accomplished for him! His vengeance—for he called it his vengeance—had been softly brought to him by the waves. He had not lain in ambush in vain.

He was the rock, Josiana was the waif. Josiana was about to be dashed against Barkilphedro, to his intense villainous ecstasy.

He was clever in the art of suggestion, which consists in making in the minds of others a little incision into which you put an idea of your own. Holding himself aloof, and without appearing to mix himself up in the matter, it was he who arranged that Josiana should go to the Green Box and see Gwynplaine. It could do no harm. The appearance of the mountebank, in his low estate, would be a good ingredient in the combination; later on it would season it.

He had quietly prepared everything beforehand. What he most desired was something unspeakably abrupt. The work on which he was engaged could only be expressed in these strange words—the construction of a thunderbolt.

All preliminaries being complete, he had watched till all the necessary legal formalities had been accomplished. The secret had not oozed out, silence being an element of law.

The confrontation of Hardquanonne with Gwynplaine had taken place. Barkilphedro had been present. We have seen the result.

The same day a post-chaise belonging to the royal household was suddenly sent by her Majesty to fetch Lady Josiana from London to Windsor, where the queen was at the time residing.

Josiana, for reasons of her own, would have been very glad to disobey, or at least to delay obedience, and put off her departure till next day; but court life does not permit of these objections. She was obliged to set out at once, and to leave her residence in London, Hunkerville House, for her residence at Windsor, Corleone Lodge.

The Duchess Josiana left London at the very moment that the wapentake appeared at the Tadcaster Inn to arrest Gwynplaine and take him to the torture cell of Southwark.

When she arrived at Windsor, the Usher of the Black Rod, who guards the door of the presence chamber, informed her that her Majesty was in audience with the Lord Chancellor, and could not receive her until the next day; that, consequently, she was to remain at Corleone Lodge, at the orders of her Majesty; and that she should receive the queen's commands direct, when her Majesty awoke the next morning. Josiana entered her house feeling very spiteful, supped in a bad humour, had the spleen, dismissed every one except her page, then dismissed him, and went to bed while it was yet daylight.

When she arrived she had learned that Lord David Dirry-Moir was expected at Windsor the next day, owing to his having, whilst at sea, received orders to return immediately and receive her Majesty's commands.

CHAPTER III.

AN AWAKENING

"No man could pass suddenly from Siberia into Senegal without losing consciousness."—HUMBOLDT.

The swoon of a man, even of one the most firm and energetic, under the sudden shock of an unexpected stroke of good fortune, is nothing wonderful. A man is knocked down by the unforeseen blow, like an ox by the poleaxe. Francis d'Albescola, he who tore from the Turkish ports their iron chains, remained a whole day without consciousness when they made him pope. Now the stride from a cardinal to a pope is less than that from a mountebank to a peer of England.

No shock is so violent as a loss of equilibrium.

When Gwynplaine came to himself and opened his eyes it was night. He was in an armchair, in the midst of a large chamber lined throughout with purple velvet, over walls, ceiling, and floor. The carpet was velvet. Standing near him, with uncovered head, was the fat man in the travelling cloak, who had emerged from behind the pillar in the cell at Southwark. Gwynplaine was alone in the chamber with him. From the chair, by extending his arms, he could reach two tables, each bearing a branch of six lighted wax candles. On one of these tables there were papers and a casket, on the other refreshments; a cold fowl, wine, and brandy, served on a silver-gilt salver.

Through the panes of a high window, reaching from the ceiling to the floor, a semicircle of pillars was to be seen, in the clear April night, encircling a courtyard with three gates, one very wide, and the other two low. The carriage gate, of great size, was in the middle; on the right, that for equestrians, smaller; on the left, that for foot passengers, still less. These gates were formed of iron railings, with glittering points. A tall piece of sculpture surmounted the central one. The columns were probably in white marble, as well as the pavement of the court, thus producing an effect like snow; and framed in its sheet of flat flags was a mosaic, the pattern of which was vaguely marked in the shadow. This mosaic, when seen by daylight, would no doubt have disclosed to the sight, with much emblazonry and many colours, a gigantic coat-of-arms, in the Florentine fashion. Zigzags of balustrades rose and fell, indicating stairs of terraces. Over the court frowned an immense pile of architecture, now shadowy and vague in the starlight. Intervals of sky, full of stars, marked out clearly the outline of the palace. An enormous roof could be seen, with the gable ends vaulted; garret windows, roofed over like visors; chimneys like towers; and entablatures covered with motionless gods and goddesses.

Beyond the colonnade there played in the shadow one of those fairy fountains in which, as the water falls from basin to basin, it combines the beauty of rain with that of the cascade, and as if scattering the contents of a jewel box, flings to the wind its diamonds and its pearls as though to divert the statues around. Long rows of windows ranged away, separated by panoplies, in relievo, and by busts on small pedestals. On the pinnacles, trophies and morions with plumes cut in stone alternated with statues of heathen deities.

In the chamber where Gwynplaine was, on the side opposite the window, was a fireplace as high as the ceiling, and on another, under a dais, one of those old spacious feudal beds which were reached by a ladder, and where you might sleep lying across; the joint-stool of the bed was at its side; a row of armchairs by the walls, and a row of ordinary chairs, in front of them, completed the furniture. The ceiling was domed. A great wood fire in the French fashion blazed in the fireplace; by the richness of the flames, variegated of rose colour and green, a judge of such things would have seen that the wood was ash—a great luxury. The room was so large that the branches of candles failed to light it up. Here and there curtains over doors, falling and swaying, indicated communications with other rooms. The style of the room was altogether that of the reign of James I.—a style square and massive, antiquated and magnificent. Like the carpet and the lining of the chamber, the dais, the baldaquin, the bed, the stool, the curtains, the mantelpiece, the coverings of the table, the sofas, the chairs, were all of purple velvet.

There was no gilding, except on the ceiling. Laid on it, at equal distance from the four angles, was a huge round shield of embossed metal, on which sparkled, in dazzling relief, various coats of arms. Amongst the devices, on two blazons, side by side, were to be distinguished the cap of a baron and the coronet of a marquis. Were they of brass or of silver-gilt? You could not tell. They seemed to be of gold. And in the centre of this lordly ceiling, like a gloomy and magnificent sky, the gleaming escutcheon was as the dark splendour of a sun shining in the night.

The savage, in whom is embodied the free man, is nearly as restless in a palace as in a prison. This magnificent chamber was depressing. So much splendour produces fear. Who could be the inhabitant of this stately palace? To what colossus did all this grandeur appertain? Of what lion is this the lair? Gwynplaine, as yet but half awake, was heavy at heart.

"Where am I?" he said.

The man who was standing before him answered,—"You are in your own house, my lord."

CHAPTER IV.

FASCINATION

It takes time to rise to the surface. And Gwynplaine had been thrown into an abyss of stupefaction.

We do not gain our footing at once in unknown depths.

There are routs of ideas, as there are routs of armies. The rally is not immediate.

We feel as it were scattered—as though some strange evaporation of self were taking place.

God is the arm, chance is the sling, man is the pebble. How are you to resist, once flung?

Gwynplaine, if we may coin the expression, ricocheted from one surprise to another. After the love letter of the duchess came the revelation in the Southwark dungeon.

In destiny, when wonders begin, prepare yourself for blow upon blow. The gloomy portals once open, prodigies pour in. A breach once made in the wall, and events rush upon us pell-mell. The marvellous never comes singly.

The marvellous is an obscurity. The shadow of this obscurity was over Gwynplaine. What was happening to him seemed unintelligible. He saw everything through the mist which a deep commotion leaves in the mind, like the dust caused by a falling ruin. The shock had been from top to bottom. Nothing was clear to him. However, light always returns by degrees. The dust settles. Moment by moment the density of astonishment decreases. Gwynplaine was like a man with his eyes open and fixed in a dream, as if trying to see what may be within it. He dispersed the mist. Then he reshaped it. He had intermittances of wandering. He underwent that oscillation of the mind in the unforeseen which alternately pushes us in the direction in which we understand, and then throws us back in that which is incomprehensible. Who has not at some time felt this pendulum in his brain?

By degrees his thoughts dilated in the darkness of the event, as the pupil of his eye had done in the underground shadows at Southwark. The difficulty was to succeed in putting a certain space between accumulated sensations. Before that combustion of hazy ideas called comprehension can take place, air must be admitted between the emotions. There air was wanting. The event, so to speak, could not be breathed.

In entering that terrible cell at Southwark, Gwynplaine had expected the iron collar of a felon; they had placed on his head the coronet of a peer. How could this be? There had not been space of time enough between what Gwynplaine had feared and what had really occurred; it had succeeded too quickly—his terror changing into other feelings too abruptly for comprehension. The contrasts were too tightly packed one against the other. Gwynplaine made an effort to withdraw his mind from the vice.

He was silent. This is the instinct of great stupefaction, which is more on the defensive than it is thought to be. Who says nothing is prepared for everything. A word of yours allowed to drop may be seized in some unknown system of wheels, and your utter destruction be compassed in its complex machinery.

The poor and weak live in terror of being crushed. The crowd ever expect to be trodden down. Gwynplaine had long been one of the crowd.

A singular state of human uneasiness can be expressed by the words: Let us see what will happen. Gwynplaine was in this state. You feel that you have not gained your equilibrium when an unexpected situation surges up under your feet. You watch for something which must produce a result. You are vaguely attentive. We will see what happens. What? You do not know. Whom? You watch.

The man with the paunch repeated, "You are in your own house, my lord."

Gwynplaine felt himself. In surprises, we first look to make sure that things exist; then we feel ourselves, to make sure that we exist ourselves. It was certainly to him that the words were spoken; but he himself was somebody else. He no longer had his jacket on, or his esclavine of leather. He had a waistcoat of cloth of silver; and a satin coat, which he touched and found to be embroidered. He felt a heavy purse in his waistcoat pocket. A pair of velvet trunk hose covered his clown's tights. He wore shoes with high red heels. As they had brought him to this palace, so had they changed his dress.

The man resumed,—

"Will your lordship deign to remember this: I am called Barkilphedro; I am clerk to the Admiralty. It was I who opened Hardquanonne's flask and drew your destiny out of it. Thus, in the 'Arabian Nights' a fisherman releases a giant from a bottle."

Gwynplaine fixed his eyes on the smiling face of the speaker.

Barkilphedro continued:—

"Besides this palace, my lord, Hunkerville House, which is larger, is yours. You own Clancharlie Castle, from which you take your title, and which was a fortress in the time of Edward the Elder. You have nineteen bailiwicks belonging to you, with their villages and their inhabitants. This puts under your banner, as a landlord and a nobleman, about eighty thousand vassals and tenants. At Clancharlie you are a judge—judge of all, both of goods and of persons—and you hold your baron's court. The king has no right which you have not, except the privilege of coining money. The king, designated by the Norman law as chief signor, has justice, court, and coin. Coin is money. So that you, excepting in this last, are as much a king in your lordship as he is in his kingdom. You have the right, as a baron, to a gibbet with four pillars in England; and, as a marquis, to a scaffold with seven posts in Sicily: that of the mere lord having two pillars; that of a lord of the manor, three; and that of a duke, eight. You are styled prince in the ancient charters of Northumberland. You are related to the Viscounts Valentia in Ireland, whose name is Power; and to the Earls of Umfraville in Scotland, whose name is Angus. You are chief of a clan, like Campbell, Ardmannach, and Macallummore. You have eight barons' courts—Reculver, Baston, Hell-Kerters, Homble, Moricambe, Grundraith, Trenwardraith, and others. You have a right over the turf-cutting of Pillinmore, and over the alabaster quarries near Trent. Moreover, you own all the country of Penneth Chase; and you have a mountain with an ancient town on it. The town is called Vinecaunton; the mountain is called Moilenlli. All which gives you an income of forty thousand pounds a year. That is to say, forty times the five-and-twenty thousand francs with which a Frenchman is satisfied."

Whilst Barkilphedro spoke, Gwynplaine, in a crescendo of stupor, remembered the past. Memory is a gulf that a word can move to its lowest depths. Gwynplaine knew all the words pronounced by Barkilphedro. They were written in the last lines of the two scrolls which lined the van in which his childhood had been passed, and, from so often letting his eyes wander over them mechanically, he knew them by heart. On reaching, a forsaken orphan, the travelling caravan at Weymouth, he had found the inventory of the inheritance which awaited him; and in the morning, when the poor little boy awoke, the first thing spelt by his careless and unconscious eyes was his own title and its possessions. It was a strange detail added to all his other surprises, that, during fifteen years, rolling from highway to highway, the clown of a travelling theatre, earning his bread day by day, picking up farthings, and living on crumbs, he should have travelled with the inventory of his fortune placarded over his misery.

Barkilphedro touched the casket on the table with his forefinger.

"My lord, this casket contains two thousand guineas which her gracious Majesty the Queen has sent you for your present wants."

Gwynplaine made a movement.

"That shall be for my Father Ursus," he said.

"So be it, my lord," said Barkilphedro. "Ursus, at the Tadcaster Inn. The Serjeant of the Coif, who accompanied us hither, and is about to return immediately, will carry them to him. Perhaps I may go to London myself. In that case I will take charge of it."

"I shall take them to him myself," said Gwynplaine.

Barkilphedro's smile disappeared, and he said,—"Impossible!"

There is an impressive inflection of voice which, as it were, underlines the words. Barkilphedro's tone was thus emphasized; he paused, so as to put a full stop after the word he had just uttered. Then he continued, with the peculiar and respectful tone of a servant who feels that he is master,—

"My lord, you are twenty-three miles from London, at Corleone Lodge, your court residence, contiguous to the Royal Castle of Windsor. You are here unknown to any one. You were brought here in a close carriage, which was awaiting you at the gate of the jail at Southwark. The servants who introduced you into this palace are ignorant who you are; but they know me, and that is sufficient. You may possibly have been brought to these apartments by means of a private key which is in my possession. There are people in the house asleep, and it is not an hour to awaken them. Hence we have time for an explanation, which, nevertheless, will be short. I have been commissioned by her Majesty—"

As he spoke, Barkilphedro began to turn over the leaves of some bundles of papers which were lying near the casket.

"My lord, here is your patent of peerage. Here is that of your Sicilian marquisate. These are the parchments and title-deeds of your eight baronies, with the seals of eleven kings, from Baldret, King of Kent, to James the Sixth of Scotland, and first of England and Scotland united. Here are your letters of precedence. Here are your rent-rolls, and titles and descriptions of your fiefs, freeholds, dependencies, lands, and domains. That which you see above your head in the emblazonment on the ceiling are your two coronets: the circlet with pearls for the baron, and the circlet with strawberry leaves for the marquis.

"Here, in the wardrobe, is your peer's robe of red velvet, bordered with ermine. To-day, only a few hours since, the Lord Chancellor and the Deputy Earl Marshal of England, informed of the result of your confrontation with the Comprachico Hardquanonne, have taken her Majesty's commands. Her Majesty has signed them, according to her royal will, which is the same as the law. All formalities have been complied with. To-morrow, and no later than to-morrow, you will take your seat in the House of Lords, where they have for some days been deliberating on a bill, presented by the crown, having for its object the augmentation, by a hundred thousand pounds sterling yearly, of the annual allowance to the Duke of Cumberland, husband of the queen. You will be able to take part in the debate."

Barkilphedro paused, breathed slowly, and resumed.

"However, nothing is yet settled. A man cannot be made a peer of England without his own consent. All can be annulled and disappear, unless you acquiesce. An event nipped in the bud ere it ripens often occurs in state policy. My lord, up to this time silence has been preserved on what has occurred. The House of Lords will not be informed of the facts until to-morrow. Secrecy has been kept about the whole matter for reasons of state, which are of such importance that the influential persons who alone are at this moment cognizant of your existence, and of your rights, will forget them immediately should reasons of state command their being forgotten. That which is in darkness may remain in darkness. It is easy to wipe you out; the more so as you have a brother, the natural son of your father and of a woman who afterwards, during the exile of your father, became mistress to King Charles II., which accounts for your brother's high position at court; for it is to this brother, bastard though he be, that your peerage would revert. Do you wish this? I cannot think so. Well, all depends on you. The queen must be obeyed. You will not quit the house till to-morrow in a royal carriage, and to go to the House of Lords. My lord, will you be a peer of England; yes or no? The queen has designs for you. She destines you for an alliance almost royal. Lord Fermain Clancharlie, this is the decisive moment. Destiny never opens one door without shutting another. After a certain step in advance, to step back is impossible. Whoso enters into transfiguration, leaves behind him evanescence. My lord, Gwynplaine is dead. Do you understand?"

Gwynplaine trembled from head to foot.

Then he recovered himself.

"Yes," he said.

Barkilphedro, smiling, bowed, placed the casket under his cloak, and left the room.

CHAPTER V.

WE THINK WE REMEMBER; WE FORGET.

Whence arise those strange, visible changes which occur in the soul of man?

Gwynplaine had been at the same moment raised to a summit and cast into an abyss.

His head swam with double giddiness—the giddiness of ascent and descent. A fatal combination.

He felt himself ascend, and felt not his fall.

It is appalling to see a new horizon.

A perspective affords suggestions,—not always good ones.

He had before him the fairy glade, a snare perhaps, seen through opening clouds, and showing the blue depths of sky; so deep, that they are obscure.

He was on the mountain, whence he could see all the kingdoms of the earth. A mountain all the more terrible that it is a visionary one. Those who are on its apex are in a dream.

Palaces, castles, power, opulence, all human happiness extending as far as eye could reach; a map of enjoyments spread out to the horizon; a sort of radiant geography of which he was the centre. A perilous mirage!

Imagine what must have been the haze of such a vision, not led up to, not attained to as by the gradual steps of a ladder, but reached without transition and without previous warning.

A man going to sleep in a mole's burrow, and awaking on the top of the Strasbourg steeple; such was the state of Gwynplaine.

Giddiness is a dangerous kind of glare, particularly that which bears you at once towards the day and towards the night, forming two whirlwinds, one opposed to the other.

He saw too much, and not enough.

He saw all, and nothing.

His state was what the author of this book has somewhere expressed as the blind man dazzled.

Gwynplaine, left by himself, began to walk with long strides. A bubbling precedes an explosion.

Notwithstanding his agitation, in this impossibility of keeping still, he meditated. His mind liquefied as it boiled. He began to recall things to his memory. It is surprising how we find that we have heard so clearly that to which we scarcely listened. The declaration of the shipwrecked men, read by the sheriff in the Southwark cell, came back to him clearly and intelligibly. He recalled every word, he saw under it his whole infancy.

Suddenly he stopped, his hands clasped behind his back, looking up to the ceilings—the sky—no matter what—whatever was above him.

"Quits!" he cried.

He felt like one whose head rises out of the water. It seemed to him that he saw everything—the past, the future, the present—in the accession of a sudden flash of light.

"Oh!" he cried, for there are cries in the depths of thought. "Oh! it was so, was it! I was a lord. All is discovered. They stole, betrayed, destroyed, abandoned, disinherited, murdered me! The corpse of my destiny floated fifteen years on the sea; all at once it touched the earth, and it started up, erect and living. I am reborn. I am born. I felt under my rags that the breast there palpitating was not that of a wretch; and when I looked on crowds of men, I felt that they were the flocks, and that I was not the dog, but the shepherd! Shepherds of the people, leaders of men, guides and masters, such were my fathers; and what they were I am! I am a gentleman, and I have a sword; I am a baron, and I have a casque; I am a marquis, and I have a plume; I am a peer, and I have a coronet. Lo! they deprived me of all this. I dwelt in light, they flung me into darkness. Those who proscribed the father, sold the son. When my father was dead, they took from beneath his head the stone of exile which he had placed for his pillow, and, tying it to my neck, they flung me into a sewer. Oh! those scoundrels who tortured my infancy! Yes, they rise and move in the depths of my memory. Yes; I see them again. I was that morsel of flesh pecked to pieces on a tomb by a flight of crows. I bled and cried under all those horrible shadows. Lo! it was there that they precipitated me, under the crush of those who come and go, under the trampling feet of men, under the undermost of the human race, lower than the serf, baser than the serving man, lower than the felon, lower than the slave, at the spot where Chaos becomes a sewer, in which I was engulfed. It is from thence that I come; it is from this that I rise; it is from this that I am risen. And here I am now. Quits!"

He sat down, he rose, clasped his head with his hands, began to pace the room again, and his tempestuous monologue continued within him.

"Where am I?—on the summit? Where is it that I have just alighted?—on the highest peak? This pinnacle, this grandeur, this dome of the world, this great power, is my home. This temple is in air. I am one of the gods. I live in inaccessible heights. This supremacy, which I looked up to from below, and from whence emanated such rays of glory that I shut my eyes; this ineffaceable peerage; this impregnable fortress of the fortunate, I enter. I am in it. I am of it. Ah, what a decisive turn of the wheel! I was below, I am on high—on high for ever! Behold me a lord! I shall have a scarlet robe. I shall have an earl's coronet on my head. I shall assist at the coronation of kings. They will take the oath from my hands. I shall judge princes and ministers. I shall exist. From the depths into which I was thrown, I have rebounded to the zenith. I have palaces in town and country: houses, gardens, chases, forests, carriages, millions. I will give fêtes. I will make laws. I shall have the choice of joys and pleasures. And the vagabond Gwynplaine, who had not the right to gather a flower in the grass, may pluck the stars from heaven!"

Melancholy overshadowing of a soul's brightness! Thus it was that in Gwynplaine, who had been a hero, and perhaps had not ceased to be one, moral greatness gave way to material splendour. A lamentable transition! Virtue broken down by a troop of passing demons. A surprise made on the weak side of man's fortress. All the inferior circumstances called by men superior, ambition, the purblind desires of instinct, passions, covetousness, driven far from Gwynplaine by the wholesome restraints of misfortune, took tumultuous possession of his generous heart. And from what had this arisen? From the discovery of a parchment in a waif drifted by the sea. Conscience may be violated by a chance attack.

Gwynplaine drank in great draughts of pride, and it dulled his soul. Such is the poison of that fatal wine.

Giddiness invaded him. He more than consented to its approach. He welcomed it. This was the effect of previous and long-continued thirst. Are we an accomplice of the cup which deprives us of reason? He had always vaguely desired this. His eyes had always turned towards the great. To watch is to wish. The eaglet is not born in the eyrie for nothing.

Now, however, at moments, it seemed to him the simplest thing in the world that he should be a lord. A few hours only had passed, and yet the past of yesterday seemed so far off! Gwynplaine had fallen into the ambuscade of Better, who is the enemy of Good.

Unhappy is he of whom we say, how lucky he is! Adversity is more easily resisted than prosperity. We rise more perfect from ill fortune than from good. There is a Charybdis in poverty, and a Scylla in riches. Those who remain erect under the thunderbolt are prostrated by the flash. Thou who standest without shrinking on the verge of a precipice, fear lest thou be carried up on the innumerable wings of mists and dreams. The ascent which elevates will dwarf thee. An apotheosis has a sinister power of degradation.

It is not easy to understand what is good luck. Chance is nothing but a disguise. Nothing deceives so much as the face of fortune. Is she Providence? Is she Fatality?

A brightness may not be a brightness, because light is truth, and a gleam may be a deceit. You believe that it lights you; but no, it sets you on fire.

At night, a candle made of mean tallow becomes a star if placed in an opening in the darkness. The moth flies to it.

In what measure is the moth responsible?

The sight of the candle fascinates the moth as the eye of the serpent fascinates the bird.

Is it possible that the bird and the moth should resist the attraction? Is it possible that the leaf should resist the wind? Is it possible that the stone should refuse obedience to the laws of gravitation?

These are material questions, which are moral questions as well.

After he had received the letter of the duchess, Gwynplaine had recovered himself. The deep love in his nature had resisted it. But the storm having wearied itself on one side of the horizon, burst out on the other; for in destiny, as in nature, there are successive convulsions. The first shock loosens, the second uproots.

Alas! how do the oaks fall?

Thus he who, when a child of ten, stood alone on the shore of Portland, ready to give battle, who had looked steadfastly at all the combatants whom he had to encounter, the blast which bore away the vessel in which he had expected to embark, the gulf which had swallowed up the plank, the yawning abyss, of which the menace was its retrocession, the earth which refused him a shelter, the sky which refused him a star, solitude without pity, obscurity without notice, ocean, sky, all the violence of one infinite space, and all the mysterious enigmas of another; he who had neither trembled nor fainted before the mighty hostility of the unknown; he who, still so young, had held his own with night, as Hercules of old had held his own with death; he who in the unequal struggle had thrown down this defiance, that he, a child, adopted a child, that he encumbered himself with a load, when tired and exhausted, thus rendering himself an easier prey to the attacks on his weakness, and, as it were, himself unmuzzling the shadowy monsters in ambush around him; he who, a precocious warrior, had immediately, and from his first steps out of the cradle, struggled breast to breast with destiny; he, whose disproportion with strife had not discouraged from striving; he who, perceiving in everything around him a frightful occultation of the human race, had accepted that eclipse, and proudly continued his journey; he who had known how to endure cold, thirst, hunger, valiantly; he who, a pigmy in stature, had been a colossus in soul: this Gwynplaine, who had conquered the great terror of the abyss under its double form, Tempest and Misery, staggered under a breath—Vanity.

Thus, when she has exhausted distress, nakedness, storms, catastrophes, agonies on an unflinching man, Fatality begins to smile, and her victim, suddenly intoxicated, staggers.

The smile of Fatality! Can anything more terrible be imagined? It is the last resource of the pitiless trier of souls in his proof of man. The tiger, lurking in destiny, caresses man with a velvet paw. Sinister preparation, hideous gentleness in the monster!

Every self-observer has detected within himself mental weakness coincident with aggrandisement. A sudden growth disturbs the system, and produces fever.

In Gwynplaine's brain was the giddy whirlwind of a crowd of new circumstances; all the light and shade of a metamorphosis; inexpressibly strange confrontations; the shock of the past against the future. Two Gwynplaines, himself doubled; behind, an infant in rags crawling through night—wandering, shivering, hungry, provoking laughter; in front, a brilliant nobleman—luxurious, proud, dazzling all London. He was casting off one form, and amalgamating himself with the other. He was casting the mountebank, and becoming the peer. Change of skin is sometimes change of soul. Now and then the past seemed like a dream. It was complex; bad and good. He thought of his father. It was a poignant anguish never to have known his father. He tried to picture him to himself. He thought of his brother, of whom he had just heard. Then he had a family! He, Gwynplaine! He lost himself in fantastic dreams. He saw visions of magnificence; unknown forms of solemn grandeur moved in mist before him. He heard flourishes of trumpets.

"And then," he said, "I shall be eloquent."

He pictured to himself a splendid entrance into the House of Lords. He should arrive full to the brim with new facts and ideas. What could he not tell them? What subjects he had accumulated! What an advantage to be in the midst of them, a man who had seen, touched, undergone, and suffered; who could cry aloud to them, "I have been near to everything, from which you are so far removed." He would hurl reality in the face of those patricians, crammed with illusions. They should tremble, for it would be the truth. They would applaud, for it would be grand. He would arise amongst those powerful men, more powerful than they. "I shall appear as a torch-bearer, to show them truth; and as a sword-bearer, to show them justice!" What a triumph!

And, building up these fantasies in his mind, clear and confused at the same time, he had attacks of delirium,—sinking on the first seat he came to; sometimes drowsy, sometimes starting up. He came and went, looked at the ceiling, examined the coronets, studied vaguely the hieroglyphics of the emblazonment, felt the velvet of the walls, moved the chairs, turned over the parchments, read the names, spelt out the titles, Buxton, Homble, Grundraith, Hunkerville, Clancharlie; compared the wax, the impression, felt the twist of silk appended to the royal privy seal, approached the window, listened to the splash of the fountain, contemplated the statues, counted, with the patience of a somnambulist, the columns of marble, and said,—

"It is real."

Then he touched his satin clothes, and asked himself,—

"Is it I? Yes."

He was torn by an inward tempest.

In this whirlwind, did he feel faintness and fatigue? Did he drink, eat, sleep? If he did so, he was unconscious of the fact. In certain violent situations instinct satisfies itself, according to its requirements, unconsciously. Besides, his thoughts were less thoughts than mists. At the moment that the black flame of an irruption disgorges itself from depths full of boiling lava, has the crater any consciousness of the flocks which crop the grass at the foot of the mountain?

The hours passed.

The dawn appeared and brought the day. A bright ray penetrated the chamber, and at the same instant broke on the soul of Gwynplaine.

And Dea! said the light.

BOOK THE SIXTH

URSUS UNDER DIFFERENT ASPECTS

CHAPTER I.

WHAT THE MISANTHROPE SAID

After Ursus had seen Gwynplaine thrust within the gates of Southwark Jail, he remained, haggard, in the corner from which he was watching. For a long time his ears were haunted by the grinding of the bolts and bars, which was like a howl of joy that one wretch more should be enclosed within them.

He waited. What for? He watched. What for? Such inexorable doors, once shut, do not re-open so soon. They are tongue-tied by their stagnation in darkness, and move with difficulty, especially when they have to give up a prisoner. Entrance is permitted. Exit is quite a different matter. Ursus knew this. But waiting is a thing which we have not the power to give up at our own will. We wait in our own despite. What we do disengages an acquired force, which maintains its action when its object has ceased, which keeps possession of us and holds us, and obliges us for some time longer to continue that which has already lost its motive. Hence the useless watch, the inert position that we have all held at times, the loss of time which every thoughtful man gives mechanically to that which has disappeared. None escapes this law. We become stubborn in a sort of vague fury. We know not why we are in the place, but we remain there. That which we have begun actively we continue passively, with an exhausting tenacity from which we emerge overwhelmed. Ursus, though differing from other men, was, as any other might have been, nailed to his post by that species of conscious reverie into which we are plunged by events all important to us, and in which we are impotent. He scrutinized by turns those two black walls, now the high one, then the low; sometimes the door near which the ladder to the gibbet stood, then that surmounted by a death's head. It was as if he were caught in a vice, composed of a prison and a cemetery. This shunned and unpopular street was so deserted that he was unobserved.

At length he left the arch under which he had taken shelter, a kind of chance sentry-box, in which he had acted the watchman, and departed with slow steps. The day was declining, for his guard had been long. From time to time he turned his head and looked at the fearful wicket through which Gwynplaine had disappeared. His eyes were glassy and dull. He reached the end of the alley, entered another, then another, retracing almost unconsciously the road which he had taken some hours before. At intervals he turned, as if he could still see the door of the prison, though he was no longer in the street in which the jail was situated.

Step by step he was approaching Tarrinzeau Field. The lanes in the neighbourhood of the fair-ground were deserted pathways between enclosed gardens. He walked along, his head bent down, by the hedges and ditches. All at once he halted, and drawing himself up, exclaimed, "So much the better!"

At the same time he struck his fist twice on his head and twice on his thigh, thus proving himself to be a sensible fellow, who saw things in their right light; and then he began to growl inwardly, yet now and then raising his voice.

"It is all right! Oh, the scoundrel! the thief! the vagabond! the worthless fellow! the seditious scamp! It is his speeches about the government that have sent him there. He is a rebel. I was harbouring a rebel. I am free of him, and lucky for me; he was compromising us. Thrust into prison! Oh, so much the better! What excellent laws! Ungrateful boy! I who brought him up! To give oneself so much trouble for this! Why should he want to speak and to reason? He mixed himself up in politics. The ass! As he handled pennies he babbled about the taxes, about the poor, about the people, about what was no business of his. He permitted himself to make reflections on pennies. He commented wickedly and maliciously on the copper money of the kingdom. He insulted the farthings of her Majesty. A farthing! Why, 'tis the same as the queen. A sacred effigy! Devil take it! a sacred effigy! Have we a queen—yes or no? Then respect her verdigris! Everything depends on the government; one ought to know that. I have experience, I have. I know something. They may say to me, 'But you give up politics, then?' Politics, my friends! I care as much for them as for the rough hide of an ass. I received, one day, a blow from a baronet's cane. I said to myself, That is enough: I understand politics. The people have but a farthing, they give it; the queen takes it, the people thank her. Nothing can be more natural. It is for the peers to arrange the rest; their lordships, the lords spiritual and temporal. Oh! so Gwynplaine is locked up! So he is in prison. That is just as it should be. It is equitable, excellent, well-merited, and legitimate. It is his own fault. To criticize is forbidden. Are you a lord, you idiot? The constable has seized him, the justice of the quorum has carried him off, the sheriff has him in custody. At this moment he is probably being examined by a serjeant of the coif. They pluck out your crimes, those clever fellows! Imprisoned, my wag! So much the worse for him, so much the better for me! Faith, I am satisfied. I own frankly that fortune favours me. Of what folly was I guilty when I picked up that little boy and girl! We were so quiet before, Homo and I! What had they to do in my caravan, the little blackguards? Didn't I brood over them when they were young! Didn't I draw them along with my harness! Pretty foundlings, indeed; he as ugly as sin, and she blind of both eyes! Where was the use of depriving myself of everything for their sakes? The beggars grow up, forsooth, and make love to each other. The flirtations of the deformed! It was to that we had come. The toad and the mole; quite an idyl! That was what went on in my household. All which was sure to end by going before the justice. The toad talked politics! But now I am free of him. When the wapentake came I was at first a fool; one always doubts one's own good luck. I believed that I did not see what I did see; that it was impossible, that it was a nightmare, that a day-dream was playing me a trick. But no! Nothing could be truer. It is all clear. Gwynplaine is really in prison. It is a stroke of Providence. Praise be to it! He was the monster who, with the row he made, drew attention to my establishment and denounced my poor wolf. Be off, Gwynplaine; and, see, I am rid of both! Two birds killed with one stone. Because Dea will die, now that she can no longer see Gwynplaine. For she sees him, the idiot! She will have no object in life. She will say, 'What am I to do in the world?' Good-bye! To the devil with both of them. I always hated the creatures! Die, Dea! Oh, I am quite comfortable!"

CHAPTER II.

WHAT HE DID

He returned to the Tadcaster Inn,

It struck half-past six. It was a little before twilight.

Master Nicless stood on his doorstep.

He had not succeeded, since the morning, in extinguishing the terror which still showed on his scared face.

He perceived Ursus from afar.

"Well!" he cried.

"Well! what?"

"Is Gwynplaine coming back? It is full time. The public will soon be coming. Shall we have the performance of 'The Laughing Man' this evening?"

"I am the laughing man," said Ursus.

And he looked at the tavern-keeper with a loud chuckle.

Then he went up to the first floor, opened the window next to the sign of the inn, leant over towards the placard about Gwynplaine, the laughing man, and the bill of "Chaos Vanquished;" unnailed the one, tore down the other, put both under his arm, and descended.

Master Nicless followed him with his eyes.

"Why do you unhook that?"

Ursus burst into a second fit of laughter.

"Why do you laugh?" said the tavern-keeper.

"I am re-entering private life."

Master Nicless understood, and gave an order to his lieutenant, the boy Govicum, to announce to every one who should come that there would be no performance that evening. He took from the door the box made out of a cask, where they received the entrance money, and rolled it into a corner of the lower sitting-room.

A moment after, Ursus entered the Green Box.

He put the two signs away in a corner, and entered what he called the woman's wing.

Dea was asleep.

She was on her bed, dressed as usual, excepting that the body of her gown was loosened, as when she was taking her siesta.

Near her Vinos and Fibi were sitting—one on a stool, the other on the ground—musing. Notwithstanding the lateness of the hour, they had not dressed themselves in their goddesses' gauze, which was a sign of deep discouragement. They had remained in their drugget petticoats and their dress of coarse cloth.

Ursus looked at Dea.

"She is rehearsing for a longer sleep," murmured he.

Then, addressing Fibi and Vinos,—

"You both know all. The music is over. You may put your trumpets into the drawer. You did well not to equip yourselves as deities. You look ugly enough as you are, but you were quite right. Keep on your petticoats. No performance to-night, nor to-morrow, nor the day after to-morrow. No Gwynplaine. Gwynplaine is clean gone."

Then he looked at Dea again.

"What a blow to her this will be! It will be like blowing out a candle."

He inflated his cheeks.

"Puff! nothing more."

Then, with a little dry laugh,—

"Losing Gwynplaine, she loses all. It would be just as if I were to lose Homo. It will be worse. She will feel more lonely than any one else could. The blind wade through more sorrow than we do."

He looked out of the window at the end of the room.

"How the days lengthen! It is not dark at seven o'clock. Nevertheless we will light up."

He struck the steel and lighted the lamp which hung from the ceiling of the Green Box.

Then he leaned over Dea.

"She will catch cold; you have unlaced her bodice too low. There is a proverb,—

"'Though April skies be bright,
Keep all your wrappers tight.'"

Seeing a pin shining on the floor, he picked it up and pinned up her sleeve. Then he paced the Green Box, gesticulating.

"I am in full possession of my faculties. I am lucid, quite lucid. I consider this occurrence quite proper, and I approve of what has happened. When she awakes I will explain everything to her clearly. The catastrophe will not be long in coming. No more Gwynplaine. Good-night, Dea. How well all has been arranged! Gwynplaine in prison, Dea in the cemetery, they will be *vis-à-vis!* A dance of death! Two destinies going off the stage at once. Pack up the dresses. Fasten the valise. For valise, read coffin. It was just what was best for them both. Dea without eyes, Gwynplaine without a face. On high the Almighty will restore sight to Dea and beauty to Gwynplaine. Death puts things to rights. All will be well. Fibi, Vinos, hang up your tambourines on the nail. Your talents for noise will go to rust, my beauties; no more playing, no more trumpeting 'Chaos Vanquished' is vanquished. 'The Laughing Man' is done for. 'Taratantara' is dead. Dea sleeps on. She does well. If I were she I would never awake. Oh! she will soon fall asleep again. A skylark like her takes very little killing. This comes of meddling with politics. What a lesson! Governments are right. Gwynplaine to the sheriff. Dea to the grave-digger. Parallel cases! Instructive symmetry! I hope the tavern-keeper has barred the door. We are going to die to-night quietly at home, between ourselves—not I, nor Homo, but Dea. As for me, I shall continue to roll on in the caravan. I belong to the meanderings of vagabond life. I shall dismiss these two women. I shall not keep even one of them. I have a tendency to become an old scoundrel. A maidservant in the house of a libertine is like a loaf of bread on the shelf. I decline the temptation. It is not becoming at my age. *Turpe senilis amor.* I will follow my way alone with Homo. How astonished Homo will be! Where is Gwynplaine? Where is Dea? Old comrade, here we are once more alone together. Plague take it! I'm delighted. Their bucolics were an encumbrance. Oh! that scamp Gwynplaine, who is never coming back. He has left us stuck here. I say 'All right.' And now 'tis Dea's turn. That won't be long. I like things to be done with. I would not snap my fingers to stop her dying—her dying, I tell you! See, she awakes!"

Dea opened her eyelids; many blind persons shut them when they sleep. Her sweet unwitting face wore all its usual radiance.

"She smiles," whispered Ursus, "and I laugh. That is as it should be."

Dea called,—

"Fibi! Vinos! It must be the time for the performance. I think I have been asleep a long time. Come and dress me."

Neither Fibi nor Vinos moved.

Meanwhile the ineffable blind look of Dea's eyes met those of Ursus. He started.

"Well!" he cried; "what are you about? Vinos! Fibi! Do you not hear your mistress? Are you deaf? Quick! the play is going to begin."

The two women looked at Ursus in stupefaction.

Ursus shouted,—

"Do you not hear the audience coming in?—Fibi, dress Dea.—Vinos, take your tambourine."

Fibi was obedient; Vinos, passive. Together, they personified submission. Their master, Ursus, had always been to them an enigma. Never to be understood is a reason for being always obeyed. They simply thought he had gone mad, and did as they were told. Fibi took down the costume, and Vinos the tambourine.

Fibi began to dress Dea. Ursus let down the door-curtain of the women's room, and from behind the curtain continued,—

"Look there, Gwynplaine! the court is already more than half full of people. They are in heaps in the passages. What a crowd! And you say that Fibi and Vinos look as if they did not see them. How stupid the gipsies are! What fools they are in Egypt! Don't lift the curtain from the door. Be decent. Dea is dressing."

He paused, and suddenly they heard an exclamation,—

"How beautiful Dea is!"

It was the voice of Gwynplaine.

Fibi and Vinos started, and turned round. It was the voice of Gwynplaine, but in the mouth of Ursus.

Ursus, by a sign which he made through the door ajar, forbade the expression of any astonishment.

Then, again taking the voice of Gwynplaine,—

"Angel!"

Then he replied in his own voice,—

"Dea an angel! You are a fool, Gwynplaine. No mammifer can fly except the bats."

And he added,—

"Look here, Gwynplaine! Let Homo loose; that will be more to the purpose."

And he descended the ladder of the Green Box very quickly, with the agile spring of Gwynplaine, imitating his step so that Dea could hear it.

In the court he addressed the boy, whom the occurrences of the day had made idle and inquisitive.

"Spread out both your hands," said he, in a loud voice.

And he poured a handful of pence into them.

Govicum was grateful for his munificence.

Ursus whispered in his ear,—

"Boy, go into the yard; jump, dance, knock, bawl, whistle, coo, neigh, applaud, stamp your feet, burst out laughing, break something."

Master Nicless, saddened and humiliated at seeing the folks who had come to see "The Laughing Man" turned back and crowding towards other caravans, had shut the door of the inn. He had even given up the idea of selling any beer or spirits that evening, that he might have to answer no awkward questions; and, quite overcome by the sudden close of the performance, was looking, with his candle in his hand, into the court from the balcony above.

Ursus, taking the precaution of putting his voice between parentheses fashioned by adjusting the palms of his hands to his mouth, cried out to him,—

"Sir! do as your boy is doing—yelp, bark, howl."

He re-ascended the steps of the Green Box, and said to the wolf,—

"*Talk* as much as you can."

Then, raising his voice,—

"What a crowd there is! We shall have a crammed performance."

In the meantime Vinos played the tambourine. Ursus went on,—

"Dea is dressed. Now we can begin. I am sorry they have admitted so many spectators. How thickly packed they are!—Look, Gwynplaine, what a mad mob it is! I will bet that to-day we shall take more money than we have ever done yet.—Come, gipsies, play up, both of you. Come here.—Fibi, take your clarion. Good.—Vinos, drum on your tambourine. Fling it up and catch it again.—Fibi, put yourself into the attitude of Fame.—Young ladies, you have too much on. Take off those jackets. Replace stuff by gauze. The public like to see the female form exposed. Let the moralists thunder. A little indecency. Devil take it! what of that? Look voluptuous, and rush into wild melodies. Snort, blow, whistle, flourish, play the tambourine.—What a number of people, my poor Gwynplaine!"

He interrupted himself.

"Gwynplaine, help me. Let down the platform." He spread out his pocket-handkerchief. "But first let me roar in my rag," and he blew his nose violently as a ventriloquist ought. Having returned his handkerchief to his pocket, he drew the pegs out of the pulleys, which creaked as usual as the platform was let down.

"Gwynplaine, do not draw the curtain until the performance begins. We are not alone.—You two come on in front. Music, ladies! turn, turn, turn.—A pretty audience we have! the dregs of the people. Good heavens!"

The two gipsies, stupidly obedient, placed themselves in their usual corners of the platform. Then Ursus became wonderful. It was no longer a man, but a crowd. Obliged to make abundance out of emptiness, he called to aid his prodigious powers of ventriloquism. The whole orchestra of human and animal voices which was within him he called into tumult at once.

He was legion. Any one with his eyes closed would have imagined that he was in a public place on some day of rejoicing, or in some sudden popular riot. A whirlwind of clamour proceeded from Ursus: he sang, he shouted, he talked, he coughed, he spat, he sneezed, took snuff, talked and responded, put questions and gave answers, all at once. The half-uttered syllables ran one into another. In the court, untenanted by a single spectator, were heard men, women, and children. It was a clear confusion of tumult. Strange laughter wound, vapour-like, through the noise, the chirping of birds, the swearing of cats, the wailings of children at the breast. The indistinct tones of drunken men were to be heard, and the growls of dogs under the feet of people who stamped on them. The cries came from far and near, from top to bottom, from the upper boxes to the pit. The whole was an uproar, the detail was a cry. Ursus clapped his hands, stamped his feet, threw his voice to the end of the court, and then made it come from underground. It was both stormy and familiar. It passed from a murmur to a noise, from a noise to a tumult, from a tumult to a tempest. He was himself, any, every one else. Alone, and polyglot. As there are optical illusions, there are also auricular illusions. That which Proteus did to sight Ursus did to hearing. Nothing could be more marvellous than his facsimile of multitude. From time to time he opened the door of the women's apartment and looked at Dea. Dea was listening. On his part the boy exerted himself to the utmost. Vinos and Fibi trumpeted conscientiously, and took turns with the tambourine. Master Nicless, the only spectator, quietly made himself the same explanation as they did—that Ursus was gone mad; which was, for that matter, but another sad item added to his misery. The good tavern-keeper growled out, "What insanity!" And he was serious as a man might well be who has the fear of the law before him.

Govicum, delighted at being able to help in making a noise, exerted himself almost as much as Ursus. It amused him, and, moreover, it earned him pence.

Homo was pensive.

In the midst of the tumult Ursus now and then uttered such words as these:—

"Just as usual, Gwynplaine. There is a cabal against us. Our rivals are undermining our success. Tumult is the seasoning of triumph. Besides, there are too many people. They are uncomfortable. The angles of their neighbours' elbows do not dispose them to good-nature. I hope the benches will not give way. We shall be the victims of an incensed population. Oh, if our friend Tom-Jim-Jack were only here! but he never comes now. Look at those heads rising one above the other. Those who are forced to stand don't look very well pleased, though the great Galen pronounced it to be strengthening. We will shorten the entertainment; as only 'Chaos Vanquished' was announced in the playbill, we will not play 'Ursus Rursus.' There will be something gained in that. What an uproar! O blind turbulence of the masses. They will do us some damage. However, they can't go on like this. We should not be able to play. No one can catch a word of the piece. I am going to address them. Gwynplaine, draw the curtain a little aside.—Gentlemen." Here Ursus addressed himself with a shrill and feeble voice,—

"Down with that old fool!"

Then he answered in his own voice,—

"It seems that the mob insult me. Cicero is right: *plebs fex urbis*. Never mind; we will admonish the mob, though I shall have a great deal of trouble to make myself heard. I will speak, notwithstanding. Man, do your duty. Gwynplaine, look at that scold grinding her teeth down there."

Ursus made a pause, in which he placed a gnashing of his teeth. Homo, provoked, added a second, and Govicum a third.

Ursus went on,—

"The women are worse than the men. The moment is unpropitious, but it doesn't matter! Let us try the power of a speech; an eloquent speech is never out of place. Listen, Gwynplaine, to my attractive exordium. Ladies and gentlemen, I am a bear. I take off my head to address you. I humbly appeal to you for silence." Ursus, lending a cry to the crowd, said, "Grumphll!"

Then he continued,—

"I respect my audience. Grumphll is an epiphonema as good as any other welcome. You growlers. That you are all of the dregs of the people, I do not doubt. That in no way diminishes my esteem for you. A well-considered esteem. I have a profound respect for the bullies who honour me with their custom. There are deformed folks amongst you. They give me no offence. The lame and the humpbacked are works of nature. The camel is gibbous. The bison's back is humped. The badger's left legs are shorter than the right, That fact is decided by Aristotle, in his treatise on the walking of animals. There are those amongst you who have but two shirts—one on his back, and the other at the pawnbroker's. I know that to be true. Albuquerque pawned his moustache, and St. Denis his glory. The Jews advanced money on the glory. Great examples. To have debts is to have something. I revere your beggardom."

Ursus cut short his speech, interrupting it in a deep bass voice by the shout,—

"Triple ass!"

And he answered in his politest accent,—

"I admit it. I am a learned man. I do my best to apologize for it. I scientifically despise science. Ignorance is a reality on which we feed; science is a reality on which we starve. In general one is obliged to choose between two things—to be learned and grow thin, or to browse and be an ass. O gentlemen, browse! Science is not worth a mouthful of anything nice. I had rather eat a sirloin of beef than know what they call the psoas muscle. I have but one merit—a dry eye. Such as you see me, I have never wept. It must be owned that I have never been satisfied—never satisfied—not even with myself. I despise myself; but I submit this to the members of the opposition here present—if Ursus is only a learned man, Gwynplaine is an artist."

He groaned again,—

"Grumphll!"

And resumed,—

"Grumphll again! it is an objection. All the same, I pass it over. Near Gwynplaine, gentlemen and ladies, is another artist, a valued and distinguished personage who accompanies us—his lordship Homo, formerly a wild dog, now a civilized wolf, and a faithful subject of her Majesty's. Homo is a mine of deep and superior talent. Be attentive and watch. You are going to set Homo play as well as Gwynplaine, and you must do honour to art. That is an attribute of great nations. Are you men of the woods? I admit the fact. In that case, *sylvæ sunt consule digna.* Two artists are well worth one consul. All right! Some one has flung a cabbage stalk at me, but did not hit me. That will not stop my speaking; on the contrary, a danger evaded makes folks garrulous. *Garrula pericula*, says Juvenal. My hearers!

there are amongst you drunken men and drunken women. Very well. The men are unwholesome. The women are hideous. You have all sorts of excellent reasons for stowing yourselves away here on the benches of the pothouse—want of work, idleness, the spare time between two robberies, porter, ale, stout, malt, brandy, gin, and the attraction of one sex for the other. What could be better? A wit prone to irony would find this a fair field. But I abstain. 'Tis luxury; so be it, but even an orgy should be kept within bounds. You are gay, but noisy. You imitate successfully the cries of beasts; but what would you say if, when you were making love to a lady, I passed my time in barking at you? It would disturb you, and so it disturbs us. I order you to hold your tongues. Art is as respectable as debauch. I speak to you civilly."

He apostrophized himself,—

"May the fever strangle you, with your eyebrows like the beard of rye."

And he replied,—

"Honourable gentlemen, let the rye alone. It is impious to insult the vegetables, by likening them either to human creatures or animals. Besides, the fever does not strangle. 'Tis a false metaphor. For pity's sake, keep silence. Allow me to tell you that you are slightly wanting in the repose which characterizes the true English gentleman. I see that some amongst you, who have shoes out of which their toes are peeping, take advantage of the circumstance to rest their feet on the shoulders of those who are in front of them, causing the ladies to remark that the soles of shoes divide always at the part at which is the head of the metatarsal bones. Show more of your hands and less of your feet. I perceive scamps who plunge their ingenious fists into the pockets of their foolish neighbours. Dear pickpockets, have a little modesty. Fight those next to you if you like; do not plunder them. You will vex them less by blackening an eye, than by lightening their purses of a penny. Break their noses if you like. The shopkeeper thinks more of his money than of his beauty. Barring this, accept my sympathies, for I am not pedantic enough to blame thieves. Evil exists. Every one endures it, every one inflicts it. No one is exempt from the vermin of his sins. That's what I keep saying. Have we not all our itch? I myself have made mistakes. *Plaudite, cives.*"

Ursus uttered a long groan, which he overpowered by these concluding words,—

"My lords and gentlemen, I see that my address has unluckily displeased you. I take leave of your hisses for a moment. I shall put on my head, and the performance is going to begin."

He dropt his oratorical tone, and resumed his usual voice.

"Close the curtains. Let me breathe. I have spoken like honey. I have spoken well. My words were like velvet; but they were useless. I called them my lords and gentlemen. What do you think of all this scum, Gwynplaine? How well may we estimate the ills which England has suffered for the last forty years through the ill-temper of these irritable and malicious spirits! The ancient Britons were warlike; these are melancholy and learned. They glory in despising the laws and contemning royal authority. I have done all that human eloquence can do. I have been prodigal of metonymics, as gracious as the blooming cheek of youth. Were they softened by them? I doubt it. What can affect a people who eat so extraordinarily, who stupefy themselves by tobacco so completely that their literary men often write their works with a pipe in their mouths? Never mind. Let us begin the play."

The rings of the curtain were heard being drawn over the rod. The tambourines of the gipsies were still. Ursus took down his instrument, executed his prelude, and said in a low tone: "Alas, Gwynplaine, how mysterious it is!" then he flung himself down with the wolf.

When he had taken down his instrument, he had also taken from the nail a rough wig which he had, and which he had thrown on the stage in a corner within his reach. The performance of "Chaos Vanquished" took place as usual, minus only the effect of the blue light and the brilliancy of the fairies. The wolf played his best. At the proper moment Dea made her appearance, and, in her voice so tremulous and heavenly, invoked Gwynplaine. She extended her arms, feeling for that head.

Ursus rushed at the wig, ruffled it, put it on, advanced softly, and holding his breath, his head bristled thus under the hand of Dea.

Then calling all his art to his aid, and copying Gwynplaine's voice, he sang with ineffable love the response of the monster to the call of the spirit. The imitation was so perfect that again the gipsies looked for Gwynplaine, frightened at hearing without seeing him.

Govicum, filled with astonishment, stamped, applauded, clapped his hands, producing an Olympian tumult, and himself laughed as if he had been a chorus of gods. This boy, it must be confessed, developed a rare talent for acting an audience.

Fibi and Vinos, being automatons of which Ursus pulled the strings, rattled their instruments, composed of copper and ass's skin—the usual sign of the performance being over and of the departure of the people.

Ursus arose, covered with perspiration. He said, in a low voice, to Homo, "You see it was necessary to gain time. I think we have succeeded. I have not acquitted myself badly—I, who have as much reason as any one to go distracted. Gwynplaine may perhaps return to-morrow. It is useless to kill Dea directly. I can explain matters to you."

He took off his wig and wiped his forehead.

"I am a ventriloquist of genius," murmured he. "What talent I displayed! I have equalled Brabant, the engastrimist of Francis I. of France. Dea is convinced that Gwynplaine is here."

"Ursus," said Dea, "where is Gwynplaine?"

Ursus started and turned round. Dea was still standing at the back of the stage, alone under the lamp which hung from the ceiling. She was pale, with the pallor of a ghost.

She added, with an ineffable expression of despair,—

"I know. He has left us. He is gone. I always knew that he had wings."

And raising her sightless eyes on high, she added,—

"When shall I follow?"

CHAPTER III.

COMPLICATIONS

Ursus was stunned.

He had not sustained the illusion.

Was it the fault of ventriloquism? Certainly not. He had succeeded in deceiving Fibi and Vinos, who had eyes, although he had not deceived Dea, who was blind. It was because Fibi and Vinos saw with their eyes, while Dea saw with her heart. He could not utter a word. He thought to himself, *Bos in lingûa.* The troubled man has an ox on his tongue.

In his complex emotions, humiliation was the first which dawned on him. Ursus, driven out of his last resource, pondered.

"I lavish my onomatopies in vain." Then, like every dreamer, he reviled himself. "What a frightful failure! I wore myself out in a pure loss of imitative harmony. But what is to be done next?"

He looked at Dea. She was silent, and grew paler every moment, as she stood perfectly motionless. Her sightless eyes remained fixed in depths of thought.

Fortunately, something happened. Ursus saw Master Nicless in the yard, with a candle in his hand, beckoning to him.

Master Nicless had not assisted at the end of the phantom comedy played by Ursus. Some one had happened to knock at the door of the inn. Master Nicless had gone to open it. There had been two knocks, and twice Master Nicless had disappeared. Ursus, absorbed by his hundred-voiced monologue, had not observed his absence.

On the mute call of Master Nicless, Ursus descended.

He approached the tavern-keeper. Ursus put his finger on his lips. Master Nicless put his finger on his lips.

The two looked at each other thus.

Each seemed to say to the other, "We will talk, but we will hold our tongues."

The tavern-keeper silently opened the door of the lower room of the tavern. Master Nicless entered. Ursus entered. There was no one there except these two. On the side looking on the street both doors and window-shutters were closed.

The tavern-keeper pushed the door behind him, and shut it in the face of the inquisitive Govicum.

Master Nicless placed the candle on the table.

A low whispering dialogue began.

"Master Ursus?"

"Master Nicless?"

"I understand at last."

"Nonsense!"

"You wished the poor blind girl to think that all going on as usual."

"There is no law against my being a ventriloquist."

"You are a clever fellow."
"No."
"It is wonderful how you manage all that you wish to do."
"I tell you it is not."
"Now, I have something to tell you."
"Is it about politics?"
"I don't know."
"Because in that case I could not listen to you."
"Look here: whilst you were playing actors and audience by yourself, some one knocked at the door of the tavern."
"Some one knocked at the door?"
"Yes."
"I don't like that."
"Nor I, either."
"And then?"
"And then I opened it."
"Who was it that knocked?"
"Some one who spoke to me."
"What did he say?"
"I listened to him."
"What did you answer?"
"Nothing. I came back to see you play."
"And—?"
"Some one knocked a second time."
"Who? the same person?"
"No, another."
"Some one else to speak to you?"
"Some one who said nothing."
"I like that better."
"I do not."
"Explain yourself, Master Nicless."
"Guess who called the first time."
"I have no leisure to be an Oedipus."
"It was the proprietor of the circus."
"Over the way?"
"Over the way."
"Whence comes all that fearful noise. Well?"
"Well, Master Ursus, he makes you a proposal."
"A proposal?"
"A proposal."
"Why?"
"Because—"
"You have an advantage over me, Master Nicless. Just now you solved my enigma, and now I cannot understand yours."
"The proprietor of the circus commissioned me to tell you that he had seen the *cortège* of police pass this morning, and that he, the proprietor of the circus, wishing to prove that he is your friend, offers to buy of you, for fifty pounds,

ready money, your caravan, the Green Box, your two horses, your trumpets, with the women that blow them, your play, with the blind girl who sings in it, your wolf, and yourself."

Ursus smiled a haughty smile.

"Innkeeper, tell the proprietor of the circus that Gwynplaine is coming back."

The innkeeper took something from a chair in the darkness, and turning towards Ursus with both arms raised, dangled from one hand a cloak, and from the other a leather esclavine, a felt hat, and a jacket.

And Master Nicless said, "The man who knocked the second time was connected with the police; he came in and left without saying a word, and brought these things."

Ursus recognized the esclavine, the jacket, the hat, and the cloak of Gwynplaine.

CHAPTER IV.

MOENIBUS SURDIS CAMPANA MUTA

Ursus smoothed the felt of the hat, touched the cloth of the cloak, the serge of the coat, the leather of the esclavine, and no longer able to doubt whose garments they were, with a gesture at once brief and imperative, and without saying a word, pointed to the door of the inn.

Master Nicless opened it.

Ursus rushed out of the tavern.

Master Nicless looked after him, and saw Ursus run, as fast as his old legs would allow, in the direction taken that morning by the wapentake who carried off Gwynplaine.

A quarter of an hour afterwards, Ursus, out of breath, reached the little street in which stood the back wicket of the Southwark jail, which he had already watched so many hours. This alley was lonely enough at all hours; but if dreary during the day, it was portentous in the night. No one ventured through it after a certain hour. It seemed as though people feared that the walls should close in, and that if the prison or the cemetery took a fancy to embrace, they should be crushed in their clasp. Such are the effects of darkness. The pollard willows of the Ruelle Vauvert in Paris were thus ill-famed. It was said that during the night the stumps of those trees changed into great hands, and caught hold of the passers-by.

By instinct the Southwark folks shunned, as we have already mentioned, this alley between a prison and a churchyard. Formerly it had been barricaded during the night by an iron chain. Very uselessly; because the strongest chain which guarded the street was the terror it inspired.

Ursus entered it resolutely.

What intention possessed him? None.

He came into the alley to seek intelligence.

Was he going to knock at the gate of the jail? Certainly not. Such an expedient, at once fearful and vain, had no place in his brain. To attempt to introduce himself to demand an explanation. What folly! Prisons do not open to those who wish to enter, any more than to those who desire to get out. Their hinges never turn except by law. Ursus knew this. Why, then, had he come there? To see. To see what? Nothing. Who can tell? Even to be opposite the gate through which Gwynplaine had disappeared was something.

Sometimes the blackest and most rugged of walls whispers, and some light escapes through a cranny. A vague glimmering is now and then to be perceived through solid and sombre piles of building. Even to examine the envelope of a fact may be to some purpose. The instinct of us all is to leave between the fact which interests us and ourselves but the thinnest possible cover. Therefore it was that Ursus returned to the alley in which the lower entrance to the prison was situated.

Just as he entered it he heard one stroke of the clock, then a second.

"Hold," thought he; "can it be midnight already?"

Mechanically he set himself to count.

"Three, four, five."

He mused.

"At what long intervals this clock strikes! how slowly! Six; seven!"

Then he remarked,—

"What a melancholy sound! Eight, nine! Ah! nothing can be more natural; it's dull work for a clock to live in a prison. Ten! Besides, there is the cemetery. This clock sounds the hour to the living, and eternity to the dead. Eleven! Alas! to strike the hour to him who is not free is also to chronicle an eternity. Twelve!"

He paused.

"Yes, it is midnight."

The clock struck a thirteenth stroke.

Ursus shuddered.

"Thirteen!"

Then followed a fourteenth; then a fifteenth.

"What can this mean?"

The strokes continued at long intervals. Ursus listened.

"It is not the striking of a clock; it is the bell Muta. No wonder I said, 'How long it takes to strike midnight!' This clock does not strike; it tolls. What fearful thing is about to take place?"

Formerly all prisons and all monasteries had a bell called Muta, reserved for melancholy occasions. La Muta (the mute) was a bell which struck very low, as if doing its best not to be heard.

Ursus had reached the corner which he had found so convenient for his watch, and whence he had been able, during a great part of the day, to keep his eye on the prison.

The strokes followed each other at lugubrious intervals.

A knell makes an ugly punctuation in space. It breaks the preoccupation of the mind into funereal paragraphs. A knell, like a man's death-rattle, notifies an agony. If in the houses about the neighbourhood where a knell is tolled there are reveries straying in doubt, its sound cuts them into rigid fragments. A vague reverie is a sort of refuge. Some indefinable diffuseness in anguish allows now and then a ray of hope to pierce through it. A knell is precise and desolating. It concentrates this diffusion of thought, and precipitates the vapours in which anxiety seeks to remain in suspense. A knell speaks to each one in the sense of his own grief or of his own fear. Tragic bell! it concerns you. It is a warning to you.

There is nothing so dreary as a monologue on which its cadence falls. The even returns of sound seem to show a purpose.

What is it that this hammer, the bell, forges on the anvil of thought?

Ursus counted, vaguely and without motive, the tolling of the knell. Feeling that his thoughts were sliding from him, he made an effort not to let them slip into conjecture. Conjecture is an inclined plane, on which we slip too far to be to our own advantage. Still, what was the meaning of the bell?

He looked through the darkness in the direction in which he knew the gate of the prison to be.

Suddenly, in that very spot which looked like a dark hole, a redness showed. The redness grew larger, and became a light.

There was no uncertainty about it. It soon took a form and angles. The gate of the jail had just turned on its hinges. The glow painted the arch and the jambs of the door. It was a yawning rather than an opening. A prison does not open; it yawns—perhaps from ennui. Through the gate passed a man with a torch in his hand.

The bell rang on. Ursus felt his attention fascinated by two objects. He watched—his ear the knell, his eye the torch. Behind the first man the gate, which had been ajar, enlarged the opening suddenly, and allowed egress to two other men; then to a fourth. This fourth was the wapentake, clearly visible in the light of the torch. In his grasp was his iron staff.

Following the wapentake, there filed and opened out below the gateway in order, two by two, with the rigidity of a series of walking posts, ranks of silent men.

This nocturnal procession stepped through the wicket in file, like a procession of penitents, without any solution of continuity, with a funereal care to make no noise—gravely, almost gently. A serpent issues from its hole with similar precautions.

The torch threw out their profiles and attitudes into relief. Fierce looks, sullen attitudes.

Ursus recognized the faces of the police who had that morning carried off Gwynplaine.

There was no doubt about it. They were the same. They were reappearing.

Of course, Gwynplaine would also reappear. They had led him to that place; they would bring him back.

It was all quite clear.

Ursus strained his eyes to the utmost. Would they set Gwynplaine at liberty?

The files of police flowed from the low arch very slowly, and, as it were, drop by drop. The toll of the bell was uninterrupted, and seemed to mark their steps. On leaving the prison, the procession turned their backs on Ursus, went to the right, into the bend of the street opposite to that in which he was posted.

A second torch shone under the gateway, announcing the end of the procession.

Ursus was now about to see what they were bringing with them. The prisoner—the man.

Ursus was soon, he thought, to see Gwynplaine.

That which they carried appeared.

It was a bier.

Four men carried a bier, covered with black cloth.

Behind them came a man, with a shovel on his shoulder.

A third lighted torch, held by a man reading a book, probably the chaplain, closed the procession.

The bier followed the ranks of the police, who had turned to the right.

Just at that moment the head of the procession stopped.

Ursus heard the grating of a key.

Opposite the prison, in the low wall which ran along the other side of the street, another opening was illuminated by a torch passing beneath it.

This gate, over which a death's-head was placed, was that of the cemetery.

The wapentake passed through it, then the men, then the second torch. The procession decreased therein, like a reptile entering his retreat.

The files of police penetrated into that other darkness which was beyond the gate; then the bier; then the man with the spade; then the chaplain with his torch and his book, and the gate closed.

There was nothing left but a haze of light above the wall.

A muttering was heard; then some dull sounds. Doubtless the chaplain and the gravedigger—the one throwing on the coffin some verses of Scripture, the other some clods of earth.

The muttering ceased; the heavy sounds ceased. A movement was made. The torches shone. The wapentake reappeared, holding high his weapon, under the reopened gate of the cemetery; then the chaplain with his book, and the gravedigger with his spade. The *cortège* reappeared without the coffin.

The files of men crossed over in the same order, with the same taciturnity, and in the opposite direction. The gate of the cemetery closed. That of the prison opened. Its sepulchral architecture stood out against the light. The obscurity of the passage became vaguely visible. The solid and deep night of the jail was revealed to sight; then the whole vision disappeared in the depths of shadow.

The knell ceased. All was locked in silence. A sinister incarceration of shadows.

A vanished vision; nothing more.

A passage of spectres, which had disappeared.

The logical arrangement of surmises builds up something which at least resembles evidence. To the arrest of Gwynplaine, to the secret mode of his capture, to the return of his garments by the police officer, to the death bell of the prison to which he had been conducted, was now added, or rather adjusted—portentous circumstance—a coffin carried to the grave.

"He is dead!" cried Ursus.

He sank down upon a stone.

"Dead! They have killed him! Gwynplaine! My child! My son!"

And he burst into passionate sobs.

CHAPTER V.

STATE POLICY DEALS WITH LITTLEMATTERS AS WELL AS WITH GREAT

Ursus, alas! had boasted that he had never wept. His reservoir of tears was full. Such plentitude as is accumulated drop on drop, sorrow on sorrow, through a long existence, is not to be poured out in a moment. Ursus wept alone.

The first tear is a letting out of waters. He wept for Gwynplaine, for Dea, for himself, Ursus, for Homo. He wept like a child. He wept like an old man. He wept for everything at which he had ever laughed. He paid off arrears. Man is never nonsuited when he pleads his right to tears.

The corpse they had just buried was Hardquanonne's; but Ursus could not know that.

The hours crept on.

Day began to break. The pale clothing of the morning was spread out, dimly creased with shadow, over the bowling-green. The dawn lighted up the front of the Tadcaster Inn. Master Nicless had not gone to bed, because sometimes the same occurrence produces sleeplessness in many.

Troubles radiate in every direction. Throw a stone in the water, and count the splashes.

Master Nicless felt himself impeached. It is very disagreeable that such things should happen in one's house. Master Nicless, uneasy, and foreseeing misfortunes, meditated. He regretted having received such people into his house. Had he but known that they would end by getting him into mischief! But the question was how to get rid of them? He had given Ursus a lease. What a blessing if he could free himself from it! How should he set to work to drive them out?

Suddenly the door of the inn resounded with one of those tumultuous knocks which in England announces "Somebody." The gamut of knocking corresponds with the ladder of hierarchy.

It was not quite the knock of a lord; but it was the knock of a justice.

The trembling innkeeper half opened his window. There was, indeed, the magistrate. Master Nicless perceived at the door a body of police, from the head of which two men detached themselves, one of whom was the justice of the quorum.

Master Nicless had seen the justice of the quorum that morning, and recognized him.

He did not know the other, who was a fat gentleman, with a waxen-coloured face, a fashionable wig, and a travelling cloak. Nicless was much afraid of the first of these persons, the justice of the quorum. Had he been of the court, he would have feared the other most, because it was Barkilphedro.

One of the subordinates knocked at the door again violently.

The innkeeper, with great drops of perspiration on his brow, from anxiety, opened it.

The justice of the quorum, in the tone of a man who is employed in matters of police, and who is well acquainted with various shades of vagrancy, raised his voice, and asked, severely, for

"Master Ursus!"

The host, cap in hand, replied,—

"Your honour; he lives here."

"I know it," said the justice.

"No doubt, your honour."

"Tell him to come down."

"Your honour, he is not here."

"Where is he?"

"I do not know."

"How is that?"

"He has not come in."

"Then he must have gone out very early?"

"No; but he went out very late."

"What vagabonds!" replied the justice.

"Your honour," said Master Nicless, softly, "here he comes."

Ursus, indeed, had just come in sight, round a turn of the wall. He was returning to the inn. He had passed nearly the whole night between the jail, where at midday he had seen Gwynplaine, and the cemetery, where at midnight he had heard the grave filled up. He was pallid with two pallors—that of sorrow and of twilight.

Dawn, which is light in a chrysalis state, leaves even those forms which are in movement in the uncertainty of night. Ursus, wan and indistinct, walked slowly, like a man in a dream. In the wild distraction produced by agony of mind, he had left the inn with his head bare. He had not even found out that he had no hat on. His spare, gray locks fluttered in the wind. His open eyes appeared sightless. Often when awake we are asleep, and as often when asleep we are awake.

Ursus looked like a lunatic.

"Master Ursus," cried the innkeeper, "come; their honours desire to speak to you."

Master Nicless, in his endeavour to soften matters down, let slip, although he would gladly have omitted, this plural, "their honours"—respectful to the group, but mortifying, perhaps, to the chief, confounded therein, to some degree, with his subordinates.

Ursus started like a man falling off a bed, on which he was sound asleep.

"What is the matter?" said he.

He saw the police, and at the head of the police the justice. A fresh and rude shock.

But a short time ago, the wapentake, now the justice of the quorum. He seemed to have been cast from one to the other, as ships by some reefs of which we have read in old stories.

The justice of the quorum made him a sign to enter the tavern. Ursus obeyed.

Govicum, who had just got up, and who was sweeping the room, stopped his work, got into a corner behind the tables, put down his broom, and held his breath. He plunged his fingers into his hair, and scratched his head, a symptom which indicated attention to what was about to occur.

The justice of the quorum sat down on a form, before a table. Barkilphedro took a chair. Ursus and Master Nicless remained standing. The police officers, left outside, grouped themselves in front of the closed door.

The justice of the quorum fixed his eye, full of the law, upon Ursus. He said,—

"You have a wolf."

Ursus answered,—

"Not exactly."

"You have a wolf," continued the justice, emphasizing "wolf" with a decided accent.

Ursus answered,—

"You see—"

And he was silent.

"A misdemeanour!" replied the justice.

Ursus hazarded an excuse,—

"He is my servant."

The justice placed his hand flat on the table, with his fingers spread out, which is a very fine gesture of authority.

"Merry-andrew! to-morrow, by this hour, you and your wolf must have left England. If not, the wolf will be seized, carried to the register office, and killed."

Ursus thought, "More murder!" but he breathed not a syllable, and was satisfied with trembling in every limb.

"You hear?" said the justice.

Ursus nodded.

The justice persisted,—

"Killed."

There was silence.

"Strangled, or drowned."

The justice of the quorum watched Ursus.

"And yourself in prison."

Ursus murmured,—

"Your worship!"

"Be off before to-morrow morning; if not, such is the order."

"Your worship!"

"What?"

"Must we leave England, he and I?"

"Yes."

"To-day?"

"To-day."

"What is to be done?"

Master Nicless was happy. The magistrate, whom he had feared, had come to his aid. The police had acted as auxiliary to him, Nicless. They had delivered him from "such people." The means he had sought were brought to him. Ursus, whom he wanted to get rid of, was being driven away by the police, a superior authority. Nothing to object to. He was delighted. He interrupted,—

"Your honour, that man—"

He pointed to Ursus with his finger.

"That man wants to know how he is to leave England to-day. Nothing can be easier. There are night and day at anchor on the Thames, both on this and on the other side of London Bridge, vessels that sail to the Continent. They go from England to Denmark, to Holland, to Spain; not to France, on account of the war, but everywhere else. To-night several ships will sail, about one o'clock in the morning, which is the hour of high tide, and, amongst others, the *Vograat* of Rotterdam."

The justice of the quorum made a movement of his shoulder towards Ursus.

"Be it so. Leave by the first ship—by the *Vograat.*"

"Your worship," said Ursus.

"Well?"

"Your worship, if I had, as formerly, only my little box on wheels, it might be done. A boat would contain that; but—"

"But what?"

"But now I have got the Green Box, which is a great caravan drawn by two horses, and however wide the ship might be, we could not get it into her."

"What is that to me?" said the justice. "The wolf will be killed."

Ursus shuddered, as if he were grasped by a hand of ice.

"Monsters!" he thought. "Murdering people is their way of settling matters."

The innkeeper smiled, and addressed Ursus.

"Master Ursus, you can sell the Green Box."

Ursus looked at Nicless.

"Master Ursus, you have the offer."

"From whom?"

"An offer for the caravan, an offer for the two horses, an offer for the two gipsy women, an offer—"

"From whom?" repeated Ursus.

"From the proprietor of the neighbouring circus."

Ursus remembered it.

"It is true."

Master Nicless turned to the justice of the quorum.

"Your honour, the bargain can be completed to-day. The proprietor of the circus close by wishes to buy the caravan and the horses."

"The proprietor of the circus is right," said the justice, "because he will soon require them. A caravan and horses will be useful to him. He, too, will depart to-day. The reverend gentlemen of the parish of Southwark have complained of the indecent riot in Tarrinzeau field. The sheriff has taken his measures. To-night there will not be a single juggler's booth in the place. There must be an end of all these scandals. The honourable gentleman who deigns to be here present—"

The justice of the quorum interrupted his speech to salute Barkilphedro, who returned the bow.

"The honourable gentleman who deigns to be present has just arrived from Windsor. He brings orders. Her Majesty has said, 'It must be swept away.'"

Ursus, during his long meditation all night, had not failed to put himself some questions. After all, he had only seen a bier. Could he be sure that it contained Gwynplaine? Other people might have died besides Gwynplaine. A coffin does not announce the name of the corpse, as it passes by. A funeral had followed the arrest of Gwynplaine. That proved nothing. *Post hoc, non propter hoc, etc.* Ursus had begun to doubt.

Hope burns and glimmers over misery like naphtha over water. Its hovering flame ever floats over human sorrow. Ursus had come to this conclusion, "It is probable that it was Gwynplaine whom they buried, but it is not certain. Who knows? Perhaps Gwynplaine is still alive."

Ursus bowed to the justice.

"Honourable judge, I will go away, we will go away, all will go away, by the *Vograat* of Rotterdam, to-day. I will sell the Green Box, the horses, the trumpets, the gipsies. But I have a comrade, whom I cannot leave behind—Gwynplaine."

"Gwynplaine is dead," said a voice.

Ursus felt a cold sensation, such as is produced by a reptile crawling over the skin. It was Barkilphedro who had just spoken.

The last gleam was extinguished. No more doubt now. Gwynplaine was dead. A person in authority must know. This one looked ill-favoured enough to do so.

Ursus bowed to him.

Master Nicless was a good-hearted man enough, but a dreadful coward. Once terrified, he became a brute. The greatest cruelty is that inspired by fear.

He growled out,—

"This simplifies matters."

And he indulged, standing behind Ursus, in rubbing his hands, a peculiarity of the selfish, signifying, "I am well out of it," and suggestive of Pontius Pilate washing his hands.

Ursus, overwhelmed, bent down his head.

The sentence on Gwynplaine had been executed—death. His sentence was pronounced—exile. Nothing remained but to obey. He felt as in a dream.

Some one touched his arm. It was the other person, who was with the justice of the quorum. Ursus shuddered.

The voice which had said, "Gwynplaine is dead," whispered in his ear,—

"Here are ten guineas, sent you by one who wishes you well."

And Barkilphedro placed a little purse on a table before Ursus. We must not forget the casket that Barkilphedro had taken with him.

Ten guineas out of two thousand! It was all that Barkilphedro could make up his mind to part with. In all conscience it was enough. If he had given more, he would have lost. He had taken the trouble of finding out a lord; and having sunk the shaft, it was but fair that the first proceeds of the mine should belong to him. Those who see meanness in the act are right, but they would be wrong to feel astonished. Barkilphedro loved money, especially money which was stolen. An envious man is an avaricious one. Barkilphedro was not without his faults. The commission of crimes does not preclude the possession of vices. Tigers have their lice.

Besides, he belonged to the school of Bacon.

Barkilphedro turned towards the justice of the quorum, and said to him,—

"Sir, be so good as to conclude this matter. I am in haste. A carriage and horses belonging to her Majesty await me. I must go full gallop to Windsor, for I must be there within two hours' time. I have intelligence to give, and orders to take."

The justice of the quorum arose.

He went to the door, which was only latched, opened it, and, looking silently towards the police, beckoned to them authoritatively. They entered with that silence which heralds severity of action.

Master Nicless, satisfied with the rapid *dénouement* which cut short his difficulties, charmed to be out of the entangled skein, was afraid, when he saw the muster of officers, that they were going to apprehend Ursus in his house. Two arrests, one after the other, made in his house—first that of Gwynplaine, then that of Ursus—might be injurious to the inn. Customers dislike police raids.

Here then was a time for a respectful appeal, suppliant and generous. Master Nicless turned toward the justice of the quorum a smiling face, in which confidence was tempered by respect.

"Your honour, I venture to observe to your honour that these honourable gentlemen, the police officers, might be dispensed with, now that the wolf is about to be carried away from England, and that this man, Ursus, makes no resistance; and since your honour's orders are being punctually carried out, your honour will consider that the respectable business of the police, so necessary to the good of the kingdom, does great harm to an establishment, and that my house is innocent. The merry-andrews of the Green Box having been swept away, as her Majesty says, there is no longer any criminal here, as I do not suppose that the blind girl and the two women are criminals; therefore, I implore your honour to deign to shorten your august visit, and to dismiss these worthy gentlemen who have just entered, because there is nothing for them to do in my house; and, if your honour will permit me to prove the justice of my speech under the form of a humble question, I will prove the inutility of these revered gentlemen's presence by asking your honour, if the man, Ursus, obeys orders and departs, who there can be to arrest here?"

"Yourself," said the justice.

A man does not argue with a sword which runs him through and through. Master Nicless subsided—he cared not on what, on a table, on a form, on anything that happened to be there—prostrate.

The justice raised his voice, so that if there were people outside, they might hear.

"Master Nicless Plumptree, keeper of this tavern, this is the last point to be settled. This mountebank and the wolf are vagabonds. They are driven away. But the person most in fault is yourself. It is in your house, and with your consent, that the law has been violated; and you, a man licensed, invested with a public responsibility, have established the scandal here. Master Nicless, your licence is taken away; you must pay the penalty, and go to prison."

The policemen surrounded the innkeeper.

The justice continued, pointing out Govicum,—

"Arrest that boy as an accomplice." The hand of an officer fell upon the collar of Govicum, who looked at him inquisitively. The boy was not much alarmed, scarcely understanding the occurrence; having already observed many things out of the way, he wondered if this were the end of the comedy.

The justice of the quorum forced his hat down on his head, crossed his hands on his stomach, which is the height of majesty, and added,—

"It is decided, Master Nicless; you are to be taken to prison, and put into jail, you and the boy; and this house, the Tadcaster Inn, is to remain shut up, condemned and closed. For the sake of example. Upon which, you will follow us."

BOOK THE SEVENTH

THE TITANESS

CHAPTER I.

THE AWAKENING

And Dea!

It seemed to Gwynplaine, as he watched the break of day at Corleone Lodge, while the things we have related were occurring at the Tadcaster Inn, that the call came from without; but it came from within.

Who has not heard the deep clamours of the soul?

Moreover, the morning was dawning.

Aurora is a voice.

Of what use is the sun if not to reawaken that dark sleeper—the conscience?

Light and virtue are akin.

Whether the god be called Christ or Love, there is at times an hour when he is forgotten, even by the best. All of us, even the saints, require a voice to remind us; and the dawn speaks to us, like a sublime monitor. Conscience calls out before duty, as the cock crows before the dawn of day.

That chaos, the human heart, hears the *fiat lux!*

Gwynplaine—we will continue thus to call him (Clancharlie is a lord, Gwynplaine is a man)—Gwynplaine felt as if brought back to life. It was time that the artery was bound up.

For a while his virtue had spread its wings and flown away.

"And Dea!" he said.

Then he felt through his veins a generous transfusion. Something healthy and tumultuous rushed upon him. The violent irruption of good thoughts is like the return home of a man who has not his key, and who forces his own look honestly. It is an escalade, but an escalade of good. It is a burglary, but a burglary of evil.

"Dea! Dea! Dea!" repeated he.

He strove to assure himself of his heart's strength. And he put the question with a loud voice—"Where are you?"

He almost wondered that no one answered him.

Then again, gazing on the walls and the ceiling, with wandering thoughts, through which reason returned.

"Where are you? Where am I?"

And in the chamber which was his cage he began to walk again, to and fro, like a wild beast in captivity.

"Where am I? At Windsor. And you? In Southwark. Alas! this is the first time that there has been distance between us. Who has dug this gulf? I here, thou there. Oh, it cannot be; it shall not be! What is this that they have done to me?"

He stopped.

"Who talked to me of the queen? What do I know of such things? *I* changed! Why? Because I am a lord. Do you know what has happened, Dea? You are a lady. What has come to pass is astounding. My business now is to get back into my right road. Who is it who led me astray? There is a man who spoke to me mysteriously. I remember the words which he addressed to me. 'My lord, when one door opens another is shut. That which you have left behind is no longer yours.' In other words, you are a coward. That man, the miserable wretch! said that to me before I was well awake. He took advantage of my first moment of astonishment. I was as it were a prey to him. Where is he, that I may insult him? He spoke to me with the evil smile of a demon. But see—I am myself again. That is well. They deceive themselves if they think that they can do what they like with Lord Clancharlie, a peer of England. Yes, with a peeress, who is Dea! Conditions! Shall I accept them? The queen! What is the queen to me? I never saw her. I am not a lord to be made a slave. I enter my position unfettered. Did they think they had unchained me for nothing? They have unmuzzled me. That is all. Dea! Ursus! we are together. That which you were, I was; that which I am, you are. Come. No. I will go to you directly—directly. I have already waited too long. What can they think, not seeing me return! That money. When I think I sent them that money! It was myself that they wanted. I remember the man said that I could not leave this place. We shall see that. Come! a carriage, a carriage! put to the horses. I am going to look for them. Where are the servants? I ought to have servants here, since I am a lord. I am master here. This is my house. I will twist off the bolts, I will break the locks, I will kick down the doors, I will run my sword through the body of any one who bars my passage. I should like to see who shall stop me. I have a wife, and she is Dea. I have a father, who is Ursus. My house is a palace, and I give it to Ursus. My name is a diadem, and I give it to Dea. Quick, directly, Dea, I am coming; yes, you may be sure that I shall soon stride across the intervening space!"

And raising the first piece of tapestry he came to, he rushed from the chamber impetuously.

He found himself in a corridor.

He went straight forward.

A second corridor opened out before him.

All the doors were open.

He walked on at random, from chamber to chamber, from passage to passage, seeking an exit.

CHAPTER II.

THE RESEMBLANCE OF A PALACE TO A WOOD

In palaces after the Italian fashion, and Corleone Lodge was one, there were very few doors, but abundance of tapestry screens and curtained doorways. In every palace of that date there was a wonderful labyrinth of chambers and corridors, where luxury ran riot; gilding, marble, carved wainscoting, Eastern silks; nooks and corners, some secret and dark as night, others light and pleasant as the day. There were attics, richly and brightly furnished; burnished recesses shining with Dutch tiles and Portuguese azulejos. The tops of the high windows were converted into small rooms and glass attics, forming pretty habitable lanterns. The thickness of the walls was such that there were rooms within them. Here and there were closets, nominally wardrobes. They were called "The Little Rooms." It was within them that evil deeds were hatched.

When a Duke of Guise had to be killed, the pretty Présidente of Sylvecane abducted, or the cries of little girls brought thither by Lebel smothered, such places were convenient for the purpose. They were labyrinthine chambers, impracticable to a stranger; scenes of abductions; unknown depths, receptacles of mysterious disappearances. In those elegant caverns princes and lords stored their plunder. In such a place the Count de Charolais hid Madame Courchamp, the wife of the Clerk of the Privy Council; Monsieur de Monthulé, the daughter of Haudry, the farmer of La Croix Saint Lenfroy; the Prince de Conti, the two beautiful baker women of L'Ile Adam; the Duke of Buckingham, poor Pennywell, etc. The deeds done there were such as were designated by the Roman law as committed *vi, clam, et precario*—by force, in secret, and for a short time. Once in, an occupant remained there till the master of the house decreed his or her release. They were gilded oubliettes, savouring both of the cloister and the harem. Their staircases twisted, turned, ascended, and descended. A zigzag of rooms, one running into another, led back to the starting-point. A gallery terminated in an oratory. A confessional was grafted on to an alcove. Perhaps the architects of "the little rooms," building for royalty and aristocracy, took as models the ramifications of coral beds, and the openings in a sponge. The branches became a labyrinth. Pictures turning on false panels were exits and entrances. They were full of stage contrivances, and no wonder—considering the dramas that were played there! The floors of these hives reached from the cellars to the attics. Quaint madrepore inlaying every palace, from Versailles downwards, like cells of pygmies in dwelling-places of Titans. Passages, niches, alcoves, and secret recesses. All sorts of holes and corners, in which was stored away the meanness of the great.

These winding and narrow passages recalled games, blindfolded eyes, hands feeling in the dark, suppressed laughter, blind man's buff, hide and seek, while, at the same time, they suggested memories of the Atrides, of the Plantagenets, of the Médicis, the brutal knights of Eltz, of Rizzio, of Monaldeschi; of naked swords, pursuing the fugitive flying from room to room.

The ancients, too, had mysterious retreats of the same kind, in which luxury was adapted to enormities. The pattern has been preserved underground in some sepulchres in Egypt, notably in the tomb of King Psammetichus, discovered by Passalacqua. The ancient poets have recorded the horrors of these suspicious buildings. *Error circumflexus, locus implicitus gyris.*

Gwynplaine was in the "little rooms" of Corleone Lodge. He was burning to be off, to get outside, to see Dea again. The maze of passages and alcoves, with secret and bewildering doors, checked and retarded his progress. He strove to run; he was obliged to wander. He thought that he had but one door to thrust open, while he had a skein of doors to unravel. To one room succeeded another. Then a crossway, with rooms on every side.

Not a living creature was to be seen. He listened. Not a sound.

At times he thought that he must be returning towards his starting-point; then, that he saw some one approaching. It was no one. It was only the reflection of himself in a mirror, dressed as a nobleman. *That* he? Impossible! Then he recognized himself, but not at once.

He explored every passage that he came to.

He examined the quaint arrangements of the rambling building, and their yet quainter fittings. Here, a cabinet, painted and carved in a sentimental but vicious style; there, an equivocal-looking chapel, studded with enamels and mother-of-pearl, with miniatures on ivory wrought out in relief, like those on old-fashioned snuff-boxes; there, one of those pretty Florentine retreats, adapted to the hypochondriasis of women, and even then called *boudoirs*. Everywhere—on the ceilings, on the walls, and on the very floors—were representations, in velvet or in metal, of birds, of trees; of luxuriant vegetation, picked out in reliefs of lacework; tables covered with jet carvings, representing warriors, queens, and tritons armed with the scaly terminations of a hydra. Cut crystals combining prismatic effects with those of reflection. Mirrors repeated the light of precious stones, and sparkles glittered in the darkest corners. It was impossible to guess whether those many-sided, shining surfaces, where emerald green mingled with the golden hues of the rising sun where floated a glimmer of ever-varying colours, like those on a pigeon's neck, were miniature mirrors or enormous beryls. Everywhere was magnificence, at once refined and stupendous; if it was not the most diminutive of palaces, it was the most gigantic of jewel-cases. A house for Mab or a jewel for Geo.

Gwynplaine sought an exit. He could not find one. Impossible to make out his way. There is nothing so confusing as wealth seen for the first time. Moreover, this was a labyrinth. At each step he was stopped by some magnificent object which appeared to retard his exit, and to be unwilling to let him pass. He was encompassed by a net of wonders. He felt himself bound and held back.

What a horrible palace! he thought. Restless, he wandered through the maze, asking himself what it all meant—whether he was in prison; chafing, thirsting for the fresh air. He repeated Dea! Dea! as if that word was the thread of the labyrinth, and must be held unbroken, to guide him out of it. Now and then he shouted, "Ho! Any one there?" No one answered. The rooms never came to an end. All was deserted, silent, splendid, sinister. It realized the fables of enchanted castles. Hidden pipes of hot air maintained a summer temperature in the building. It was as if some magician had caught up the month of June and imprisoned it in a labyrinth. There were pleasant odours now and then, and he crossed currents of perfume, as though passing by invisible flowers. It was warm. Carpets everywhere. One might have walked about there, unclothed.

Gwynplaine looked out of the windows. The view from each one was different. From one he beheld gardens, sparkling with the freshness of a spring morning; from another a plot decked with statues; from a third, a patio in the Spanish style, a little square, flagged, mouldy, and cold. At times he saw a river—it was the Thames; sometimes a great tower—it was Windsor.

It was still so early that there were no signs of life without.

He stood still and listened.

"Oh! I will get out of this place," said he. "I will return to Dea! They shall not keep me here by force. Woe to him who bars my exit! What is that great tower yonder? If there was a giant, a hell-hound, a minotaur, to keep the gate of this enchanted palace, I would annihilate him. If an army, I would exterminate it. Dea! Dea!"

Suddenly he heard a gentle noise, very faint. It was like dropping water. He was in a dark narrow passage, closed, some few paces further on, by a curtain. He advanced to the curtain, pushed it aside, entered. He leaped before he looked.

CHAPTER III.

EVE

An octagon room, with a vaulted ceiling, without windows but lighted by a skylight; walls, ceiling, and floors faced with peach-coloured marble; a black marble canopy, like a pall, with twisted columns in the solid but pleasing Elizabethan style, overshadowing a vase-like bath of the same black marble—this was what he saw before him. In the centre of the bath arose a slender jet of tepid and perfumed water, which, softly and slowly, was filling the tank. The bath was black to augment fairness into brilliancy.

It was the water which he had heard. A waste-pipe, placed at a certain height in the bath, prevented it from overflowing. Vapour was rising from the water, but not sufficient to cause it to hang in drops on the marble. The slender jet of water was like a supple wand of steel, bending at the slightest current of air. There was no furniture, except a chair-bed with pillows, long enough for a woman to lie on at full length, and yet have room for a dog at her feet. The French, indeed, borrow their word *canapé* from *can-al-pié*. This sofa was of Spanish manufacture. In it silver took the place of woodwork. The cushions and coverings were of rich white silk.

On the other side of the bath, by the wall, was a lofty dressing-table of solid silver, furnished with every requisite for the table, having in its centre, and in imitation of a window, eight small Venetian mirrors, set in a silver frame. In a panel on the wall was a square opening, like a little window, which was closed by a door of solid silver. This door was fitted with hinges, like a shutter. On the shutter there glistened a chased and gilt royal crown. Over it, and affixed to the wall, was a bell, silver gilt, if not of pure gold.

Opposite the entrance of the chamber, in which Gwynplaine stood as if transfixed, there was an opening in the marble wall, extending to the ceiling, and closed by a high and broad curtain of silver tissue. This curtain, of fairy-like tenuity, was transparent, and did not interrupt the view. Through the centre of this web, where one might expect a spider, Gwynplaine saw a more formidable object—a woman. Her dress was a long chemise—so long that it floated over her feet, like the dresses of angels in holy pictures; but so fine that it seemed liquid.

The silver tissue, transparent as glass and fastened only at the ceiling, could be lifted aside. It separated the marble chamber, which was a bathroom, from the adjoining apartment, which was a bedchamber. This tiny dormitory was as a grotto of mirrors. Venetian glasses, close together, mounted with gold mouldings, reflected on every side the bed in the centre of the room. On the bed, which, like the toilet-table, was of silver, lay the woman; she was asleep.

The crumpled clothes bore evidence of troubled sleep. The beauty of the folds was proof of the quality of the material.

It was a period when a queen, thinking that she should be damned, pictured hell to herself as a bed with coarse sheets.[20]

A dressing-gown, of curious silk, was thrown over the foot of the couch. It was apparently Chinese; for a great golden lizard was partly visible in between the folds.

Beyond the couch, and probably masking a door, was a large mirror, on which were painted peacocks and swans.

Shadow seemed to lose its nature in this apartment, and glistened. The spaces between the mirrors and the gold work were lined with that sparkling material called at Venice thread of glass—that is, spun glass.

At the head of the couch stood a reading desk, on a movable pivot, with candles, and a book lying open, bearing this title, in large red letters, "Alcoranus Mahumedis."

Gwynplaine saw none of these details. He had eyes only for the woman. He was at once stupefied and filled with tumultuous emotions, states apparently incompatible, yet sometimes co-existent. He recognized her. Her eyes were closed, but her face was turned towards him. It was the duchess—she, the mysterious being in whom all the splendours of the unknown were united; she who had occasioned him so many unavowable dreams; she who had written him so strange a letter! The only woman in the world of whom he could say, "She has seen me, and she desires me!"

He had dismissed the dreams from his mind; he had burnt the letter. He had, as far as lay in his power, banished the remembrance of her from his thoughts and dreams. He no longer thought of her. He had forgotten her....

Again he saw her, and saw her terrible in power. His breath came in short catches. He felt as if he were in a storm-driven cloud. He looked. This woman before him! Was it possible? At the theatre a duchess; here a nereid, a nymph, a fairy. Always an apparition. He tried to fly, but felt the futility of the attempt. His eyes were riveted on the vision, as though he were bound. Was she a woman? Was she a maiden? Both. Messalina was perhaps present, though invisible, and smiled, while Diana kept watch.

Over all her beauty was the radiance of inaccessibility. No purity could compare with her chaste and haughty form. Certain snows, which have never been touched, give an idea of it—such as the sacred whiteness of the Jungfrau. Immodesty was merged in splendour. She felt the security of an Olympian, who knew that she was daughter of the depths, and might say to the ocean, "Father!" And she exposed herself, unattainable and proud, to everything that should pass—to looks, to desires, to ravings, to dreams; as proud in her languor, on her boudoir couch, as Venus in the immensity of the sea-foam.

She had slept all night, and was prolonging her sleep into the daylight; her boldness, begun in shadow, continued in light.

Gwynplaine shuddered. He admired her with an unhealthy and absorbing admiration, which ended in fear. Misfortunes never come singly. Gwynplaine thought he had drained to the dregs the cup of his ill-luck. Now it was refilled. Who was it who was hurling all those unremitting thunderbolts on his devoted head, and who had now thrown against him, as he stood trembling there, a sleeping goddess? What! was the dangerous and desirable object of his dream lurking all the while behind these successive glimpses of heaven? Did these favours of the mysterious tempter tend to inspire him with vague aspirations and confused ideas, and overwhelm him with an intoxicating series of realities proceeding from apparent impossibilities? Wherefore did all the shadows conspire against him, a wretched man; and what would become of him, with all those evil smiles of fortune beaming on him? Was his temptation prearranged? This woman, how and why was she there? No explanation! Why him? Why her? Was he made a peer of England expressly for this duchess? Who had brought them together? Who was the dupe? Who the victim? Whose simplicity was being abused? Was it God who was being deceived? All these undefined thoughts passed confusedly, like a flight of dark shadows, through his brain. That magical and malevolent abode, that strange and prison-like palace, was it also in the plot? Gwynplaine suffered a partial unconsciousness. Suppressed emotions threatened to strangle him. He was weighed down by an overwhelming force. His will became powerless. How could he resist? He was incoherent and entranced. This time he felt he was becoming irremediably insane. His dark, headlong fall over the precipice of stupefaction continued.

But the woman slept on.

What aggravated the storm within him was, that he saw not the princess, not the duchess, not the lady, but the woman.

Gwynplaine, losing all self-command, trembled. What could he do against such a temptation? Here were no skilful effects of dress, no silken folds, no complex and coquettish adornments, no affected exaggeration of concealment or of exhibition, no cloud. It was fearful simplicity—a sort of mysterious summons—the shameless audacity of Eden. The whole of the dark side of human nature was there. Eve worse than Satan; the human and the superhuman commingled. A perplexing ecstasy, winding up in a brutal triumph of instinct over duty. The sovereign contour of beauty is imperious. When it leaves the ideal and condescends to be real, its proximity is fatal to man.

Now and then the duchess moved softly on the bed, with the vague movement of a cloud in the heavens, changing as a vapour changes its form. Absurd as it may appear, though he saw her present in the flesh before him, yet she seemed a chimera; and, palpable as she was, she seemed to him afar off. Scared and livid, he gazed on. He listened for her breathing, and fancied he heard only a phantom's respiration. He was attracted, though against his will. How arm himself against her—or against himself? He had been prepared for everything except this danger. A savage doorkeeper, a raging monster of a jailer—such were his expected antagonists. He looked for Cerberus; he saw Hebe. A sleeping woman! What an opponent! He closed his eyes. Too bright a dawn blinds the eyes. But through his closed eyelids there penetrated at once the woman's form—not so distinct, but beautiful as ever.

Fly! Easier said than done. He had already tried and failed. He was rooted to the ground, as if in a dream. When we try to draw back, temptation clogs our feet and glues them to the earth. We can still advance, but to retire is impossible. The invisible arms of sin rise from below and drag us down.

There is a commonplace idea, accepted by every one, that feelings become blunted by experience. Nothing can be more untrue. You might as well say that by dropping nitric acid slowly on a sore it would heal and become sound, and that torture dulled the sufferings of Damiens. The truth is, that each fresh application intensifies the pain.

From one surprise after another, Gwynplaine had become desperate. That cup, his reason, under this new stupor, was overflowing. He felt within him a terrible awakening. Compass he no longer possessed. One idea only was before him—the woman. An indescribable happiness appeared, which threatened to overwhelm him. He could no longer decide for himself. There was an irresistible current and a reef. The reef was not a rock, but a siren—a magnet at the bottom of the abyss. He wished to tear himself away from this magnet; but how was he to carry out his wish? He had ceased to feel any basis of support. Who can foresee the fluctuations of the human mind! A man may be wrecked, as is a ship. Conscience is an anchor. It is a terrible thing, but, like the anchor, conscience may be carried away.

He had not even the chance of being repulsed on account of his terrible disfigurement. The woman had written to say that she loved him.

In every crisis there is a moment when the scale hesitates before kicking the beam. When we lean to the worst side of our nature, instead of strengthening our better qualities, the moral force which has been preserving the balance gives way, and down we go. Had this critical moment in Gwynplaine's life arrived?

How could he escape?

So it is she—the duchess, the woman! There she was in that lonely room—asleep, far from succour, helpless, alone, at his mercy; yet he was in her power! The duchess! We have, perchance, observed a star in the distant firmament. We have admired it. It is so far off. What can there be to make us shudder in a fixed star? Well, one day—one night, rather—it moves. We perceive a trembling gleam around it. The star which we imagined to be immovable is in motion. It is no longer a star, but a comet—the incendiary giant of the skies. The luminary moves on, grows bigger, shakes off a shower of sparks and fire, and becomes enormous. It advances towards us. Oh, horror, it is coming our way! The comet recognizes us, marks us for its own, and will not be turned aside. Irresistible attack of the heavens! What is it which is bearing down on us? An excess of light, which blinds us; an excess of life, which kills us. That proposal which the heavens make we refuse; that unfathomable love we reject. We close our eyes; we hide; we tear ourselves away; we imagine the danger is past. We open our eyes: the formidable star is still before us; but, no longer a star, it has become a world—a world unknown, a world of lava and ashes; the devastating prodigy of space. It fills the sky, allowing no compeers. The carbuncle of the firmament's depths, a diamond in the distance, when drawn close to us becomes a furnace. You are caught in its flames. And the first sensation of burning is that of a heavenly warmth.

CHAPTER IV.

SATAN

Suddenly the sleeper awoke. She sat up with a sudden and gracious dignity of movement, her fair silken tresses falling in soft disorder. Then stretching herself, she yawned like a tigress in the rising sun.

Perhaps Gwynplaine breathed heavily, as we do when we endeavour to restrain our respiration.

"Is any one there?" said she.

She yawned as she spoke, and her very yawn was graceful. Gwynplaine listened to the unfamiliar voice—the voice of a charmer, its accents exquisitely haughty, its caressing intonation softening its native arrogance. Then rising on her knees—there is an antique statue kneeling thus in the midst of a thousand transparent folds—she drew the dressing-gown towards her, and springing from the couch stood upright. In the twinkling of an eye the silken robe was around her. The trailing sleeve concealed her hands; only the tips of her toes, with little pink nails like those of an infant, were left visible. Having drawn from underneath the dressing-gown a mass of hair which had been imprisoned by it, she crossed behind the couch to the end of the room, and placed her ear to the painted mirror, which was, apparently, a door. Tapping the glass with her finger, she called, "Is any one there? Lord David? Are you come already? What time is it then? Is that you, Barkilphedro?" She turned from the glass. "No! it was not there. Is there any one in the bathroom? Will you answer? Of course not. No one could come that way."

Going to the silver lace curtain, she raised it with her foot, thrust it aside with her shoulder, and entered the marble room. An agonized numbness fell upon Gwynplaine. No possibility of concealment. It was too late to fly. Moreover, he was no longer equal to the exertion. He wished that the earth might open and swallow him up. Anything to hide him.

She saw him. She stared, immensely astonished, but without the slightest nervousness. Then, in a tone of mingled pleasure and contempt, she said, "Why, it is Gwynplaine!" Suddenly with a rapid spring, for this cat was a panther, she flung herself on his neck.

Suddenly, pushing him back, and holding him by both shoulders with her small claw-like hands, she stood up face to face with him, and began to gaze at him with a strange expression.

It was a fatal glance she gave him with her Aldebaran-like eyes—a glance at once equivocal and starlike. Gwynplaine watched the blue eye and the black eye, distracted by the double ray of heaven and of hell that shone in the orbs thus fixed on him. The man and the woman threw a malign dazzling reflection one on the other. Both were fascinated—he by her beauty, she by his deformity. Both were in a measure awe-stricken. Pressed down, as by an overwhelming weight, he was speechless.

"Oh!" she cried. "How clever you are! You are come. You found out that I was obliged to leave London. You followed me. That was right. Your being here proves you to be a wonder."

The simultaneous return of self-possession acts like a flash of lightning. Gwynplaine, indistinctly warned by a vague, rude, but honest misgiving, drew back, but the pink nails clung to his shoulders and restrained him. Some inexorable power proclaimed its sway over him. He himself, a wild beast, was caged in a wild beast's den. She continued, "Anne, the fool—you know whom I mean—the queen—ordered me to Windsor without giving any reason. When I arrived she was closeted with her idiot of a Chancellor. But how did you contrive to obtain access to me? That's what I call being a man. Obstacles, indeed! there are no such things. You come at a call. You found things out. My name, the Duchess Josiana, you knew, I fancy. Who was it brought you in? No doubt it was the page. Oh, he is clever! I will give him a hundred guineas. Which way did you get in? Tell me! No, don't tell me; I don't want to know. Explanations diminish interest. I prefer the marvellous, and you are hideous enough to be wonderful. You have fallen from the highest heavens, or you have risen from the depths of hell through the devil's trap-door. Nothing can be more natural. The ceiling opened or the floor yawned. A descent in a cloud, or an ascent in a mass of fire and brimstone, that is how you have travelled. You have a right to enter like the gods. Agreed; you are my lover."

Gwynplaine was scared, and listened, his mind growing more irresolute every moment. Now all was certain. Impossible to have any further doubt. That letter! the woman confirmed its meaning. Gwynplaine the lover and the beloved of a duchess! Mighty pride, with its thousand baleful heads, stirred his wretched heart. Vanity, that powerful agent within us, works us measureless evil.

The duchess went on, "Since you are here, it is so decreed. I ask nothing more. There is some one on high, or in hell, who brings us together. The betrothal of Styx and Aurora! Unbridled ceremonies beyond all laws! The very day I first saw you I said, 'It is he!' I recognize him. He is the monster of my dreams. He shall be mine. We should give destiny a helping hand. Therefore I wrote to you. One question, Gwynplaine: do you believe in predestination? For my part, I have believed in it since I read, in Cicero, Scipio's dream. Ah! I did not observe it. Dressed like a gentleman! You in fine clothes! Why not? You are a mountebank. All the more reason. A juggler is as good as a lord. Moreover, what are lords? Clowns. You have a noble figure; you are magnificently made. It is wonderful that you should be here. When did you arrive? How long have you been here? Did you see me naked? I am beautiful, am I not? I was going to take my bath. Oh, how I love you! You read my letter! Did you read it yourself? Did any one read it to you? Can you read? Probably you are ignorant. I ask questions, but don't answer them. I don't like the sound of your voice. It is soft. An extraordinary thing like you should snarl, and not speak. You sing harmoniously. I hate it. It is the only thing about you that I do not like. All the rest is terrible—is grand. In India you would be a god. Were you born with that frightful laugh on your face? No! No doubt it is a penal brand. I do hope you have committed some crime. Come to my arms."

She sank on the couch, and made him sit beside her. They found themselves close together unconsciously. What she said passed over Gwynplaine like a mighty storm. He hardly understood the meaning of her whirlwind of words. Her eyes were full of admiration. She spoke tumultuously, frantically, with a voice broken and tender. Her words were music, but their music was to Gwynplaine as a hurricane. Again she fixed her gaze upon him and continued,—

"I feel degraded in your presence, and oh, what happiness that is! How insipid it is to be a grandee! I am noble; what can be more tiresome? Disgrace is a comfort. I am so satiated with respect that I long for contempt. We are all a little erratic, from Venus, Cleopatra, Mesdames de Chevreuse and de Longueville, down to myself. I will make a display of you, I declare. Here's a love affair which will be a blow to my family, the Stuarts. Ah! I breathe again. I have discovered a secret. I am clear of royalty. To be free from its trammels is indeed deliverance. To break down, defy, make and destroy at will, that is true enjoyment. Listen, I love you."

She paused; then with a frightful smile went on, "I love you, not only because you are deformed, but because you are low. I love monsters, and I love mountebanks. A lover despised, mocked, grotesque, hideous, exposed to laughter on that pillory called a theatre, has for me an extraordinary attraction. It is tasting the fruit of hell. An infamous lover, how exquisite! To taste the apple, not of Paradise, but of hell—such is my temptation. It is for that I hunger and thirst. I am that Eve, the Eve of the depths. Probably you are, unknown to yourself, a devil. I am in love with a nightmare. You are a moving puppet, of which the strings are pulled by a spectre. You are the incarnation of infernal mirth. You are the master I require. I wanted a lover such as those of Medea and Canidia. I felt sure that some night would bring me such a one. You are all that I want. I am talking of a heap of things of which you probably know nothing. Gwynplaine, hitherto I have remained untouched; I give myself to you, pure as a burning ember. You evidently do not believe me; but if you only knew how little I care!"

Her words flowed like a volcanic eruption. Pierce Mount Etna, and you may obtain some idea of that jet of fiery eloquence.

Gwynplaine stammered, "Madame—"

She placed her hand on his mouth. "Silence," she said. "I am studying you. I am unbridled desire, immaculate. I am a vestal bacchante. No man has known me, and I might be the virgin pythoness at Delphos, and have under my naked foot the bronze tripod, where the priests lean their elbows on the skin of the python, whispering questions to the invisible god. My heart is of stone, but it is like those mysterious pebbles which the sea washes to the foot of the rock called Huntly Nabb, at the mouth of the Tees, and which if broken are found to contain a serpent. That serpent is my love—a love which is all-powerful, for it has brought you to me. An impossible distance was between us. I was in Sirius, and you were in Allioth. You have crossed the immeasurable space, and here you are. 'Tis well. Be silent. Take me."

She ceased; he trembled. Then she went on, smiling, "You see, Gwynplaine, to dream is to create; to desire is to summon. To build up the chimera is to provoke the reality. The all-powerful and terrible mystery will not be defied. It produces result. You are here. Do I dare to lose caste? Yes. Do I dare to be your mistress—your concubine—your slave—your chattel? Joyfully. Gwynplaine, I am woman. Woman is clay longing to become mire. I want to despise myself. That lends a zest to pride. The alloy of greatness is baseness. They combine in perfection.

Despise me, you who are despised. Nothing can be better. Degradation on degradation. What joy! I pluck the double blossom of ignominy. Trample me under foot. You will only love me the more. I am sure of it. Do you understand why I idolize you? Because I despise you. You are so immeasurably below me that I place you on an altar. Bring the highest and lowest depths together, and you have Chaos, and I delight in Chaos—Chaos, the beginning and end of everything. What is Chaos? A huge blot. Out of that blot God made light, and out of that sink the world. You don't know how perverse I can be. Knead a star in mud, and you will have my likeness."

She went on,—

"A wolf to all beside; a faithful dog to you. How astonished they will all be! The astonishment of fools is amusing. I understand myself. Am I a goddess? Amphitrite gave herself to the Cyclops. *Fluctivoma Amphitrite.* Am I a fairy? Urgele gave herself to Bugryx, a winged man, with eight webbed hands. Am I a princess? Marie Stuart had Rizzio. Three beauties, three monsters. I am greater than they, for you are lower than they. Gwynplaine, we were made for one another. The monster that you are outwardly, I am within. Thence my love for you. A caprice? Just so. What is a hurricane but a caprice? Our stars have a certain affinity. Together we are things of night—you in your face, I in my mind. As your countenance is defaced, so is my mind. You, in your turn, create me. You come, and my real soul shows itself. I did not know it. It is astonishing. Your coming has evoked the hydra in me, who am a goddess. You reveal my real nature. See how I resemble you. Look at me as if I were a mirror. Your face is my mind. I did not know I was so terrible. I am also, then, a monster. O Gwynplaine, you do amuse me!"

She laughed, a strange and childlike laugh; and, putting her mouth close to his ear, whispered,—

"Do you want to see a mad woman? look at me."

She poured her searching look into Gwynplaine. A look is a philtre. Her loosened robe provoked a thousand dangerous feelings. Blind, animal ecstasy was invading his mind—ecstasy combined with agony. Whilst she spoke, though he felt her words like burning coals, his blood froze within his veins. He had not strength to utter a word.

She stopped, and looked at him.

"O monster!" she cried. She grew wild.

Suddenly she seized his hands.

"Gwynplaine, I am the throne; you are the footstool. Let us join on the same level. Oh, how happy I am in my fall! I wish all the world could know how abject I am become. It would bow down all the lower. The more man abhors, the more does he cringe. It is human nature. Hostile, but reptile; dragon, but worm. Oh, I am as depraved as are the gods! They can never say that I am not a king's bastard. I act like a queen. Who was Rodope but a queen loving Pteh, a man with a crocodile's head? She raised the third pyramid in his honour. Penthesilea loved the centaur, who, being now a star, is named Sagittarius. And what do you say about Anne of Austria? Mazarin was ugly enough! Now, you are not only ugly; you are deformed. Ugliness is mean, deformity is grand. Ugliness is the devil's grin behind beauty; deformity is the reverse of sublimity. It is the back view. Olympus has two aspects. One, by day, shows Apollo; the other, by night, shows Polyphemus. You—you are a Titan. You would be Behemoth in the forests, Leviathan in the deep, and Typhon in the sewer. You surpass everything. There is the trace of lightning in your deformity; your face has been battered by the thunderbolt. The jagged contortion of forked lightning has imprinted its mark on your face. It struck you and passed on. A mighty and mysterious wrath has, in a fit of passion, cemented your spirit in a terrible and superhuman form. Hell is a penal furnace, where the iron called Fatality is raised to a white heat. You have been branded with it. To love you is to understand grandeur. I enjoy that triumph. To be in love with Apollo—a fine effort, forsooth! Glory is to be measured by the astonishment it creates. I love you. I have dreamt of you night after night. This is my palace. You shall see my gardens. There are fresh springs under the shrubs; arbours for lovers; and beautiful groups of marble statuary by Bernini. Flowers! there are too many—during the spring the place is on fire with roses. Did I tell you that the queen is my sister? Do what you like with me. I am made for Jupiter to kiss my feet, and for Satan to spit in my face. Are you of any religion? I am a Papist. My father, James II., died in France, surrounded by Jesuits. I have never felt before as I feel now that I am near you. Oh, how I should like to pass the evening with you, in the midst of music, both reclining on the same cushion, under a purple awning, in a gilded gondola on the soft expanse of ocean! Insult me, beat me, kick me, cuff me, treat me like a brute! I adore you."

Caresses can roar. If you doubt it, observe the lion's. The woman was horrible, and yet full of grace. The effect was tragic. First he felt the claw, then the velvet of the paw. A feline attack, made up of advances and retreats. There was death as well as sport in this game of come and go. She idolized him, but arrogantly. The result was contagious frenzy. Fatal language, at once inexpressible, violent, and sweet. The insulter did not insult; the adorer outraged the object of adoration. She, who buffeted, deified him. Her tones imparted to her violent yet amorous words an indescribable Promethean grandeur. According to Æschylus, in the orgies in honour of the great goddess the women were smitten by this evil frenzy when they pursued the satyrs under the stars. Such paroxysms raged in the mysterious dances in the grove of Dodona. This woman was as if transfigured—if, indeed, we can term that transfiguration which is the antithesis of heaven.

Her hair quivered like a mane; her robe opened and closed. The sunshine of the blue eye mingled with the fire of the black one. She was unearthly.

Gwynplaine, giving way, felt himself vanquished by the deep subtilty of this attack.

"I love you!" she cried. And she bit him with a kiss.

Homeric clouds were, perhaps, about to be required to encompass Gwynplaine and Josiana, as they did Jupiter and Juno. For Gwynplaine to be loved by a woman who could see and who saw him, to feel on his deformed mouth the pressure of divine lips, was exquisite and maddening. Before this woman, full of enigmas, all else faded away in his mind. The remembrance of Dea struggled in the shadows with weak cries. There is an antique bas-relief representing the Sphinx devouring a Cupid. The wings of the sweet celestial are bleeding between the fierce, grinning fangs.

Did Gwynplaine love this woman? Has man, like the globe, two poles? Are we, on our inflexible axis, a moving sphere, a star when seen from afar, mud when seen more closely, in which night alternates with day? Has the heart two aspects—one on which its love is poured forth in light; the other in darkness? Here a woman of light, there a woman of the sewer. Angels are necessary. Is it possible that demons are also essential? Has the soul the wings of the bat? Does twilight fall fatally for all? Is sin an integral and inevitable part of our destiny? Must we accept evil as part and portion of our whole? Do we inherit sin as a debt? What awful subjects for thought!

Yet a voice tells us that weakness is a crime. Gwynplaine's feelings are not to be described. The flesh, life, terror, lust, an overwhelming intoxication of spirit, and all the shame possible to pride. Was he about to succumb?

She repeated, "I love you!" and flung her frenzied arms around him. Gwynplaine panted.

Suddenly close at hand there rang, clear and distinct, a little bell. It was the little bell inside the wall. The duchess, turning her head, said,—

"What does she want of me?"

Quickly, with the noise of a spring door, the silver panel, with the golden crown chased on it, opened. A compartment of a shaft, lined with royal blue velvet, appeared, and on a golden salver a letter. The letter, broad and weighty, was placed so as to exhibit the seal, which was a large impression in red wax. The bell continued to tinkle. The open panel almost touched the couch where the duchess and Gwynplaine were sitting.

Leaning over, but still keeping her arm round his neck, she took the letter from the plate, and touched the panel. The compartment closed in, and the bell ceased ringing.

The duchess broke the seal, and, opening the envelope, drew out two documents contained therein, and flung it on the floor at Gwynplaine's feet. The impression of the broken seal was still decipherable, and Gwynplaine could distinguish a royal crown over the initial A. The torn envelope lay open before him, so that he could read, "To Her Grace the Duchess Josiana." The envelope had contained both vellum and parchment. The former was a small, the latter a large document. On the parchment was a large Chancery seal in green wax, called Lords' sealing-wax.

The face of the duchess, whose bosom was palpitating, and whose eyes were swimming with passion, became overspread with a slight expression of dissatisfaction.

"Ah!" she said. "What does she send me? A lot of papers! What a spoil-sport that woman is!"

Pushing aside the parchment, she opened the vellum.

"It is her handwriting. It is my sister's hand. It is quite provoking. Gwynplaine, I asked you if you could read. Can you?"

Gwynplaine nodded assent.

She stretched herself at full length on the couch, carefully drew her feet and arms under her robe, with a whimsical affectation of modesty, and, giving Gwynplaine the vellum, watched him with an impassioned look.

"Well, you are mine. Begin your duties, my beloved. Read me what the queen writes."

Gwynplaine took the vellum, unfolded it, and, in a voice tremulous with many emotions, began to read:—

"MADAM,—We are graciously pleased to send to you herewith, sealed and signed by our trusty and well-beloved William Cowper, Lord High Chancellor of England, a copy of a report showing forth the very important fact that the legitimate son of Linnæus Lord Clancharlie has just been discovered and recognized, bearing the name of Gwynplaine, in the lowest rank of a wandering and vagabond life, among strollers and mountebanks. His false position dates from his earliest days. In accordance with the laws of the country, and in virtue of his hereditary rights, Lord Fermain Clancharlie, son of Lord Linnæus, will be this day admitted, and installed in his position in the House of Lords. Therefore, having regard to your welfare, and wishing to preserve for your use the property and estates of Lord Clancharlie of Hunkerville, we substitute him in the place of Lord David Dirry-Moir, and recommend him to your good graces. We have caused Lord Fermain to be conducted to Corleone Lodge. We will and command, as sister and as Queen, that the said Fermain Lord Clancharlie, hitherto called Gwynplaine, shall be your husband, and that you shall marry him. Such is our royal pleasure."

While Gwynplaine, in tremulous tones which varied at almost every word, was reading the document, the duchess, half risen from the couch, listened with fixed attention. When Gwynplaine finished, she snatched the letter from his hands.

"Anne R," she murmured in a tone of abstraction. Then picking up from the floor the parchment she had thrown down, she ran her eye over it. It was the confession of the shipwrecked crew of the *Matutina*, embodied in a report signed by the sheriff of Southwark and by the lord chancellor.

Having perused the report, she read the queen's letter over again. Then she said, "Be it so." And calmly pointing with her finger to the door of the gallery through which he had entered, she added, "Begone."

Gwynplaine was petrified, and remained immovable. She repeated, in icy tones, "Since you are my husband, begone." Gwynplaine, speechless, and with eyes downcast like a criminal, remained motionless. She added, "You have no right to be here; it is my lover's place." Gwynplaine was like a man transfixed. "Very well," said she; "I must go myself. So you are my husband. Nothing can be better. I hate you." She rose, and with an indescribably haughty gesture of adieu left the room. The curtain in the doorway of the gallery fell behind her.

CHAPTER V.

THEY RECOGNIZE, BUT DO NOT KNOW, EACH OTHER

Gwynplaine was alone—alone, and in the presence of the tepid bath and the deserted couch. The confusion in his mind had reached its culminating point. His thoughts no longer resembled thoughts. They overflowed and ran riot; it was the anguish of a creature wrestling with perplexity. He felt as if he were awaking from a horrid nightmare. The entrance into unknown spheres is no simple matter.

From the time he had received the duchess's letter, brought by the page, a series of surprising adventures had befallen Gwynplaine, each one less intelligible than the other. Up to this time, though in a dream, he had seen things clearly. Now he could only grope his way. He no longer thought, nor even dreamed. He collapsed. He sank down upon the couch which the duchess had vacated.

Suddenly he heard a sound of footsteps, and those of a man. The noise came from the opposite side of the gallery to that by which the duchess had departed. The man approached, and his footsteps, though deadened by the carpet, were clear and distinct. Gwynplaine, in spite of his abstraction, listened.

Suddenly, beyond the silver web of curtain which the duchess had left partly open, a door, evidently concealed by the painted glass, opened wide, and there came floating into the room the refrain of an old French song, carolled at the top of a manly and joyous voice,—

"Trois petits gorets sur leur fumier
Juraient comme de porteurs de chaise,"

and a man entered. He wore a sword by his side, a magnificent naval uniform, covered with gold lace, and held in his hand a plumed hat with loops and cockade. Gwynplaine sprang up erect as if moved by springs. He recognized the man, and was, in turn, recognized by him. From their astonished lips came, simultaneously, this double exclamation:—

"Gwynplaine!"

"Tom-Jim-Jack!"

The man with the plumed hat advanced towards Gwynplaine, who stood with folded arms.

"What are you doing here, Gwynplaine?"

"And you, Tom-Jim-Jack, what are you doing here?"

"Oh! I understand. Josiana! a caprice. A mountebank and a monster! The double attraction is too powerful to be resisted. You disguised yourself in order to get here, Gwynplaine?"

"And you, too, Tom-Jim-Jack?"

"Gwynplaine, what does this gentleman's dress mean?"

"Tom-Jim-Jack, what does that officer's uniform mean?"

"Gwynplaine, I answer no questions."

"Neither do I, Tom-Jim-Jack."

"Gwynplaine, my name is not Tom-Jim-Jack."

"Tom-Jim-Jack, my name is not Gwynplaine."

"Gwynplaine, I am here in my own house."

"I am here in my own house, Tom-Jim-Jack."

"I will not have you echo my words. You are ironical; but I've got a cane. An end to your jokes, you wretched fool."

Gwynplaine became ashy pale. "You are a fool yourself, and you shall give me satisfaction for this insult."

"In your booth as much as you like, with fisticuffs."

"Here, and with swords?"

"My friend Gwynplaine, the sword is a weapon for gentlemen. With it I can only fight my equals. At fisticuffs we are equal, but not so with swords. At the Tadcaster Inn Tom-Jim-Jack could box with Gwynplaine; at Windsor the case is altered. Understand this: I am a rear-admiral."

"And I am a peer of England."

The man whom Gwynplaine recognized as Tom-Jim-Jack burst out laughing. "Why not a king? Indeed, you are right. An actor plays every part. You'll tell me next that you are Theseus, Duke of Athens."

"I am a peer of England, and we are going to fight."

"Gwynplaine, this becomes tiresome. Don't play with one who can order you to be flogged. I am Lord David Dirry-Moir."

"And I am Lord Clancharlie."

Again Lord David burst out laughing.

"Well said! Gwynplaine is Lord Clancharlie. That is indeed the name the man must bear who is to win Josiana. Listen. I forgive you; and do you know the reason? It's because we are both lovers of the same woman."

The curtain in the door was lifted, and a voice exclaimed, "You are the two husbands, my lords."

They turned.

"Barkilphedro!" cried Lord David.

It was indeed he; he bowed low to the two lords, with a smile on his face. Some few paces behind him was a gentleman with a stern and dignified countenance, who carried in his hand a black wand. This gentleman advanced, and, bowing three times to Gwynplaine, said, "I am the Usher of the Black Rod. I come to fetch your lordship, in obedience to her Majesty's commands."

BOOK THE EIGHTH

THE CAPITOL AND THINGS AROUND IT

CHAPTER I.

ANALYSIS OF MAJESTIC MATTERS

Irresistible Fate ever carrying him forward, which had now for so many hours showered its surprises on Gwynplaine, and which had transported him to Windsor, transferred him again to London. Visionary realities succeeded each other without a moment's intermission. He could not escape from their influence. Freed from one he met another. He had scarcely time to breathe. Any one who has seen a juggler throwing and catching balls can judge the nature of fate. Those rising and falling projectiles are like men tossed in the hands of Destiny—projectiles and playthings.

On the evening of the same day, Gwynplaine was an actor in an extraordinary scene. He was seated on a bench covered with fleurs-de-lis; over his silken clothes he wore a robe of scarlet velvet, lined with white silk, with a cape of ermine, and on his shoulders two bands of ermine embroidered with gold. Around him were men of all ages, young and old, seated like him on benches covered with fleurs-de-lis, and dressed like him in ermine and purple. In front of him other men were kneeling, clothed in black silk gowns. Some of them were writing; opposite, and a short distance from him, he observed steps, a raised platform, a dais, a large escutcheon glittering between a lion and a unicorn, and at the top of the steps, on the platform under the dais, resting against the escutcheon, was a gilded chair with a crown over it. This was a throne—the throne of Great Britain.

Gwynplaine, himself a peer of England, was in the House of Lords. How Gwynplaine's introduction to the House of Lords came about, we will now explain. Throughout the day, from morning to night, from Windsor to London, from Corleone Lodge to Westminster Hall, he had step by step mounted higher in the social grade. At each step he grew giddier. He had been conveyed from Windsor in a royal carriage with a peer's escort. There is not much difference between a guard of honour and a prisoner's. On that day, travellers on the London and Windsor road saw a galloping cavalcade of gentlemen pensioners of her Majesty's household escorting two carriages drawn at a rapid pace. In the first carriage sat the Usher of the Black Rod, his wand in his hand. In the second was to be seen a large hat with white plumes, throwing into shadow and hiding the face underneath it. Who was it who was thus being hurried on—a prince, a prisoner? It was Gwynplaine.

It looked as if they were conducting some one to the Tower, unless, indeed, they were escorting him to the House of Lords. The queen had done things well. As it was for her future brother-in-law, she had provided an escort from her own household. The officer of the Usher of the Black Rod rode on horseback at the head of the cavalcade. The Usher of the Black Rod carried, on a cushion placed on a seat of the carriage, a black portfolio stamped with the royal crown. At Brentford, the last relay before London, the carriages and escort halted. A four-horse carriage of tortoise-shell, with two postilions, a coachman in a wig, and four footmen, was in waiting. The wheels, steps, springs, pole, and all the fittings of this carriage were gilt. The horses' harness was of silver. This state coach was of an ancient and extraordinary shape, and would have been distinguished by its grandeur among the fifty-one celebrated carriages of which Roubo has left us drawings.

The Usher of the Black Rod and his officer alighted. The latter, having lifted the cushion, on which rested the royal portfolio, from the seat in the postchaise, carried it on outstretched hands, and stood behind the Usher. He first opened the door of the empty carriage, then the door of that occupied by Gwynplaine, and, with downcast eyes, respectfully invited him to descend. Gwynplaine left the chaise, and took his seat in the carriage. The Usher carrying the rod, and the officer supporting the cushion, followed, and took their places on the low front seat provided for pages in old state coaches. The inside of the carriage was lined with white satin trimmed with Binche silk, with tufts and tassels of silver. The roof was painted with armorial bearings. The postilions of the chaises they were leaving were dressed in the royal livery. The attendants of the carriage they now entered wore a different but very magnificent livery.

Gwynplaine, in spite of his bewildered state, in which he felt quite overcome, remarked the gorgeously-attired footmen, and asked the Usher of the Black Rod,—

"Whose livery is that?"

He answered,—

"Yours, my lord."

The House of Lords was to sit that evening. *Curia erat serena*, run the old records. In England parliamentary work is by preference undertaken at night. It once happened that Sheridan began a speech at midnight and finished it at sunrise.

The two postchaises returned to Windsor. Gwynplaine's carriage set out for London. This ornamented four-horse carriage proceeded at a walk from Brentford to London, as befitted the dignity of the coachman. Gwynplaine's servitude to ceremony was beginning in the shape of his solemn-looking coachman. The delay was, moreover, apparently prearranged; and we shall see presently its probable motive.

Night was falling, though it was not quite dark, when the carriage stopped at the King's Gate, a large sunken door between two turrets connecting Whitehall with Westminster. The escort of gentlemen pensioners formed a circle around the carriage. A footman jumped down from behind it and opened the door. The Usher of the Black Rod, followed by the officer carrying the cushion, got out of the carriage, and addressed Gwynplaine.

"My lord, be pleased to alight. I beg your lordship to keep your hat on."

Gwynplaine wore under his travelling cloak the suit of black silk, which he had not changed since the previous evening. He had no sword. He left his cloak in the carriage. Under the arched way of the King's Gate there was a small side door raised some few steps above the road. In ceremonial processions the greatest personage never walks first.

The Usher of the Black Rod, followed by his officer, walked first; Gwynplaine followed. They ascended the steps, and entered by the side door. Presently they were in a wide, circular room, with a pillar in the centre, the lower part of a turret. The room, being on the ground floor, was lighted by narrow windows in the pointed arches, which served but to make darkness visible. Twilight often lends solemnity to a scene. Obscurity is in itself majestic.

In this room, thirteen men, disposed in ranks, were standing—three in the front row, six in the second row, and four behind. In the front row one wore a crimson velvet gown; the other two, gowns of the same colour, but of satin. All three had the arms of England embroidered on their shoulders. The second rank wore tunics of white silk, each one having a different coat of arms emblazoned in front. The last row were clad in black silk, and were thus distinguished. The first wore a blue cape. The second had a scarlet St. George embroidered in front. The third, two embroidered crimson crosses, in front and behind. The fourth had a collar of black sable fur. All were uncovered, wore wigs, and carried swords. Their faces were scarcely visible in the dim light, neither could they see Gwynplaine's face.

The Usher of the Black Rod, raising his wand, said,—

"My Lord Fermain Clancharlie, Baron Clancharlie and Hunkerville, I, the Usher of the Black Rod, first officer of the presence chamber, hand your lordship over to Garter King-at-Arms."

The person clothed in velvet, quitting his place in the ranks, bowed to the ground before Gwynplaine, and said,—

"My Lord Fermain Clancharlie, I am Garter, Principal King-at-Arms of England. I am the officer appointed and installed by his grace the Duke of Norfolk, hereditary Earl Marshal. I have sworn obedience to the king, peers, and knights of the garter. The day of my installation, when the Earl Marshal of England anointed me by pouring a goblet of wine on my head, I solemnly promised to be attentive to the nobility; to avoid bad company; to excuse, rather than accuse, gentlefolks; and to assist widows and virgins. It is I who have the charge of arranging the funeral ceremonies of peers, and the supervision of their armorial bearings. I place myself at the orders of your lordship."

The first of those wearing satin tunics, having bowed deeply, said,—

"My lord, I am Clarenceaux, Second King-at-Arms of England. I am the officer who arranges the obsequies of nobles below the rank of peers. I am at your lordship's disposal."

The other wearer of the satin tunic bowed and spoke thus,—

"My lord, I am Norroy, Third King-at-Arms of England. Command me."

The second row, erect and without bowing, advanced a pace. The right-hand man said,—

"My lord, we are the six Dukes-at-Arms of England. I am York."

Then each of the heralds, or Dukes-at-Arms, speaking in turn, proclaimed his title.

"I am Lancaster."

"I am Richmond."

"I am Chester."

"I am Somerset."

"I am Windsor."

The coats of arms embroidered on their breasts were those of the counties and towns from which they took their names.

The third rank, dressed in black, remained silent. Garter King-at-Arms, pointing them out to Gwynplaine, said,—

"My lord, these are the four Pursuivants-at-Arms. Blue Mantle."

The man with the blue cape bowed.

"Rouge Dragon."

He with the St. George inclined his head.

"Rouge Croix."

He with the scarlet crosses saluted.

"Portcullis."

He with the sable fur collar made his obeisance.

On a sign from the King-at-Arms, the first of the pursuivants, Blue Mantle, stepped forward and received from the officer of the Usher the cushion of silver cloth and crown-emblazoned portfolio. And the King-at-Arms said to the Usher of the Black Rod,—

"Proceed; I leave in your hands the introduction of his lordship!"

The observance of these customs, and also of others which will now be described, were the old ceremonies in use prior to the time of Henry VIII., and which Anne for some time attempted to revive. There is nothing like it in existence now. Nevertheless, the House of Lords thinks that it is unchangeable; and, if Conservatism exists anywhere, it is there.

It changes, nevertheless. *E pur si muove.* For instance, what has become of the may-pole, which the citizens of London erected on the 1st of May, when the peers went down to the House? The last one was erected in 1713. Since then the may-pole has disappeared. Disuse.

Outwardly, unchangeable; inwardly, mutable. Take, for example, the title of Albemarle. It sounds eternal. Yet it has been through six different families—Odo, Mandeville, Bethune, Plantagenet, Beauchamp, Monck. Under the title of Leicester five different names have been merged—Beaumont, Breose, Dudley, Sydney, Coke. Under Lincoln, six; under Pembroke, seven. The families change, under unchanging titles. A superficial historian believes in immutability. In reality it does not exist. Man can never be more than a wave; humanity is the ocean.

Aristocracy is proud of what women consider a reproach—age! Yet both cherish the same illusion, that they do not change. It is probable the House of Lords will not recognize itself in the foregoing description, nor yet in that which follows, thus resembling the once pretty woman, who objects to having any wrinkles. The mirror is ever a scapegoat, yet its truths cannot be contested. To portray exactly, constitutes the duty of a historian. The King-at-Arms, turning to Gwynplaine, said,—

"Be pleased to follow me, my lord." And added, "You will be saluted. Your lordship, in returning the salute, will be pleased merely to raise the brim of your hat."

They moved off, in procession, towards a door at the far side of the room. The Usher of the Black Rod walked in front; then Blue Mantle, carrying the cushion; then the King-at-Arms; and after him came Gwynplaine, wearing his hat. The rest, kings-at-arms, heralds, and pursuivants, remained in the circular room. Gwynplaine, preceded by the Usher of the Black Rod, and escorted by the King-at-Arms, passed from room to room, in a direction which it would now be impossible to trace, the old Houses of Parliament having been pulled down. Amongst others, he crossed that Gothic state chamber in which took place the last meeting of James II. and Monmouth, and whose walls witnessed the useless debasement of the cowardly nephew at the feet of his vindictive uncle. On the walls of this chamber hung, in chronological order, nine fell-length portraits of former peers, with their dates—Lord Nansladron, 1305; Lord Baliol, 1306; Lord Benestede, 1314; Lord Cantilupe, 1356; Lord Montbegon, 1357; Lord Tibotot, 1373; Lord Zouch of Codnor, 1615; Lord Bella-Aqua, with no date; Lord Harren and Surrey, Count of Blois, also without date.

It being now dark, lamps were burning at intervals in the galleries. Brass chandeliers, with wax candles, illuminated the rooms, lighting them like the side aisles of a church. None but officials were present. In one room, which the procession crossed, stood, with heads respectfully lowered, the four clerks of the signet, and the Clerk of the Council. In another room stood the distinguished Knight Banneret, Philip Sydenham of Brympton in Somersetshire. The Knight Banneret is a title conferred in time of war, under the unfurled royal standard. In another room was the senior baronet of England, Sir Edmund Bacon of Suffolk, heir of Sir Nicholas Bacon, styled, *Primus baronetorum Anglicæ*. Behind Sir Edmund was an armour-bearer with an arquebus, and an esquire carrying the arms of Ulster, the baronets being the hereditary defenders of the province of Ulster in Ireland. In another room was the Chancellor of the Exchequer, with his four accountants, and the two deputies of the Lord Chamberlain, *appointed to cleave the tallies*.[21]

At the entrance of a corridor covered with matting, which was the communication between the Lower and the Upper House, Gwynplaine was saluted by Sir Thomas Mansell of Margam, Comptroller of the Queen's Household and Member for Glamorgan; and at the exit from the corridor by a deputation of one for every two of the Barons of the Cinque Ports, four on the right and four on the left, the Cinque Ports being eight in number. William Hastings did obeisance for Hastings; Matthew Aylmor, for Dover; Josias Burchett, for Sandwich; Sir Philip Boteler, for Hythe; John Brewer, for New Rumney; Edward Southwell, for the town of Rye; James Hayes, for Winchelsea; George Nailor, for Seaford. As Gwynplaine was about to return the salute, the King-at-Arms reminded him in a low voice of the etiquette, "Only the brim of your hat, my lord." Gwynplaine did as directed. He now entered the so-called Painted Chamber, in which there was no painting, except a few of saints, and amongst them St. Edward, in the high arches of the long and deep-pointed windows, which were divided by what formed the ceiling of Westminster Hall and the floor of the Painted Chamber. On the far side of the wooden barrier which divided the room from end to end, stood the three Secretaries of State, men of mark. The functions of the first of these officials comprised the supervision of all affairs relating to the south of England, Ireland, the Colonies, France, Switzerland, Italy, Spain, Portugal, and Turkey. The second had charge of the north of England, and watched affairs in the Low Countries, Germany, Denmark, Sweden, Poland, and Russia. The third, a Scot, had charge of Scotland. The two first-mentioned were English, one of them being the Honourable Robert Harley, Member for the borough of New Radnor. A Scotch member, Mungo Graham, Esquire, a relation of the Duke of Montrose, was present. All bowed, without speaking, to Gwynplaine, who returned the salute by touching his hat. The barrier-keeper lifted the wooden arm which, pivoting on a hinge, formed the entrance to the far side of the Painted Chamber, where stood the long table, covered with green cloth, reserved for peers. A branch of lighted candles stood on the table. Gwynplaine, preceded by the Usher of the Black Rod, Garter King-at-Arms, and Blue Mantle, penetrated into this privileged compartment. The barrier-keeper closed the opening immediately Gwynplaine had passed. The King-at-Arms, having entered the precincts of the privileged compartment, halted. The Painted Chamber was a spacious apartment. At the farther end, upright, beneath the royal escutcheon which was placed between the two windows, stood two old men, in red velvet robes, with two rows of ermine trimmed with gold lace on their shoulders, and wearing wigs, and hats with white plumes. Through the openings of their robes might be detected silk garments and sword hilts. Motionless behind them stood a man dressed in black silk, holding on high a great mace of gold surmounted by a crowned lion. It was the Mace-bearer of the Peers of England. The lion is their crest. *Et les Lions ce sont les Barons et li Per*, runs the manuscript chronicle of Bertrand Duguesclin.

The King-at-Arms pointed out the two persons in velvet, and whispered to Gwynplaine,—

"My lord, these are your equals. Be pleased to return their salute exactly as they make it. These two peers are barons, and have been named by the Lord Chancellor as your sponsors. They are very old, and almost blind. They will, themselves, introduce you to the House of Lords. The first is Charles Mildmay, Lord Fitzwalter, sixth on the roll of barons; the second is Augustus Arundel, Lord Arundel of Trerice, thirty-eighth on the roll of barons." The King-at-Arms having advanced a step towards the two old men, proclaimed "Fermain Clancharlie, Baron Clancharlie, Baron Hunkerville, Marquis of Corleone in Sicily, greets your lordships!" The two peers raised their hats to the full extent of the arm, and then replaced them. Gwynplaine did the same. The Usher of the Black Rod stepped forward, followed by Blue Mantle and Garter King at-Arms. The Mace-bearer took up his post in front of Gwynplaine, the two peers at his side, Lord Fitzwalter on the right, and Lord Arundel of Trerice on the left. Lord Arundel, the elder of the two, was very feeble. He died the following year, bequeathing to his grandson John, a minor, the title which became extinct in 1768. The procession, leaving the Painted Chamber, entered a gallery in which were rows of pilasters, and between the spaces were sentinels, alternately pike-men of England and halberdiers of Scotland. The Scotch halberdiers were magnificent kilted soldiers, worthy to encounter later on at Fontenoy the French cavalry, and the royal cuirassiers, whom their colonel thus addressed: "*Messieurs les maitres, assurez vos chapeaux. Nous allons avoir l'honneur de charger.*" The captain of these soldiers saluted Gwynplaine, and the peers, his sponsors, with their swords. The men saluted with their pikes and halberds.

At the end of the gallery shone a large door, so magnificent that its two folds seemed to be masses of gold. On each side of the door there stood, upright and motionless, men who were called doorkeepers. Just before you came to this door, the gallery widened out into a circular space. In this space was an armchair with an immense back, and on it, judging by his wig and from the amplitude of his robes, was a distinguished person. It was William Cowper, Lord Chancellor of England. To be able to cap a royal infirmity with a similar one has its advantages. William Cowper was short-sighted. Anne had also defective sight, but in a lesser degree. The near-sightedness of William Cowper found favour in the eyes of the short-sighted queen, and induced her to appoint him Lord Chancellor, and Keeper of the Royal Conscience. William Cowper's upper lip was thin, and his lower one thick—a sign of semi-good-nature.

This circular space was lighted by a lamp hung from the ceiling. The Lord Chancellor was sitting gravely in his large armchair; at his right was the Clerk of the Crown, and at his left the Clerk of the Parliaments.

Each of the clerks had before him an open register and an inkhorn.

Behind the Lord Chancellor was his mace-bearer, holding the mace with the crown on the top, besides the train-bearer and purse-bearer, in large wigs.

All these officers are still in existence. On a little stand, near the woolsack, was a sword, with a gold hilt and sheath, and belt of crimson velvet.

Behind the Clerk of the Crown was an officer holding in his hands the coronation robe.

Behind the Clerk of the Parliaments another officer held a second robe, which was that of a peer.

The robes, both of scarlet velvet, lined with white silk, and having bands of ermine trimmed with gold lace over the shoulders, were similar, except that the ermine band was wider on the coronation robe.

The third officer, who was the librarian, carried on a square of Flanders leather the red book, a little volume, bound in red morocco, containing a list of the peers and commons, besides a few blank leaves and a pencil, which it was the custom to present to each new member on his entering the House.

Gwynplaine, between the two peers, his sponsors, brought up the procession, which stopped before the woolsack.

The two peers, who introduced him, uncovered their heads, and Gwynplaine did likewise.

The King-at-Arms received from the hands of Blue Mantle the cushion of silver cloth, knelt down, and presented the black portfolio on the cushion to the Lord Chancellor.

The Lord Chancellor took the black portfolio, and handed it to the Clerk of the Parliament.

The Clerk received it ceremoniously, and then sat down.

The Clerk of the Parliament opened the portfolio, and arose.

The portfolio contained the two usual messages—the royal patent addressed to the House of Lords, and the writ of summons.

The Clerk read aloud these two messages, with respectful deliberation, standing.

The writ of summons, addressed to Fermain Lord Clancharlie, concluded with the accustomed formalities,—

"We strictly enjoin you, on the faith and allegiance that you owe, to come and take your place in person among the prelates and peers sitting in our Parliament at Westminster, for the purpose of giving your advice, in all honour and conscience, on the business of the kingdom and of the church."

The reading of the messages being concluded, the Lord Chancellor raised his voice,—

"The message of the Crown has been read. Lord Clancharlie, does your lordship renounce transubstantiation, adoration of saints, and the mass?"

Gwynplaine bowed.

"The test has been administered," said the Lord Chancellor.

And the Clerk of the Parliament resumed,—

"His lordship has taken the test."

The Lord Chancellor added,—

"My Lord Clancharlie, you can take your seat."

"So be it," said the two sponsors.

The King-at-Arms rose, took the sword from the stand, and buckled it round Gwynplaine's waist.

"Ce faict," says the old Norman charter, "le pair prend son espée, et monte aux hauts siéges, et assiste a l'audience."

Gwynplaine heard a voice behind him which said,—

"I array your lordship in a peer's robe."

At the same time, the officer who spoke to him, who was holding the robe, placed it on him, and tied the black strings of the ermine cape round his neck.

Gwynplaine, the scarlet robe on his shoulders, and the golden sword by his side, was attired like the peers on his right and left.

The librarian presented to him the red book, and put it in the pocket of his waistcoat.

The King-at-Arms murmured in his ear,—

"My lord, on entering, will bow to the royal chair."

The royal chair is the throne.

Meanwhile the two clerks were writing, each at his table—one on the register of the Crown, the other on the register of the House.

Then both—the Clerk of the Crown preceding the other—brought their books to the Lord Chancellor, who signed them. Having signed the two registers, the Lord Chancellor rose.

"Fermain Lord Clancharlie, Baron Clancharlie, Baron Hunkerville, Marquis of Corleone in Sicily, be you welcome among your peers, the lords spiritual and temporal of Great Britain."

Gwynplaine's sponsors touched his shoulder.

He turned round.

The folds of the great gilded door at the end of the gallery opened.

It was the door of the House of Lords.

Thirty-six hours only had elapsed since Gwynplaine, surrounded by a different procession, had entered the iron door of Southwark Jail.

What shadowy chimeras had passed, with terrible rapidity through his brain—chimeras which were hard facts; rapidity, which was a capture by assault!

CHAPTER II.

IMPARTIALITY

The creation of an equality with the king, called Peerage, was, in barbarous epochs, a useful fiction. This rudimentary political expedient produced in France and England different results. In France, the peer was a mock king; in England, a real prince—less grand than in France, but more genuine: we might say less, but worse.

Peerage was born in France; the date is uncertain—under Charlemagne, says the legend; under Robert le Sage, says history, and history is not more to be relied on than legend. Favin writes: "The King of France wished to attach to himself the great of his kingdom, by the magnificent title of peers, as if they were his equals."

Peerage soon thrust forth branches, and from France passed over to England.

The English peerage has been a great fact, and almost a mighty institution. It had for precedent the Saxon wittenagemote. The Danish thane and the Norman vavassour commingled in the baron. Baron is the same as vir, which is translated into Spanish by *varon*, and which signifies, *par excellence*, "Man." As early as 1075, the barons made themselves felt by the king—and by what a king! By William the Conqueror. In 1086 they laid the foundation of feudality, and its basis was the "Doomsday Book." Under John Lackland came conflict. The French peerage took the high hand with Great Britain, and demanded that the king of England should appear at their bar. Great was the indignation of the English barons. At the coronation of Philip Augustus, the King of England, as Duke of Normandy, carried the first square banner, and the Duke of Guyenne the second. Against this king, a vassal of the foreigner, the War of the Barons burst forth. The barons imposed on the weak-minded King John Magna Charta, from which sprang the House of Lords. The pope took part with the king, and excommunicated the lords. The date was 1215, and the pope was Innocent III., who wrote the "Veni, Sancte Spiritus," and who sent to John Lackland the four cardinal virtues in the shape of four gold rings. The Lords persisted. The duel continued through many generations. Pembroke struggled. 1248 was the year of "the provisions of Oxford." Twenty-four barons limited the king's powers, discussed him, and called a knight from each county to take part in the widened breach. Here was the dawn of the Commons. Later on, the Lords added two citizens from each city, and two burgesses from each borough. It arose from this, that up to the time of Elizabeth the peers were judges of the validity of elections to the House of Commons. From their jurisdiction sprang the proverb that the members returned ought to be without the three P's—*sine Prece, sine Pretio, sine Poculo.* This did not obviate rotten boroughs. In 1293, the Court of Peers in France had still the King of England under their jurisdiction; and Philippe le Bel cited Edward I. to appear before him. Edward I. was the king who ordered his son to boil him down after death, and to carry his bones to the wars. Under the follies of their kings the Lords felt the necessity of fortifying Parliament. They divided it into two chambers, the upper and the lower. The Lords arrogantly kept the supremacy. "If it happens that any member of the Commons should be so bold as to speak to the prejudice of the House of Lords, he is called to the bar of the House to be reprimanded, and, occasionally, to be sent to the Tower." There is the same distinction in voting. In the House of Lords they vote one by one, beginning with the junior, called the puisne baron. Each peer answers "*Content*," or "*Non-content*." In the Commons they vote together, by "Aye," or "No," in a crowd. The Commons accuse, the peers judge. The peers, in their disdain of figures, delegated to the Commons, who were to profit by it, the superintendence of the Exchequer—thus named, according to some, after the table-cover, which was like a chess-board; and according to others, from the drawers of the old safe, where was kept, behind an iron grating, the treasure of the kings of England. The "Year-Book" dates from the end of the thirteenth century. In the War of the Roses the weight of the Lords was thrown, now on the side of John of Gaunt, Duke of Lancaster, now on the side of Edmund, Duke of York. Wat Tyler, the Lollards, Warwick the King-maker, all that anarchy from which freedom is to spring, had for foundation, avowed or secret, the English feudal system. The Lords were usefully jealous of the Crown; for to be jealous is to be watchful. They circumscribed the royal initiative, diminished the category of cases of high treason, raised up pretended Richards against Henry IV., appointed themselves arbitrators, judged the question of the three crowns between the Duke of York and Margaret of Anjou, and at need levied armies, and fought their battles of Shrewsbury, Tewkesbury, and St. Albans, sometimes winning, sometimes losing. Before this, in the thirteenth century, they had gained the battle of Lewes, and had driven from the kingdom the four brothers of the king, bastards of Queen Isabella by the Count de la Marche; all four usurers, who extorted money from Christians by means of the Jews; half princes, half sharpers—a thing common enough in more recent times, but not held in good odour in those days. Up to the fifteenth century the Norman Duke peeped out in the King of England, and the acts of Parliament were written in French. From the reign of Henry VII., by the will of the Lords, these were written in English. England, British under Uther Pendragon; Roman under Cæsar; Saxon under the Heptarchy; Danish under Harold; Norman after William; then became, thanks to the Lords, English. After that she became Anglican. To have one's religion at home is a great power. A foreign pope drags down the national life. A Mecca is an octopus, and devours it. In 1534, London bowed out Rome. The peerage adopted the reformed religion, and the Lords accepted Luther. Here we have the answer to the excommunication of 1215. It was agreeable to Henry VIII.; but, in other respects, the Lords were a trouble to him. As a bulldog to a bear, so was the House of Lords to Henry VIII. When Wolsey robbed the nation of Whitehall, and when Henry robbed Wolsey of it, who complained? Four lords—Darcie, of Chichester; Saint John of Bletsho; and (two Norman names) Mountjoie and Mounteagle. The king usurped. The peerage encroached. There is something in hereditary power which is incorruptible. Hence the insubordination of the Lords. Even in Elizabeth's reign the barons were restless. From this resulted the tortures at Durham. Elizabeth was as a farthingale over an executioner's block. Elizabeth assembled Parliament as seldom as possible, and reduced the House of

Lords to sixty-five members, amongst whom there was but one marquis (Winchester), and not a single duke. In France the kings felt the same jealousy and carried out the same elimination. Under Henry III. there were no more than eight dukedoms in the peerage, and it was to the great vexation of the king that the Baron de Mantes, the Baron de Courcy, the Baron de Coulommiers, the Baron de Chateauneuf-en-Thimerais, the Baron de la Fère-en-Lardenois, the Baron de Mortagne, and some others besides, maintained themselves as barons—peers of France. In England the crown saw the peerage diminish with pleasure. Under Anne, to quote but one example, the peerages become extinct since the twelfth century amounted to five hundred and sixty-five. The War of the Roses had begun the extermination of dukes, which the axe of Mary Tudor completed. This was, indeed, the decapitation of the nobility. To prune away the dukes was to cut off its head. Good policy, perhaps; but it is better to corrupt than to decapitate. James I. was of this opinion. He restored dukedoms. He made a duke of his favourite Villiers, who had made him a pig;[22] a transformation from the duke feudal to the duke courtier. This sowing was to bring forth a rank harvest: Charles II. was to make two of his mistresses duchesses—Barbara of Southampton, and Louise de la Querouel of Portsmouth. Under Anne there were to be twenty-five dukes, of whom three were to be foreigners, Cumberland, Cambridge, and Schomberg. Did this court policy, invented by James I., succeed? No. The House of Peers was irritated by the effort to shackle it by intrigue. It was irritated against James I., it was irritated against Charles I., who, we may observe, may have had something to do with the death of his father, just as Marie de Medicis may have had something to do with the death of her husband. There was a rupture between Charles I. and the peerage. The lords who, under James I., had tried at their bar extortion, in the person of Bacon, under Charles I. tried treason, in the person of Stratford. They had condemned Bacon; they condemned Stratford. One had lost his honour, the other lost his life. Charles I. was first beheaded in the person of Stratford. The Lords lent their aid to the Commons. The king convokes Parliament to Oxford; the revolution convokes it to London. Forty-four peers side with the King, twenty-two with the Republic. From this combination of the people with the Lords arose the Bill of Rights—a sketch of the French *Droits de l'homme*, a vague shadow flung back from the depths of futurity by the revolution of France on the revolution of England.

Such were the services of the peerage. Involuntary ones, we admit, and dearly purchased, because the said peerage is a huge parasite. But considerable services, nevertheless.

The despotic work of Louis XI., of Richelieu, and of Louis XIV., the creation of a sultan, levelling taken for true equality, the bastinado given by the sceptre, the common abasement of the people, all these Turkish tricks in France the peers prevented in England. The aristocracy was a wall, banking up the king on one side, sheltering the people on the other. They redeemed their arrogance towards the people by their insolence towards the king. Simon, Earl of Leicester, said to Henry III., "*King, thou hast lied!*" The Lords curbed the crown, and grated against their kings in the tenderest point, that of venery. Every lord, passing through a royal park, had the right to kill a deer: in the house of the king the peer was at home; in the Tower of London the scale of allowance for the king was no more than that for a peer—namely, twelve pounds sterling per week. This was the House of Lords' doing.

Yet more. We owe to it the deposition of kings. The Lords ousted John Lackland, degraded Edward II., deposed Richard II., broke the power of Henry VI., and made Cromwell a possibility. What a Louis XIV. there was in Charles I.! Thanks to Cromwell, it remained latent. By-the-bye, we may here observe that Cromwell himself, though no historian seems to have noticed the fact, aspired to the peerage. This was why he married Elizabeth Bouchier, descendant and heiress of a Cromwell, Lord Bouchier, whose peerage became extinct in 1471, and of a Bouchier, Lord Robesart, another peerage extinct in 1429. Carried on with the formidable increase of important events, he found the suppression of a king a shorter way to power than the recovery of a peerage. A ceremonial of the Lords, at times ominous, could reach even to the king. Two men-at-arms from the Tower, with their axes on their shoulders, between whom an accused peer stood at the bar of the house, might have been there in like attendance on the king as on any other nobleman. For five centuries the House of Lords acted on a system, and carried it out with determination. They had their days of idleness and weakness, as, for instance, that strange time when they allowed themselves to be seduced by the vessels loaded with cheeses, hams, and Greek wines sent them by Julius II. The English aristocracy was restless, haughty, ungovernable, watchful, and patriotically mistrustful. It was that aristocracy which, at the end of the seventeenth century, by act the tenth of the year 1694, deprived the borough of Stockbridge, in Hampshire, of the right of sending members to Parliament, and forced the Commons to declare null the election for that borough, stained by papistical fraud. It imposed the test on James, Duke of York, and, on his refusal to take it, excluded him from the throne. He reigned, notwithstanding; but the Lords wound up by calling him to account and banishing him. That aristocracy has had, in its long duration, some instinct of progress. It has always given out a certain quantity of appreciable light, except now towards its end, which is at hand. Under James II. it maintained in the Lower House the proportion of three hundred and forty-six burgesses against ninety-two knights. The sixteen barons, by courtesy, of the Cinque Ports were more than counterbalanced by the fifty citizens of the twenty-five cities. Though corrupt and egotistic, that aristocracy was, in some instances, singularly impartial. It is harshly judged. History keeps all its compliments for the Commons. The justice of this is doubtful. We consider the part played by the Lords a very great one. Oligarchy is the independence of a barbarous state, but it is an independence. Take Poland, for instance, nominally a kingdom, really a republic. The peers of England held the throne in suspicion and guardianship. Time after time they have made their power more felt than that of the Commons. They gave check to the king. Thus, in that remarkable year, 1694, the Triennial Parliament Bill, rejected by the Commons, in consequence of the objections of William III., was passed by the Lords. William III., in his irritation, deprived the Earl of Bath of the governorship of Pendennis Castle, and Viscount Mordaunt of all his offices. The House of Lords was the republic of Venice in the heart of the royalty of England. To reduce the king to a doge was its object; and in proportion as it decreased the power of the crown it increased that of the people. Royalty knew this, and hated the peerage. Each endeavoured to lessen the other. What was thus lost by each was proportionate profit to the people. Those two blind powers, monarchy and oligarchy, could not see that they were working for the benefit of a third, which was democracy. What a delight it was to the crown, in the last century, to be able to hang a peer, Lord Ferrers!

However, they hung him with a silken rope. How polite!

"They would not have hung a peer of France," the Duke of Richelieu haughtily remarked. Granted. They would have beheaded him. Still more polite!

Montmorency Tancarville signed himself *peer of France and England;* thus throwing the English peerage into the second rank. The peers of France were higher and less powerful, holding to rank more than to authority, and to precedence more than to domination. There was between them and the Lords that shade of difference which separates vanity from pride. With the peers of France, to take precedence of foreign princes, of Spanish grandees, of Venetian patricians; to see seated on the lower benches the Marshals of France, the Constable and the Admiral of France, were he even Comte de Toulouse and son of Louis XIV.; to draw a distinction between duchies in the male and female line; to maintain the proper distance between a simple *comté*, like Armagnac or Albret, and a *comté pairie*, like Evreux; to wear by right, at five-and-twenty, the blue ribbon of the Golden Fleece; to counterbalance the Duke de la Tremoille, the most ancient peer of the court, with the Duke Uzès, the most ancient peer of the Parliament; to claim as many pages and horses to their carriages as an elector; to be called *monseigneur* by the first President; to discuss whether the Duke de Maine dates his peerage as the Comte d'Eu, from 1458; to cross the grand chamber diagonally, or by the side—such things were grave matters. Grave matters with the Lords were the Navigation Act, the Test Act, the enrolment of Europe in the service of England, the command of the sea, the expulsion of the Stuarts, war with France. On one side, etiquette above all; on the other, empire above all. The peers of England had the substance, the peers of France the shadow.

To conclude, the House of Lords was a starting-point; towards civilization this is an immense thing. It had the honour to found a nation. It was the first incarnation of the unity of the people: English resistance, that obscure but all-powerful force, was born in the House of Lords. The barons, by a series of acts of violence against royalty, have paved the way for its eventual downfall. The House of Lords at the present day is somewhat sad and astonished at what it has unwillingly and unintentionally done, all the more that it is irrevocable.

What are concessions? Restitutions;—and nations know it.

"I grant," says the king.

"I get back my own," says the people.

The House of Lords believed that it was creating the privileges of the peerage, and it has produced the rights of the citizen. That vulture, aristocracy, has hatched the eagle's egg of liberty.

And now the egg is broken, the eagle is soaring, the vulture dying.

Aristocracy is at its last gasp; England is growing up.

Still, let us be just towards the aristocracy. It entered the scale against royalty, and was its counterpoise. It was an obstacle to despotism. It was a barrier. Let us thank and bury it.

CHAPTER III.

THE OLD HALL

Near Westminster Abbey was an old Norman palace which was burnt in the time of Henry VIII. Its wings were spared. In one of them Edward VI. placed the House of Lords, in the other the House of Commons. Neither the two wings nor the two chambers are now in existence. The whole has been rebuilt.

We have already said, and we must repeat, that there is no resemblance between the House of Lords of the present day and that of the past. In demolishing the ancient palace they somewhat demolished its ancient usages. The strokes of the pickaxe on the monument produce their counter-strokes on customs and charters. An old stone cannot fall without dragging down with it an old law. Place in a round room a parliament which has been hitherto held in a square room, and it will no longer be the same thing. A change in the shape of the shell changes the shape of the fish inside.

If you wish to preserve an old thing, human or divine, a code or a dogma, a nobility or a priesthood, never repair anything about it thoroughly, even its outside cover. Patch it up, nothing more. For instance, Jesuitism is a piece added to Catholicism. Treat edifices as you would treat institutions. Shadows should dwell in ruins. Worn-out powers are uneasy in chambers freshly decorated. Ruined palaces accord best with institutions in rags. To attempt to describe the House of Lords of other days would be to attempt to describe the unknown. History is night. In history there is no second tier. That which is no longer on the stage immediately fades into obscurity. The scene is shifted, and all is at once forgotten. The past has a synonym, the unknown.

The peers of England sat as a court of justice in Westminster Hall, and as the higher legislative chamber in a chamber specially reserved for the purpose, called *The House of Lords.*

Besides the house of peers of England, which did not assemble as a court unless convoked by the crown, two great English tribunals, inferior to the house of peers, but superior to all other jurisdiction, sat in Westminster Hall. At the end of that hall they occupied adjoining compartments. The first was the Court of King's Bench, in which the king was supposed to preside; the second, the Court of Chancery, in which the Chancellor presided. The one was a court of justice, the other a court of mercy. It was the Chancellor who counselled the king to pardon; only rarely, though.

These two courts, which are still in existence, interpreted legislation, and reconstructed it somewhat, for the art of the judge is to carve the code into jurisprudence; a task from which equity results as it best may. Legislation was worked up and applied in the severity of the great hall of Westminster, the rafters of which were of chestnut wood, over which spiders could not spread their webs. There are enough of them in all conscience in the laws.

To sit as a court and to sit as a chamber are two distinct things. This double function constitutes supreme power. The Long Parliament, which began in November 1640, felt the revolutionary necessity for this two-edged sword. So it declared that, as House of Lords, it possessed judicial as well as legislative power.

This double power has been, from time immemorial, vested in the House of Peers. We have just mentioned that as judges they occupied Westminster Hall; as legislators, they had another chamber. This other chamber, properly called the House of Lords, was oblong and narrow. All the light in it came from four windows in deep embrasures, which received their light through the roof, and a bull's-eye, composed of six panes with curtains, over the throne. At night there was no other light than twelve half candelabra, fastened to the wall. The chamber of Venice was darker still. A certain obscurity is pleasing to those owls of supreme power.

A high ceiling adorned with many-faced relievos and gilded cornices, circled over the chamber where the Lords assembled. The Commons had but a flat ceiling. There is a meaning in all monarchical buildings. At one end of the long chamber of the Lords was the door; at the other, opposite to it, the throne. A few paces from the door, the bar, a transverse barrier, and a sort of frontier, marked the spot where the people ended and the peerage began. To the right of the throne was a fireplace with emblazoned pinnacles, and two bas-reliefs of marble, representing, one, the victory of Cuthwolf over the Britons, in 572; the other, the geometrical plan of the borough of Dunstable, which had four streets, parallel to the four quarters of the world. The throne was approached by three steps. It was called the royal chair. On the two walls, opposite each other, were displayed in successive pictures, on a huge piece of tapestry given to the Lords by Elizabeth, the adventures of the Armada, from the time of its leaving Spain until it was wrecked on the coasts of Great Britain. The great hulls of the ships were embroidered with threads of gold and silver, which had become blackened by time. Against this tapestry, cut at intervals by the candelabra fastened in the wall, were placed, to the right of the throne, three rows of benches for the bishops, and to the left three rows of benches for the dukes, marquises, and earls, in tiers, and separated by gangways. On the three benches of the first section sat the dukes; on those of the second, the marquises; on those of the third, the earls. The viscounts' bench was placed across, opposite the throne, and behind, between the viscounts and the bar, were two benches for the barons.

On the highest bench to the right of the throne sat the two archbishops of Canterbury and York; on the middle bench three bishops, London, Durham, and Winchester, and the other bishops on the lowest bench. There is between the Archbishop of Canterbury and the other bishops this considerable difference, that he is bishop "by divine providence," whilst the others are only so "by divine permission." On the right of the throne was a chair for the Prince of Wales, and on the left, folding chairs for the royal dukes, and behind the latter, a raised seat for minor peers, who had not the privilege of voting. Plenty of fleurs-de-lis everywhere, and the great escutcheon of England over the four walls, above the peers, as well as above the king.

The sons of peers and the heirs to peerages assisted at the debates, standing behind the throne, between the daïs and the wall. A large square space was left vacant between the tiers of benches placed along three sides of the chamber and the throne. In this space, which was covered with the state carpet, interwoven with the arms of Great Britain, were four woolsacks—one in front of the throne, on which sat the Lord Chancellor, between the mace and the seal; one in front of the bishops, on which sat the judges, counsellors of state, who had the right to vote, but not to speak; one in front of the dukes, marquises, and earls, on which sat the Secretaries of State; and one in front of the viscounts and barons, on which sat the Clerk of the Crown and the Clerk of the Parliament, and on which the two under-clerks wrote, kneeling.

In the middle of the space was a large covered table, heaped with bundles of papers, registers, and summonses, with magnificent inkstands of chased silver, and with high candlesticks at the four corners.

The peers took their seats in chronological order, each according to the date of the creation of his peerage. They ranked according to their titles, and within their grade of nobility according to seniority. At the bar stood the Usher of the Black Rod, his wand in his hand. Inside the door was the Deputy-Usher; and outside, the Crier of the Black Rod, whose duty it was to open the sittings of the Courts of Justice with the cry, "Oyez!" in French, uttered thrice, with a solemn accent upon the first syllable. Near the Crier stood the Serjeant Mace-Bearer of the Chancellor.

In royal ceremonies the temporal peers wore coronets on their heads, and the spiritual peers, mitres. The archbishops wore mitres, with a ducal coronet; and the bishops, who rank after viscounts, mitres, with a baron's cap.

It is to be remarked, as a coincidence at once strange and instructive, that this square formed by the throne, the bishops, and the barons, with kneeling magistrates within it, was in form similar to the ancient parliament in France under the two first dynasties. The aspect of authority was the same in France as in England. Hincmar, in his treatise, "De Ordinatione Sacri Palatii," described in 853 the sittings of the House of Lords at Westminster in the eighteenth century. Strange, indeed! a description given nine hundred years before the existence of the thing described.

But what is history? An echo of the past in the future; a reflex from the future on the past.

The assembly of Parliament was obligatory only once in every seven years.

The Lords deliberated in secret, with closed doors. The debates of the Commons were public. Publicity entails diminution of dignity.

The number of the Lords was unlimited. To create Lords was the menace of royalty; a means of government.

At the beginning of the eighteenth century the House of Lords already contained a very large number of members. It has increased still further since that period. To dilute the aristocracy is politic. Elizabeth most probably erred in condensing the peerage into sixty-five lords. The less numerous, the more intense is a peerage. In assemblies, the more numerous the members, the fewer the heads. James II. understood this when he increased the Upper House to a hundred and eighty-eight lords; a hundred and eighty-six if we subtract from the peerages the two duchies of royal favourites, Portsmouth and Cleveland. Under Anne the total number of the lords, including bishops, was two hundred and seven. Not counting the Duke of Cumberland, husband of the queen, there were twenty-five dukes, of whom the premier, Norfolk, did not take his seat, being a Catholic; and of whom the junior, Cambridge, the Elector of Hanover, did, although a foreigner. Winchester, termed first and sole marquis of England, as Astorga was termed sole Marquis of Spain, was absent, being a Jacobite; so that there were only five marquises, of whom the premier was Lindsay, and the junior Lothian; seventy-nine earls, of whom Derby was premier and Islay junior; nine viscounts, of whom Hereford was premier and Lonsdale junior; and sixty-two barons, of whom Abergavenny was premier and Hervey junior. Lord Hervey, the junior baron, was what was called the "Puisné of the House." Derby, of whom Oxford, Shrewsbury, and Kent took precedence, and who was therefore but the fourth under James II., became (under Anne) premier earl. Two chancellors' names had disappeared from the list of barons—Verulam, under which designation history finds us Bacon; and Wem, under which it finds us Jeffreys. Bacon and Jeffreys! both names overshadowed, though by different crimes. In 1705, the twenty-six bishops were reduced to twenty-five, the see of Chester being vacant. Amongst the bishops some were peers of high rank, such as William Talbot, Bishop of Oxford, who was head of the Protestant branch of that family. Others were eminent Doctors, like John Sharp, Archbishop of York, formerly Dean of Norwich; the poet, Thomas Spratt, Bishop of Rochester, an apoplectic old man; and that Bishop of Lincoln, who was to die Archbishop of Canterbury, Wake, the adversary of Bossuet. On important occasions, and when a message from the Crown to the House was expected, the whole of this august assembly—in robes, in wigs, in mitres, or plumes—formed out, and displayed their rows of heads, in tiers, along the walls of the House, where the storm was vaguely to be seen exterminating the Armada—almost as much as to say, "The storm is at the orders of England."

CHAPTER IV.

THE OLD CHAMBER

The whole ceremony of the investiture of Gwynplaine, from his entry under the King's Gate to his taking the test under the nave window, was enacted in a sort of twilight.

Lord William Cowper had not permitted that he, as Lord Chancellor of England, should receive too many details of circumstances connected with the disfigurement of the young Lord Fermain Clancharlie, considering it below his dignity to know that a peer was not handsome; and feeling that his dignity would suffer if an inferior should venture to intrude on him information of such a nature. We know that a common fellow will take pleasure in saying, "That prince is humpbacked;" therefore, it is abusive to say that a lord is deformed. To the few words dropped on the subject by the queen the Lord Chancellor had contented himself with replying, "The face of a peer is in his peerage!"

Ultimately, however, the affidavits he had read and certified enlightened him. Hence the precautions which he took. The face of the new lord, on his entrance into the House, might cause some sensation. This it was necessary to prevent; and the Lord Chancellor took his measures for the purpose. It is a fixed idea, and a rule of conduct in grave personages, to allow as little disturbance as possible. Dislike of incident is a part of their gravity. He felt the necessity of so ordering matters that the admission of Gwynplaine should take place without any hitch, and like that of any other successor to the peerage.

It was for this reason that the Lord Chancellor directed that the reception of Lord Fermain Clancharlie should take place at the evening sitting. The Chancellor being the doorkeeper—"*Quodammodo ostiarus*," says the Norman charter; "*Januarum cancellorumque*," says Tertullian—he can officiate outside the room on the threshold; and Lord William Cowper had used his right by carrying out under the nave the formalities of the investiture of Lord Fermain Clancharlie. Moreover, he had brought forward the hour for the ceremonies; so that the new peer actually made his entrance into the House before the House had assembled.

For the investiture of a peer on the threshold, and not in the chamber itself, there were precedents. The first hereditary baron, John de Beauchamp, of Holt Castle, created by patent by Richard II., in 1387, Baron Kidderminster, was thus installed. In renewing this precedent the Lord Chancellor was creating for himself a future cause for embarrassment, of which he felt the inconvenience less than two years afterwards on the entrance of Viscount Newhaven into the House of Lords.

Short-sighted as we have already stated him to be, Lord William Cowper scarcely perceived the deformity of Gwynplaine; while the two sponsors, being old and nearly blind, did not perceive it at all.

The Lord Chancellor had chosen them for that very reason.

More than this, the Lord Chancellor, having only seen the presence and stature of Gwynplaine, thought him a fine-looking man. When the door-keeper opened the folding doors to Gwynplaine there were but few peers in the house; and these few were nearly all old men. In assemblies the old members are the most punctual, just as towards women they are the most assiduous.

On the dukes' benches there were but two, one white-headed, the other gray—Thomas Osborne, Duke of Leeds, and Schomberg, son of that Schomberg, German by birth, French by his marshal's bâton, and English by his peerage, who was banished by the edict of Nantes, and who, having fought against England as a Frenchman, fought against France as an Englishman. On the benches of the lords spiritual there sat only the Archbishopof Canterbury, Primate of England, above; and below, Dr. Simon Patrick, Bishop of Ely, in conversation with Evelyn Pierrepoint, Marquis of Dorchester, who was explaining to him the difference between a gabion considered singly and when used in the parapet of a field work, and between palisades and fraises; the former being a row of posts driven info the ground in front of the tents, for the purpose of protecting the camp; the latter sharp-pointed stakes set up under the wall of a fortress, to prevent the escalade of the besiegers and the desertion of the besieged; and the marquis was explaining further the method of placing fraises in the ditches of redoubts, half of each stake being buried and half exposed. Thomas Thynne, Viscount Weymouth, having approached the light of a chandelier, was examining a plan of his architect's for laying out his gardens at Longleat, in Wiltshire, in the Italian style—as a lawn, broken up into plots, with squares of turf alternating with squares of red and yellow sand, of river shells, and of fine coal dust. On the viscounts' benches was a group of old peers, Essex, Ossulstone, Peregrine, Osborne, William Zulestein, Earl of Rochford, and amongst them, a few more youthful ones, of the faction which did not wear wigs, gathered round Prince Devereux, Viscount Hereford, and discussing the question whether an infusion of apalaca holly was tea. "Very nearly," said Osborne. "Quite," said Essex. This discussion was attentively listened to by Paulet St. John, a cousin of Bolingbroke, of whom Voltaire was, later on, in some degree the pupil; for Voltaire's education, commenced by Père Porée, was finished by Bolingbroke. On the marquises' benches, Thomas de Grey, Marquis of Kent, Lord Chamberlain to the Queen, was informing Robert Bertie, Marquis of Lindsay, Lord Chamberlain of England, that the first prize in the great English lottery of 1694 had been won by two French refugees, Monsieur Le Coq, formerly councillor in the parliament of Paris, and Monsieur Ravenel, a gentleman of Brittany. The Earl of Wemyss was reading a book, entitled "Pratique Curieuse des Oracles des Sybilles." John Campbell, Earl of Greenwich, famous for his long chin, his gaiety, and his eighty-seven years, was writing to his mistress. Lord Chandos was trimming his nails.

The sitting which was about to take place, being a royal one, where the crown was to be represented by commissioners, two assistant door-keepers were placing in front of the throne a bench covered with purple velvet. On the second woolsack sat the Master of the Rolls, *sacrorum scriniorum magister*, who had then for his residence the house formerly belonging to the converted Jews. Two under-clerks were kneeling, and turning over the leaves of the registers which lay on the fourth woolsack. In the meantime the Lord Chancellor took his place on the first woolsack. The members of the chamber took theirs, some sitting, others standing; when the Archbishop of Canterbury rose and read the prayer, and the sitting of the house began.

Gwynplaine had already been there for some time without attracting any notice. The second bench of barons, on which was his place, was close to the bar, so that he had had to take but a few steps to reach it. The two peers, his sponsors, sat, one on his right, the other on his left, thus almost concealing the presence of the new-comer.

No one having been furnished with any previous information, the Clerk of the Parliament had read in a low voice, and as it were, mumbled through the different documents concerning the new peer, and the Lord Chancellor had proclaimed his admission in the midst of what is called, in the reports, "general inattention." Every one was talking. There buzzed through the House that cheerful hum of voices during which assemblies pass things which will not bear the light, and at which they wonder when they find out what they have done, too late.

Gwynplaine was seated in silence, with his head uncovered, between the two old peers, Lord Fitzwalter and Lord Arundel. On entering, according to the instructions of the King-at-Arms—afterwards renewed by his sponsors—he had bowed to the throne.

Thus all was over. He was a peer. That pinnacle, under the glory of which he had, all his life, seen his master, Ursus, bow himself down in fear—that prodigious pinnacle was under his feet. He was in that place, so dark and yet so dazzling in England. Old peak of the feudal mountain, looked up to for six centuries by Europe and by history! Terrible nimbus of a world of shadow! He had entered into the brightness of its glory, and his entrance was irrevocable.

He was there in his own sphere, seated on his throne, like the king on his. He was there and nothing in the future could obliterate the fact. The royal crown, which he saw under the daïs, was brother to his coronet. He was a peer of that throne. In the face of majesty he was peerage; less, but like. Yesterday, what was he? A player. To-day, what was he? A prince.

Yesterday, nothing; to-day, everything.

It was a sudden confrontation of misery and power, meeting face to face, and resolving themselves at once into the two halves of a conscience. Two spectres, Adversity and Prosperity, were taking possession of the same soul, and each drawing that soul towards itself.

Oh, pathetic division of an intellect, of a will, of a brain, between two brothers who are enemies! the Phantom of Poverty and the Phantom of Wealth! Abel and Cain in the same man!

CHAPTER V.

ARISTOCRATIC GOSSIP

By degrees the seats of the House filled as the Lords arrived. The question was the vote for augmenting, by a hundred thousand pounds sterling, the annual income of George of Denmark, Duke of Cumberland, the queen's husband. Besides this, it was announced that several bills assented to by her Majesty were to be brought back to the House by the Commissioners of the Crown empowered and charged to sanction them. This raised the sitting to a royal one. The peers all wore their robes over their usual court or ordinary dress. These robes, similar to that which had been thrown over Gwynplaine, were alike for all, excepting that the dukes had five bands of ermine, trimmed with gold; marquises, four; earls and viscounts, three; and barons, two. Most of the lords entered in groups. They had met in the corridors, and were continuing the conversations there begun. A few came in alone. The costumes of all were solemn; but neither their attitudes nor their words corresponded with them. On entering, each one bowed to the throne.

The peers flowed in. The series of great names marched past with scant ceremonial, the public not being present. Leicester entered, and shook Lichfield's hand; then came Charles Mordaunt, Earl of Peterborough and Monmouth, the friend of Locke, under whose advice he had proposed the recoinage of money; then Charles Campbell, Earl of Loudoun, listening to Fulke Greville, Lord Brooke; then Dorme, Earl of Carnarvon; then Robert Sutton, Baron Lexington, son of that Lexington who recommended Charles II. to banish Gregorio Leti, the historiographer, who was so ill-advised as to try to become a historian; then Thomas Bellasys, Viscount Falconberg, a handsome old man; and the three cousins, Howard, Earl of Bindon, Bowes Howard, Earl of Berkshire, and Stafford Howard, Earl of Stafford—all together; then John Lovelace, Baron Lovelace, which peerage became extinct in 1736, so that Richardson was enabled to introduce Lovelace in his book, and to create a type under the name. All these personages—celebrated each in his own way, either in politics or in war, and of whom many were an honour to England—were laughing and talking.

It was history, as it were, seen in undress.

In less than half an hour the House was nearly full. This was to be expected, as the sitting was a royal one. What was more unusual was the eagerness of the conversations. The House, so sleepy not long before, now hummed like a hive of bees.

The arrival of the peers who had come in late had wakened them up. These lords had brought news. It was strange that the peers who had been there at the opening of the sitting knew nothing of what had occurred, while those who had not been there knew all about it. Several lords had come from Windsor.

For some hours past the adventures of Gwynplaine had been the subject of conversation. A secret is a net; let one mesh drop, and the whole goes to pieces.

In the morning, in consequence of the incidents related above, the whole story of a peer found on the stage, and of a mountebank become a lord, had burst forth at Windsor in Royal places. The princes had talked about it, and then the lackeys. From the Court the news soon reached the town. Events have a weight, and the mathematical rule of velocity, increasing in proportion to the squares of the distance, applies to them. They fall upon the public, and work themselves through it with the most astounding rapidity. At seven o'clock no one in London had caught wind of the story; by eight Gwynplaine was the talk of the town. Only the lords who had been so punctual that they were present before the assembling of the House were ignorant of the circumstances, not having been in the town when the matter was talked of by every one, and having been in the House, where nothing had been perceived. Seated quietly on their benches, they were addressed by the eager newcomers.

"Well!" said Francis Brown, Viscount Montacute, to the Marquis of Dorchester.

"What?"

"Is it possible?"

"What?"

"The Laughing Man!"

"Who is the Laughing Man?"

"Don't you know the Laughing Man?"

"No."

"He is a clown, a fellow performing at fairs. He has an extraordinary face, which people gave a penny to look at. A mountebank."

"Well, what then?"

"You have just installed him as a peer of England."

"You are the laughing man, my Lord Montacute!"

"I am not laughing, my Lord Dorchester."

Lord Montacute made a sign to the Clerk of the Parliament, who rose from his woolsack, and confirmed to their lordships the fact of the admission of the new peer. Besides, he detailed the circumstances.

"How wonderful!" said Lord Dorchester. "I was talking to the Bishop of Ely all the while."

The young Earl of Annesley addressed old Lord Eure, who had but two years more to live, as he died in 1707.

"My Lord Eure."

"My Lord Annesley."

"Did you know Lord Linnæus Clancharlie?"

"A man of bygone days. Yes I did."

"He died in Switzerland?"

"Yes; we were relations."

"He was a republican under Cromwell, and remained a republican under Charles II.?"

"A republican? Not at all! He was sulking. He had a personal quarrel with the king. I know from good authority that Lord Clancharlie would have returned to his allegiance, if they had given him the office of Chancellor, which Lord Hyde held."

"You astonish me, Lord Eure. I had heard that Lord Clancharlie was an honest politician."

"An honest politician! does such a thing exist? Young man, there is no such thing."

"And Cato?"

"Oh, you believe in Cato, do you?"

"And Aristides?"

"They did well to exile him."

"And Thomas More?"

"They did well to cut off his head."

"And in your opinion Lord Clancharlie was a man as you describe. As for a man remaining in exile, why, it is simply ridiculous."

"He died there."

"An ambitious man disappointed?"

"You ask if I knew him? I should think so indeed. I was his dearest friend."

"Do you know, Lord Eure, that he married when in Switzerland?"

"I am pretty sure of it."

"And that he had a lawful heir by that marriage?"

"Yes; who is dead."

"Who is living."

"Living?"

"Living."

"Impossible!"

"It is a fact—proved, authenticated, confirmed, registered."

"Then that son will inherit the Clancharlie peerage?"

"He is not going to inherit it."

"Why?"

"Because he has inherited it. It is done."

"Done?"

"Turn your head, Lord Eure; he is sitting behind you, on the barons' benches."

Lord Eure turned, but Gwynplaine's face was concealed under his forest of hair.

"So," said the old man, who could see nothing but his hair, "he has already adopted the new fashion. He does not wear a wig."

Grantham accosted Colepepper.

"Some one is finely sold."

"Who is that?"

"David Dirry-Moir."

"How is that?"

"He is no longer a peer."

"How can that be?"

And Henry Auverquerque, Earl of Grantham, told John Baron Colepepper the whole anecdote—how the waif-flask had been carried to the Admiralty, about the parchment of the Comprachicos, the *jussu regis*, countersigned *Jeffreys*, and the confrontation in the torture-cell at Southwark, the proof of all the facts acknowledged by the Lord Chancellor and by the Queen; the taking the test under the nave, and finally the admission of Lord Fermain Clancharlie at the commencement of the sitting. Both the lords endeavoured to distinguish his face as he sat between Lord Fitzwalter and Lord Arundel, but with no better success than Lord Eure and Lord Annesley.

Gwynplaine, either by chance or by the arrangement of his sponsors, forewarned by the Lord Chancellor, was so placed in shadow as to escape their curiosity.

"Who is it? Where is he?"

Such was the exclamation of all the new-comers, but no one succeeded in making him out distinctly. Some, who had seen Gwynplaine in the Green Box, were exceedingly curious, but lost their labour: as it sometimes happens that a young lady is entrenched within a troop of dowagers, Gwynplaine was, as it were, enveloped in several layers of lords, old, infirm, and indifferent. Good livers, with the gout, are marvellously indifferent to stories about their neighbours.

There passed from hand to hand copies of a letter three lines in length, written, it was said, by the Duchess Josiana to the queen, her sister, in answer to the injunction made by her Majesty, that she should espouse the new peer, the lawful heir of the Clancharlies, Lord Fermain. This letter was couched in the following terms:—

"MADAM,—The arrangement will suit me just as well. I can have Lord David for my lover.—(Signed) JOSIANA."

This note, whether a true copy or a forgery, was received by all with the greatest enthusiasm. A young lord, Charles Okehampton, Baron Mohun, who belonged to the wigless faction, read and re-read it with delight. Lewis de Duras, Earl of Faversham, an Englishman with a Frenchman's wit, looked at Mohun and smiled.

"That is a woman I should like to marry!" exclaimed Lord Mohun.

The lords around them overheard the following dialogue between Duras and Mohun:—

"Marry the Duchess Josiana, Lord Mohun!"

"Why not?"

"Plague take it."

"She would make one very happy."

"She would make many very happy."

"But is it not always a question of many?"

"Lord Mohun, you are right. With regard to women, we have always the leavings of others. Has any one ever had a beginning?"

"Adam, perhaps."

"Not he."

"Then Satan."

"My dear lord," concluded Lewis de Duras, "Adam only lent his name. Poor dupe! He endorsed the human race. Man was begotten on the woman by the devil."

Hugh Cholmondeley, Earl of Cholmondeley, strong in points of law, was asked from the bishops' benches by Nathaniel Crew, who was doubly a peer, being a temporal peer, as Baron Crew, and a spiritual peer, as Bishop of Durham.

"Is it possible?" said Crew.

"Is it regular?" said Cholmondeley.

"The investiture of this peer was made outside the House," replied the bishop; "but it is stated that there are precedents for it."

"Yes. Lord Beauchamp, under Richard II.; Lord Chenay, under Elizabeth: and Lord Broghill, under Cromwell."

"Cromwell goes for nothing."

"What do you think of it all?"

"Many different things."

"My Lord Cholmondeley, what will be the rank of this young Lord Clancharlie in the House?"

"My Lord Bishop, the interruption of the Republic having displaced ancient rights of precedence, Clancharlie now ranks in the peerage between Barnard and Somers, so that should each be called upon to speak in turn, Lord Clancharlie would be the eighth in rotation."

"Really! he—a mountebank from a public show!"

"The act, *per se*, does not astonish me, my Lord Bishop. We meet with such things. Still more wonderful circumstances occur. Was not the War of the Roses predicted by the sudden drying up of the river Ouse, in Bedfordshire, on January 1st, 1399. Now, if a river dries up, a peer may, quite as naturally, fall into a servile condition. Ulysses, King of Ithaca, played all kinds of different parts. Fermain Clancharlie remained a lord under his player's garb. Sordid garments touch not the soul's nobility. But taking the test and the investiture outside the sitting, though strictly legal, might give rise to objections. I am of opinion that it will be necessary to look into the matter, to see if there be any ground to question the Lord Chancellor in Privy Council later on. We shall see in a week or two what is best to be done."

And the Bishop added,—

"All the same. It is an adventure such as has not occurred since Earl Gesbodus's time."

Gwynplaine, the Laughing Man; the Tadcaster Inn; the Green Box; "Chaos Vanquished;" Switzerland; Chillon; the Comprachicos; exile; mutilation; the Republic; Jeffreys; James II.; the *jussu regis;* the bottle opened at the Admiralty; the father, Lord Linnæus; the legitimate son, Lord Fermain; the bastard son, Lord David; the probable lawsuits; the Duchess Josiana; the Lord Chancellor; the Queen;—all these subjects of conversation ran from bench to bench.

Whispering is like a train of gunpowder.

They seized on every incident. All the details of the occurrence caused an immense murmur through the House. Gwynplaine, wandering in the depths of his reverie, heard the buzzing, without knowing that he was the cause of it. He was strangely attentive to the depths, not to the surface. Excess of attention becomes isolation.

The buzz of conversation in the House impedes its usual business no more than the dust raised by a troop impedes its march. The judges—who in the Upper House were mere assistants, without the privilege of speaking, except when questioned—had taken their places on the second woolsack; and the three Secretaries of State theirs on the third.

The heirs to peerages flowed into their compartment, at once without and within the House, at the back of the throne.

The peers in their minority were on their own benches. In 1705 the number of these little lords amounted to no less than a dozen—Huntingdon, Lincoln, Dorset, Warwick, Bath, Barlington, Derwentwater—destined to a tragical death—Longueville, Lonsdale, Dudley, Ward, and Carteret: a troop of brats made up of eight earls, two viscounts, and two barons.

In the centre, on the three stages of benches, each lord had taken his seat. Almost all the bishops were there. The dukes mustered strong, beginning with Charles Seymour, Duke of Somerset; and ending with George Augustus, Elector of Hanover, and Duke of Cambridge, junior in date of creation, and consequently junior in rank. All were in order, according to right of precedence: Cavendish, Duke of Devonshire, whose grandfather had sheltered Hobbes, at Hardwicke, when he was ninety-two; Lennox, Duke of Richmond; the three Fitzroys, the Duke of Southampton, the Duke of Grafton, and the Duke of Northumberland; Butler, Duke of Ormond; Somerset, Duke of Beaufort; Beauclerk, Duke of St. Albans; Paulet, Duke of Bolton; Osborne, Duke of Leeds; Wrottesley Russell, Duke of Bedford, whose motto and device was *Che sarà sarà*, which expresses a determination to take things as they come; Sheffield, Duke of Buckingham; Manners, Duke of Rutland; and others. Neither Howard, Duke of Norfolk, nor Talbot, Duke of Shrewsbury, was present, being Catholics; nor Churchill, Duke of Marlborough, the French Malbrouck, who was at that time fighting the French and beating them. There were no Scotch dukes then—Queensberry, Montrose, and Roxburgh not being admitted till 1707.

CHAPTER VI.

THE HIGH AND THE LOW

All at once a bright light broke upon the House. Four doorkeepers brought and placed on each side of the throne four high candelabra filled with wax-lights. The throne, thus illuminated, shone in a kind of purple light. It was empty but august. The presence of the queen herself could not have added much majesty to it.

The Usher of the Black Rod entered with his wand and announced,—

"The Lords Commissioners of her Majesty."

The hum of conversation immediately subsided.

A clerk, in a wig and gown, appeared at the great door, holding a cushion worked with *fleurs de lis*, on which lay parchment documents. These documents were bills. From each hung the *bille*, or *bulle*, by a silken string, from which laws are called bills in England and bulls at Rome. Behind the clerk walked three men in peers' robes, and wearing plumed hats.

These were the Royal Commissioners. The first was the Lord High Treasurer of England, Godolphin; the second, the Lord President of the Council, Pembroke; the third, the Lord of the Privy Seal, Newcastle.

They walked one by one, according to precedence, not of their rank, but of their commission—Godolphin first, Newcastle last, although a duke.

They reached the bench in front of the throne, to which they bowed, took off and replaced their hats, and sat down on the bench.

The Lord Chancellor turned towards the Usher of the Black Rod, and said,—

"Order the Commons to the bar of the House."

The Usher of the Black Rod retired.

The clerk, who was one of the clerks of the House of Lords, placed on the table, between the four woolsacks, the cushion on which lay the bills.

Then there came an interruption, which continued for some minutes.

Two doorkeepers placed before the bar a stool with three steps.

This stool was covered with crimson velvet, on which *fleurs de lis* were designed in gilt nails.

The great door, which had been closed, was reopened; and a voice announced,—

"The faithful Commons of England."

It was the Usher of the Black Rod announcing the other half of Parliament.

The lords put on their hats.

The members of the House of Commons entered, preceded by their Speaker, all with uncovered heads.

They stopped at the bar. They were in their ordinary garb; for the most part dressed in black, and wearing swords. The Speaker, the Right Honourable John Smith, an esquire, member for the borough of Andover, got up on the stool which was at the centre of the bar. The Speaker of the Commons wore a robe of black satin, with large hanging sleeves, embroidered before and behind with brandenburgs of gold, and a wig smaller than that of the Lord Chancellor. He was majestic, but inferior.

The Commons, both Speaker and members, stood waiting with uncovered heads, before the peers, who were seated, with their hats on.

Amongst the members of Commons might have been remarked the Chief Justice of Chester, Joseph Jekyll; the Queen's three Serjeants-at-Law—Hooper, Powys, and Parker; James Montagu, Solicitor-General; and the Attorney-General, Simon Harcourt. With the exception of a few baronets and knights, and nine lords by courtesy—Hartington, Windsor, Woodstock, Mordaunt, Granby, Scudamore, Fitzharding, Hyde, and Berkeley—sons of peers and heirs to peerages—all were of the people, a sort of gloomy and silent crowd.

When the noise made by the trampling of feet had ceased, the Crier of the Black Rod, standing by the door, exclaimed:—

"Oyez!"

The Clerk of the Crown arose. He took, unfolded, and read the first of the documents on the cushion. It was a message from the Queen, naming three commissioners to represent her in Parliament, with power to sanction the bills.

"To wit—"

Here the Clerk raised his voice.

"Sidney Earl Godolphin."

The Clerk bowed to Lord Godolphin. Lord Godolphin raised his hat.

The Clerk continued,—

"Thomas Herbert, Earl of Pembroke and Montgomery."

The Clerk bowed to Lord Pembroke. Lord Pembroke touched his hat.

The Clerk resumed,—

"John Holles, Duke of Newcastle."

The Duke of Newcastle nodded.

The Clerk of the Crown resumed his seat.

The Clerk of the Parliaments arose. His under-clerk, who had been on his knees behind him, got up also. Both turned their faces to the throne, and their backs to the Commons.

There were five bills on the cushion. These five bills, voted by the Commons and agreed to by the Lords, awaited the royal sanction.

The Clerk of the Parliaments read the first bill.

It was a bill passed by the Commons, charging the country with the costs of the improvements made by the Queen to her residence at Hampton Court, amounting to a million sterling.

The reading over, the Clerk bowed low to the throne. The under-clerk bowed lower still; then, half turning his head towards the Commons, he said,—

"The Queen accepts your bounty—*et ainsi le veut.*"

The Clerk read the second bill.

It was a law condemning to imprisonment and fine whosoever withdrew himself from the service of the trainbands. The trainbands were a militia, recruited from the middle and lower classes, serving gratis, which in Elizabeth's reign furnished, on the approach of the Armada, one hundred and eighty-five thousand foot-soldiers and forty thousand horse.

The two clerks made a fresh bow to the throne, after which the under-clerk, again half turning his face to the Commons, said,—

"*La Reine le veut.*"

The third bill was for increasing the tithes and prebends of the Bishopric of Lichfield and Coventry, which was one of the richest in England; for making an increased yearly allowance to the cathedral, for augmenting the number of its canons, and for increasing its deaneries and benefices, "to the benefit of our holy religion," as the preamble set forth. The fourth bill added to the budget fresh taxes—one on marbled paper; one on hackney coaches, fixed at the number of eight hundred in London, and taxed at a sum equal to fifty-two francs yearly each; one on barristers, attorneys, and solicitors, at forty-eight francs a year a head; one on tanned skins, notwithstanding, said the preamble, the complaints of the workers in leather; one on soap, notwithstanding the petitions of the City of Exeter and of the whole of Devonshire, where great quantities of cloth and serge were manufactured; one on wine at four shillings; one on flour; one on barley and hops; and one renewing for four years "the necessities of the State," said the preamble, "requiring to be attended to before the remonstrances of commerce"—tonnage-dues, varying from six francs per ton, for ships coming from the westward, to eighteen francs on those coming from the eastward. Finally, the bill, declaring the sums already levied for the current year insufficient, concluded by decreeing a poll-tax on each subject throughout the kingdom of four shillings per head, adding that a double tax would be levied on every one who did not take the fresh oath to Government. The fifth bill forbade the admission into the hospital of any sick person who on entering did not deposit a pound sterling to pay for his funeral, in case of death. These last three bills, like the first two, were one after the other sanctioned and made law by a bow to the throne, and the four words pronounced by the under-clerk, "*la Reine le veut*," spoken over his shoulder to the Commons. Then the under-clerk knelt down again before the fourth woolsack, and the Lord Chancellor said,—

"*Soit fait comme il est désiré.*"

This terminated the royal sitting. The Speaker, bent double before the Chancellor, descended from the stool, backwards, lifting up his robe behind him; the members of the House of Commons bowed to the ground, and as the Upper House resumed the business of the day, heedless of all these marks of respect, the Commons departed.

CHAPTER VII.

STORMS OF MEN ARE WORSE THAN STORMS OF OCEANS

The doors were closed again, the Usher of the Black Rod re-entered; the Lords Commissioners left the bench of State, took their places at the top of the dukes' benches, by right of their commission, and the Lord Chancellor addressed the House:—

"My Lords, the House having deliberated for several days on the Bill which proposes to augment by £100,000 sterling the annual provision for his Royal Highness the Prince, her Majesty's Consort, and the debate having been exhausted and closed, the House will proceed to vote; the votes will be taken according to custom, beginning with the puisne Baron. Each Lord, on his name being called, will rise and answer *content*, or *non-content*, and will be at liberty to explain the motives of his vote, if he thinks fit to do so.—Clerk, take the vote."

The Clerk of the House, standing up, opened a large folio, and spread it open on a gilded desk. This book was the list of the Peerage.

The puisne of the House of Lords at that time was John Hervey, created Baron and Peer in 1703, from whom is descended the Marquis of Bristol.

The clerk called,—

"My Lord John, Baron Hervey."

An old man in a fair wig rose, and said, "Content."

Then he sat down.

The Clerk registered his vote.

The Clerk continued,—

"My Lord Francis Seymour, Baron Conway, of Killultagh."

"Content," murmured, half rising, an elegant young man, with a face like a page, who little thought that he was to be ancestor to the Marquises of Hertford.

"My Lord John Leveson, Baron Gower," continued the Clerk.

This Baron, from whom were to spring the Dukes of Sutherland, rose, and, as he reseated himself, said "Content."

The Clerk went on.

"My Lord Heneage Finch, Baron Guernsey."

The ancestor of the Earls of Aylesford, neither older nor less elegant than the ancestor of the Marquises of Hertford, justified his device, *Aperto vivere voto*, by the proud tone in which he exclaimed, "Content."

Whilst he was resuming his seat, the Clerk called the fifth Baron,—

"My Lord John, Baron Granville."

Rising and resuming his seat quickly, "Content," exclaimed Lord Granville, of Potheridge, whose peerage was to become extinct in 1709.

The Clerk passed to the sixth.

"My Lord Charles Montague, Baron Halifax."

"Content," said Lord Halifax, the bearer of a title which had become extinct in the Saville family, and was destined to become extinct again in that of Montague. Montague is distinct from Montagu and Montacute. And Lord Halifax added, "Prince George has an allowance as Her Majesty's Consort; he has another as Prince of Denmark; another as Duke of Cumberland; another as Lord High Admiral of England and Ireland; but he has not one as Commander-in-Chief. This is an injustice and a wrong which must be set right, in the interest of the English people."

Then Lord Halifax passed a eulogium on the Christian religion, abused popery, and voted the subsidy.

Lord Halifax sat down, and the Clerk resumed,—

"My Lord Christopher, Baron Barnard."

Lord Barnard, from whom were to descend the Dukes of Cleveland, rose to answer to his name.

"Content."

He took some time in reseating himself, for he wore a lace band which was worth showing. For all that, Lord Barnard was a worthy gentleman and a brave officer.

While Lord Barnard was resuming his seat, the Clerk, who read by routine, hesitated for an instant; he readjusted his spectacles, and leaned over the register with renewed attention; then, lifting up his head, he said,—

"My Lord Fermain Clancharlie, Baron Clancharlie and Hunkerville."

Gwynplaine arose.

"Non-content," said he.

Every face was turned towards him. Gwynplaine remained standing. The branches of candles, placed on each side of the throne, lighted up his features, and marked them against the darkness of the august chamber in the relief with which a mask might show against a background of smoke.

Gwynplaine had made that effort over himself which, it may be remembered, was possible to him in extremity. By a concentration of will equal to that which would be needed to cow a tiger, he had succeeded in obliterating for a moment the fatal grin upon his face. For an instant he no longer laughed. This effort could not last long. Rebellion against that which is our law or our fatality must be short-lived; at times the waters of the sea resist the power of gravitation, swell into a waterspout and become a mountain, but only on the condition of falling back again.

Such a struggle was Gwynplaine's. For an instant, which he felt to be a solemn one, by a prodigious intensity of will, but for not much longer than a flash of lightning lasts, he had thrown over his brow the dark veil of his soul—he held in suspense his incurable laugh. From that face upon which it had been carved he had withdrawn the joy. Now it was nothing but terrible.

"Who is this man?" exclaimed all.

That forest of hair, those dark hollows under the brows, the deep gaze of eyes which they could not see, that head, on the wild outlines of which light and darkness mingled weirdly, were a wonder indeed. It was beyond all understanding; much as they had heard of him, the sight of Gwynplaine was a terror. Even those who expected much found their expectations surpassed. It was as though on the mountain reserved for the gods, during the banquet on a serene evening, the whole of the all-powerful body being gathered together, the face of Prometheus, mangled by the vulture's beak, should have suddenly appeared before them, like a blood-coloured moon on the horizon. Olympus looking on Caucasus! What a vision! Old and young, open-mouthed with surprise, fixed their eyes upon Gwynplaine.

An old man, respected by the whole House, who had seen many men and many things, and who was intended for a dukedom—Thomas, Earl of Wharton—rose in terror.

"What does all this mean?" he cried. "Who has brought this man into the House? Let him be put out."

And addressing Gwynplaine haughtily,—

"Who are you? Whence do you come?"

Gwynplaine answered,—

"Out of the depths."

And folding his arms, he looked at the lords.

"Who am I? I am wretchedness. My lords, I have a word to say to you."

A shudder ran through the House. Then all was silence. Gwynplaine continued,—

"My lords, you are highly placed. It is well. We must believe that God has His reasons that it should be so. You have power, opulence, pleasure, the sun ever shining in your zenith; authority unbounded, enjoyment without a sting, and a total forgetfulness of others. So be it. But there is something below you—above you, it may be. My lords, I bring you news—news of the existence of mankind."

Assemblies are like children. A strange occurrence is as a Jack-in-the-Box to them. It frightens them; but they like it. It is as if a spring were touched and a devil jumps up. Mirabeau, who was also deformed, was a case in point in France.

Gwynplaine felt within himself, at that moment, a strange elevation. In addressing a body of men, one's foot seems to rest on them; to rest, as it were, on a pinnacle of souls—on human hearts, that quiver under one's heel. Gwynplaine was no longer the man who had been, only the night before, almost mean. The fumes of the sudden elevation which had disturbed him had cleared off and become transparent, and in the state in which Gwynplaine had been seduced by a vanity he now saw but a duty. That which had at first lessened now elevated him. He was illuminated by one of those great flashes which emanate from duty.

All round Gwynplaine arose cries of "Hear, hear!"

Meanwhile, rigid and superhuman, he succeeded in maintaining on his features that severe and sad contraction under which the laugh was fretting like a wild horse struggling to escape.

He resumed,—

"I am he who cometh out of the depths. My lords, you are great and rich. There lies your danger. You profit by the night; but beware! The dawn is all-powerful. You cannot prevail over it. It is coming. Nay! it is come. Within it is the day-spring of irresistible light. And who shall hinder that sling from hurling the sun into the sky? The sun I speak of is Right. You are Privilege. Tremble! The real master of the house is about to knock at the door. What is the father of Privilege? Chance. What is his son? Abuse. Neither Chance nor Abuse are abiding. For both a dark morrow is at hand. I am come to warn you. I am come to impeach your happiness. It is fashioned out of the misery of your neighbour. You have everything, and that everything is composed of the nothing of others. My lords, I am an advocate without hope, pleading a cause that is lost; but that cause God will gain on appeal. As for me, I am but a voice. Mankind is a mouth, of which I am the cry. You shall hear me! I am about to open before you, peers of England, the great assize of the people; of that sovereign who is the subject; of that criminal who is the judge. I am weighed down under the load of all that I have to say. Where am I to begin? I know not. I have gathered together, in the vast diffusion of suffering, my innumerable and scattered pleas. What am I to do with them now? They overwhelm me, and I must cast them to you in a confused mass. Did I foresee this? No. You are astonished. So am I. Yesterday I was a mountebank; to-day I am a peer. Deep play. Of whom? Of the Unknown. Let us all tremble. My lords, all the blue sky is for you. Of this immense universe you see but the sunshine. Believe me, it has its shadows. Amongst you I am called Lord Fermain Clancharlie; but my true name is one of poverty—Gwynplaine. I am a wretched thing carved out of the stuff of which the great are made, for such was the pleasure of a king. That is my history. Many amongst you knew my father. I knew him not. His connection with you was his feudal descent; his outlawry is the bond between him and me. What God willed was well. I was cast into the abyss. For what end? To search its depths. I am a diver, and I have brought back the pearl, truth. I speak, because I know. You shall hear me, my lords. I have seen, I have felt! Suffering is not a mere word, ye happy ones! Poverty I grew up in; winter has frozen me; hunger I have tasted; contempt I have suffered; pestilence I have undergone; shame I have drunk of. And I will vomit all these up before you, and this ejection of all misery shall sully your feet and flame about them. I hesitated before I allowed myself to be brought to the place where I now stand, because I have duties to others elsewhere, and my heart is not here. What passed within me has nothing to do with you. When the man whom you call Usher of the Black Rod came to seek me by order of the woman whom you call the Queen, the idea struck me for a moment that I would refuse to come. But it seemed to me that the hidden hand of God pressed me to the spot, and I obeyed. I felt that I must come amongst you. Why? Because of my rags of yesterday. It is to raise my voice among those who have eaten their fill that God mixed me up with the famished. Oh, have pity! Of this fatal world to which you believe yourselves to belong you know nothing. Placed so high, you are out of it. But I will tell you what it is. I have had experience enough. I come from beneath the pressure of your feet. I can tell you your weight. Oh, you who are masters, do you know what you are? do you see what you are doing? No. Oh, it is dreadful! One night, one night of storm, a little deserted child, an orphan alone in the immeasurable creation, I made my entrance into that darkness which you call society. The first thing that I saw was the law, under the form of a gibbet; the second was riches, your riches, under the form of a woman dead of cold and hunger; the third, the future, under the form of a child left to die; the fourth, goodness, truth, and justice, under the figure of a vagabond, whose sole friend and companion was a wolf."

Just then Gwynplaine, stricken by a sudden emotion, felt the sobs rising in his throat, causing him, most unfortunately, to burst into an uncontrollable fit of laughter.

The contagion was immediate. A cloud had hung over the assembly. It might have broken into terror; it broke into delight. Mad merriment seized the whole House. Nothing pleases the great chambers of sovereign man so much as buffoonery. It is their revenge upon their graver moments.

The laughter of kings is like the laughter of the gods. There is always a cruel point in it. The lords set to play. Sneers gave sting to their laughter. They clapped their hands around the speaker, and insulted him. A volley of merry exclamations assailed him like bright but wounding hailstones.

"Bravo, Gwynplaine!"—"Bravo, Laughing Man!"—"Bravo, Snout of the Green Box!"—"Mask of Tarrinzeau Field!"—"You are going to give us a performance."—"That's right; talk away!"—"There's a funny fellow!"—"How the beast does laugh, to be sure!"—"Good-day, pantaloon!"—"How d'ye do, my lord clown!"—"Go on with your speech!"—"That fellow a peer of England?"—"Go on!"—"No, no!"—"Yes, yes!"

The Lord Chancellor was much disturbed.

A deaf peer, James Butler, Duke of Ormond, placing his hand to his ear like an ear trumpet, asked Charles Beauclerk, Duke of St. Albans,—

"How has he voted?"

"Non-content."

"By heavens!" said Ormond, "I can understand it, with such a face as his."

Do you think that you can ever recapture a crowd once it has escaped your grasp? And all assemblies are crowds alike. No, eloquence is a bit; and if the bit breaks, the audience runs away, and rushes on till it has thrown the orator. Hearers naturally dislike the speaker, which is a fact not as clearly understood as it ought to be. Instinctively he pulls the reins, but that is a useless expedient. However, all orators try it, as Gwynplaine did.

He looked for a moment at those men who were laughing at him. Then he cried,—

"So, you insult misery! Silence, Peers of England! Judges, listen to my pleading! Oh, I conjure you, have pity. Pity for whom? Pity for yourselves. Who is in danger? Yourselves! Do you not see that you are in a balance, and that there is in one scale your power, and in the other your responsibility? It is God who is weighing you. Oh, do not laugh. Think. The trembling of your consciences is the oscillation of the balance in which God is weighing your actions. You are not wicked; you are like other men, neither better nor worse. You believe yourselves to be gods; but be ill to-morrow, and see your divinity shivering in fever! We are worth one as much as the other. I address myself to honest men; there are such here. I address myself to lofty intellects; there are such here. I address myself to generous souls; there are such here. You are fathers, sons, and brothers; therefore you are often touched. He amongst you who has this morning watched the awaking of his little child is a good man. Hearts are all alike. Humanity is nothing but a heart. Between those who oppress and those who are oppressed there is but a difference of place. Your feet tread on the heads of men. The fault is not yours; it is that of the social Babel. The building is faulty, and out of the perpendicular.

One floor bears down the other. Listen, and I will tell you what to do. Oh! as you are powerful, be brotherly; as you are great, be tender. If you only knew what I have seen! Alas, what gloom is there beneath! The people are in a dungeon. How many are condemned who are innocent! No daylight, no air, no virtue! They are without hope, and yet—there is the danger—they expect something. Realize all this misery. There are beings who live in death. There are little girls who at twelve begin by prostitution, and who end in old age at twenty. As to the severities of the criminal code, they are fearful. I speak somewhat at random, and do not pick my words. I say everything that comes into my head. No later than yesterday I who stand here saw a man lying in chains, naked, with stones piled on his chest, expire in torture. Do you know of these things? No. If you knew what goes on, you would not dare to be happy. Who of you have been to Newcastle-upon-Tyne? There, in the mines, are men who chew coals to fill their stomachs and deceive hunger. Look here! in Lancashire, Ribblechester has sunk, by poverty, from a town to a village. I do not see that Prince George of Denmark requires a hundred thousand pounds extra. I should prefer receiving a poor sick man into the hospital, without compelling him to pay his funeral expenses in advance. In Carnarvon, and at Strathmore, as well as at Strathbickan, the exhaustion of the poor is horrible. At Stratford they cannot drain the marsh for want of money. The manufactories are shut up all over Lancashire. There is forced idleness everywhere. Do you know that the herring fishers at Harlech eat grass when the fishery fails? Do you know that at Burton-Lazars there are still lepers confined, on whom they fire if they leave their tan houses! At Ailesbury, a town of which one of you is lord, destitution is chronic. At Penkridge, in Coventry, where you have just endowed a cathedral and enriched a bishop, there are no beds in the cabins, and they dig holes in the earth in which to put the little children to lie, so that instead of beginning life in the cradle, they begin it in the grave. I have seen these things! My lords, do you know who pays the taxes you vote? The dying! Alas! you deceive yourselves. You are going the wrong road. You augment the poverty of the poor to increase the riches of the rich. You should do the reverse. What! take from the worker to give to the idle, take from the tattered to give to the well-clad; take from the beggar to give to the prince! Oh yes! I have old republican blood in my veins. I have a horror of these things. How I execrate kings! And how shameless are the women! I have been told a sad story. How I hate Charles II.! A woman whom my father loved gave herself to that king whilst my father was dying in exile. The prostitute! Charles II., James II.! After a scamp, a scoundrel. What is there in a king? A man, feeble and contemptible, subject to wants and infirmities. Of what good is a king? You cultivate that parasite royalty; you make a serpent of that worm, a dragon of that insect. O pity the poor! You increase the weight of the taxes for the profit of the throne. Look to the laws which you decree. Take heed of the suffering swarms which you crush. Cast your eyes down. Look at what is at your feet. O ye great, there are the little. Have pity! yes, have pity on yourselves; for the people is in its agony, and when the lower part of the trunk dies, the higher parts die too. Death spares no limb. When night comes no one can keep his corner of daylight. Are you selfish? then save others. The destruction of the vessel cannot be a matter of indifference to any passenger.

There can be no wreck for some that is not wreck for all. O believe it, the abyss yawns for all!"

The laughter increased, and became irresistible. For that matter, such extravagance as there was in his words was sufficient to amuse any assembly. To be comic without and tragic within, what suffering can be more humiliating? what pain deeper? Gwynplaine felt it. His words were an appeal in one direction, his face in the other. What a terrible position was his!

Suddenly his voice rang out in strident bursts.

"How gay these men are! Be it so. Here is irony face to face with agony; a sneer mocking the death-rattle. They are all-powerful. Perhaps so; be it so. We shall see. Behold! I am one of them; but I am also one of you, O ye poor! A king sold me. A poor man sheltered me. Who mutilated me? A prince. Who healed and nourished me? A pauper. I am Lord Clancharlie; but I am still Gwynplaine. I take my place amongst the great; but I belong to the mean. I am amongst those who rejoice; but I am with those who suffer. Oh, this system of society is false! Some day will come that which is true. Then there will be no more lords, and there shall be free and living men. There will be no more masters; there will be fathers. Such is the future. No more prostration; no more baseness; no more ignorance; no more human beasts of burden; no more courtiers; no more toadies; no more kings; but Light! In the meantime, see me here. I have a right, and I will use it. Is it a right? No, if I use it for myself; yes, if I use it for all. I will speak to you, my lords, being one of you. O my brothers below, I will tell them of your nakedness. I will rise up with a bundle of the people's rags in my hand. I will shake off over the masters the misery of the slaves; and these favoured and arrogant ones shall no longer be able to escape the remembrance of the wretched, nor the princes the itch of the poor; and so much the worse, if it be the bite of vermin; and so much the better, if it awake the lions from their slumber."

Here Gwynplaine turned towards the kneeling under-clerks, who were writing on the fourth woolsack.

"Who are those fellows kneeling down?—What are you doing? Get up; you are men."

These words, suddenly addressed to inferiors whom a lord ought not even to perceive, increased the merriment to the utmost.

They had cried, "Bravo!" Now they shouted, "Hurrah!" From clapping their hands they proceeded to stamping their feet. One might have been back in the Green Box, only that there the laughter applauded Gwynplaine; here it exterminated him. The effort of ridicule is to kill. Men's laughter sometimes exerts all its power to murder.

The laughter proceeded to action. Sneering words rained down upon him. Humour is the folly of assemblies. Their ingenious and foolish ridicule shuns facts instead of studying them, and condemns questions instead of solving them. Any extraordinary occurrence is a point of interrogation; to laugh at it is like laughing at an enigma. But the Sphynx, which never laughs, is behind it.

Contradictory shouts arose,—

"Enough! enough!" "Encore! encore!"

William Farmer, Baron Leimpster, flung at Gwynplaine the insult cast by Ryc Quiney at Shakespeare,—

"Histrio, mima!"

Lord Vaughan, a sententious man, twenty-ninth on the barons' bench, exclaimed,—

"We must be back in the days when animals had the gift of speech. In the midst of human tongues the jaw of a beast has spoken."

"Listen to Balaam's ass," added Lord Yarmouth.

Lord Yarmouth presented that appearance of sagacity produced by a round nose and a crooked mouth.

"The rebel Linnæus is chastised in his tomb. The son is the punishment of the father," said John Hough, Bishop of Lichfield and Coventry, whose prebendary Gwynplaine's attack had glanced.

"He lies!" said Lord Cholmondeley, the legislator so well read up in the law. "That which he calls torture is only the *peine forte et dure*, and a very good thing, too. Torture is not practised in England."

Thomas Wentworth, Baron Raby, addressed the Chancellor.

"My Lord Chancellor, adjourn the House."

"No, no. Let him go on. He is amusing. Hurrah! hip! hip! hip!"

Thus shouted the young lords, their fun amounting to fury. Four of them especially were in the full exasperation of hilarity and hate. These were Laurence Hyde, Earl of Rochester; Thomas Tufton, Earl of Thanet; Viscount Hatton; and the Duke of Montagu.

"To your tricks, Gwynplaine!" cried Rochester.

"Put him out, put him out!" shouted Thanet.

Viscount Hatton drew from his pocket a penny, which he flung to Gwynplaine.

And John Campbell, Earl of Greenwich; Savage, Earl Rivers; Thompson, Baron Haversham; Warrington, Escrick Rolleston, Rockingham, Carteret, Langdale, Barcester, Maynard, Hunsdon, Cäernarvon, Cavendish, Burlington, Robert Darcy, Earl of Holderness, Other Windsor, Earl of Plymouth, applauded.

There was a tumult as of pandemonium or of pantheon, in which the words of Gwynplaine were lost.

Amidst it all, there was heard but one word of Gwynplaine's: "Beware!"

Ralph, Duke of Montagu, recently down from Oxford, and still a beardless youth, descended from the bench of dukes, where he sat the nineteenth in order, and placed himself in front of Gwynplaine, with his arms folded. In a sword there is a spot which cuts sharpest, and in a voice an accent which insults most keenly. Montagu spoke with that accent, and sneering with his face close to that of Gwynplaine, shouted,—"What are you talking about?"

"I am prophesying," said Gwynplaine.

The laughter exploded anew; and below this laughter, anger growled its continued bass. One of the minors, Lionel Cranfield Sackville, Earl of Dorset and Middlesex, stood upon his seat, not smiling, but grave as became a future legislator, and, without saying a word, looked at Gwynplaine with his fresh twelve-year old face, and shrugged his shoulders. Whereat the Bishop of St. Asaph's whispered in the ear of the Bishop of St. David's, who was sitting beside him, as he pointed to Gwynplaine, "There is the fool;" then pointing to the child, "there is the sage."

A chaos of complaint rose from amidst the confusion of exclamations:—

"Gorgon's face!"—"What does it all mean?"—"An insult to the House!"—"The fellow ought to be put out!"—"What a madman!"—"Shame! shame!"—"Adjourn the House!"—"No; let him finish his speech!"—"Talk away, you buffoon!"

Lord Lewis of Duras, with his arms akimbo, shouted,—

"Ah! it does one good to laugh. My spleen is cured. I propose a vote of thanks in these terms: 'The House of Lords returns thanks to the Green Box.'"

Gwynplaine, it may be remembered, had dreamt of a different welcome.

A man who, climbing up a steep and crumbling acclivity of sand above a giddy precipice, has felt it giving way under his hands, his nails, his elbows, his knees, his feet; who—losing instead of gaining on his treacherous way, a prey to every terror of the danger, slipping back instead of ascending, increasing the certainty of his fall by his very efforts to gain the summit, and losing ground in every struggle for safety—has felt the abyss approaching nearer and nearer, until the certainty of his coming fall into the yawning jaws open to receive him, has frozen the marrow of his bones;—that man has experienced the sensations of Gwynplaine.

He felt the ground he had ascended crumbling under him, and his audience was the precipice.

There is always some one to say the word which sums all up.

Lord Scarsdale translated the impression of the assembly in one exclamation,—

"What is the monster doing here?"

Gwynplaine stood up, dismayed and indignant, in a sort of final convulsion. He looked at them all fixedly.

"What am I doing here? I have come to be a terror to you! I am a monster, do you say? No! I am the people! I am an exception? No! I am the rule; you are the exception! You are the chimera; I am the reality! I am the frightful man who laughs! Who laughs at what? At you, at himself, at everything! What is his laugh? Your crime and his torment! That crime he flings at your head! That punishment he spits in your face! I laugh, and that means I weep!"

He paused. There was less noise. The laughter continued, but it was more subdued. He may have fancied that he had regained a certain amount of attention. He breathed again, and resumed,—

"This laugh which is on my face a king placed there. This laugh expresses the desolation of mankind. This laugh means hate, enforced silence, rage, despair. This laugh is the production of torture. This laugh is a forced laugh. If Satan were marked with this laugh, it would convict God. But the Eternal is not like them that perish. Being absolute, he is just; and God hates the acts of kings. Oh! you take me for an exception; but I am a symbol. Oh, all-powerful men, fools that you are! open your eyes. I am the incarnation of All. I represent humanity, such as its masters have made it. Mankind is mutilated. That which has been done to me has been done to it. In it have been deformed right, justice, truth, reason, intelligence, as eyes, nostrils, and ears have been deformed in me; its heart has been made a sink of passion and pain, like mine, and, like mine, its features have been hidden in a mask of joy. Where God had placed his finger, the king set his sign-manual. Monstrous superposition! Bishops, peers, and princes, the people is a sea of suffering, smiling on the surface. My lords, I tell you that the people are as I am.

To-day you oppress them; to-day you hoot at me. But the future is the ominous thaw, in which that which was as stone shall become wave. The appearance of solidity melts into liquid. A crack in the ice, and all is over. There will come an hour when convulsion shall break down your oppression; when an angry roar will reply to your jeers. Nay, that hour did come! Thou wert of it, O my father! That hour of God did come, and was called the Republic! It was destroyed, but it will return. Meanwhile, remember that the line of kings armed with the sword was broken by Cromwell, armed with the axe. Tremble! Incorruptible solutions are at hand: the talons which were cut are growing again; the tongues which were torn out are floating away, they are turning to tongues of fire, and, scattered by the breath of darkness, are shouting through infinity; those who hunger are showing their idle teeth; false heavens, built over real hells, are tottering. The people are suffering—they are suffering; and that which is on high totters, and that which is below yawns. Darkness demands its change to light; the damned discuss the elect. Behold! it is the coming of the people, the ascent of mankind, the beginning of the end, the red dawn of the catastrophe! Yes, all these things are in this laugh of mine, at which you laugh to-day! London is one perpetual fête. Be it so. From one end to the other, England rings with acclamation. Well! but listen. All that you see is I. You have your fêtes—they are my laugh; you have your public rejoicings—they are my laugh; you have your weddings, consecrations, and coronations—they are my laugh. The births of your princes are my laugh. But above you is the thunderbolt—it is my laugh."

How could they stand such nonsense? The laughter burst out afresh; and now it was overwhelming. Of all the lava which that crater, the human mouth, ejects, the most corrosive is joy. To inflict evil gaily is a contagion which no crowd can resist. All executions do not take place on the scaffold; and men, from the moment they are in a body, whether in mobs or in senates, have always a ready executioner amongst them, called sarcasm. There is no torture to be compared to that of the wretch condemned to execution by ridicule. This was Gwynplaine's fate. He was stoned with their jokes, and riddled by the scoffs shot at him. He stood there a mark for all. They sprang up; they cried, "Encore;" they shook with laughter; they stamped their feet; they pulled each other's bands. The majesty of the place, the purple of the robes, the chaste ermine, the dignity of the wigs, had no effect. The lords laughed, the bishops laughed, the judges laughed, the old men's benches derided, the children's benches were in convulsions. The Archbishop of Canterbury nudged the Archbishop of York; Henry Compton, Bishop of London, brother of Lord Northampton, held his sides; the Lord Chancellor bent down his head, probably to conceal his inclination to laugh; and, at the bar, that statue of respect, the Usher of the Black Rod, was laughing also.

Gwynplaine, become pallid, had folded his arms; and, surrounded by all those faces, young and old, in which had burst forth this grand Homeric jubilee; in that whirlwind of clapping hands, of stamping feet, and of hurrahs; in that mad buffoonery, of which he was the centre; in that splendid overflow of hilarity; in the midst of that unmeasured gaiety, he felt that the sepulchre was within him. All was over. He could no longer master the face which betrayed nor the audience which insulted him.

That eternal and fatal law by which the grotesque is linked with the sublime—by which the laugh re-echoes the groan, parody rides behind despair, and seeming is opposed to being—had never found more terrible expression. Never had a light more sinister illumined the depths of human darkness.

Gwynplaine was assisting at the final destruction of his destiny by a burst of laughter. The irremediable was in this. Having fallen, we can raise ourselves up; but, being pulverized, never. And the insult of their sovereign mockery had reduced him to dust. From thenceforth nothing was possible. Everything is in accordance with the scene. That which was triumph in the Green Box was disgrace and catastrophe in the House of Lords. What was applause there, was insult here. He felt something like the reverse side of his mask. On one side of that mask he had the sympathy of the people, who welcomed Gwynplaine; on the other, the contempt of the great, rejecting Lord Fermain Clancharlie. On one side, attraction; on the other, repulsion; both leading him towards the shadows. He felt himself, as it were, struck from behind. Fate strikes treacherous blows. Everything will be explained hereafter, but, in the meantime, destiny is a snare, and man sinks into its pitfalls. He had expected to rise, and was welcomed by laughter. Such apotheoses have lugubrious terminations. There is a dreary expression—to be sobered; tragical wisdom born of drunkenness! In the midst of that tempest of gaiety commingled with ferocity, Gwynplaine fell into a reverie.

An assembly in mad merriment drifts as chance directs, and loses its compass when it gives itself to laughter. None knew whither they were tending, or what they were doing. The House was obliged to rise, adjourned by the Lord Chancellor, "owing to extraordinary circumstances," to the next day. The peers broke up. They bowed to the royal throne and departed. Echoes of prolonged laughter were heard losing themselves in the corridors.

Assemblies, besides their official doors, have—under tapestry, under projections, and under arches—all sorts of hidden doors, by which the members escape like water through the cracks in a vase. In a short time the chamber was deserted. This takes place quickly and almost imperceptibly, and those places, so lately full of voices, are suddenly given back to silence.

Reverie carries one far; and one comes by long dreaming to reach, as it were, another planet.

Gwynplaine suddenly awoke from such a dream. He was alone. The chamber was empty. He had not even observed that the House had been adjourned. All the peers had departed, even his sponsors. There only remained here and there some of the lower officers of the House, waiting for his lordship to depart before they put the covers on and extinguished the lights.

Mechanically he placed his hat on his head, and, leaving his place, directed his steps to the great door opening into the gallery. As he was passing through the opening in the bar, a doorkeeper relieved him of his peer's robes. This he scarcely felt. In another instant he was in the gallery.

The officials who remained observed with astonishment that the peer had gone out without bowing to the throne!

CHAPTER VIII.

HE WOULD BE A GOOD BROTHER, WERE HE NOT A GOOD SON

There was no one in the gallery.

Gwynplaine crossed the circular space, from whence they had removed the arm-chair and the tables, and where there now remained no trace of his investiture. Candelabra and lustres, placed at certain intervals, marked the way out. Thanks to this string of light, he retraced without difficulty, through the suite of saloons and galleries, the way which he had followed on his arrival with the King-at-Arms and the Usher of the Black Rod. He saw no one, except here and there some old lord with tardy steps, plodding along heavily in front of him.

Suddenly, in the silence of those great deserted rooms, bursts of indistinct exclamations reached him, a sort of nocturnal clatter unusual in such a place. He directed his steps to the place whence this noise proceeded, and found himself in a spacious hall, dimly lighted, which was one of the exits from the House of Lords. He saw a great glass door open, a flight of steps, footmen and links, a square outside, and a few coaches waiting at the bottom of the steps.

This was the spot from which the noise which he had heard had proceeded.

Within the door, and under the hall lamp, was a noisy group in a storm of gestures and of voices.

Gwynplaine approached in the gloom.

They were quarrelling. On one side there were ten or twelve young lords, who wanted to go out; on the other, a man, with his hat on, like themselves, upright and with a haughty brow, who barred their passage.

Who was this man? Tom-Jim-Jack.

Some of these lords were still in their robes, others had thrown them off, and were in their usual attire. Tom-Jim-Jack wore a hat with plumes—not white, like the peers; but green tipped with orange. He was embroidered and laced from head to foot, had flowing bows of ribbon and lace round his wrists and neck, and was feverishly fingering with his left hand the hilt of the sword which hung from his waistbelt, and on the billets and scabbard of which were embroidered an admiral's anchors.

It was he who was speaking and addressing the young lords; and Gwynplaine overheard the following:—

"I have told you you are cowards. You wish me to withdraw my words. Be it so. You are not cowards; you are idiots. You all combined against one man. That was not cowardice. All right. Then it was stupidity. He spoke to you, and you did not understand him. Here, the old are hard of hearing, the young devoid of intelligence. I am one of your own order to quite sufficient extent to tell you the truth. This new-comer is strange, and he has uttered a heap of nonsense, I admit; but amidst all that nonsense there were some things which were true. His speech was confused, undigested, ill-delivered. Be it so. He repeated, 'You know, you know,' too often; but a man who was but yesterday a clown at a fair cannot be expected to speak like Aristotle or like Doctor Gilbert Burnet, Bishop of Salisbury. The vermin, the lions, the address to the under-clerks—all that was in bad taste. Zounds! who says it wasn't? It was a senseless and fragmentary and topsy-turvy harangue; but here and there came out facts which were true. It is no small thing to speak even as he did, seeing it is not his trade. I should like to see you do it. Yes, you! What he said about the lepers at Burton Lazars is an undeniable fact. Besides, he is not the first man who has talked nonsense. In fine, my lords, I do not like to see many set upon one. Such is my humour; and I ask your lordships' permission to take offence. You have displeased me; I am angry. I am grateful to God for having drawn up from the depth of his low existence this peer of England, and for having given back his inheritance to the heir; and, without heeding whether it will or will not affect my own affairs, I consider it a beautiful sight to see an insect transformed into an eagle, and Gwynplaine into Lord Clancharlie. My lords, I forbid you holding any opinion but mine. I regret that Lord Lewis Duras should not be here. I should like to insult him. My lords, it is Fermain Clancharlie who has been the peer, and you who have been the mountebanks. As to his laugh, it is not his fault. You have laughed at that laugh; men should not laugh at misfortune. If you think that people cannot laugh at you as well, you are very much mistaken. You are ugly. You are badly dressed. My Lord Haversham, I saw your mistress the other day; she is hideous—a duchess, but a monkey. Gentlemen who laugh, I repeat that I should like to hear you try to say four words running! Many men jabber; very few speak. You imagine you know something, because you have kept idle terms at Oxford or Cambridge, and because, before being peers of England on the benches of Westminster, you have been asses on the benches at Gonville and Caius. Here I am; and I choose to stare you in the face. You have just been impudent to this new peer. A monster, certainly; but a monster given up to beasts. I had rather be that man than you. I was present at the sitting, in my place as a possible heir to a peerage. I heard all. I have not the right to speak; but I have the right to be a gentleman. Your jeering airs annoyed me. When I am angry I would go up to Mount Pendlehill, and pick the cloudberry which brings the thunderbolt down on the gatherer. That is the reason why I have waited for you at the door. We must have a few words, for we have arrangements to make. Did it strike you that you failed a little in respect towards myself? My lords, I entertain a firm determination to kill a few of you. All you who are here—Thomas Tufton, Earl of Thanet; Savage, Earl Rivers; Charles Spencer, Earl of Sunderland; Laurence Hyde, Earl of Rochester; you Barons, Gray of Rolleston, Cary Hunsdon, Escrick, Rockingham, little Carteret; Robert Darcy, Earl of Holderness; William, Viscount Hutton; and Ralph, Duke of Montagu; and any who choose—I, David Dirry-Moir, an officer of the fleet, summon, call, and command you to provide yourselves, in all haste, with seconds and umpires, and I will meet you face to face and hand to hand, to-night, at once, to-morrow, by day or night, by sunlight or by candlelight, where, when, or how you please, so long as there is two sword-lengths' space; and you will do well to look to the flints of your pistols and the edges of your rapiers, for it is my firm intention to cause vacancies in your peerages.—Ogle Cavendish, take your measures, and think of your motto, *Cavendo tutus*.—Marmaduke Langdale, you will do well, like your ancestor, Grindold, to order a coffin to be brought with you.—George Booth, Earl of Warrington, you will never again see the County Palatine of Chester, or your labyrinth like that of Crete, or the high towers of Dunham Massy!—As to Lord Vaughan, he is young enough to talk impertinently, and too old to answer for it. I shall demand satisfaction for his words of his nephew Richard Vaughan, Member of Parliament for the Borough of Merioneth.—As for you, John Campbell, Earl of Greenwich, I will kill you as Achon killed Matas; but with a fair cut, and not from behind, it being my custom to present my heart and not my back to the point of the sword.—I have spoken my mind, my lords. And so use witchcraft if you like. Consult the fortune-tellers. Grease your skins with ointments and drugs to make them invulnerable; hang round your necks charms of the devil or the Virgin. I will fight you blest or curst, and I will not have you searched to see if you are wearing any wizard's tokens. On foot or on horseback, on the highroad if you wish it, in Piccadilly, or at Charing Cross; and they shall take up the pavement for our meeting, as they unpaved the court of the Louvre for the duel between Guise and Bassompierre. All of you! Do you hear? I mean to fight you all.—Dorme, Earl of Caernarvon, I will make you swallow my sword up to the hilt, as Marolles did to Lisle Mariveaux, and then we shall see, my lord, whether you will laugh or not.—You, Burlington, who look like a girl of seventeen—you shall choose between the lawn of your house in Middlesex, and your beautiful garden at Londesborough in Yorkshire, to be buried in.—I beg to inform your lordships that it does not suit me to allow your insolence in my presence. I will chastise you, my lords. I take it ill that you should have ridiculed Lord Fermain Clancharlie. He is worth more than you. As Clancharlie, he has nobility, which you have; as Gwynplaine, he has intellect, which you have not. I make his cause my cause, insult to him insult to me, and your ridicule my wrath. We shall see who will come out of this affair alive, because I challenge you to the death. Do you understand? With any arm, in any fashion, and you shall choose the death that pleases you best; and since you are clowns as well as gentlemen, I proportion my defiance to your qualities, and I give you your choice of any way in which a man can be killed, from the sword of the prince to the fist of the blackguard."

To this furious onslaught of words the whole group of young noblemen answered by a smile. "Agreed," they said.

"I choose pistols," said Burlington.

"I," said Escrick, "the ancient combat of the lists, with the mace and the dagger."

"I," said Holderness, "the duel with two knives, long and short, stripped to the waist, and breast to breast."

"Lord David," said the Earl of Thanet, "you are a Scot. I choose the claymore."

"I the sword," said Rockingham.

"I," said Duke Ralph, "prefer the fists; 'tis noblest."

Gwynplaine came out from the shadow. He directed his steps towards him whom he had hitherto called Tom-Jim-Jack, but in whom now, however, he began to perceive something more. "I thank you," said he, "but this is my business."

Every head turned towards him.

Gwynplaine advanced. He felt himself impelled towards the man whom he heard called Lord David—his defender, and perhaps something nearer. Lord David drew back.

"Oh!" said he. "It is you, is it? This is well-timed. I have a word for you as well. Just now you spoke of a woman who, after having loved Lord Linnæus Clancharlie, loved Charles II."

"It is true."

"Sir, you insulted my mother."

"Your mother!" cried Gwynplaine. "In that case, as I guessed, we are—"

"Brothers," answered Lord David, and he struck Gwynplaine. "We are brothers," said he; "so we can fight. One can only fight one's equal; who is one's equal if not one's brother? I will send you my seconds; to-morrow we will cut each other's throats."

BOOK THE NINTH

IN RUINS

CHAPTER I.

IT IS THROUGH EXCESS OF GREATNESS THAT MAN REACHES EXCESS OF MISERY

As midnight tolled from St. Paul's, a man who had just crossed London Bridge struck into the lanes of Southwark. There were no lamps lighted, it being at that time the custom in London, as in Paris, to extinguish the public lamps at eleven o'clock—that is, to put them out just as they became necessary. The streets were dark and deserted. When the lamps are out men stay in. He whom we speak of advanced with hurried strides. He was strangely dressed for walking at such an hour. He wore a coat of embroidered silk, a sword by his side, a hat with white plumes, and no cloak. The watchmen, as they saw him pass, said, "It is a lord walking for a wager," and they moved out of his way with the respect due to a lord and to a better.

The man was Gwynplaine. He was making his escape. Where was he? He did not know. We have said that the soul has its cyclones—fearful whirlwinds, in which heaven, the sea, day, night, life, death, are all mingled in unintelligible horror. It can no longer breathe Truth; it is crushed by things in which it does not believe. Nothingness becomes hurricane. The firmament pales. Infinity is empty. The mind of the sufferer wanders away. He feels himself dying. He craves for a star. What did Gwynplaine feel? a thirst—a thirst to see Dea.

He felt but that. To reach the Green Box again, and the Tadcaster Inn, with its sounds and light—full of the cordial laughter of the people; to find Ursus and Homo, to see Dea again, to re-enter life. Disillusion, like a bow, shoots its arrow, man, towards the True. Gwynplaine hastened on. He approached Tarrinzeau Field. He walked no longer now; he ran. His eyes pierced the darkness before him. His glance preceded him, eagerly seeking the harbour on the horizon. What a moment for him when he should see the lighted windows of Tadcaster Inn!

He reached the bowling-green. He turned the corner of the wall, and saw before him, at the other end of the field, some distance off, the inn—the only house, it may be remembered, in the field where the fair was held.

He looked. There was no light; nothing but a black mass.

He shuddered. Then he said to himself that it was late; that the tavern was shut up; that it was very natural; that every one was asleep; that he had only to awaken Nicless or Govicum; that he must go up to the inn and knock at the door. He did so, running no longer now, but rushing.

He reached the inn, breathless. It is when, storm-beaten and struggling in the invisible convulsions of the soul until he knows not whether he is in life or in death, that all the delicacy of a man's affection for his loved ones, being yet unimpaired, proves a heart true. When all else is swallowed up, tenderness still floats unshattered. Not to awaken Dea too suddenly was Gwynplaine's first thought. He approached the inn with as little noise as possible. He recognized the nook, the old dog kennel, where Govicum used to sleep. In it, contiguous to the lower room, was a window opening on to the field. Gwynplaine tapped softly at the pane. It would be enough to awaken Govicum, he thought.

There was no sound in Govicum's room.

"At his age," said Gwynplaine, "a boy sleeps soundly."

With the back of his hand he knocked against the window gently. Nothing stirred.

He knocked louder twice. Still nothing stirred. Then, feeling somewhat uneasy, he went to the door of the inn and knocked. No one answered. He reflected, and began to feel a cold shudder come over him.

"Master Nicless is old, children sleep soundly, and old men heavily. Courage! louder!"

He had tapped, he had knocked, he had kicked the door; now he flung himself against it.

This recalled to him a distant memory of Weymouth, when, a little child, he had carried Dea, an infant, in his arms.

He battered the door again violently, like a lord, which, alas! he was.

The house remained silent. He felt that he was losing his head. He no longer thought of caution. He shouted,—

"Nicless! Govicum!"

At the same time he looked up at the windows, to see if any candle was lighted. But the inn was blank. Not a voice, not a sound, not a glimmer of light. He went to the gate and knocked at it, kicked against it, and shook it, crying out wildly,—

"Ursus! Homo!"

The wolf did not bark.

A cold sweat stood in drops upon his brow. He cast his eyes around. The night was dark; but there were stars enough to render the fair-green visible. He saw—a melancholy sight to him—that everything on it had vanished.

There was not a single caravan. The circus was gone. Not a tent, not a booth, not a cart, remained. The strollers, with their thousand noisy cries, who had swarmed there, had given place to a black and sullen void.

All were gone.

The madness of anxiety took possession of him. What did this mean? What had happened? Was no one left? Could it be that life had crumbled away behind him? What had happened to them all? Good heavens! Then he rushed like a tempest against the house. He struck the small door, the gate, the windows, the window-shutters, the walls, with fists and feet, furious with terror and agony of mind.

He called Nicless, Govicum, Fibi, Vinos, Ursus, Homo. He tried every shout and every sound against this wall. At times he waited and listened; but the house remained mute and dead. Then, exasperated, he began again with blows, shouts, and repeated knockings, re-echoed all around. It might have been thunder trying to awake the grave.

There is a certain stage of fright in which a man becomes terrible. He who fears everything fears nothing. He would strike the Sphynx. He defies the Unknown.

Gwynplaine renewed the noise in every possible form—stopping, resuming, unwearying in the shouts and appeals by which he assailed the tragic silence. He called a thousand times on the names of those who should have been there. He shrieked out every name except that of Dea—a precaution of which he could not have explained the reason himself, but which instinct inspired even in his distraction.

Having exhausted calls and cries, nothing was left but to break in.

"I must enter the house," he said to himself; "but how?"

He broke a pane of glass in Govicum's room by thrusting his hand through it, tearing the flesh; he drew the bolt of the sash and opened the window. Perceiving that his sword was in the way, he tore it off angrily, scabbard, blade, and belt, and flung it on the pavement. Then he raised himself by the inequalities in the wall, and though the window was narrow, he was able to pass through it. He entered the inn. Govicum's bed, dimly visible in its nook, was there; but Govicum was not in it. If Govicum was not in his bed, it was evident that Nicless could not be in his.

The whole house was dark. He felt in that shadowy interior the mysterious immobility of emptiness, and that vague fear which signifies—"There is no one here."

Gwynplaine, convulsed with anxiety, crossed the lower room, knocking against the tables, upsetting the earthenware, throwing down the benches, sweeping against the jugs, and, striding over the furniture, reached the door leading into the court, and broke it open with one blow from his knee, which sprung the lock. The door turned on its hinges. He looked into the court. The Green Box was no longer there.

CHAPTER II.

THE DREGS

Gwynplaine left the house, and began to explore Tarrinzeau Field in every direction. He went to every place where, the day before, the tents and caravans had stood. He knocked at the stalls, though he knew well that they were uninhabited. He struck everything that looked like a door or a window. Not a voice arose from the darkness. Something like death had been there.

The ant-hill had been razed. Some measures of police had apparently been carried out. There had been what, in our days, would be called a *razzia*. Tarrinzeau Field was worse than a desert; it had been scoured, and every corner of it scratched up, as it were, by pitiless claws. The pocket of the unfortunate fair-green had been turned inside out, and completely emptied.

Gwynplaine, after having searched every yard of ground, left the green, struck into the crooked streets abutting on the site called East Point, and directed his steps towards the Thames. He had threaded his way through a network of lanes, bounded only by walls and hedges, when he felt the fresh breeze from the water, heard the dull lapping of the river, and suddenly saw a parapet in front of him. It was the parapet of the Effroc stone.

This parapet bounded a block of the quay, which was very short and very narrow. Under it the high wall, the Effroc stone, buried itself perpendicularly in the dark water below.

Gwynplaine stopped at the parapet, and, leaning his elbows on it, laid his head in his hands and set to thinking, with the water beneath him.

Did he look at the water? No. At what then? At the shadow; not the shadow without, but within him. In the melancholy night-bound landscape, which he scarcely marked, in the outer depths, which his eyes did not pierce, were the blurred sketches of masts and spars. Below the Effroc stone there was nothing on the river; but the quay sloped insensibly downwards till, some distance off, it met a pier, at which several vessels were lying, some of which had just arrived, others which were on the point of departure. These vessels communicated with the shore by little jetties, constructed for the purpose, some of stone, some of wood, or by movable gangways. All of them, whether moored to the jetties or at anchor, were wrapped in silence. There was neither voice nor movement on board, it being a good habit of sailors to sleep when they can, and awake only when wanted. If any of them were to sail during the night at high tide, the crews were not yet awake. The hulls, like large black bubbles, and the rigging, like threads mingled with ladders, were barely visible. All was livid and confused. Here and there a red cresset pierced the haze.

Gwynplaine saw nothing of all this. What he was musing on was destiny.

He was in a dream—a vision—giddy in presence of an inexorable reality.

He fancied that he heard behind him something like an earthquake. It was the laughter of the Lords.

From that laughter he had just emerged. He had come out of it, having received a blow, and from whom?

From his own brother!

Flying from the laughter, carrying with him the blow, seeking refuge, a wounded bird, in his nest, rushing from hate and seeking love, what had he found?

Darkness.

No one.

Everything gone.

He compared that darkness to the dream he had indulged in.

What a crumbling away!

Gwynplaine had just reached that sinister bound—the void. The Green Box gone was his universe vanished.

His soul had been closed up.

He reflected.

What could have happened? Where were they? They had evidently been carried away. Destiny had given him, Gwynplaine, a blow, which was greatness; its reaction had struck them another, which was annihilation. It was clear that he would never see them again. Precautions had been taken against that. They had scoured the fair-green, beginning by Nicless and Govicum, so that he should gain no clue through them. Inexorable dispersion! That fearful social system, at the same time that it had pulverized him in the House of Lords, had crushed them in their little cabin. They were lost; Dea was lost—lost to him for ever. Powers of heaven! where was she? And he had not been there to defend her!

To have to make guesses as to the absent whom we love is to put oneself to the torture. He inflicted this torture on himself. At every thought that he fathomed, at every supposition which he made, he felt within him a moan of agony.

Through a succession of bitter reflections he remembered a man who was evidently fatal to him, and who had called himself Barkilphedro. That man had inscribed on his brain a dark sentence which reappeared now; he had written it in such terrible ink that every letter had turned to fire; and Gwynplaine saw flaming at the bottom of his thought the enigmatical words, the meaning of which was at length solved: "Destiny never opens one door without closing another."

All was over. The final shadows had gathered about him. In every man's fate there may be an end of the world for himself alone. It is called despair. The soul is full of falling stars.

This, then, was what he had come to.

A vapour had passed. He had been mingled with it. It had lain heavily on his eyes; it had disordered his brain. He had been outwardly blinded, intoxicated within. This had lasted the time of a passing vapour. Then everything melted away, the vapour and his life. Awaking from the dream, he found himself alone.

All vanished, all gone, all lost—night—nothingness. Such was his horizon.

He was alone.

Alone has a synonym, which is Dead. Despair is an accountant. It sets itself to find its total; it adds up everything, even to the farthings. It reproaches Heaven with its thunderbolts and its pinpricks. It seeks to find what it has to expect from fate. It argues, weighs, and calculates, outwardly cool, while the burning lava is still flowing on within.

Gwynplaine examined himself, and examined his fate.

The backward glance of thought; terrible recapitulation!

When at the top of a mountain, we look down the precipice; when at the bottom, we look up at heaven. And we say, "I was there."

Gwynplaine was at the very bottom of misfortune. How sudden, too, had been his fall!

Such is the hideous swiftness of misfortune, although it is so heavy that we might fancy it slow. But no! It would likewise appear that snow, from its coldness, ought to be the paralysis of winter, and, from its whiteness, the immobility of the winding-sheet. Yet this is contradicted by the avalanche.

The avalanche is snow become a furnace. It remains frozen, but it devours. The avalanche had enveloped Gwynplaine. He had been torn like a rag, uprooted like a tree, precipitated like a stone. He recalled all the circumstances of his fall. He put himself questions, and returned answers. Grief is an examination. There is no judge so searching as conscience conducting its own trial.

What amount of remorse was there in his despair? This he wished to find out, and dissected his conscience. Excruciating vivisection!

His absence had caused a catastrophe. Had this absence depended on him? In all that had happened, had he been a free agent? No! He had felt himself captive. What was that which had arrested and detained him—a prison? No. A chain? No. What then? Sticky slime! He had sunk into the slough of greatness.

To whom has it not happened to be free in appearance, yet to feel that his wings are hampered?

There had been something like a snare spread for him. What is at first temptation ends by captivity.

Nevertheless—and his conscience pressed him on this point—had he merely submitted to what had been offered him? No; he had accepted it.

Violence and surprise had been used with him in a certain measure, it was true; but he, in a certain measure, had given in. To have allowed himself to be carried off was not his fault; but to have allowed himself to be inebriated was his weakness. There had been a moment—a decisive moment—when the question was proposed. This Barkilphedro had placed a dilemma before Gwynplaine, and had given him clear power to decide his fate by a word. Gwynplaine might have said, "No." He had said, "Yes."

From that "Yes," uttered in a moment of dizziness, everything had sprung. Gwynplaine realized this now in the bitter aftertaste of that consent.

Nevertheless—for he debated with himself—was it then so great a wrong to take possession of his right, of his patrimony, of his heritage, of his house; and, as a patrician, of the rank of his ancestors; as an orphan, of the name of his father? What had he accepted? A restitution. Made by whom? By Providence.

Then his mind revolted. Senseless acceptance! What a bargain had he struck! what a foolish exchange! He had trafficked with Providence at a loss. How now! For an income of £80,000 a year; for seven or eight titles; for ten or twelve palaces; for houses in town, and castles in the country; for a hundred lackeys; for packs of hounds, and carriages, and armorial bearings; to be a judge and legislator; for a coronet and purple robes, like a king; to be a baron and a marquis; to be a peer of England, he had given the hut of Ursus and the smile of Dea. For shipwreck and destruction in the surging immensity of greatness, he had bartered happiness. For the ocean he had given the pearl. O madman! O fool! O dupe!

Yet nevertheless—and here the objection reappeared on firmer ground—in this fever of high fortune which had seized him all had not been unwholesome. Perhaps there would have been selfishness in renunciation; perhaps he had done his duty in the acceptance. Suddenly transformed into a lord, what ought he to have done? The complication of events produces perplexity of mind. This had happened to him. Duty gave contrary orders. Duty on all sides at once, duty multiple and contradictory—this was the bewilderment which he had suffered. It was this that had paralyzed him, especially when he had not refused to take the journey from Corleone Lodge to the House of Lords. What we call rising in life is leaving the safe for the dangerous path. Which is, thenceforth, the straight line? Towards whom is our first duty? Is it towards those nearest to ourselves, or is it towards mankind generally? Do we not cease to belong to our own circumscribed circle, and become part of the great family of all? As we ascend we feel an increased pressure on our virtue. The higher we rise, the greater is the strain. The increase of right is an increase of duty. We come to many cross-ways, phantom roads perchance, and we imagine that we see the finger of conscience pointing each one of them out to us. Which shall we take? Change our direction, remain where we are, advance, go back? What are we to do? That there should be cross-roads in conscience is strange enough; but responsibility may be a labyrinth. And when a man contains an idea, when he is the incarnation of a fact—when he is a symbolical man, at the same time that he is a man of flesh and blood—is not the responsibility still more oppressive? Thence the care-laden docility and the dumb anxiety of Gwynplaine; thence his obedience when summoned to take his seat. A pensive man is often a passive man. He had heard what he fancied was the command of duty itself. Was not that entrance into a place where oppression could be discussed and resisted the realization of one of his deepest aspirations? When he had been called upon to speak—he the fearful human scantling, he the living specimen of the despotic whims under which, for six thousand years, mankind has groaned in agony—had he the right to refuse? Had he the right to withdraw his head from under the tongue of fire descending from on high to rest upon him?

In the obscure and giddy debate of conscience, what had he said to himself? This: "The people are a silence. I will be the mighty advocate of that silence; I will speak for the dumb; I will speak of the little to the great—of the weak to the powerful. This is the purpose of my fate. God wills what He wills, and does it. It was a wonder that Hardquanonne's flask, in which was the metamorphosis of Gwynplaine into Lord Clancharlie, should have floated for fifteen years on the ocean, on the billows, in the surf, through the storms, and that all the raging of the sea did it no harm. But I can see the reason. There are destinies with secret springs. I have the key of mine, and know its enigma. I am predestined; I have a mission. I will be the poor man's lord; I will speak for the speechless with despair; I will translate inarticulate remonstrance; I will translate the mutterings, the groans, the murmurs, the voices of the crowd, their ill-spoken complaints, their unintelligible words, and those animal-like cries which ignorance and suffering put into men's mouths. The clamour of men is as inarticulate as the howling of the wind. They cry out, but they are understood; so that cries become equivalent to silence, and silence with them means throwing down their arms. This forced disarmament calls for help. I will be their help; I will be the Denunciation; I will be the Word of the people. Thanks to me, they shall be understood. I will be the bleeding mouth from which the gag has been torn. I will tell everything. This will be great indeed."

Yes; it is fine to speak for the dumb, but to speak to the deaf is sad. And that was his second part in the drama.

Alas! he had failed irremediably. The elevation in which he had believed, the high fortune, had melted away like a mirage. And what a fall! To be drowned in a surge of laughter!

He had believed himself strong—he who, during so many years, had floated with observant mind on the wide sea of suffering; he who had brought back out of the great shadow so touching a cry. He had been flung against that huge rock the frivolity of the fortunate. He believed himself an avenger; he was but a clown. He thought that he wielded the thunderbolt; he did but tickle. In place of emotion, he met with mockery. He sobbed; they burst into gaiety, and under that gaiety he had sunk fatally submerged.

And what had they laughed at? At his laugh. So that trace of a hateful act, of which he must keep the mark for ever—mutilation carved in everlasting gaiety; the stigmata of laughter, image of the sham contentment of nations under their oppressors; that mask of joy produced by torture; that abyss of grimace which he carried on his features; the scar which signified *Jussu regis*, the attestation of a crime committed by the king towards him, and the symbol of crime committed by royalty towards the people;—that it was which had triumphed over him; that it was which had overwhelmed him; so that the accusation against the executioner turned into sentence upon the victim. What a prodigious denial of justice! Royalty, having had satisfaction of his father, had had satisfaction of him! The evil that had been done had served as pretext and as motive for the evil which remained to be done. Against whom were the lords angered? Against the torturer? No; against the tortured. Here is the throne; there, the people. Here, James II.; there, Gwynplaine. That confrontation, indeed, brought to light an outrage and a crime. What was the outrage? Complaint. What was the crime? Suffering. Let misery hide itself in silence, otherwise it becomes treason. And those men who had dragged Gwynplaine on the hurdle of sarcasm, were they wicked? No; but they, too, had their fatality—they were happy. They were executioners, ignorant of the fact. They were good-humoured; they saw no use in Gwynplaine. He opened himself to them. He tore out his heart to show them, and they cried, "Go on with your play!" But, sharpest sting! he had laughed himself. The frightful chain which tied down his soul hindered his thoughts from rising to his face. His disfigurement reached even his senses; and, while his conscience was indignant, his face gave it the lie, and jested. Then all was over. He was the laughing man, the caryatid of the weeping world. He was an agony petrified in hilarity, carrying the weight of a universe of calamity, and walled up for ever with the gaiety, the ridicule, and the amusement of others; of all the oppressed, of whom he was the incarnation, he partook the hateful fate, to be a desolation not believed in; they jeered at his distress; to them he was but an extraordinary buffoon lifted out of some frightful condensation of misery, escaped from his prison, changed to a deity, risen from the dregs of the people to the foot of the throne, mingling with the stars, and who, having once amused the damned, now amused the elect. All that was in him of generosity, of enthusiasm, of eloquence, of heart, of soul, of fury, of anger, of love, of inexpressible grief, ended in—a burst of laughter! And he proved, as he had told the lords, that this was not the exception; but that it was the normal, ordinary, universal, unlimited, sovereign fact, so amalgamated with the routine of life that they took no account of it. The hungry pauper laughs, the beggar laughs, the felon laughs, the prostitute laughs, the orphan laughs to gain his bread; the slave laughs, the soldier laughs, the people laugh. Society is so constituted that every perdition, every indigence, every catastrophe, every fever, every ulcer, every agony, is resolved on the surface of the abyss into one frightful grin of joy. Now he was that universal grin, and that grin was himself. The law of heaven, the unknown power which governs, had willed that a spectre visible and palpable, a spectre of flesh and bone, should be the synopsis of the monstrous parody which we call the world; and he was that spectre, immutable fate!

He had cried, "Pity for those who suffer." In vain! He had striven to awake pity; he had awakened horror. Such is the law of apparitions.

But while he was a spectre, he was also a man; here was the heartrending complication. A spectre without, a man within. A man more than any other, perhaps, since his double fate was the synopsis of all humanity. And he felt that humanity was at once present in him and absent from him. There was in his existence something insurmountable. What was he? A disinherited heir? No; for he was a lord. Was he a lord? No; for he was a rebel. He was the light-bearer; a terrible spoil-sport. He was not Satan, certainly; but he was Lucifer. His entrance, with his torch in his hand, was sinister.

Sinister for whom? for the sinister. Terrible to whom? to the terrible. Therefore they rejected him. Enter their order? be accepted by them? Never. The obstacle which he carried in his face was frightful; but the obstacle which he carried in his ideas was still more insurmountable. His speech was to them more deformed than his face. He had no possible thought in common with the world of the great and powerful, in which he had by a freak of fate been born, and from which another freak of fate had driven him out. There was between men and his face a mask, and between society and his mind a wall. In mixing, from infancy, a wandering mountebank, with that vast and tough substance which is called the crowd, in saturating himself with the attraction of the multitude, and impregnating himself with the great soul of mankind, he had lost, in the common sense of the whole of mankind, the particular sense of the reigning classes. On their heights he was impossible. He had reached them wet with water from the well of Truth; the odour of the abyss was on him. He was repugnant to those princes perfumed with lies. To those who live on fiction, truth is disgusting; and he who thirsts for flattery vomits the real, when he has happened to drink it by mistake. That which Gwynplaine brought was not fit for their table. For what was it? Reason, wisdom, justice; and they rejected them with disgust.

There were bishops there. He brought God into their presence. Who was this intruder?

The two poles repel each other. They can never amalgamate, for transition is wanting. Hence the result—a cry of anger—when they were brought together in terrible juxtaposition: all misery concentrated in a man, face to face with all pride concentrated in a caste.

To accuse is useless. To state is sufficient. Gwynplaine, meditating on the limits of his destiny, proved the total uselessness of his effort. He proved the deafness of high places. The privileged have no hearing on the side next the disinherited. Is it their fault? Alas! no. It is their law. Forgive them! To be moved would be to abdicate. Of lords and princes expect nothing. He who is satisfied is inexorable. For those that have their fill the hungry do not exist. The happy ignore and isolate themselves. On the threshold of their paradise, as on the threshold of hell, must be written, "Leave all hope behind."

Gwynplaine had met with the reception of a spectre entering the dwelling of the gods.

Here all that was within him rose in rebellion. No, he was no spectre; he was a man. He told them, he shouted to them, that he was Man.

He was not a phantom. He was palpitating flesh. He had a brain, and he thought; he had a heart, and he loved; he had a soul, and he hoped. Indeed, to have hoped overmuch was his whole crime.

Alas! he had exaggerated hope into believing in that thing at once so brilliant and so dark which is called Society. He who was without had re-entered it. It had at once, and at first sight, made him its three offers, and given him its three gifts—marriage, family, and caste. Marriage? He had seen prostitution on the threshold. Family? His brother had struck him, and was awaiting him the next day, sword in hand. Caste? It had burst into laughter in his face, at him the patrician, at him the wretch. It had rejected, almost before it had admitted him. So that his first three steps into the dense shadow of society had opened three gulfs beneath him.

And it was by a treacherous transfiguration that his disaster had begun; and catastrophe had approached him with the aspect of apotheosis!

Ascend had signified Descend!

His fate was the reverse of Job's. It was through prosperity that adversity had reached him.

O tragical enigma of life! Behold what pitfalls! A child, he had wrestled against the night, and had been stronger than it; a man, he had wrestled against destiny, and had overcome it. Out of disfigurement he had created success; and out of misery, happiness. Of his exile he had made an asylum. A vagabond, he had wrestled against space; and, like the birds of the air, he had found his crumb of bread. Wild and solitary, he had wrestled against the crowd, and had made it his friend. An athlete, he had wrestled against that lion, the people; and he had tamed it. Indigent, he had wrestled against distress, he had faced the dull necessity of living, and from amalgamating with misery every joy of his heart, he had at length made riches out of poverty. He had believed himself the conqueror of life. Of a sudden he was attacked by fresh forces, reaching him from unknown depths; this time, with menaces no longer, but with smiles and caresses. Love, serpent-like and sensual, had appeared to him, who was filled with angelic love. The flesh had tempted him, who had lived on the ideal. He had heard words of voluptuousness like cries of rage; he had felt the clasp of a woman's arms, like the convolutions of a snake; to the illumination of truth had succeeded the fascination of falsehood; for it is not the flesh that is real, but the soul. The flesh is ashes, the soul is flame. For the little circle allied to him by the relationship of poverty and toil, which was his true and natural family, had been substituted the social family—his family in blood, but of tainted blood; and even before he had entered it, he found himself face to face with an intended fractricide. Alas! he had allowed himself to be thrown back into that society of which Brantôme, whom he had not read, wrote: "*The son has a right to challenge his father!*" A fatal fortune had cried to him, "Thou art not of the crowd; thou art of the chosen!" and had opened the ceiling above his head, like a trap in the sky, and had shot him up, through this opening, causing him to appear, wild, and unexpected, in the midst of princes and masters. Then suddenly he saw around him, instead of the people who applauded him, the lords who cursed him. Mournful metamorphosis! Ignominious ennobling! Rude spoliation of all that had been his happiness! Pillage of his life by derision! Gwynplaine, Clancharlie, the lord, the mountebank, torn out of his old lot, out of his new lot, by the beaks of those eagles!

What availed it that he had commenced life by immediate victory over obstacle? Of what good had been his early triumphs? Alas! the fall must come, ere destiny be complete.

So, half against his will, half of it—because after he had done with the wapentake he had to do with Barkilphedro, and he had given a certain amount of consent to his abductions—he had left the real for the chimerical; the true for the false; Dea for Josiana; love for pride; liberty for power; labour proud and poor for opulence full of unknown responsibilities; the shade in which is God for the lurid flames in which the devils dwell; Paradise for Olympus!

He had tasted the golden fruit. He was now spitting out the ashes to which it turned.

Lamentable result! Defeat, failure, fall into ruin, insolent expulsion of all his hopes, frustrated by ridicule. Immeasurable disillusion! And what was there for him in the future? If he looked forward to the morrow, what did he see? A drawn sword, the point of which was against his breast, and the hilt in the hand of his brother. He could see nothing but the hideous flash of that sword. Josiana and the House of Lords made up the background in a monstrous chiaroscuro full of tragic shadows.

And that brother seemed so brave and chivalrous! Alas! he had hardly seen the Tom-Jim-Jack who had defended Gwynplaine, the Lord David who had defended Lord Clancharlie; but he had had time to receive a blow from him and to love him.

He was crushed.

He felt it impossible to proceed further. Everything had crumbled about him. Besides, what was the good of it? All weariness dwells in the depths of despair.

The trial had been made. It could not be renewed.

Gwynplaine was like a gamester who has played all his trumps away, one after the other. He had allowed himself to be drawn to a fearful gambling-table, without thinking what he was about; for, so subtle is the poison of illusion, he had staked

Dea against Josiana, and had gained a monster; he had staked Ursus against a family, and had gained an insult; he had played his mountebank platform against his seat in the Lords; for the applause which was his he had gained insult. His last card had fallen on that fatal green cloth, the deserted bowling-green. Gwynplaine had lost. Nothing remained but to pay. Pay up, wretched man!

The thunder-stricken lie still. Gwynplaine remained motionless. Anybody perceiving him from afar, in the shadow, stiff, and without movement, might have fancied that he saw an upright stone.

Hell, the serpent, and reverie are tortuous. Gwynplaine was descending the sepulchral spirals of the deepest thought.

He reflected on that world of which he had just caught a glimpse with the icy contemplation of a last look. Marriage, but no love; family, but no brotherly affection; riches, but no conscience; beauty, but no modesty; justice, but no equity; order, but no equilibrium; authority, but no right; power, but no intelligence; splendour, but no light. Inexorable balance-sheet! He went throughout the supreme vision in which his mind had been plunged. He examined successively destiny, situation, society, and himself. What was destiny? A snare. Situation? Despair. Society? Hatred. And himself? A defeated man. In the depths of his soul he cried. Society is the stepmother, Nature is the mother. Society is the world of the body, Nature is the world of the soul. The one tends to the coffin, to the deal box in the grave, to the earth-worms, and ends there. The other tends to expanded wings, to transformation into the morning light, to ascent into the firmament, and there revives into new life.

By degrees a paroxysm came over him, like a sweeping surge. At the close of events there is always a last flash, in which all stands revealed once more.

He who judges meets the accused face to face. Gwynplaine reviewed all that society and all that nature had done for him. How kind had nature been to him! How she, who is the soul, had succoured him! All had been taken from him, even his features. The soul had given him all back—all, even his features; because there was on earth a heavenly blind girl made expressly for him, who saw not his ugliness, and who saw his beauty.

And it was from this that he had allowed himself to be separated—from that adorable girl, from his own adopted one, from her tenderness, from her divine blind gaze, the only gaze on earth that saw him, that he had strayed! Dea was his sister, because he felt between them the grand fraternity of above—the mystery which contains the whole of heaven. Dea, when he was a little child, was his virgin; because every child has his virgin, and at the commencement of life a marriage of souls is always consummated in the plenitude of innocence. Dea was his wife, for theirs was the same nest on the highest branch of the deep-rooted tree of Hymen. Dea was still more—she was his light, for without her all was void, and nothingness; and for him her head was crowned with rays. What would become of him without Dea? What could he do with all that was himself? Nothing in him could live without her. How, then, could he have lost sight of her for a moment? O unfortunate man! He allowed distance to intervene between himself and his star and, by the unknown and terrible laws of gravitation in such things, distance is immediate loss.

Where was she, the star? Dea! Dea! Dea! Dea! Alas! he had lost her light. Take away the star, and what is the sky? A black mass. But why, then, had all this befallen him? Oh, what happiness had been his! For him God had remade Eden. Too close was the resemblance, alas! even to allowing the serpent to enter; but this time it was the man who had been tempted. He had been drawn without, and then, by a frightful snare, had fallen into a chaos of murky laughter, which was hell. O grief! O grief! How frightful seemed all that had fascinated him! That Josiana, fearful creature!—half beast, half goddess! Gwynplaine was now on the reverse side of his elevation, and he saw the other aspect of that which had dazzled him. It was baleful. His peerage was deformed, his coronet was hideous; his purple robe, a funeral garment; those palaces, infected; those trophies, those statues, those armorial bearings, sinister; the unwholesome and treacherous air poisoned those who breathed it, and turned them mad. How brilliant the rags of the mountebank, Gwynplaine, appeared to him now! Alas! where was the Green Box, poverty, joy, the sweet wandering life—wandering together, like the swallows? They never left each other then; he saw her every minute, morning, evening. At table their knees, their elbows, touched; they drank from the same cup; the sun shone through the pane, but it was only the sun, and Dea was Love. At night they slept not far from each other; and the dream of Dea came and hovered over Gwynplaine, and the dream of Gwynplaine spread itself mysteriously above the head of Dea. When they awoke they could be never quite sure that they had not exchanged kisses in the azure mists of dreams. Dea was all innocence; Ursus, all wisdom. They wandered from town to town; and they had for provision and for stimulant the frank, loving gaiety of the people. They were angel vagabonds, with enough of humanity to walk the earth and not enough of wings to fly away; and now all had disappeared! Where was it gone? Was it possible that it was all effaced? What wind from the tomb had swept over them? All was eclipsed! All was lost! Alas! power, irresistible and deaf to appeal, which weighs down the poor, flings its shadow over all, and is capable of anything. What had been done to them? And he had not been there to protect them, to fling himself in front of them, to defend them, as a lord, with his title, his peerage, and his sword; as a mountebank, with his fists and his nails!

And here arose a bitter reflection, perhaps the most bitter of all. Well, no; he could not have defended them. It was he himself who had destroyed them; it was to save him, Lord Clancharlie, from them; it was to isolate his dignity from contact with them, that the infamous omnipotence of society had crushed them. The best way in which he could protect them would be to disappear, and then the cause of their persecution would cease. He out of the way, they would be allowed to remain in peace. Into what icy channel was his thought beginning to run! Oh! why had he allowed himself to be separated from Dea? Was not his first duty towards her? To serve and to defend the people? But Dea was the people. Dea was an orphan. She was blind; she represented humanity. Oh! what had they done to them? Cruel smart of regret! His absence had left the field free for the catastrophe. He would have shared their fate; either they would have been taken and carried away with him, or he would have been swallowed up with them. And, now, what would become of him without them? Gwynplaine without Dea! Was it possible? Without Dea was to be without everything. It was all over now. The beloved group was for ever buried in irreparable disappearance. All was spent. Besides, condemned and damned as Gwynplaine was, what was the good of further struggle? He had nothing more to expect either of men or of heaven. Dea! Dea! Where is Dea? Lost! What? lost? He who has lost his soul can regain it but through one outlet—death.

Gwynplaine, tragically distraught, placed his hand firmly on the parapet, as on a solution, and looked at the river.

It was his third night without sleep. Fever had come over him. His thoughts, which he believed to be clear, were blurred. He felt an imperative need of sleep. He remained for a few instants leaning over the water. Its darkness offered him a bed of boundless tranquillity in the infinity of shadow. Sinister temptation!

He took off his coat, which he folded and placed on the parapet; then he unbuttoned his waistcoat. As he was about to take it off, his hand struck against something in the pocket. It was the red book which had been given him by the librarian of the House of Lords: he drew it from the pocket, examined it in the vague light of the night, and found a pencil in it, with which he wrote on the first blank that he found these two lines,—

"I depart. Let my brother David take my place, and may he be happy!"

Then he signed, "Fermain Clancharlie, peer of England."

He took off his waistcoat and placed it upon the coat; then his hat, which he placed upon the waistcoat. In the hat he laid the red book open at the page on which he had written. Seeing a stone lying on the ground, he picked it up and placed it in the hat. Having done all this, he looked up into the deep shadow above him. Then his head sank slowly, as if drawn by an invisible thread towards the abyss.

There was a hole in the masonry near the base of the parapet; he placed his foot in it, so that his knee stood higher than the top, and scarcely an effort was necessary to spring over it. He clasped his hands behind his back and leaned over. "So be it," said he.

And he fixed his eyes on the deep waters. Just then he felt a tongue licking his hands.

He shuddered, and turned round.

Homo was behind him.

CONCLUSION

THE NIGHT AND THE SEA

CHAPTER I.

A WATCH-DOG MAY BE A GUARDIAN ANGEL

Gwynplaine uttered a cry.

"Is that you, wolf?"

Homo wagged his tail. His eyes sparkled in the darkness. He was looking earnestly at Gwynplaine.

Then he began to lick his hands again. For a moment Gwynplaine was like a drunken man, so great is the shock of Hope's mighty return.

Homo! What an apparition! During the last forty-eight hours he had exhausted what might be termed every variety of the thunder-bolt. But one was left to strike him—the thunderbolt of joy. And it had just fallen upon him. Certainty, or at least the light which leads to it, regained; the sudden intervention of some mysterious clemency possessed, perhaps, by destiny; life saying, "Behold me!" in the darkest recess of the grave; the very moment in which all expectation has ceased bringing back health and deliverance; a place of safety discovered at the most critical instant in the midst of crumbling ruins—Homo was all this to Gwynplaine. The wolf appeared to him in a halo of light.

Meanwhile, Homo had turned round. He advanced a few steps, and then looked back to see if Gwynplaine was following him.

Gwynplaine was doing so. Homo wagged his tail, and went on.

The road taken by the wolf was the slope of the quay of the Effroc-stone. This slope shelved down to the Thames; and Gwynplaine, guided by Homo, descended it.

Homo turned his head now and then, to make sure that Gwynplaine was behind him.

In some situations of supreme importance nothing approaches so near an omniscient intelligence as the simple instinct of a faithful animal. An animal is a lucid somnambulist.

There are cases in which the dog feels that he should follow his master; others, in which he should precede him. Then the animal takes the direction of sense. His imperturbable scent is a confused power of vision in what is twilight to us. He feels a vague obligation to become a guide. Does he know that there is a dangerous pass, and that he can help his master to surmount it? Probably not. Perhaps he does. In any case, some one knows it for him. As we have already said, it often happens in life that some mighty help which we have held to have come from below has, in reality, come from above. Who knows all the mysterious forms assumed by God?

What was this animal? Providence.

Having reached the river, the wolf led down the narrow tongue of land which bordered the Thames.

Without noise or bark he pushed forward on his silent way. Homo always followed his instinct and did his duty, but with the pensive reserve of an outlaw.

Some fifty paces more, and he stopped. A wooden platform appeared on the right. At the bottom of this platform, which was a kind of wharf on piles, a black mass could be made out, which was a tolerably large vessel. On the deck of the vessel, near the prow, was a glimmer, like the last flicker of a night-light.

The wolf, having finally assured himself that Gwynplaine was there, bounded on to the wharf. It was a long platform, floored and tarred, supported by a network of joists, and under which flowed the river. Homo and Gwynplaine shortly reached the brink.

The ship moored to the wharf was a Dutch vessel, of the Japanese build, with two decks, fore and aft, and between them an open hold, reached by an upright ladder, in which the cargo was laden. There was thus a forecastle and an afterdeck, as in our old river boats, and a space between them ballasted by the freight. The paper boats made by children are of a somewhat similar shape. Under the decks were the cabins, the doors of which opened into the hold and were lighted by glazed portholes. In stowing the cargo a passage was left between the packages of which it consisted. These vessels had a mast on each deck. The foremast was called Paul, the mainmast Peter—the ship being sailed by these two masts, as the Church was guided by her two apostles. A gangway was thrown, like a Chinese bridge, from one deck to the other, over the centre of the hold. In bad weather, both flaps of the gangway were lowered, on the right and left, on hinges, thus making a roof over the hold; so that the ship, in heavy seas, was hermetically closed. These sloops, being of very massive construction, had a beam for a tiller, the strength of the rudder being necessarily proportioned to the height of the vessel. Three men, the skipper and two sailors, with a cabin-boy, sufficed to navigate these ponderous sea-going machines. The decks, fore and aft, were, as we have already said, without bulwarks. The great lumbering hull of this particular vessel was painted black, and on it, visible even in the night, stood out, in white letters, the words, *Vograat, Rotterdam.*

About that time many events had occurred at sea, and amongst others, the defeat of the Baron de Pointi's eight ships off Cape Carnero, which had driven the whole French fleet into refuge at Gibraltar; so that the Channel was swept of every man-of-war, and merchant vessels were able to sail backwards and forwards between London and Rotterdam, without a convoy.

The vessel on which was to be read the word *Vograat*, and which Gwynplaine was now close to, lay with her main-deck almost level with the wharf. But one step to descend, and Homo in a bound, and Gwynplaine in a stride, were on board.

The deck was clear, and no stir was perceptible. The passengers, if, as was likely, there were any, were already on board, the vessel being ready to sail, and the cargo stowed, as was apparent from the state of the hold, which was full of bales and cases. But they were, doubtless, lying asleep in the cabins below, as the passage was to take place during the night. In such cases the passengers do not appear on deck till they awake the following morning. As for the crew, they were probably having their supper in the men's cabin, whilst awaiting the hour fixed for sailing, which was now rapidly approaching. Hence the silence on the two decks connected by the gangway.

The wolf had almost run across the wharf; once on board, he slackened his pace into a discreet walk. He still wagged his tail—no longer joyfully, however, but with the sad and feeble wag of a dog troubled in his mind. Still preceding Gwynplaine, he passed along the after-deck, and across the gangway.

Gwynplaine, having reached the gangway, perceived a light in front of him. It was the same that he had seen from the shore. There was a lantern on the deck, close to the foremast, by the gleam of which was sketched in black, on the dim background of the night, what Gwynplaine recognized to be Ursus's old four-wheeled van.

This poor wooden tenement, cart and hut combined, in which his childhood had rolled along, was fastened to the bottom of the mast by thick ropes, of which the knots were visible at the wheels. Having been so long out of service, it had become dreadfully rickety; it leant over feebly on one side; it had become quite paralytic from disuse; and, moreover, it was suffering from that incurable malady—old age. Mouldy and out of shape, it tottered in decay. The materials of which it was built were all rotten. The iron was rusty, the leather torn, the wood-work worm-eaten. There were lines of cracks across the window in front, through which shone a ray from the lantern. The wheels were warped. The lining, the floor, and the axletrees seemed worn out with fatigue. Altogether, it presented an indescribable appearance of beggary and prostration. The shafts, stuck up, looked like two arms raised to heaven. The whole thing was in a state of dislocation. Beneath it was hanging Homo's chain.

Does it not seem that the law and the will of nature would have dictated Gwynplaine's headlong rush to throw himself upon life, happiness, love regained? So they would, except in some case of deep terror such as his. But he who comes forth, shattered in nerve and uncertain of his way, from a series of catastrophes, each one like a fresh betrayal, is prudent even in his joy; hesitates, lest he should bear the fatality of which he has been the victim to those whom he loves; feels that some evil contagion may still hang about him, and advances towards happiness with wary steps. The gates of Paradise reopen; but before he enters he examines his ground.

Gwynplaine, staggering under the weight of his emotion, looked around him, while the wolf went and lay down silently by his chain.

CHAPTER II.

BARKILPHEDRO, HAVING AIMED AT THE EAGLE, BRINGS DOWN THE DOVE

The step of the little van was down—the door ajar—there was no one inside. The faint light which broke through the pane in front sketched the interior of the caravan vaguely in melancholy chiaroscuro. The inscriptions of Ursus, gloryifying the grandeur of Lords, showed distinctly on the worn-out boards, which were both the wall without and the wainscot within. On a nail, near the door, Gwynplaine saw his esclavine and his cape hung up, as they hang up the clothes of a corpse in a dead-house. Just then he had neither waistcoat nor coat on.

Behind the van something was laid out on the deck at the foot of the mast, which was lighted by the lantern. It was a mattress, of which he could make out one corner. On this mattress some one was probably lying, for he could see a shadow move.

Some one was speaking. Concealed by the van, Gwynplaine listened. It was Ursus's voice. That voice, so harsh in its upper, so tender in its lower, pitch; that voice, which had so often upbraided Gwynplaine, and which had taught him so well, had lost the life and clearness of its tone. It was vague and low, and melted into a sigh at the end of every sentence. It bore but a confused resemblance to his natural and firm voice of old. It was the voice of one in whom happiness is dead. A voice may become a ghost.

He seemed to be engaged in monologue rather than in conversation. We are already aware, however, that soliloquy was a habit with him. It was for that reason that he passed for a madman.

Gwynplaine held his breath, so as not to lose a word of what Ursus said, and this was what he heard.

"This is a very dangerous kind of craft, because there are no bulwarks to it. If we were to slip, there is nothing to prevent our going overboard. If we have bad weather, we shall have to take her below, and that will be dreadful. An awkward step, a fright, and we shall have a rupture of the aneurism. I have seen instances of it. O my God! what is to become of us? Is she asleep? Yes. She is asleep. Is she in a swoon? No. Her pulse is pretty strong. She is only asleep. Sleep is a reprieve. It is the happy blindness. What can I do to prevent people walking about here? Gentlemen, if there be anybody on deck, I beg of you to make no noise. Do not come near us, if you do not mind. You know a person in delicate health requires a little attention. She is feverish, you see. She is very young. 'Tis a little creature who is rather feverish. I put this mattress down here so that she may have a little air. I explain all this so that you should be careful. She fell down exhausted on the mattress as if she had fainted. But she is asleep. I do hope that no one will awake her. I address myself to the ladies, if there are any present. A young girl, it is pitiful! We are only poor mountebanks, but I beg a little kindness, and if there is anything to pay for not making a noise, I will pay it. I thank you, ladies and gentlemen. Is there any one there? No? I don't think there is. My talk is mere loss of breath. So much the better. Gentlemen, I thank you, if you are there; and I thank you still more if you are not. Her forehead is all in perspiration. Come, let us take our places in the galleys again. Put on the chain. Misery is come back. We are sinking again. A hand, the fearful hand which we cannot see, but the weight of which we feel ever upon us, has suddenly struck us back towards the dark point of our destiny. Be it so. We will bear up. Only I will not have her ill. I must seem a fool to talk aloud like this, when I am alone; but she must feel she has some one near her when she awakes. What shall I do if somebody awakes her suddenly! No noise, in the name of Heaven! A sudden shock which would awake her suddenly would be of no use. It will be a pity if anybody comes by. I believe that every one on board is asleep. Thanks be to Providence for that mercy. Well, and Homo? Where is he, I wonder? In all this confusion I forgot to tie him up. I do not know what I am doing. It is more than an hour since I have seen him. I suppose he has been to look for his supper somewhere ashore. I hope nothing has happened to him. Homo! Homo!"

Homo struck his tail softly on the planks of the deck.

"You are there. Oh! you are there! Thank God for that. If Homo had been lost, it would have been too much to bear. She has moved her arm. Perhaps she is going to awake. Quiet, Homo! The tide is turning. We shall sail directly. I think it will be a fine night. There is no wind: the flag droops. We shall have a good passage. I do not know what moon it is, but there is scarcely a stir in the clouds. There will be no swell. It will be a fine night. Her cheek is pale; it is only weakness! No, it is flushed; it is only the fever. Stay! It is rosy. She is well! I can no longer see clearly. My poor Homo, I no longer see distinctly. So we must begin life afresh. We must set to work again. There are only we two left, you see. We will work for her, both of us! She is our child, Ah! the vessel moves! We are off! Good-bye, London! Good evening! good-night! To the devil with horrible London!"

He was right. He heard the dull sound of the unmooring as the vessel fell away from the wharf. Abaft on the poop a man, the skipper, no doubt, just come from below, was standing. He had slipped the hawser and was working the tiller. Looking only to the rudder, as befitted the combined phlegm of a Dutchman and a sailor, listening to nothing but the wind and the water, bending against the resistance of the tiller, as he worked it to port or starboard, he looked in the gloom of the after-deck like a phantom bearing a beam upon its shoulder. He was alone there. So long as they were in the river the other sailors were not required. In a few minutes the vessel was in the centre of the current, with which she drifted without rolling or pitching. The Thames, little disturbed by the ebb, was calm. Carried onwards by the tide, the vessel made rapid way. Behind her the black scenery of London was fading in the mist.

Ursus went on talking.

"Never mind, I will give her digitalis. I am afraid that delirium will supervene. She perspires in the palms of her hands. What sin can we have committed in the sight of God? How quickly has all this misery come upon us! Hideous rapidity of evil! A stone falls. It has claws. It is the hawk swooping on the lark. It is destiny. There you lie, my sweet child! One comes to London. One says: What a fine city!

What fine buildings! Southwark is a magnificent suburb. One settles there. But now they are horrid places. What would you have me do there? I am going to leave. This is the 30th of April. I always distrusted the month of April. There are but two lucky days in April, the 5th and the 27th; and four unlucky ones—the 10th, the 20th, the 29th, and the 30th. This has been placed beyond doubt by the calculations of Cardan. I wish this day were over. Departure is a comfort. At dawn we shall be at Gravesend, and to-morrow evening at Rotterdam. Zounds! I will begin life again in the van. We will draw it, won't we, Homo?"

A light tapping announced the wolf's consent.

Ursus continued,—

"If one could only get out of a grief as one gets out of a city! Homo, we must yet be happy. Alas! there must always be the one who is no more. A shadow remains on those who survive. You know whom I mean, Homo. We were four, and now we are but three. Life is but a long loss of those whom we love. They leave behind them a train of sorrows. Destiny amazes us by a prolixity of unbearable suffering; who then can wonder that the old are garrulous? It is despair that makes the dotard, old fellow! Homo, the wind continues favourable. We can no longer see the dome of St. Paul's. We shall pass Greenwich presently. That will be six good miles over. Oh! I turn my back for ever on those odious capitals, full of priests, of magistrates, and of people. I prefer looking at the leaves rustling in the woods. Her forehead is still in perspiration. I don't like those great violet veins in her arm. There is fever in them. Oh! all this is killing me. Sleep, my child. Yes; she sleeps."

Here a voice spoke: an ineffable voice, which seemed from afar, and appeared to come at once from the heights and the depths—a voice divinely fearful, the voice of Dea.

All that Gwynplaine had hitherto felt seemed nothing. His angel spoke. It seemed as though he heard words spoken from another world in a heaven-like trance.

The voice said,—

"He did well to go. This world was not worthy of him. Only I must go with him. Father! I am not ill; I heard you speak just now. I am very well, quite well. I was asleep. Father, I am going to be happy."

"My child," said Ursus in a voice of anguish, "what do you mean by that?"

The answer was,—

"Father, do not be unhappy."

There was a pause, as if to take breath, and then these few words, pronounced slowly, reached Gwynplaine.

"Gwynplaine is no longer here. It is now that I am blind. I knew not what night was. Night is absence."

The voice stopped once more, and then continued,—

"I always feared that he would fly away. I felt that he belonged to heaven. He has taken flight suddenly. It was natural that it should end thus. The soul flies away like a bird. But the nest of the soul is in the height, where dwells the Great Loadstone, who draws all towards Him. I know where to find Gwynplaine. I have no doubt about the way. Father, it is yonder. Later on, you will rejoin us, and Homo, too."

Homo, hearing his name pronounced, wagged his tail softly against the deck.

"Father!" resumed the voice, "you understand that once Gwynplaine is no longer here, all is over. Even if I would remain, I could not, because one must breathe. We must not ask for that which is impossible. I was with Gwynplaine. It was quite natural, I lived. Now Gwynplaine is no more, I die. The two things are alike: either he must come or I must go. Since he cannot come back, I am going to him. It is good to die. It is not at all difficult. Father, that which is extinguished here shall be rekindled elsewhere. It is a heartache to live in this world. It cannot be that we shall always be unhappy. When we go to what you call the stars, we shall marry, we shall never part again, and we shall love, love, love; and that is what is God."

"There, there, do not agitate yourself," said Ursus.

The voice continued,—

"Well, for instance; last year. In the spring of last year we were together, and we were happy. How different it is now! I forget what little village we were in, but there were trees, and I heard the linnets singing. We came to London; all was changed. This is no reproach, mind. When one comes to a fresh place, how is one to know anything about it? Father, do you remember that one day there was a woman in the great box; you said: 'It is a duchess.' I felt sad. I think it might have been better had we kept to the little towns. Gwynplaine has done right, withal. Now my turn has come. Besides, you have told me yourself, that when I was very little, my mother died, and that I was lying on the ground with the snow falling upon me, and that he, who was also very little then, and alone, like myself, picked me up, and that it was thus that I came to be alive; so you cannot wonder that now I should feel it absolutely necessary to go and search the grave to see if Gwynplaine be in it. Because the only thing which exists in life is the heart; and after life, the soul. You take notice of what I say, father, do you not? What is moving? It seems as if we are in something that is moving, yet I do not hear the sound of the wheels."

After a pause the voice added,—

"I cannot exactly make out the difference between yesterday and to-day. I do not complain. I do not know what has occurred, but something must have happened."

These words, uttered with deep and inconsolable sweetness, and with a sigh which Gwynplaine heard, wound up thus,—

"I must go, unless he should return."

Ursus muttered gloomily: "I do not believe in ghosts."

He went on,—

"This is a ship. You ask why the house moves; it is because we are on board a vessel. Be calm; you must not talk so much. Daughter, if you have any love for me, do not agitate yourself, it will make you feverish. I am so old, I could not bear it if you were to have an illness. Spare me! do not be ill!"

Again the voice spoke,—

"What is the use of searching the earth, when we can only find in heaven?"

Ursus replied, with a half attempt at authority,—

"Be calm. There are times when you have no sense at all. I order you to rest. After all, you cannot be expected to know what it is to rupture a blood-vessel. I should be easy if you were easy. My child, do something for me as well. If he picked you up, I took you in. You will make me ill. That is wrong. You must calm yourself, and go to sleep. All will come right. I give you my word of honour, all will come right. Besides, it is very fine weather. The night might have been made on purpose. To-morrow we shall be at Rotterdam, which is a city in Holland, at the mouth of the Meuse."

"Father," said the voice, "look here; when two beings have always been together from infancy, their state should not be disturbed, or death must come, and it cannot be otherwise. I love you all the same, but I feel that I am no longer altogether with you, although I am as yet not altogether with him."

"Come! try to sleep," repeated Ursus.

The voice answered,—

"I shall have sleep enough soon."

Ursus replied, in trembling tones,—

"I tell you that we are going to Holland, to Rotterdam, which is a city."

"Father," continued the voice, "I am not ill; if you are anxious about that, you may rest easy. I have no fever. I am rather hot; it is nothing more."

Ursus stammered out,—

"At the mouth of the Meuse—"

"I am quite well, father; but look here! I feel that I am going to die!"

"Do nothing so foolish," said Ursus. And he added, "Above all, God forbid she should have a shock!"

There was a silence. Suddenly Ursus cried out,—

"What are you doing? Why are you getting up? Lie down again, I implore of you."

Gwynplaine shivered, and stretched out his head.

CHAPTER III.

PARADISE REGAINED BELOW

He saw Dea. She had just raised herself up on the mattress. She had on a long white dress, carefully closed, and showing only the delicate form of her neck. The sleeves covered her arms; the folds, her feet. The branch-like tracery of blue veins, hot and swollen with fever, were visible on her hands. She was shivering and rocking, rather than reeling, to and fro, like a reed. The lantern threw up its glancing light on her beautiful face. Her loosened hair floated over her shoulders. No tears fell on her cheeks. In her eyes there was fire, and darkness. She was pale, with that paleness which is like the transparency of a divine life in an earthly face. Her fragile and exquisite form was, as it were, blended and interfused with the folds of her robe. She wavered like the flicker of a flame, while, at the same time, she was dwindling into shadow. Her eyes, opened wide, were resplendent. She was as one just freed from the sepulchre; a soul standing in the dawn.

Ursus, whose back only was visible to Gwynplaine, raised his arms in terror. "O my child! O heavens! she is delirious. Delirium is what I feared worst of all. She must have no shock, for that might kill her; yet nothing but a shock can prevent her going mad. Dead or mad! what a situation. O God! what can I do? My child, lie down again."

Meanwhile, Dea spoke. Her voice was almost indistinct, as if a cloud already interposed between her and earth.

"Father, you are wrong. I am not in the least delirious. I hear all you say to me, distinctly. You tell me that there is a great crowd of people, that they are waiting, and that I must play to-night. I am quite willing. You see that I have my reason; but I do not know what to do, since I am dead, and Gwynplaine is dead. I am coming all the same. I am ready to play. Here I am; but Gwynplaine is no longer here."

"Come, my child," said Ursus, "do as I bid you. Lie down again."

"He is no longer here, no longer here. Oh! how dark it is!"

"Dark!" muttered Ursus. "This is the first time she has ever uttered that word!"

Gwynplaine, with as little noise as he could help making as he crept, mounted the step of the caravan, entered it, took from the nail the cape and the esclavine, put the esclavine round his neck, and redescended from the van, still concealed by the projection of the cabin, the rigging, and the mast.

Dea continued murmuring. She moved her lips, and by degrees the murmur became a melody. In broken pauses, and with the interrupted cadences of delirium, her voice broke into the mysterious appeal she had so often addressed to Gwynplaine in *Chaos Vanquished*. She sang, and her voice was low and uncertain as the murmur of the bee,—

"Noche, quita te de allí.

El alba canta...."[23]

She stopped. "No, it is not true. I am not dead. What was I saying? Alas! I am alive. I am alive. He is dead. I am below. He is above. He is gone. I remain. I shall hear his voice no more, nor his footstep. God, who had given us a little Paradise on earth, has taken it away. Gwynplaine, it is over. I shall never feel you near me again. Never! And his voice! I shall never hear his voice again. And she sang:—

"Es menester a cielos ir—
Deja, quiero,
A tu negro
Caparazon."

"We must go to heaven.
Take off, I entreat thee,
Thy black cloak."

She stretched out her hand, as if she sought something in space on which she might rest.

Gwynplaine, rising by the side of Ursus, who had suddenly become as though petrified, knelt down before her.

"Never," said Dea, "never shall I hear him again."

She began, wandering, to sing again:—

"Deja, quiero,
A tu negro
Caparazon."

Then she heard a voice—even the beloved voice—answering:—

"O ven! ama!
Eres alma,
Soy corazon."

"O come and love
Thou art the soul,
I am the heart."

And at the same instant Dea felt under her hand the head of Gwynplaine. She uttered an indescribable cry.

"Gwynplaine!"

A light, as of a star, shone over her pale face, and she tottered. Gwynplaine received her in his arms.

"Alive!" cried Ursus.

Dea repeated "Gwynplaine;" and with her head bowed against Gwynplaine's cheek, she whispered faintly,—

"You have come down to me again. I thank you, Gwynplaine."

And seated on his knee, she lifted up her head. Wrapt in his embrace, she turned her sweet face towards him, and fixed on him those eyes so full of light and shadow, as though she could see him.

"It is you," she said.

Gwynplaine covered her sobs with kisses. There are words which are at once words, cries, and sobs, in which all ecstasy and all grief are mingled and burst forth together. They have no meaning, and yet tell all.

"Yes, it is! It is I, Gwynplaine, of whom you are the soul. Do you hear me? I, of whom you are the child, the wife, the star, the breath of life; I, to whom you are eternity. It is I. I am here. I hold you in my arms. I am alive. I am yours. Oh, when I think that in a moment all would have been over—one minute more, but for Homo! I will tell you everything. How near is despair to joy! Dea, we live! Dea, forgive me. Yes—yours for ever. You are right. Touch my forehead. Make sure that it is I. If you only knew—but nothing can separate us now. I rise out of hell, and ascend into heaven. Am I not with you? You said that I descended. Not so; I reascend. Once more with you! For ever! I tell you for ever! Together! We are together! Who would have believed it? We have found each other again. All our troubles are past. Before us now there is nothing but enchantment. We will renew our happy life, and we will shut the door so fast that misfortune shall never enter again. I will tell you all. You will be astonished. The vessel has sailed. No one can prevent that now. We are on our voyage, and at liberty. We are going to Holland. We will marry. I have no fear about gaining a livelihood. What can hinder it? There is nothing to fear. I adore you!"

"Not so quick!" stammered Ursus.

Dea, trembling, and with the rapture of an angelic touch, passed her hand over Gwynplaine's profile. He overheard her say to herself, "It is thus that gods are made."

Then she touched his clothes.

"The esclavine," she said, "the cape. Nothing changed; all as it was before."

Ursus, stupefied, delighted, smiling, drowned in tears, looked at them, and addressed an aside to himself.

"I don't understand it in the least. I am a stupid idiot—I, who saw him carried to the grave! I cry and I laugh. That is all I know. I am as great a fool as if I were in love myself. But that is just what I am. I am in love with them both. Old fool! Too much emotion—too much emotion. It is what I was afraid of. No; it is that I wished for. Gwynplaine, be careful of her. Yes, let them kiss; it is no affair of mine. I am but a spectator. What I feel is droll. I am the parasite of their happiness, and I am nourished by it."

Whilst Ursus was talking to himself, Gwynplaine exclaimed,—

"Dea, you are too beautiful! I don't know where my wits were gone these last few days. Truly, there is but you on earth. I see you again, but as yet I can hardly believe it. In this ship! But tell me, how did it all happen? To what a state have they reduced you! But where is the Green Box? They have robbed you. They have driven you away. It is infamous. Oh, I will avenge you—I will avenge you, Dea! They shall answer for it. I am a peer of England."

Ursus, as if stricken by a planet full in his breast, drew back, and looked at Gwynplaine attentively.

"It is clear that he is not dead; but can he have gone mad?" and he listened to him doubtfully.

Gwynplaine resumed.

"Be easy, Dea; I will carry my complaint to the House of Lords."

Ursus looked at him again, and struck his forehead with the tip of his forefinger. Then making up his mind,—

"It is all one to me," he said. "It will be all right, all the same. Be as mad as you like, my Gwynplaine. It is one of the rights of man. As for me, I am happy. But how came all this about?"

The vessel continued to sail smoothly and fast. The night grew darker and darker. The mists, which came inland from the ocean, were invading the zenith, from which no wind blew them away. Only a few large stars were visible, and they disappeared one after another, so that soon there were none at all, and the whole sky was dark, infinite, and soft. The river broadened until the banks on each side were nothing but two thin brown lines mingling with the gloom. Out of all this shadow rose a profound peace. Gwynplaine, half seated, held Dea in his embrace. They spoke, they cried, they babbled, they murmured in a mad dialogue of joy! How are we to paint thee, O joy!

"My life!"

"My heaven!"

"My love!"

"My whole happiness!"

"Gwynplaine!"

"Dea, I am drunk. Let me kiss your feet."

"Is it you, then, for certain?"

"I have so much to say to you now that I do not know where to begin."

"One kiss!"

"O my wife!"

"Gwynplaine, do not tell me that I am beautiful. It is you who are handsome."

"I have found you again. I hold you to my heart. This is true. You are mine. I do not dream. Is it possible? Yes, it is. I recover possession of life. If you only knew! I have met with all sorts of adventures. Dea!"

"Gwynplaine, I love you!"

And Ursus murmured,—

"Mine is the joy of a grandfather."

Homo, having come from under the van, was going from one to the other discreetly, exacting no attention, licking them left and right—now Ursus's thick shoes, now Gwynplaine's cape, now Dea's dress, now the mattress. This was his way of giving his blessing.

They had passed Chatham and the mouth of the Medway. They were approaching the sea. The shadowy serenity of the atmosphere was such that the passage down the Thames was being made without trouble: no manoeuvre was needful, nor was any sailor called on deck. At the other end of the vessel the skipper, still alone, was steering. There was only this man aft. At the bow the lantern lighted up the happy group of beings who, from the depths of misery, had suddenly been raised to happiness by a meeting so unhoped for.

CHAPTER IV.

NAY; ON HIGH!

Suddenly Dea, disengaging herself from Gwynplaine's embrace, arose. She pressed both her hands against her heart, as if to still its throbbings.

"What is wrong with me?" said she. "There is something the matter. Joy is suffocating. No, it is nothing! That is lucky. Your reappearance, O my Gwynplaine, has given me a blow—a blow of happiness. All this heaven of joy which you have put into my heart has intoxicated me. You being absent, I felt myself dying. The true life which was leaving me you have brought back. I felt as if something was being torn away within me. It is the shadows that have been torn away, and I feel life dawn in my brain—a glowing life, a life of fever and delight. This life which you have just given me is wonderful. It is so heavenly that it makes me suffer somewhat. It seems as though my soul is enlarged, and can scarcely be contained in my body. This life of seraphim, this plenitude, flows into my brain and penetrates it. I feel like a beating of wings within my breast. I feel strangely, but happy. Gwynplaine, you have been my resurrection."

She flushed, became pale, then flushed again, and fell.

"Alas!" said Ursus, "you have killed her."

Gwynplaine stretched his arms towards Dea. Extremity of anguish coming upon extremity of ecstasy, what a shock! He would himself have fallen, had he not had to support her.

"Dea!" he cried, shuddering, "what is the matter?"

"Nothing," said she—"I love you!"

She lay in his arms, lifeless, like a piece of linen; her hands were hanging down helplessly.

Gwynplaine and Ursus placed Dea on the mattress. She said, feebly,—

"I cannot breathe lying down."

They lifted her up.

Ursus said,—

"Fetch a pillow."

She replied,—

"What for? I have Gwynplaine!"

She laid her head on Gwynplaine's shoulder, who was sitting behind, and supporting her, his eyes wild with grief.

"Oh," said she, "how happy I am!"

Ursus took her wrist, and counted the pulsation of the artery. He did not shake his head. He said nothing, nor expressed his thought except by the rapid movement of his eyelids, which were opening and closing convulsively, as if to prevent a flood of tears from bursting out.

"What is the matter?" asked Gwynplaine.

Ursus placed his ear against Dea's left side.

Gwynplaine repeated his question eagerly, fearful of the answer.

Ursus looked at Gwynplaine, then at Dea. He was livid. He said,—

"We ought to be parallel with Canterbury. The distance from here to Gravesend cannot be very great. We shall have fine weather all night. We need fear no attack at sea, because the fleets are all on the coast of Spain. We shall have a good passage."

Dea, bent, and growing paler and paler, clutched her robe convulsively. She heaved a sigh of inexpressible sadness, and murmured,—

"I know what this is. I am dying!"

Gwynplaine rose in terror. Ursus held Dea.

"Die! You die! No; it shall not be! You cannot die! Die now! Die at once! It is impossible! God is not ferociously cruel—to give you and to take you back in the same moment. No; such a thing cannot be. It would make one doubt in Him. Then, indeed, would everything be a snare—the earth, the sky, the cradles of infants, the human heart, love, the stars. God would be a traitor and man a dupe. There would be nothing in which to believe. It would be an insult to the creation. Everything would be an abyss. You know not what you say, Dea. You shall live! I command you to live! You must obey me! I am your husband and your master; I forbid you to leave me! O heavens! O wretched Man! No, it cannot be—I to remain in the world after you! Why, it is as monstrous as that there should be no sun! Dea! Dea! recover! It is but a moment of passing pain. One feels a shudder at times, and thinks no more about it. It is absolutely necessary that you should get well and cease to suffer. *You* die! What have I done to you? The very thought of it drives me mad. We belong to each other, and we love each other. You have no reason for going! It would be unjust! Have I committed crimes? Besides, you have forgiven me. Oh, you would not make me desperate—have me become a villain, a madman, drive me to perdition? Dea, I entreat you! I conjure you! I supplicate you! Do not die!"

And clenching his hands in his hair, agonized with fear, stifled with tears, he threw himself at her feet.

"My Gwynplaine," said Dea, "it is no fault of mine."

There then rose to her lips a red froth, which Ursus wiped away with the fold of her robe, before Gwynplaine, who was prostrate at her feet, could see it.

Gwynplaine took her feet in his hands, and implored her in all kinds of confused words.

"I tell you, I will not have it! *You* die? I have no strength left to bear it. Die? Yes; but both of us together—not otherwise. *You* die, my Dea? I will never consent to it! My divinity, my love! Do you understand that I am with you? I swear that you shall live! Oh, but you cannot have thought what would become of me after you were gone. If you had an idea of the necessity which you are to me, you would see that it is absolutely impossible! Dea! you see I have but you! The most extraordinary things have happened to me. You will hardly believe that I have just explored the whole of life in a few hours! I have found out one thing—that there is nothing in it! You exist! if you did not, the universe would have no meaning. Stay with me! Have pity on me! Since you love me, live on! If I have just found you again, it is to keep you. Wait a little longer; you cannot leave me like this, now that we have been together but a few minutes! Do not be impatient! O Heaven, how I suffer! You are not angry with me, are you? You know that I could not help going when the wapentake came for me. You will breathe more easily presently, you will see. Dea, all has been put right. We are going to be happy. Do not drive me to despair, Dea! I have done nothing to you."

These words were not spoken, but sobbed out. They rose from his breast—now in a lament which might have attracted the dove, now in a roar which might have made lions recoil.

Dea answered him in a voice growing weaker and weaker, and pausing at nearly every word.

"Alas! it is of no use, my beloved. I see that you are doing all you can. An hour ago I wanted to die; now I do not. Gwynplaine—my adored Gwynplaine—how happy we have been! God placed you in my life, and He takes me out of yours. You see, I am going. You will remember the Green Box, won't you, and poor blind little Dea? You will remember my song? Do not forget the sound of my voice, and the way in which I said, 'I love you!' I will come back and tell it to you again, in the night while you are asleep. Yes, we found each other again; but it was too much joy. It was to end at once. It is decreed that I am to go first. I love my father, Ursus, and my brother, Homo, very dearly. You are all so good. There is no air here. Open the window. My Gwynplaine, I did not tell you, but I was jealous of a woman who came one day. You do not even know of whom I speak. Is it not so? Cover my arms; I am rather cold. And Fibi and Vinos, where are they? One comes to love everybody. One feels a friendship for all those who have been mixed up in one's happiness. We have a kindly feeling towards them for having been present in our joys. Why has it all passed away? I have not clearly understood what has happened during the last two days. Now I am dying. Leave me in my dress. When I put it on I foresaw that it would be my shroud. I wish to keep it on. Gwynplaine's kisses are upon it. Oh, what would I not have given to have lived on! What a happy life we led in our poor caravan! How we sang! How I listened to the applause! What joy it was never to be separated from each other! It seemed to me that I was living in a cloud with you; I knew one day from another, although I was blind. I knew that it was morning, because I heard Gwynplaine; I felt that it was night, because I dreamed of Gwynplaine. I felt that I was wrapped up in something which was his soul. We adored each other so sweetly. It is all fading away; and there will be no more songs. Alas that I cannot live on! You will think of me, my beloved!"

Her voice was growing fainter. The ominous waning, which was death, was stealing away her breath. She folded her thumbs within her fingers—a sign that her last moments were approaching. It seemed as though the first uncertain words of an angel just created were blended with the last failing accents of the dying girl.

She murmured,—

"You will think of me, won't you? It would be very sad to be dead, and to be remembered by no one. I have been wayward at times; I beg pardon of you all. I am sure that, if God had so willed it, we might yet have been happy, my Gwynplaine; for we take up but very little room, and we might have earned our bread together in another land. But God has willed it otherwise. I cannot make out in the least why I am dying. I never complained of being blind, so that I cannot have offended any one. I should never have asked for anything, but always to be blind as I was, by your side. Oh, how sad it is to have to part!"

Her words were more and more inarticulate, evaporating into each other, as if they were being blown away. She had become almost inaudible.

"Gwynplaine," she resumed, "you will think of me, won't you? I shall crave it when I am dead."

And she added,—

"Oh, keep me with you!"

Then, after a pause, she said,—

"Come to me as soon as you can. I shall be very unhappy without you, even in heaven. Do not leave me long alone, my sweet Gwynplaine! My paradise was here; above there is only heaven! Oh! I cannot breathe! My beloved! My beloved! My beloved!"

"Mercy!" cried Gwynplaine.

"Farewell!" murmured Dea.

And he pressed his mouth to her beautiful icy hands. For a moment it seemed as if she had ceased to breathe. Then she raised herself on her elbows, and an intense splendour flashed across her eyes, and through an ineffable smile her voice rang out clearly.

"Light!" she cried. "I see!"

And she expired. She fell back rigid and motionless on the mattress.

"Dead!" said Ursus.

And the poor old man, as if crushed by his despair, bowed his bald head and buried his swollen face in the folds of the gown which covered Dea's feet. He lay there in a swoon.

Then Gwynplaine became awful. He arose, lifted his eyes, and gazed into the vast gloom above him. Seen by none on earth, but looked down upon, perhaps, as he stood in the darkness, by some invisible presence, he stretched his hands on high, and said,—

"I come!"

And he strode across the deck, towards the side of the vessel, as if beckoned by a vision.

A few paces off was the abyss. He walked slowly, never casting down his eyes. A smile came upon his face, such as Dea's had just worn. He advanced straight before him, as if watching something. In his eyes was a light like the reflection of a soul perceived from afar off. He cried out, "Yes!" At every step he was approaching nearer to the side of the vessel. His gait was rigid, his arms were lifted up, his head was thrown back, his eyeballs were fixed. His movement was ghost-like. He advanced without haste and without hesitation, with fatal precision, as though there were before him no yawning gulf and open grave. He murmured, "Be easy. I follow you. I understand the sign that you are making me." His eyes were fixed upon a certain spot in the sky, where the shadow was deepest. The smile was still upon his face. The sky was perfectly black; there was no star visible in it, and yet he evidently saw one. He crossed the deck. A few stiff and ominous steps, and he had reached the very edge.

"I come," said he; "Dea, behold, I come!"

One step more; there was no bulwark; the void was before him; he strode into it. He fell. The night was thick and dull, the water deep. It swallowed him up. He disappeared calmly and silently. None saw nor heard him. The ship sailed on, and the river flowed.

Shortly afterwards the ship reached the sea.

When Ursus returned to consciousness, he found that Gwynplaine was no longer with him, and he saw Homo by the edge of the deck baying in the shadow and looking down upon the water.

THE END.

[Footnote 1: As much as to say, the other daughters are provided for as best may be. (Note by Ursus on the margin of the wall.)]

[Footnote 2: *Una nube salida del malo lado del diablo.*]

[Footnote 3: Tiller of the mountain, who is that man?—A man.

What tongue does he speak?—All.

What things does he know?—All.

What is his country?—None and all.

Who is his God?—God.

What do you call him?—The madman.

What do you say you call him?—The wise man.

In your band, what is he?—He is what he is.

The chief?—No.

Then what is he?—The soul.]

[Footnote 4: Traitors.]

[Footnote 5: The above is a very inefficient and rather absurd translation of the French. It turns upon the fact that in the French language the word for darkness is plural—*ténèbres.*—TRANSLATOR.]

[Footnote 6: Transcriber's note: The original text refers to "vitres épaisses", thick panes, without specific dimensions. Glass only a millimetre thick would have been rather flimsy.]

[Footnote 7: *Gaufrier*, the iron with which a pattern is traced on stuff.]

[Footnote 8: Art thou near me?]

[Footnote 9: Côtes, coasts, costa, ribs.]

[Footnote 10:

"Their lips were four red roses on a stem,

Which in their summer beauty kissed each other."

Shakespeare.]

[Footnote 11: Regina Saba coram rege crura denudavit.—*Schicklardus in Proemio Tarich Jersici, F.* 65.]

[Footnote 12: Book I., p. 196.]

[Footnote 13: Pray! weep! Reason is born of the word. Song creates light.]

[Footnote 14: Night, away! the dawn sings hallali.]

[Footnote 15: Thou must go to heaven and smile, thou that weepest.]

[Footnote 16: Break the yoke; throw off, monster, thy dark clothing.]

[Footnote 17: O come and love! thou art soul, I am heart.]

[Footnote 18: The Fenian, Burke.]

[Footnote 19: The life and the limbs of subjects depend on the king. Chamberlayne, Part 2, chap. iv., p. 76.]

[Footnote 20: This fashion of sleeping partly undrest came from Italy, and was derived from the Romans. "*Sub clarâ nuda lacernâ,*" says Horace.]

[Footnote 21: The author is apparently mistaken. The Chamberlains of the Exchequer divided the wooden laths into tallies, which were given out when disbursing coin, and checked or tallied when accounting for it. It was in burning the old tallies in an oven that the Houses of Parliament were destroyed by fire.—TRANSLATOR.]

[Footnote 22: Villiers called James I., "*Votre cochonnerie.*"]

[Footnote 23: "Depart, O night! sings the dawn."]

AUTHOR BIOGRAPHY

Victor-Marie Hugo (1802–1885) was a Romantic period French poet, novelist, essayist, playwright, and dramatist. Over the course of a more than sixty-year literary career, he wrote prolifically in an extraordinary variety of genres: lyrics, satires, epics, philosophical poems, epigrams, novels, history, critical essays, political speeches, funeral orations, diaries, public and private letters, as well as verse and prose dramas.

Hugo is frequently regarded as one of the greatest and most renowned writers in France. Outside of France, his most famous works are Les Misérables (1862) and The Hunchback of Notre-Dame (French: Notre-Dame de Paris), both of which were published in 1831. Hugo's poetry collections, such as Les Contemplations and La Légende des siècles, are widely known in France (The Legend of the Ages). Hugo was a pioneer of the Romantic literary movement with his plays Cromwell and Hernani. Numerous his works, particularly the musicals Les Misérables and Notre-Dame de Paris, inspired music during and after his lifetime. Throughout his life, he created over 4,000 drawings and campaigned for women's rights.

Though a devout royalist as a child, Hugo's views shifted over the decades, and he became an outspoken supporter of republicanism, serving in politics as a deputy and senator. His work addressed the majority of the era's political and social issues, as well as artistic trends. His opposition to absolutism and his magnum opus of literature elevated him to the status of national hero. He was buried in the Panthéon.

Early life

Victor-Marie Hugo was born in Besançon, Eastern France, on 26 February 1802. Joseph Léopold Sigisbert Hugo (1774–1828) was the youngest son of Joseph Léopold Sigisbert Hugo (1774–1828) and Sophie Trébuchet (1772–1821); the couple had two additional sons: Abel Joseph (1798–1855) and Eugène (1800–1837). Victor Hugo's family originated in Nancy, Lorraine, where his grandfather was a wood merchant. Léopold enlisted in the Revolutionary French army at the age of fourteen; he was an atheist and ardent supporter of the republic established following the monarchy's abolition in 1792. Sophie, Victor's mother, was a devout Catholic who remained a stalwart supporter of the deposed dynasty. They met in 1796 in Châteaubriant, a small town near Nantes, and married the following year.

Due to Hugo's father's position as an officer in Napoleon's army, the family moved frequently; Sophie gave birth to three children in four years. Léopold Hugo wrote to his son that he was conceived on one of the Vosges Mountains' highest peaks while travelling from Lunéville to Besançon. "This elevated origin" he continued, "seems to have had effects on you so that your muse is now continually sublime." Hugo believed he was born on 24 June 1801, which corresponds to Jean Valjean's prisoner number 24601.

In 1810, then-King of Spain Joseph Bonaparte created Hugo's father Count Hugo de Cogolludo y Sigüenza, though it appears that the Spanish title was not legally recognised in France. Hugo later adopted the title of viscount, and on 13 April 1845, he was appointed a peer of France as "Vicomte Victor Hugo"

Sophie left Léopold temporarily in 1803 and settled in Paris with her sons; she began seeing General Victor Fanneau de La Horie, Hugo's godfather, who had been a comrade of General Hugo's during the Vendee campaign. The family rejoined Leopold, now Colonel Hugo, as Governor of the province of Avellino in October 1807. Victor studied mathematics in that city under the tutelage of Giuseppe de Samuele Cagnazzi, the elder brother of Italian scientist Luca de Samuele Cagnazzi. Sophie discovered that Leopold was secretly cohabiting with an Englishwoman named Catherine Thomas.

Hugo's father was summoned to Spain shortly thereafter to fight in the Peninsular War. Madame Hugo and her children were returned to Paris in 1808 and settled in an old convent at 12 Impasse des Feuillantines, a remote mansion on the left bank of the Seine. Victor Fanneau de La Horie, who had conspired to restore the Bourbons and had been sentenced to death a few years earlier, was hiding in a chapel at the back of the garden. He became Victor and his brothers' mentor.

In 1811, the family moved to Spain to join their father. Victor and his brothers were sent to the Real Colegio de San Antonio de Abad in Madrid, while Sophie returned to Paris on her own, now legally divorced from her husband. Victor Fanneau de La Horie was apprehended and executed in 1812. Victor and Eugene were taken from their mother in February 1815 and placed in the Pension Cordier, a private boarding school in Paris, where they stayed for three years while also attending lectures at Lycée Louis le Grand.

Hugo wrote in his diary on 10 July 1816, "I shall be Chateaubriand or nothing." In 1817, he submitted a poem to the Academie Française's competition, for which he received an honourable mention. Academicians refused to believe he was only fifteen years old. The following year, Victor moved in with his mother at 18 rue des Petits-Augustins and enrolled in law school. Victor fell in love and secretly married his childhood friend Adèle Foucher, against his mother's wishes. Sophie Trebuchet died in June 1821, and Léopold married Catherine Thomas, his long-time mistress, a month later. The following year, Victor married Adèle. Victor and his brothers founded the periodical Le Conservateur littéraire in 1819.

Career

Hugo published his first novel the year following his marriage (*Han d'Islande*, 1823), and his second three years later (*Bug-Jargal*, 1826). Between 1829 and 1840, he published five more volumes of poetry (*Les Orientales*, 1829; *Les Feuilles d'automne*, 1831; *Les Chants du crépuscule*, 1835; *Les Voix intérieures*, 1837; and *Les Rayons et les Ombres*, 1840), cementing his reputation as one of the greatest elegiac and lyric poets of his time.

Like many young writers of his generation, Hugo was profoundly influenced by François-René de Chateaubriand, the famous figure in the literary movement of Romanticism and France's pre-eminent literary figure during the early 19th century. In his youth, Hugo resolved to be "Chateaubriand or nothing", and his life would come to parallel that of his predecessor in many ways. Like Chateaubriand, Hugo furthered the cause of Romanticism, became involved in politics (though mostly as a champion of Republicanism), and was forced into exile due to his political stances.

The precocious passion and eloquence of Hugo's early work brought success and fame at an early age. His first collection of poetry (*Odes et poésies diverses*) was published in 1822 when he was only 20 years old and earned him a royal pension from Louis XVIII. Though the poems were admired for their spontaneous fervor and fluency, the collection that followed four years later in 1826 (*Odes et Ballades*) revealed Hugo to be a great poet, a natural master of lyric and creative song.

Victor Hugo's first mature work of fiction was first published in February 1829 by Charles Gosselin without the author's name and reflected the acute social conscience that would infuse his later work. *Le Dernier jour d'un condamné* (*The Last Day of a Condemned Man*) would have a profound influence on later writers such as Albert Camus, Charles Dickens, and Fyodor Dostoyevsky. Claude Gueux, a documentary short story about a real-life murderer who had been executed in France, appeared in 1834 and was later considered by Hugo himself to be a precursor to his great work on social injustice, *Les Misérables*.

Hugo became the figurehead of the Romantic literary movement with the plays *Cromwell* (1827) and *Hernani* (1830). *Hernani* announced the arrival of French romanticism: performed at the Comédie-Française, it was greeted with several nights of rioting as romantics and traditionalists clashed over the play's deliberate disregard for neo-classical rules. Hugo's popularity as a playwright grew with subsequent plays, such as *Marion Delorme* (1831), *The King Amuses Himself* (1832), and *Ruy Blas* (1838). Hugo's novel *Notre-Dame de Paris* (*The Hunchback of Notre-Dame*) was published in 1831 and quickly translated into other languages across Europe. One of the effects of the novel was to shame the City of Paris into restoring the much-neglected Cathedral of Notre Dame, which was attracting thousands of tourists who had read the popular novel. The book also inspired a renewed appreciation for pre-Renaissance buildings, which thereafter began to be actively preserved.

Hugo began planning a major novel about social misery and injustice as early as the 1830s, but a full 17 years were needed for *Les Misérables* to be realised and finally published in 1862. Hugo had used the departure of prisoners for the Bagne of Toulon in one of his early stories, "Le Dernier Jour d'un condamné" He went to Toulon to visit the Bagne in 1839 and took extensive notes, though he did not start writing the book until 1845. On one of the pages of his notes about the prison, he wrote in large block letters a possible name for his hero: " JEAN TRÉJEAN". When the book was finally written, Tréjean became Jean Valjean.

Hugo was acutely aware of the quality of the novel, as evidenced in a letter he wrote to his publisher, Albert Lacroix, on 23 March 1862, "My conviction is that this book is going to be one of the peaks, if not the crowning point of my work." Publication of *Les Misérables* went to the highest bidder. The Belgian publishing house Lacroix and *Verboeckhoven* undertook a marketing campaign unusual for the time, issuing press releases about the work a full six months before the launch. It also initially published only the first part of the novel ("Fantine"), which was launched simultaneously in major cities. Installments of the book sold out within hours and had enormous impact on French society.

The critical establishment was generally hostile to the novel; Taine found it insincere, Barbey d'Aurevilly complained of its vulgarity, Gustave Flaubert found within it "neither truth nor greatness", the *Goncourt* brothers lambasted its artificiality, and Baudelaire – despite giving favourable reviews in newspapers – castigated it in private as "repulsive and inept". *Les Misérables* proved popular enough with the masses that the issues it highlighted were soon on the agenda of the National Assembly of France. Today, the novel remains his most well-known work. It is popular worldwide and has been adapted for cinema, television, and stage shows.

An apocryphal tale about the shortest correspondence in history is said to have been between Hugo and his publisher Hurst and Blackett in 1862. Hugo was on vacation when *Les Misérables* was published. He queried the reaction to the work by sending a single-character telegram to his publisher, asking ?. The publisher replied with a single ! to indicate its success. Hugo turned away from social/political issues in his next novel, *Les Travailleurs de la Mer* (*Toilers of the Sea*), published in 1866. The book was well received, perhaps due to the previous success of *Les Misérables*. Dedicated to the channel island of Guernsey, where he spent 15 years of exile, Hugo tells of a man who attempts to win the approval of his beloved's father by rescuing his ship, intentionally marooned by its captain who hopes to escape with a treasure of money it is transporting, through an exhausting battle of human engineering against the force of the sea and a battle against an almost mythical beast of the sea, a giant squid. Superficially an adventure, one of Hugo's biographers calls it a "metaphor for the 19th century–technical progress, creative genius and hard work overcoming the immanent evil of the material world."

The word used in Guernsey to refer to squid (*pieuvre*, also sometimes applied to octopus) was to enter the French language as a result of its use in the book. Hugo returned to political and social issues in his next novel, *L'Homme Qui Rit* (*The Man Who Laughs*), which was published in 1869 and painted a critical picture of the aristocracy. The novel was not as successful as his previous efforts, and Hugo himself began to comment on the growing distance between himself and literary contemporaries such as Flaubert and Émile Zola, whose realist and naturalist novels were now exceeding the popularity of his own work.

His last novel, *Quatre-vingt-treize* (*Ninety-Three*), published in 1874, dealt with a subject that Hugo had previously avoided: the Reign of Terror during the French Revolution. Though Hugo's popularity was on the decline at the time of its publication, many now consider *Ninety-Three* to be a work on par with Hugo's better-known novels.

Political life and exile

Hugo published his first novel (Han d'Islande, 1823) the year after his marriage, and his second three years later (Bug-Jargal, 1826). Between 1829 and 1840, he published five additional volumes of poetry (Les Orientales, 1829; Les Feuilles d'automne, 1831; Les Chants du crépuscule, 1835; Les Voix intérieures, 1837; and Les Rayons et les Ombres, 1840), establishing himself as one of the greatest elegiac and lyric poets of his generation.

Hugo, like many of his generation's young writers, was profoundly influenced by François-René de Chateaubriand, a celebrated figure in the Romantic literary movement and France's preeminent literary figure during the early nineteenth century. Hugo resolved in his youth to be "Chateaubriand or nothing" and his life would come to parallel his predecessor's in numerous ways. As with Chateaubriand, Hugo promoted Romanticism, became involved in politics (though primarily as a Republican supporter), and was forced into exile as a result of his political stances.

Hugo's early work, with its precocious passion and eloquence, brought him success and fame at a young age. When he was only twenty years old, his first collection of poetry (Odes et poésies diverses) was published, earning him a royal pension from Louis XVIII. Though the poems were praised for their spontaneity and fluency, the collection that followed in 1826 (Odes et Ballades) established Hugo as a great poet, a natural master of lyric and creative song.

Victor Hugo's first mature work of fiction, published anonymously in February 1829 by Charles Gosselin, reflected the acute social conscience that would pervade his subsequent work. Le Dernier jour d'un condamné influenced subsequent writers such as Albert Camus, Charles Dickens, and Fyodor Dostoyevsky. Claude Gueux, a documentary short storey about a real-life murderer executed in France in 1834, was later considered by Hugo to be a precursor to his magnum opus on social injustice, Les Misérables.

With the plays Cromwell (1827) and Hernani (1828), Hugo established himself as a figurehead of the Romantic literary movement (1830). Hernani heralded the arrival of French romanticism: when it was performed at the Comédie-Française, it sparked several nights of rioting between romantics and traditionalists over the play's deliberate disregard for neo-classical conventions. Hugo's popularity as a playwright increased with the publication of subsequent works such as Marion Delorme (1831), The King Amuses Himself (1832), and Ruy Blas (1833). (1838). Hugo's novel Notre-Dame de Paris (The Hunchback of Notre-Dame) was published in 1831 and was immediately translated into several other European languages. One of the novel's effects was to shame the City of Paris into restoring the Cathedral of Notre Dame, which attracted thousands of tourists who had read the popular novel. Additionally, the book rekindled an appreciation for pre-

Renaissance structures, which have since been actively preserved.

Hugo began planning a major novel about social misery and injustice as early as the 1830s, but it took him 17 years to complete and publish Les Misérables in 1862. Hugo used the departure of prisoners for Toulon's Bagne in one of his early stories, "Le Dernier Jour d'un condamné" He visited Toulon in 1839 to visit the Bagne and took copious notes, though he did not begin writing the book until 1845. On one of the pages of his prison notes, he scribbled a possible name for his hero in large block letters: " JEAN TRÉJEAN". When the novel was completed, Tréjean assumed the identity of Jean Valjean.

Hugo was acutely aware of the novel's quality, as evidenced by a letter he wrote to his publisher, Albert Lacroix, on 23 March 1862, in which he stated, "My conviction is that this book is going to be one of the peaks, if not the crowning point of my work." Les Misérables was sold to the highest bidder. Lacroix and Verboeckhoven, a Belgian publishing house, launched an unusual marketing campaign for the time period, issuing press releases about the work six months in advance of its publication. Additionally, it initially published only the first chapter ("Fantine") of the novel, which was simultaneously launched in major cities. The book's instalments sold out within hours and had a profound effect on French society.

The critical establishment was generally hostile to the novel; Taine found it insincere, Barbey d'Aurevilly lamented its vulgarity, Gustave Flaubert decried its artificiality, and Baudelaire – despite favourable newspaper reviews – castigated it in private as "repulsive and inept." Les Misérables was so popular with the public that the issues it raised were quickly brought to the attention of France's National Assembly. The novel remains his most well-known work to this day. It is popular throughout the world and has been adapted for film, television, and stage productions.

According to an apocryphal storey, Hugo and his publisher Hurst and Blackett had the shortest correspondence in history in 1862. Hugo was on vacation at the time of the publication of Les Misérables. He enquired about the work's reception by sending a single-character telegram to his publisher, inquiring? The publisher responded with a single! to indicate that the submission was successful. Hugo's subsequent novel, Les Travailleurs de la Mer (Toilers of the Sea), published in 1866, shifted away from social/political issues. The book received favourable reviews, possibly as a result of the previous success of Les Misérables. Hugo's novel is dedicated to the channel island of Guernsey, where he spent 15 years in exile. It tells the storey of a man attempting to win the approval of his beloved's father by rescuing his ship, which has been intentionally marooned by its captain in order to escape with the treasure of money it is transporting, through an exhausting battle of human engineering against the force of the sea and a battle against an almost mythical sea creature, a giant s Although it appears to be an adventure, one of Hugo's biographers describes it as a "metaphor for the 19th century–technical progress, creative genius and hard work overcoming the immanent evil of the material world."

The word for squid used in Guernsey (pieuvre, also applied to octopus on occasion) was to enter the French language as a result of its use in the book. Hugo returned to political and social issues in his subsequent novel, L'Homme Qui Rit (The Man Who Laughs), published in 1869 and depicting the aristocracy in a critical light. The novel did not fare as well as his previous efforts, and Hugo began to lament the growing gap between himself and literary contemporaries such as Flaubert and Émile Zola, whose realist and naturalist novels were now outselling his own.

His final novel, Quatre-vingt-treize (Ninety-Three), published in 1874, addressed a subject Hugo had previously avoided: the French Revolution's Reign of Terror. Though Hugo's popularity was waning at the time of its publication, many now regard Ninety-Three as a novel on a par with his more well-known works.

Religious views

Hugo's religious views shifted dramatically throughout his life. He identified as a Catholic in his youth, influenced by his mother, and professed respect for Church hierarchy and authority. From there, he became a devout Catholic who expressed increasingly anti-Catholic and anti-clerical views. During his exile (during which he also participated in numerous séances conducted by Madame Delphine de Girardin), he frequented spiritism and later settled into a rationalist deism similar to that of Voltaire. In 1872, when a census taker inquired about Hugo's religion, he responded, "No. A Freethinker."

Hugo's hostility toward the Catholic Church remained constant after 1872. He believed the Church was callous to the plight of the working class under monarchical oppression. Perhaps he was also displeased with the frequency with which his work was included on the Church's list of prohibited books. Hugo determined that the Catholic press had published 740 attacks on Les Misérables. Hugo insisted that his sons Charles and François-Victor be buried without a crucifix or priest. He made the same provision in his will regarding his own death and funeral.

Nonetheless, he believed in life after death and prayed daily, convinced, as he wrote in The Man Who Laughs, that "Thanksgiving is a bird with wings that flies to its proper destination. Your prayer is more astute than you are in determining its path "'.

Hugo's rationalism is evident in poems such as Torquemada (1869), The Pope (1878), Religions and Religion (1880), and, posthumously published, The End of Satan and God (1886 and 1891 respectively, in which he represents Christianity as a gryphon and rationalism as an angel). Vincent van Gogh ascribed to Hugo the proverb "Religions pass away, but God remains" which was actually written by Jules Michelet.

Relationship with music

Although Hugo lacked exceptional musical ability, he had a significant impact on the music world through the inspiration his works provided for composers of the nineteenth and twentieth centuries. Hugo was particularly fond of Gluck and Weber's music. In Les Misérables, he refers to Weber's Euryanthe's huntsman's chorus as "perhaps the most beautiful piece of music ever composed" He also admired Beethoven and, somewhat unusually for his time, composers from earlier centuries such as Palestrina and Monteverdi.

Hugo was acquainted with two prominent nineteenth-century musicians: Hector Berlioz and Franz Liszt. The latter performed Beethoven in Hugo's home, and Hugo joked in a letter to a friend that he learned to play a favourite song on the piano – using only one finger – as a result of Liszt's piano lessons. Hugo also collaborated with composer Louise Bertin, writing the libretto for her 1836 opera La Esmeralda, based on the character from The Hunchback of Notre Dame. Although the opera was closed shortly after its fifth performance and is little known today for a variety of reasons, it has recently been revived, both in a piano/song concert version by Liszt at the 2007 Festival international Victor Hugo et Égaux and in a full orchestral version presented in July 2008 at Le Festival de Radio France et Montpellier Languedoc-Roussillon.

On the other hand, he despised Richard Wagner, whom he described as "a man of talent coupled with imbecility."

Hugo's works have inspired well over a thousand musical compositions from the nineteenth century to the present day. Hugo's plays, in which he defied classical theatre's rules in favour of romantic drama, piqued the interest of numerous composers, who adapted them into operas. Numerous operas are based on Hugo's works, including Donizetti's Lucrezia Borgia (1833), Verdi's Rigoletto (1851) and Ernani (1844), as well as Ponchielli's La Gioconda (1876).

Hugo's novels, as well as his plays, have inspired musicians to create not only opera and ballet, but also musical theatre, such as Notre-Dame de Paris and the ever-popular Les Misérables, the longest-running musical in London's West End. Additionally, Hugo's beautiful poems have piqued the interest of musicians, with composers such as Berlioz, Bizet, Fauré, Franck, Lalo, Liszt, Massenet, Saint-Saens, Rachmaninoff, and Wagner creating numerous melodies based on his poetry.

Hugo's work continues to inspire musicians to create new compositions to this day. For example, David Alagna adapted Hugo's novel The Last Day of a Condemned Man into an opera with a libretto by Frédérico Alagna, which was premiered in 2007 by their brother, tenor Roberto Alagna. Every two years in Guernsey, the Victor Hugo International Music Festival brings together a diverse group of musicians and features the world premieres of songs based on Hugo's poetry by composers such as Guillaume Connesson, Richard Dubugnon, Olivier Kaspar, and Thierry Escaich.

Not only has Hugo's literary work inspired musical works, but also his political writings have garnered attention from musicians and been adapted to music. For example, in 2009, the Italian composer Matteo Sommacal was commissioned by the Festival "Bagliori d'autore" to compose Actes et paroles, a work for speaker and chamber ensemble based on a text by Chiara Piola Caselli on Victor Hugo's final political speech to the Assemblée législative, "Sur la Revision de la Constitution" (18 July 1851), and premiered in Rome on 19 November 2009, in the auditorium of the

Declining years and death

When Hugo returned to Paris in 1870, he was hailed as a national hero by the country. As evidenced by the notes he kept at the time, he was confident he would be offered the dictatorship: "Dictatorship is a heinous offence. This is the offence I intend to commit ", but he felt compelled to take on that role. Hugo lost his bid for re-election to the National Assembly in 1872, despite his popularity.

Hugo believed in unstoppable humanistic progress throughout his life. On 3 August 1879, in his final public address, he prophesied overly optimistically, "In the twentieth century war will be dead, the scaffold will be dead, hatred will be dead, frontier boundaries will be dead, dogmas will be dead; man will live."

Within a short period of time, he suffered a mild stroke, his daughter Adèle was committed to a mental institution, and both of his sons died. (Adèle's biography served as the inspiration for the film The Story of Adele H.) Adèle, his wife, died in 1868.

Juliette Drouet, his devoted mistress, died in 1883, only two years before he died. Hugo remained committed to the cause of political change despite his personal loss. He was elected to the newly formed Senate on 30 January 1876. This final phase of his political career was deemed unsuccessful. Hugo was a lone wolf in the Senate, accomplishing little.

On 27 June 1878, Hugo suffered a mild stroke.

To commemorate his upcoming 80th birthday, one of the greatest tributes to a living writer was held. Hugo was presented with a Sèvres vase, the traditional gift for sovereigns, on 25 June 1881. On 27 June, France witnessed one of the largest parades in its history.

Marchers extended from the author's residence on the Avenue d'Eylau, down the Champs-Élysées, and all the way to the heart of Paris. The paraders marched past Hugo for six hours as he sat at his house's window. Hugo was involved in every inch and detail of the event; the official guides even wore cornflowers in reference to Fantine's song in Les Misérables. The city of Paris renamed the Avenue d'Eylau Avenue Victor-Hugo on 28 June. From that point forward, letters addressed to the author were labelled "To Mister Victor Hugo, In his avenue, Paris"

He left a note two days before he died with these final words: "To love is to act"

Le Petit Journal published an official medical bulletin on Hugo's health condition on 20 May 1885. "The illustrious patient" was fully conscious and cognizant of the fact that he had no hope. Additionally, they reported from a reliable source that he whispered the following alexandrin at one point during the night: "En moi c'est le combat du jour et de la nuit" – "In me, this is the battle between day and night" "Here is the battle between day and night," Le Matin published a slightly different version, "Here is the battle between day and night."

Hugo's pneumonia-related death on 22 May 1885, at the age of 83, sparked widespread national mourning. He was not only revered as a literary giant; he was also a statesman who shaped France's Third Republic and democracy. Throughout his life, he was a staunch defender of liberty, equality, and fraternity, as well as a staunch defender of French culture. He wrote, in 1877, at the age of 75, "I am not one of these mild-mannered senior citizens. I remain enraged and violent. I scream, I am incensed, and I cry. Whoever harms France, woe to him! I declare that I will die a zealous patriot "'.

Although he requested a pauper's funeral, President Jules Grévy granted him a state funeral. Over two million people attended his funeral procession in Paris, which began at the Arc de Triomphe and ended at the Panthéon, where he was laid to rest. Alexandre Dumas and Émile Zola share a crypt in the Panthéon. In the majority of large French towns and cities, he is commemorated with a street or square.

Hugo stipulated in his last will and testament that the following five sentences be published:
Je donne cinquante mille francs aux pauvres. Je veux être enterré dans leur corbillard.
Je refuse l'oraison de toutes les Églises. Je demande une prière à toutes les âmes.
Je crois en Dieu.
I leave 50,000 francs to the poor. I wish to be buried in their hearse.
I refuse [funeral] orations from all Churches. I ask [for] a prayer to all souls.
I believe in God.

Made in the USA
Coppell, TX
17 April 2026

76029327R00256